MIKE MAIHACK

CLEOPATRA
IN SPACE

BOOK SIX
QUEEN OF THE NILE

graphix
AN IMPRINT OF
■SCHOLASTIC

All rights reserved. Published by Graphix, an imprint of Scholastic Inc.,
Publishers since 1920. SCHOLASTIC, GRAPHIX, and associated logos are
trademarks and/or registered trademarks of Scholastic Inc.

Library of Congress Control Number: 2019933612

ISBN 978-1-338-20416-2 (hardcover)
ISBN 978-1-338-20415-5 (paperback)

10 9 8 7 6 5 4 3 2   21 22 23 24

Printed in China   62
First edition, August 2020
Edited by Cassandra Pelham Fulton
Book design by Phil Falco
Publisher: David Saylor

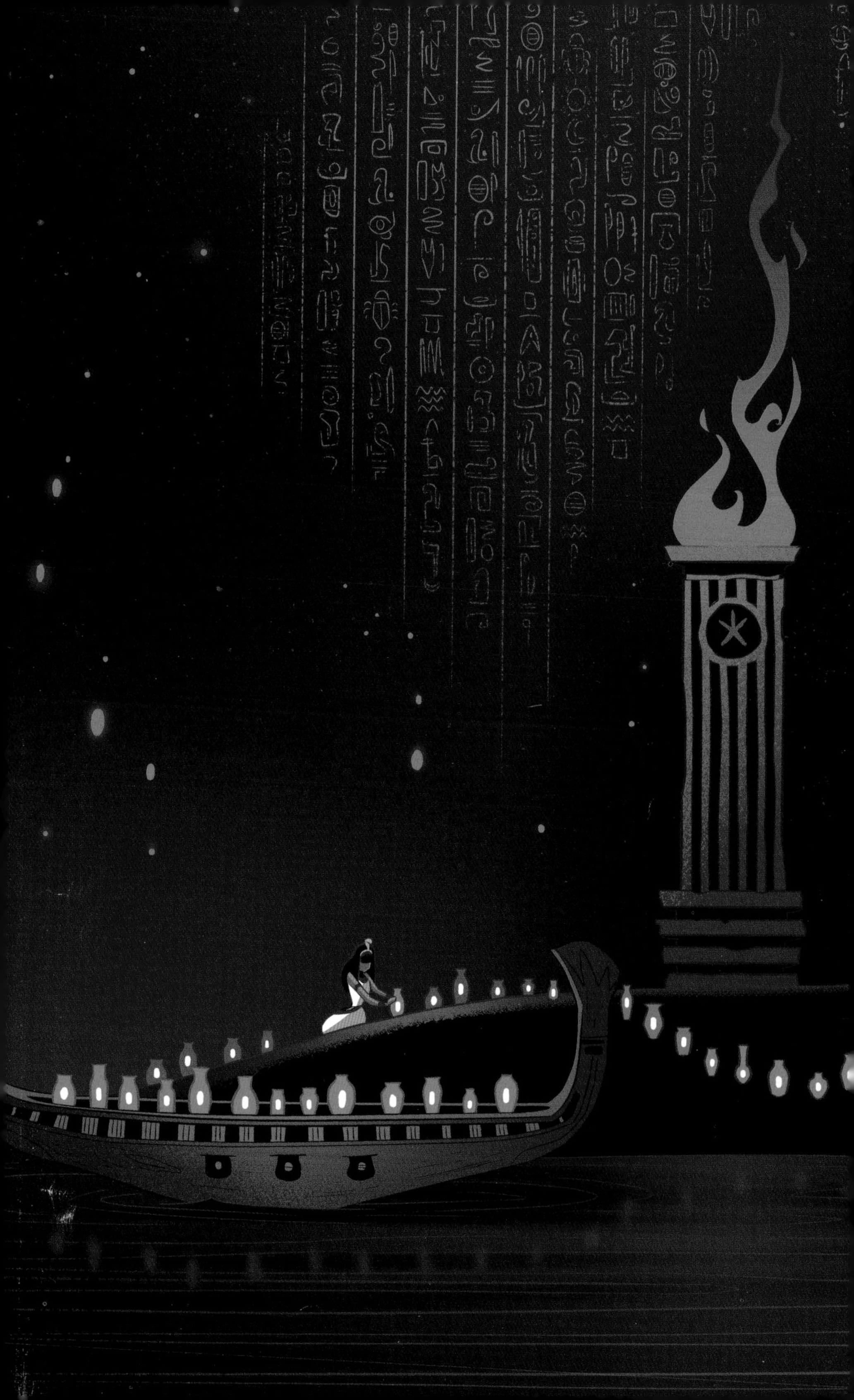

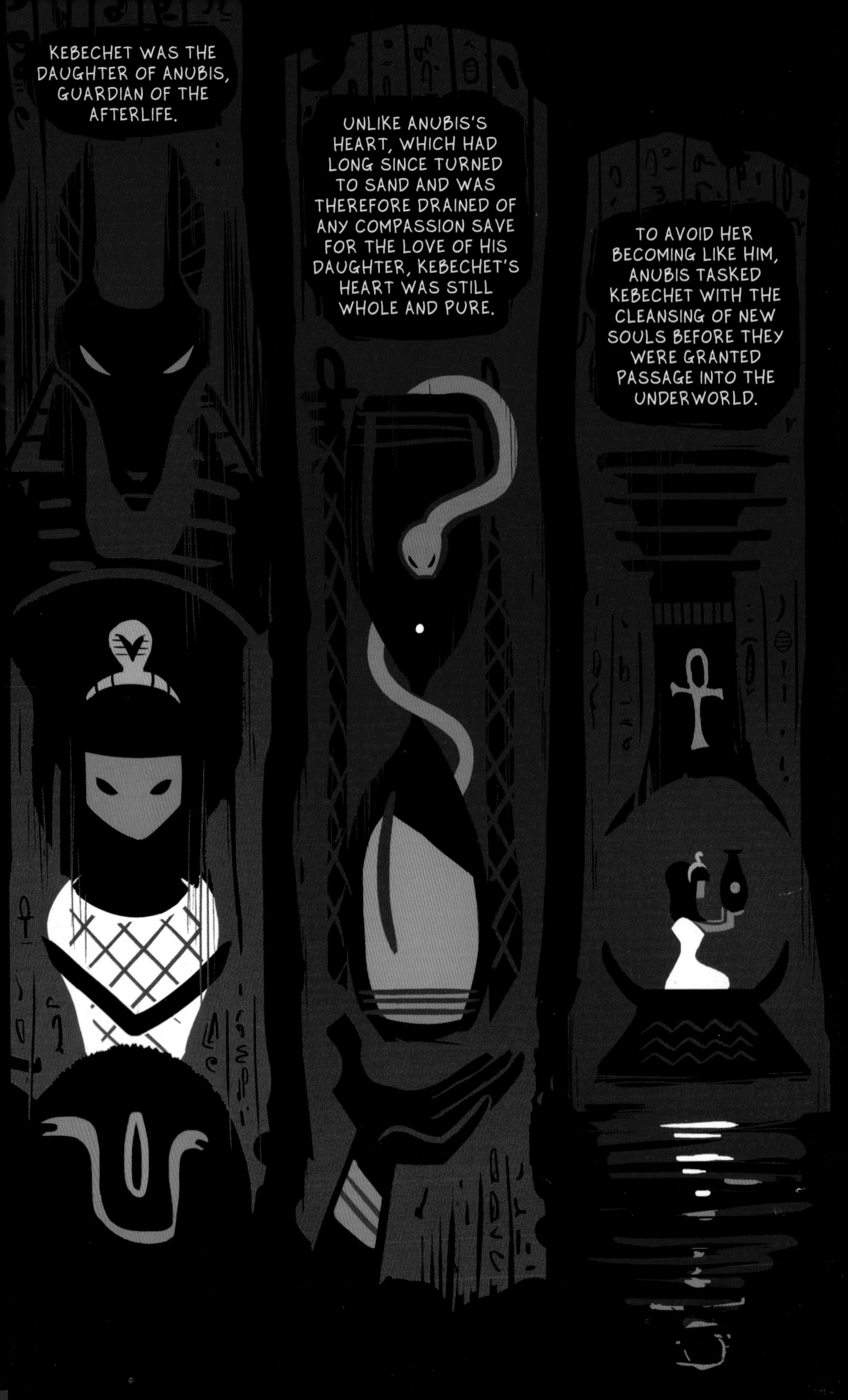
KEBECHET WAS THE DAUGHTER OF ANUBIS, GUARDIAN OF THE AFTERLIFE.
UNLIKE ANUBIS'S HEART, WHICH HAD LONG SINCE TURNED TO SAND AND WAS THEREFORE DRAINED OF ANY COMPASSION SAVE FOR THE LOVE OF HIS DAUGHTER, KEBECHET'S HEART WAS STILL WHOLE AND PURE.
TO AVOID HER BECOMING LIKE HIM, ANUBIS TASKED KEBECHET WITH THE CLEANSING OF NEW SOULS BEFORE THEY WERE GRANTED PASSAGE INTO THE UNDERWORLD.

BEFORE MEETING ANUBIS, EVERY SOUL WAS GIVEN A SMALL VASE OF WATER; THE AMOUNT OF WATER BROUGHT BEFORE ANUBIS WOULD HELP HIM DETERMINE IF THAT SOUL WAS MEANT FOR THE AFTERLIFE OR IF THEIR TIME WAS BETTER SUITED FOR A LATER DATE.

KNOWING THAT HIS DAUGHTER COULD BE USED AS A BARGAINING CHIP FOR IMMORTALITY, ANUBIS GIFTED KEBECHET WITH A SWORD: A BLACK-BLADED KHOPESH THAT SHE WAS REQUIRED TO KEEP BY HER SIDE AT ALL TIMES.

IF EVER THREATENED OR ATTACKED, KEBECHET WAS TO USE THE SWORD TO DEFEND HERSELF, SENDING THAT SOUL DIRECTLY TO ANUBIS WITH NO WATER. ANY SOUL BROUGHT TO ANUBIS WITH A VASE AS DRY AS HIS HEART WAS DENIED PASSAGE INTO THE UNDERWORLD AND INSTEAD CAST OUT INTO THE NOTHINGNESS.

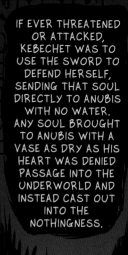

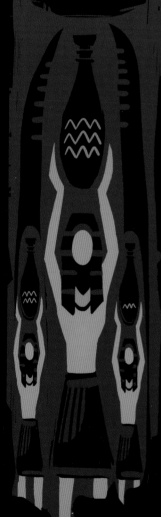

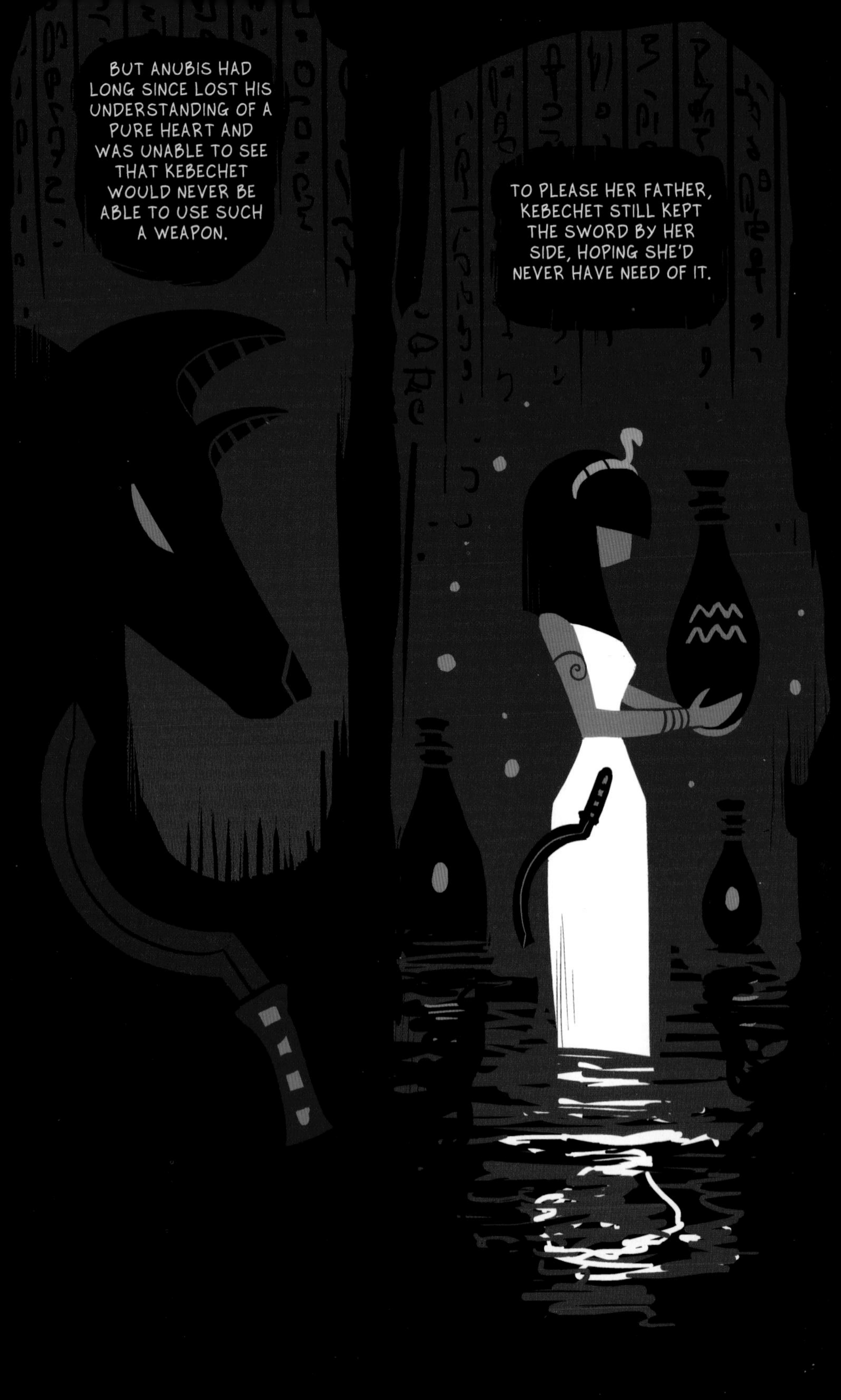
BUT ANUBIS HAD LONG SINCE LOST HIS UNDERSTANDING OF A PURE HEART AND WAS UNABLE TO SEE THAT KEBECHET WOULD NEVER BE ABLE TO USE SUCH A WEAPON.
TO PLEASE HER FATHER, KEBECHET STILL KEPT THE SWORD BY HER SIDE, HOPING SHE'D NEVER HAVE NEED OF IT.

IT HAS BEEN SAID THAT IF THE
SWORD OF KEBECHET IS EVER
FOUND, IT MEANS KEBECHET NO
LONGER CLEANSES THE SOULS OF
THE AFTERLIFE AND AN IMMORTAL
NOW WALKS AMONG THE LIVING.

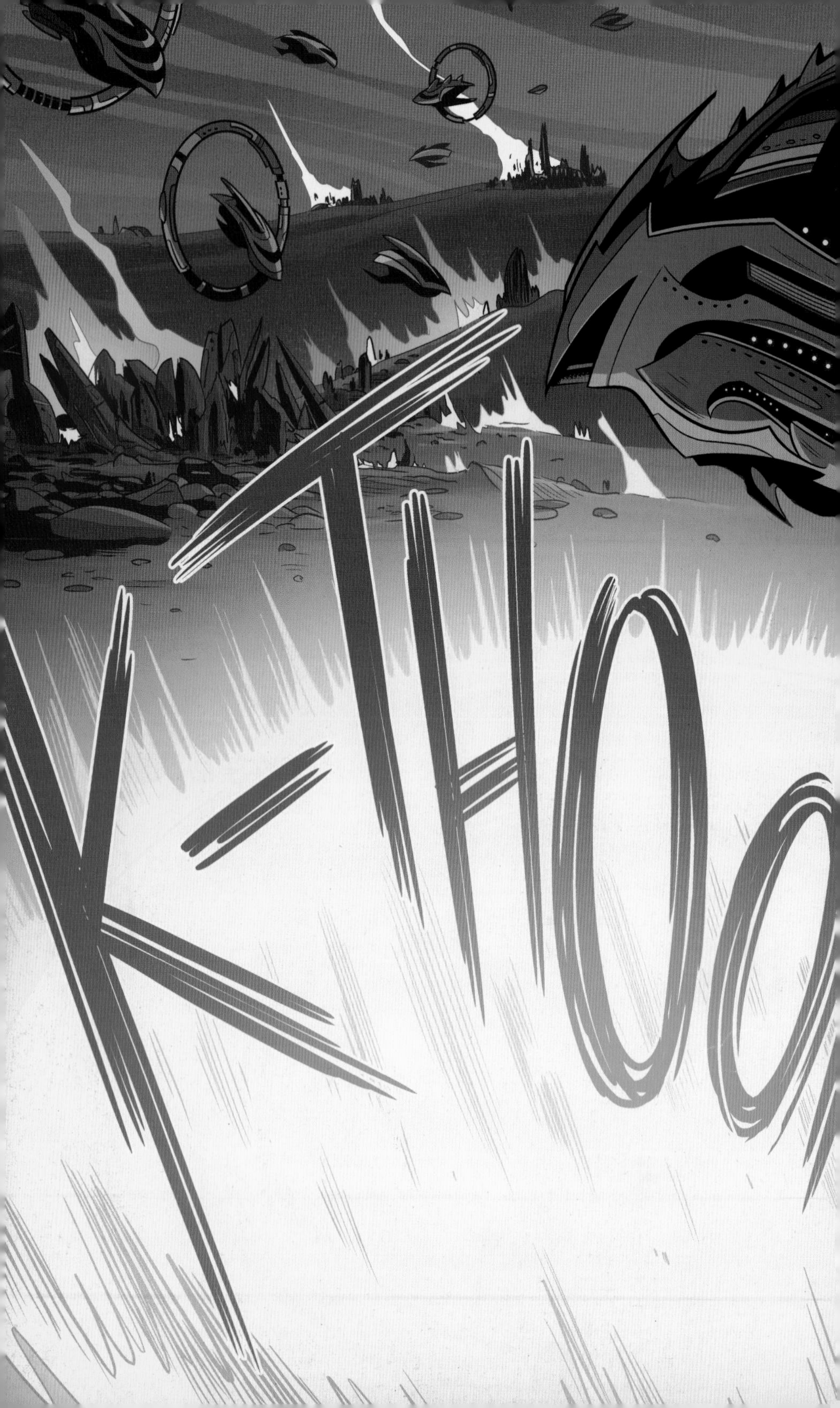
K-THOO

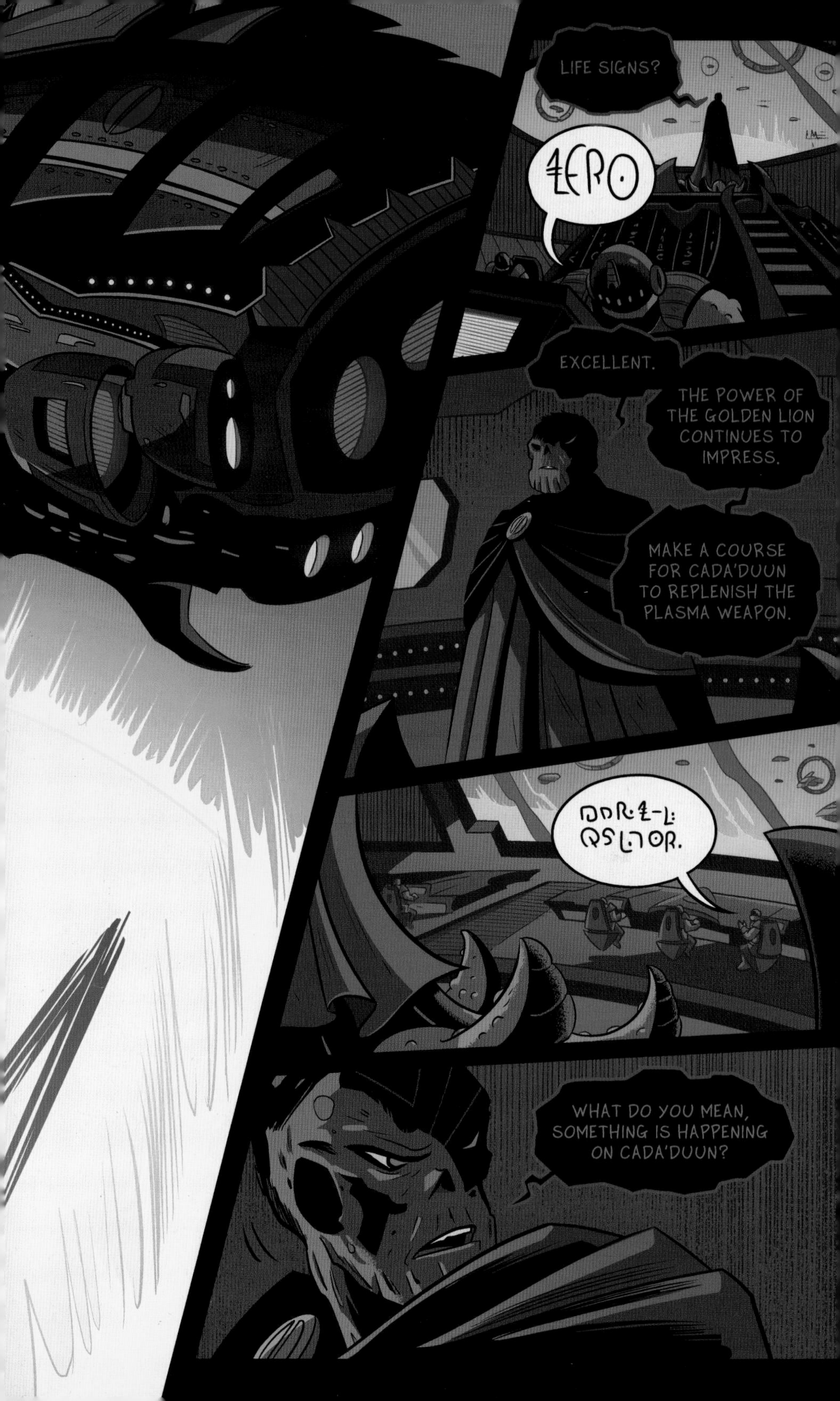
LIFE SIGNS?
ZERO
EXCELLENT.
THE POWER OF THE GOLDEN LION CONTINUES TO IMPRESS.
MAKE A COURSE FOR CADA'DUUN TO REPLENISH THE PLASMA WEAPON.
WHAT DO YOU MEAN, SOMETHING IS HAPPENING ON CADA'DUUN?

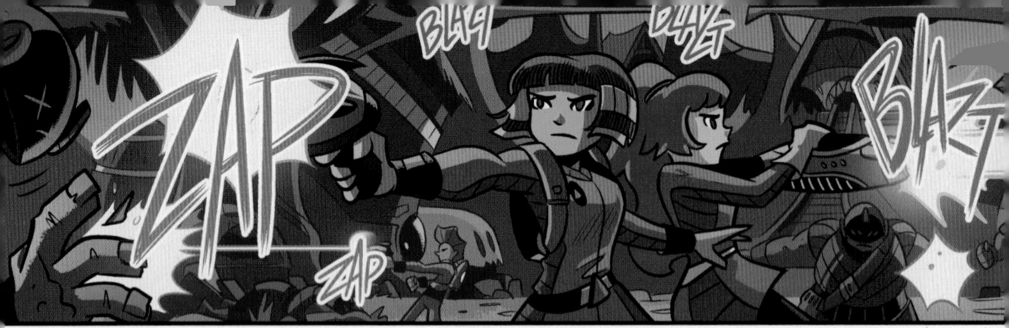
ZAP
ZAP
BLAZT

CHAPTER ONE

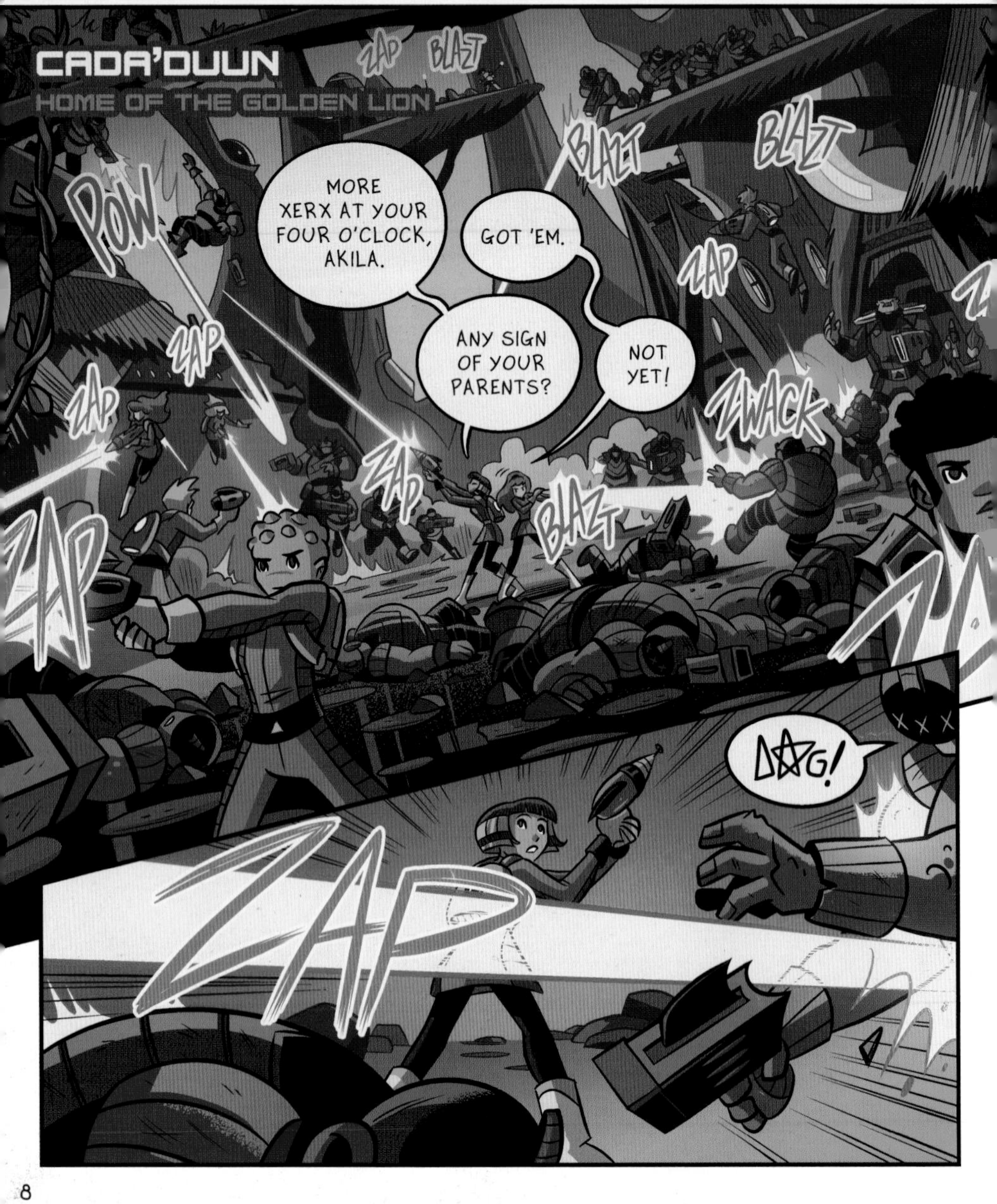
CADA'DUUN
HOME OF THE GOLDEN LION
ZAP
BLAZT
BLAZT
BLAZT
POW
MORE XERX AT YOUR FOUR O'CLOCK, AKILA.
GOT 'EM.
ANY SIGN OF YOUR PARENTS?
NOT YET!
ZAP
ZAP
ZAP
ZWACK
ZAP
BLAZT
ZAP
ZAP

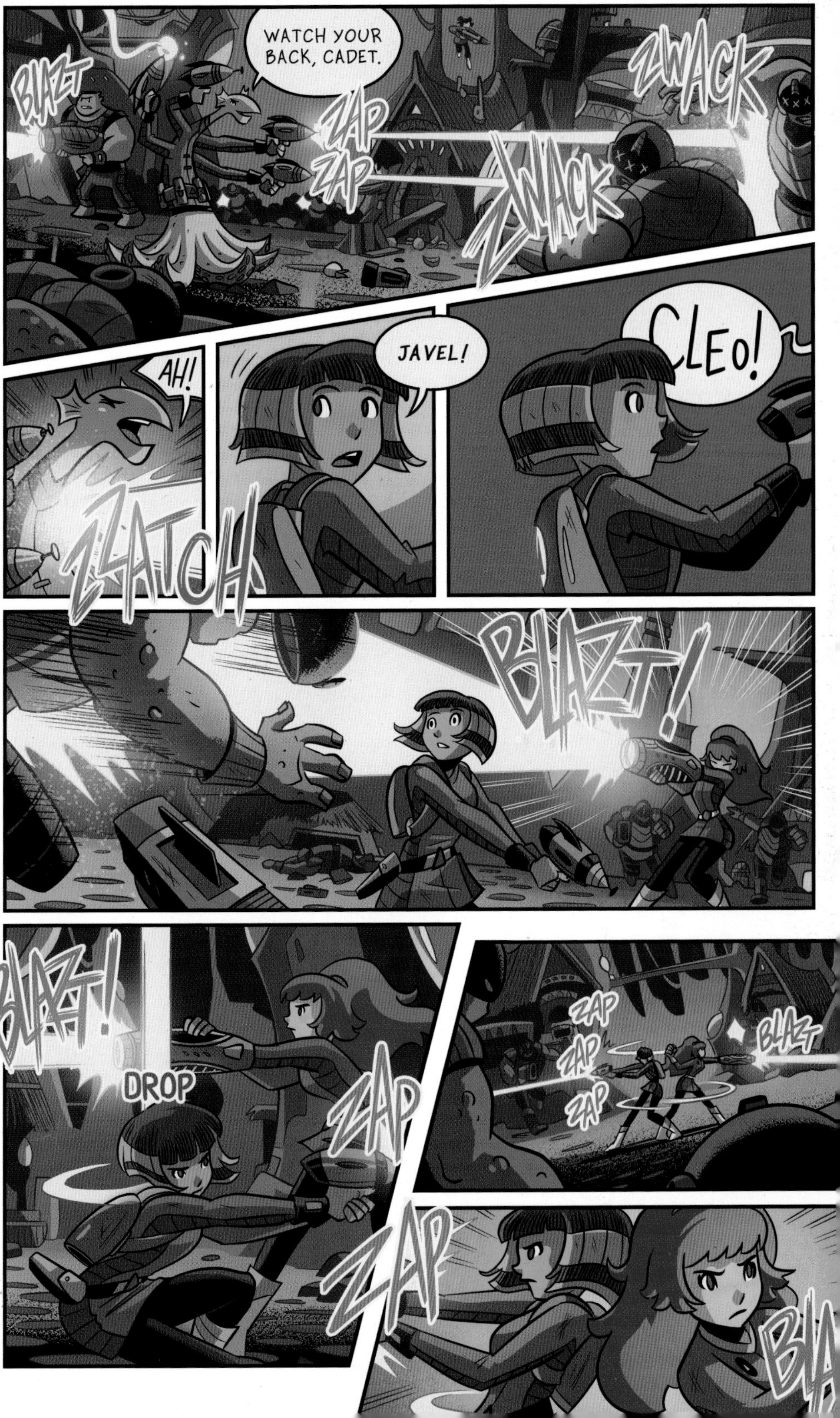
BLAZT
WATCH YOUR BACK, CADET.
ZAP
ZAP
ZWACK
ZWACK
AH!
ZZATCH
JAVEL!
CLEO!
BLAZT!
BLAZT!
DROP
ZAP
ZAP
ZAP
ZAP
BLAZT
ZAP

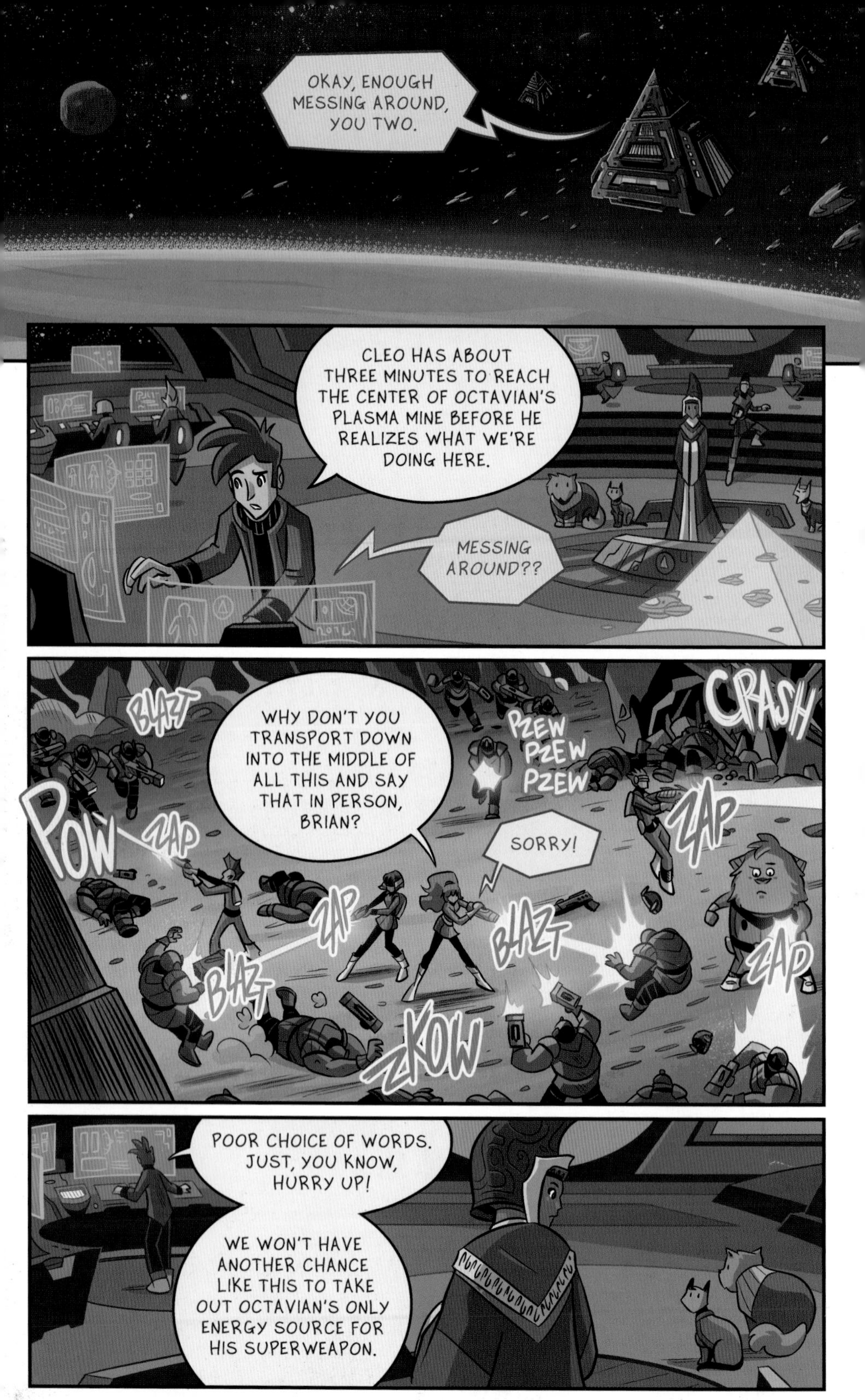
OKAY, ENOUGH MESSING AROUND, YOU TWO.
CLEO HAS ABOUT THREE MINUTES TO REACH THE CENTER OF OCTAVIAN'S PLASMA MINE BEFORE HE REALIZES WHAT WE'RE DOING HERE.
MESSING AROUND??
BLAZT
POW
ZAP
WHY DON'T YOU TRANSPORT DOWN INTO THE MIDDLE OF ALL THIS AND SAY THAT IN PERSON, BRIAN?
PZEW PZEW PZEW
CRASH
ZAP
SORRY!
ZAP
BLAZT
BLAZT
ZAP
ZKOW
POOR CHOICE OF WORDS. JUST, YOU KNOW, HURRY UP!
WE WON'T HAVE ANOTHER CHANCE LIKE THIS TO TAKE OUT OCTAVIAN'S ONLY ENERGY SOURCE FOR HIS SUPERWEAPON.

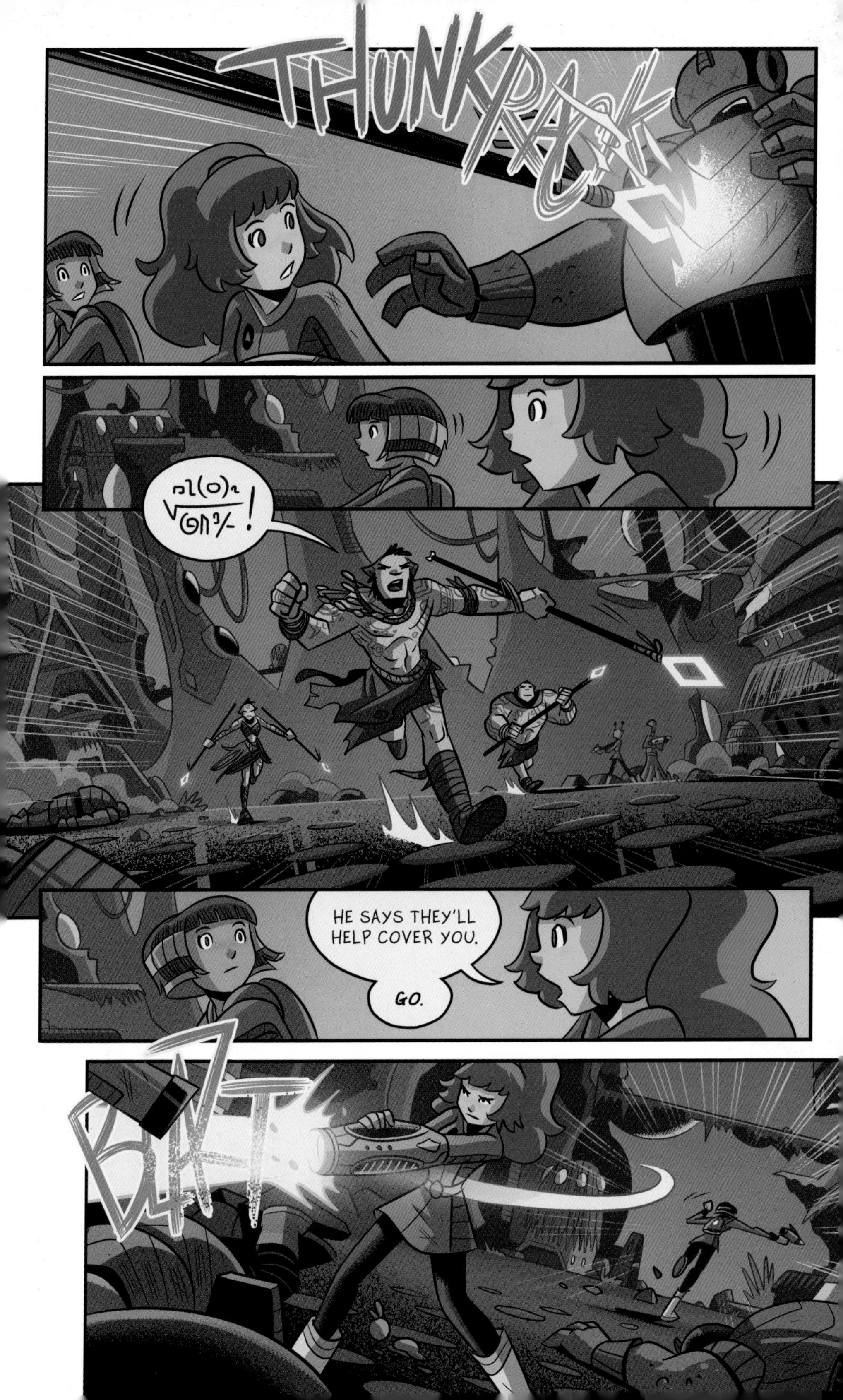
THUNKRACK
HE SAYS THEY'LL HELP COVER YOU.
GO.
BZZT

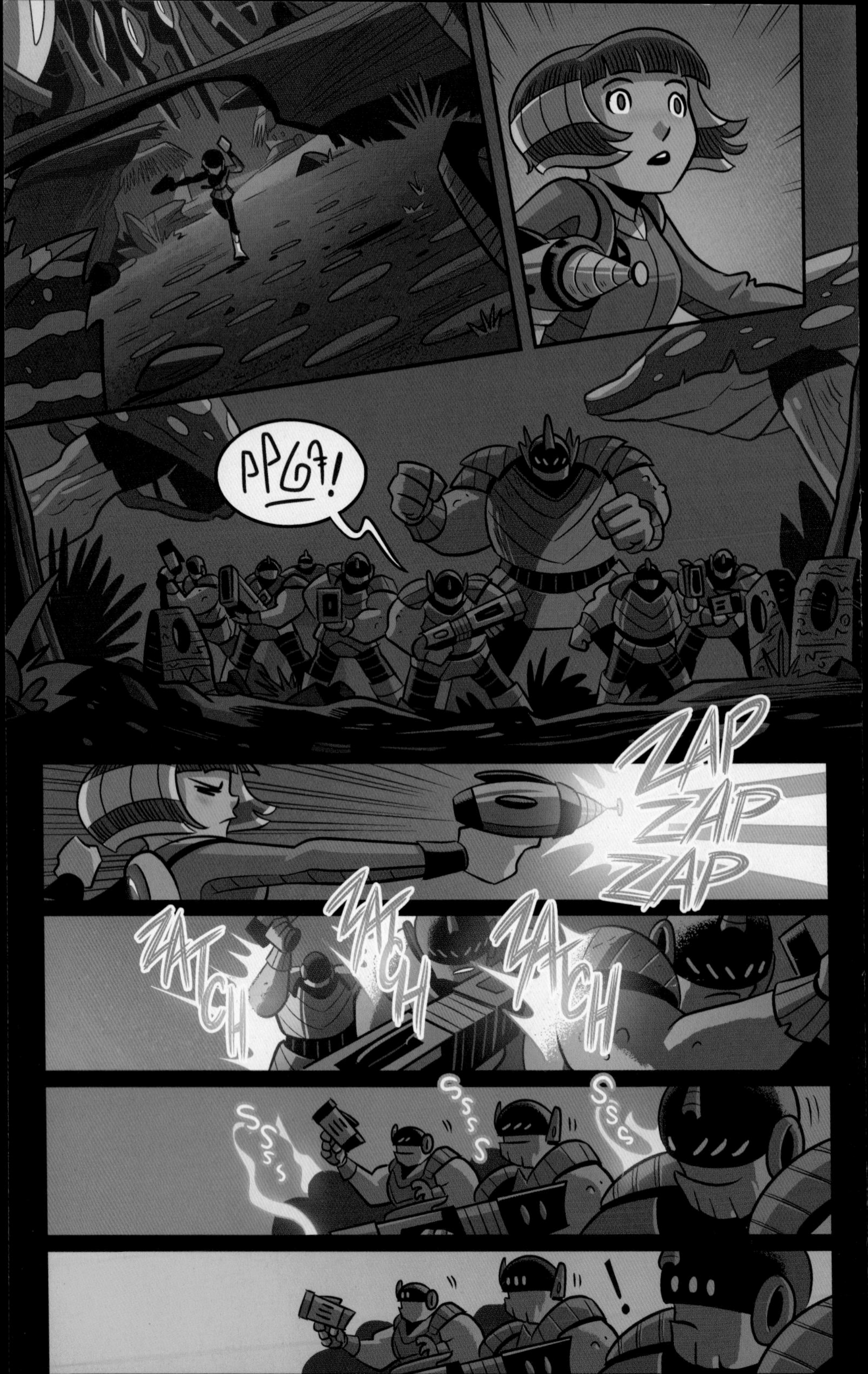
ZAP ZAP ZAP
ZATCH
ZATCH
ZATCH
Ssss
Ssss
Ssss
!

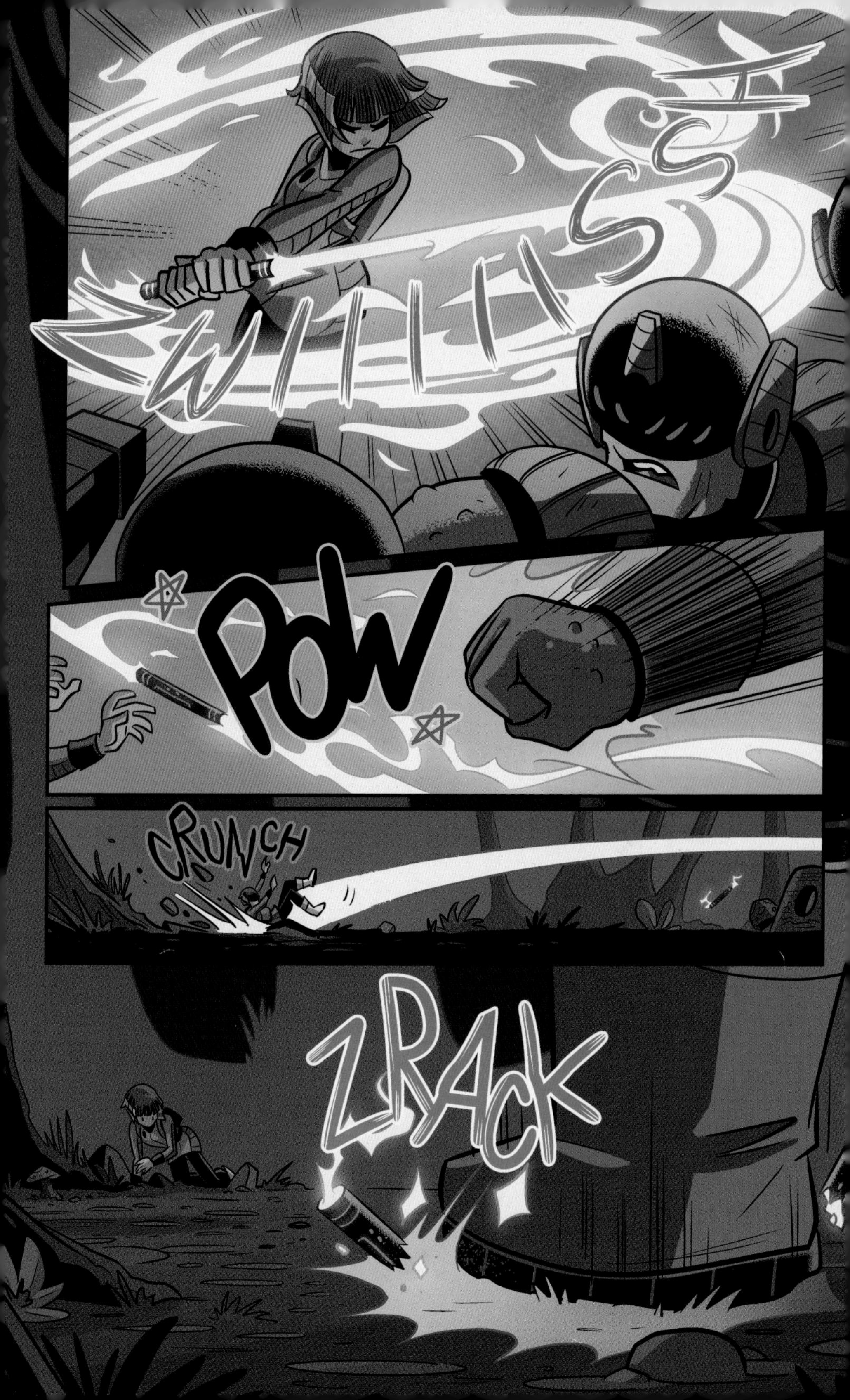
ZWIIIISSH
POW
CRUNCH
ZRACK

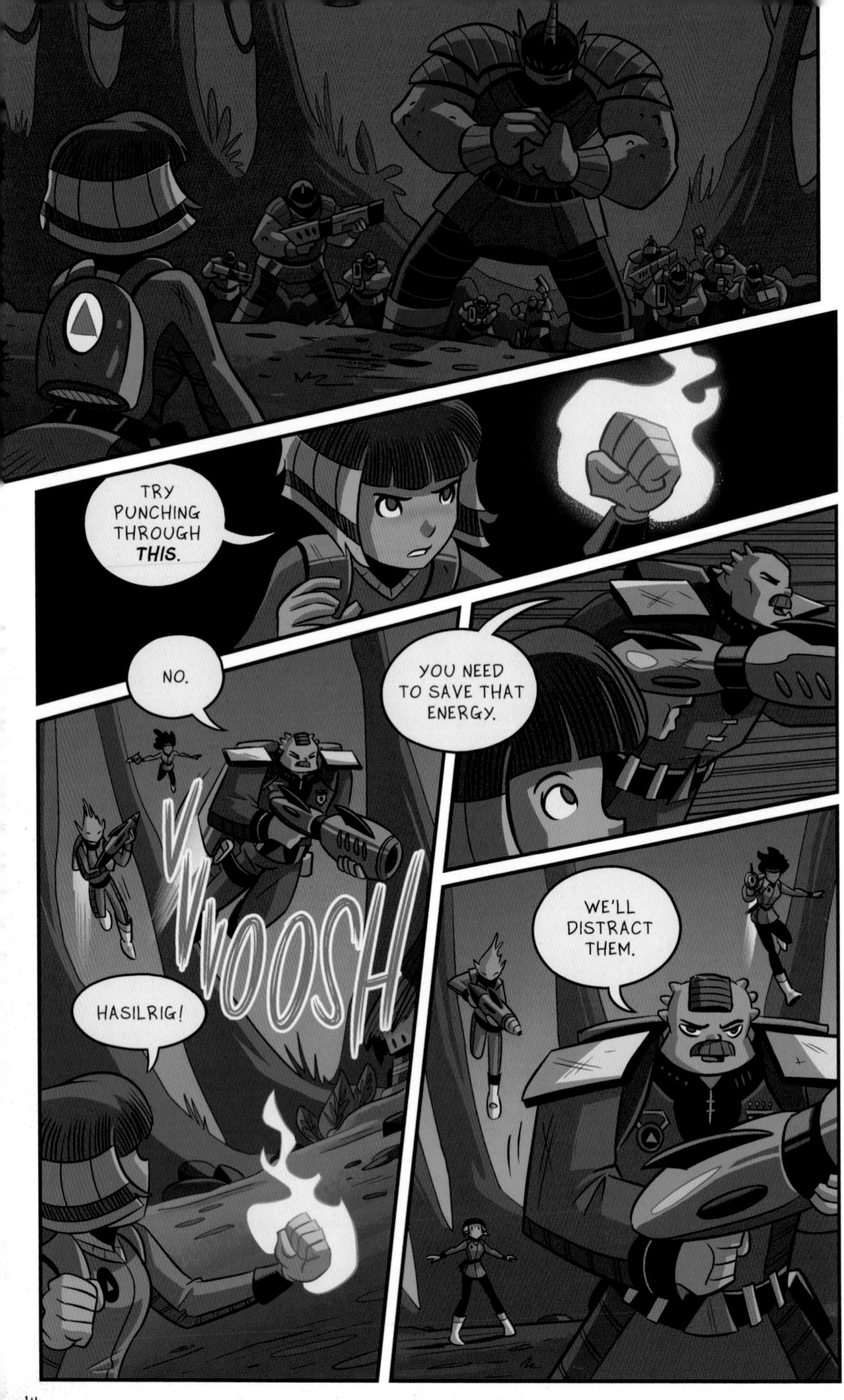
TRY PUNCHING THROUGH THIS.
NO.
YOU NEED TO SAVE THAT ENERGY.
VVWOOSH
HASILRIG!
WE'LL DISTRACT THEM.

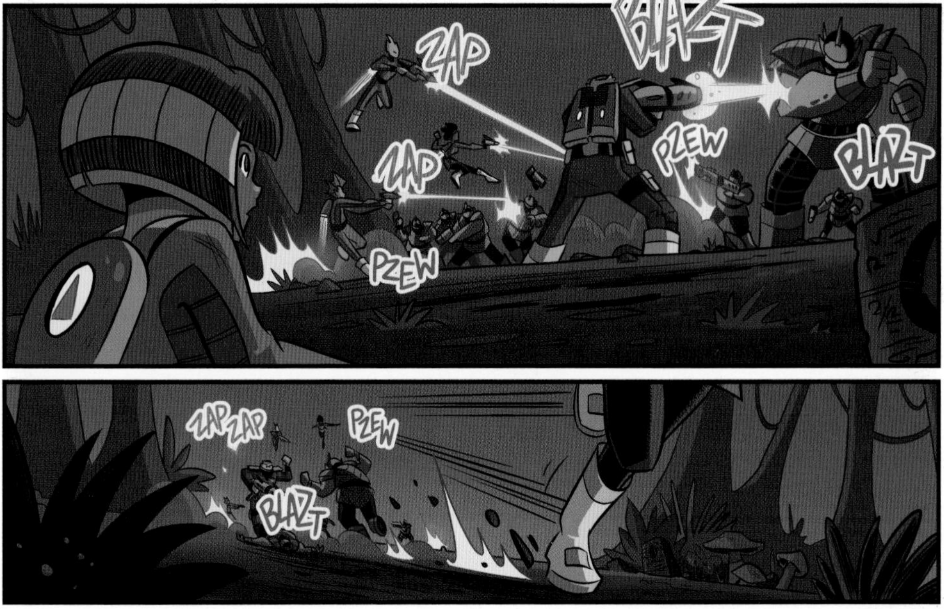
ZAP
BLAZT
ZAP
PZEW
BLAZT
PZEW
ZAP ZAP
PZEW
BLAZT

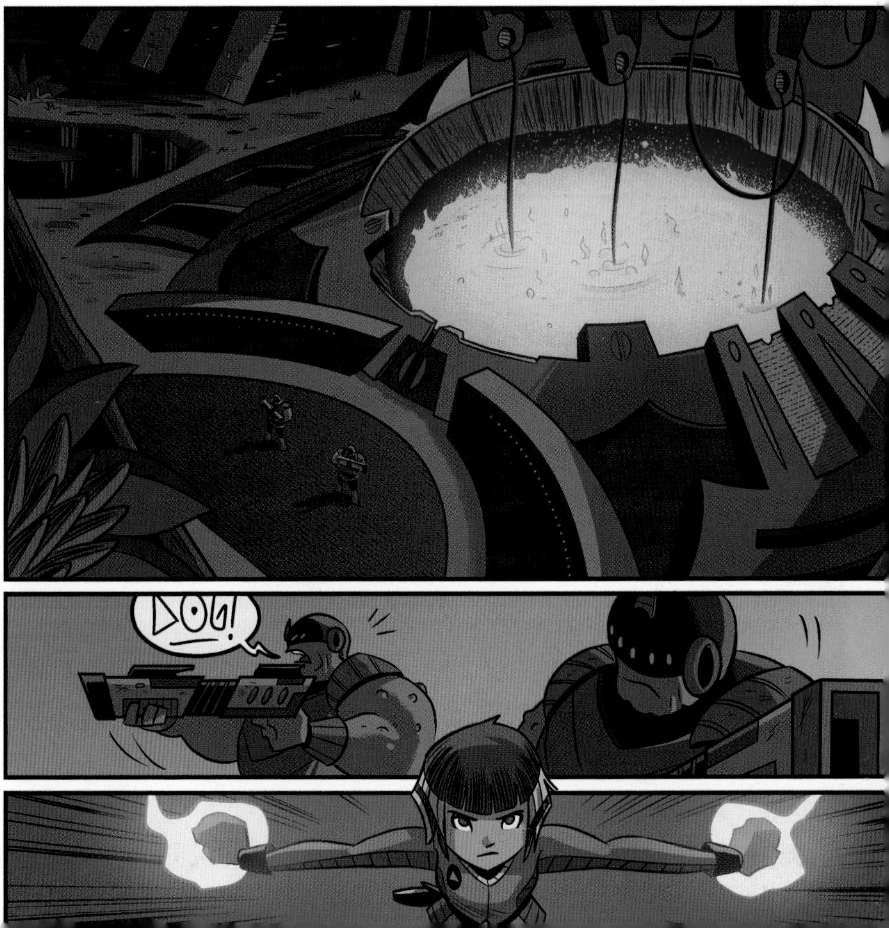
DOG!

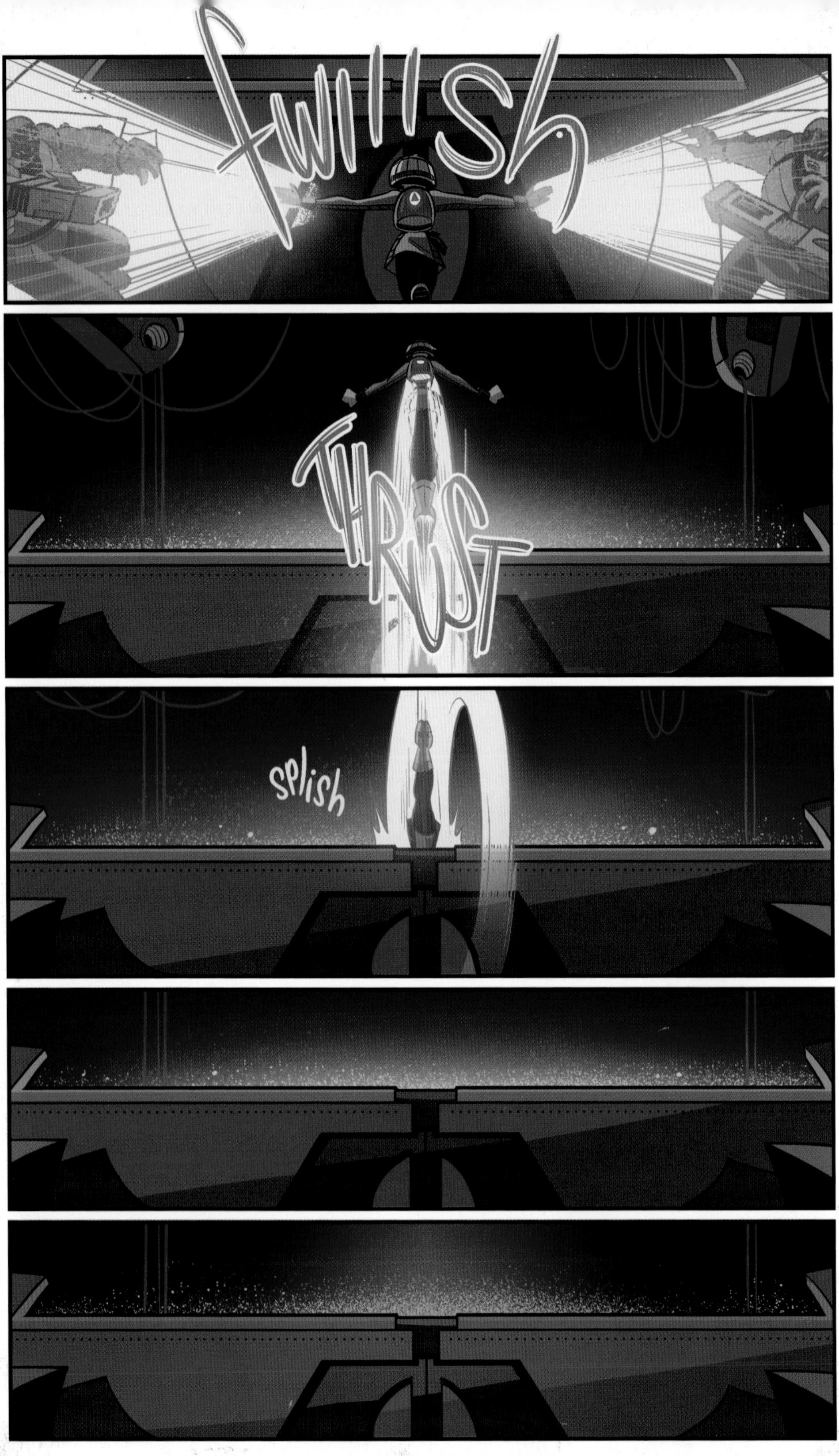
fwiiish
THRUST
splish

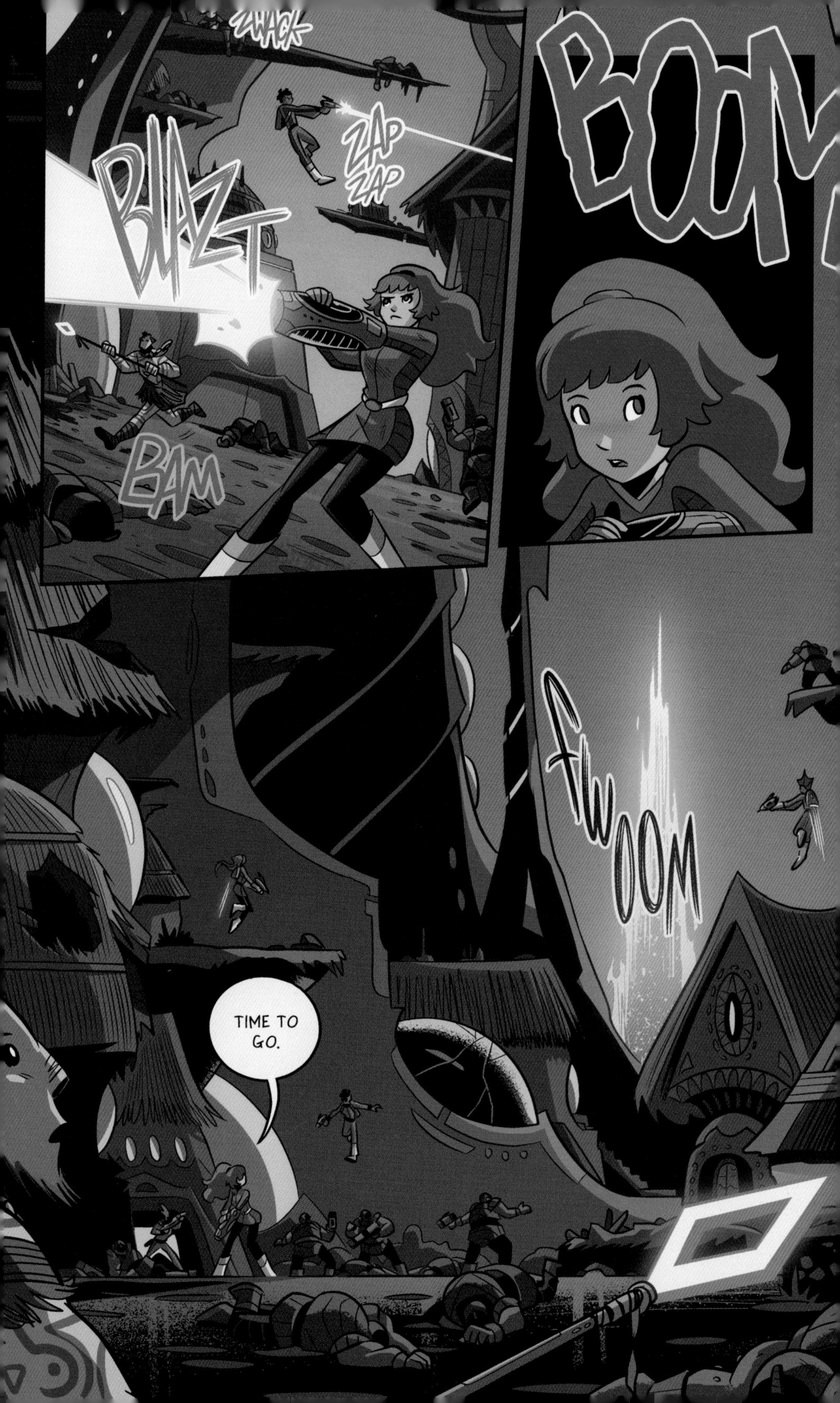
ZWACK
ZAP
ZAP
BLAZT
BAM
BOOM
FWOOM
TIME TO GO.

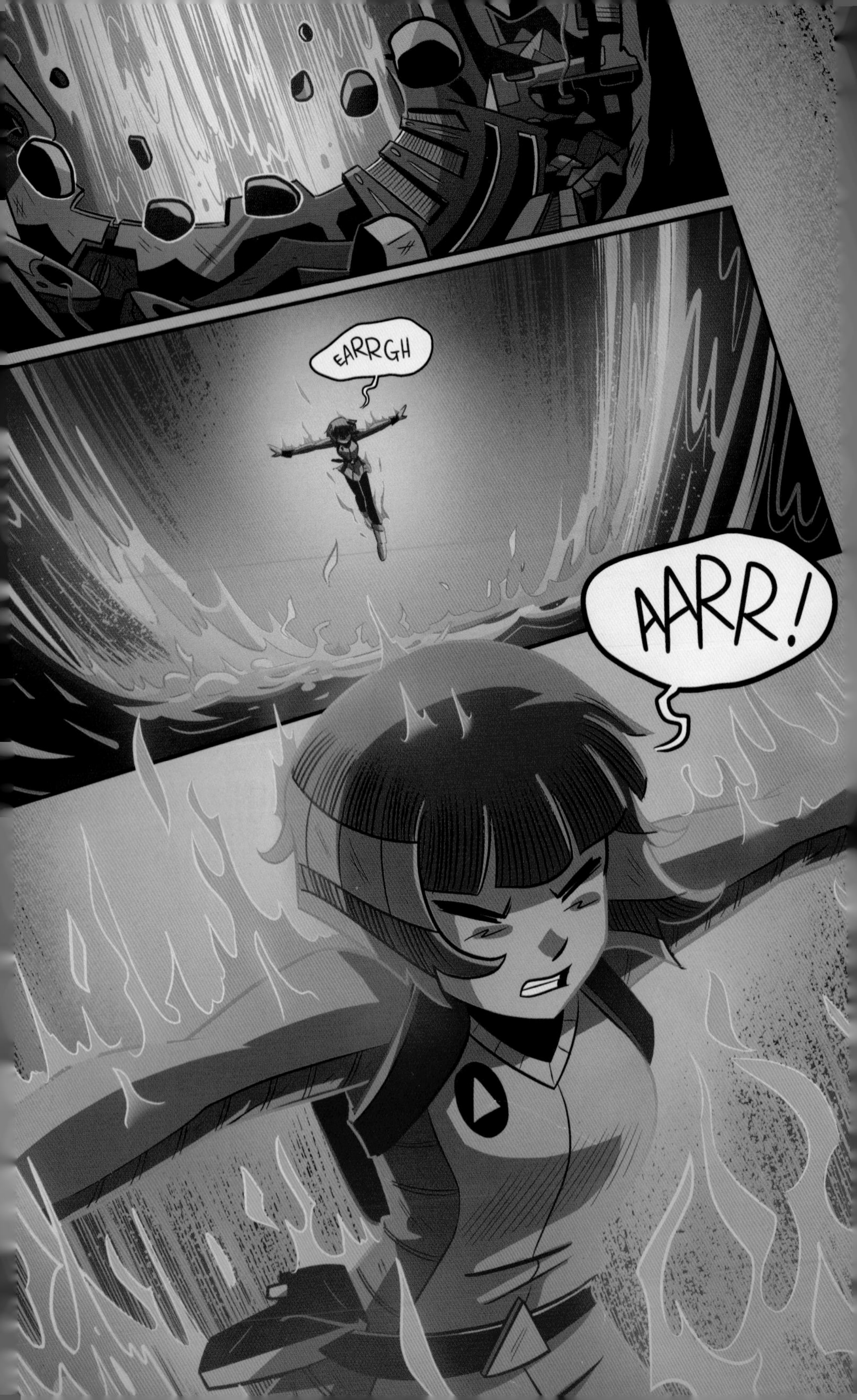
EARRGH
AARR!

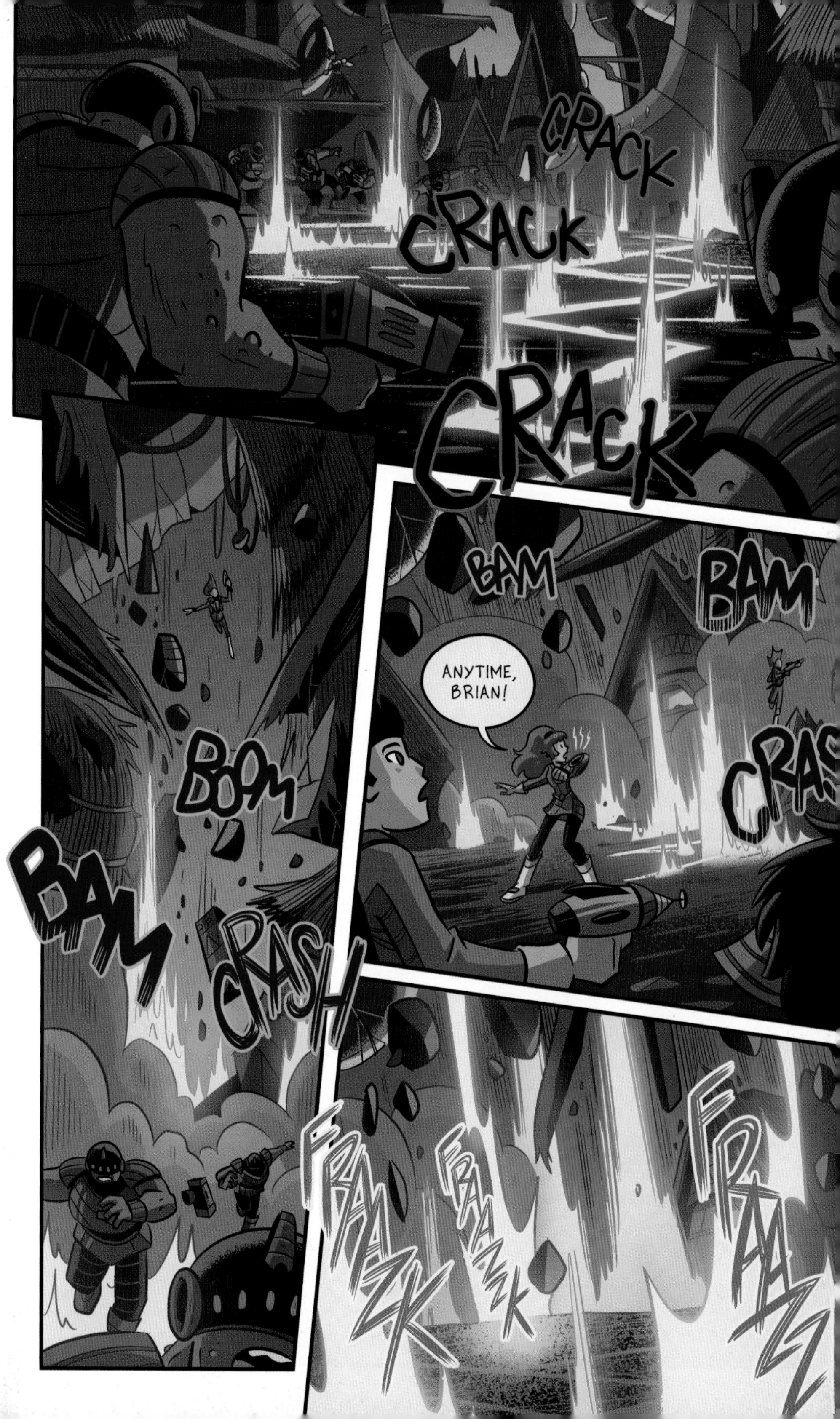
CRACK
CRACK
CRACK
BOOM
BAM
CRASH
BAM
BAM
ANYTIME, BRIAN!
CRAS
FRAAZK
FRAAZZK
FRAAZ

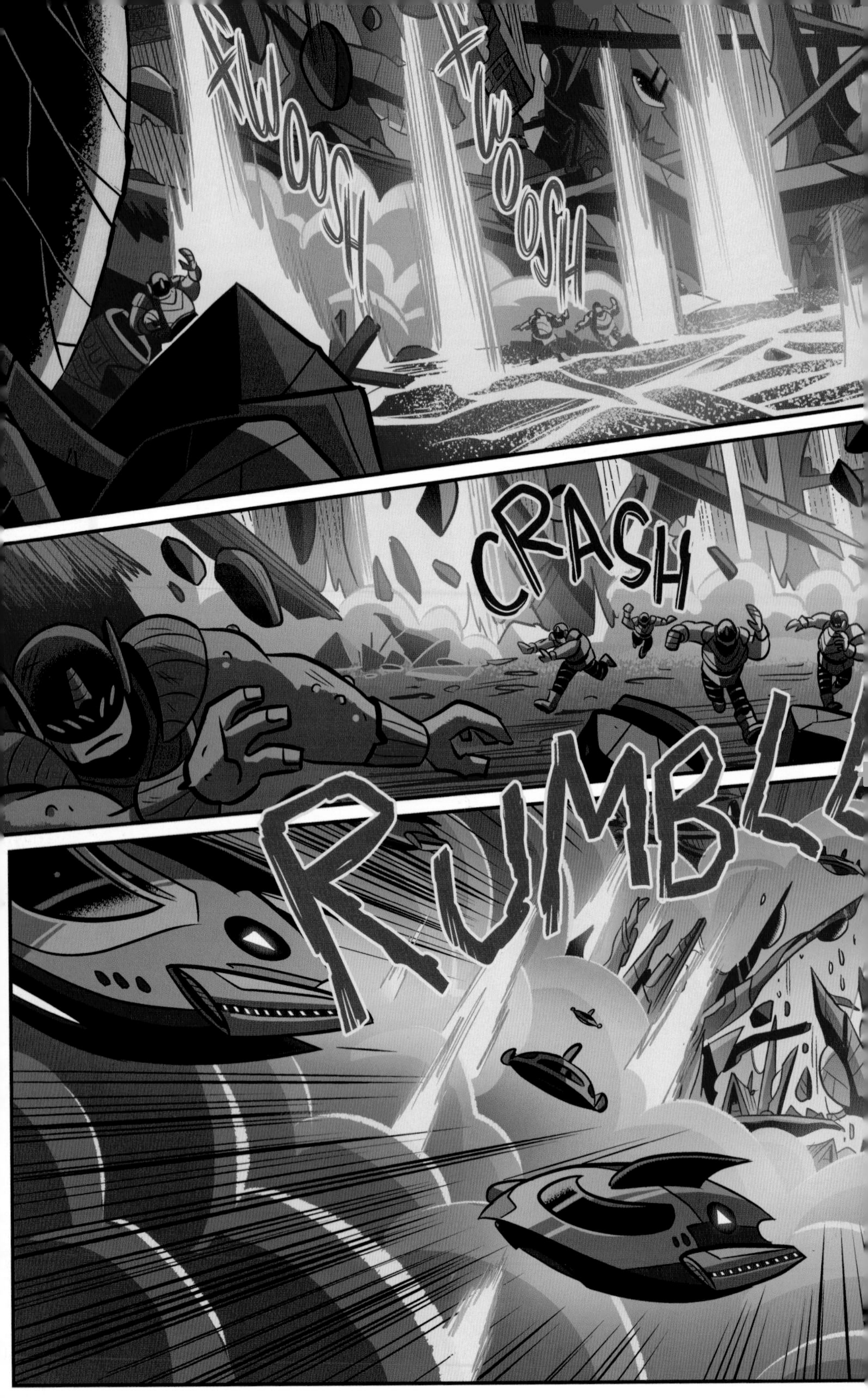
FWOOSH
FWOOSH
CRASH
RUMBL

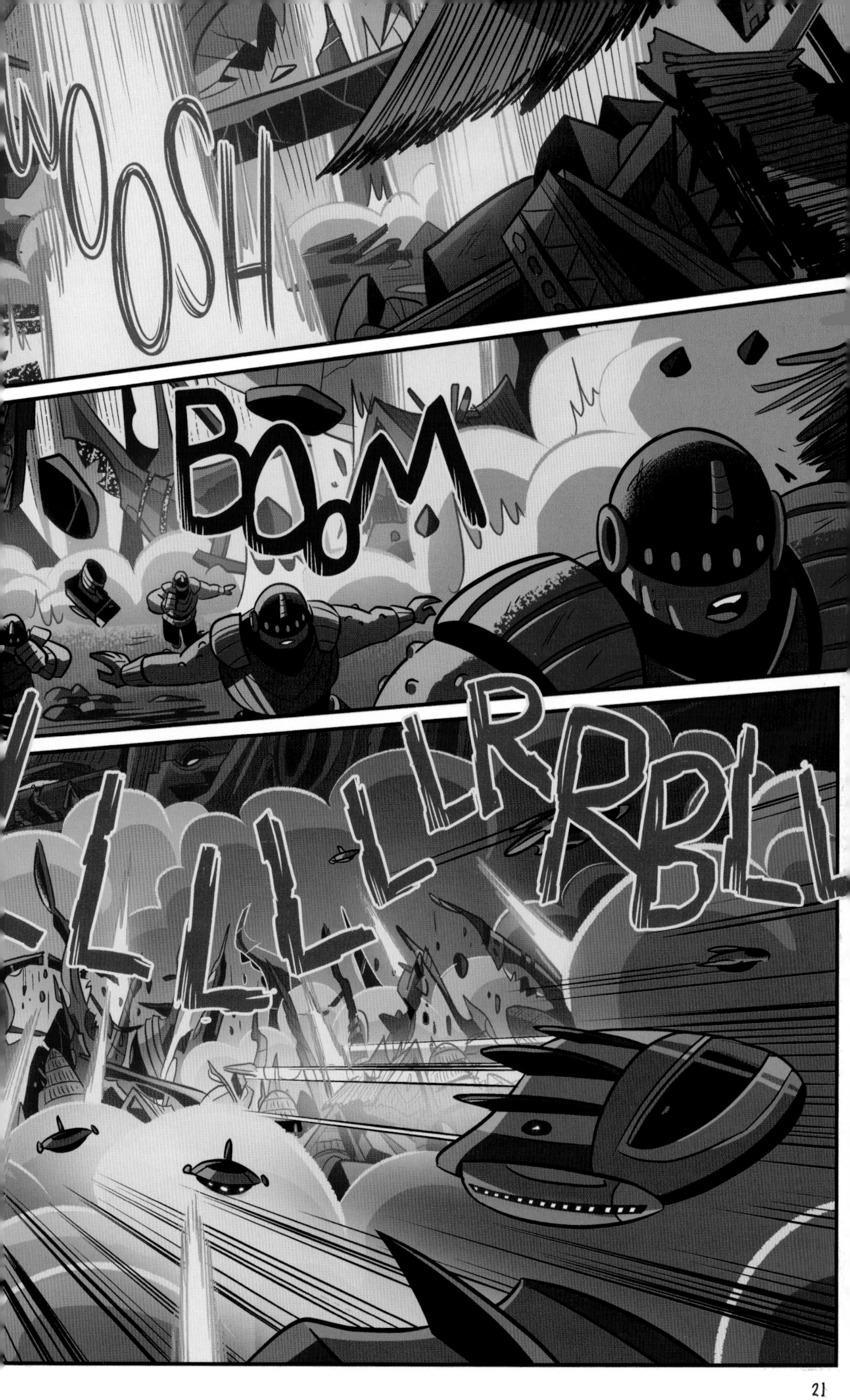
WOOSH
BOOM
LLLLLRRBLL

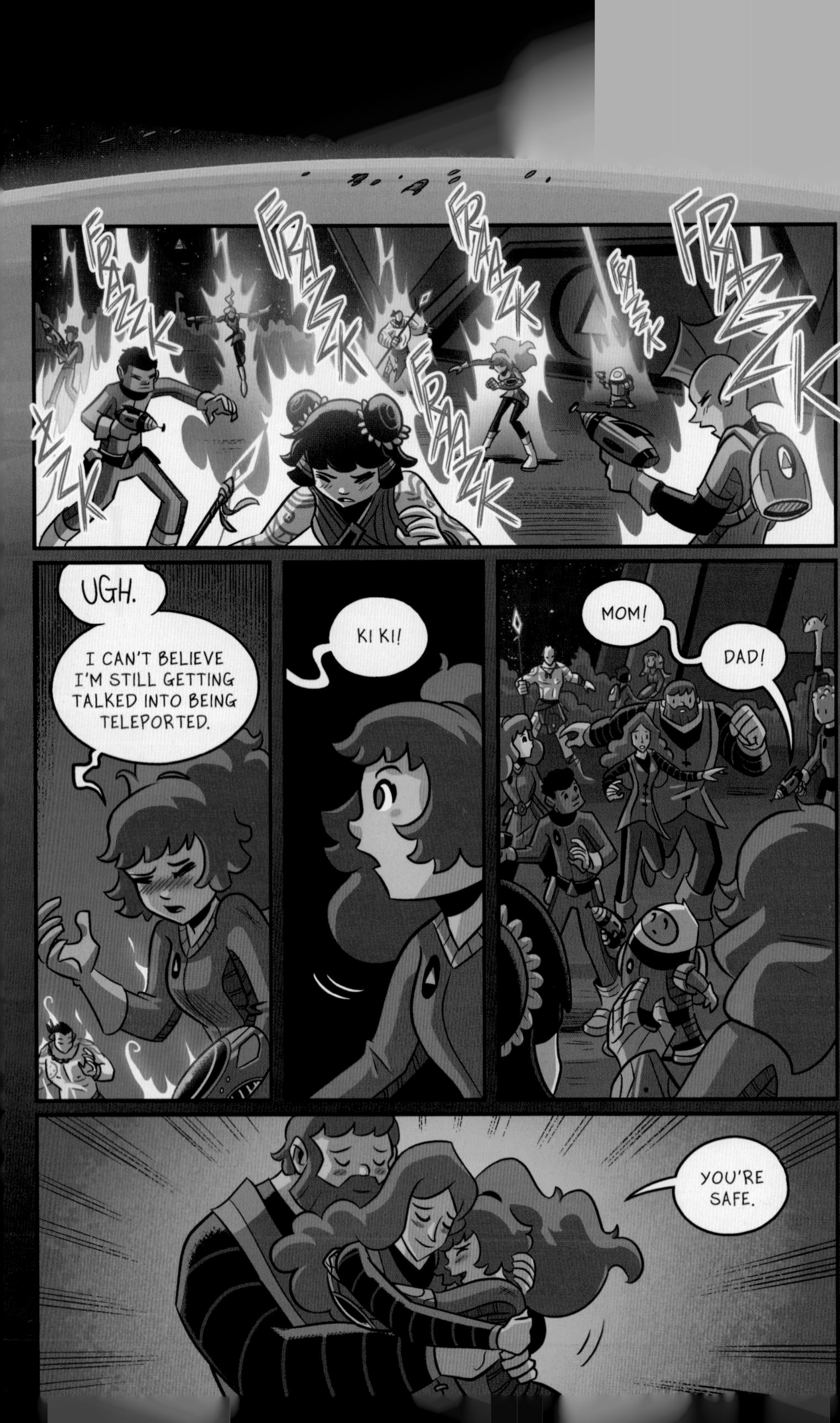
FRAZZZK
FRAAZZZK
FRAAZZK
FRAZZK
FRAAAZZK
FRAZZZK
ZZK
UGH.
I CAN'T BELIEVE I'M STILL GETTING TALKED INTO BEING TELEPORTED.
KI KI!
MOM!
DAD!
YOU'RE SAFE.

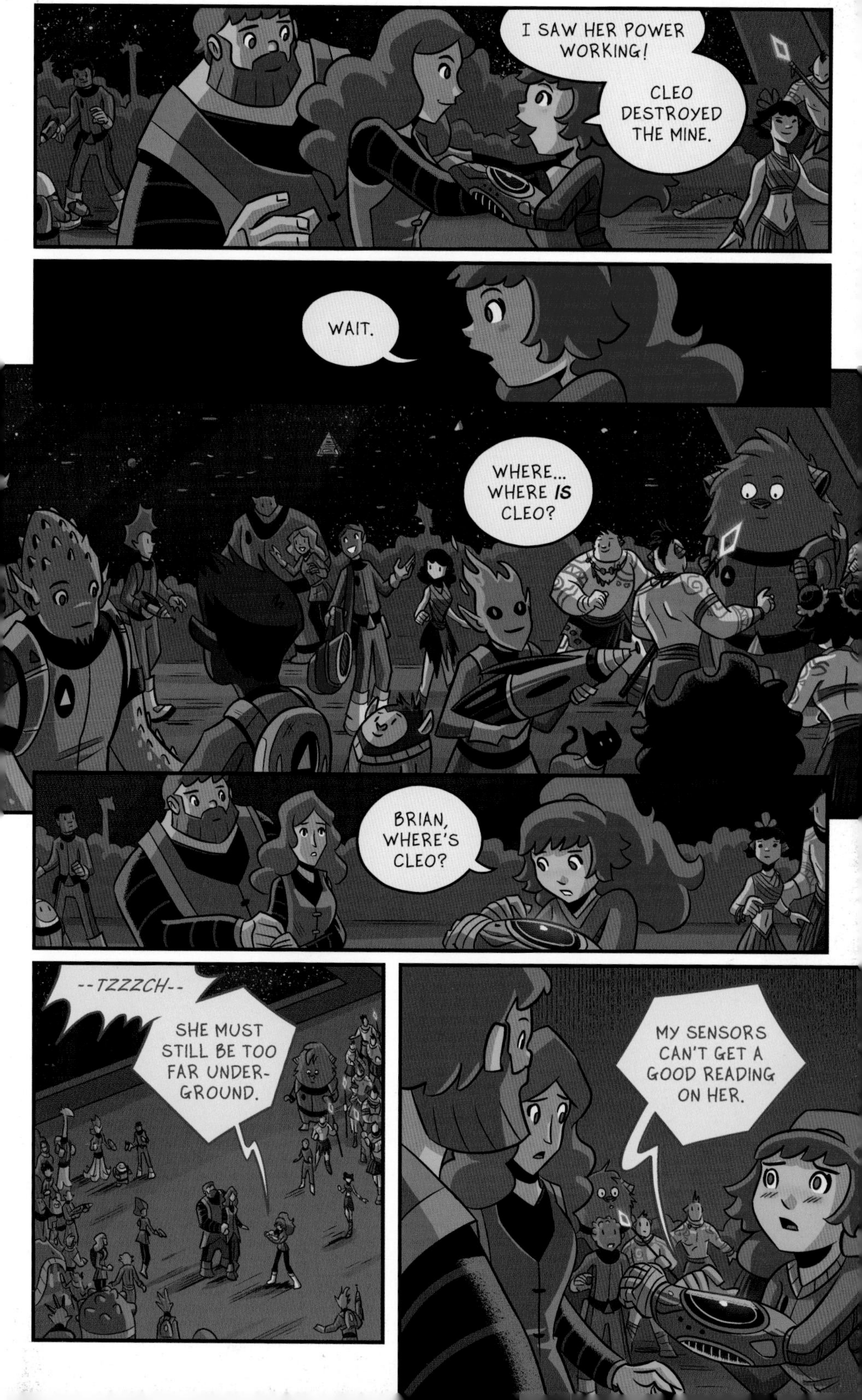
I SAW HER POWER WORKING!
CLEO DESTROYED THE MINE.
WAIT.
WHERE... WHERE *IS* CLEO?
BRIAN, WHERE'S CLEO?
--TZZZCH--
SHE MUST STILL BE TOO FAR UNDER-GROUND.
MY SENSORS CAN'T GET A GOOD READING ON HER.

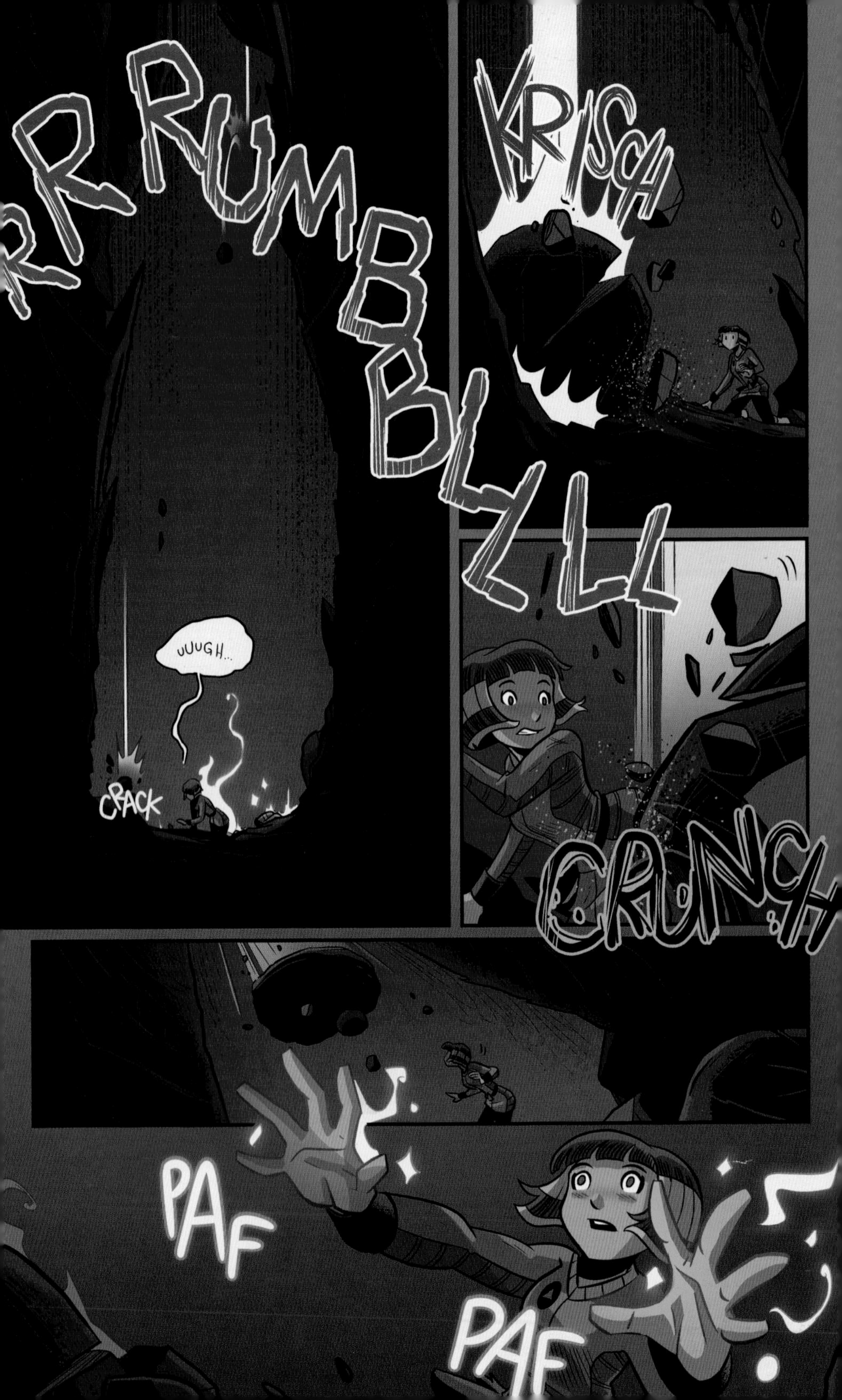
RRRUMBBLLLL
KRISCH
UUUGH...
CRACK
CRUNCH
PAF
PAF

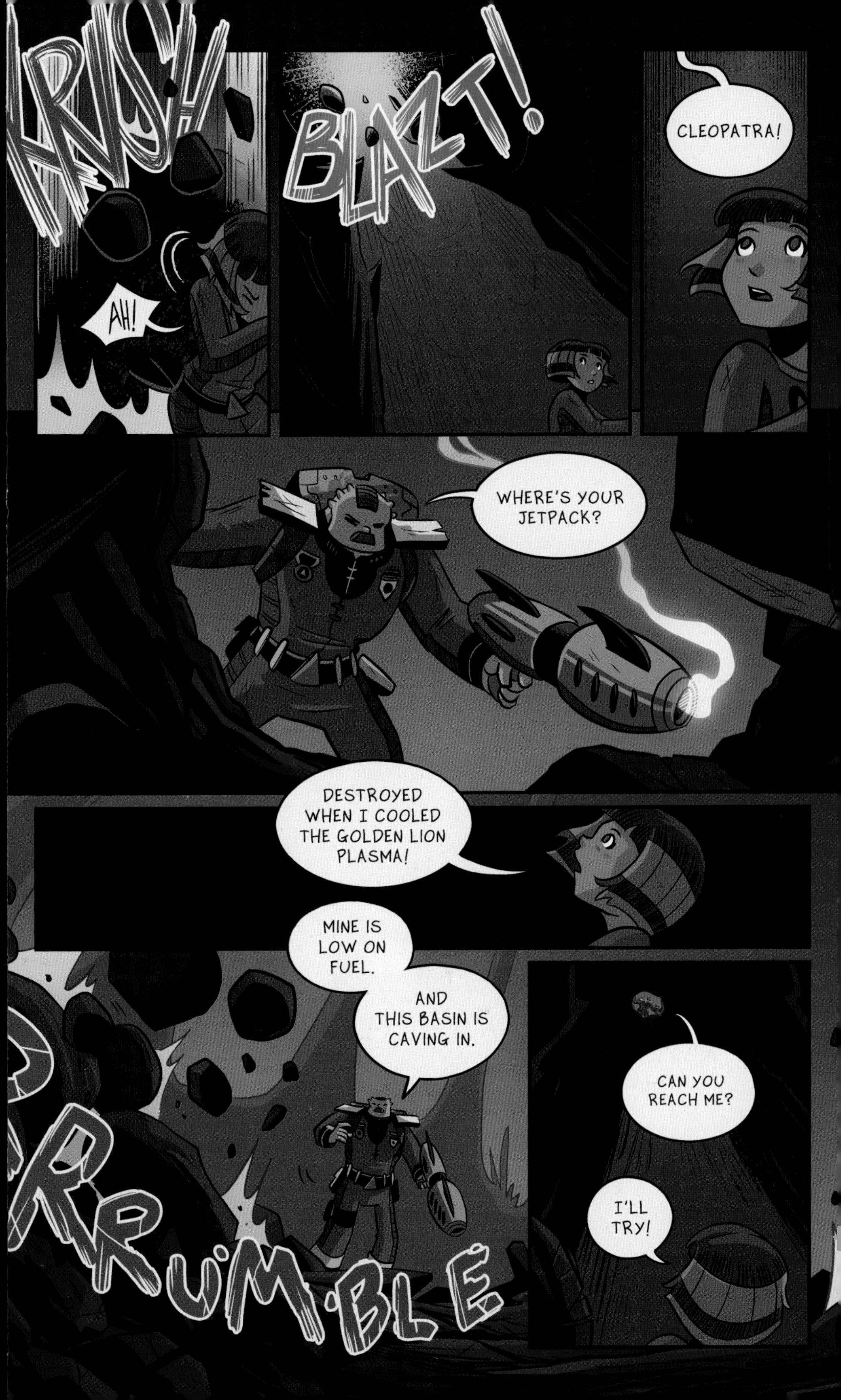
KRISH!
AH!
BLAZT!
CLEOPATRA!
WHERE'S YOUR JETPACK?
DESTROYED WHEN I COOLED THE GOLDEN LION PLASMA!
MINE IS LOW ON FUEL.
AND THIS BASIN IS CAVING IN.
RRRUMBLE
CAN YOU REACH ME?
I'LL TRY!

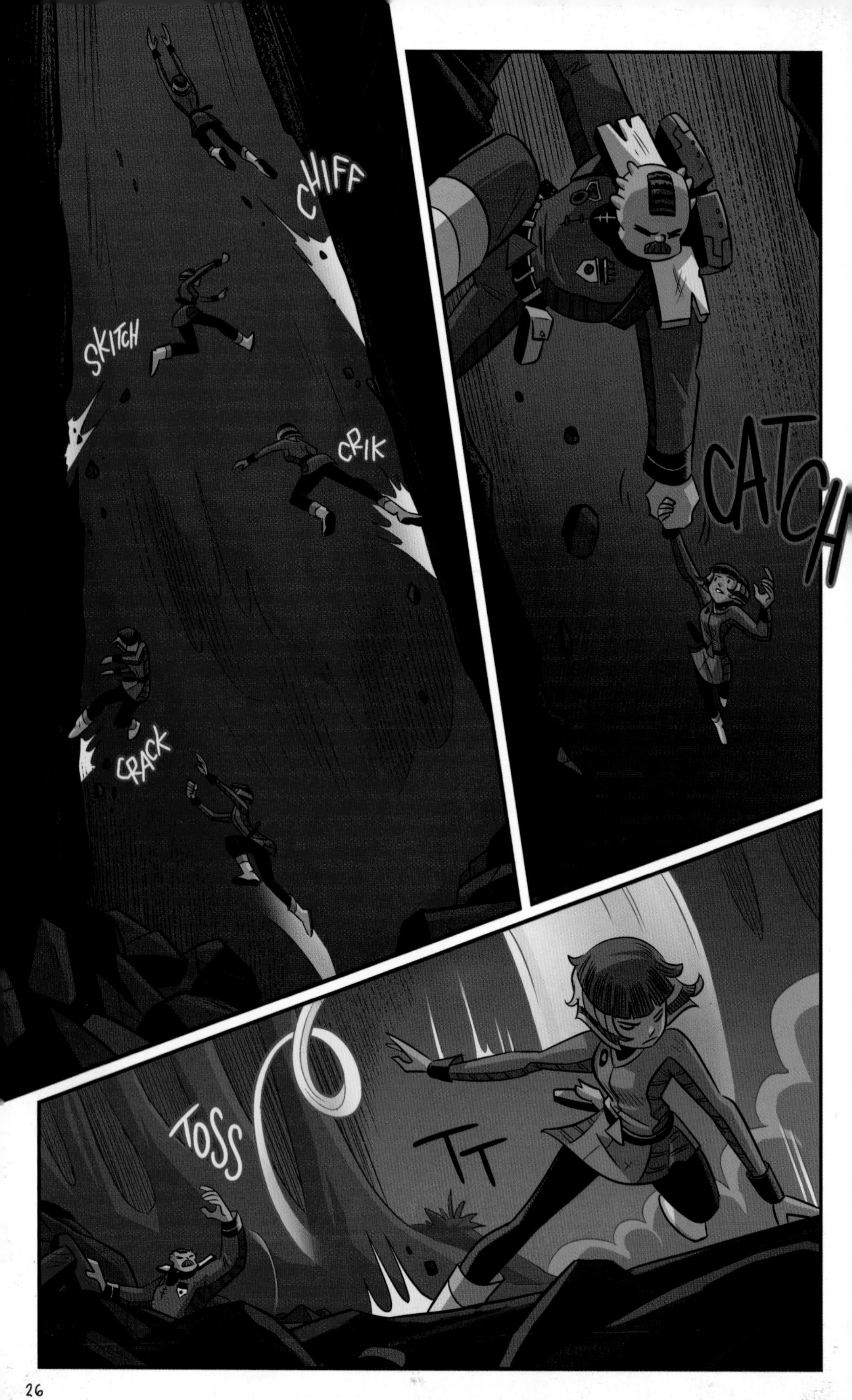
CHIFF
SKITCH
CRIK
CRACK
CATCH
TOSS
TT

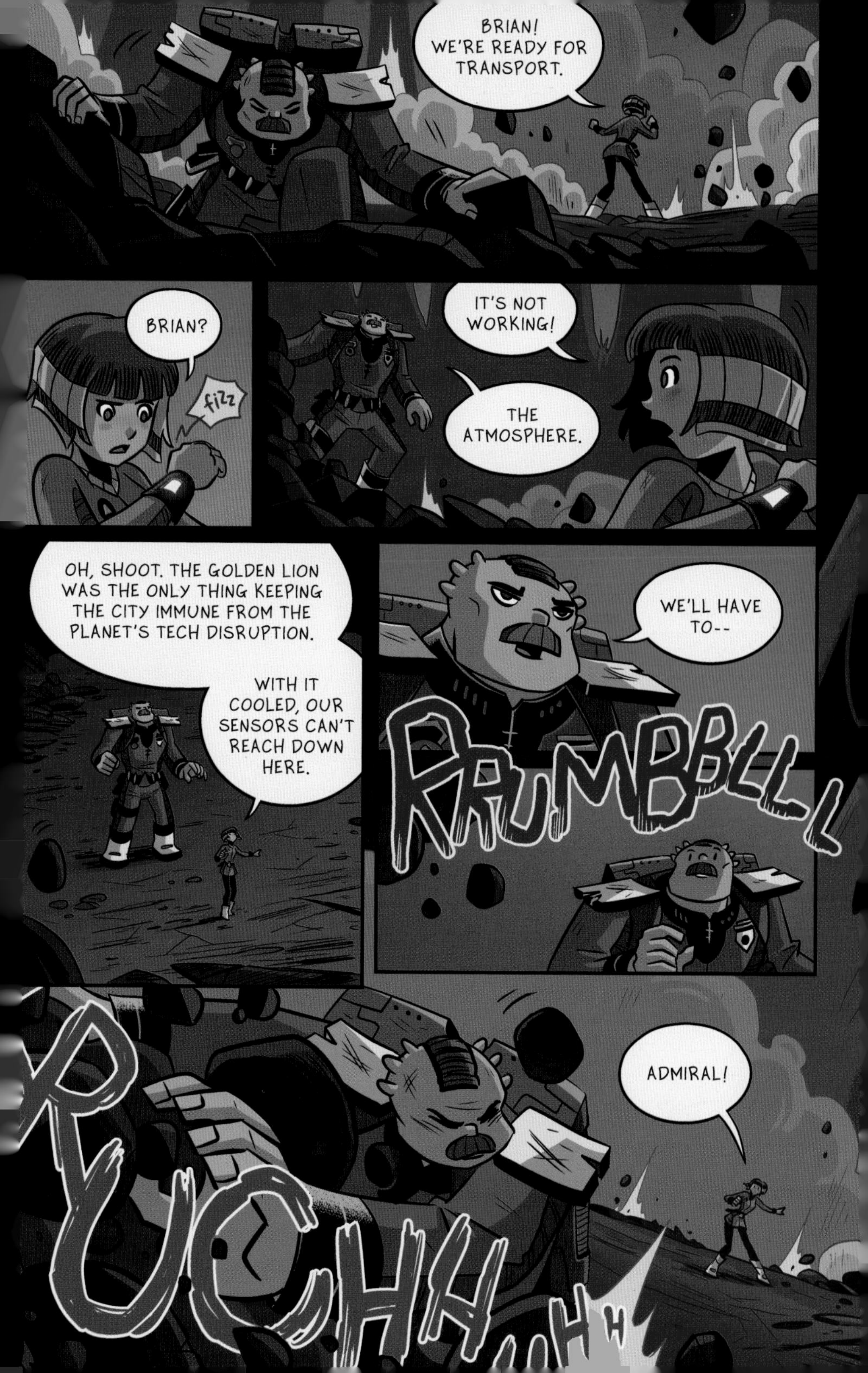
BRIAN! WE'RE READY FOR TRANSPORT.
BRIAN?
fizz
IT'S NOT WORKING!
THE ATMOSPHERE.
OH, SHOOT. THE GOLDEN LION WAS THE ONLY THING KEEPING THE CITY IMMUNE FROM THE PLANET'S TECH DISRUPTION.
WITH IT COOLED, OUR SENSORS CAN'T REACH DOWN HERE.
WE'LL HAVE TO--
RRUMBBLLL
ADMIRAL!
RUCHH...HH

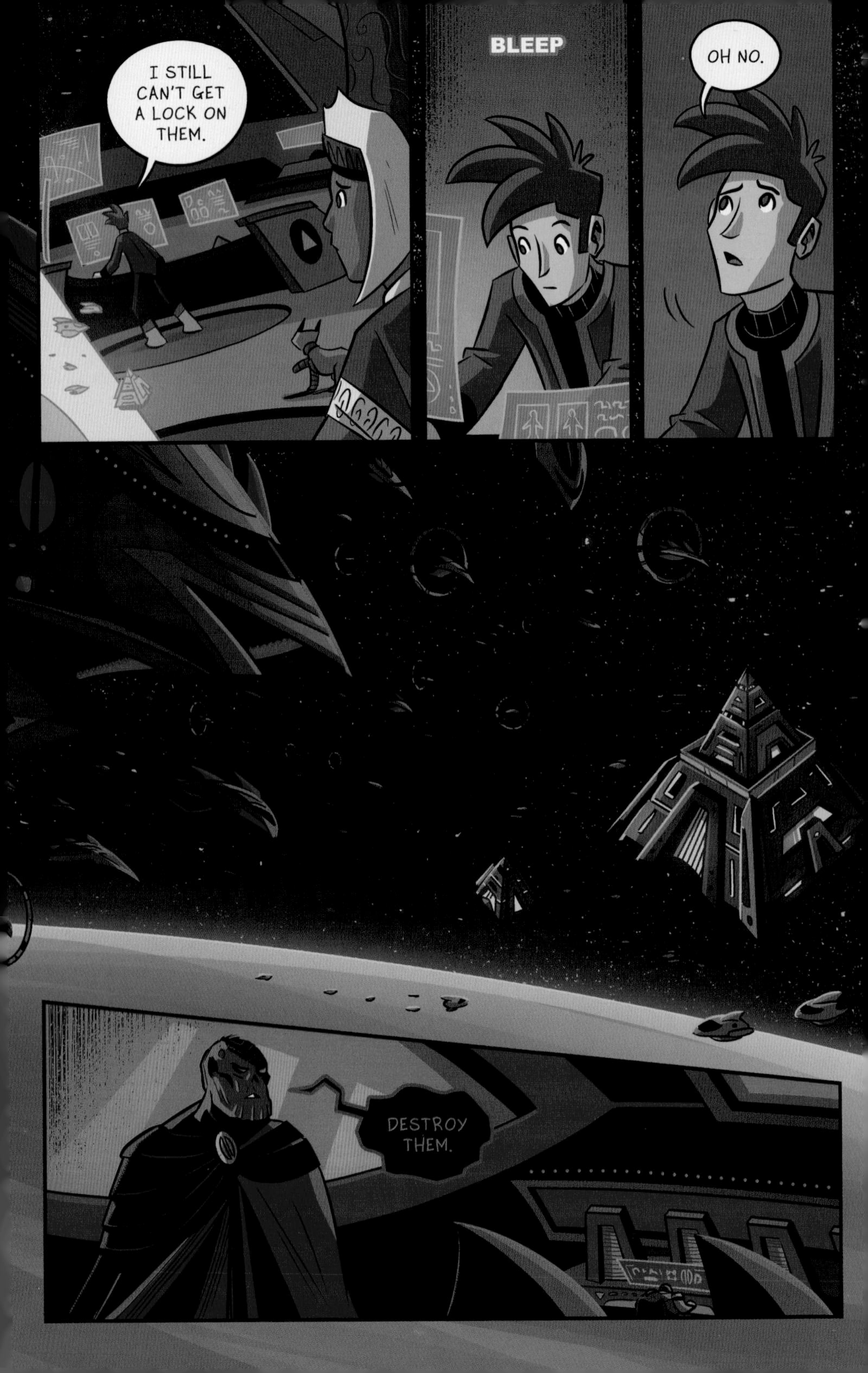
I STILL CAN'T GET A LOCK ON THEM.
BLEEP
OH NO.
DESTROY THEM.

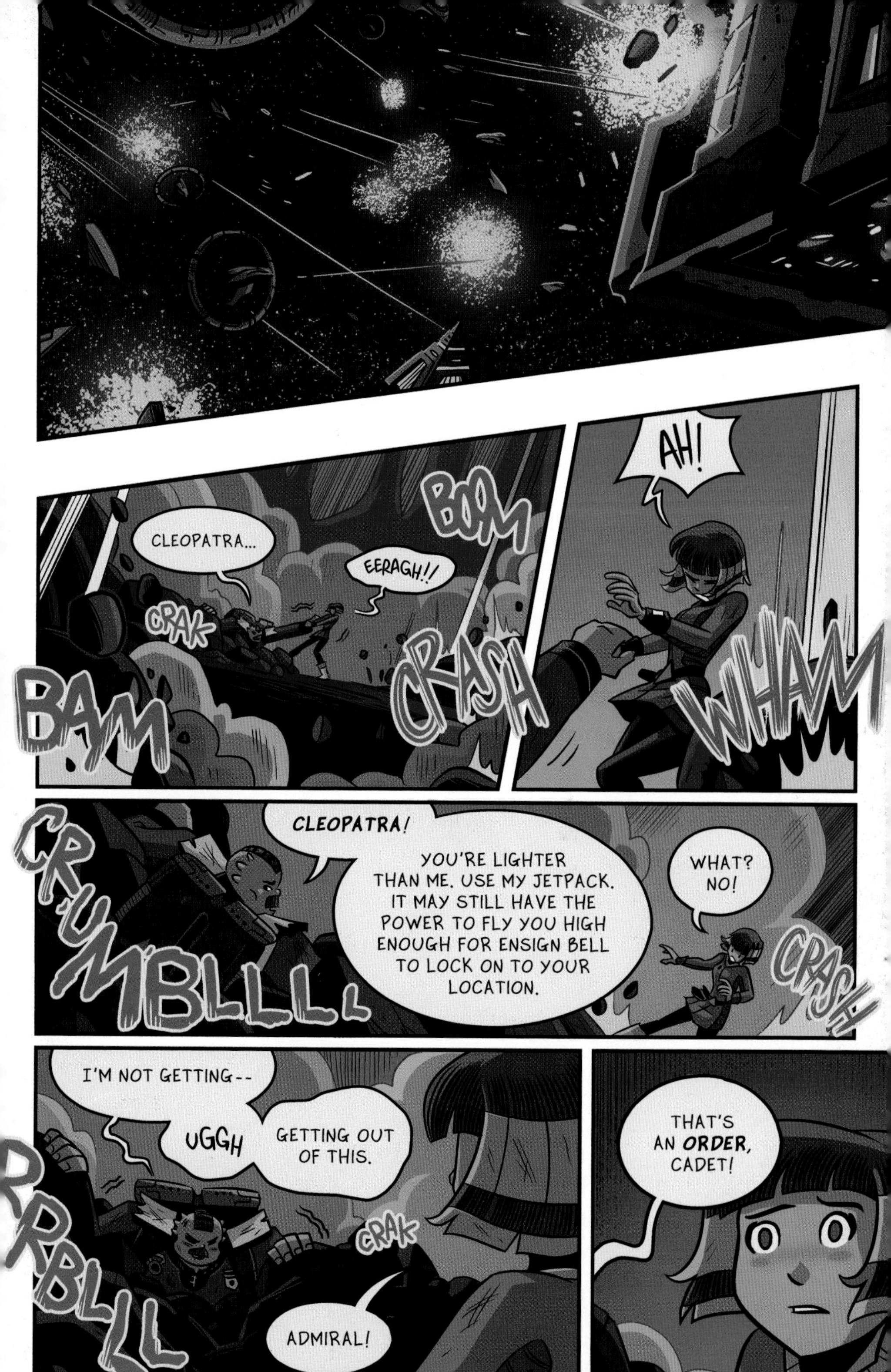
CLEOPATRA...
EERAGH!!
BOOM
CRAK
BAM
CRASH
AH!
WHAM
CLEOPATRA!
YOU'RE LIGHTER THAN ME. USE MY JETPACK. IT MAY STILL HAVE THE POWER TO FLY YOU HIGH ENOUGH FOR ENSIGN BELL TO LOCK ON TO YOUR LOCATION.
CRUMBLLLL
WHAT? NO!
CRASH
I'M NOT GETTING--
UGGH
GETTING OUT OF THIS.
RRBLLL
CRAK
ADMIRAL!
THAT'S AN ORDER, CADET!

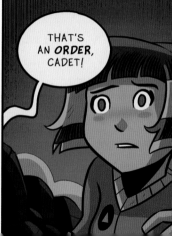

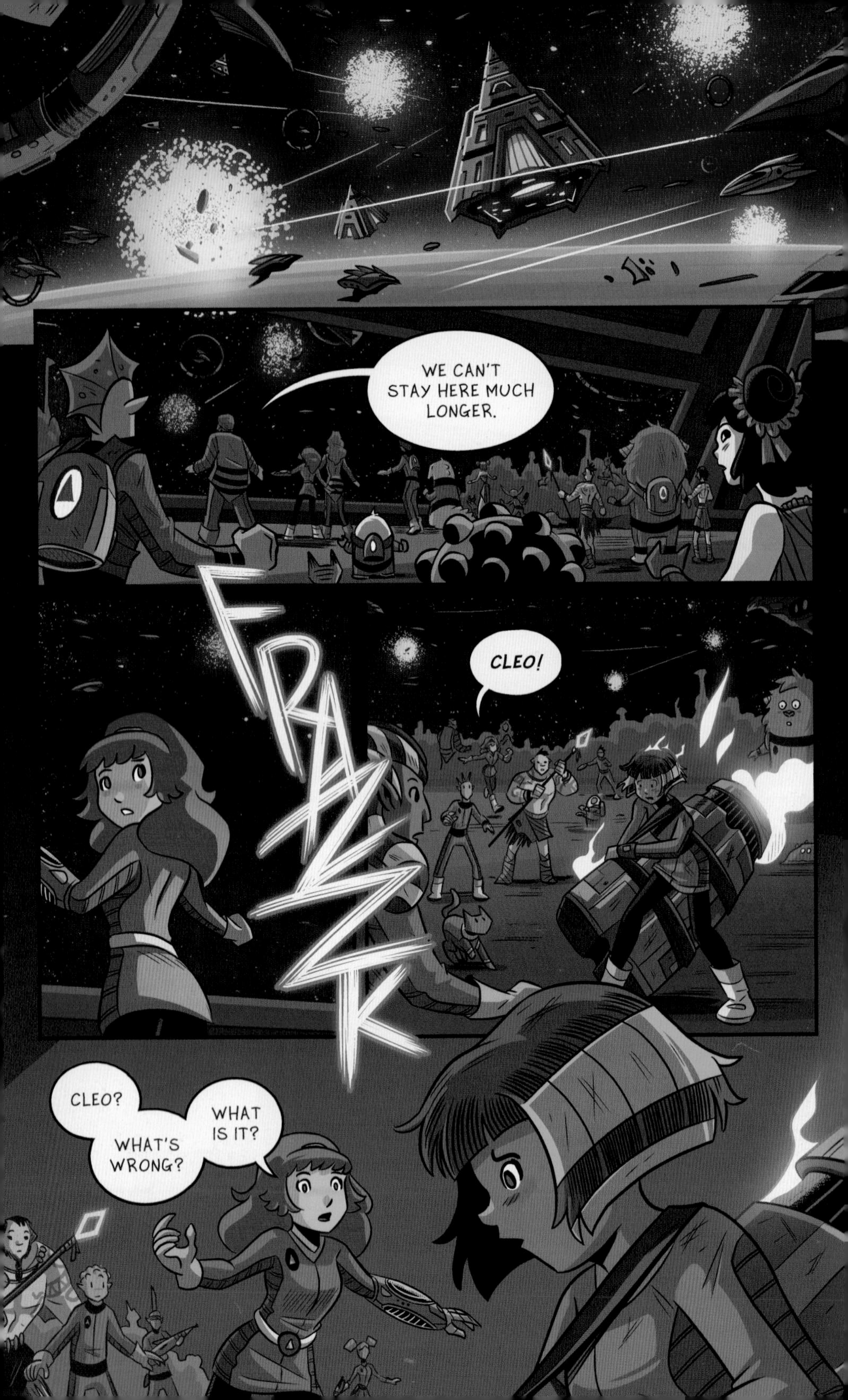
WE CAN'T STAY HERE MUCH LONGER.
FRAZZZK
CLEO!
CLEO?
WHAT'S WRONG?
WHAT IS IT?

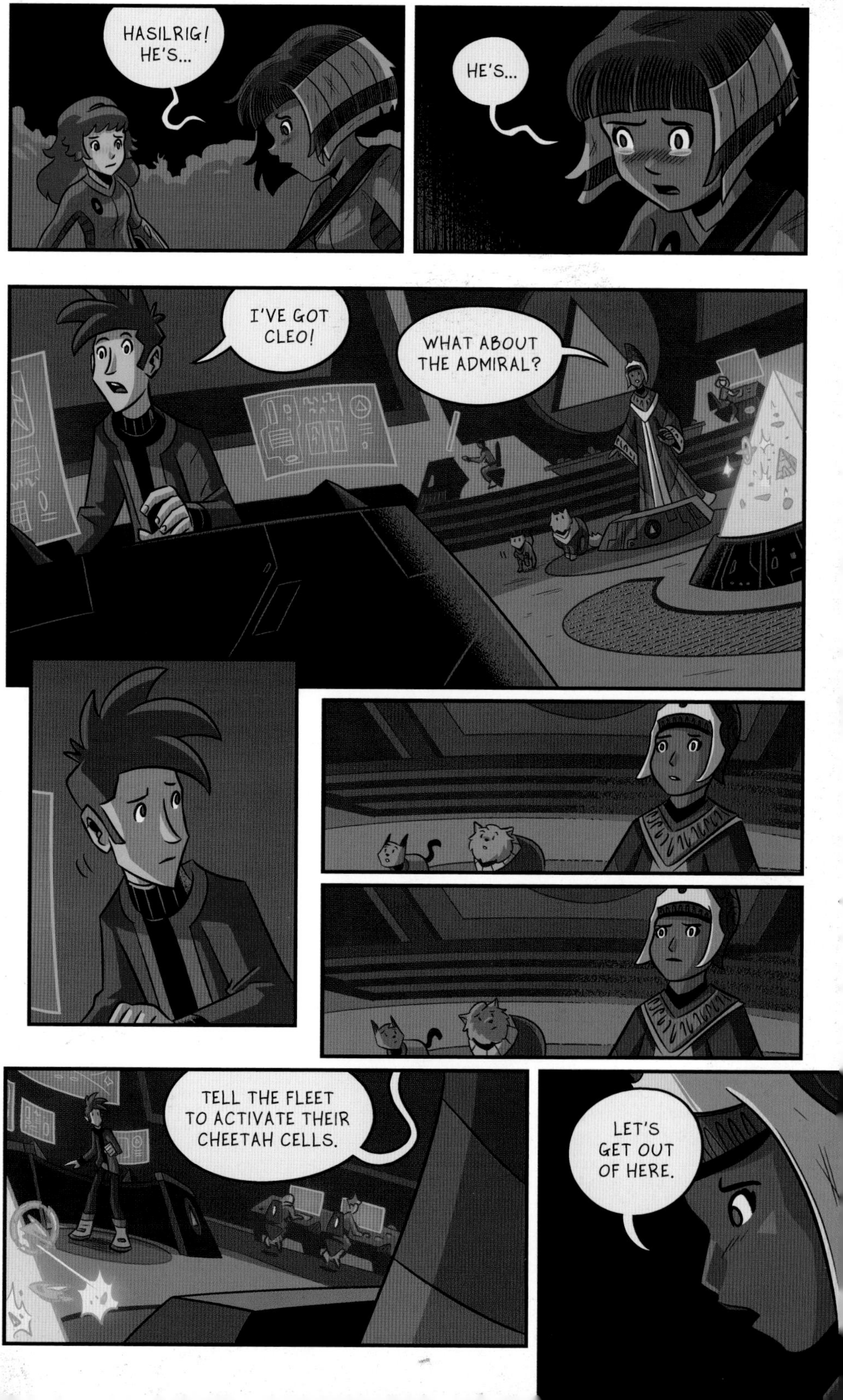
HASILRIG! HE'S...
HE'S...
I'VE GOT CLEO!
WHAT ABOUT THE ADMIRAL?
TELL THE FLEET TO ACTIVATE THEIR CHEETAH CELLS.
LET'S GET OUT OF HERE.

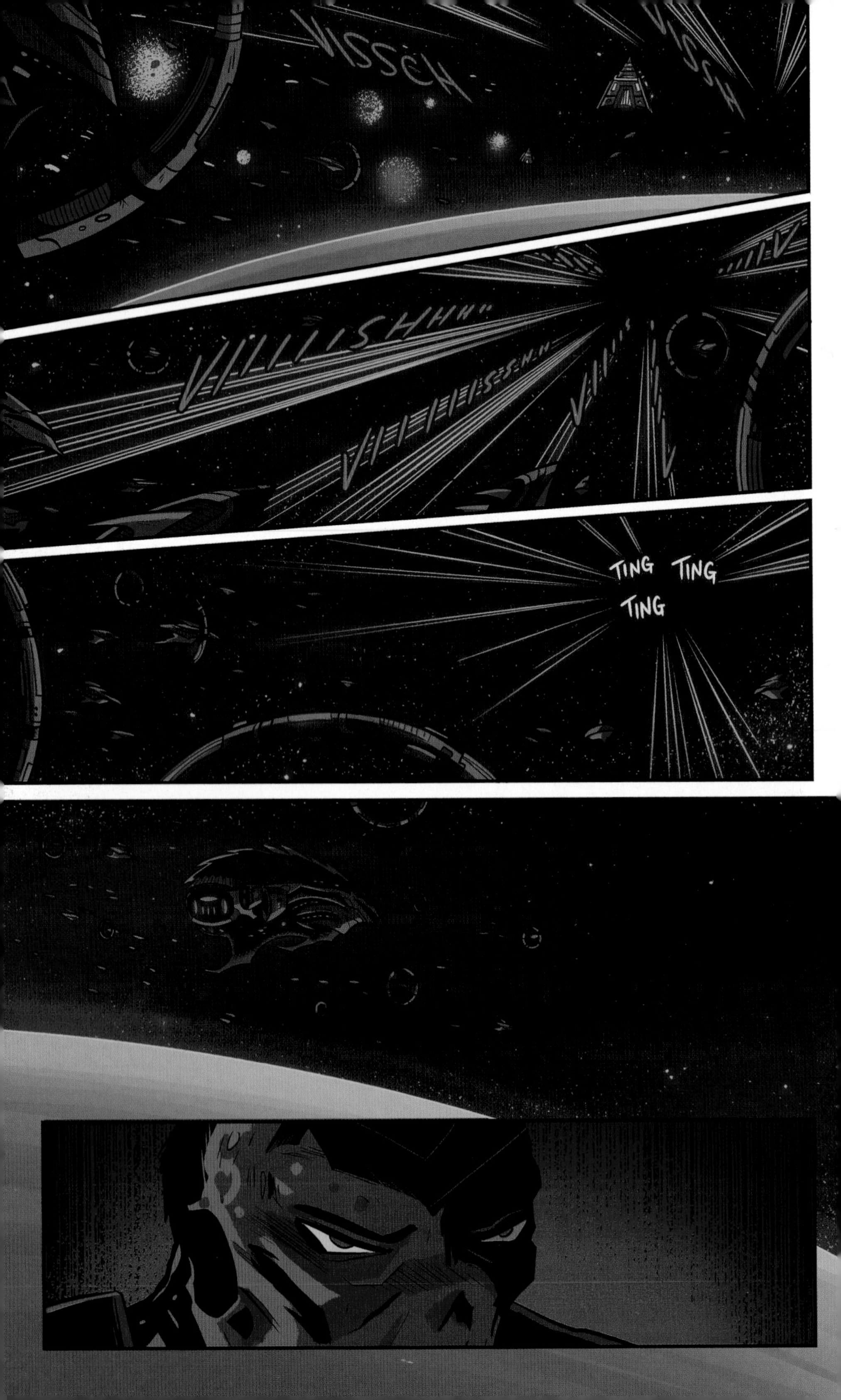
VISSCH
VISSCH
VIIIIISHHH
VIIIIIISSHH
TING TING
TING

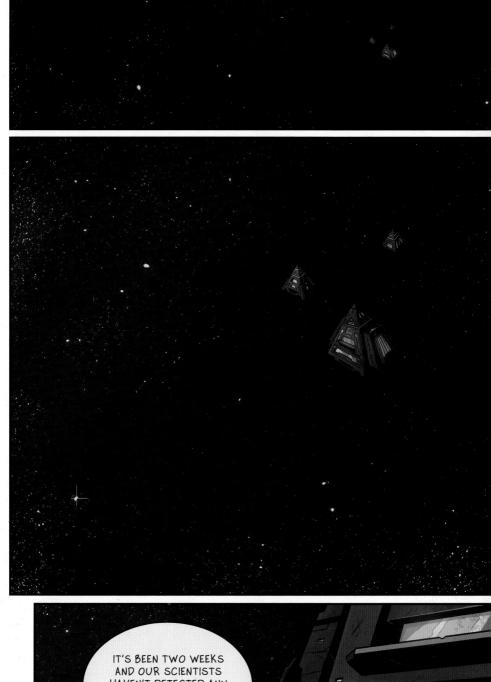

IT'S BEEN TWO WEEKS AND OUR SCIENTISTS HAVEN'T DETECTED ANY TRACE OF THE GOLDEN LION PLASMA LEFT ON CADA'DUUN.

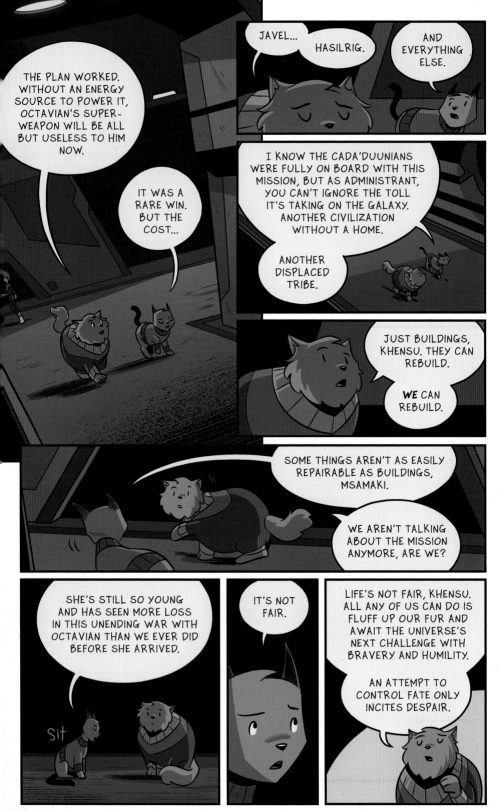

THE PLAN WORKED. WITHOUT AN ENERGY SOURCE TO POWER IT, OCTAVIAN'S SUPER-WEAPON WILL BE ALL BUT USELESS TO HIM NOW.

IT WAS A RARE WIN. BUT THE COST...

JAVEL...

HASILRIG.

AND EVERYTHING ELSE.

I KNOW THE CADA'DUUNIANS WERE FULLY ON BOARD WITH THIS MISSION, BUT AS ADMINISTRANT, YOU CAN'T IGNORE THE TOLL IT'S TAKING ON THE GALAXY. ANOTHER CIVILIZATION WITHOUT A HOME.

ANOTHER DISPLACED TRIBE.

JUST BUILDINGS, KHENSU. THEY CAN REBUILD.

WE CAN REBUILD.

SOME THINGS AREN'T AS EASILY REPAIRABLE AS BUILDINGS, MSAMAKI.

WE AREN'T TALKING ABOUT THE MISSION ANYMORE, ARE WE?

SHE'S STILL SO YOUNG AND HAS SEEN MORE LOSS IN THIS UNENDING WAR WITH OCTAVIAN THAN WE EVER DID BEFORE SHE ARRIVED.

Sit

IT'S NOT FAIR.

LIFE'S NOT FAIR, KHENSU. ALL ANY OF US CAN DO IS FLUFF UP OUR FUR AND AWAIT THE UNIVERSE'S NEXT CHALLENGE WITH BRAVERY AND HUMILITY.

AN ATTEMPT TO CONTROL FATE ONLY INCITES DESPAIR.

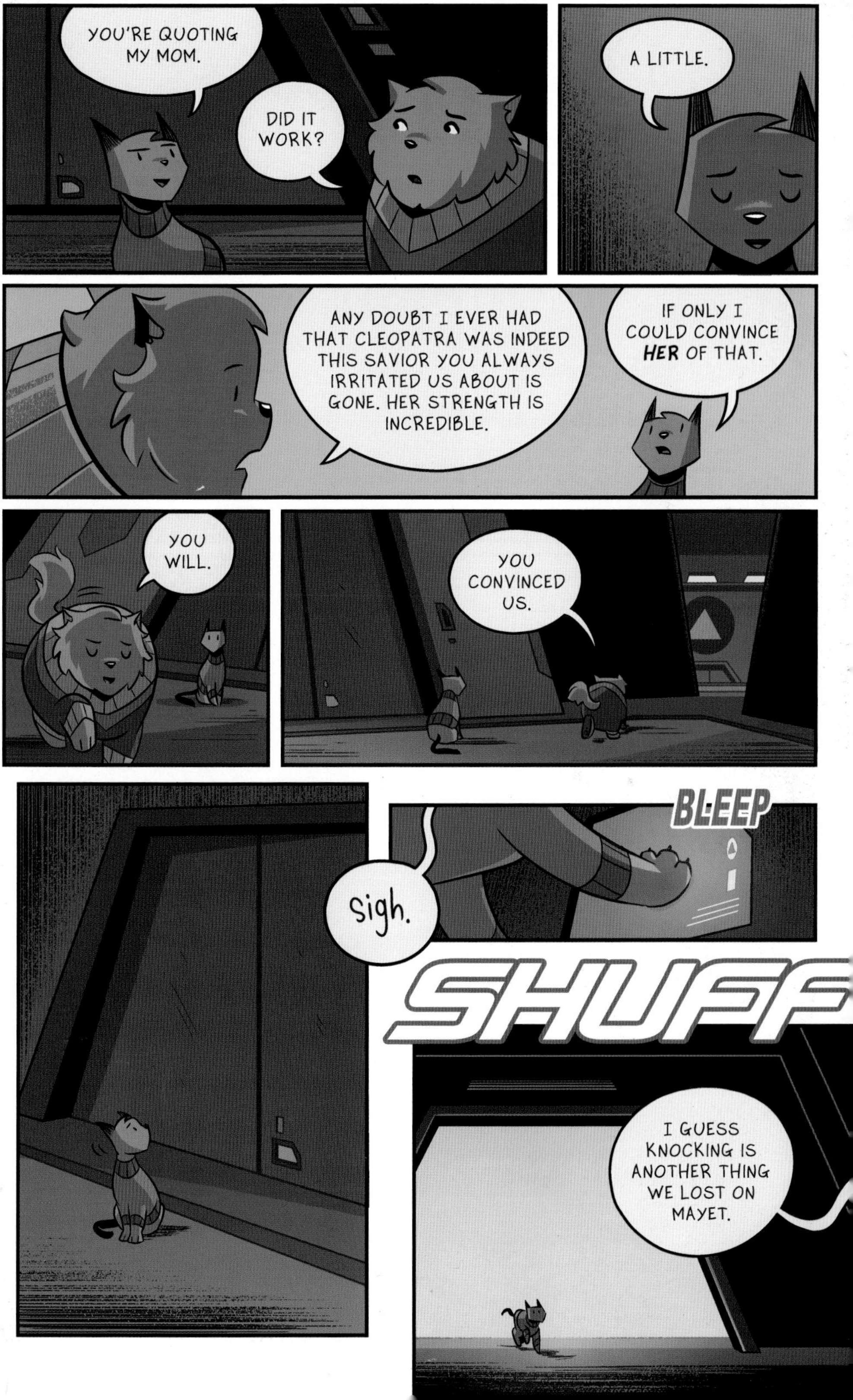
YOU'RE QUOTING MY MOM.
DID IT WORK?
A LITTLE.
ANY DOUBT I EVER HAD THAT CLEOPATRA WAS INDEED THIS SAVIOR YOU ALWAYS IRRITATED US ABOUT IS GONE. HER STRENGTH IS INCREDIBLE.
IF ONLY I COULD CONVINCE **HER** OF THAT.
YOU WILL.
YOU CONVINCED US.
BLEEP
sigh.
SHUFF
I GUESS KNOCKING IS ANOTHER THING WE LOST ON MAYET.

YOU...UM... MISSED ANOTHER ONE OF MY HISTORY LESSONS.

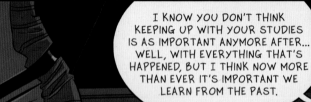

I KNOW YOU DON'T THINK KEEPING UP WITH YOUR STUDIES IS AS IMPORTANT ANYMORE AFTER... WELL, WITH EVERYTHING THAT'S HAPPENED, BUT I THINK NOW MORE THAN EVER IT'S IMPORTANT WE LEARN FROM THE PAST.

SHIFF

THERE ARE MANY OF US-- MOST OF US, ACTUALLY-- WHO FEEL WE CAN LEARN A LOT FROM YOU AS WELL.

THE PROPHECY STILL STATES THAT THE QUEEN OF THE NILE WILL LIGHT THE DARKNESS THAT--

STOP IT!

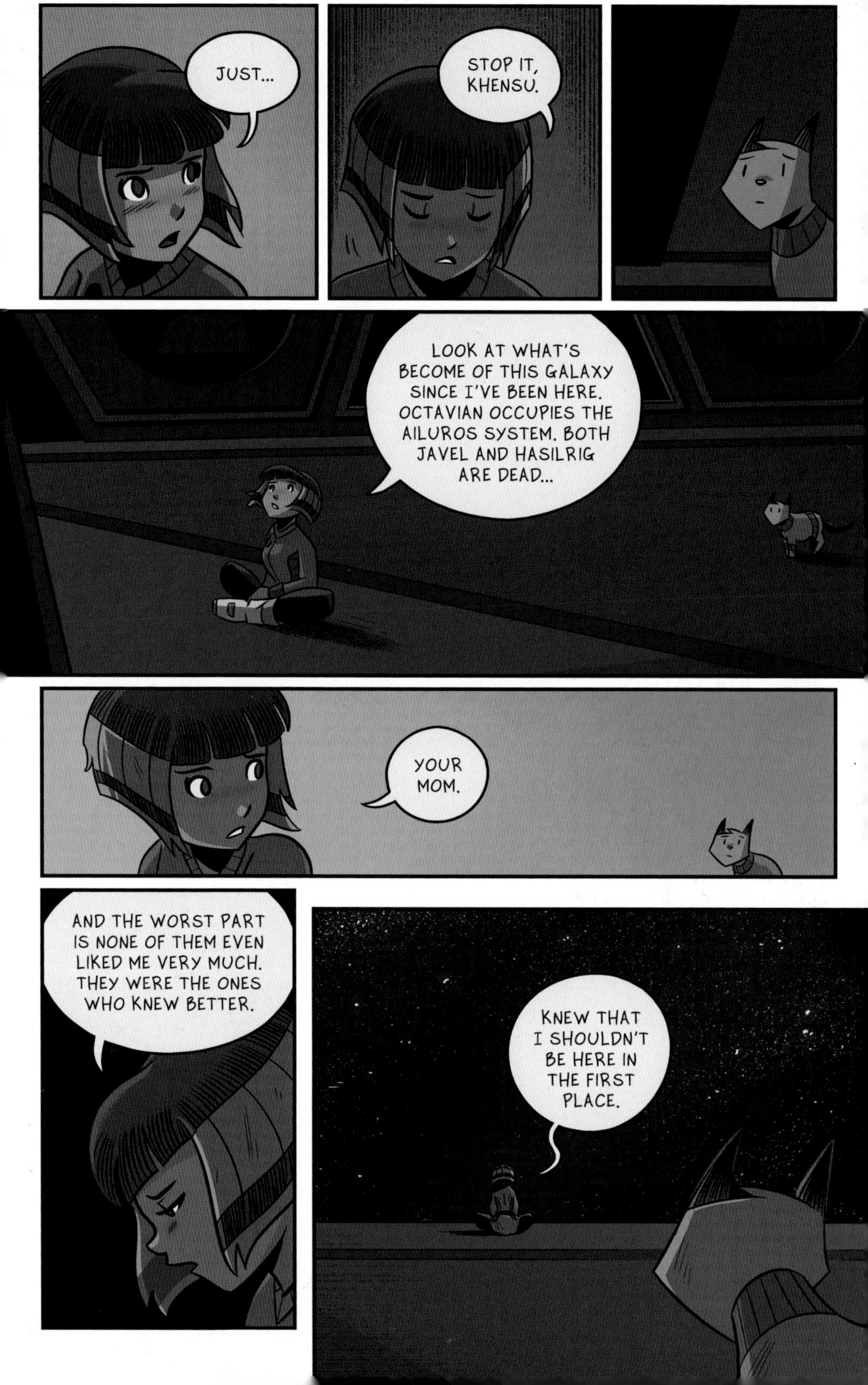
JUST...
STOP IT, KHENSU.
LOOK AT WHAT'S BECOME OF THIS GALAXY SINCE I'VE BEEN HERE. OCTAVIAN OCCUPIES THE AILUROS SYSTEM. BOTH JAVEL AND HASILRIG ARE DEAD...
YOUR MOM.
AND THE WORST PART IS NONE OF THEM EVEN LIKED ME VERY MUCH. THEY WERE THE ONES WHO KNEW BETTER.
KNEW THAT I SHOULDN'T BE HERE IN THE FIRST PLACE.

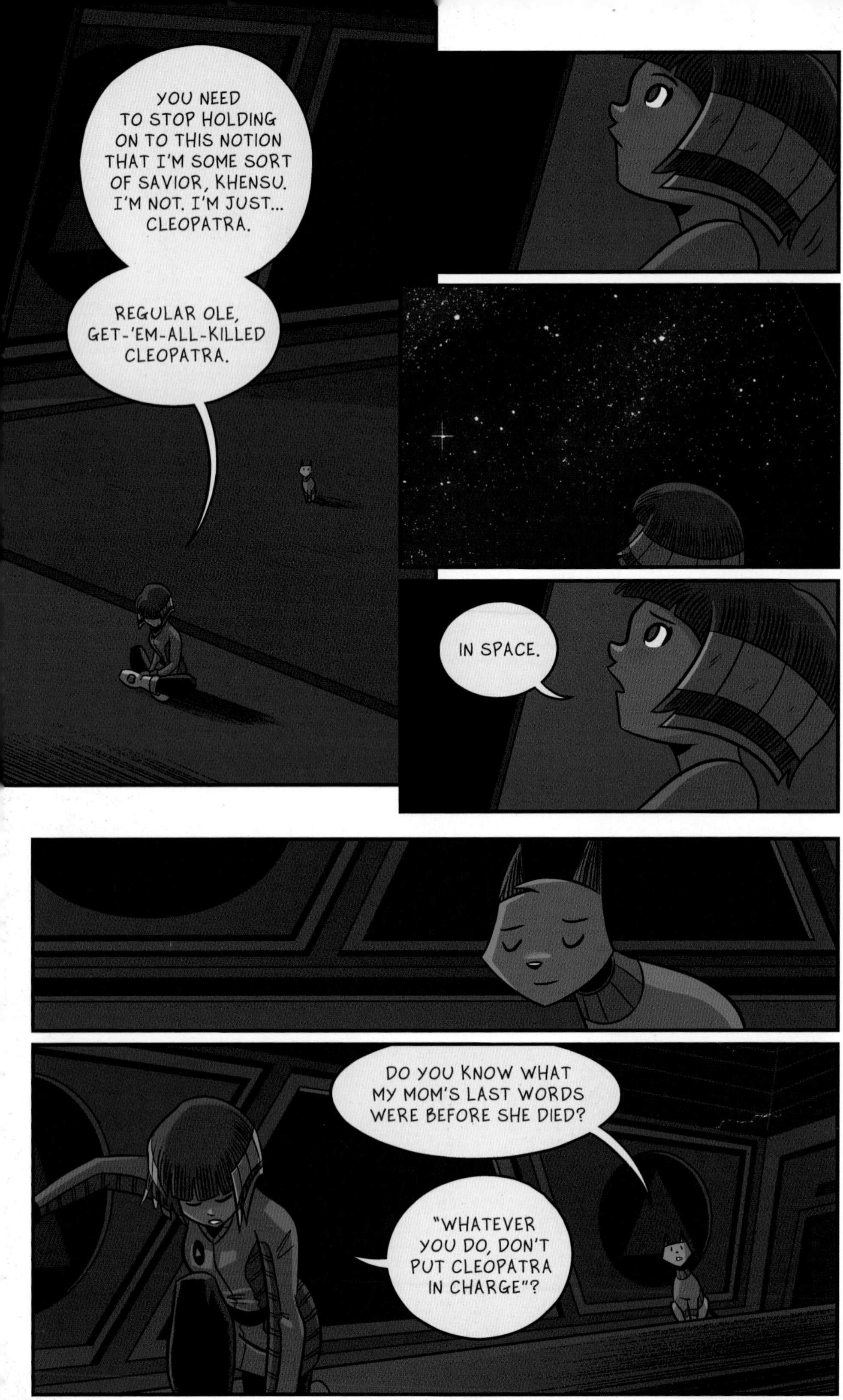
YOU NEED TO STOP HOLDING ON TO THIS NOTION THAT I'M SOME SORT OF SAVIOR, KHENSU. I'M NOT. I'M JUST... CLEOPATRA.
REGULAR OLE, GET-'EM-ALL-KILLED CLEOPATRA.
IN SPACE.
DO YOU KNOW WHAT MY MOM'S LAST WORDS WERE BEFORE SHE DIED?
"WHATEVER YOU DO, DON'T PUT CLEOPATRA IN CHARGE"?

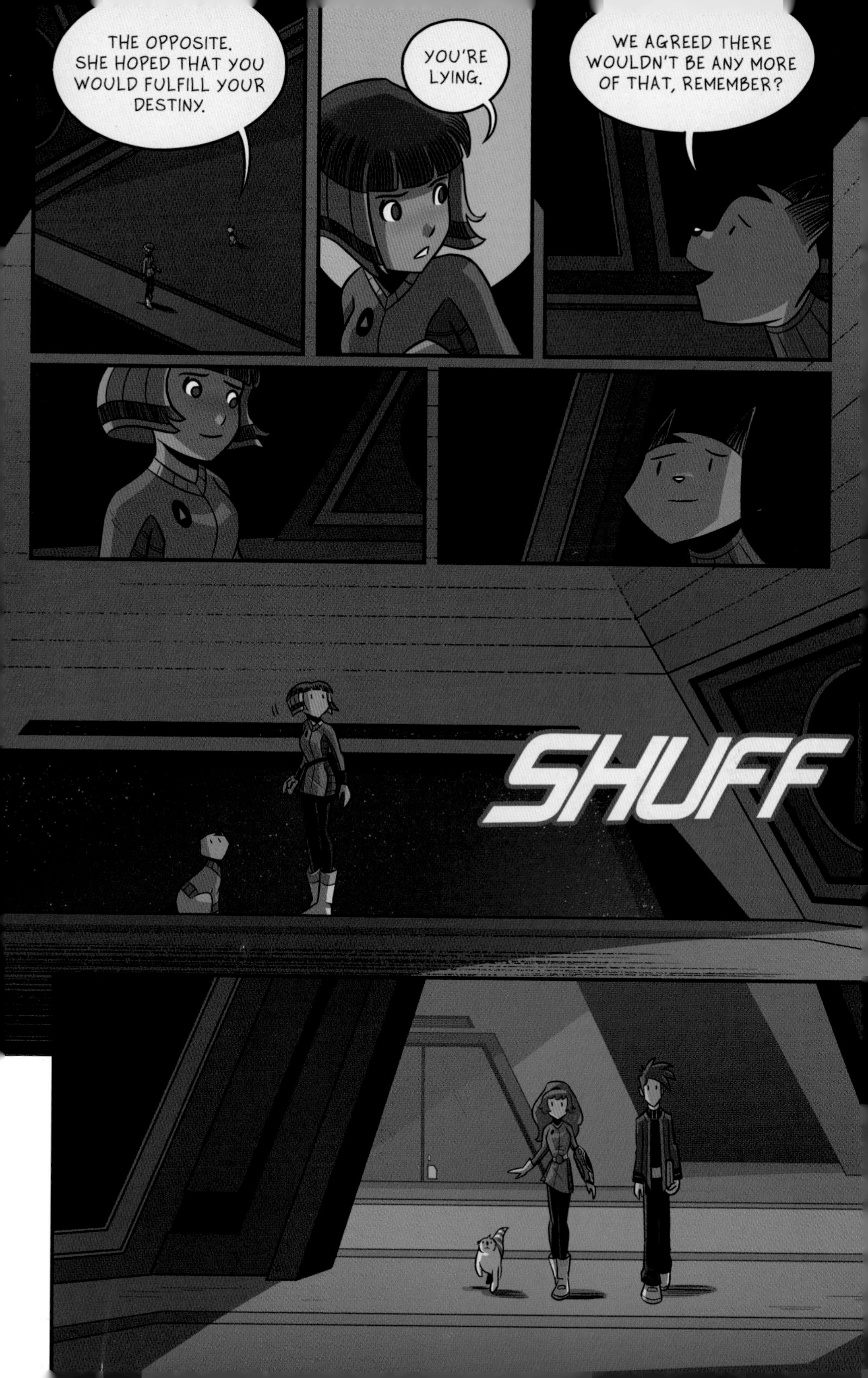
THE OPPOSITE. SHE HOPED THAT YOU WOULD FULFILL YOUR DESTINY.
YOU'RE LYING.
WE AGREED THERE WOULDN'T BE ANY MORE OF THAT, REMEMBER?
SHUFF

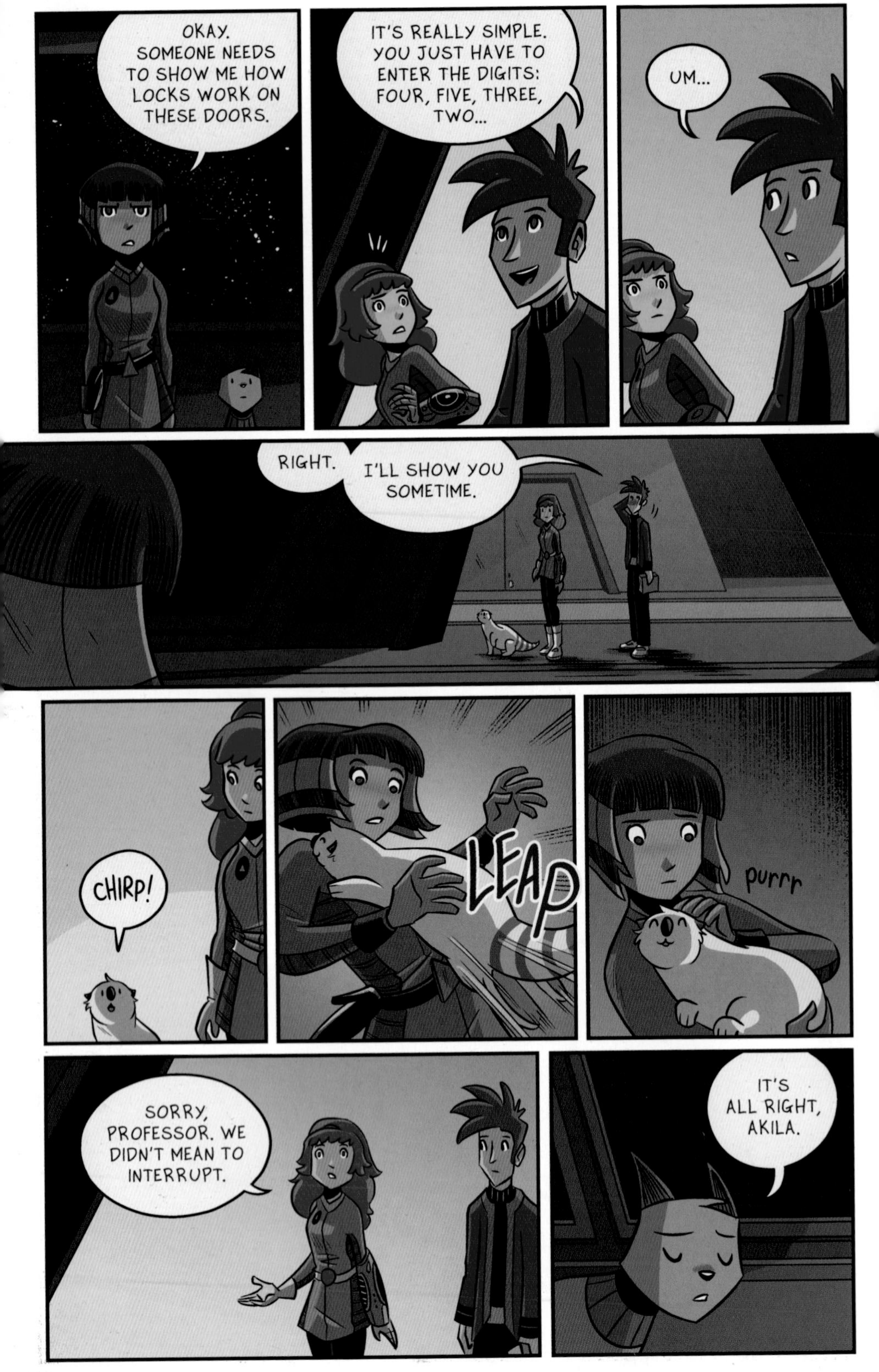
OKAY. SOMEONE NEEDS TO SHOW ME HOW LOCKS WORK ON THESE DOORS.
IT'S REALLY SIMPLE. YOU JUST HAVE TO ENTER THE DIGITS: FOUR, FIVE, THREE, TWO...
UM...
RIGHT.
I'LL SHOW YOU SOMETIME.
CHIRP!
LEAP
purrr
SORRY, PROFESSOR. WE DIDN'T MEAN TO INTERRUPT.
IT'S ALL RIGHT, AKILA.

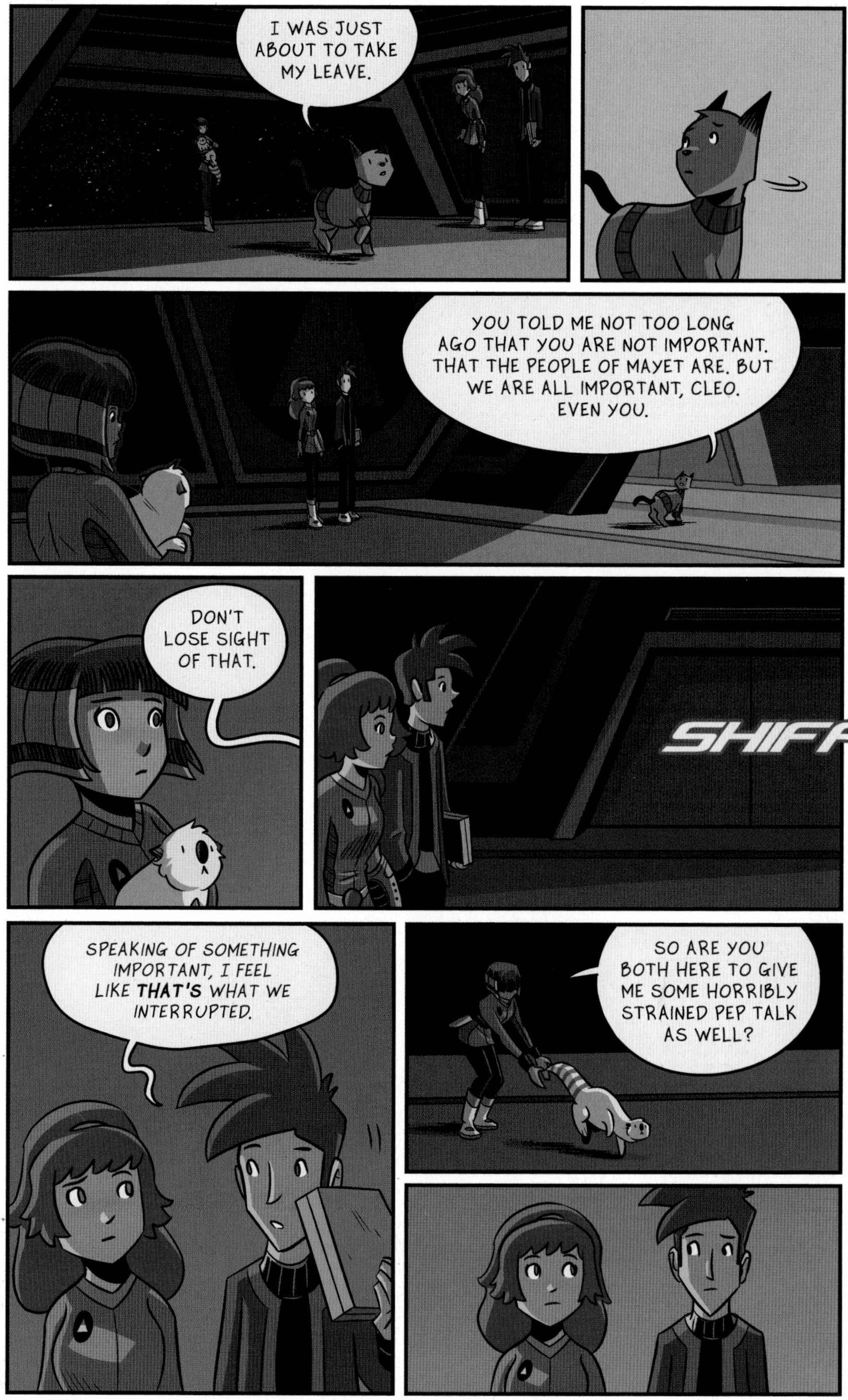
I WAS JUST ABOUT TO TAKE MY LEAVE.
YOU TOLD ME NOT TOO LONG AGO THAT YOU ARE NOT IMPORTANT. THAT THE PEOPLE OF MAYET ARE. BUT WE ARE ALL IMPORTANT, CLEO. EVEN YOU.
DON'T LOSE SIGHT OF THAT.
SHIFF
SPEAKING OF SOMETHING IMPORTANT, I FEEL LIKE THAT'S WHAT WE INTERRUPTED.
SO ARE YOU BOTH HERE TO GIVE ME SOME HORRIBLY STRAINED PEP TALK AS WELL?

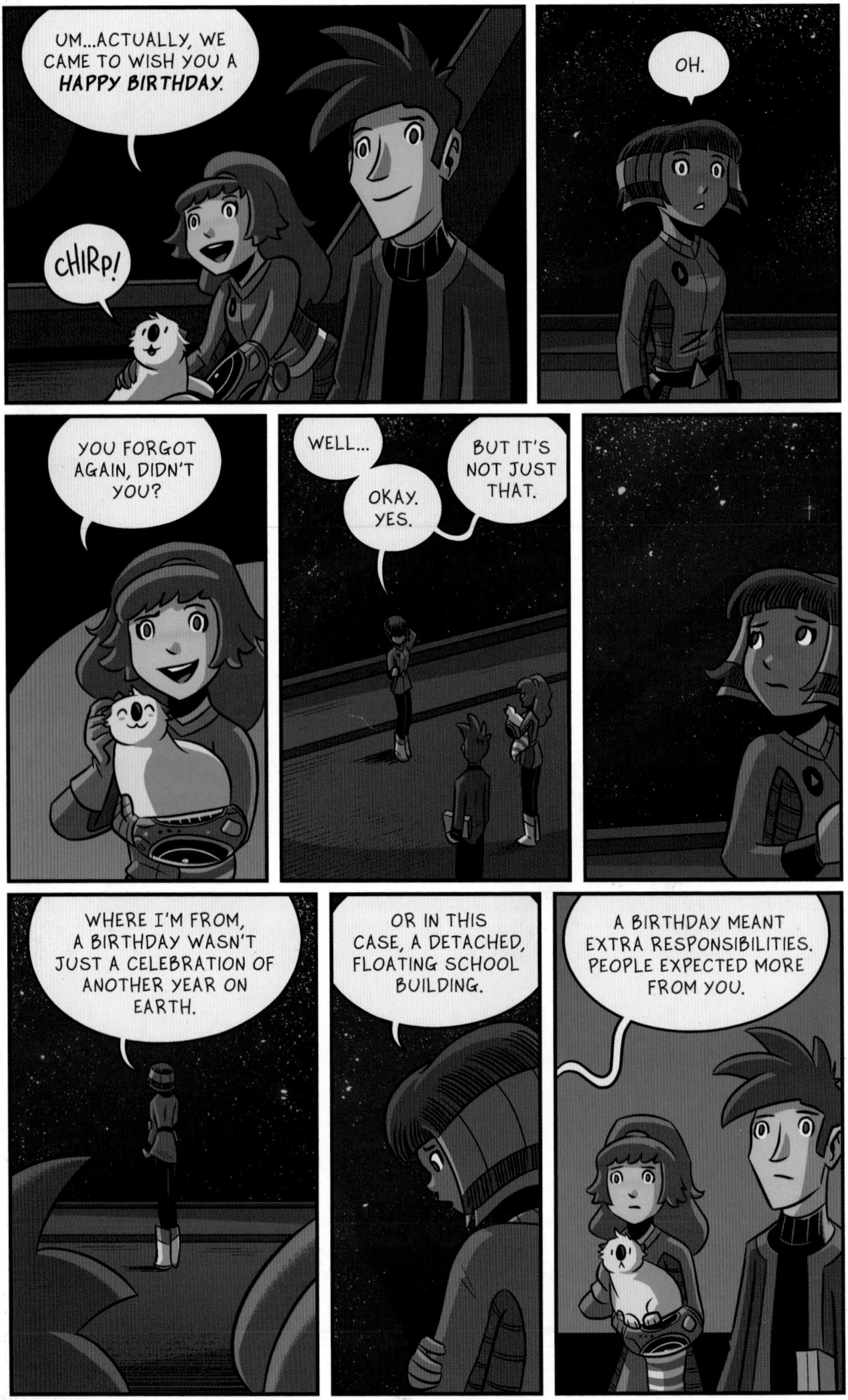
UM...ACTUALLY, WE CAME TO WISH YOU A HAPPY BIRTHDAY.
CHIRP!
OH.
YOU FORGOT AGAIN, DIDN'T YOU?
WELL...
OKAY. YES.
BUT IT'S NOT JUST THAT.
WHERE I'M FROM, A BIRTHDAY WASN'T JUST A CELEBRATION OF ANOTHER YEAR ON EARTH.
OR IN THIS CASE, A DETACHED, FLOATING SCHOOL BUILDING.
A BIRTHDAY MEANT EXTRA RESPONSIBILITIES. PEOPLE EXPECTED MORE FROM YOU.

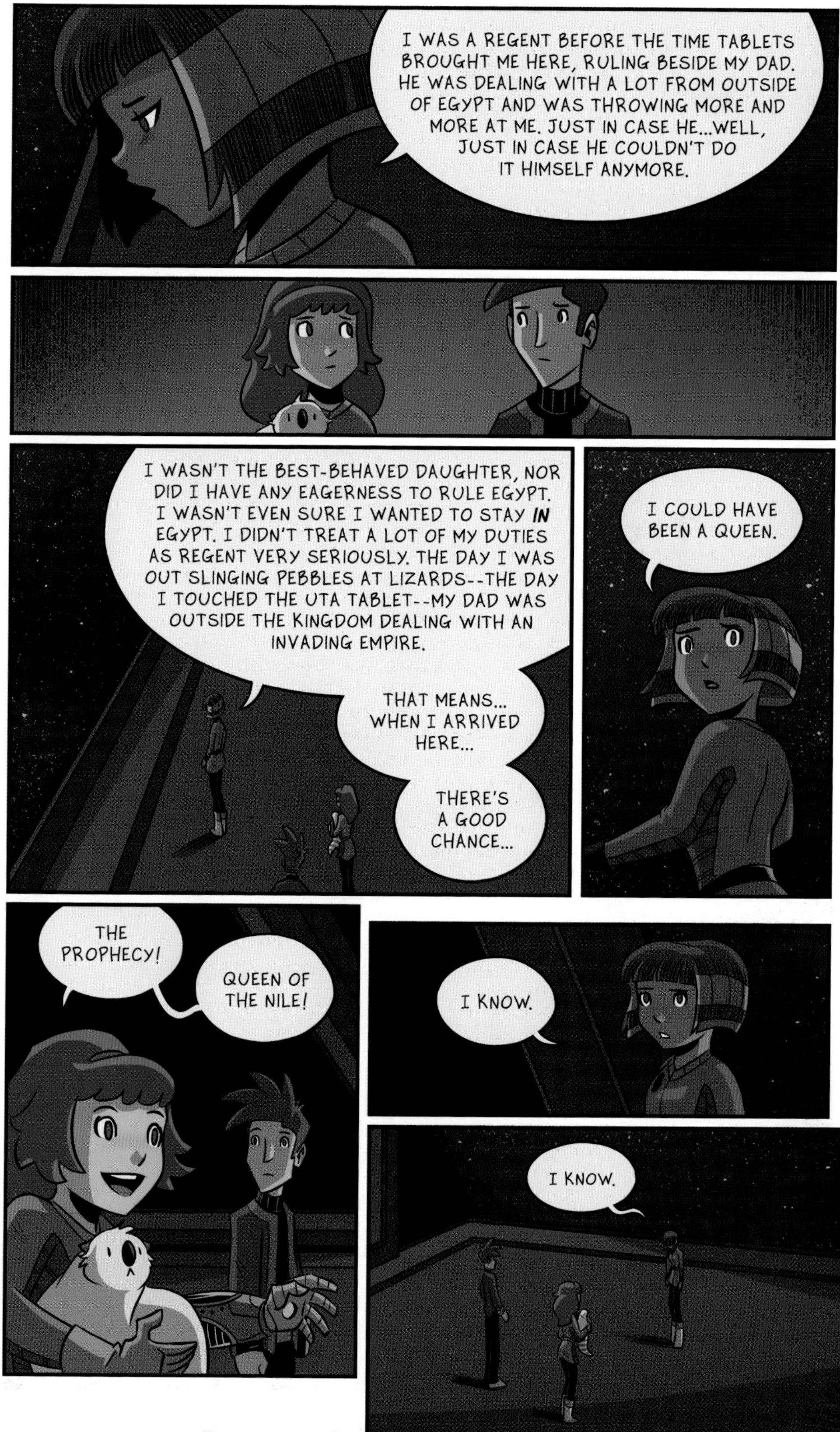
I WAS A REGENT BEFORE THE TIME TABLETS BROUGHT ME HERE, RULING BESIDE MY DAD. HE WAS DEALING WITH A LOT FROM OUTSIDE OF EGYPT AND WAS THROWING MORE AND MORE AT ME. JUST IN CASE HE...WELL, JUST IN CASE HE COULDN'T DO IT HIMSELF ANYMORE.
I WASN'T THE BEST-BEHAVED DAUGHTER, NOR DID I HAVE ANY EAGERNESS TO RULE EGYPT. I WASN'T EVEN SURE I WANTED TO STAY *IN* EGYPT. I DIDN'T TREAT A LOT OF MY DUTIES AS REGENT VERY SERIOUSLY. THE DAY I WAS OUT SLINGING PEBBLES AT LIZARDS--THE DAY I TOUCHED THE UTA TABLET--MY DAD WAS OUTSIDE THE KINGDOM DEALING WITH AN INVADING EMPIRE.
THAT MEANS... WHEN I ARRIVED HERE...
THERE'S A GOOD CHANCE...
I COULD HAVE BEEN A QUEEN.
THE PROPHECY!
QUEEN OF THE NILE!
I KNOW.
I KNOW.

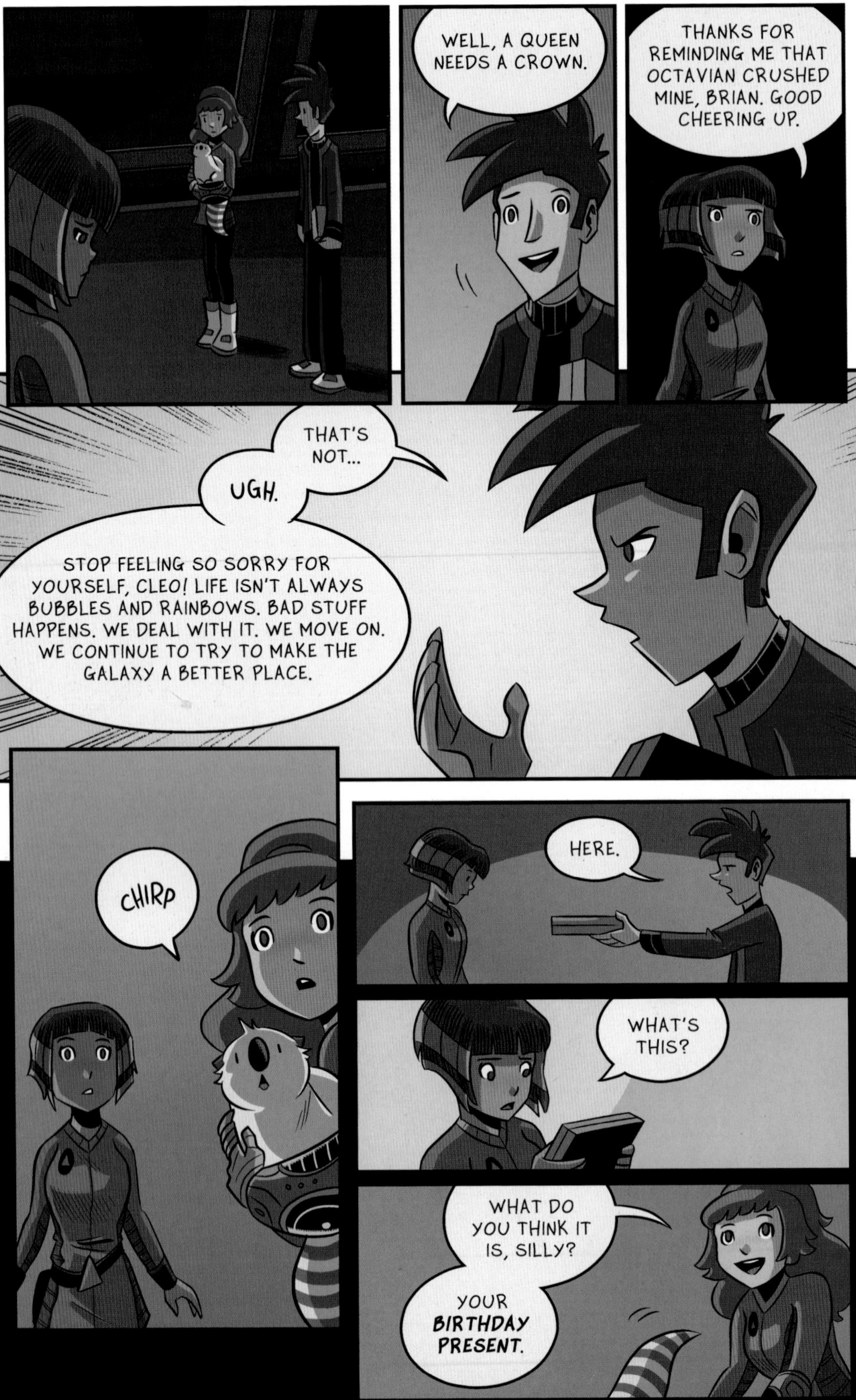
WELL, A QUEEN NEEDS A CROWN.
THANKS FOR REMINDING ME THAT OCTAVIAN CRUSHED MINE, BRIAN. GOOD CHEERING UP.
THAT'S NOT...
UGH.
STOP FEELING SO SORRY FOR YOURSELF, CLEO! LIFE ISN'T ALWAYS BUBBLES AND RAINBOWS. BAD STUFF HAPPENS. WE DEAL WITH IT. WE MOVE ON. WE CONTINUE TO TRY TO MAKE THE GALAXY A BETTER PLACE.
CHIRP
HERE.
WHAT'S THIS?
WHAT DO YOU THINK IT IS, SILLY?
YOUR **BIRTHDAY PRESENT.**

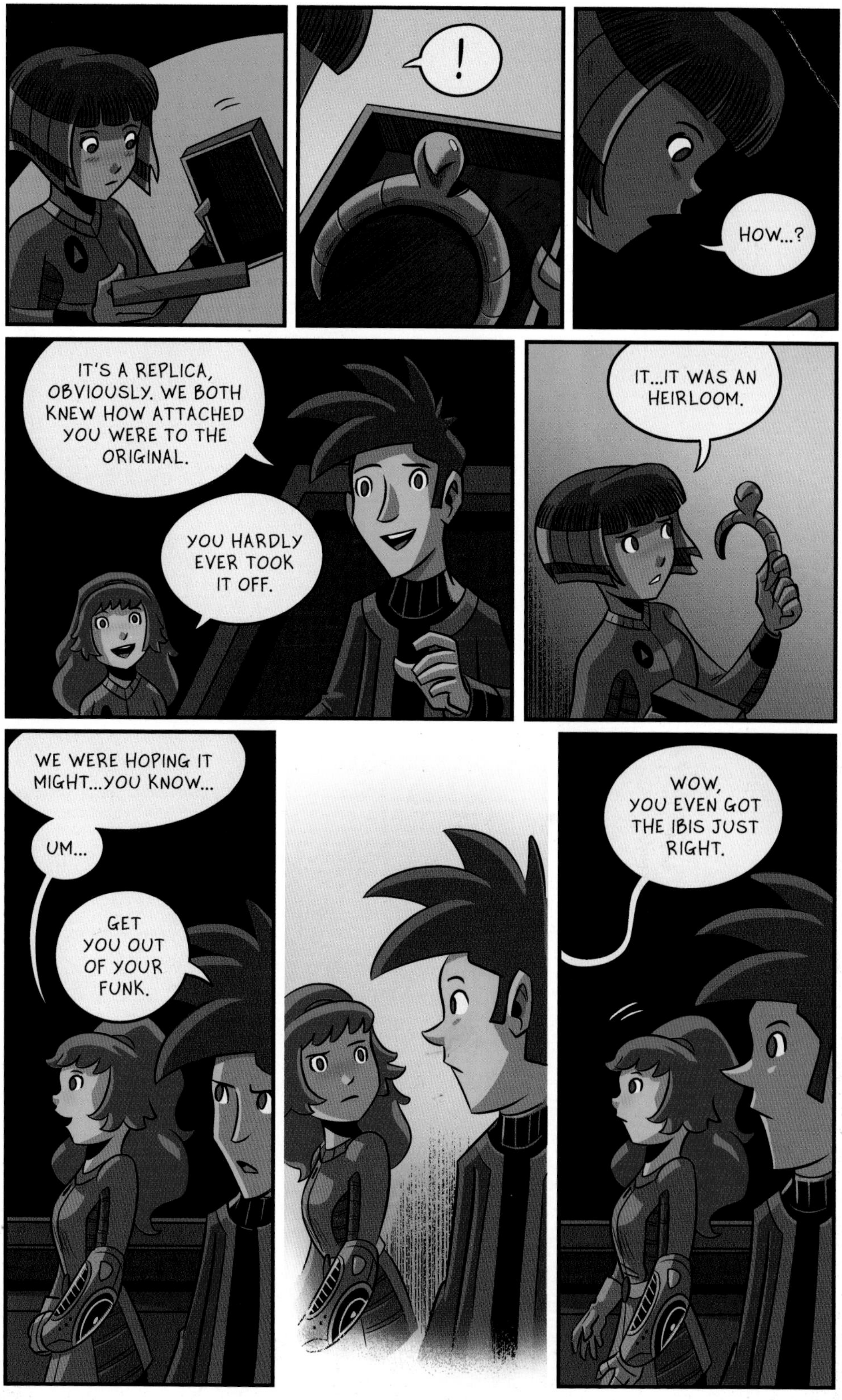
!
HOW...?
IT'S A REPLICA, OBVIOUSLY. WE BOTH KNEW HOW ATTACHED YOU WERE TO THE ORIGINAL.
YOU HARDLY EVER TOOK IT OFF.
IT...IT WAS AN HEIRLOOM.
WE WERE HOPING IT MIGHT...YOU KNOW...
UM...
GET YOU OUT OF YOUR FUNK.
WOW, YOU EVEN GOT THE IBIS JUST RIGHT.

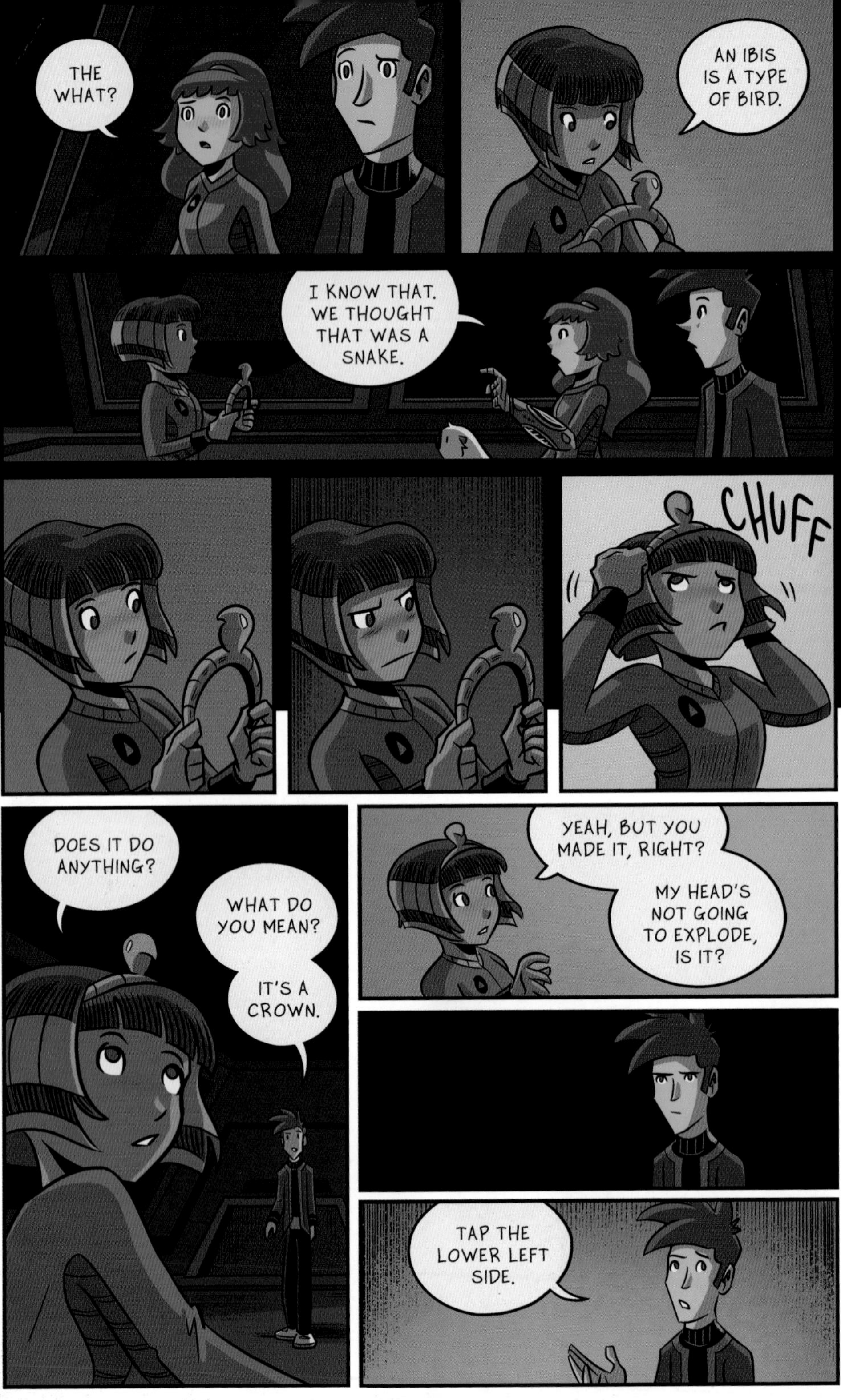
THE WHAT?
AN IBIS IS A TYPE OF BIRD.
I KNOW THAT. WE THOUGHT THAT WAS A SNAKE.
CHUFF
DOES IT DO ANYTHING?
WHAT DO YOU MEAN?
IT'S A CROWN.
YEAH, BUT YOU MADE IT, RIGHT?
MY HEAD'S NOT GOING TO EXPLODE, IS IT?
TAP THE LOWER LEFT SIDE.

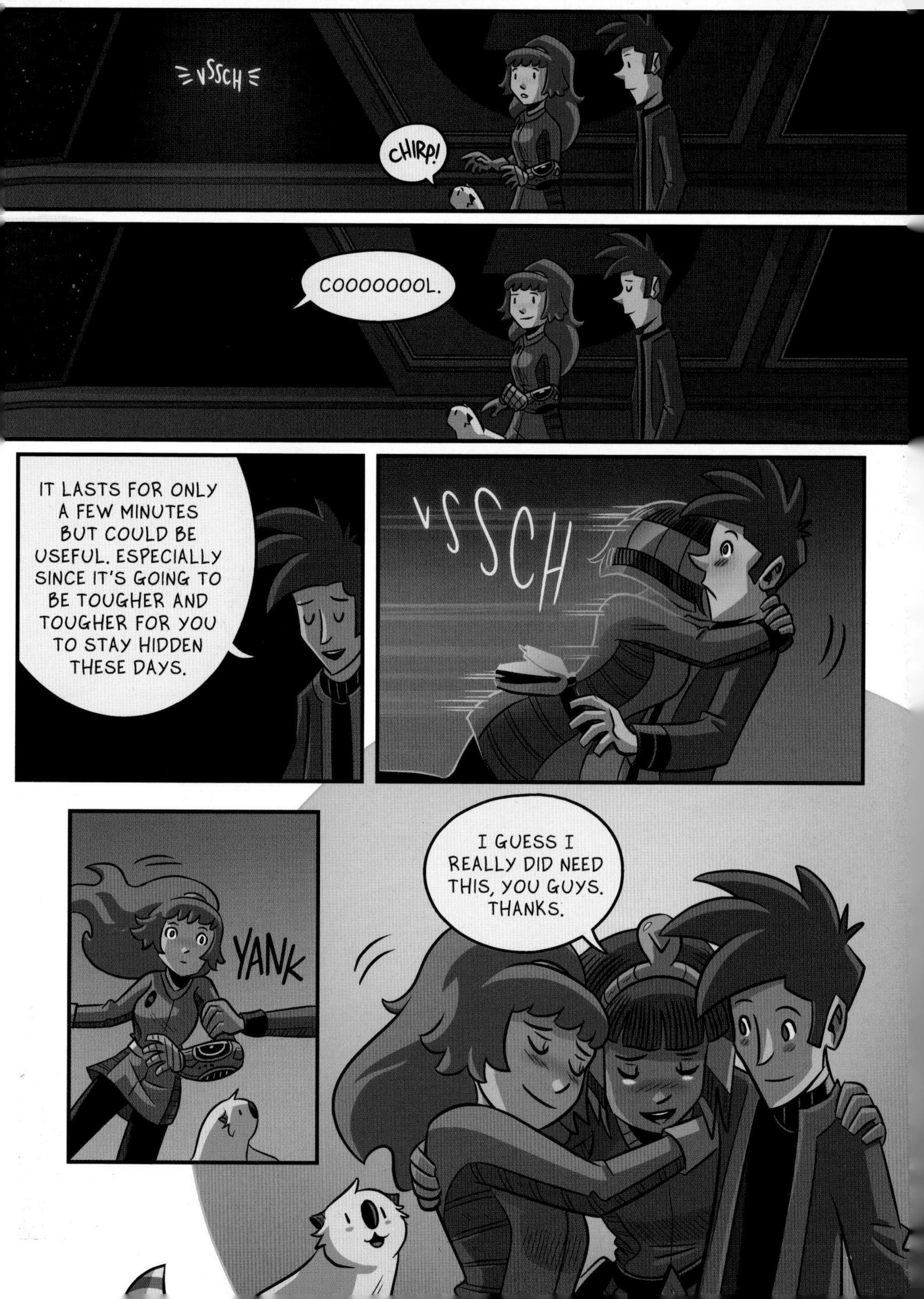
VSSCH
CHIRP!
COOOOOOOL.
IT LASTS FOR ONLY A FEW MINUTES BUT COULD BE USEFUL. ESPECIALLY SINCE IT'S GOING TO BE TOUGHER AND TOUGHER FOR YOU TO STAY HIDDEN THESE DAYS.
VSSCH
YANK
I GUESS I REALLY DID NEED THIS, YOU GUYS. THANKS.

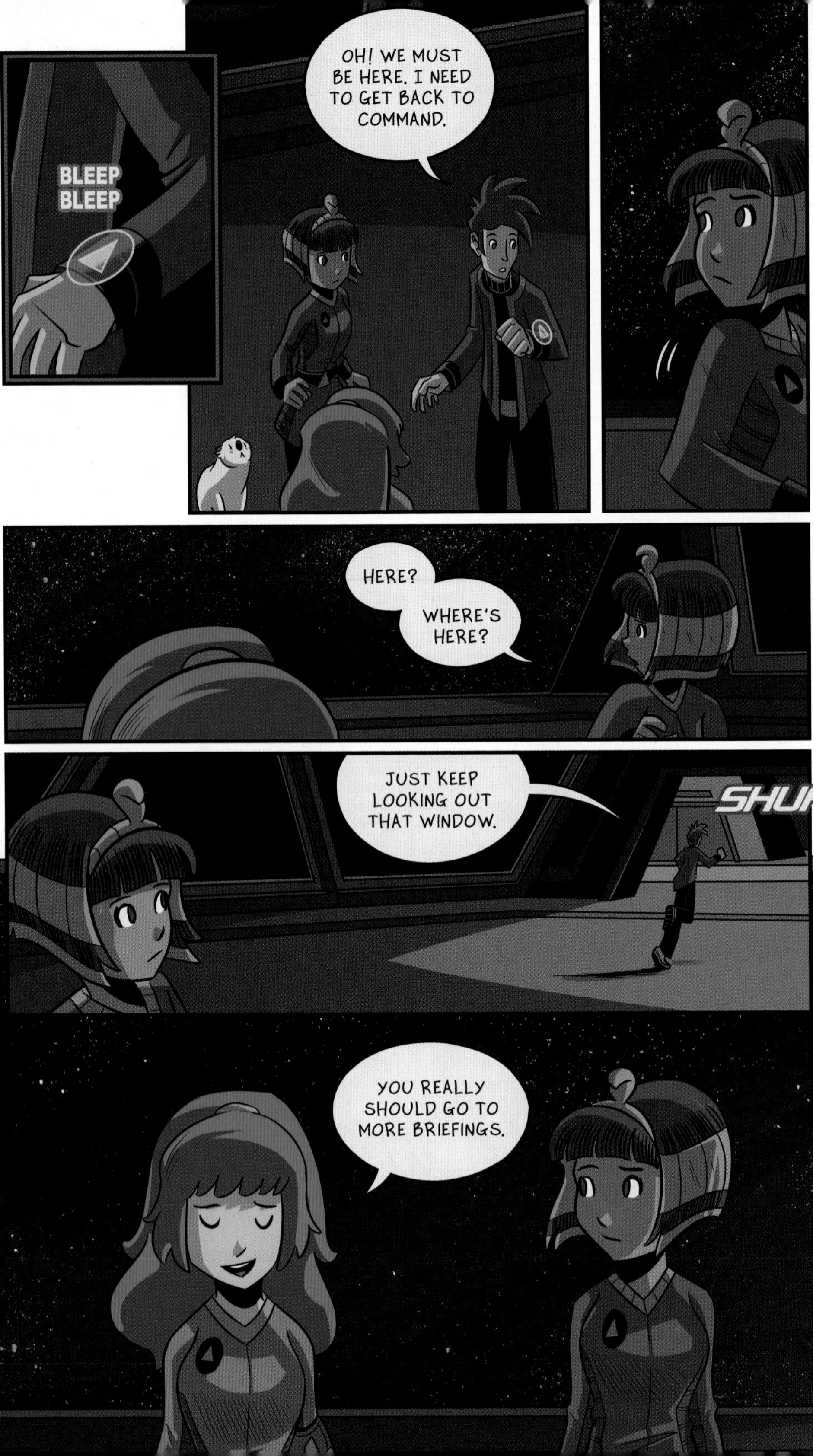
BLEEP
BLEEP
OH! WE MUST BE HERE. I NEED TO GET BACK TO COMMAND.
HERE?
WHERE'S HERE?
JUST KEEP LOOKING OUT THAT WINDOW.
SHUF
YOU REALLY SHOULD GO TO MORE BRIEFINGS.

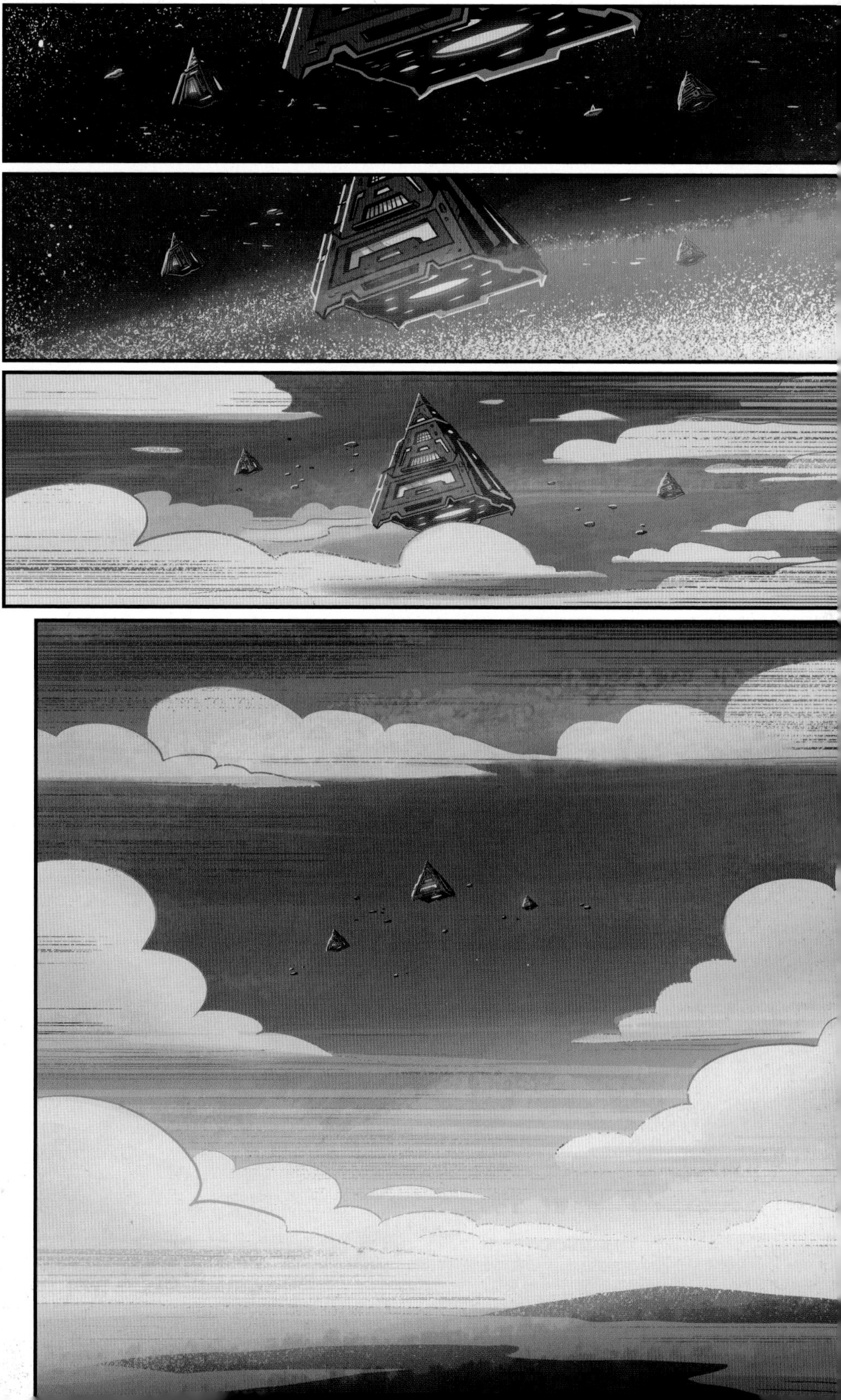

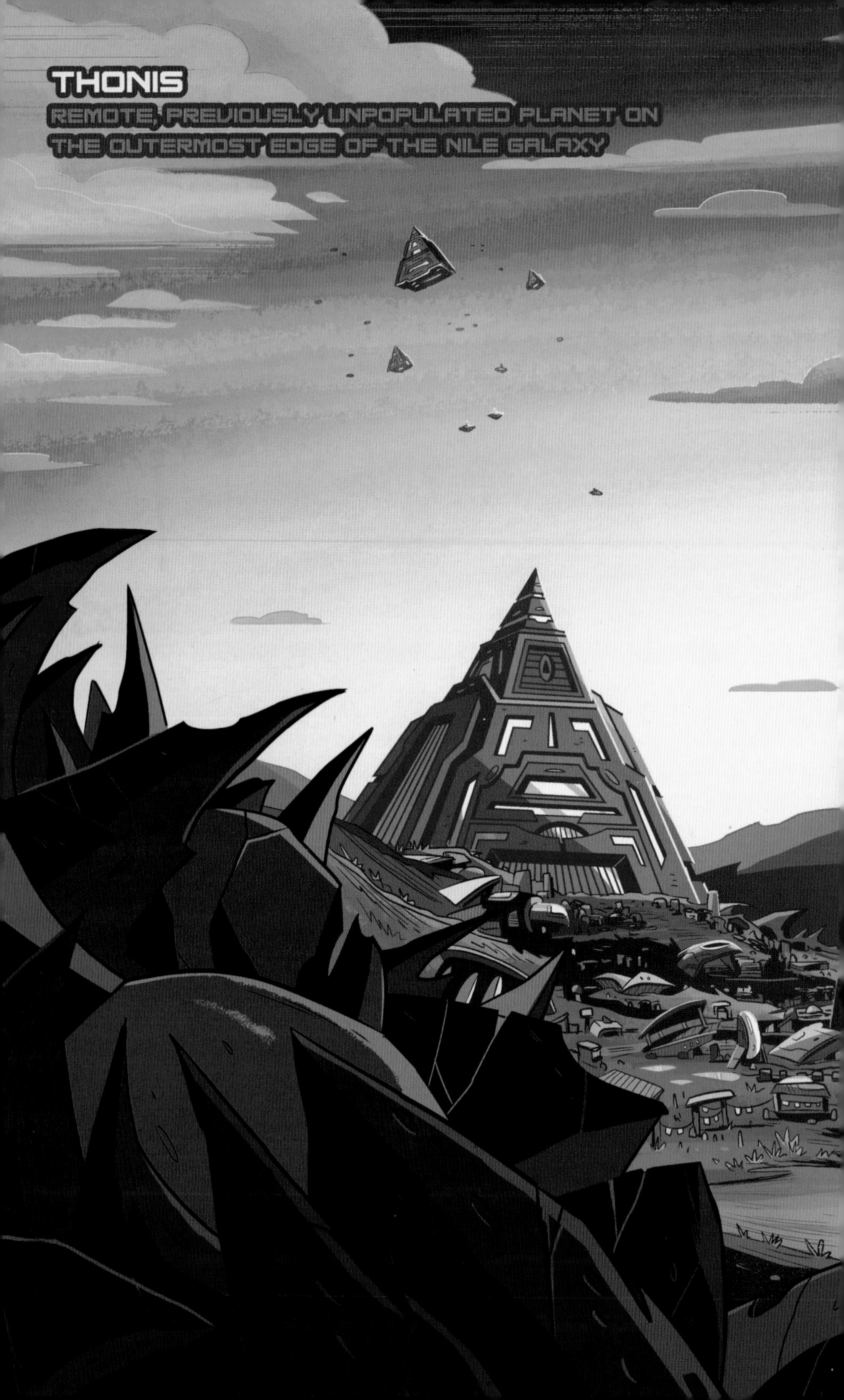
THONIS
REMOTE, PREVIOUSLY UNPOPULATED PLANET ON THE OUTERMOST EDGE OF THE NILE GALAXY

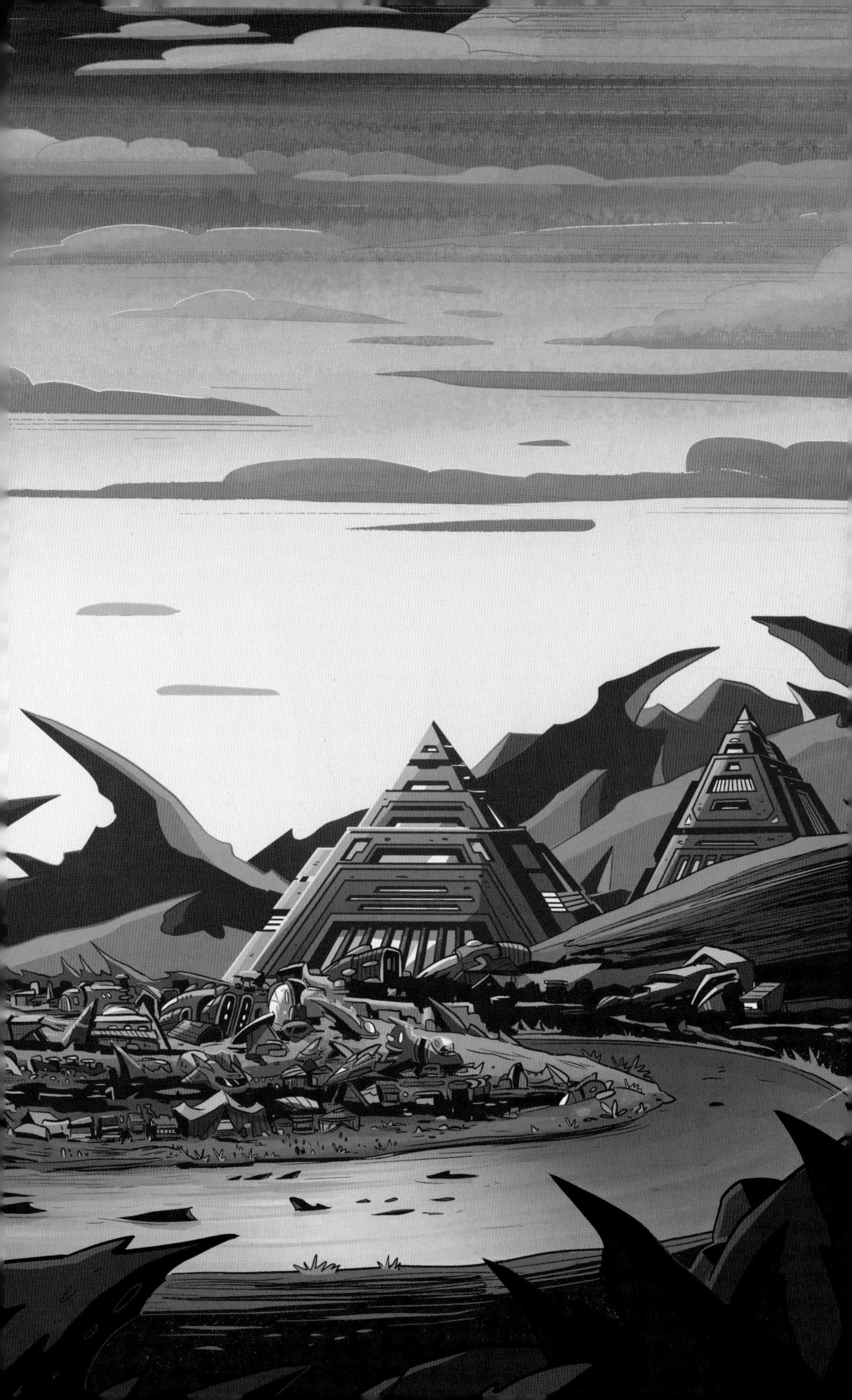

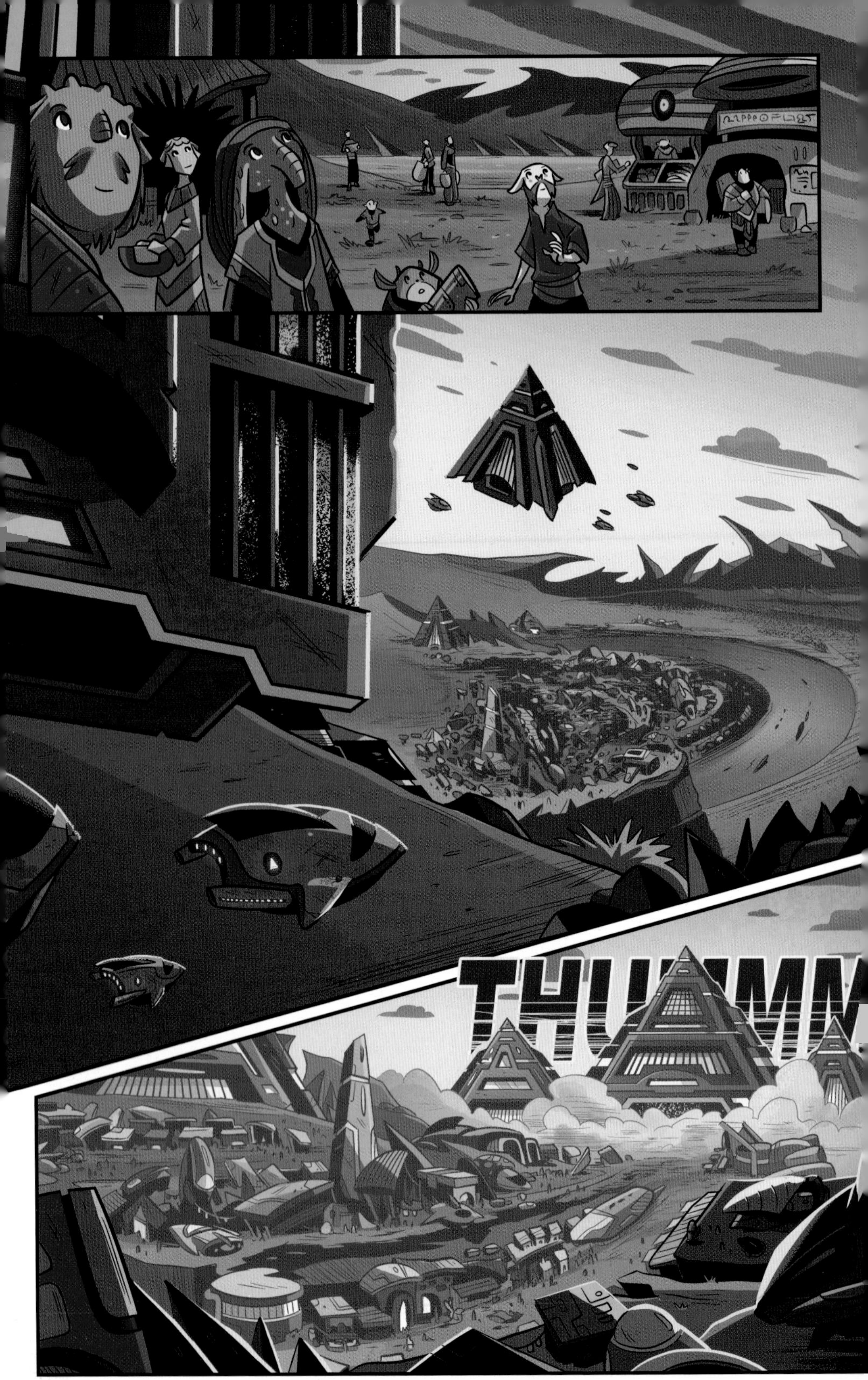
THUMM

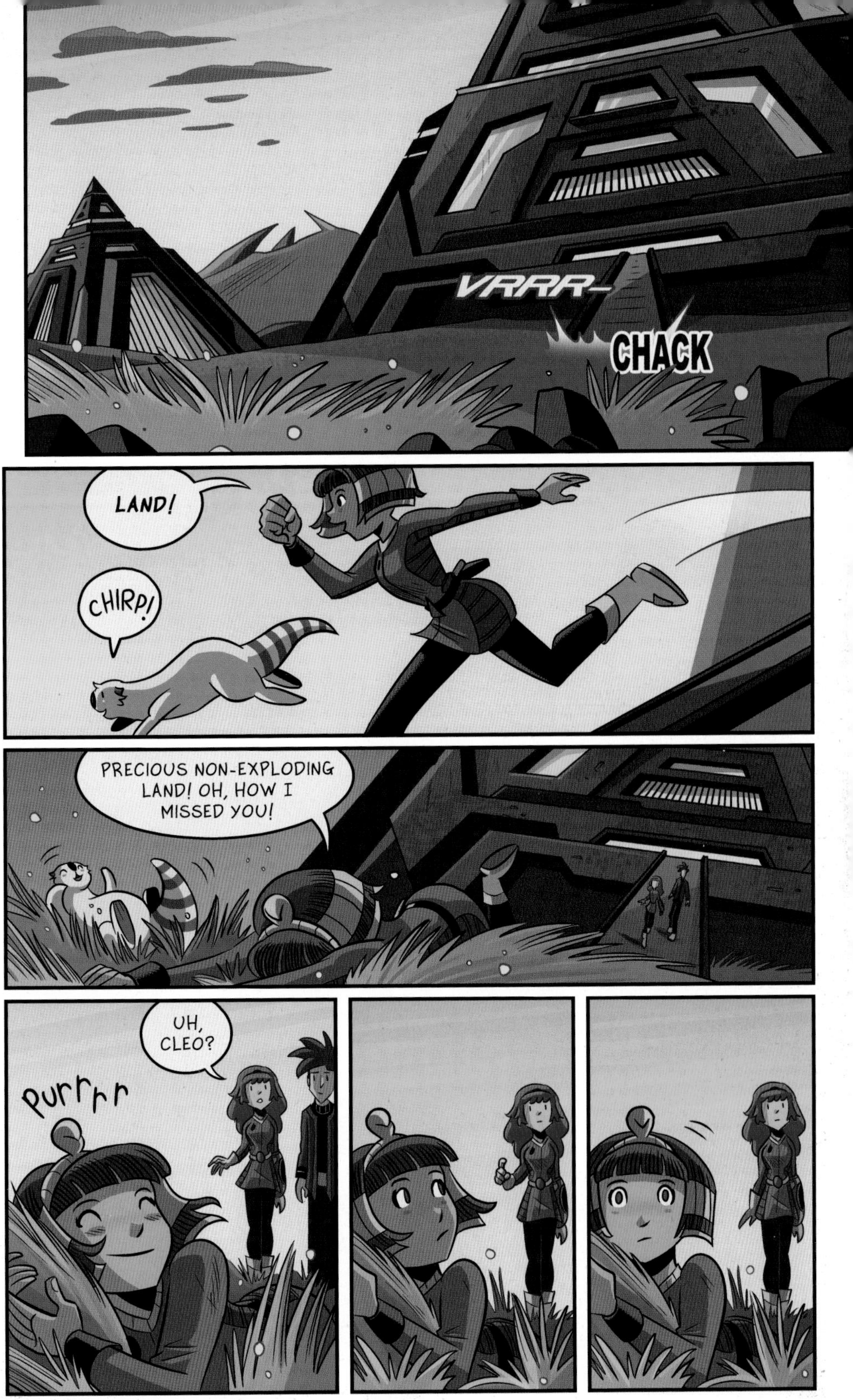
VRRR-
CHACK
LAND!
CHIRP!
PRECIOUS NON-EXPLODING LAND! OH, HOW I MISSED YOU!
UH, CLEO?
purrrr

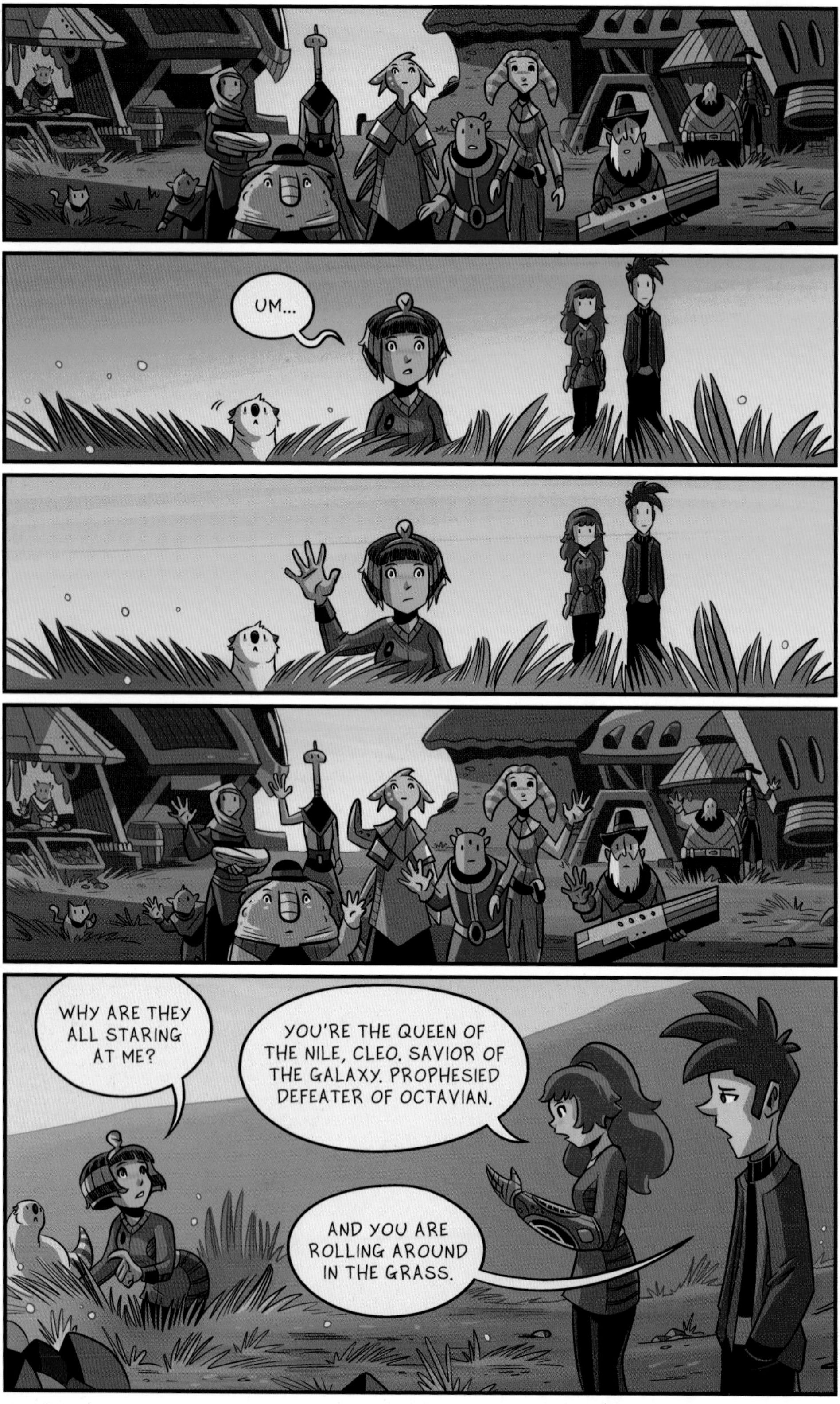
UM...
WHY ARE THEY ALL STARING AT ME?
YOU'RE THE QUEEN OF THE NILE, CLEO. SAVIOR OF THE GALAXY. PROPHESIED DEFEATER OF OCTAVIAN.
AND YOU ARE ROLLING AROUND IN THE GRASS.

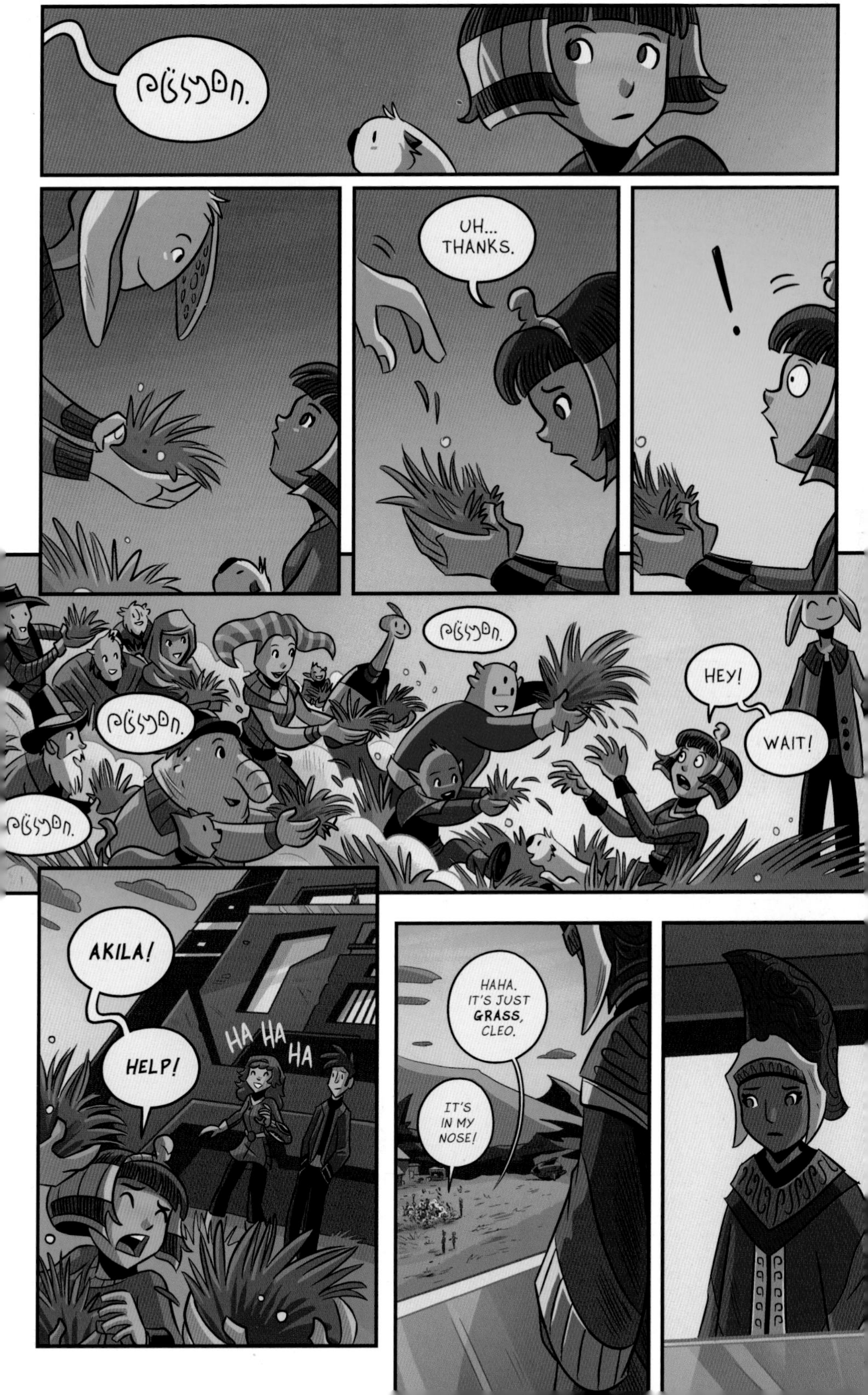
UH... THANKS.
!
HEY!
WAIT!
AKILA!
HELP!
HA HA HA
HAHA. IT'S JUST GRASS, CLEO.
IT'S IN MY NOSE!

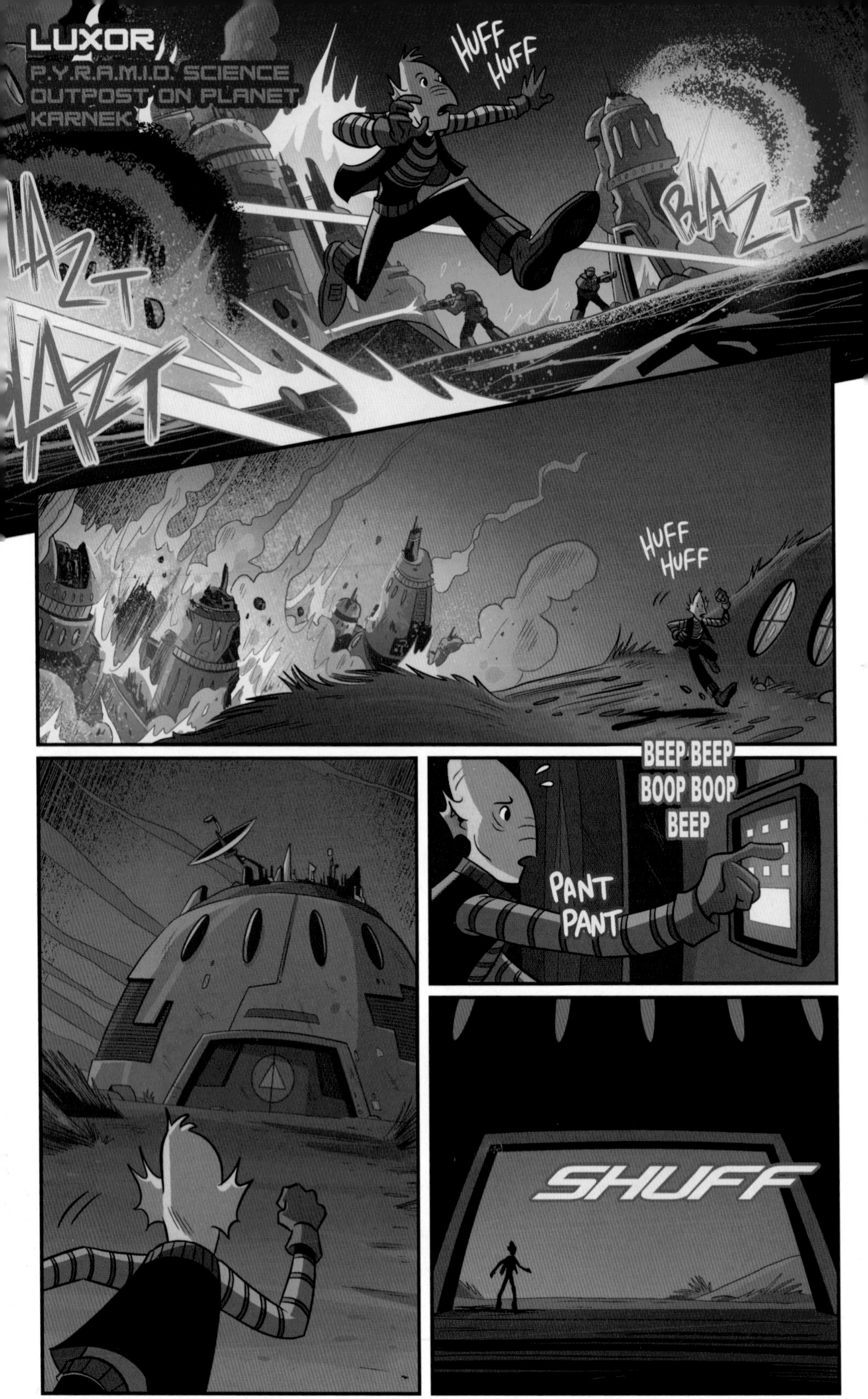
LUXOR
P.Y.R.A.M.I.D. SCIENCE OUTPOST ON PLANET KARNEK
HUFF HUFF
BLAZT
BLAZT
BLAZT
HUFF HUFF
BEEP BEEP BOOP BOOP BEEP
PANT PANT
SHUFF

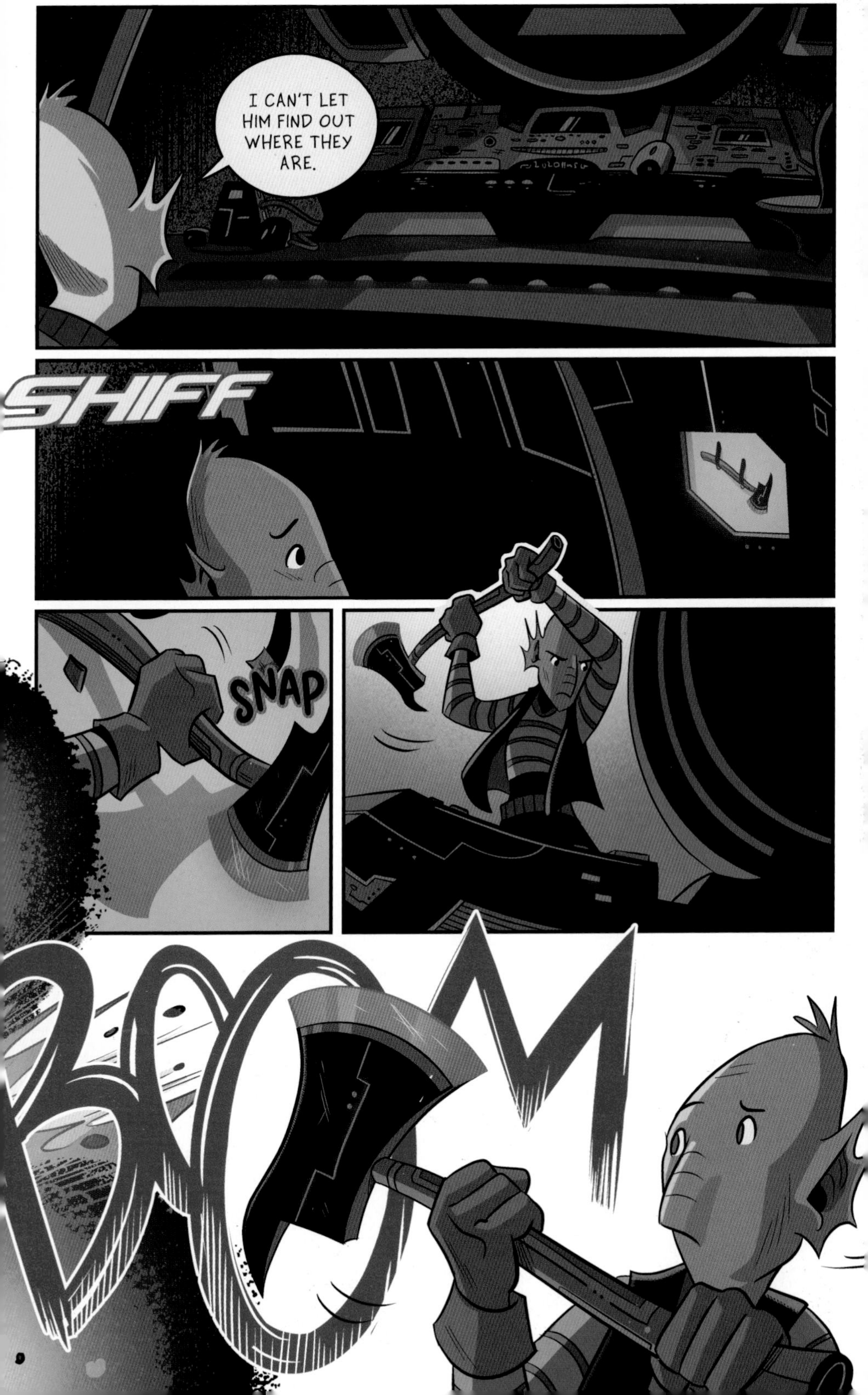

I CAN'T LET HIM FIND OUT WHERE THEY ARE.
SHIFF
SNAP
BOOM

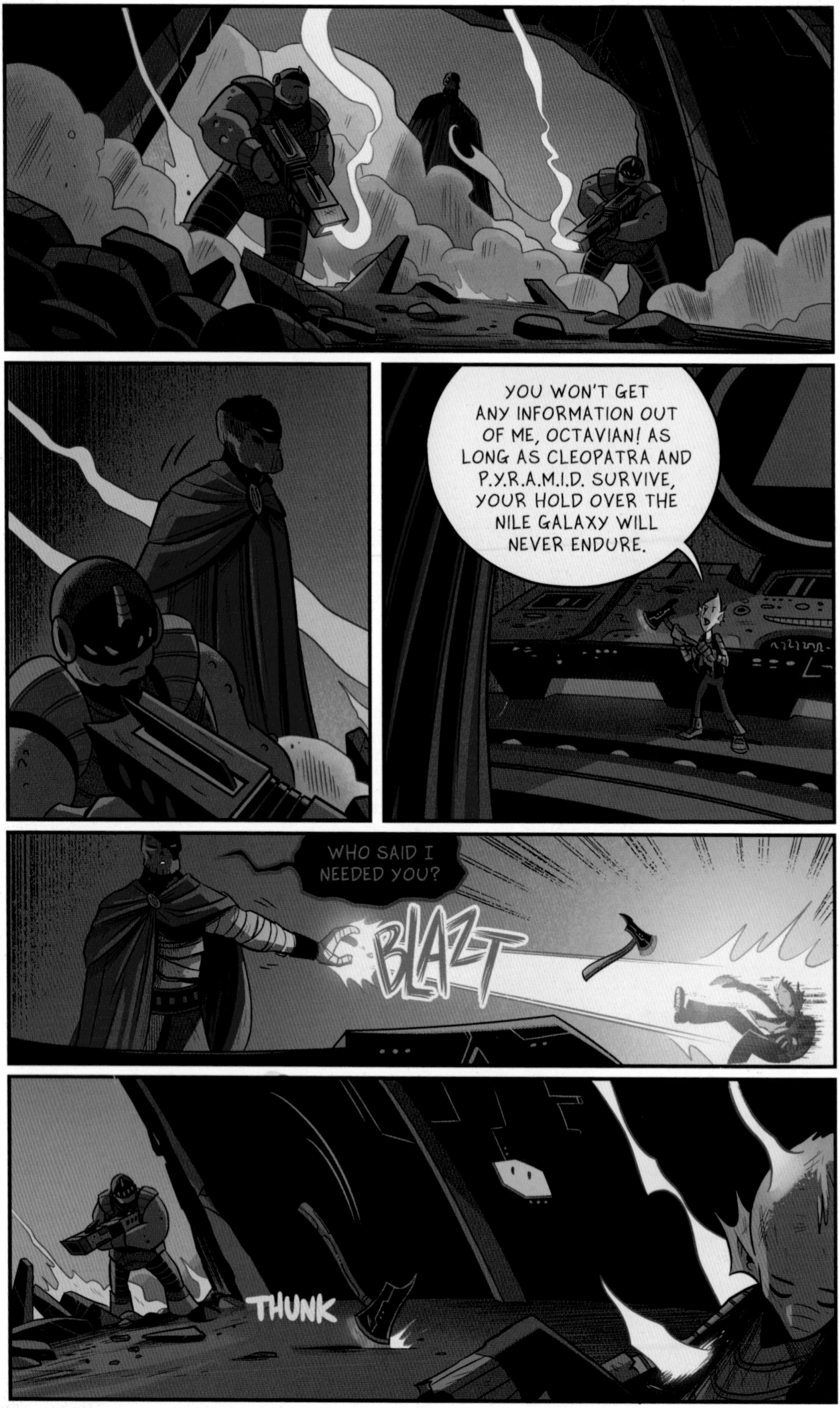
YOU WON'T GET ANY INFORMATION OUT OF ME, OCTAVIAN! AS LONG AS CLEOPATRA AND P.Y.R.A.M.I.D. SURVIVE, YOUR HOLD OVER THE NILE GALAXY WILL NEVER ENDURE.
WHO SAID I NEEDED YOU?
BLAZT
THUNK

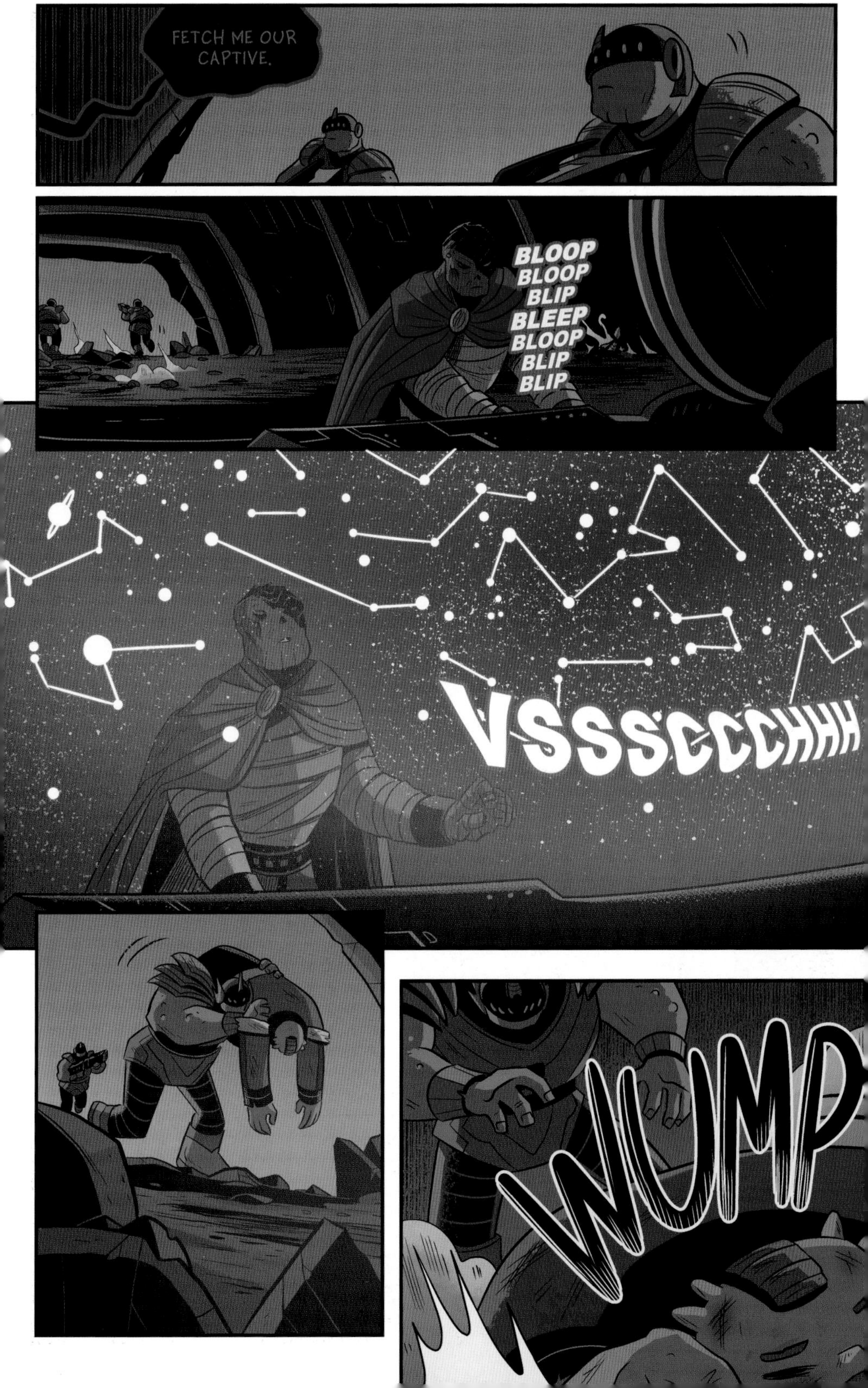
FETCH ME OUR CAPTIVE.
BLOOP BLOOP BLIP BLEEP BLOOP BLIP BLIP
VSSSCCCHHH
WUMP

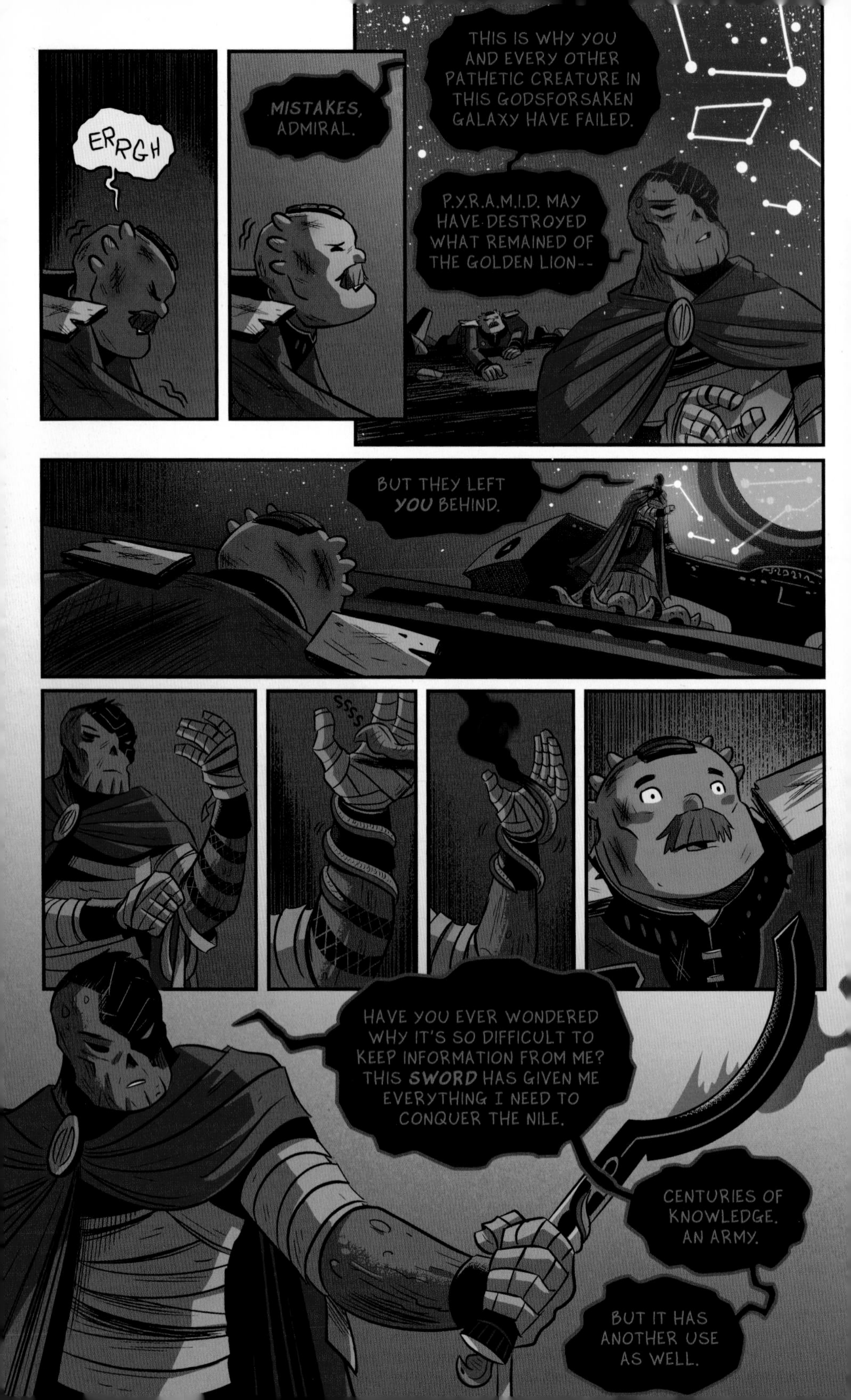
ERRGH
MISTAKES, ADMIRAL.
THIS IS WHY YOU AND EVERY OTHER PATHETIC CREATURE IN THIS GODSFORSAKEN GALAXY HAVE FAILED.
P.Y.R.A.M.I.D. MAY HAVE DESTROYED WHAT REMAINED OF THE GOLDEN LION--
BUT THEY LEFT *YOU* BEHIND.
SSSS
HAVE YOU EVER WONDERED WHY IT'S SO DIFFICULT TO KEEP INFORMATION FROM ME? THIS **SWORD** HAS GIVEN ME EVERYTHING I NEED TO CONQUER THE NILE.
CENTURIES OF KNOWLEDGE. AN ARMY.
BUT IT HAS ANOTHER USE AS WELL.

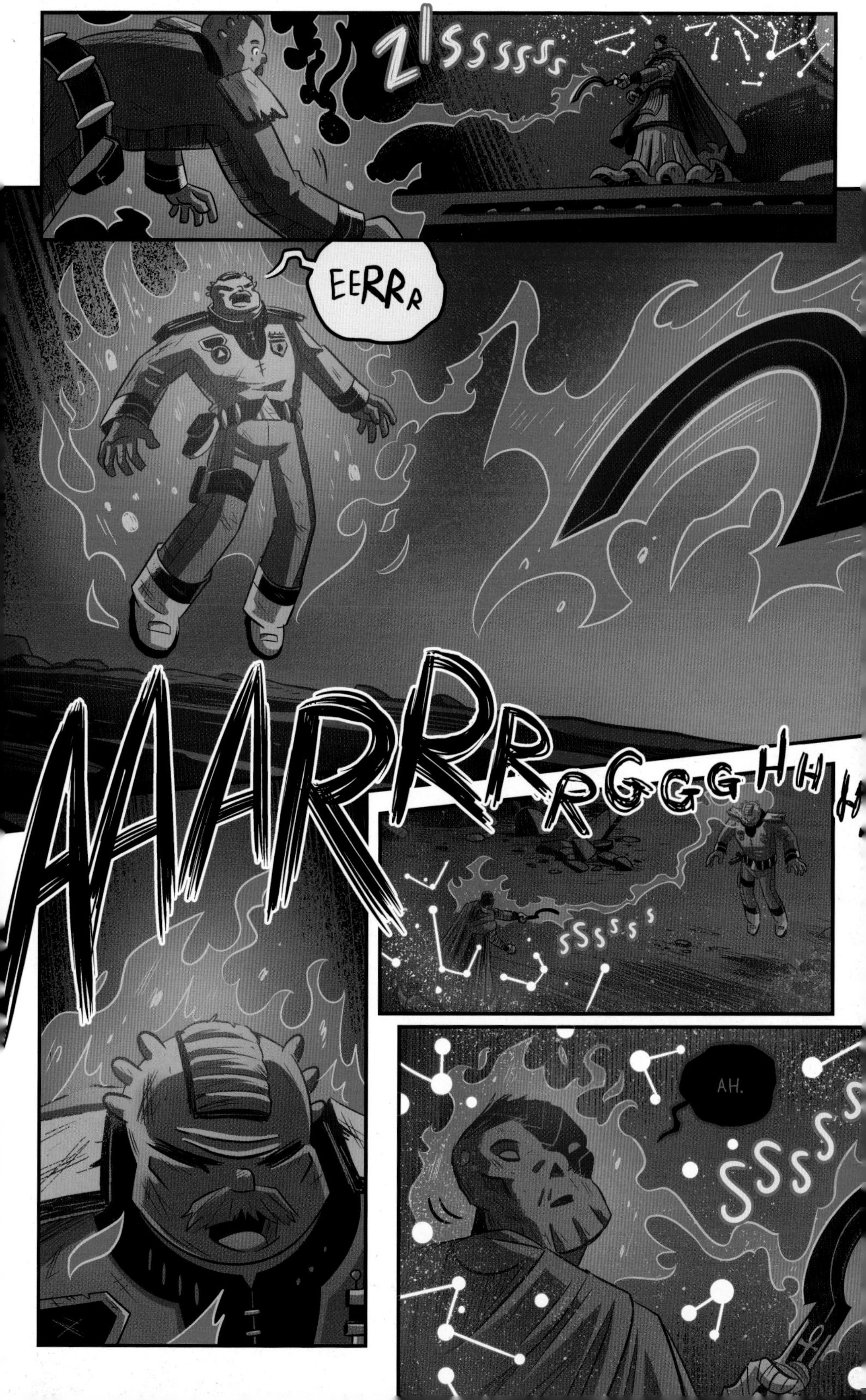

ZISSSSSS
EERRR
AAARRRRGGGHHH
SSSSSS
AH.
SSSS

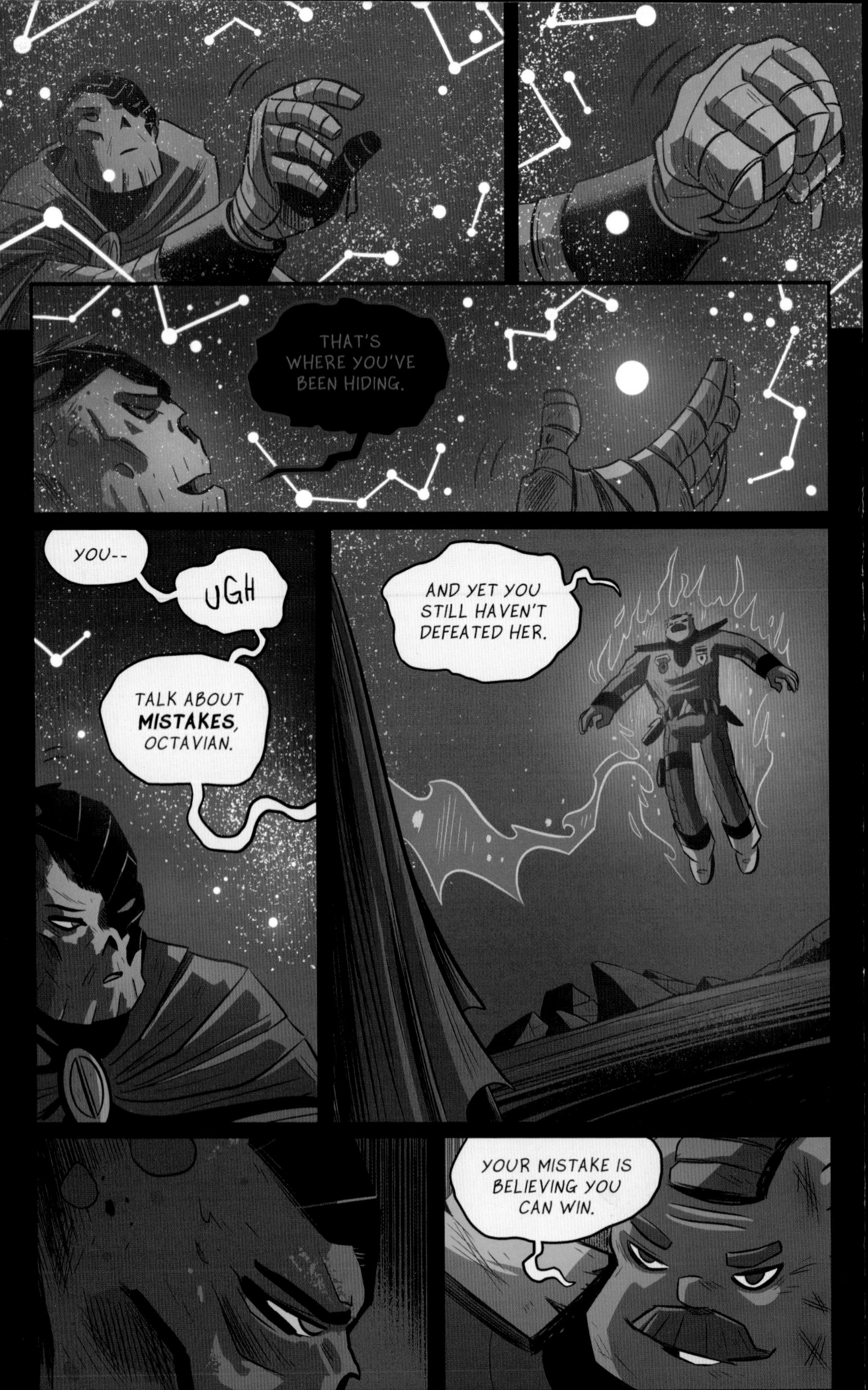
THAT'S WHERE YOU'VE BEEN HIDING.
YOU--
UGH
TALK ABOUT **MISTAKES**, OCTAVIAN.
AND YET YOU STILL HAVEN'T DEFEATED HER.
YOUR MISTAKE IS BELIEVING YOU CAN WIN.

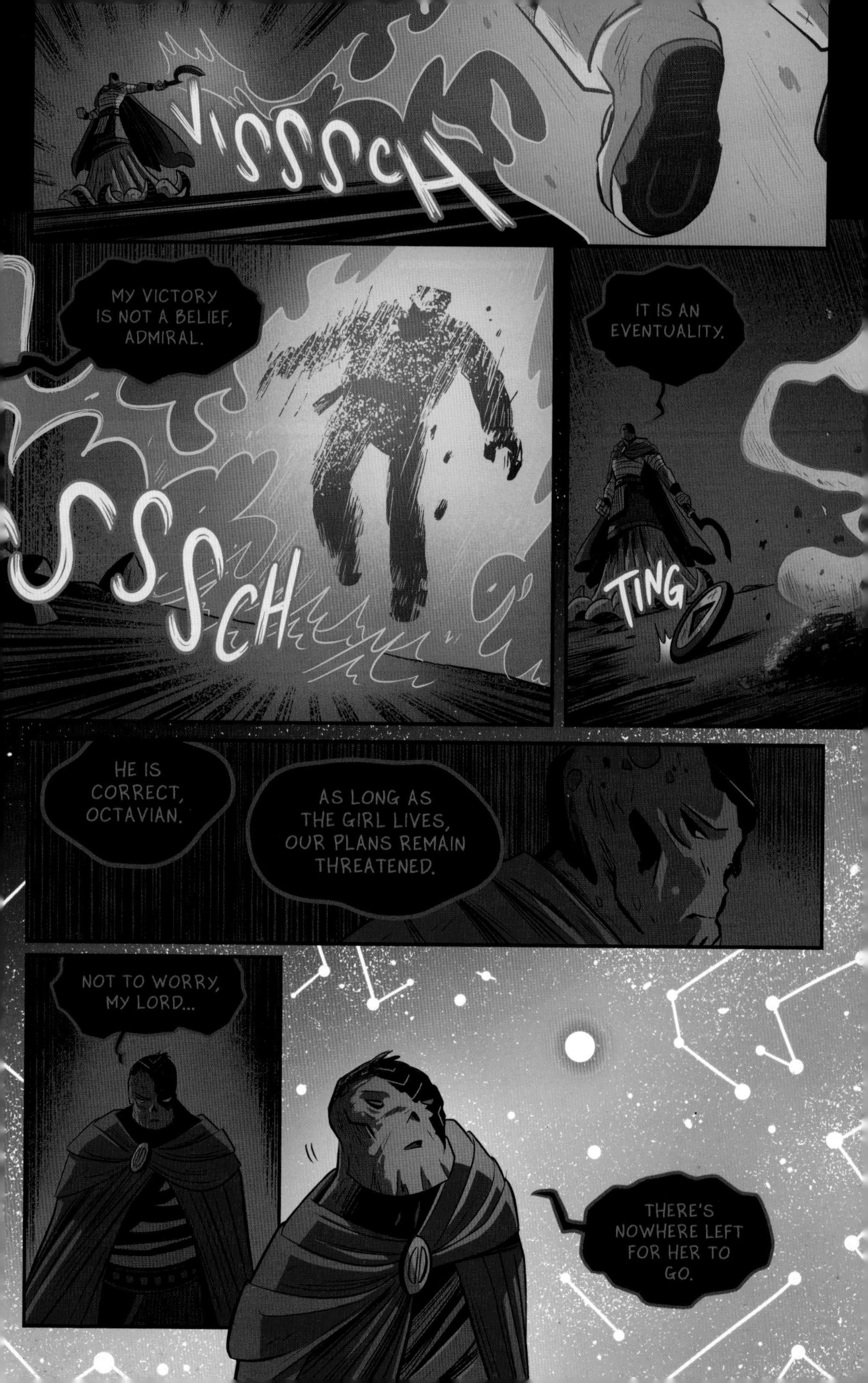
VISSSCH
MY VICTORY IS NOT A BELIEF, ADMIRAL.
SSSCH
IT IS AN EVENTUALITY.
TING
HE IS CORRECT, OCTAVIAN.
AS LONG AS THE GIRL LIVES, OUR PLANS REMAIN THREATENED.
NOT TO WORRY, MY LORD...
THERE'S NOWHERE LEFT FOR HER TO GO.

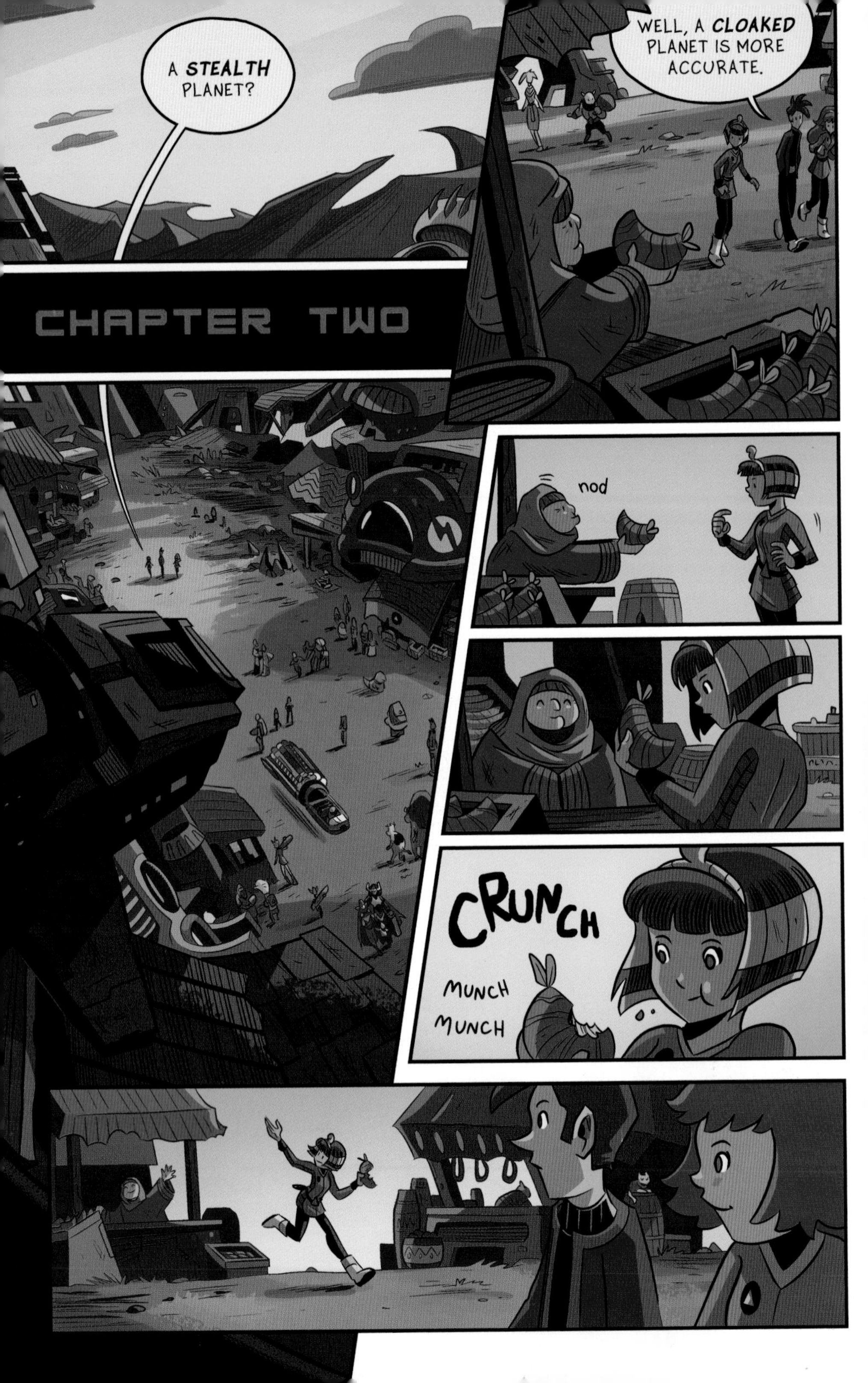
A STEALTH PLANET?
CHAPTER TWO
WELL, A CLOAKED PLANET IS MORE ACCURATE.
nod
CRUNCH
MUNCH
MUNCH

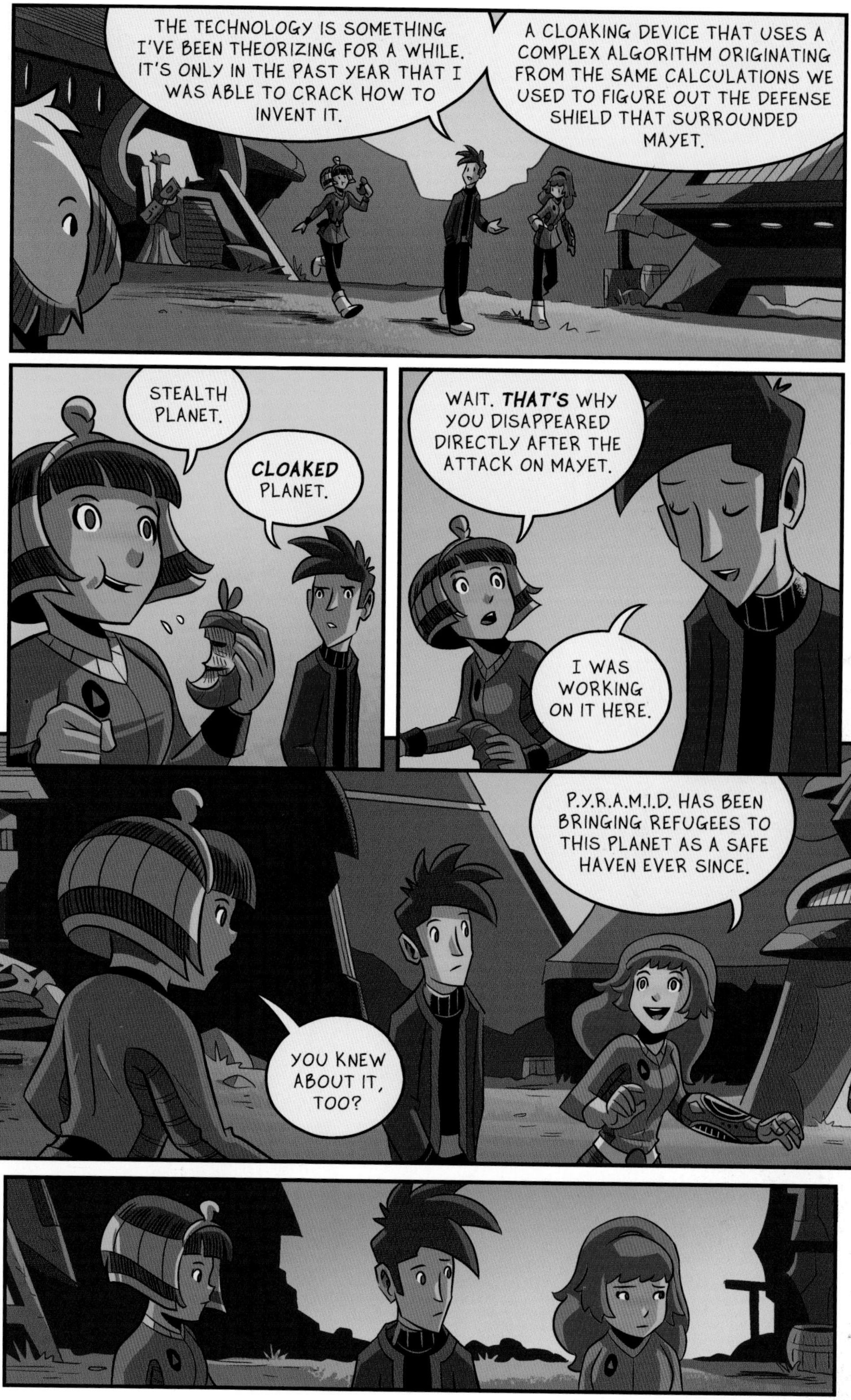
THE TECHNOLOGY IS SOMETHING I'VE BEEN THEORIZING FOR A WHILE. IT'S ONLY IN THE PAST YEAR THAT I WAS ABLE TO CRACK HOW TO INVENT IT.
A CLOAKING DEVICE THAT USES A COMPLEX ALGORITHM ORIGINATING FROM THE SAME CALCULATIONS WE USED TO FIGURE OUT THE DEFENSE SHIELD THAT SURROUNDED MAYET.
STEALTH PLANET.
CLOAKED PLANET.
WAIT. **THAT'S** WHY YOU DISAPPEARED DIRECTLY AFTER THE ATTACK ON MAYET.
I WAS WORKING ON IT HERE.
P.Y.R.A.M.I.D. HAS BEEN BRINGING REFUGEES TO THIS PLANET AS A SAFE HAVEN EVER SINCE.
YOU KNEW ABOUT IT, TOO?

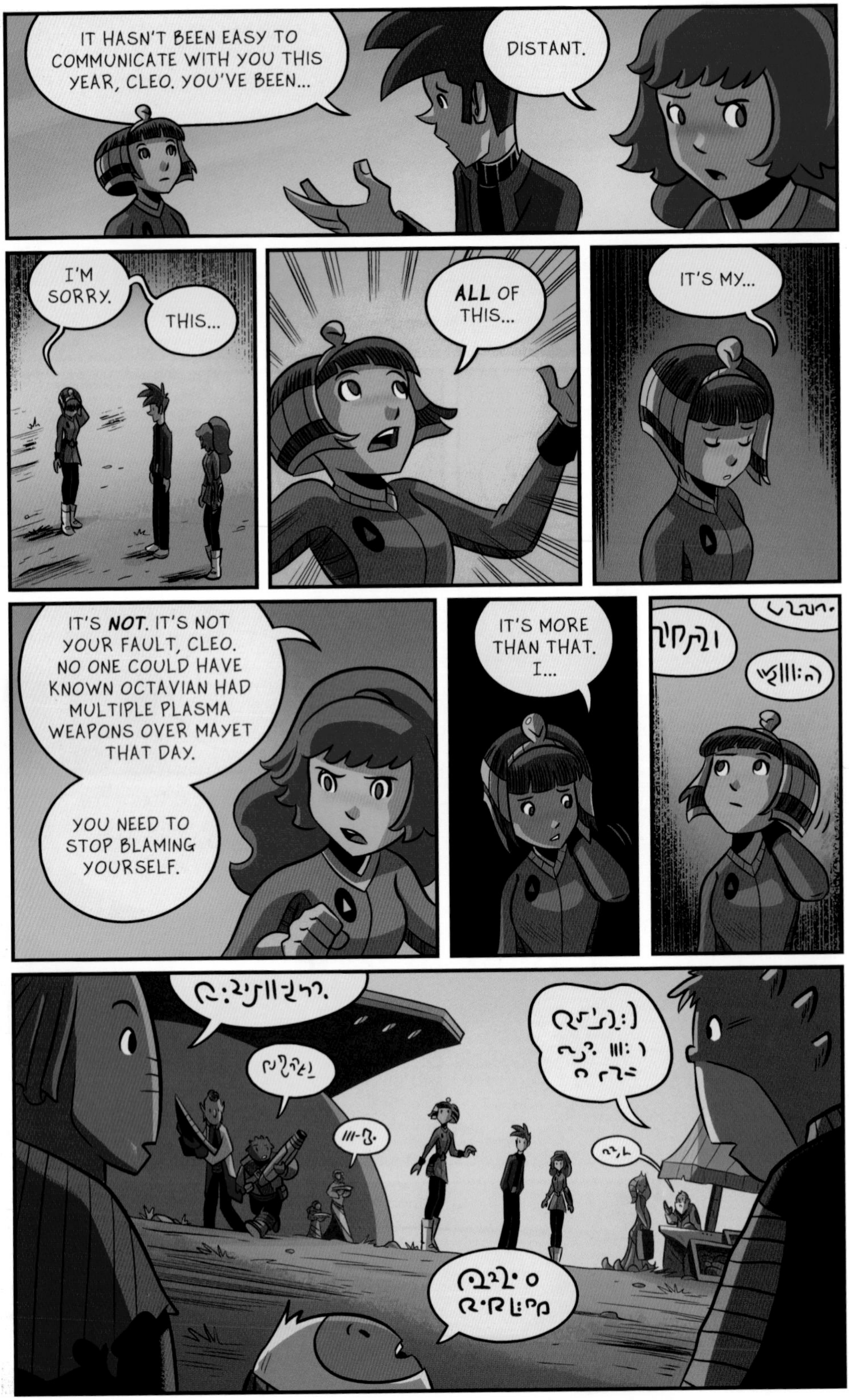
IT HASN'T BEEN EASY TO COMMUNICATE WITH YOU THIS YEAR, CLEO. YOU'VE BEEN...
DISTANT.
I'M SORRY.
THIS...
ALL OF THIS...
IT'S MY...
IT'S **NOT**. IT'S NOT YOUR FAULT, CLEO. NO ONE COULD HAVE KNOWN OCTAVIAN HAD MULTIPLE PLASMA WEAPONS OVER MAYET THAT DAY.
YOU NEED TO STOP BLAMING YOURSELF.
IT'S MORE THAN THAT. I...

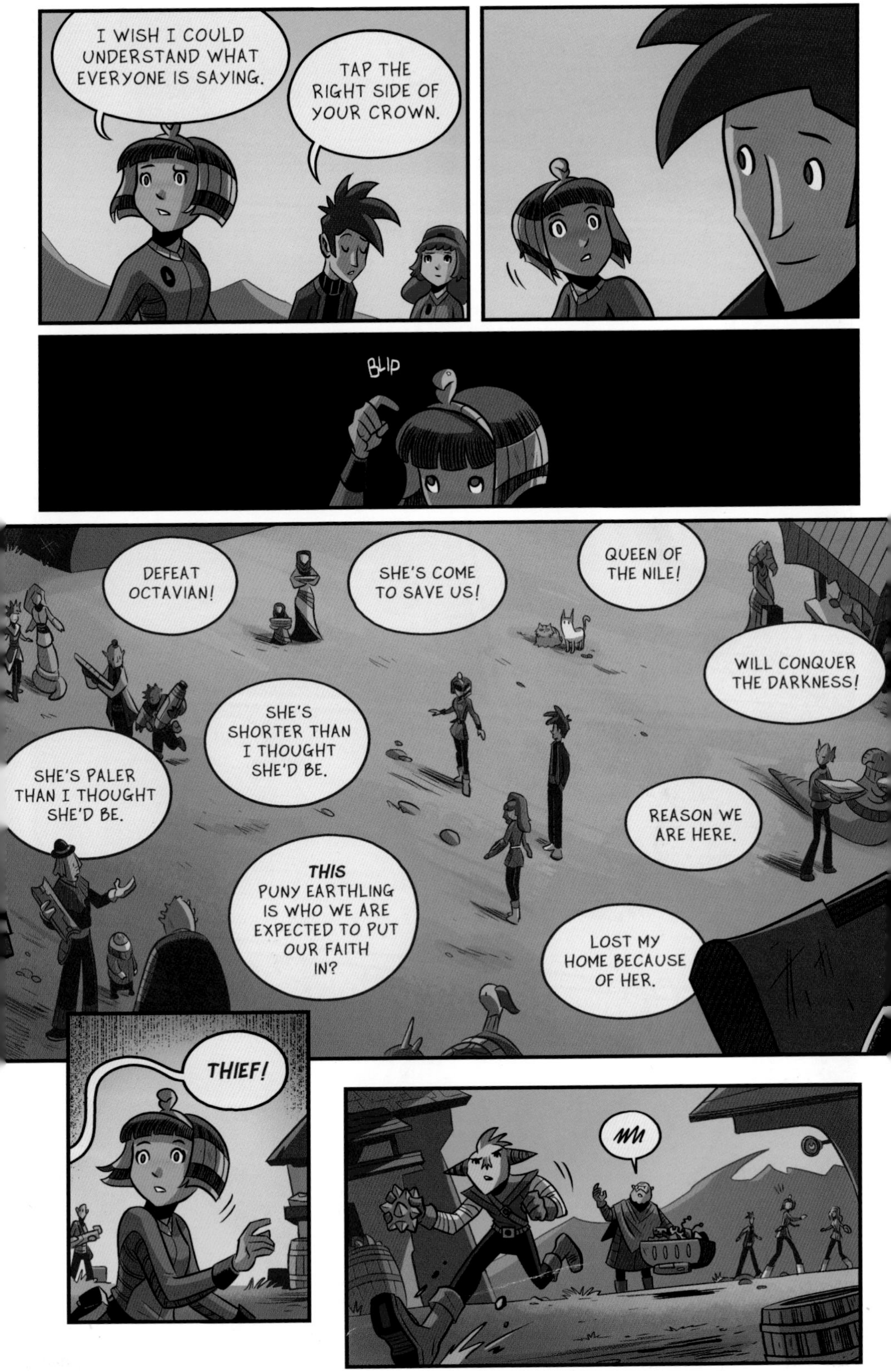
I WISH I COULD UNDERSTAND WHAT EVERYONE IS SAYING.
TAP THE RIGHT SIDE OF YOUR CROWN.
BLIP
DEFEAT OCTAVIAN!
SHE'S COME TO SAVE US!
QUEEN OF THE NILE!
WILL CONQUER THE DARKNESS!
SHE'S SHORTER THAN I THOUGHT SHE'D BE.
SHE'S PALER THAN I THOUGHT SHE'D BE.
REASON WE ARE HERE.
THIS PUNY EARTHLING IS WHO WE ARE EXPECTED TO PUT OUR FAITH IN?
LOST MY HOME BECAUSE OF HER.
THIEF!

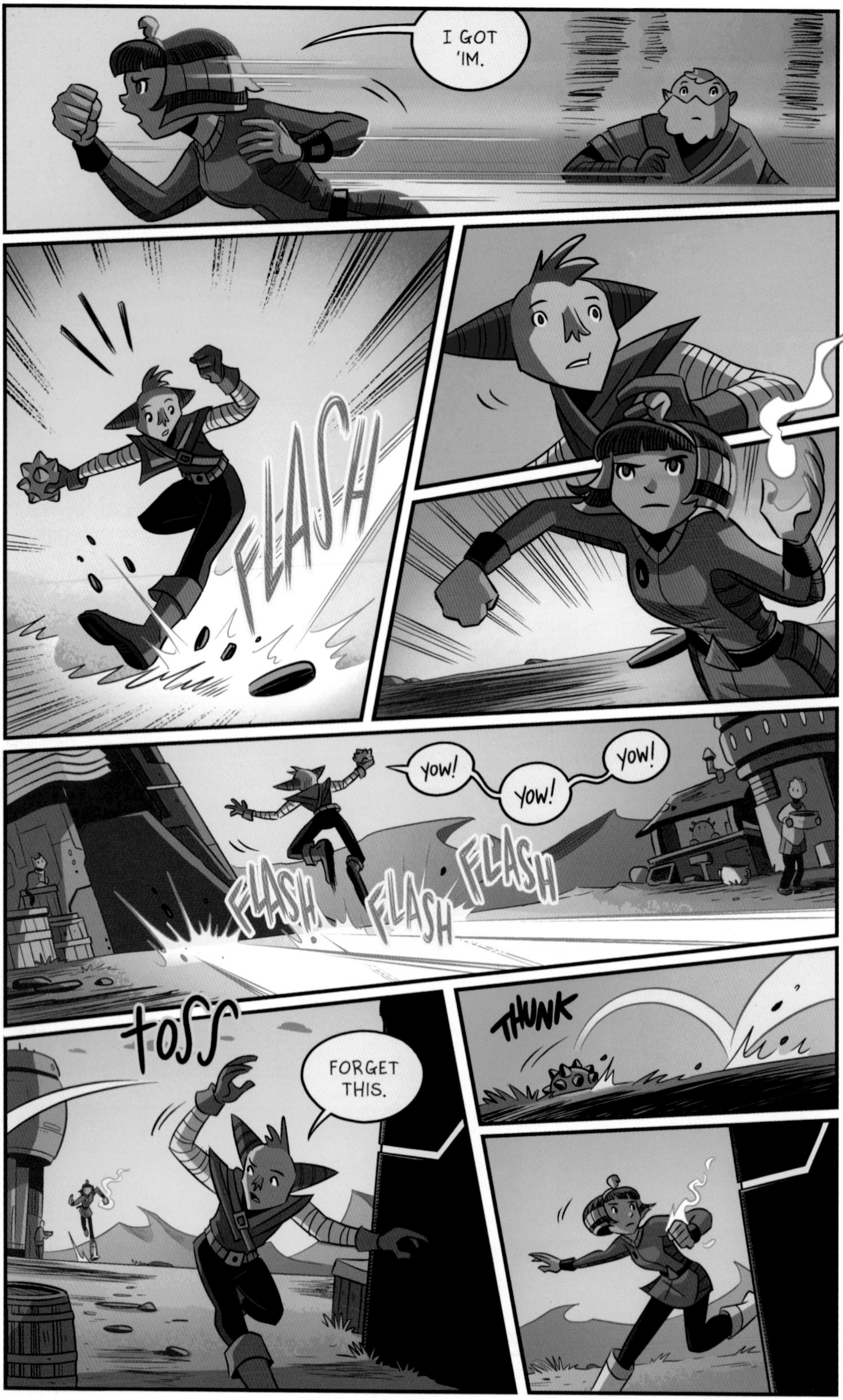
I GOT 'IM.
FLASH
YOW!
YOW!
YOW!
FLASH
FLASH
FLASH
TOSS
FORGET THIS.
THUNK

HERE'S YOUR, UM...THING.

THINGS WERE BETTER ON HYKOSIS.

CLINK

HYKOSIS?

HUFF
HUFF

THERE'S PEOPLE FROM HYKOSIS HERE?

SURVIVORS?

THERE'S PEOPLE FROM **EVERYWHERE** HERE.

I KNOW WHAT YOU'RE HOPING, CLEO, BUT P.Y.R.A.M.I.D. KEEPS A PRETTY THOROUGH LOG OF WHO LANDS ON THIS PLANET. NO ONE MATCHING ANTONY'S PROFILE HAS COME THROUGH THAT ATMOSPHERE.

BELIEVE ME. I'VE CHECKED.

EVERY DAY.

NOT **EVERY** DAY, BRIAN.

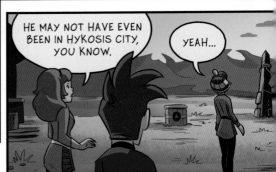

HE MAY NOT HAVE EVEN BEEN IN HYKOSIS CITY, YOU KNOW.

YEAH...

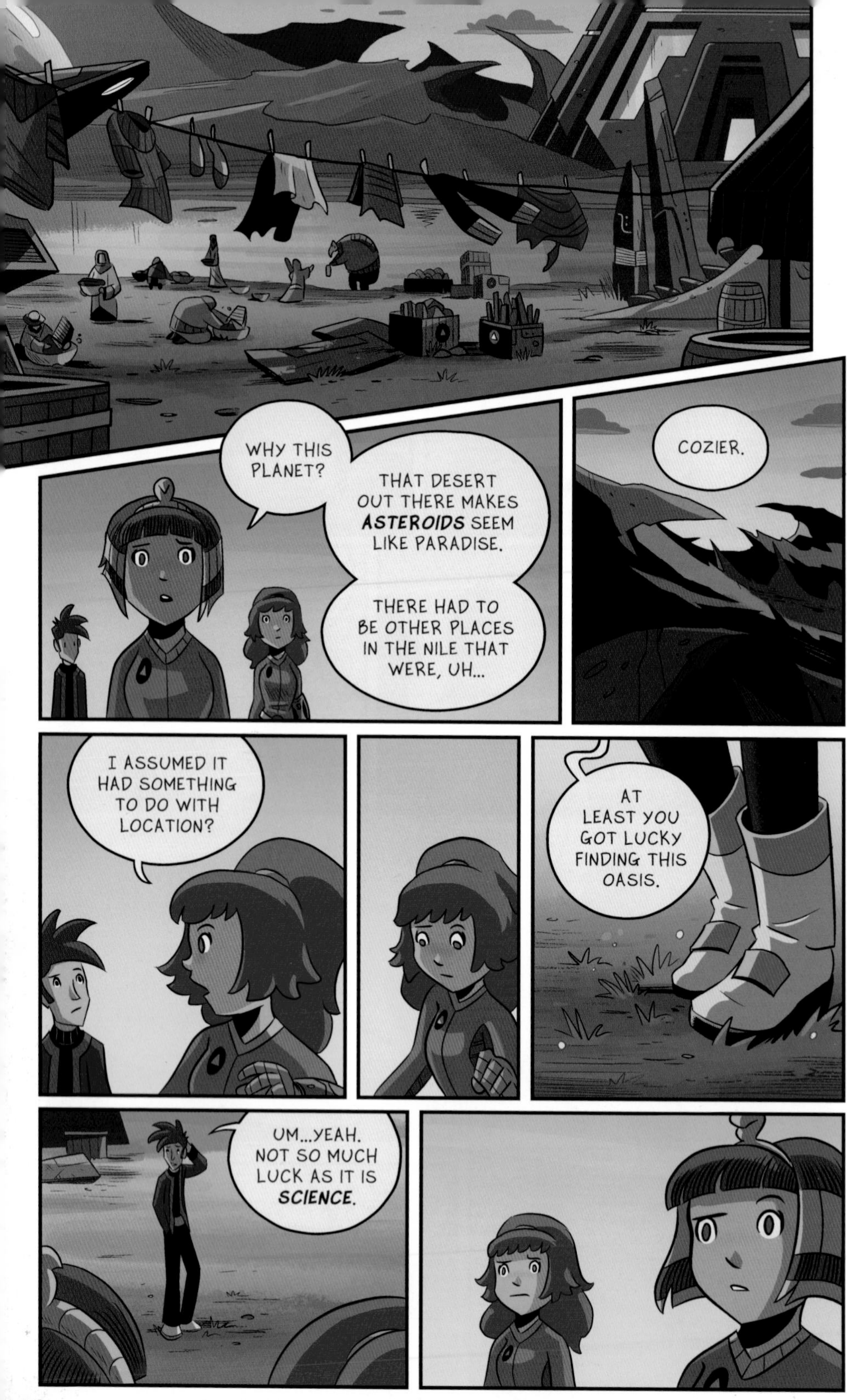
WHY THIS PLANET?
THAT DESERT OUT THERE MAKES **ASTEROIDS** SEEM LIKE PARADISE.
THERE HAD TO BE OTHER PLACES IN THE NILE THAT WERE, UH...
COZIER.
I ASSUMED IT HAD SOMETHING TO DO WITH LOCATION?
AT LEAST YOU GOT LUCKY FINDING THIS OASIS.
UM...YEAH. NOT SO MUCH LUCK AS IT IS **SCIENCE**.

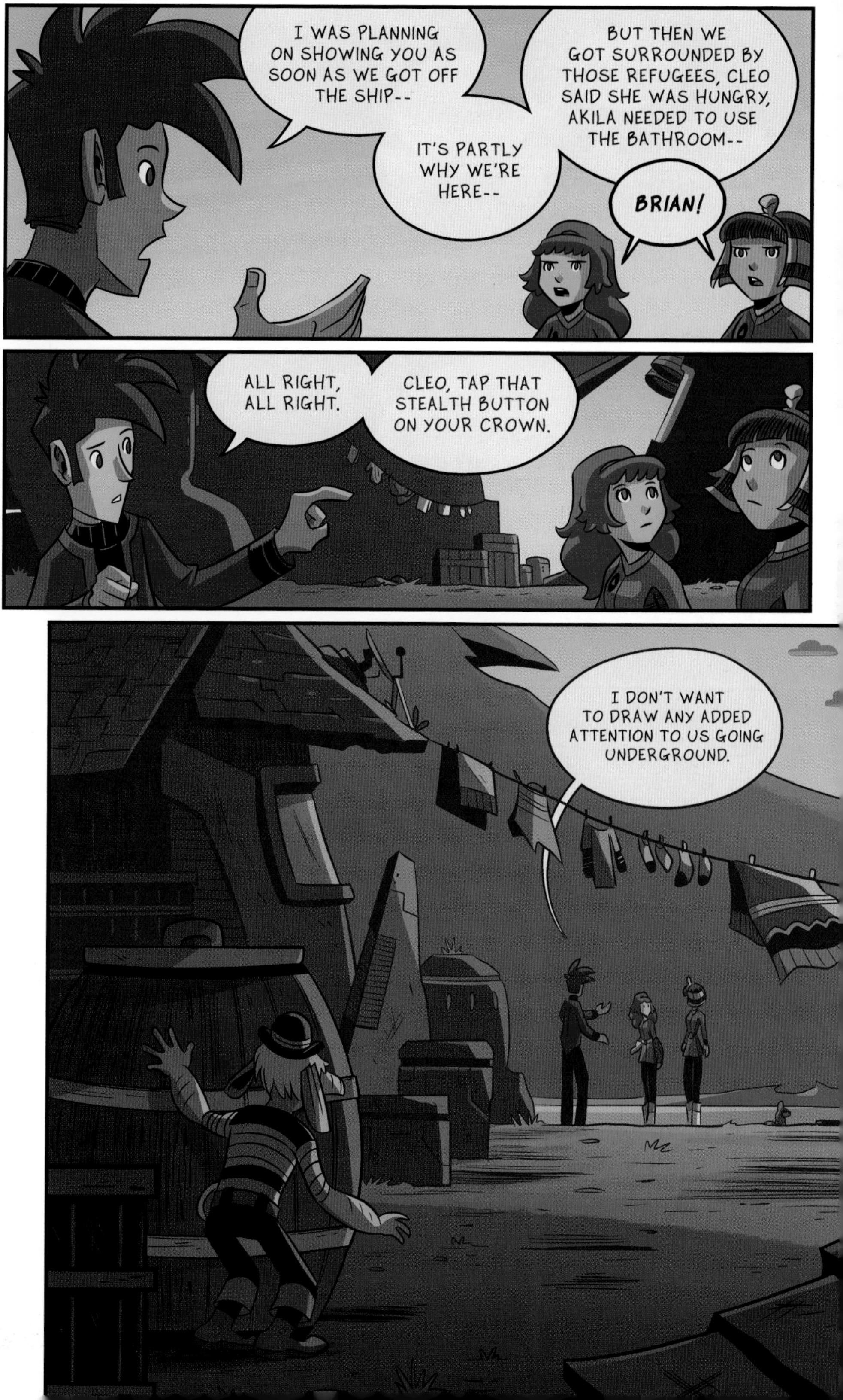
I WAS PLANNING ON SHOWING YOU AS SOON AS WE GOT OFF THE SHIP--
IT'S PARTLY WHY WE'RE HERE--
BUT THEN WE GOT SURROUNDED BY THOSE REFUGEES, CLEO SAID SHE WAS HUNGRY, AKILA NEEDED TO USE THE BATHROOM--
BRIAN!
ALL RIGHT, ALL RIGHT.
CLEO, TAP THAT STEALTH BUTTON ON YOUR CROWN.
I DON'T WANT TO DRAW ANY ADDED ATTENTION TO US GOING UNDERGROUND.

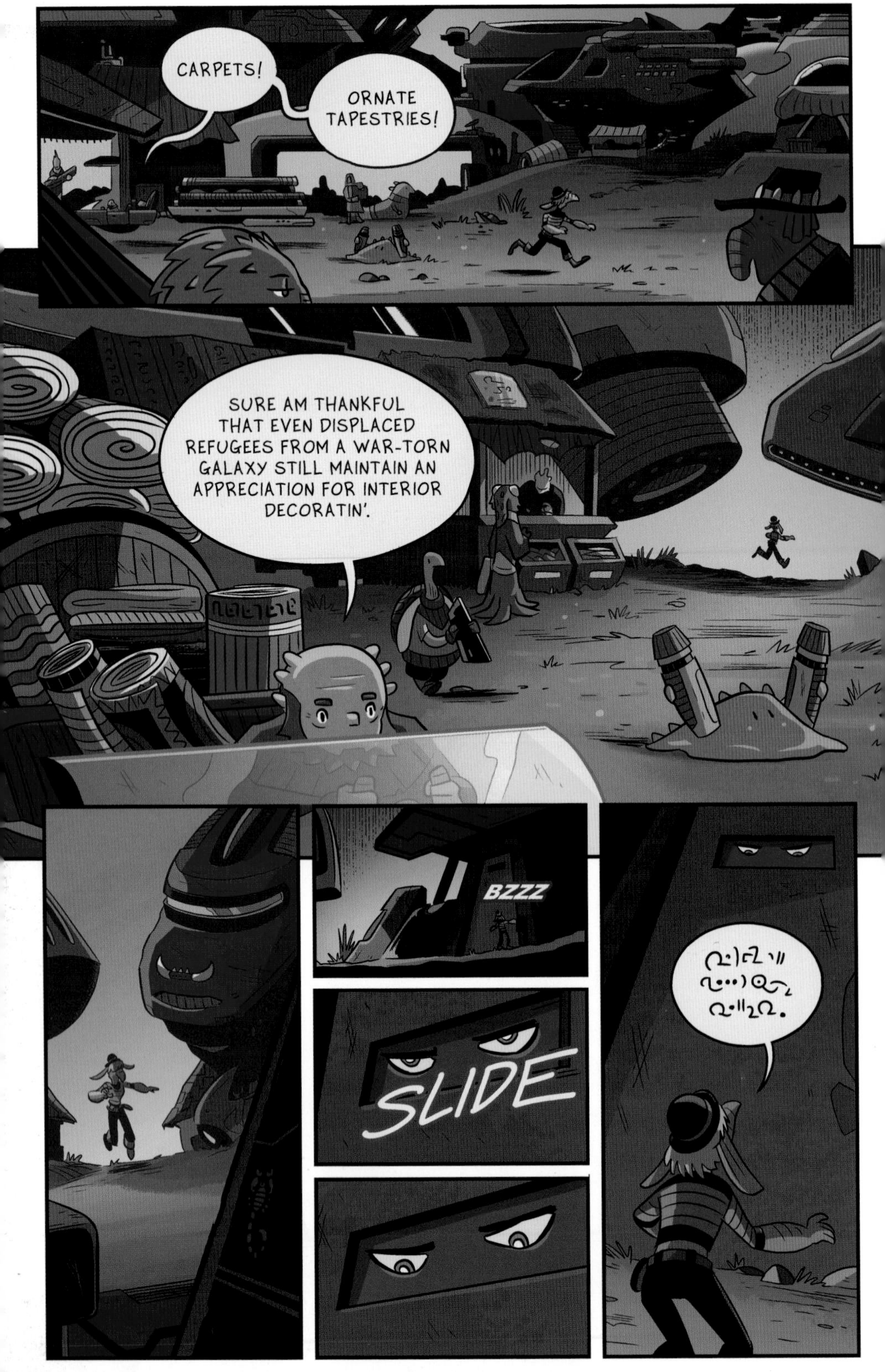

CARPETS!
ORNATE TAPESTRIES!
SURE AM THANKFUL THAT EVEN DISPLACED REFUGEES FROM A WAR-TORN GALAXY STILL MAINTAIN AN APPRECIATION FOR INTERIOR DECORATIN'.
BZZZ
SLIDE

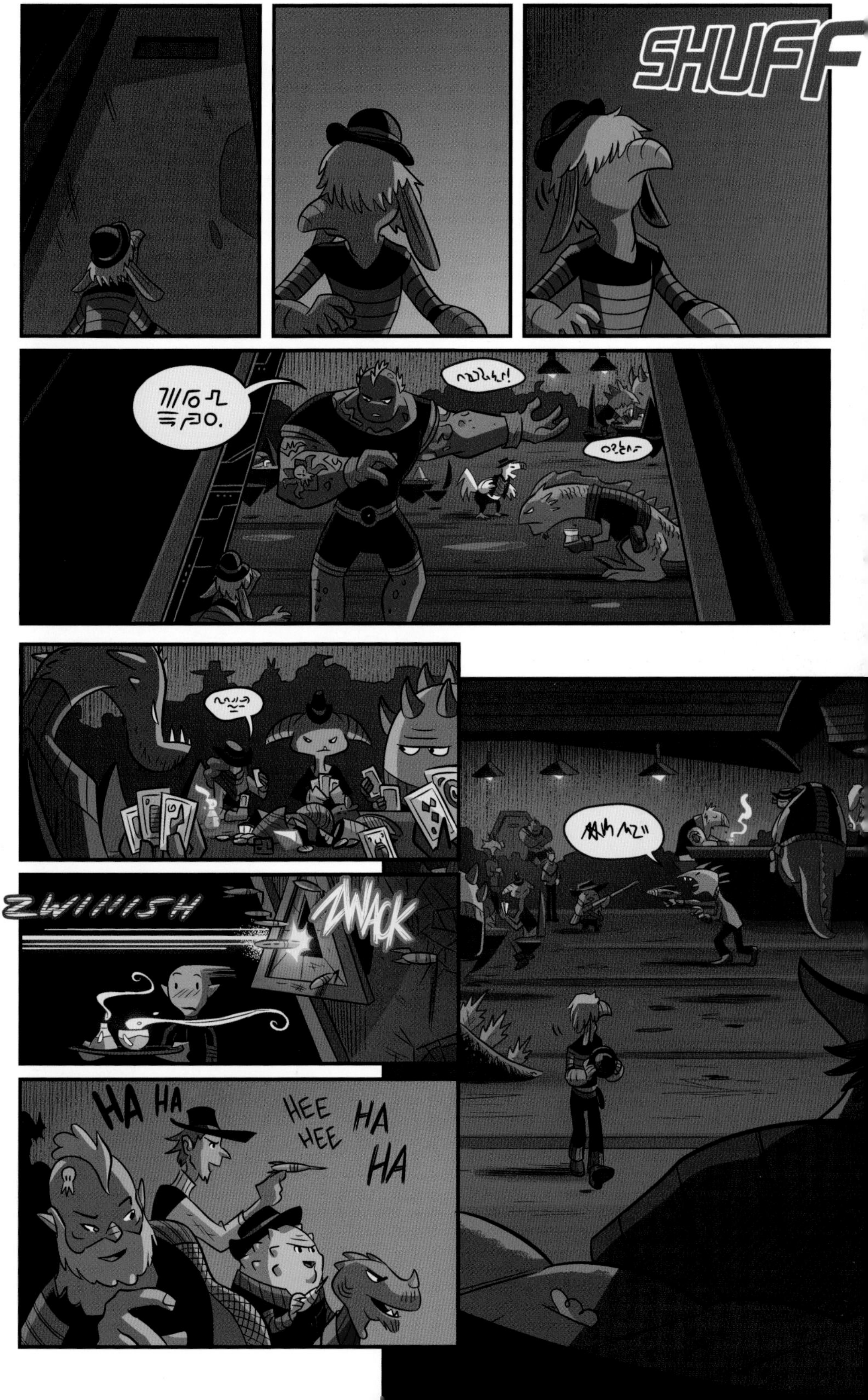
SHUFF
ZWIIIISH
ZWACK
HA HA
HEE HEE
HA HA

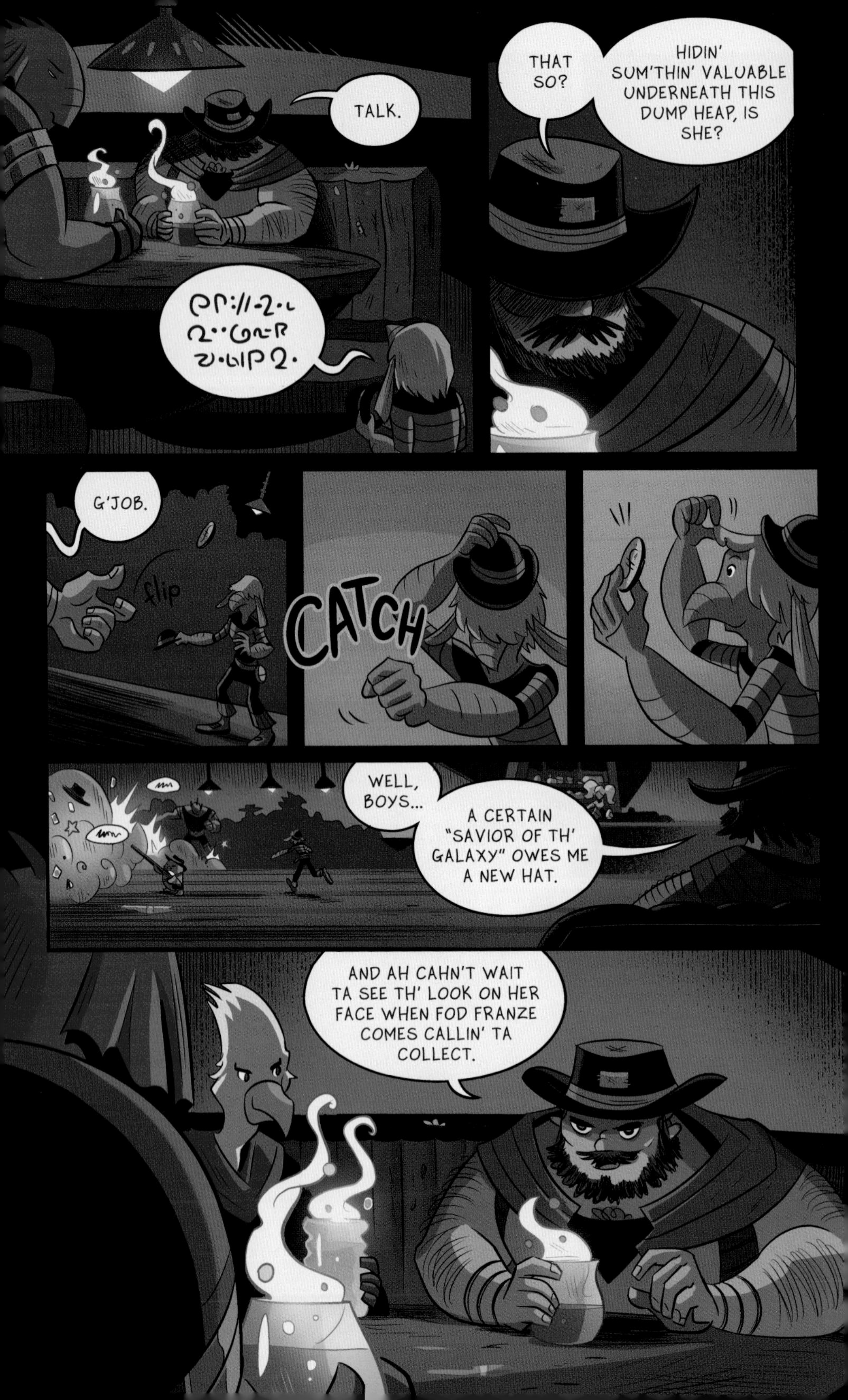
TALK.
THAT SO?
HIDIN' SUM'THIN' VALUABLE UNDERNEATH THIS DUMP HEAP, IS SHE?
G'JOB.
flip
CATCH
WELL, BOYS...
A CERTAIN "SAVIOR OF TH' GALAXY" OWES ME A NEW HAT.
AND AH CAHN'T WAIT TA SEE TH' LOOK ON HER FACE WHEN FOD FRANZE COMES CALLIN' TA COLLECT.

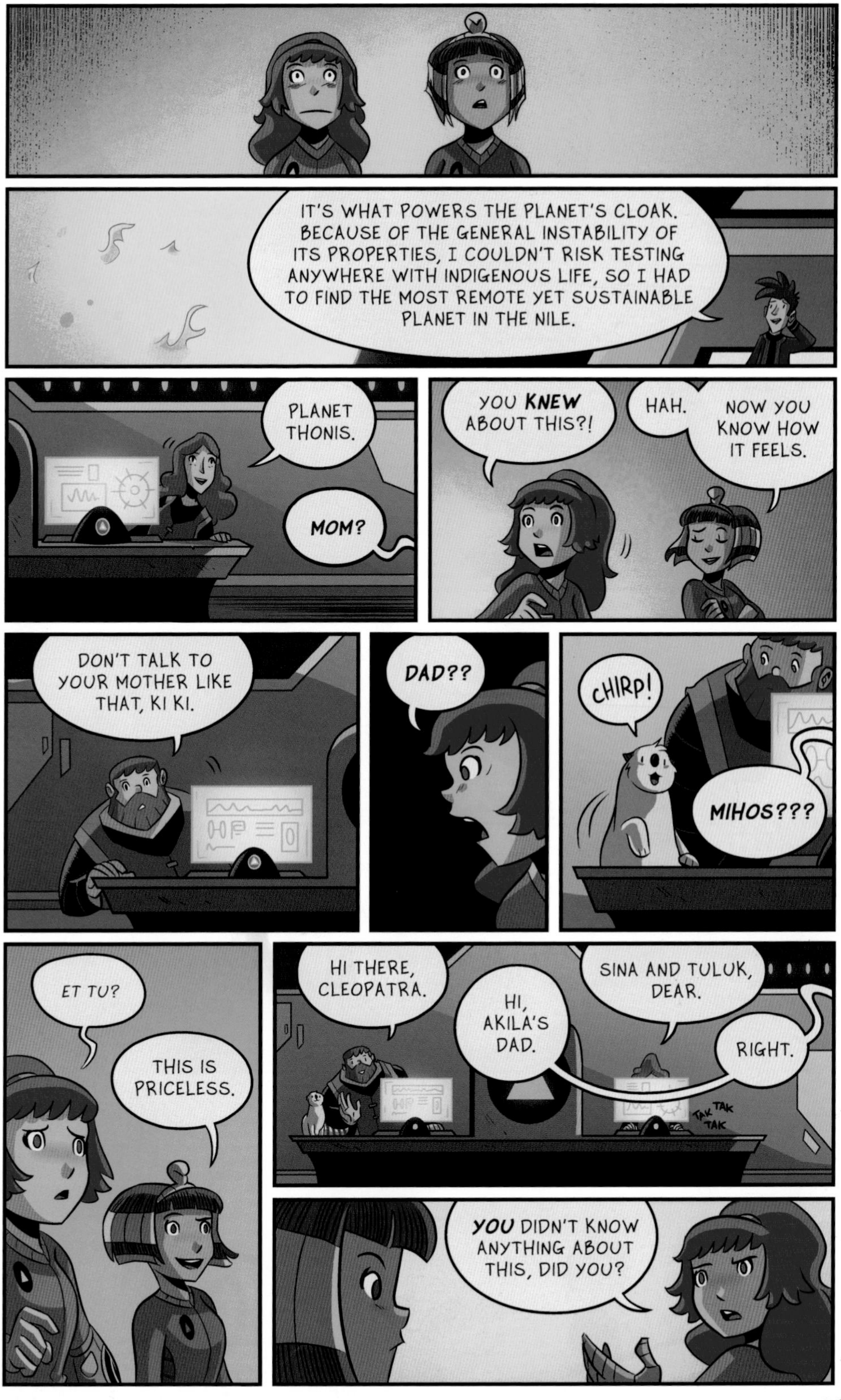
IT'S WHAT POWERS THE PLANET'S CLOAK. BECAUSE OF THE GENERAL INSTABILITY OF ITS PROPERTIES, I COULDN'T RISK TESTING ANYWHERE WITH INDIGENOUS LIFE, SO I HAD TO FIND THE MOST REMOTE YET SUSTAINABLE PLANET IN THE NILE.
PLANET THONIS.
MOM?
YOU KNEW ABOUT THIS?!
HAH.
NOW YOU KNOW HOW IT FEELS.
DON'T TALK TO YOUR MOTHER LIKE THAT, KI KI.
DAD??
CHIRP!
MIHOS???
ET TU?
THIS IS PRICELESS.
HI THERE, CLEOPATRA.
HI, AKILA'S DAD.
SINA AND TULUK, DEAR.
RIGHT.
TAK TAK TAK
YOU DIDN'T KNOW ANYTHING ABOUT THIS, DID YOU?

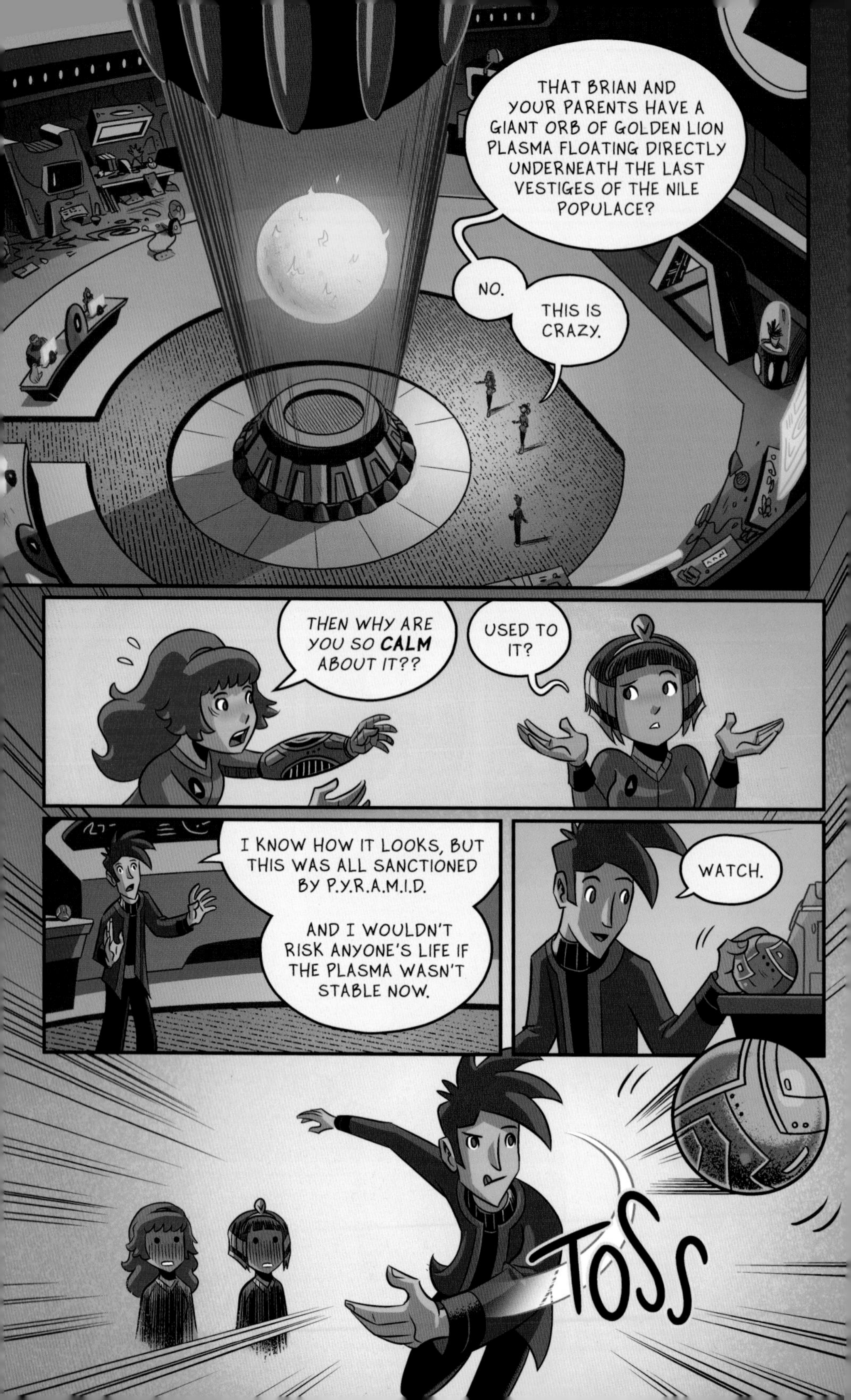
THAT BRIAN AND YOUR PARENTS HAVE A GIANT ORB OF GOLDEN LION PLASMA FLOATING DIRECTLY UNDERNEATH THE LAST VESTIGES OF THE NILE POPULACE?
NO.
THIS IS CRAZY.
THEN WHY ARE YOU SO **CALM** ABOUT IT??
USED TO IT?
I KNOW HOW IT LOOKS, BUT THIS WAS ALL SANCTIONED BY P.Y.R.A.M.I.D.
AND I WOULDN'T RISK ANYONE'S LIFE IF THE PLASMA WASN'T STABLE NOW.
WATCH.
TOSS

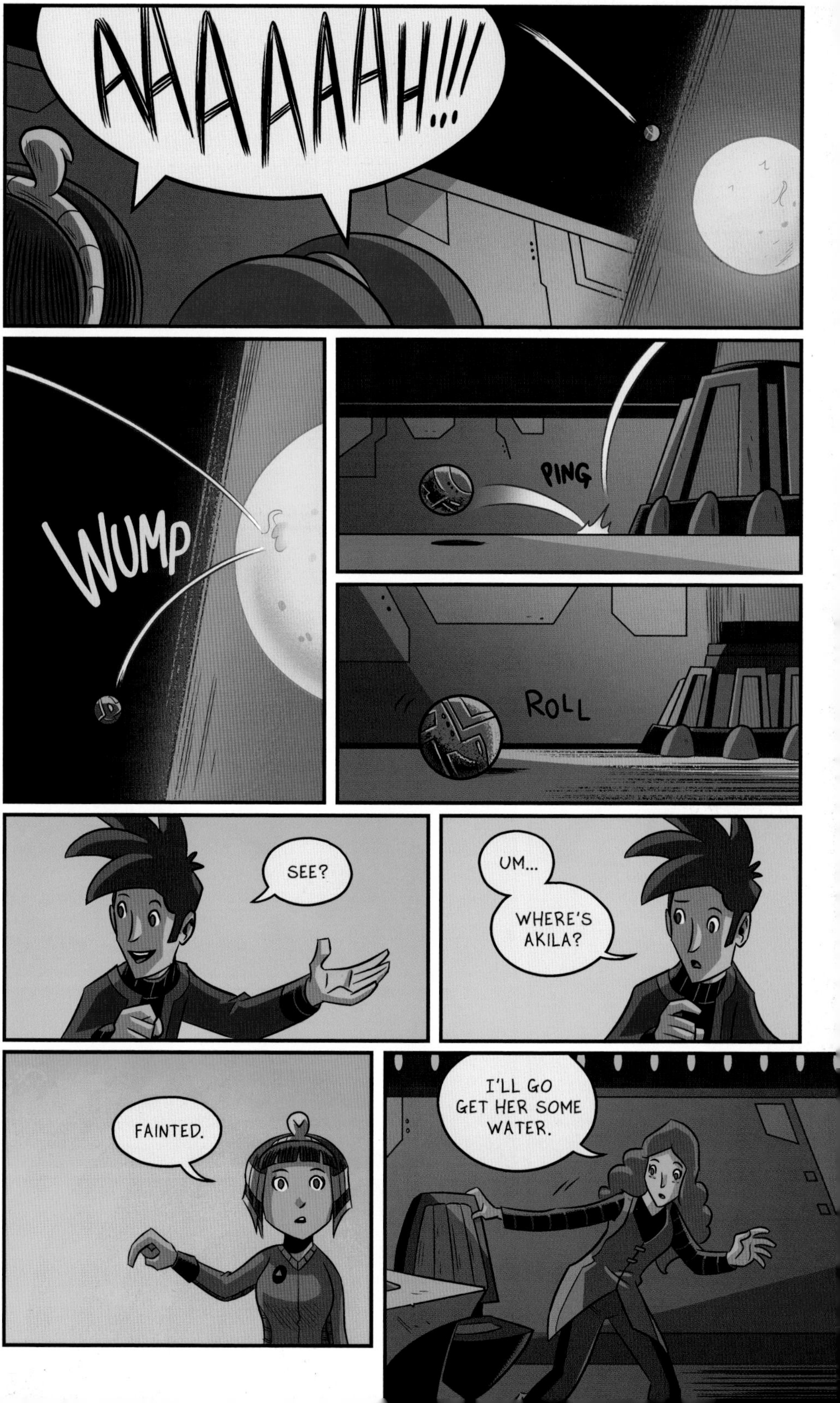
AAAAAAH!!!
WUMP
PING
ROLL
SEE?
UM...
WHERE'S AKILA?
FAINTED.
I'LL GO GET HER SOME WATER.

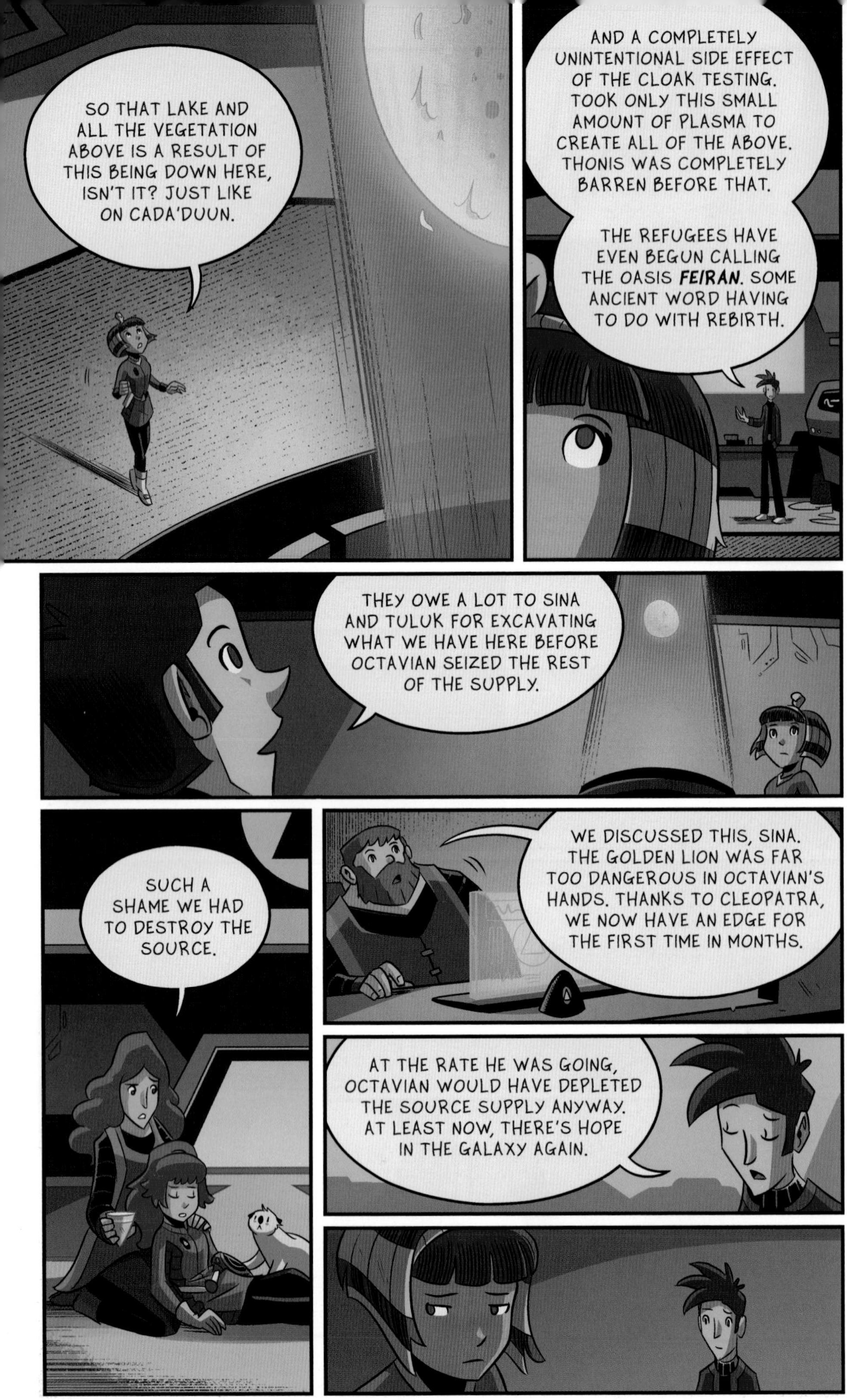
SO THAT LAKE AND ALL THE VEGETATION ABOVE IS A RESULT OF THIS BEING DOWN HERE, ISN'T IT? JUST LIKE ON CADA'DUUN.
AND A COMPLETELY UNINTENTIONAL SIDE EFFECT OF THE CLOAK TESTING. TOOK ONLY THIS SMALL AMOUNT OF PLASMA TO CREATE ALL OF THE ABOVE. THONIS WAS COMPLETELY BARREN BEFORE THAT.
THE REFUGEES HAVE EVEN BEGUN CALLING THE OASIS **FEIRAN**. SOME ANCIENT WORD HAVING TO DO WITH REBIRTH.
THEY OWE A LOT TO SINA AND TULUK FOR EXCAVATING WHAT WE HAVE HERE BEFORE OCTAVIAN SEIZED THE REST OF THE SUPPLY.
SUCH A SHAME WE HAD TO DESTROY THE SOURCE.
WE DISCUSSED THIS, SINA. THE GOLDEN LION WAS FAR TOO DANGEROUS IN OCTAVIAN'S HANDS. THANKS TO CLEOPATRA, WE NOW HAVE AN EDGE FOR THE FIRST TIME IN MONTHS.
AT THE RATE HE WAS GOING, OCTAVIAN WOULD HAVE DEPLETED THE SOURCE SUPPLY ANYWAY. AT LEAST NOW, THERE'S HOPE IN THE GALAXY AGAIN.

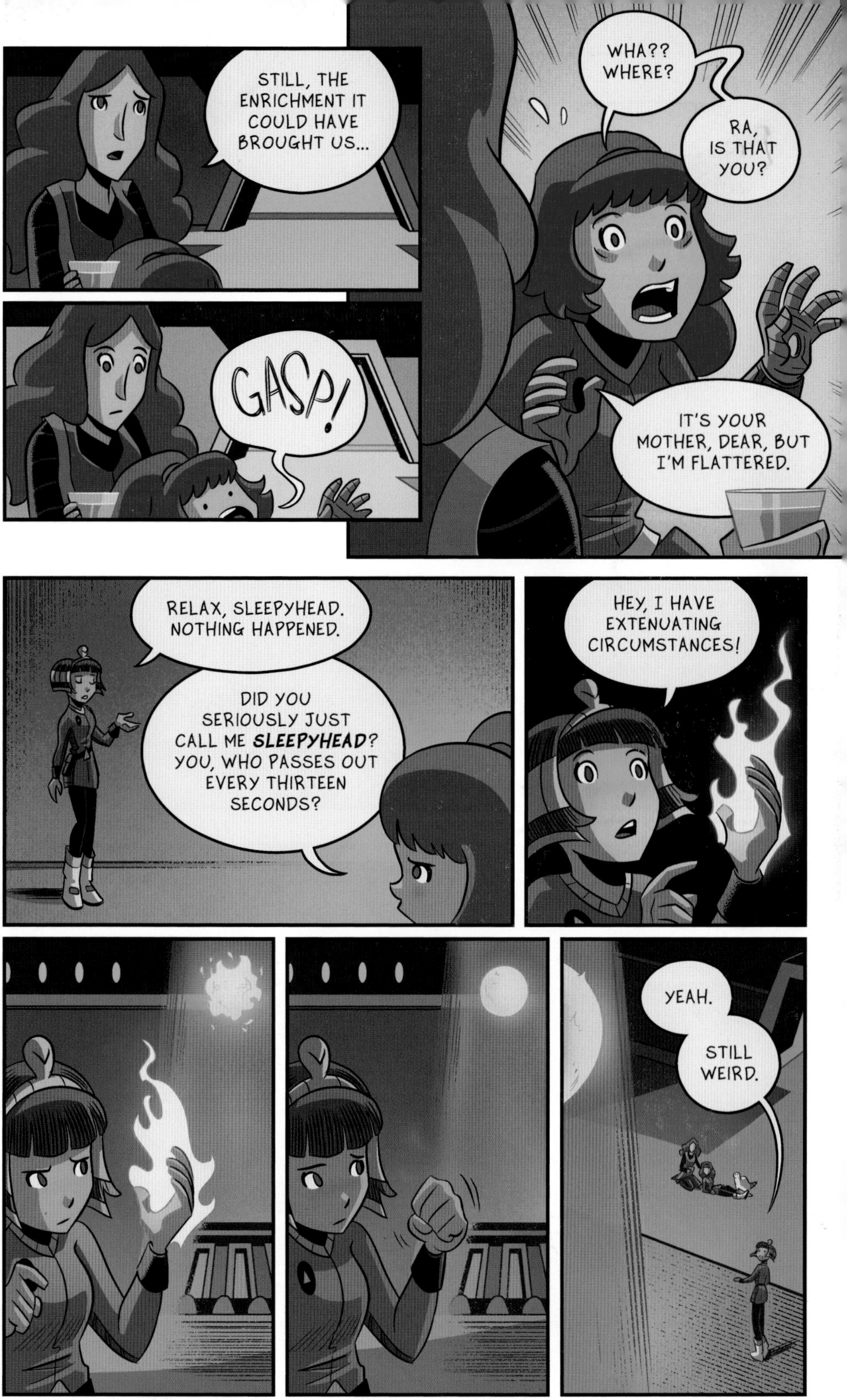

STILL, THE ENRICHMENT IT COULD HAVE BROUGHT US...
GASP!
WHA?? WHERE?
RA, IS THAT YOU?
IT'S YOUR MOTHER, DEAR, BUT I'M FLATTERED.
RELAX, SLEEPYHEAD. NOTHING HAPPENED.
DID YOU SERIOUSLY JUST CALL ME **SLEEPYHEAD**? YOU, WHO PASSES OUT EVERY THIRTEEN SECONDS?
HEY, I HAVE EXTENUATING CIRCUMSTANCES!
YEAH.
STILL WEIRD.

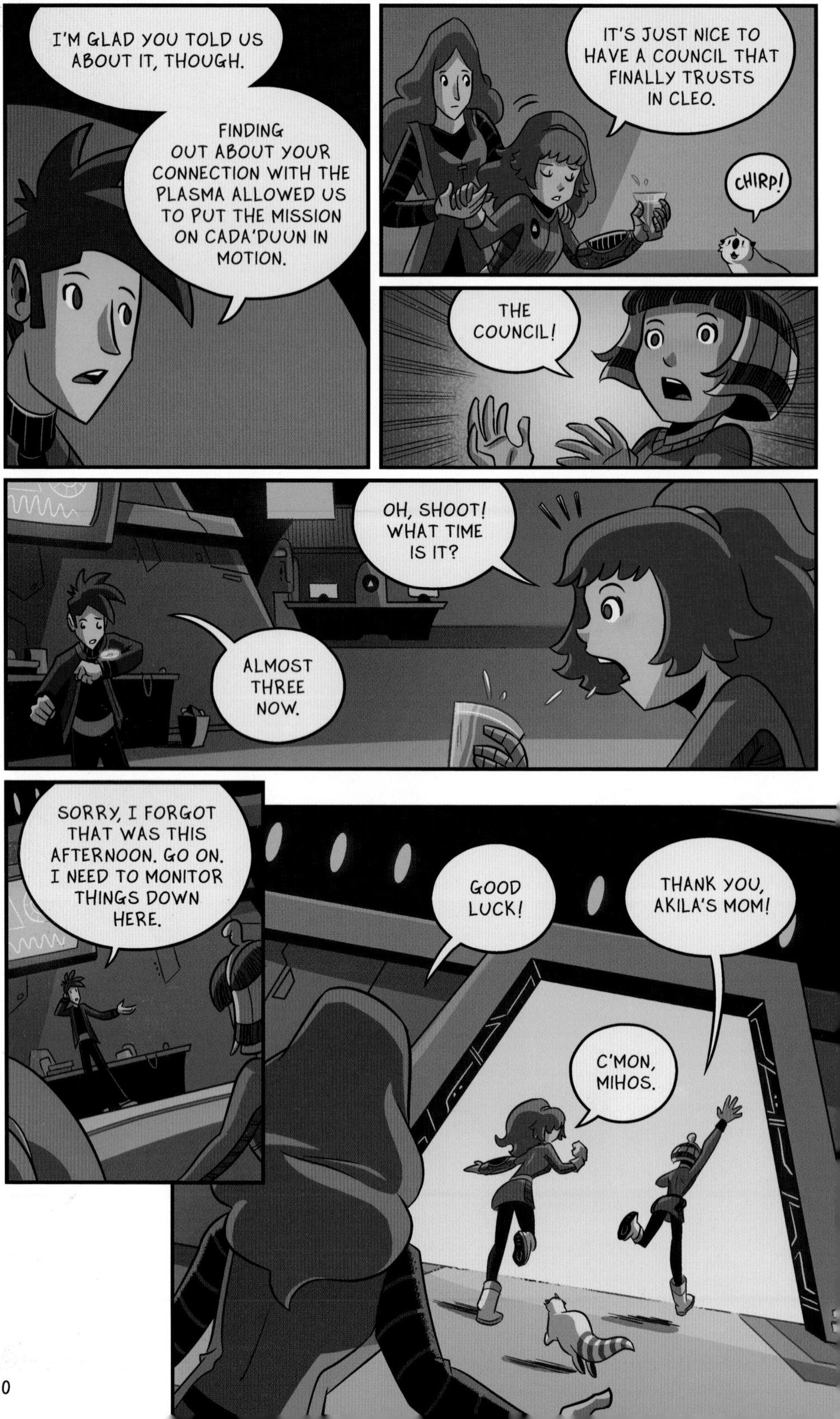
I'M GLAD YOU TOLD US ABOUT IT, THOUGH.
FINDING OUT ABOUT YOUR CONNECTION WITH THE PLASMA ALLOWED US TO PUT THE MISSION ON CADA'DUUN IN MOTION.
IT'S JUST NICE TO HAVE A COUNCIL THAT FINALLY TRUSTS IN CLEO.
CHIRP!
THE COUNCIL!
OH, SHOOT! WHAT TIME IS IT?
ALMOST THREE NOW.
SORRY, I FORGOT THAT WAS THIS AFTERNOON. GO ON. I NEED TO MONITOR THINGS DOWN HERE.
GOOD LUCK!
THANK YOU, AKILA'S MOM!
C'MON, MIHOS.

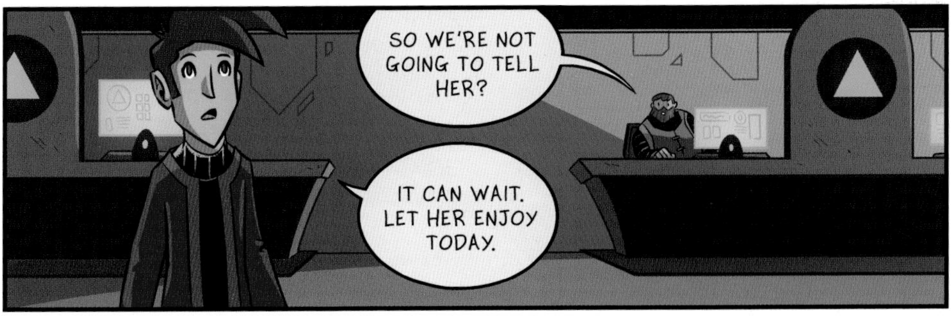
SO WE'RE NOT GOING TO TELL HER?
IT CAN WAIT. LET HER ENJOY TODAY.

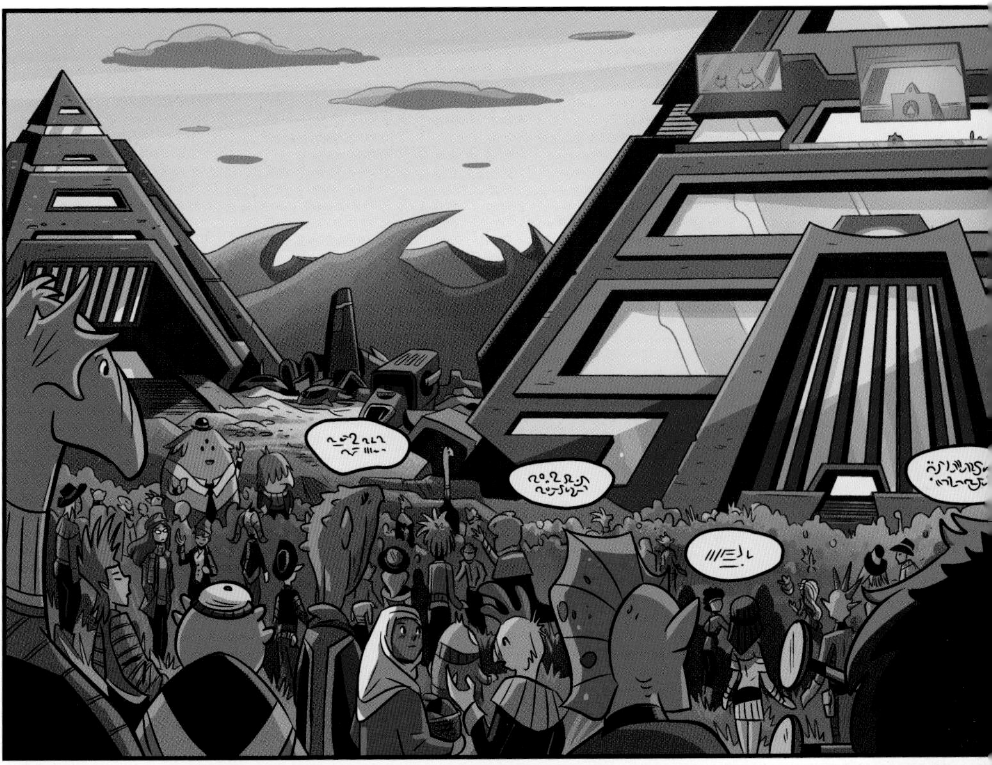

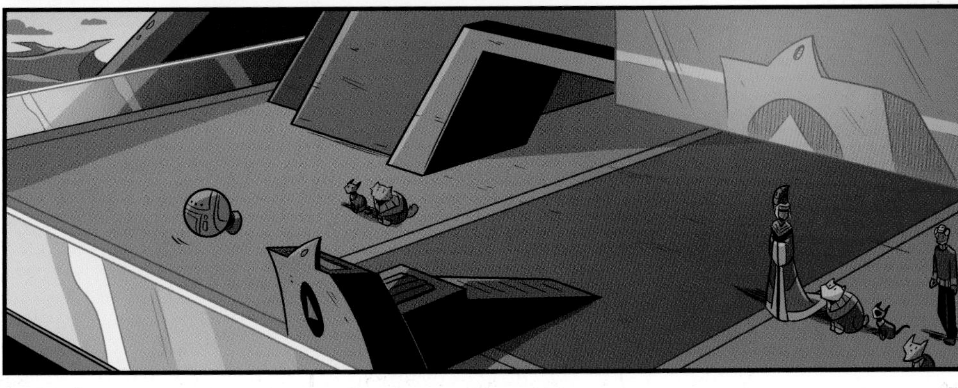

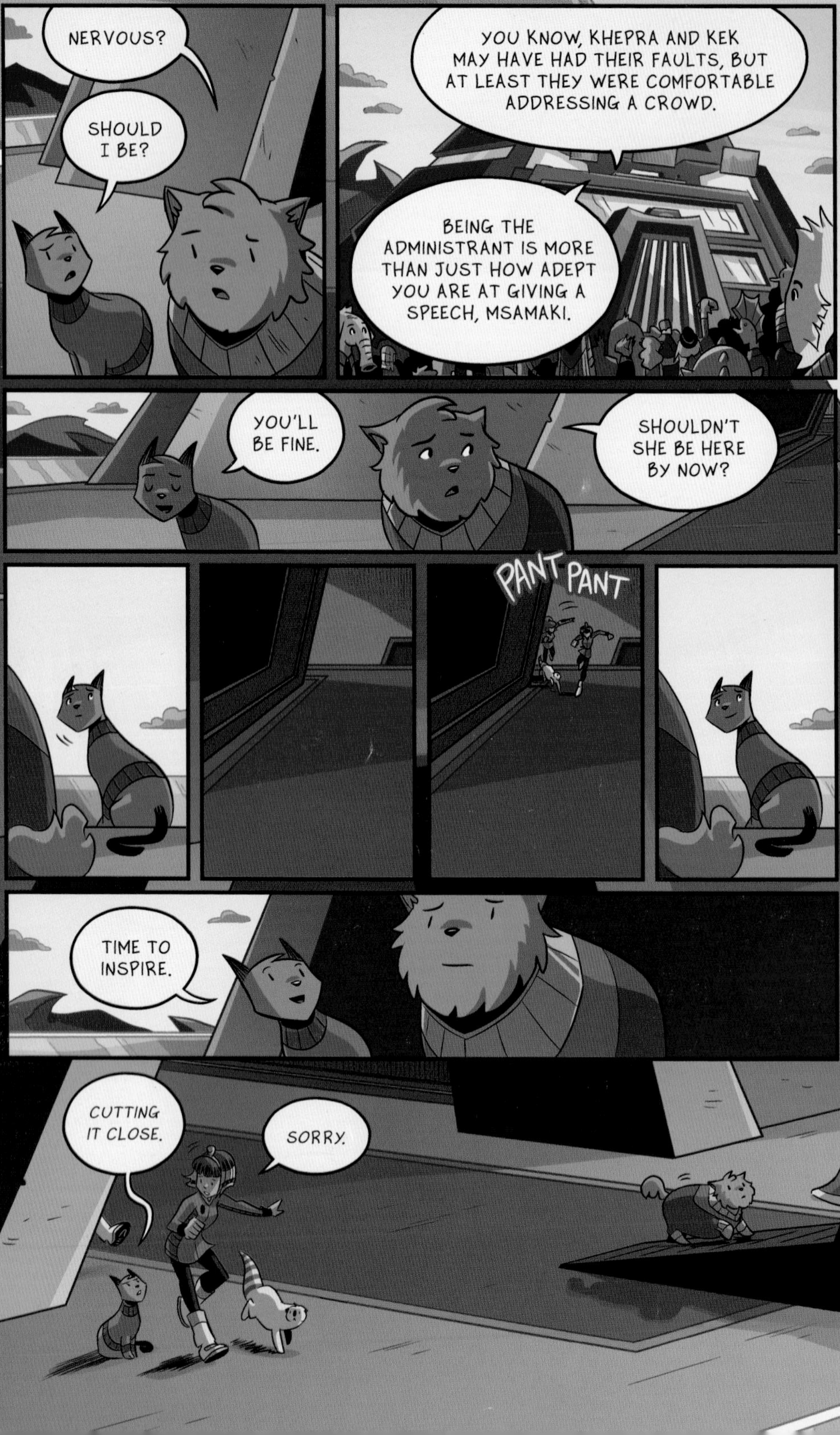
NERVOUS?
SHOULD I BE?
YOU KNOW, KHEPRA AND KEK MAY HAVE HAD THEIR FAULTS, BUT AT LEAST THEY WERE COMFORTABLE ADDRESSING A CROWD.
BEING THE ADMINISTRANT IS MORE THAN JUST HOW ADEPT YOU ARE AT GIVING A SPEECH, MSAMAKI.
YOU'LL BE FINE.
SHOULDN'T SHE BE HERE BY NOW?
PANT PANT
TIME TO INSPIRE.
CUTTING IT CLOSE.
SORRY.

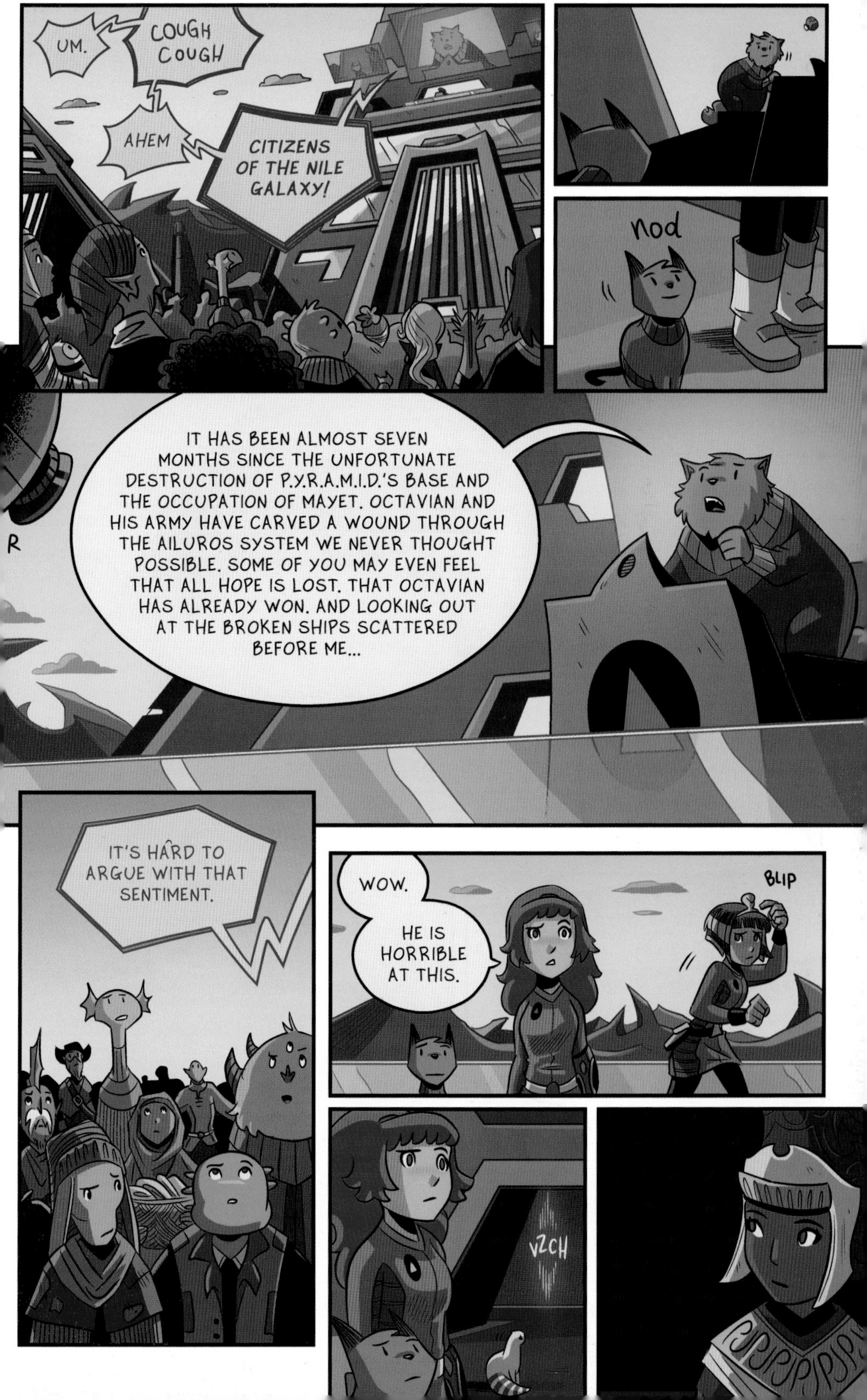
UM.
COUGH COUGH
AHEM
CITIZENS OF THE NILE GALAXY!
nod
IT HAS BEEN ALMOST SEVEN MONTHS SINCE THE UNFORTUNATE DESTRUCTION OF P.Y.R.A.M.I.D.'S BASE AND THE OCCUPATION OF MAYET. OCTAVIAN AND HIS ARMY HAVE CARVED A WOUND THROUGH THE AILUROS SYSTEM WE NEVER THOUGHT POSSIBLE. SOME OF YOU MAY EVEN FEEL THAT ALL HOPE IS LOST. THAT OCTAVIAN HAS ALREADY WON. AND LOOKING OUT AT THE BROKEN SHIPS SCATTERED BEFORE ME...
IT'S HARD TO ARGUE WITH THAT SENTIMENT.
WOW.
HE IS HORRIBLE AT THIS.
BLIP
VZCH

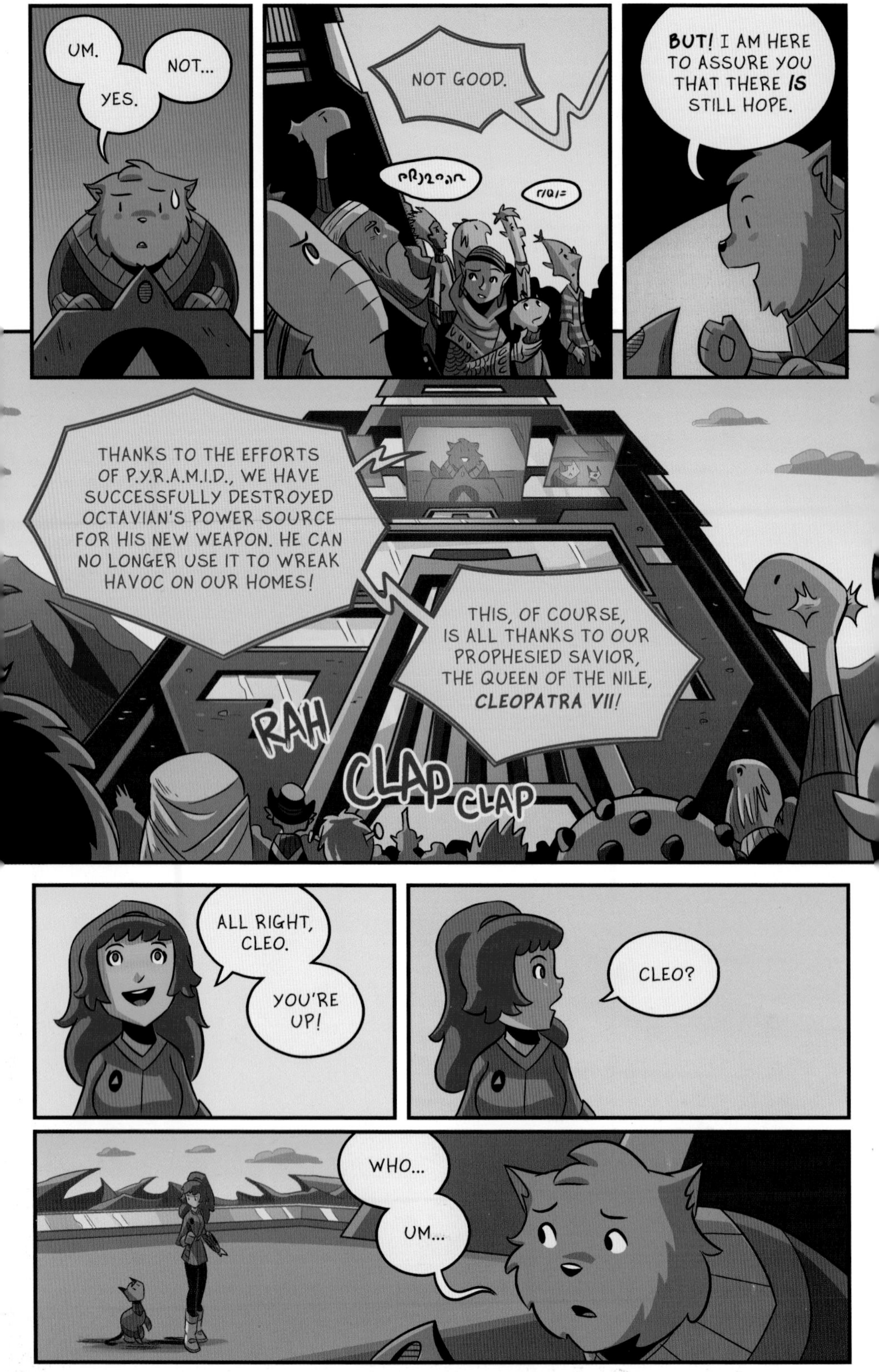
UM.
NOT...
YES.
NOT GOOD.
BUT! I AM HERE TO ASSURE YOU THAT THERE IS STILL HOPE.
THANKS TO THE EFFORTS OF P.Y.R.A.M.I.D., WE HAVE SUCCESSFULLY DESTROYED OCTAVIAN'S POWER SOURCE FOR HIS NEW WEAPON. HE CAN NO LONGER USE IT TO WREAK HAVOC ON OUR HOMES!
THIS, OF COURSE, IS ALL THANKS TO OUR PROPHESIED SAVIOR, THE QUEEN OF THE NILE, CLEOPATRA VII!
RAH
CLAP CLAP
ALL RIGHT, CLEO.
YOU'RE UP!
CLEO?
WHO...
UM...

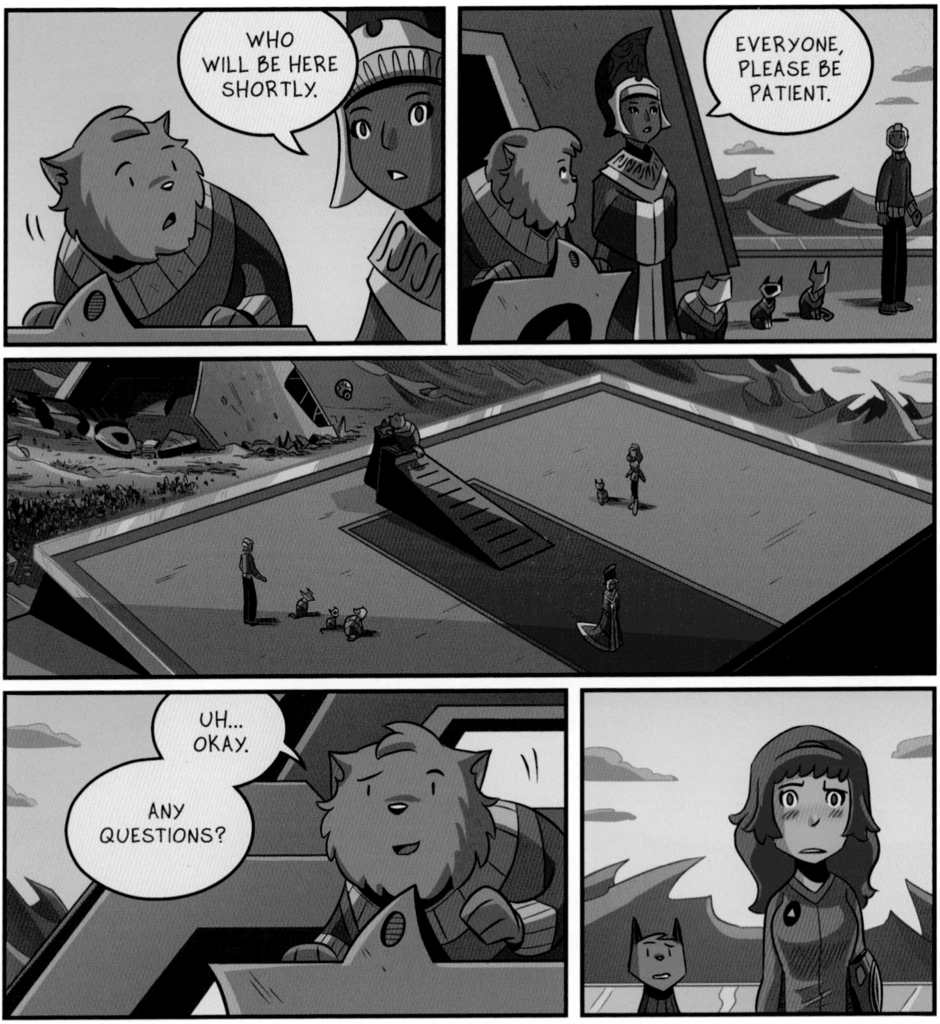
WHO WILL BE HERE SHORTLY.
EVERYONE, PLEASE BE PATIENT.
UH... OKAY.
ANY QUESTIONS?

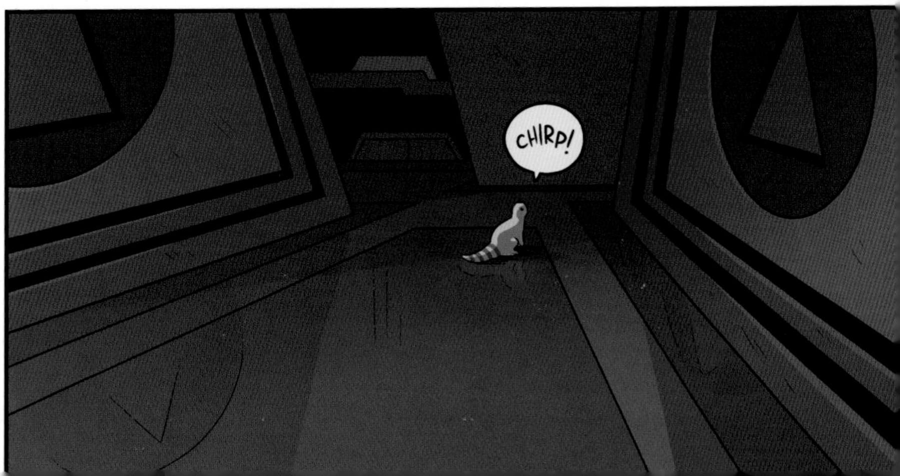
CHIRP!

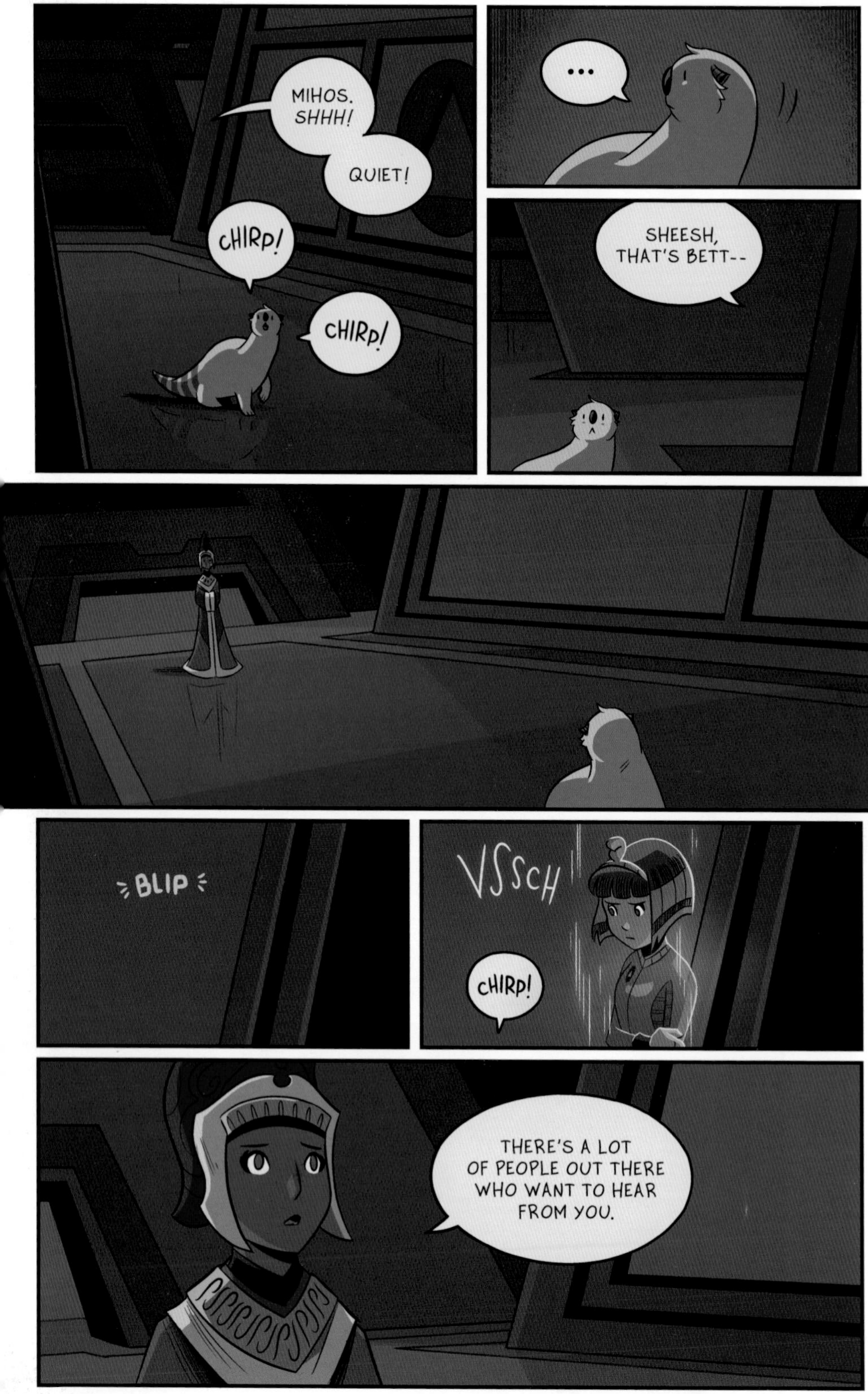

MIHOS. SHHH!
QUIET!
CHIRP!
CHIRP!
...
SHEESH, THAT'S BETT--
BLIP
VSSCH
CHIRP!
THERE'S A LOT OF PEOPLE OUT THERE WHO WANT TO HEAR FROM YOU.

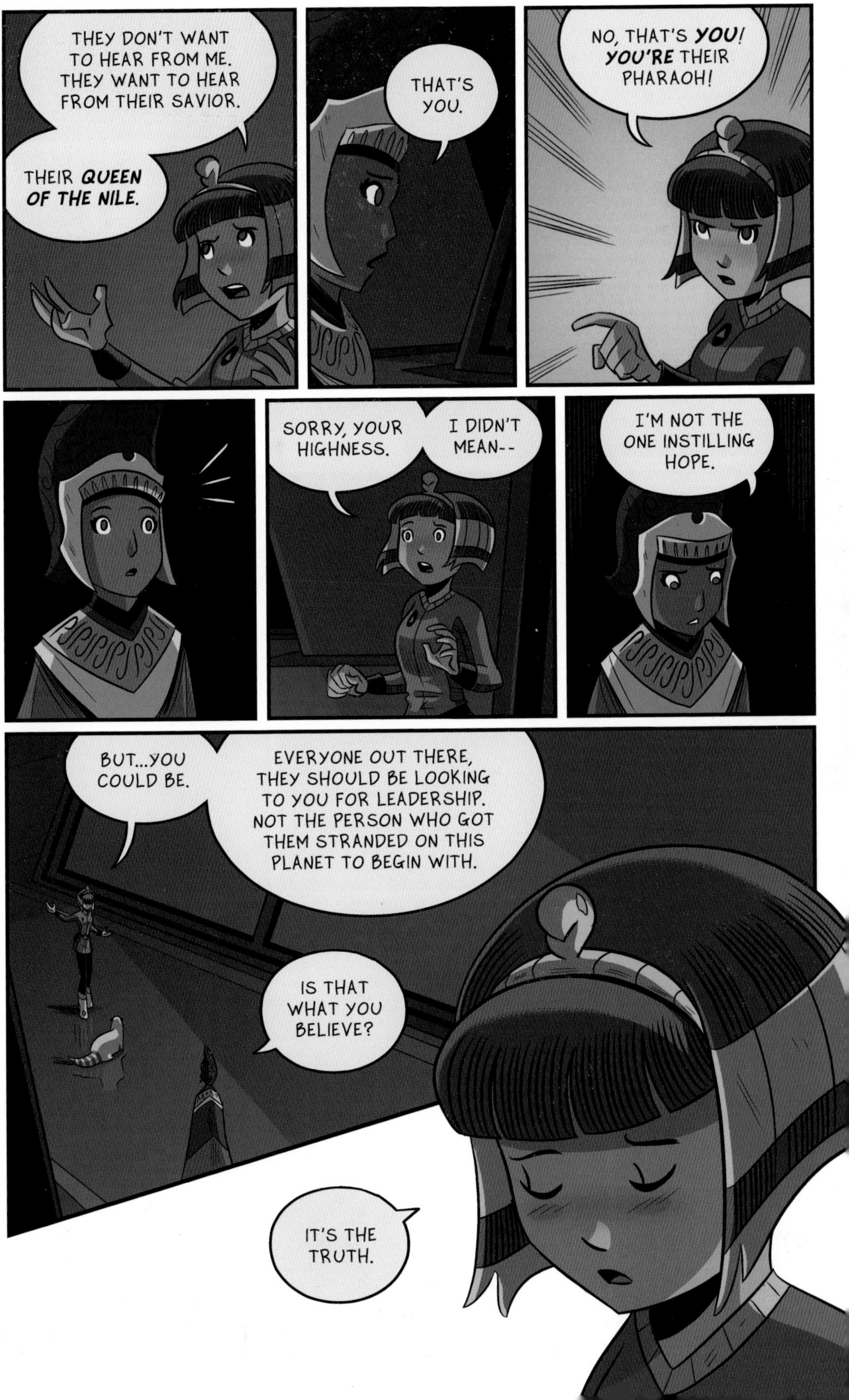

THEY DON'T WANT TO HEAR FROM ME. THEY WANT TO HEAR FROM THEIR SAVIOR.
THEIR **QUEEN OF THE NILE.**
THAT'S YOU.
NO, THAT'S **YOU**! **YOU'RE** THEIR PHARAOH!
SORRY, YOUR HIGHNESS.
I DIDN'T MEAN--
I'M NOT THE ONE INSTILLING HOPE.
BUT...YOU COULD BE.
EVERYONE OUT THERE, THEY SHOULD BE LOOKING TO YOU FOR LEADERSHIP. NOT THE PERSON WHO GOT THEM STRANDED ON THIS PLANET TO BEGIN WITH.
IS THAT WHAT YOU BELIEVE?
IT'S THE TRUTH.

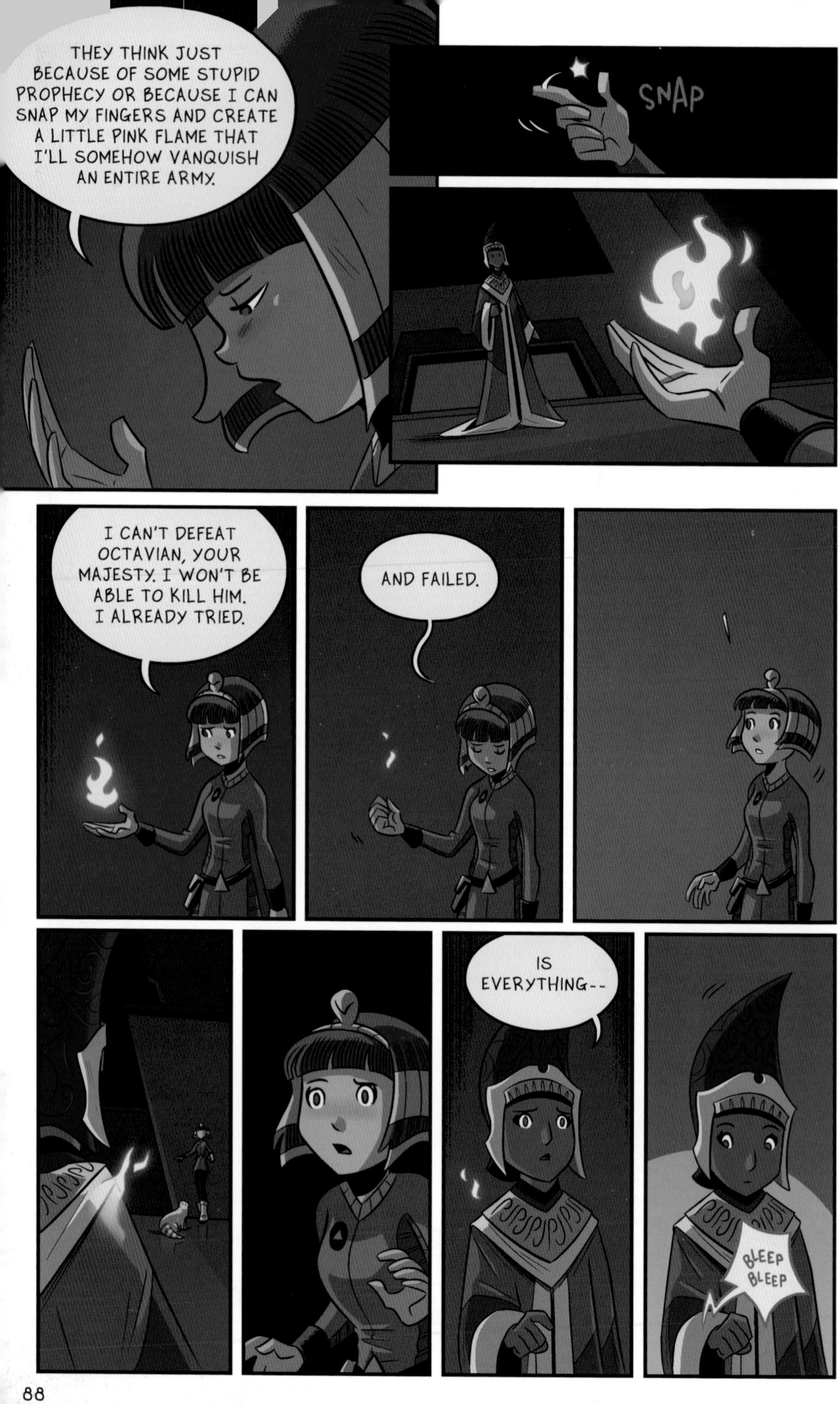
THEY THINK JUST BECAUSE OF SOME STUPID PROPHECY OR BECAUSE I CAN SNAP MY FINGERS AND CREATE A LITTLE PINK FLAME THAT I'LL SOMEHOW VANQUISH AN ENTIRE ARMY.
SNAP
I CAN'T DEFEAT OCTAVIAN, YOUR MAJESTY. I WON'T BE ABLE TO KILL HIM. I ALREADY TRIED.
AND FAILED.
IS EVERYTHING--
BLEEP BLEEP

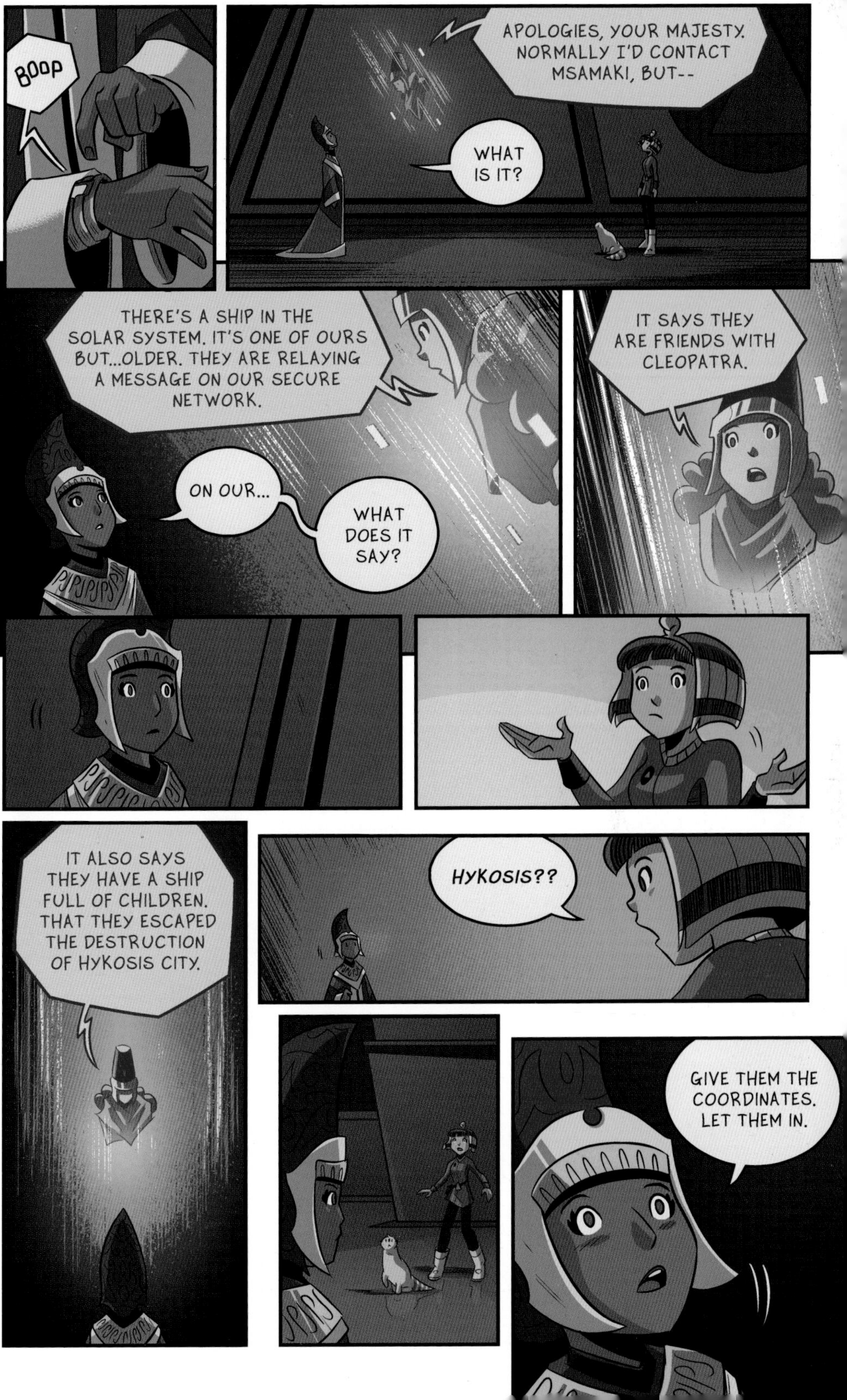
BOOP
APOLOGIES, YOUR MAJESTY. NORMALLY I'D CONTACT MSAMAKI, BUT--
WHAT IS IT?
THERE'S A SHIP IN THE SOLAR SYSTEM. IT'S ONE OF OURS BUT...OLDER. THEY ARE RELAYING A MESSAGE ON OUR SECURE NETWORK.
ON OUR...
WHAT DOES IT SAY?
IT SAYS THEY ARE FRIENDS WITH CLEOPATRA.
IT ALSO SAYS THEY HAVE A SHIP FULL OF CHILDREN. THAT THEY ESCAPED THE DESTRUCTION OF HYKOSIS CITY.
HYKOSIS??
GIVE THEM THE COORDINATES. LET THEM IN.

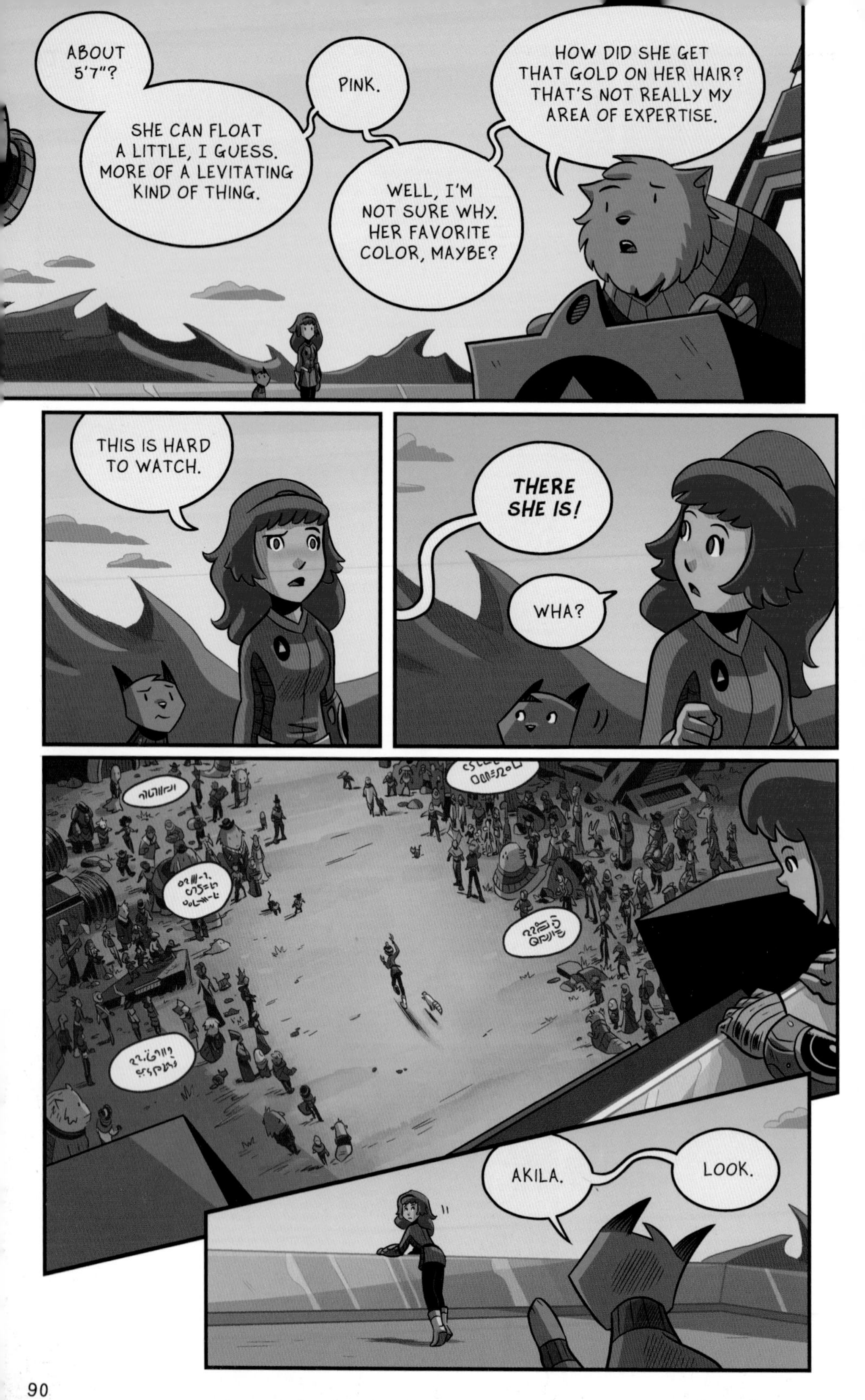
ABOUT 5'7"?
SHE CAN FLOAT A LITTLE, I GUESS. MORE OF A LEVITATING KIND OF THING.
PINK.
WELL, I'M NOT SURE WHY. HER FAVORITE COLOR, MAYBE?
HOW DID SHE GET THAT GOLD ON HER HAIR? THAT'S NOT REALLY MY AREA OF EXPERTISE.
THIS IS HARD TO WATCH.
THERE SHE IS!
WHA?
AKILA.
LOOK.

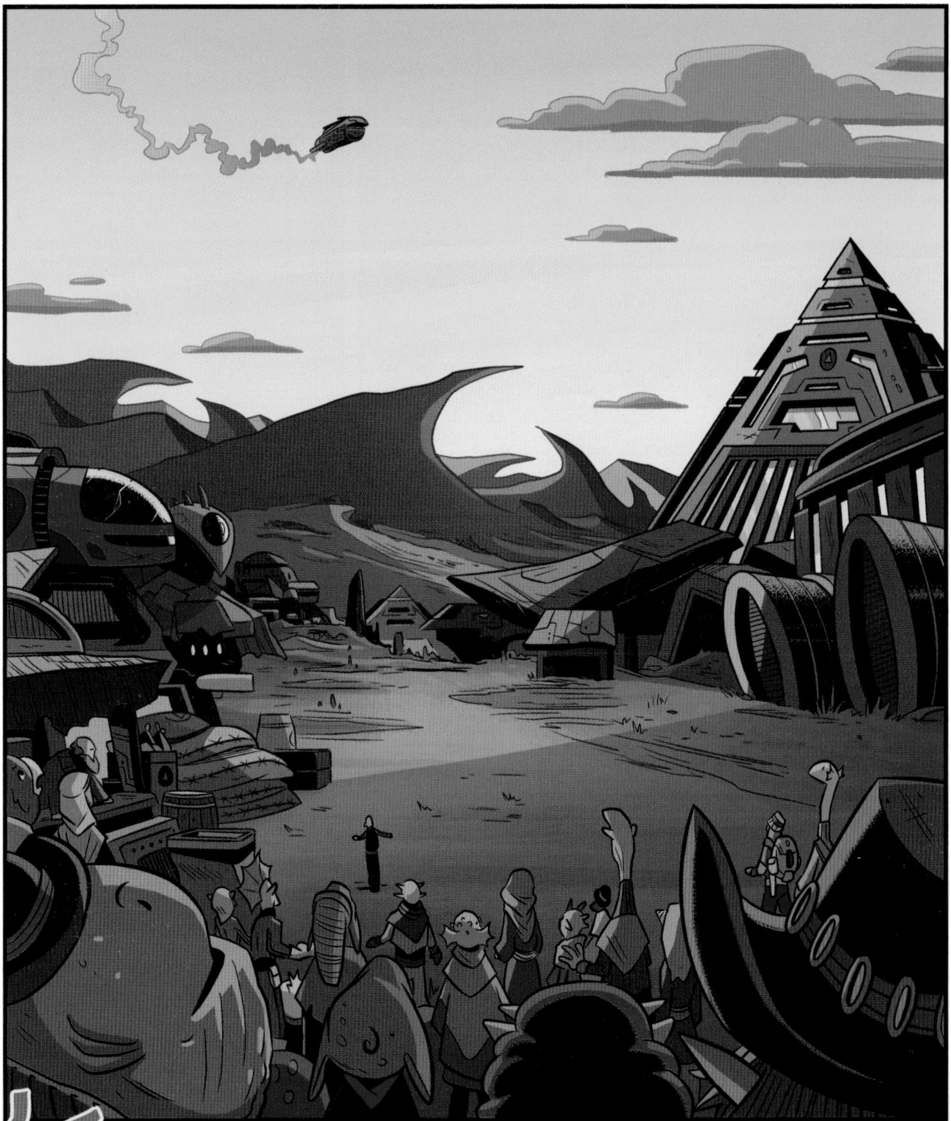

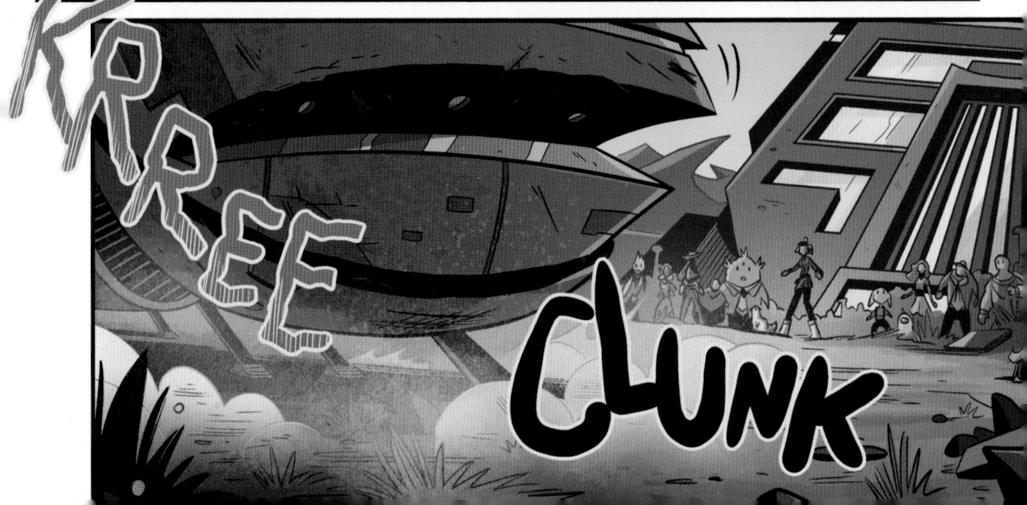
KRREE
CLUNK

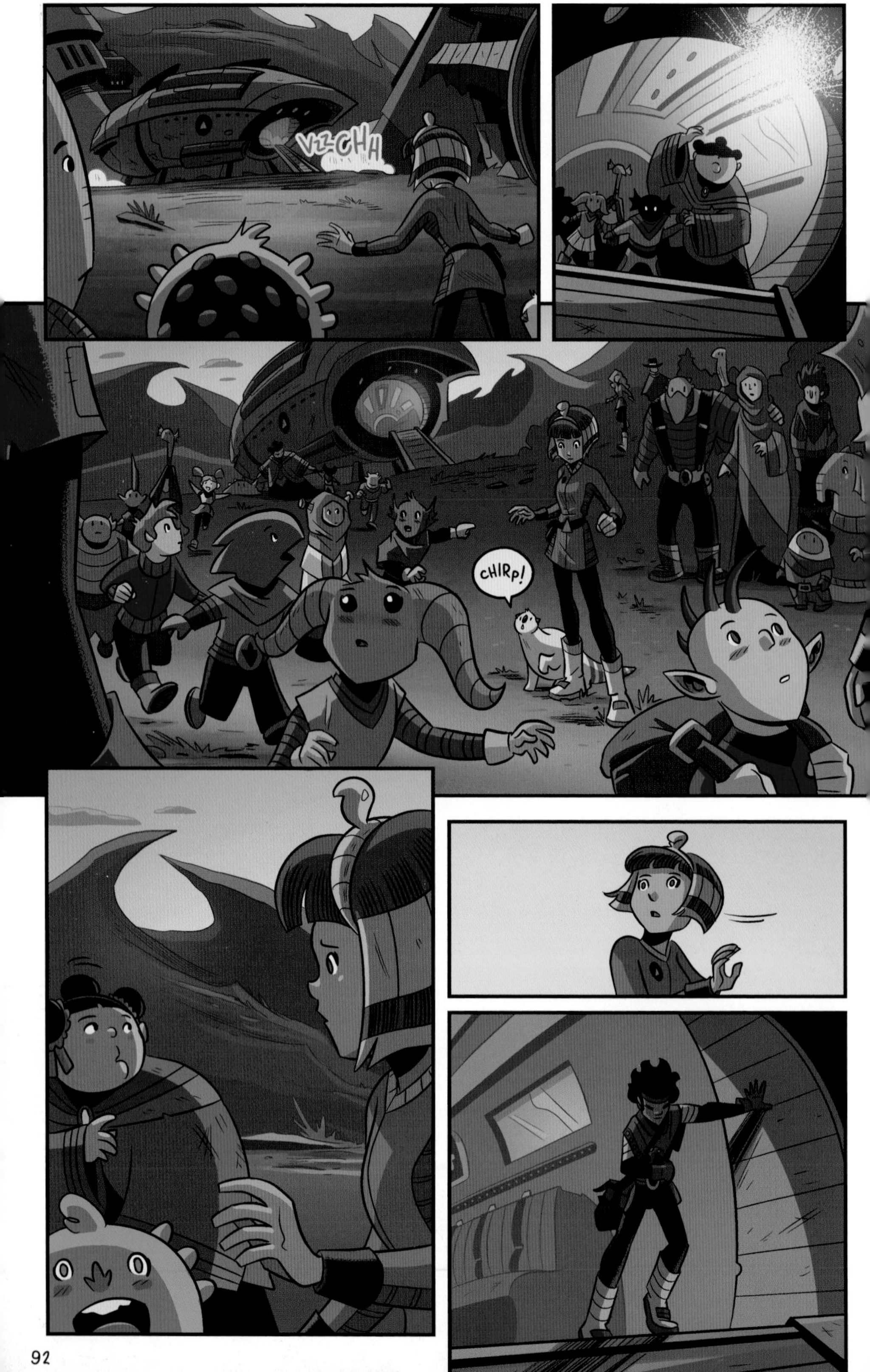
VZ-CHH
CHIRP!

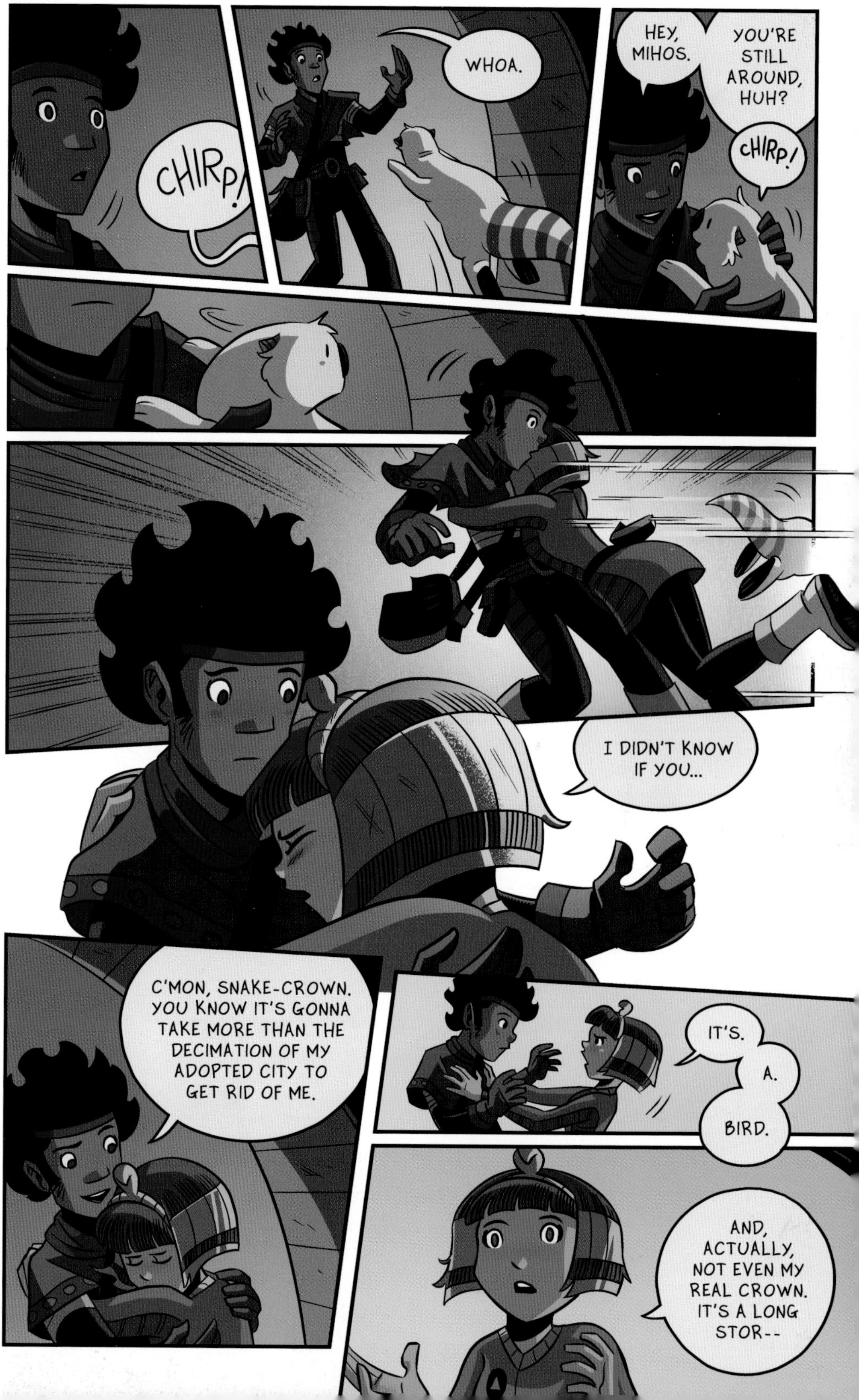
CHIRP!
WHOA.
HEY, MIHOS.
YOU'RE STILL AROUND, HUH?
CHIRP!
I DIDN'T KNOW IF YOU...
C'MON, SNAKE-CROWN. YOU KNOW IT'S GONNA TAKE MORE THAN THE DECIMATION OF MY ADOPTED CITY TO GET RID OF ME.
IT'S.
A.
BIRD.
AND, ACTUALLY, NOT EVEN MY REAL CROWN. IT'S A LONG STOR--

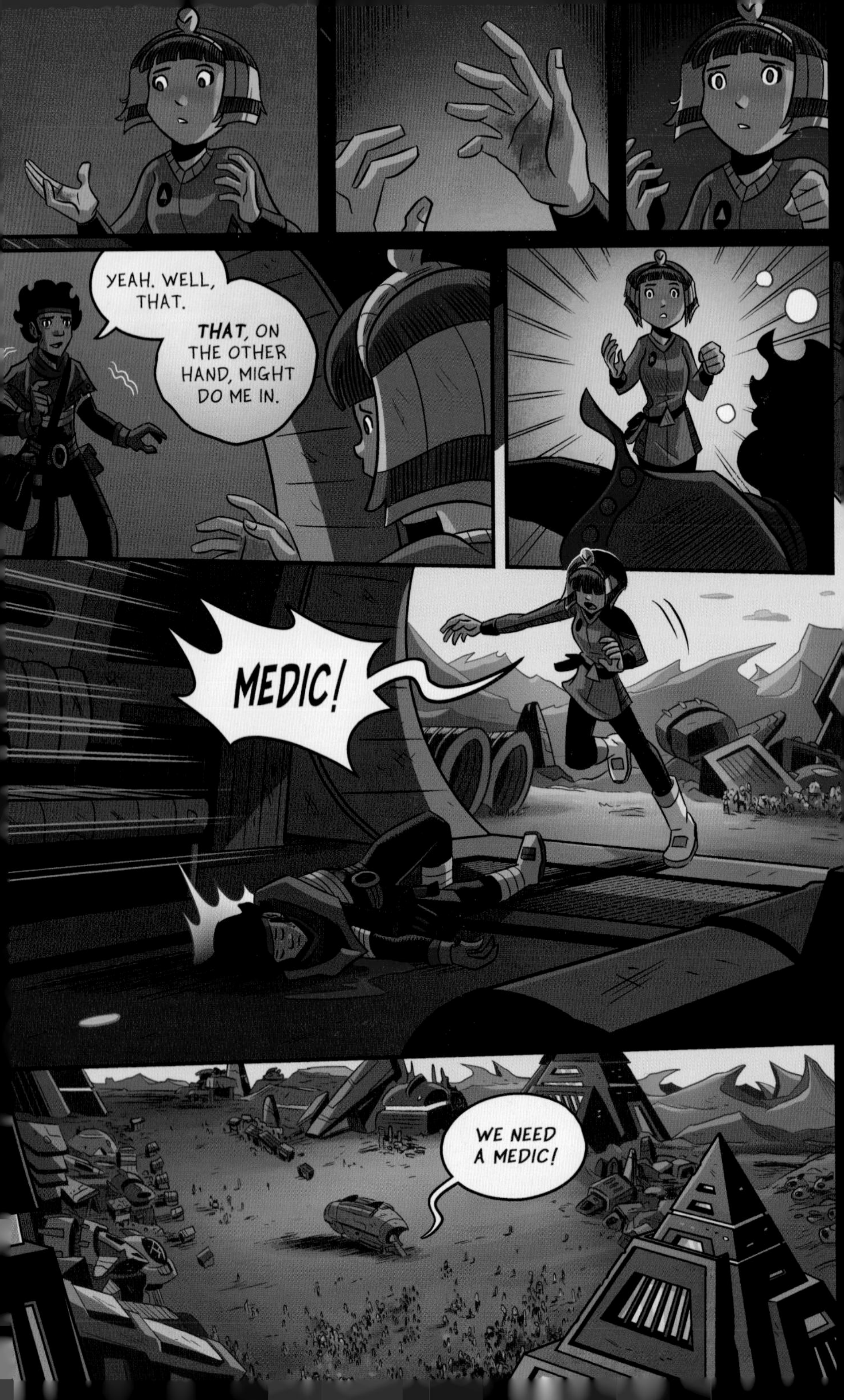
YEAH. WELL, THAT.
THAT, ON THE OTHER HAND, MIGHT DO ME IN.
MEDIC!
WE NEED A MEDIC!

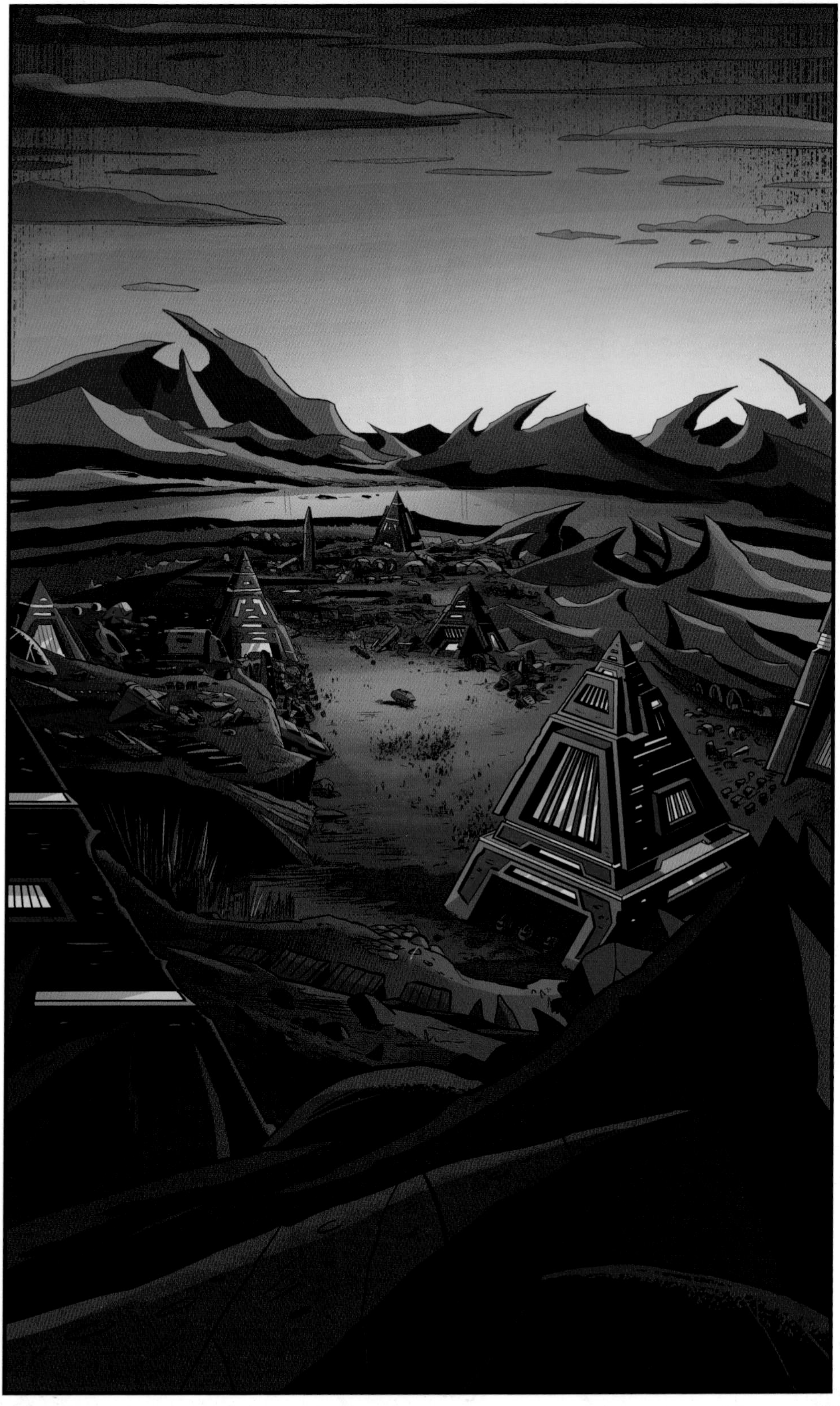

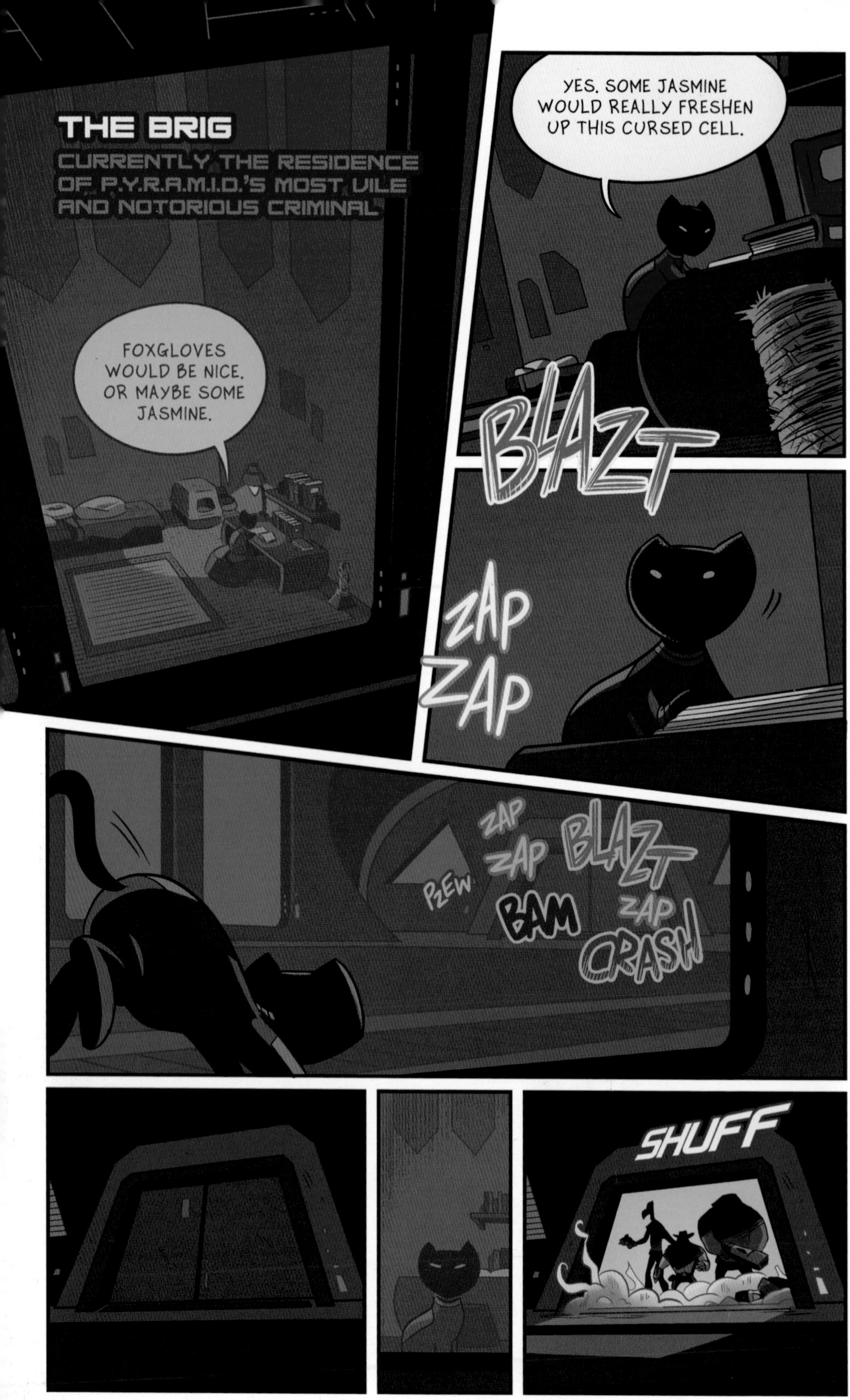
THE BRIG
CURRENTLY THE RESIDENCE OF P.Y.R.A.M.I.D.'S MOST VILE AND NOTORIOUS CRIMINAL
FOXGLOVES WOULD BE NICE. OR MAYBE SOME JASMINE.
YES. SOME JASMINE WOULD REALLY FRESHEN UP THIS CURSED CELL.
BLAZT
ZAP
ZAP
ZAP
ZAP
BLAZT
PZEW
BAM
ZAP
CRASH
SHUFF

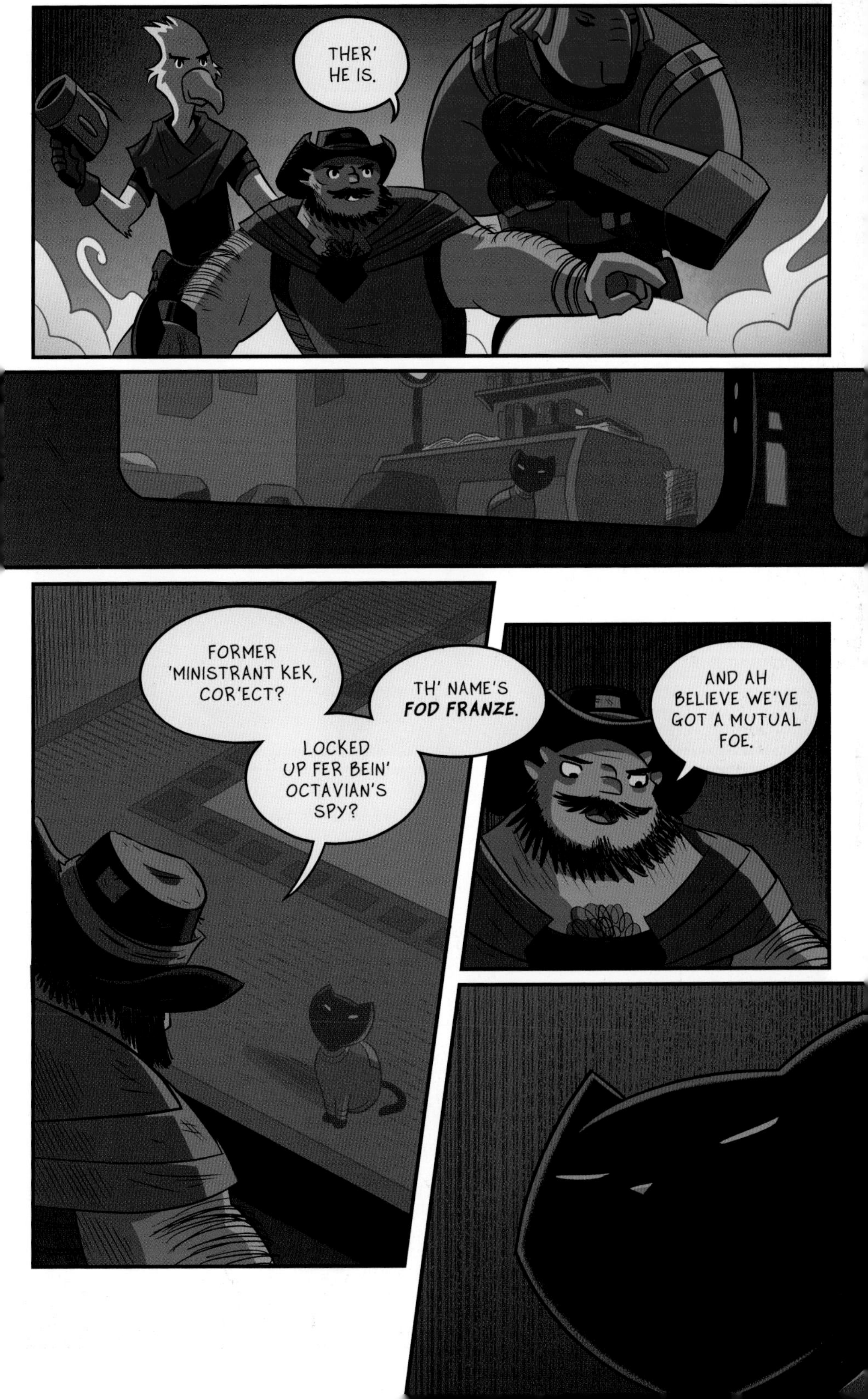
THER' HE IS.
FORMER 'MINISTRANT KEK, COR'ECT?
LOCKED UP FER BEIN' OCTAVIAN'S SPY?
TH' NAME'S **FOD FRANZE.**
AND AH BELIEVE WE'VE GOT A MUTUAL FOE.

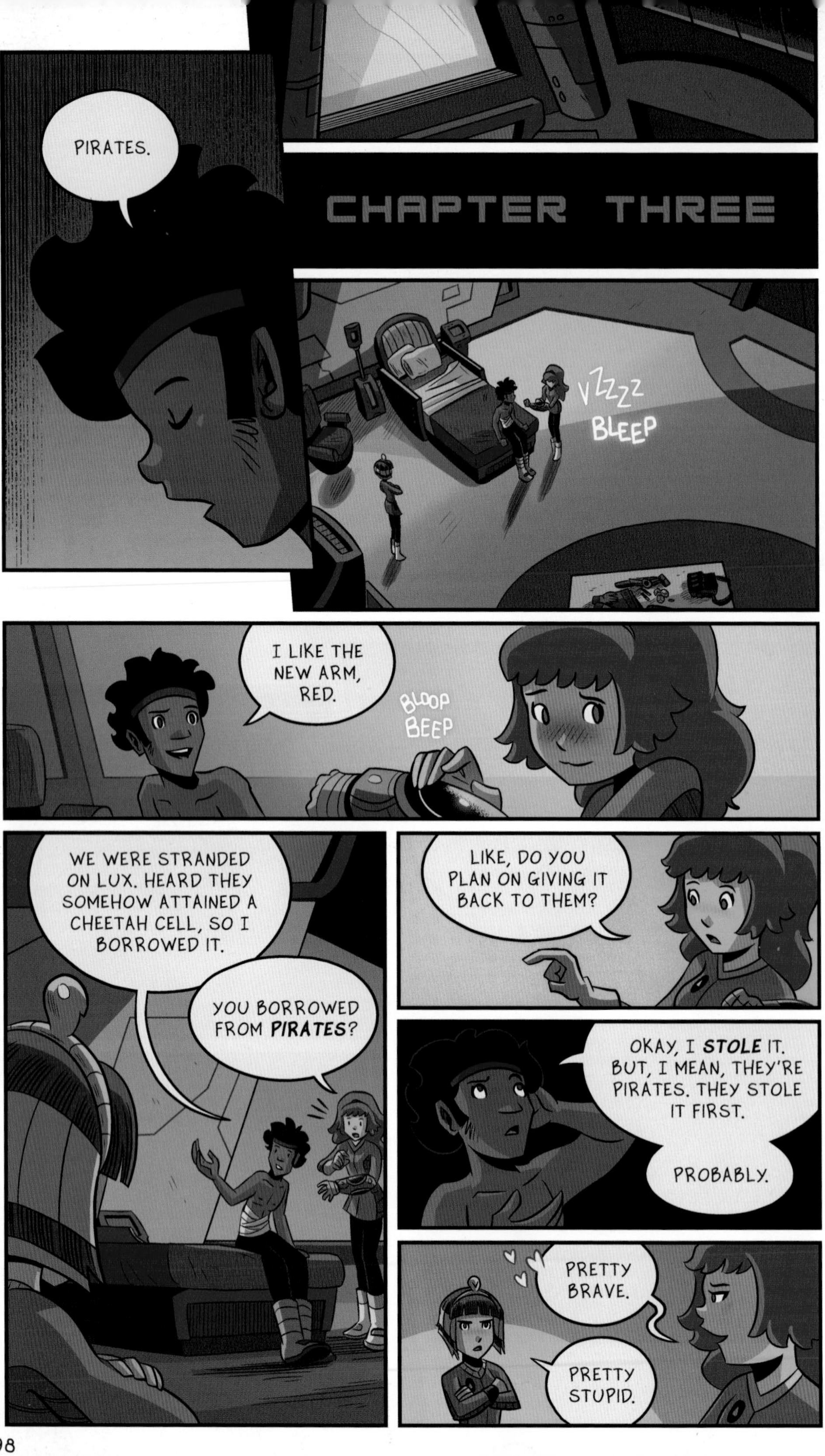
PIRATES.
CHAPTER THREE
VZZZZ
BLEEP
I LIKE THE NEW ARM, RED.
BLOOP BEEP
WE WERE STRANDED ON LUX. HEARD THEY SOMEHOW ATTAINED A CHEETAH CELL, SO I BORROWED IT.
YOU BORROWED FROM PIRATES?
LIKE, DO YOU PLAN ON GIVING IT BACK TO THEM?
OKAY, I STOLE IT. BUT, I MEAN, THEY'RE PIRATES. THEY STOLE IT FIRST.
PROBABLY.
PRETTY BRAVE.
PRETTY STUPID.

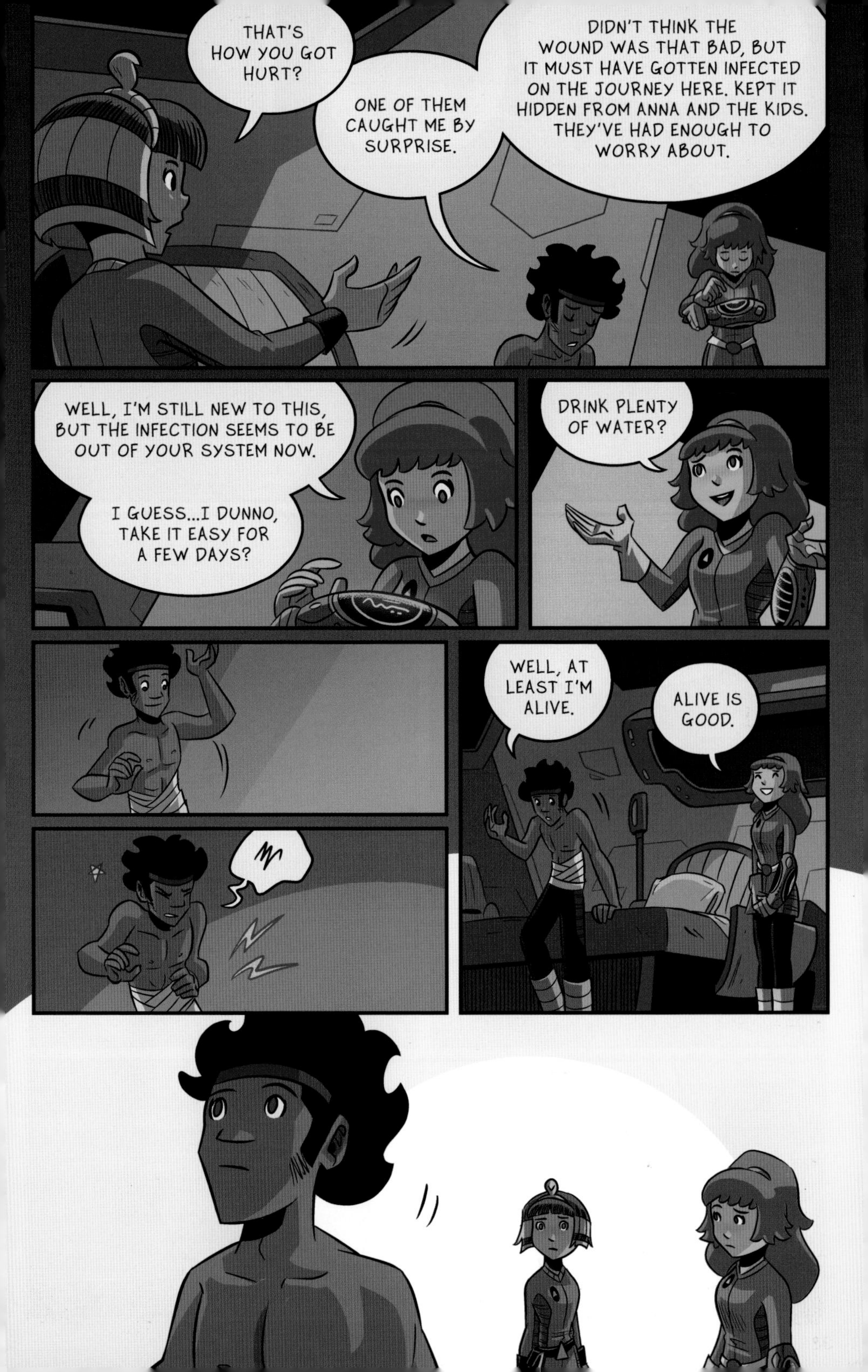
THAT'S HOW YOU GOT HURT?
ONE OF THEM CAUGHT ME BY SURPRISE.
DIDN'T THINK THE WOUND WAS THAT BAD, BUT IT MUST HAVE GOTTEN INFECTED ON THE JOURNEY HERE. KEPT IT HIDDEN FROM ANNA AND THE KIDS. THEY'VE HAD ENOUGH TO WORRY ABOUT.
WELL, I'M STILL NEW TO THIS, BUT THE INFECTION SEEMS TO BE OUT OF YOUR SYSTEM NOW.
I GUESS...I DUNNO, TAKE IT EASY FOR A FEW DAYS?
DRINK PLENTY OF WATER?
WELL, AT LEAST I'M ALIVE.
ALIVE IS GOOD.

SOOO YOU'VE JUST, WHAT? BEEN FLYING AROUND IN THAT BUS ALL YEAR?

WE INITIALLY WERE EN ROUTE TO MAYET, BUT AFTER WE HEARD WHAT HAPPENED...

ANYWAY, WE BRIEFLY FOUND SHELTER ON KHARTOUM UNTIL OCTAVIAN OBLITERATED THAT CITY, TOO. WE'VE ESSENTIALLY BEEN PLANET-HOPPING TILL WE CAUGHT WIND OF THIS PLACE.

IT HASN'T BEEN EASY, BUT THOSE ARE STRONG KIDS. THEY'VE BEEN HANDLING THINGS BETTER THAN MOST OF THE TRIBES WE'VE COME ACROSS.

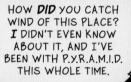

EVEN HELPED US GET OUT OF A TIGHT SPOT OR TWO.

HOW *DID* YOU CATCH WIND OF THIS PLACE? *I* DIDN'T EVEN KNOW ABOUT IT, AND I'VE BEEN WITH P.Y.R.A.M.I.D. THIS WHOLE TIME.

YOU DON'T FLY AROUND IN A STEALTH SHIP FOR AS LONG AS I HAVE WITHOUT PICKING UP ON CERTAIN TRAILS. STEALTH TECH LEAVES A RESIDUE.

I INVESTIGATED A FEW LOCATION RUMORS AND--

VOILÀ.

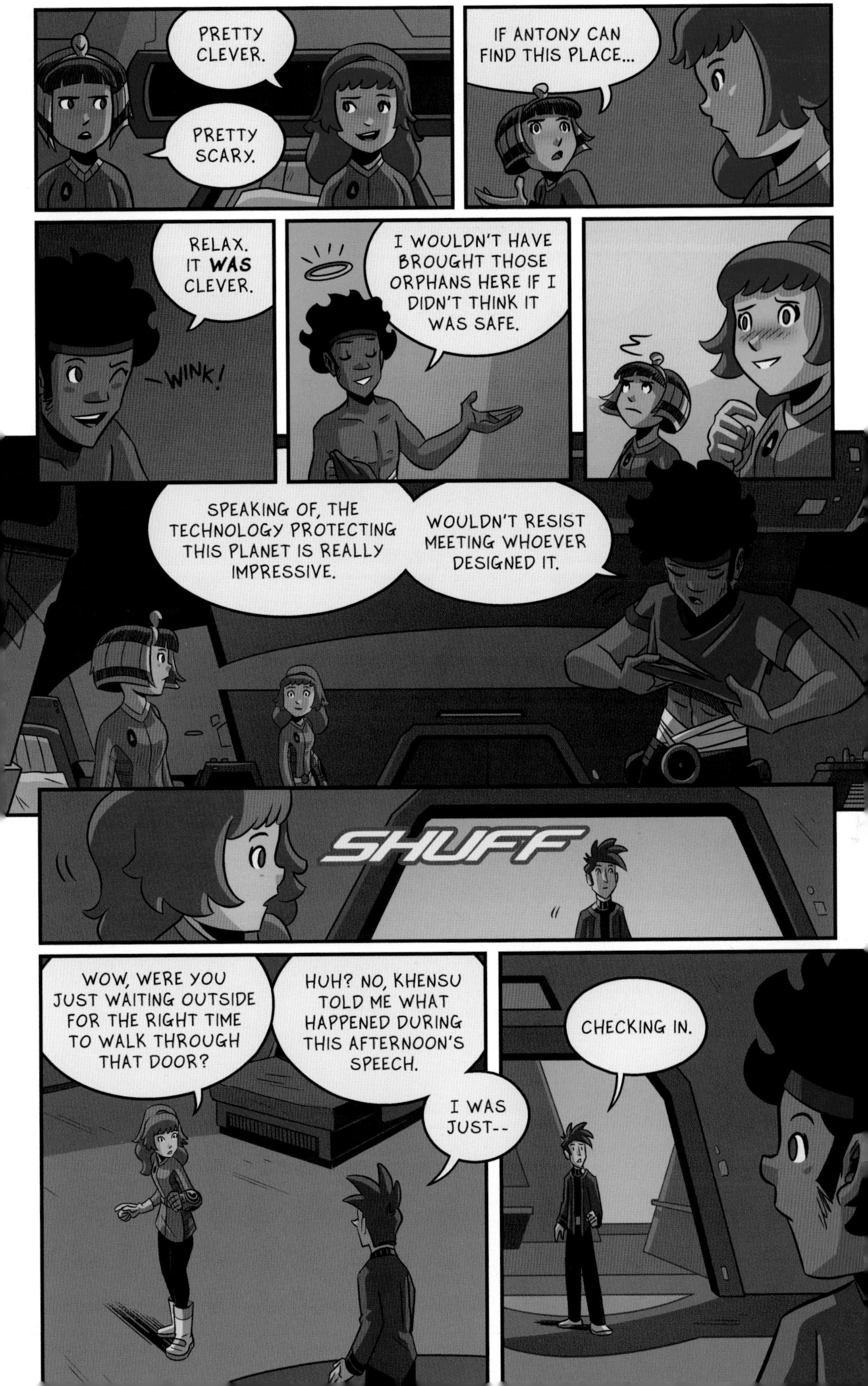
PRETTY CLEVER.
PRETTY SCARY.
IF ANTONY CAN FIND THIS PLACE...
RELAX. IT **WAS** CLEVER.
WINK!
I WOULDN'T HAVE BROUGHT THOSE ORPHANS HERE IF I DIDN'T THINK IT WAS SAFE.
SPEAKING OF, THE TECHNOLOGY PROTECTING THIS PLANET IS REALLY IMPRESSIVE.
WOULDN'T RESIST MEETING WHOEVER DESIGNED IT.
SHUFF
WOW, WERE YOU JUST WAITING OUTSIDE FOR THE RIGHT TIME TO WALK THROUGH THAT DOOR?
HUH? NO, KHENSU TOLD ME WHAT HAPPENED DURING THIS AFTERNOON'S SPEECH.
I WAS JUST--
CHECKING IN.

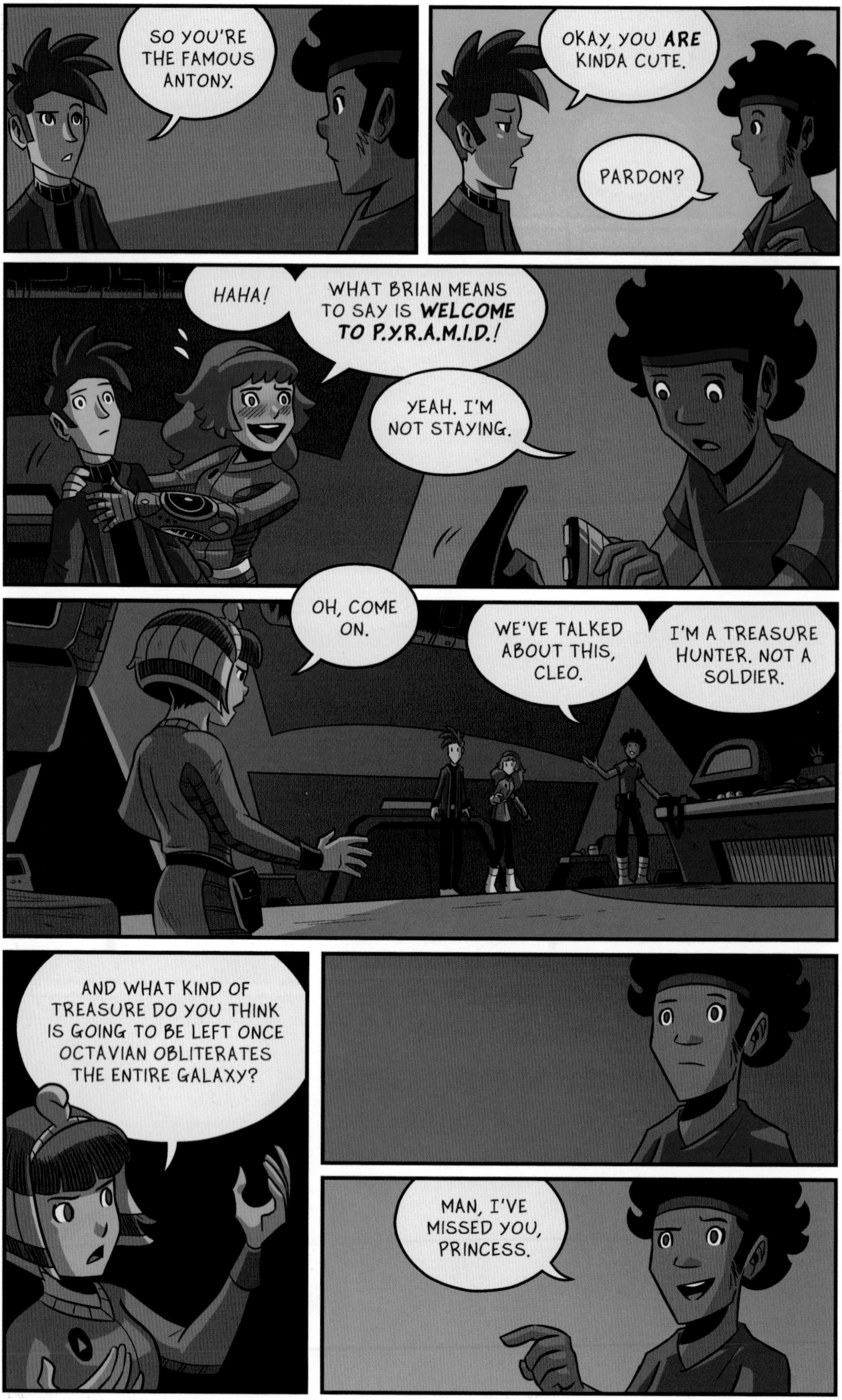
SO YOU'RE THE FAMOUS ANTONY.
OKAY, YOU **ARE** KINDA CUTE.
PARDON?
HAHA!
WHAT BRIAN MEANS TO SAY IS ***WELCOME TO P.Y.R.A.M.I.D.!***
YEAH. I'M NOT STAYING.
OH, COME ON.
WE'VE TALKED ABOUT THIS, CLEO.
I'M A TREASURE HUNTER. NOT A SOLDIER.
AND WHAT KIND OF TREASURE DO YOU THINK IS GOING TO BE LEFT ONCE OCTAVIAN OBLITERATES THE ENTIRE GALAXY?
MAN, I'VE MISSED YOU, PRINCESS.

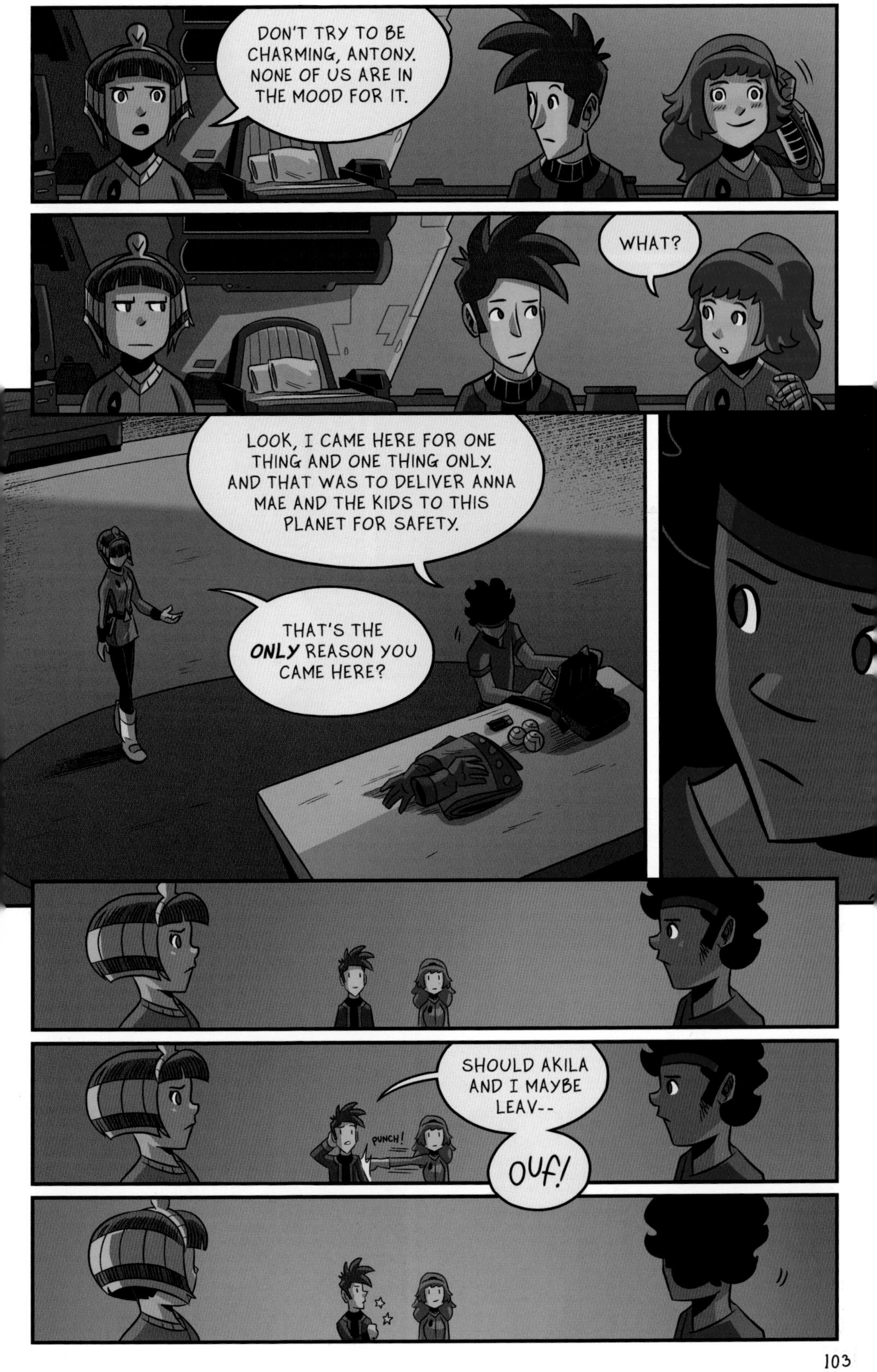
DON'T TRY TO BE CHARMING, ANTONY. NONE OF US ARE IN THE MOOD FOR IT.
WHAT?
LOOK, I CAME HERE FOR ONE THING AND ONE THING ONLY. AND THAT WAS TO DELIVER ANNA MAE AND THE KIDS TO THIS PLANET FOR SAFETY.
THAT'S THE ***ONLY*** REASON YOU CAME HERE?
SHOULD AKILA AND I MAYBE LEAV--
PUNCH!
OUF!

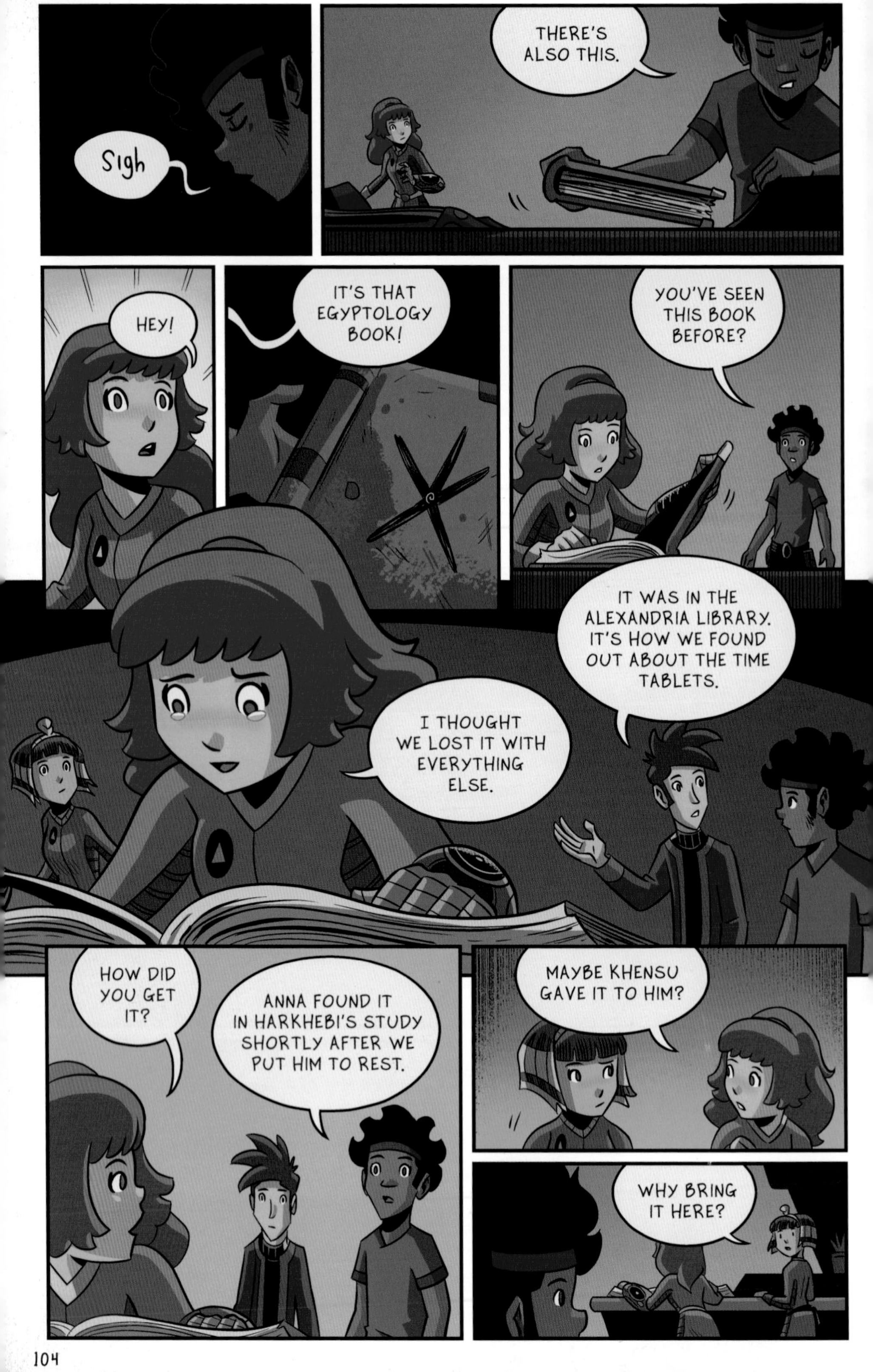
Sigh
THERE'S ALSO THIS.
HEY!
IT'S THAT EGYPTOLOGY BOOK!
YOU'VE SEEN THIS BOOK BEFORE?
IT WAS IN THE ALEXANDRIA LIBRARY. IT'S HOW WE FOUND OUT ABOUT THE TIME TABLETS.
I THOUGHT WE LOST IT WITH EVERYTHING ELSE.
HOW DID YOU GET IT?
ANNA FOUND IT IN HARKHEBI'S STUDY SHORTLY AFTER WE PUT HIM TO REST.
MAYBE KHENSU GAVE IT TO HIM?
WHY BRING IT HERE?

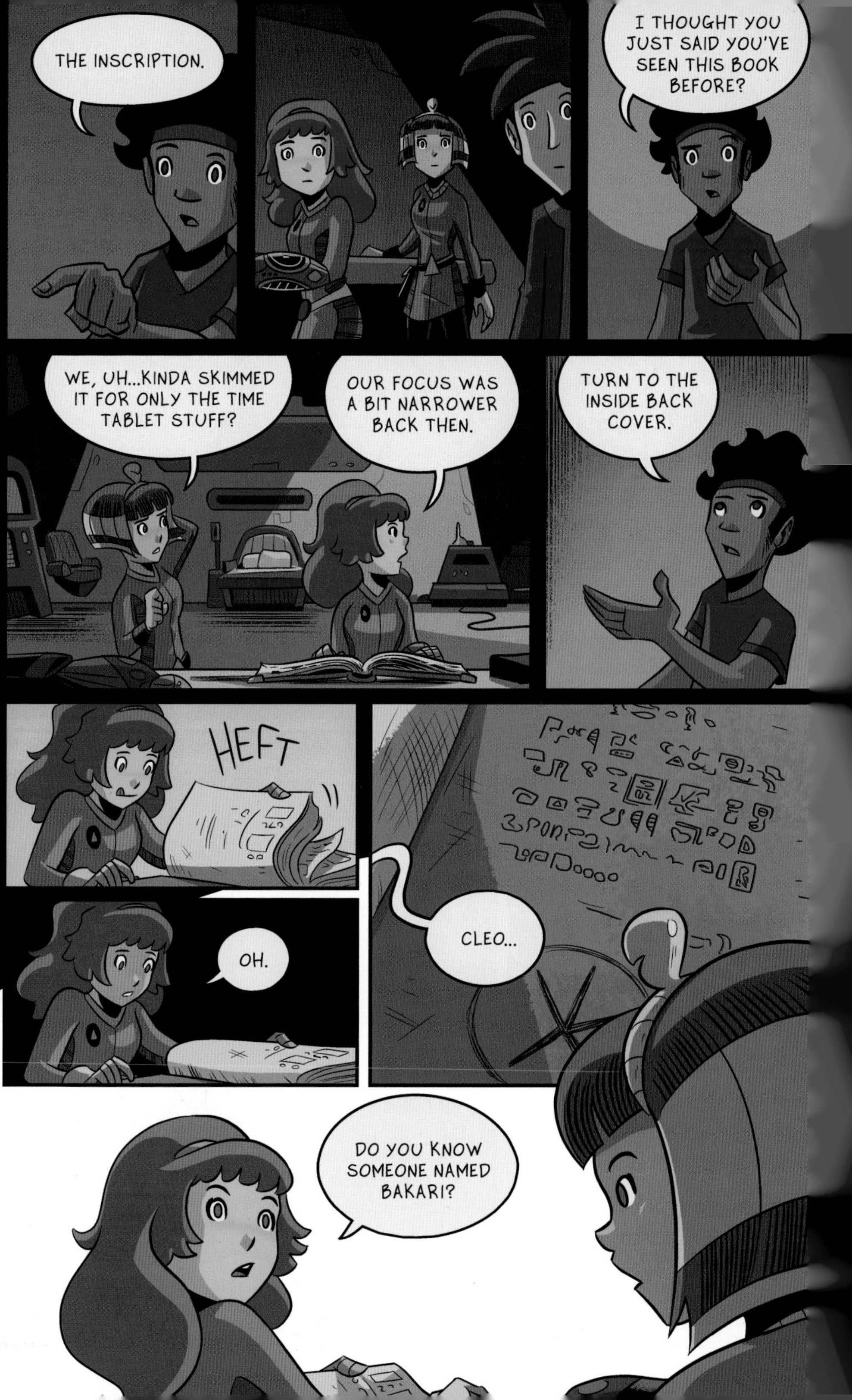
THE INSCRIPTION.
I THOUGHT YOU JUST SAID YOU'VE SEEN THIS BOOK BEFORE?
WE, UH...KINDA SKIMMED IT FOR ONLY THE TIME TABLET STUFF?
OUR FOCUS WAS A BIT NARROWER BACK THEN.
TURN TO THE INSIDE BACK COVER.
HEFT
OH.
CLEO...
DO YOU KNOW SOMEONE NAMED BAKARI?

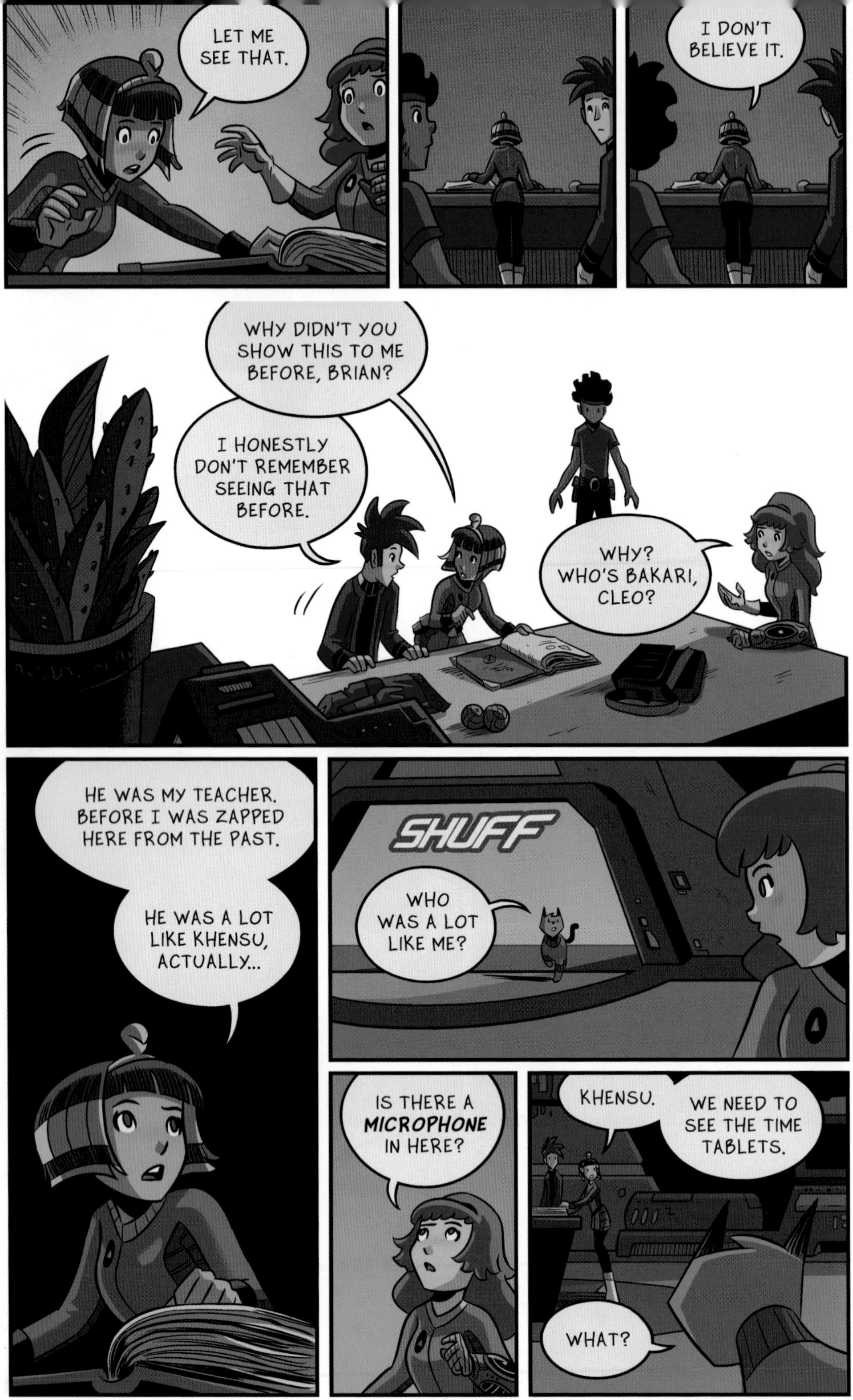
LET ME SEE THAT.
I DON'T BELIEVE IT.
WHY DIDN'T YOU SHOW THIS TO ME BEFORE, BRIAN?
I HONESTLY DON'T REMEMBER SEEING THAT BEFORE.
WHY? WHO'S BAKARI, CLEO?
HE WAS MY TEACHER. BEFORE I WAS ZAPPED HERE FROM THE PAST.
HE WAS A LOT LIKE KHENSU, ACTUALLY...
SHUFF
WHO WAS A LOT LIKE ME?
IS THERE A **MICROPHONE** IN HERE?
KHENSU.
WE NEED TO SEE THE TIME TABLETS.
WHAT?

WHY?

YEAH, WHERE DID **THAT** COME FROM?

YOU READ THE INSCRIPTION.

ALL I COULD READ WAS YOUR NAME AND THAT TEACHER OF YOURS. THE REST WAS JUST...SHAPES.

DON'T LOOK AT **ME**.

I COULDN'T MAKE HEADS OR TAILS OUT OF IT, EITHER. PARTLY WHY I BROUGHT IT TO YOU.

WHAT ARE YOU ALL--

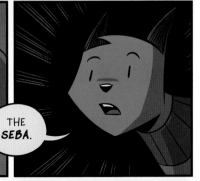

THE **SEBA**.

I HAVEN'T SEEN THIS SINCE I WAS A KITTEN.

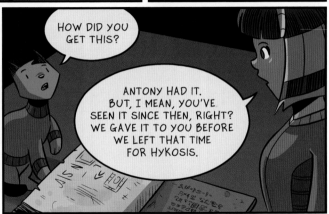

HOW DID YOU GET THIS?

ANTONY HAD IT. BUT, I MEAN, YOU'VE SEEN IT SINCE THEN, RIGHT? WE GAVE IT TO YOU BEFORE WE LEFT THAT TIME FOR HYKOSIS.

NOT THE ORIGINAL. THE ONE YOU FOUND IN THE LIBRARY WAS A COPY.

A COPY?

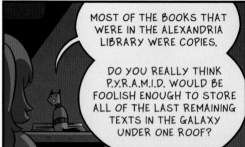

MOST OF THE BOOKS THAT WERE IN THE ALEXANDRIA LIBRARY WERE COPIES.

DO YOU REALLY THINK P.Y.R.A.M.I.D. WOULD BE FOOLISH ENOUGH TO STORE ALL OF THE LAST REMAINING TEXTS IN THE GALAXY UNDER ONE ROOF?

WELL, THEY DO SEEM TO BE GATHERING THE LAST REMAINING GOOD GUYS IN THE GALAXY ON ONE PLANET.

OH, *THAT'S* WHERE CLEO GETS IT.

YOU ARE MUCH SCARIER.

ARE YOU SAYING YOU CAN READ THIS, CLEO? NO ONE HAS EVER BEEN ABLE TO DECIPHER WHAT THAT INSCRIPTION SAYS.

WELL, SURE.

WOW, IS THIS WHAT IT FEELS LIKE TO BE BRIAN?

OR AKILA?

ANTONY.

ANYONE IN THIS ROOM, I GUESS...

JUST READ IT, CLEO.

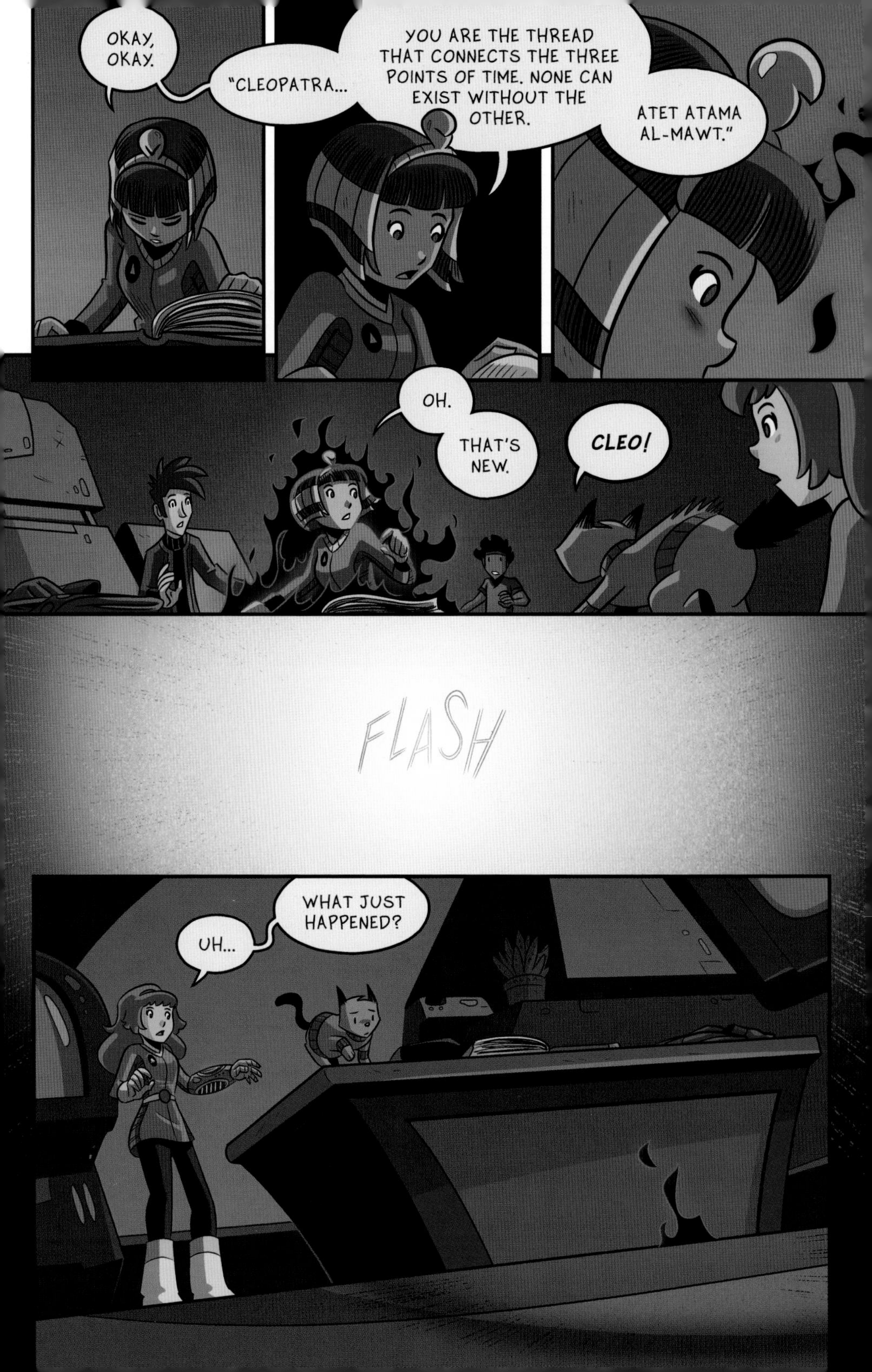
OKAY, OKAY.
"CLEOPATRA...
YOU ARE THE THREAD THAT CONNECTS THE THREE POINTS OF TIME. NONE CAN EXIST WITHOUT THE OTHER.
ATET ATAMA AL-MAWT."
OH.
THAT'S NEW.
CLEO!
FLASH
UH...
WHAT JUST HAPPENED?

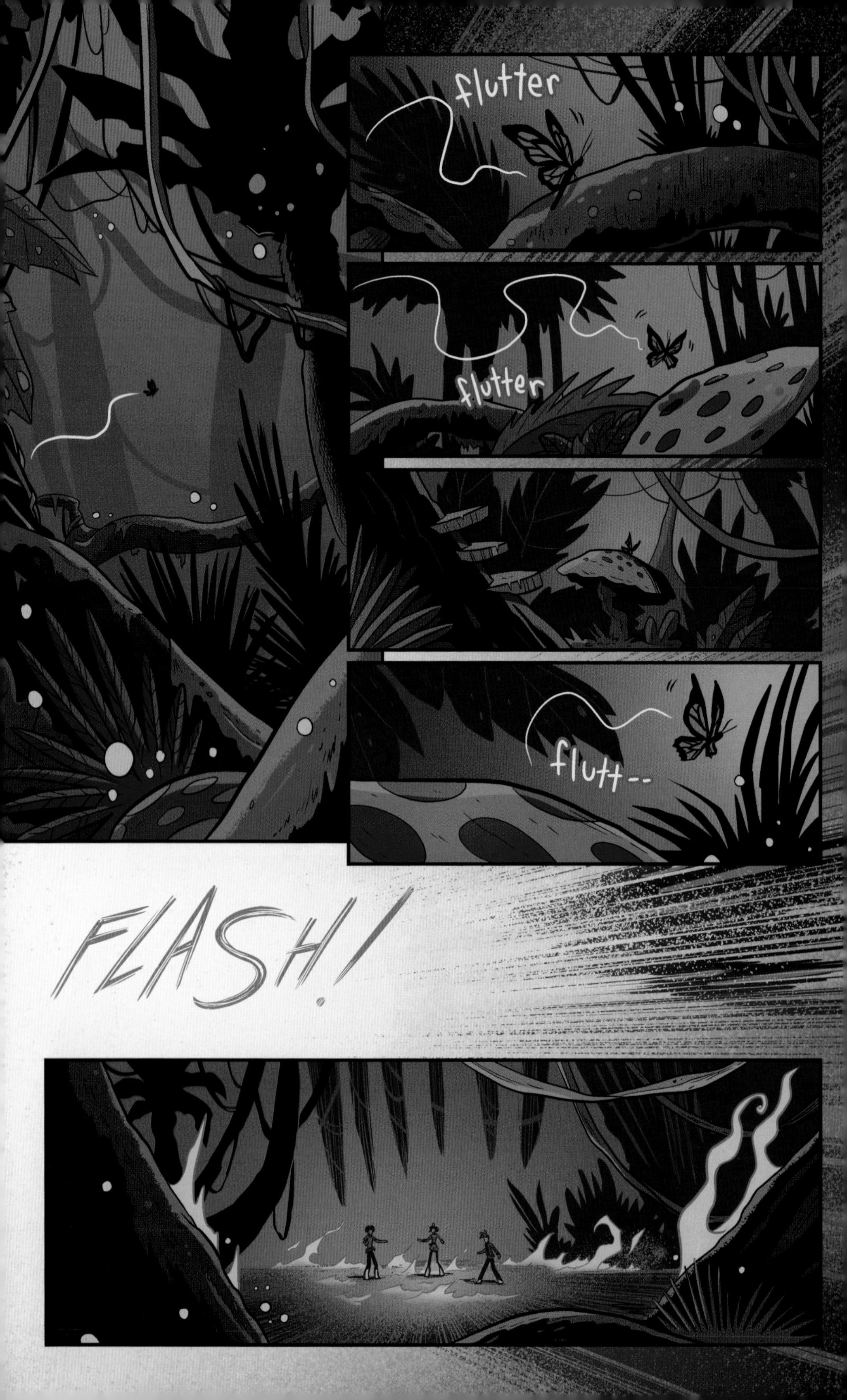
flutter
flutter
flutt--
FLASH!

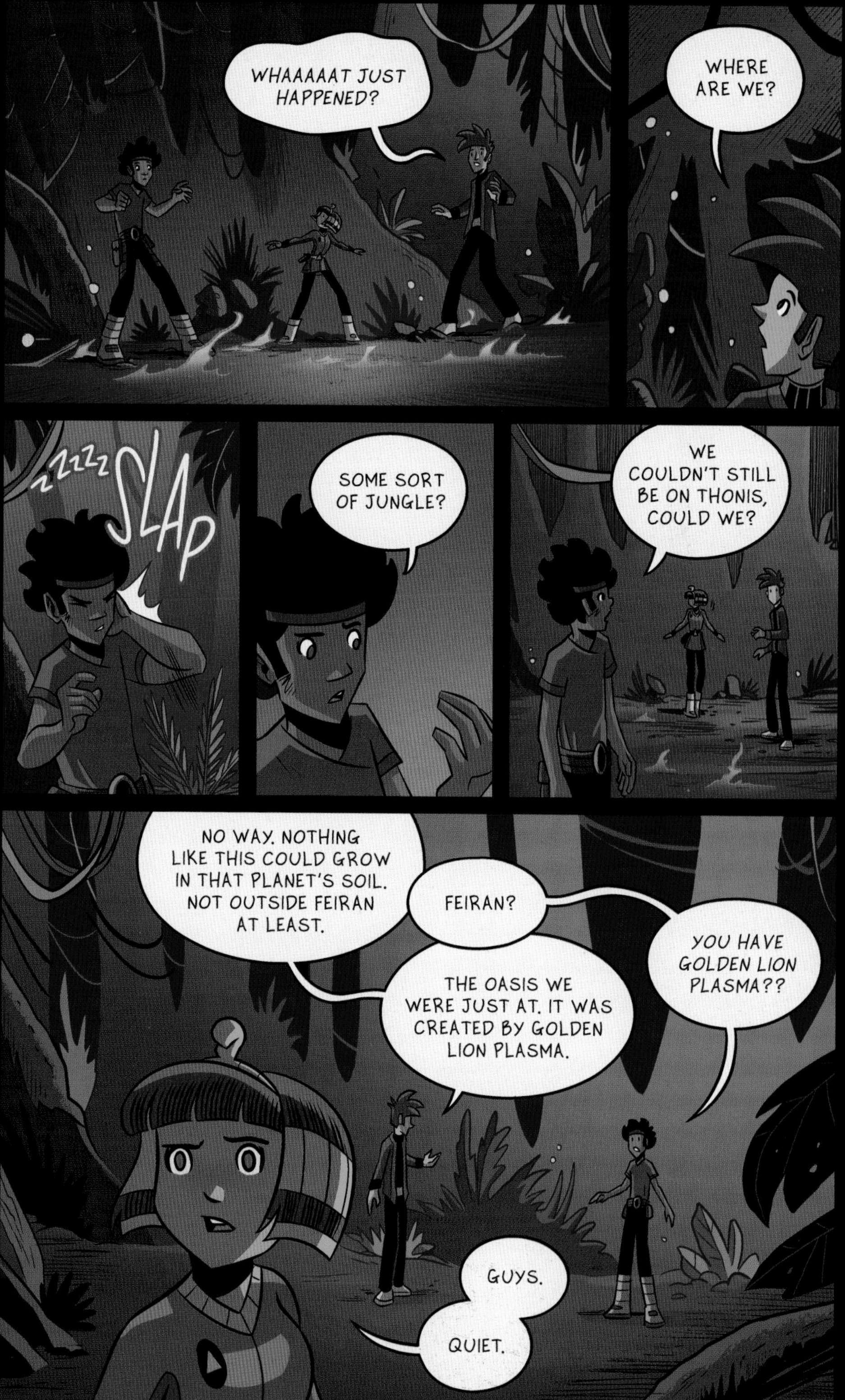
WHAAAAAT JUST HAPPENED?
WHERE ARE WE?
ZZZZZ
SLAP
SOME SORT OF JUNGLE?
WE COULDN'T STILL BE ON THONIS, COULD WE?
NO WAY. NOTHING LIKE THIS COULD GROW IN THAT PLANET'S SOIL. NOT OUTSIDE FEIRAN AT LEAST.
FEIRAN?
THE OASIS WE WERE JUST AT. IT WAS CREATED BY GOLDEN LION PLASMA.
YOU HAVE GOLDEN LION PLASMA??
GUYS.
QUIET.

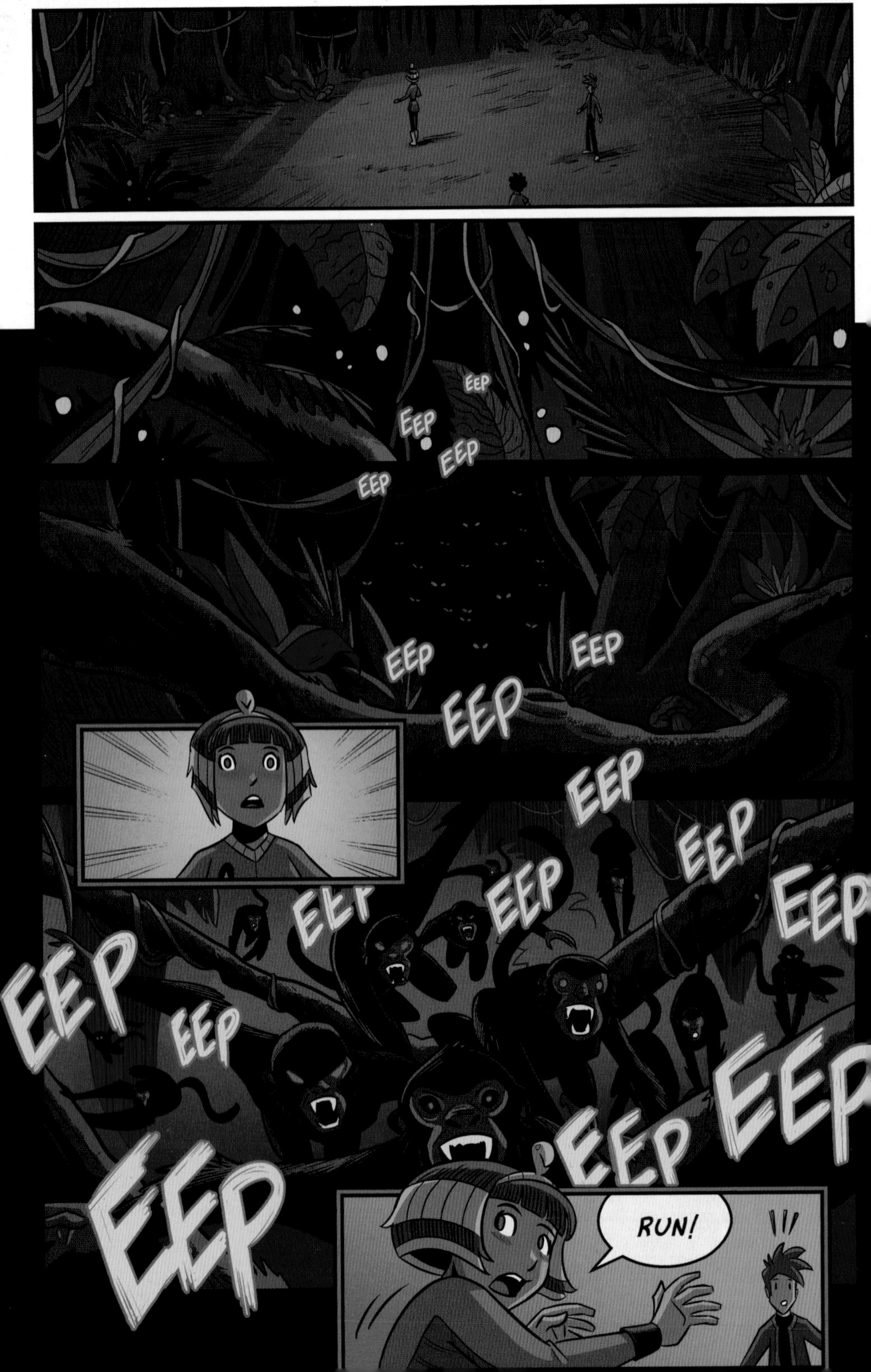
EEP
EEP
EEP
EEP
EEP
EEP
EEP
EEP
EEP
EEP
EEP
EEP
EEP
EEP
EEP
EEP
EEP
RUN!

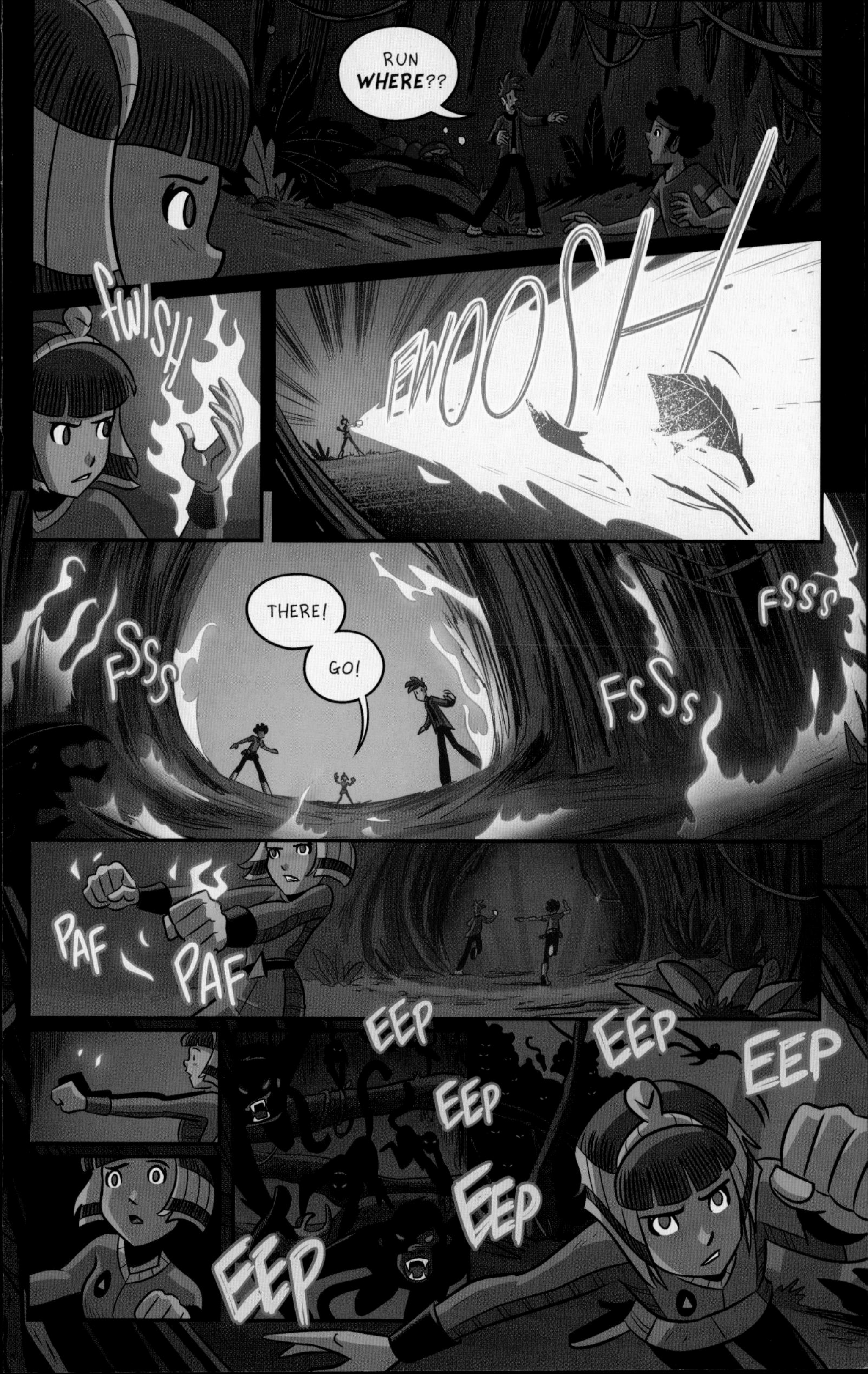
RUN WHERE??
FWISH
FWOOSH
FSSS
THERE!
GO!
FSSS
FSSS
PAF
PAF
EEP
EEP
EEP
EEP
EEP
EEP

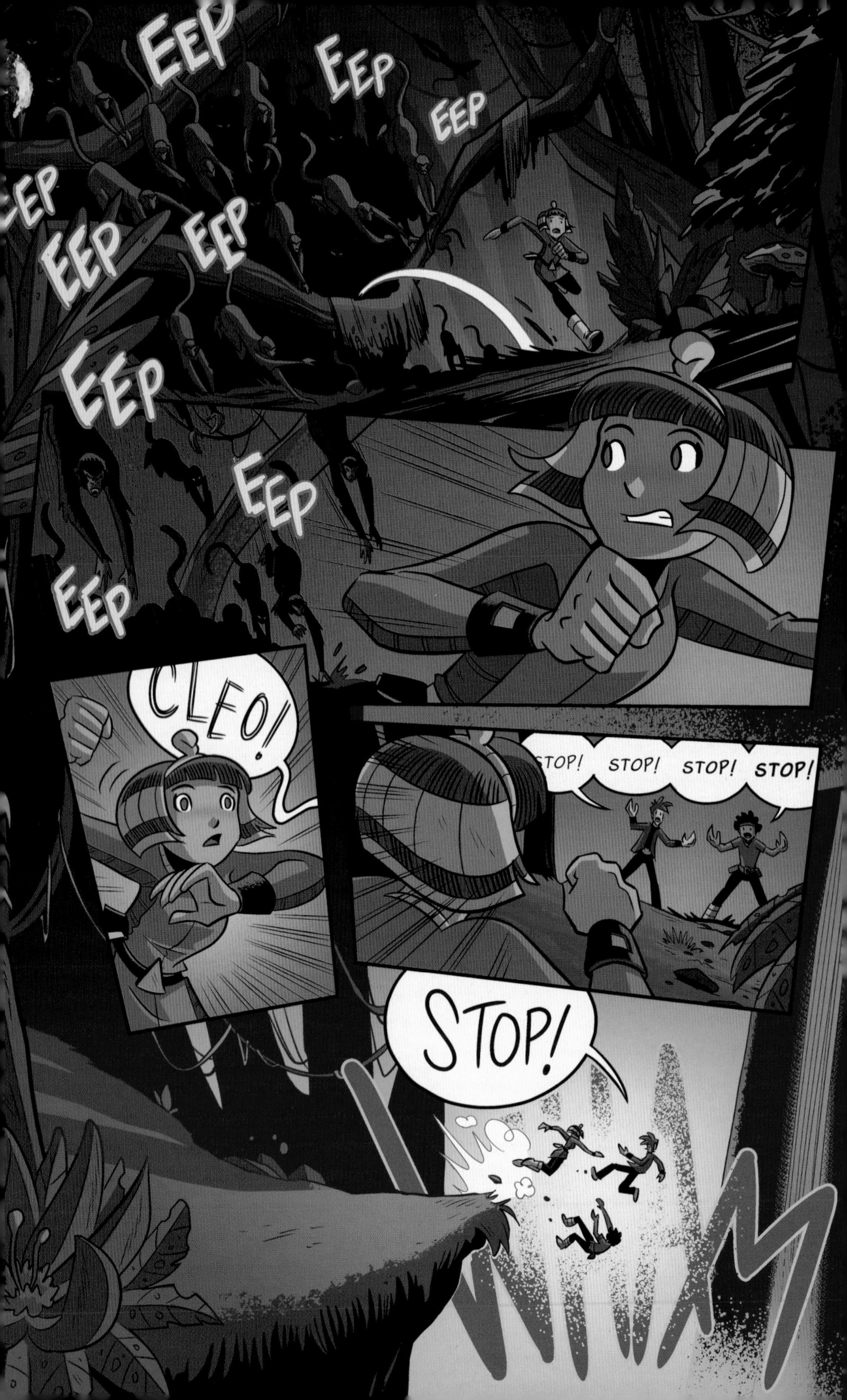
EEP
EEP
EEP
EEP
EEP
EEP
EEP
EEP
EEP
CLEO!
STOP!
STOP!
STOP!
STOP!
STOP!

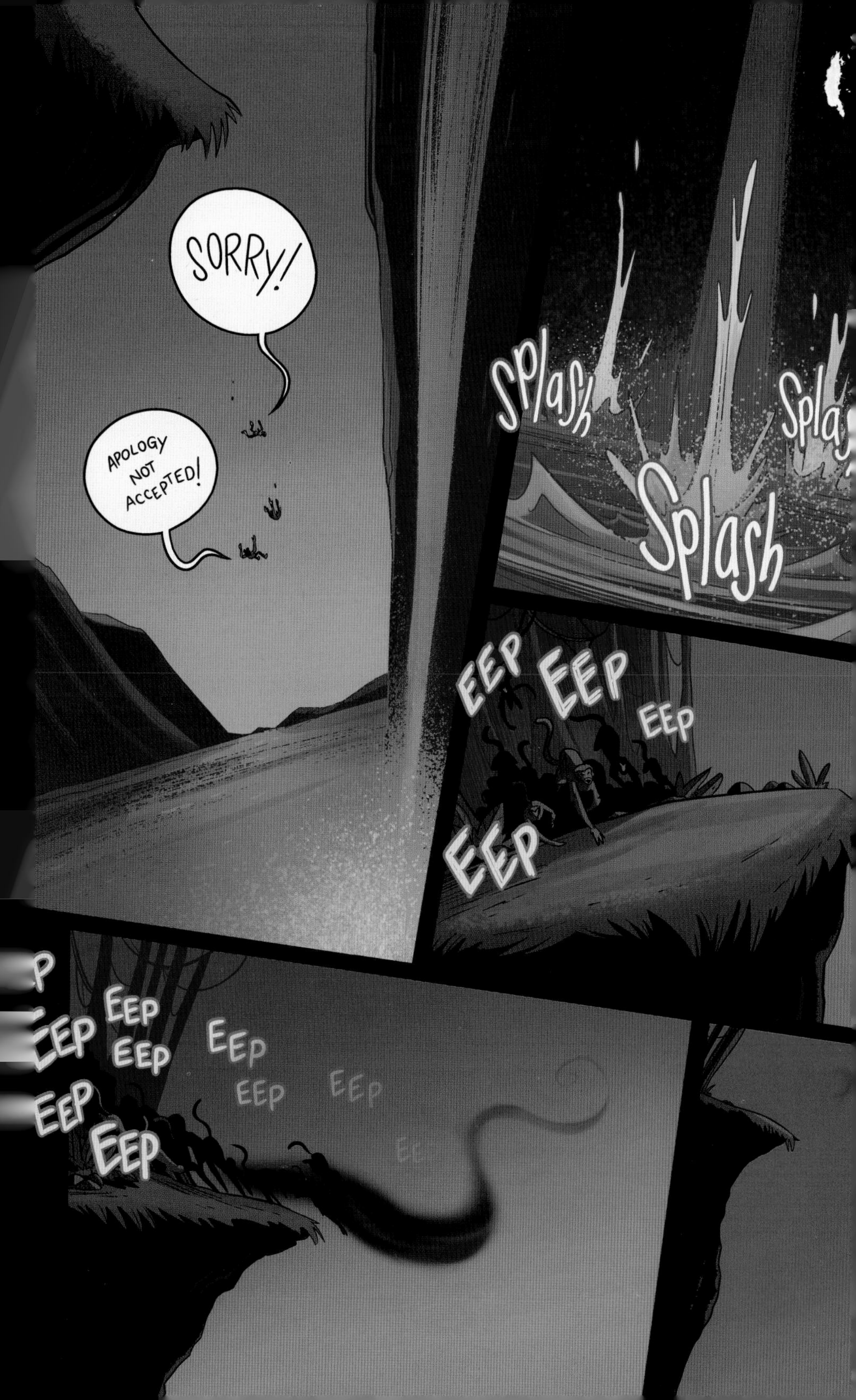
SORRY!
APOLOGY NOT ACCEPTED!
Splash
Splash
Splash
EEP
EEP
EEP
EEP
EEP
EEP
EEP
EEP
EEP
EEP
EEP

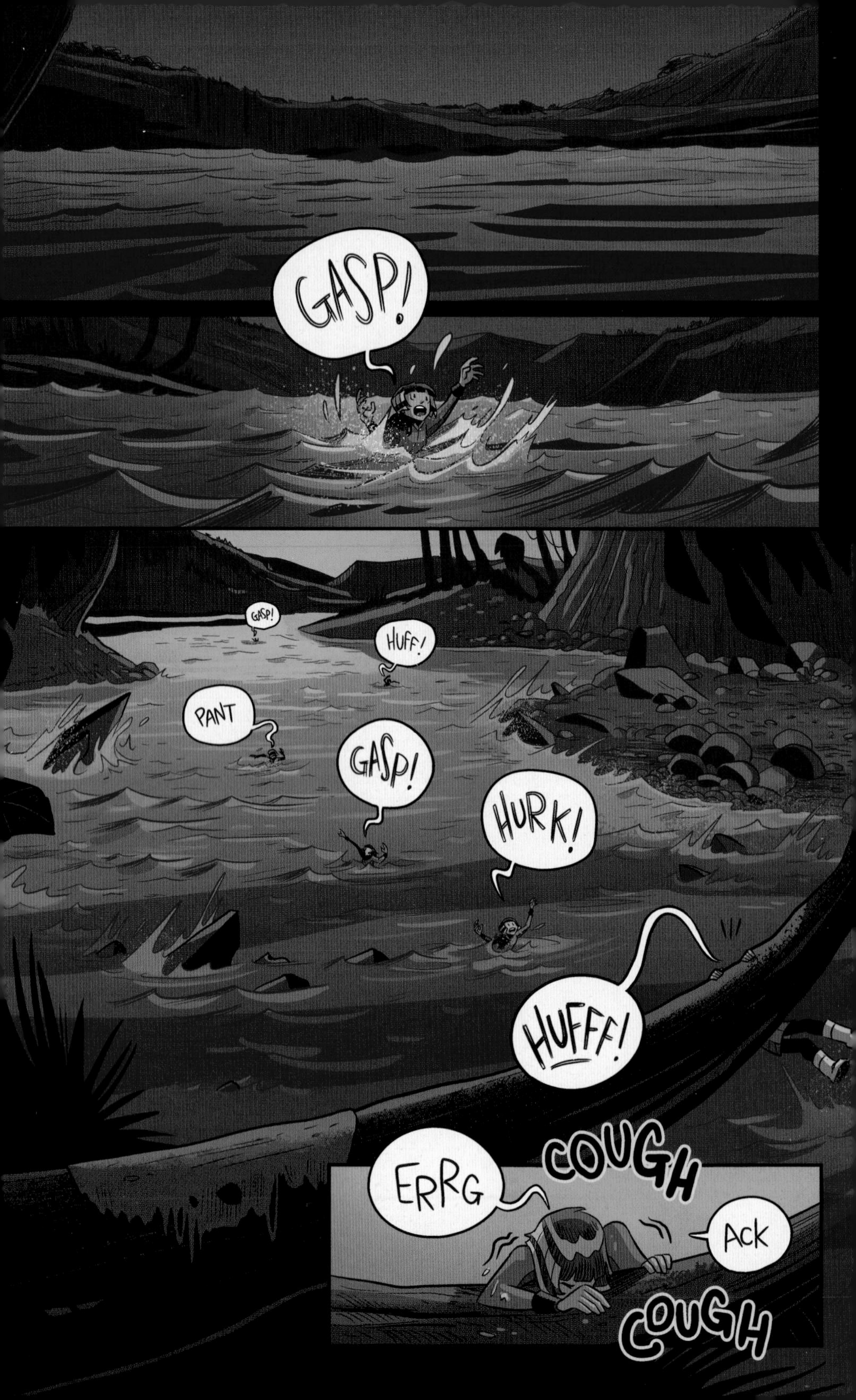
GASP!
GASP!
HUFF!
PANT
GASP!
HURK!
HUFFF!
ERRG
COUGH
ACK
COUGH

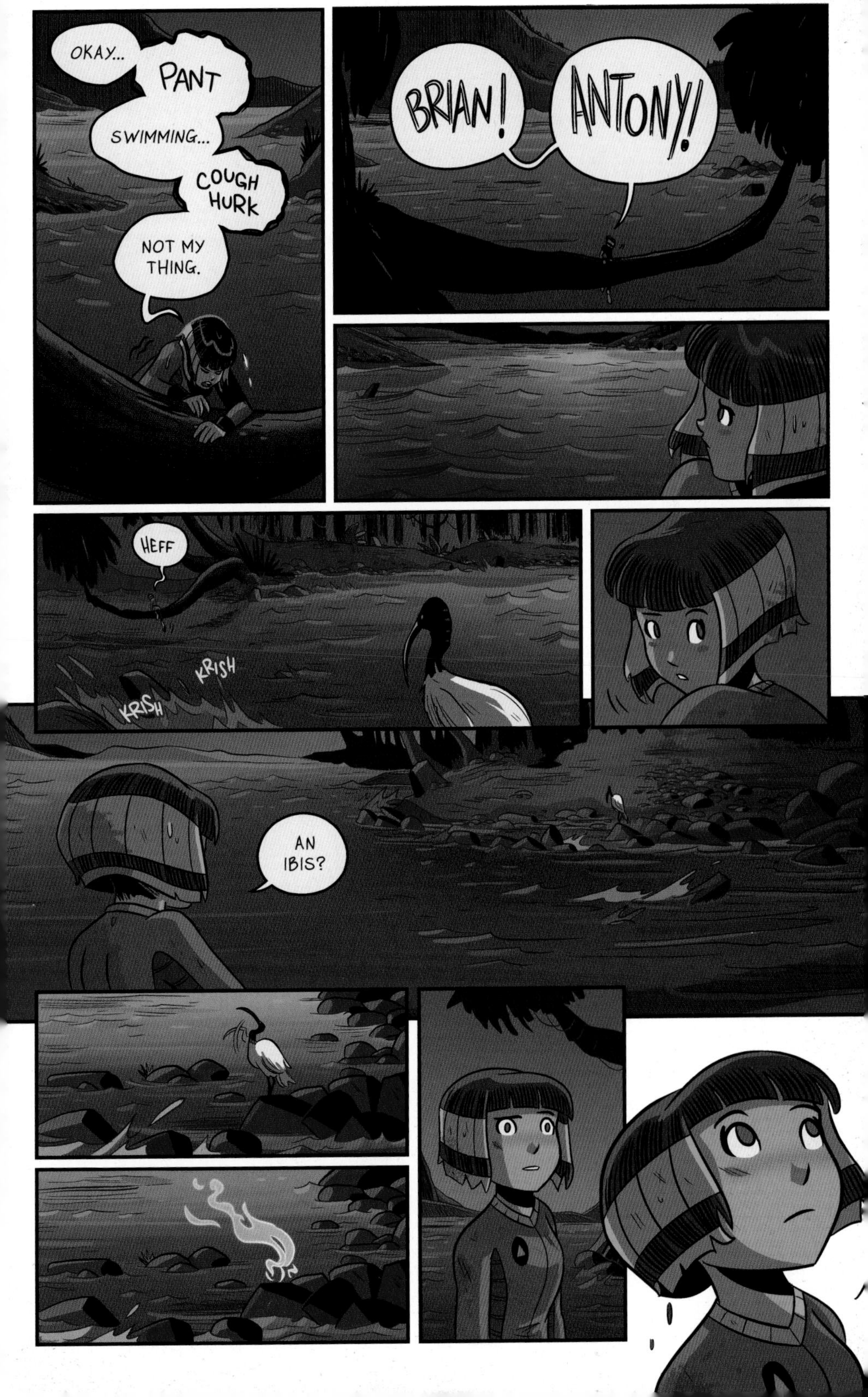
OKAY...
PANT
SWIMMING...
COUGH HURK
NOT MY THING.
BRIAN!
ANTONY!
HEFF
KRISH
KRISH
AN IBIS?

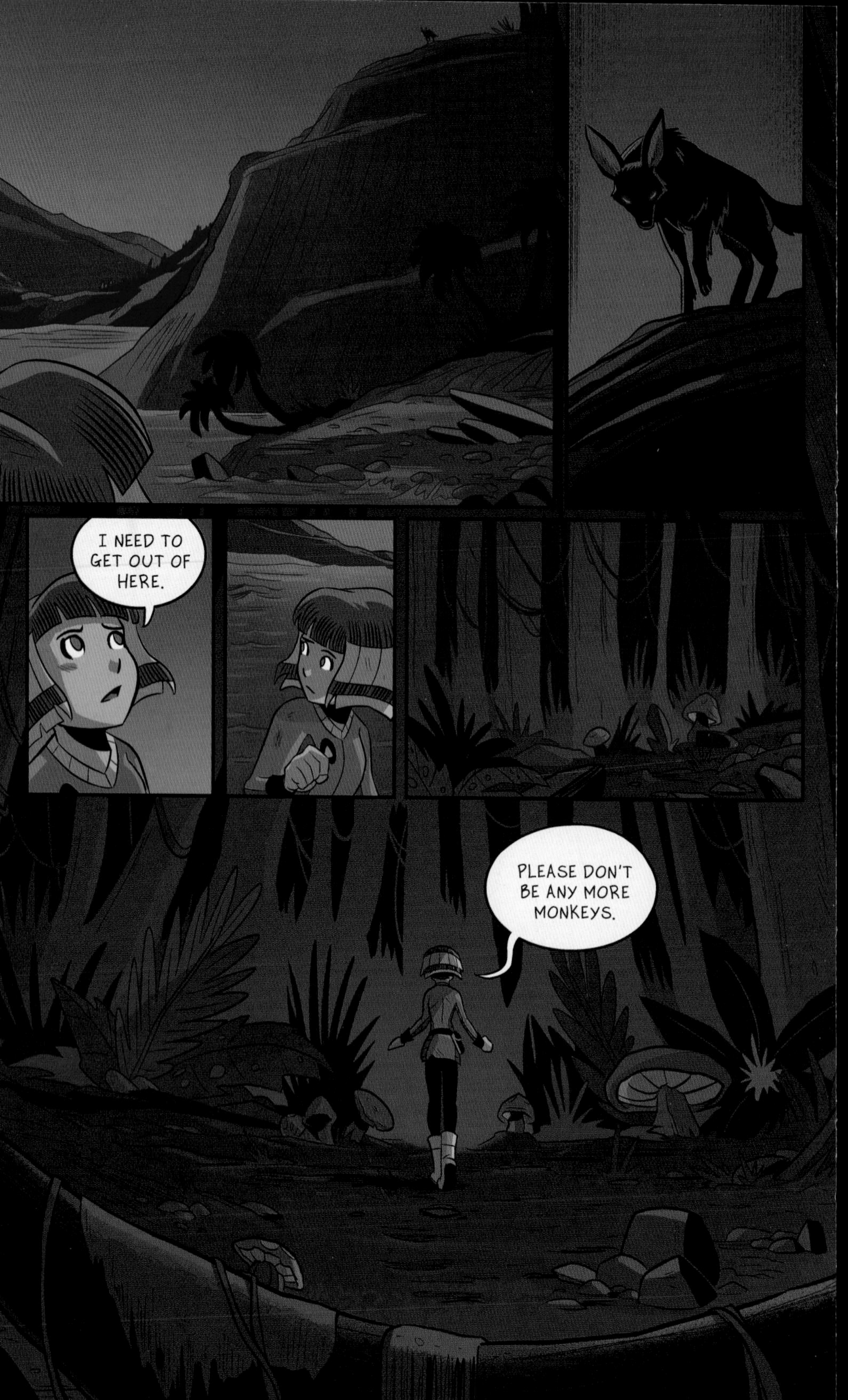
I NEED TO GET OUT OF HERE.
PLEASE DON'T BE ANY MORE MONKEYS.

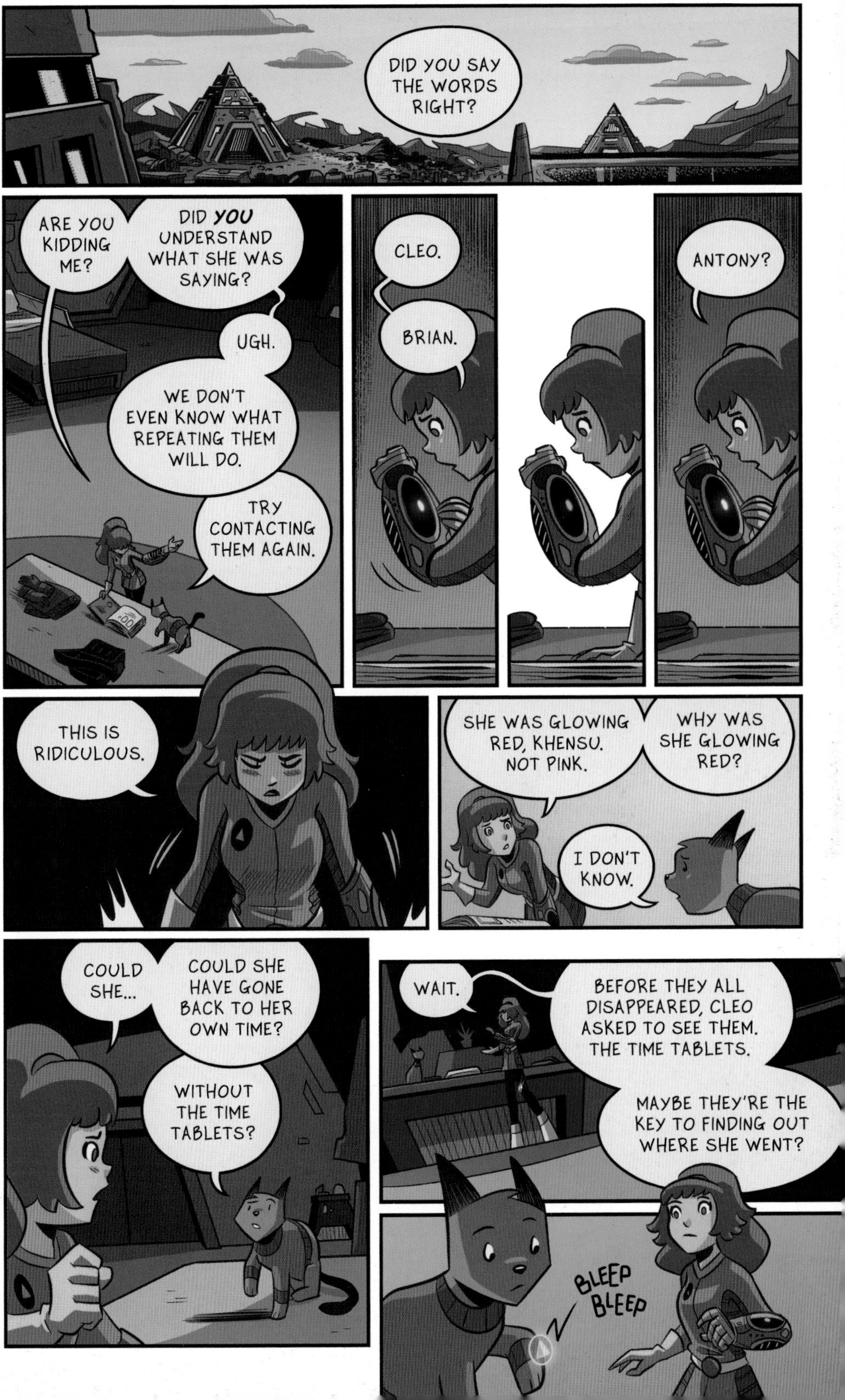

DID YOU SAY THE WORDS RIGHT?
ARE YOU KIDDING ME?
DID YOU UNDERSTAND WHAT SHE WAS SAYING?
UGH.
WE DON'T EVEN KNOW WHAT REPEATING THEM WILL DO.
TRY CONTACTING THEM AGAIN.
CLEO.
BRIAN.
ANTONY?
THIS IS RIDICULOUS.
SHE WAS GLOWING RED, KHENSU. NOT PINK.
WHY WAS SHE GLOWING RED?
I DON'T KNOW.
COULD SHE...
COULD SHE HAVE GONE BACK TO HER OWN TIME?
WITHOUT THE TIME TABLETS?
WAIT.
BEFORE THEY ALL DISAPPEARED, CLEO ASKED TO SEE THEM. THE TIME TABLETS.
MAYBE THEY'RE THE KEY TO FINDING OUT WHERE SHE WENT?
BLEEP BLEEP

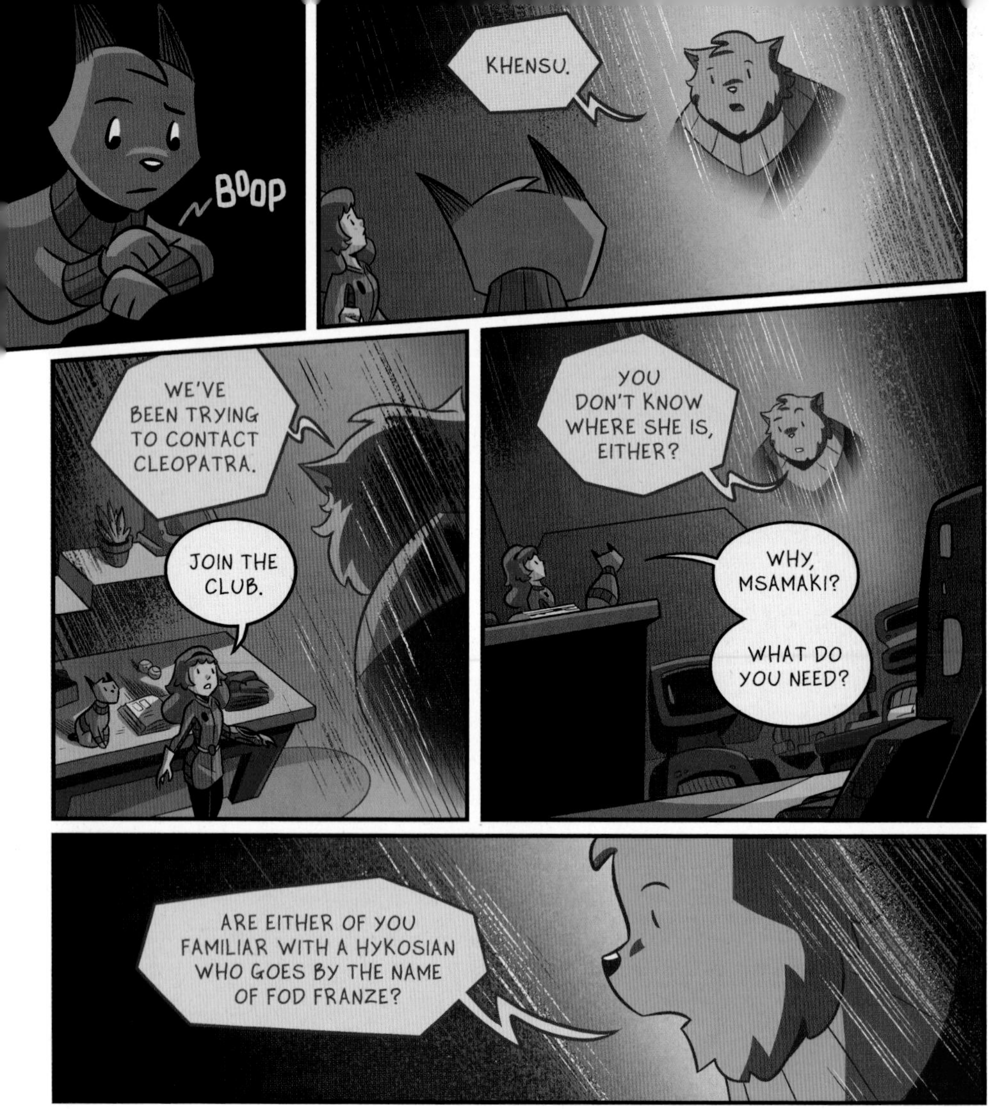
BOOP
KHENSU.
WE'VE BEEN TRYING TO CONTACT CLEOPATRA.
JOIN THE CLUB.
YOU DON'T KNOW WHERE SHE IS, EITHER?
WHY, MSAMAKI?
WHAT DO YOU NEED?
ARE EITHER OF YOU FAMILIAR WITH A HYKOSIAN WHO GOES BY THE NAME OF FOD FRANZE?

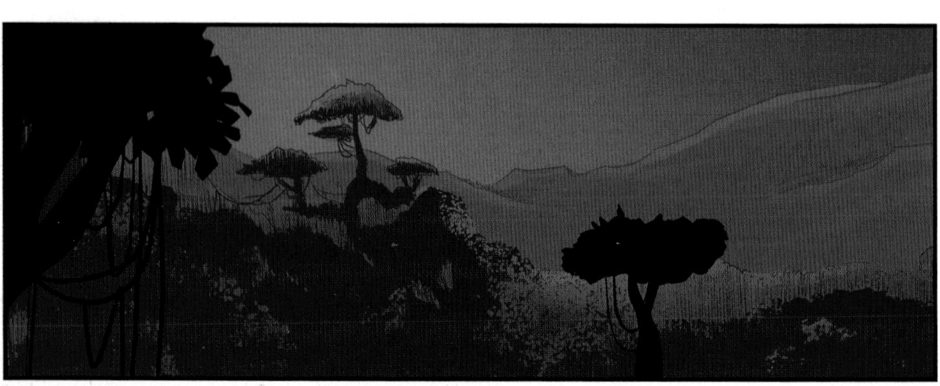

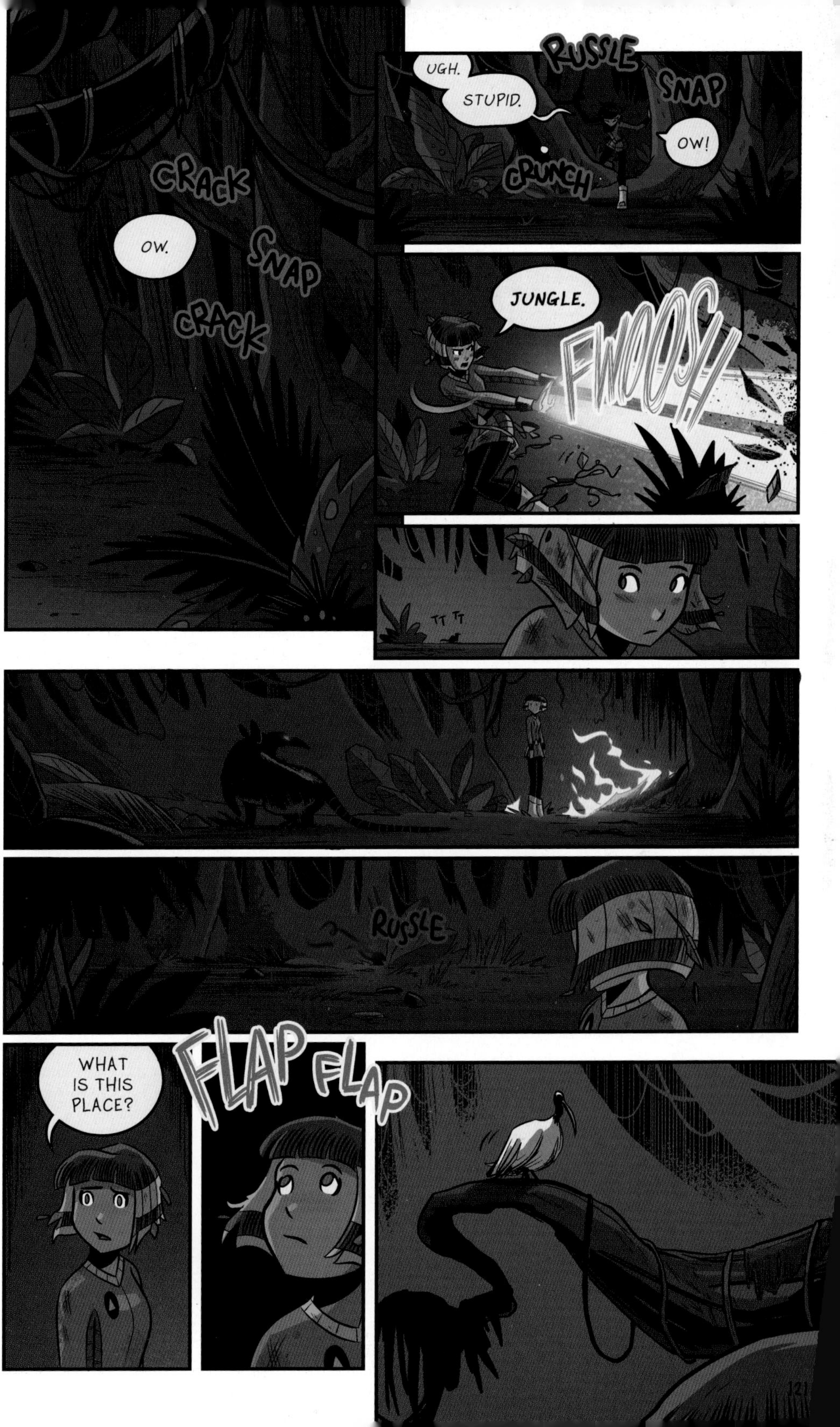
CRACK
OW.
SNAP
CRACK
UGH.
STUPID.
RUSSLE
SNAP
OW!
CRUNCH
JUNGLE.
FWOOSH
TT TT
RUSSLE
WHAT IS THIS PLACE?
FLAP FLAP

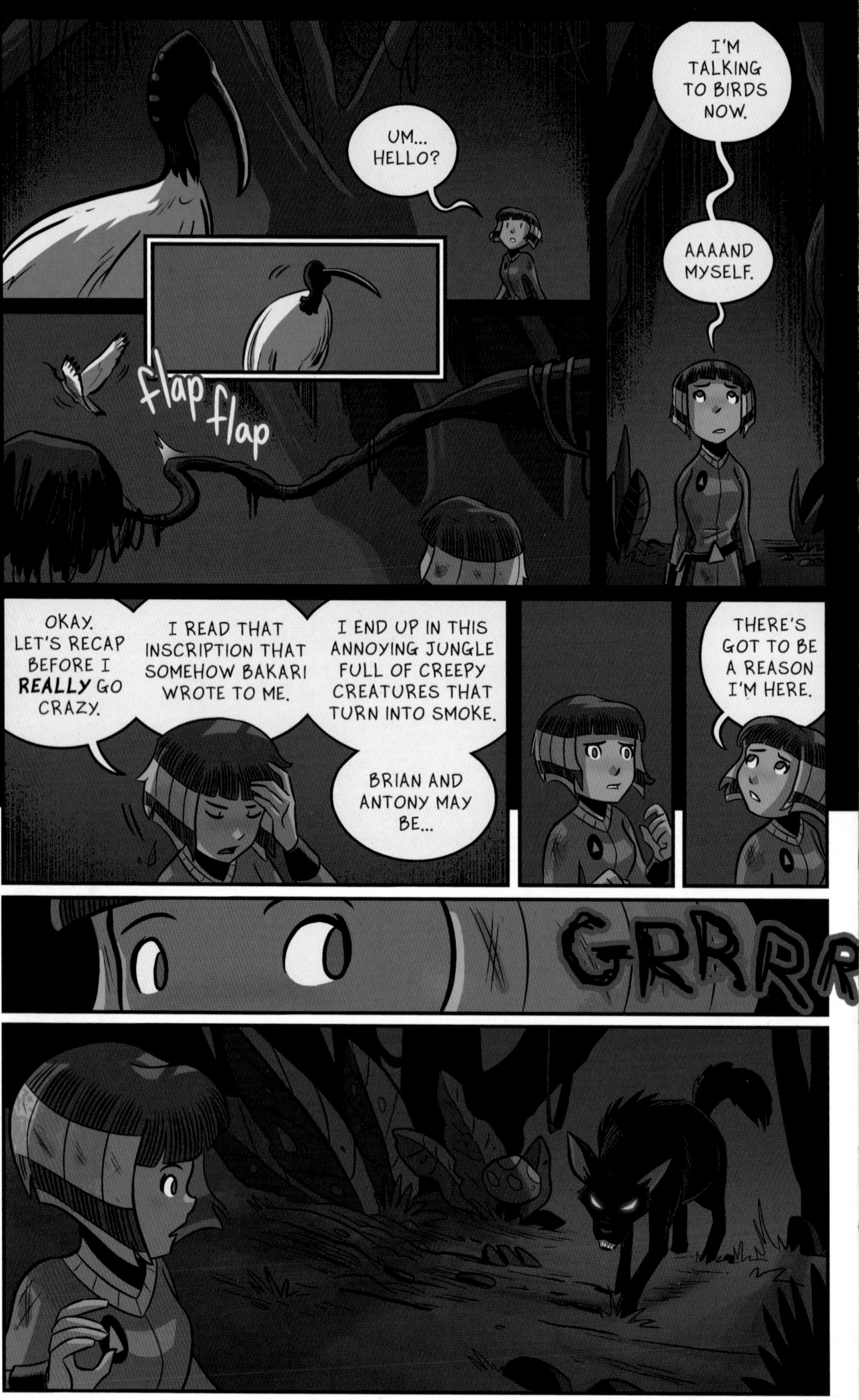
UM... HELLO?
flap flap
I'M TALKING TO BIRDS NOW.
AAAAND MYSELF.
OKAY. LET'S RECAP BEFORE I **REALLY** GO CRAZY.
I READ THAT INSCRIPTION THAT SOMEHOW BAKARI WROTE TO ME.
I END UP IN THIS ANNOYING JUNGLE FULL OF CREEPY CREATURES THAT TURN INTO SMOKE.
BRIAN AND ANTONY MAY BE...
THERE'S GOT TO BE A REASON I'M HERE.
GRRRR

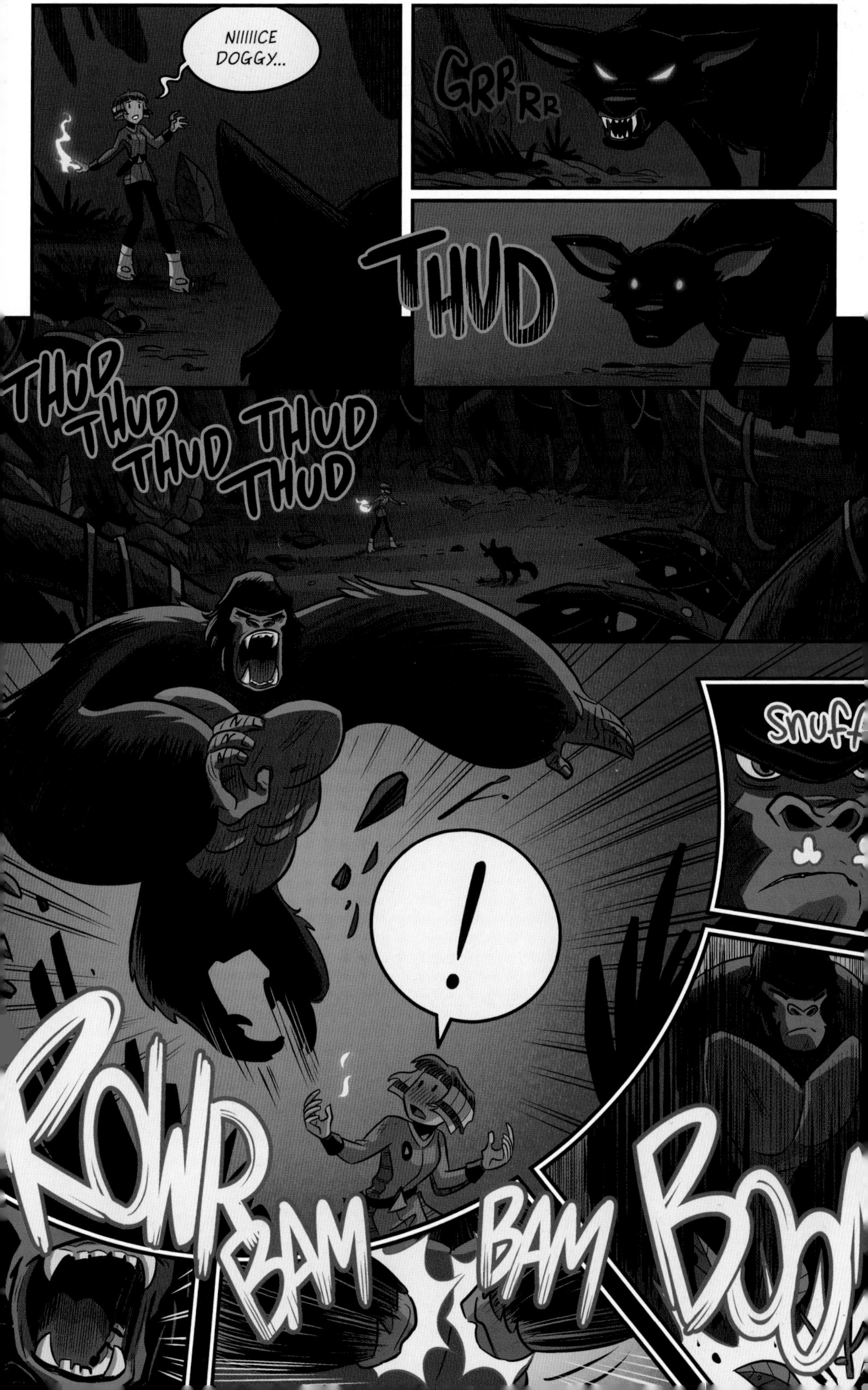
NIIIIICE DOGGY...
GRRRRR
THUD
THUD THUD THUD THUD THUD
snuff
!
ROWR
BAM
BAM
BOO

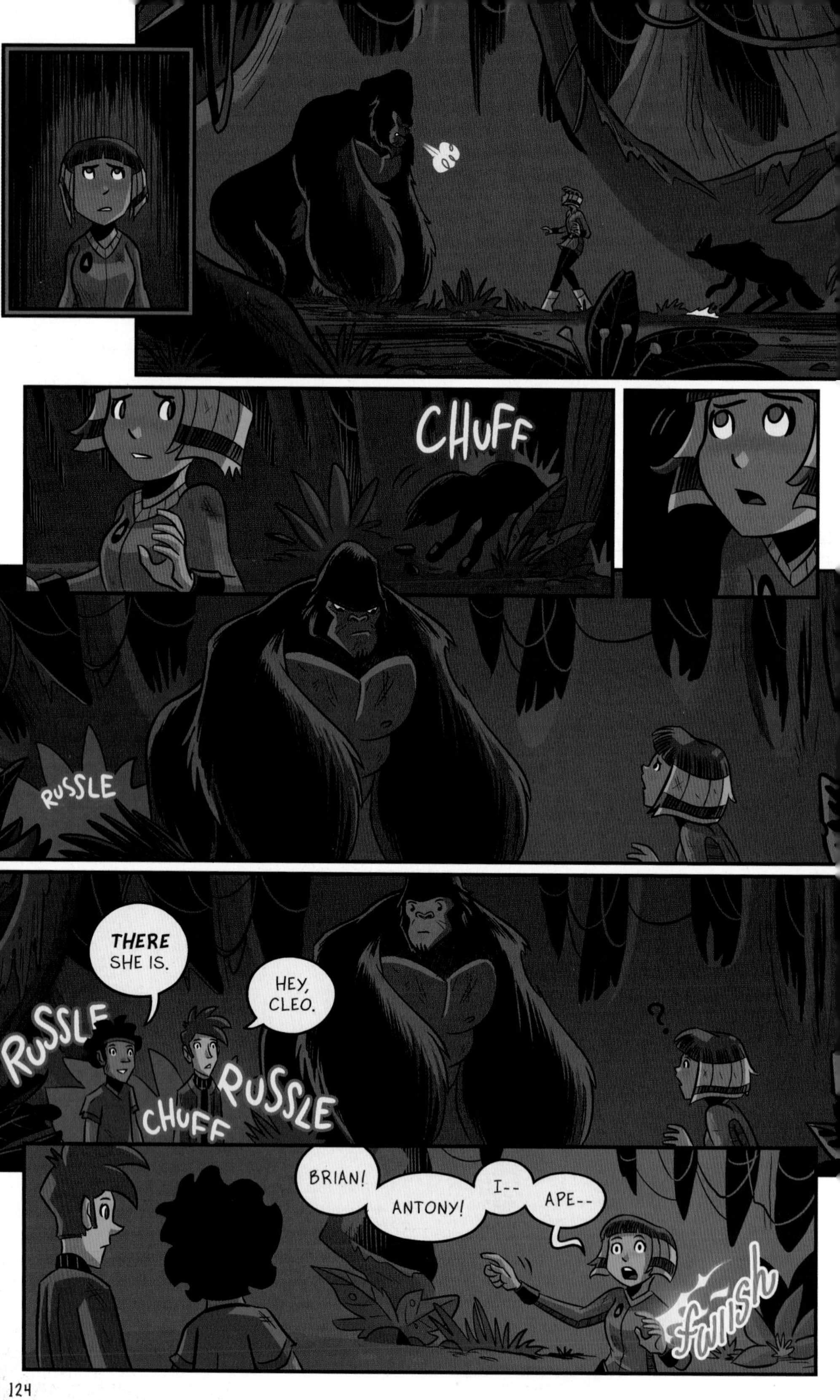
CHUFF
RUSSLE
THERE SHE IS.
HEY, CLEO.
RUSSLE
RUSSLE
CHUFF
BRIAN!
ANTONY!
I--
APE--

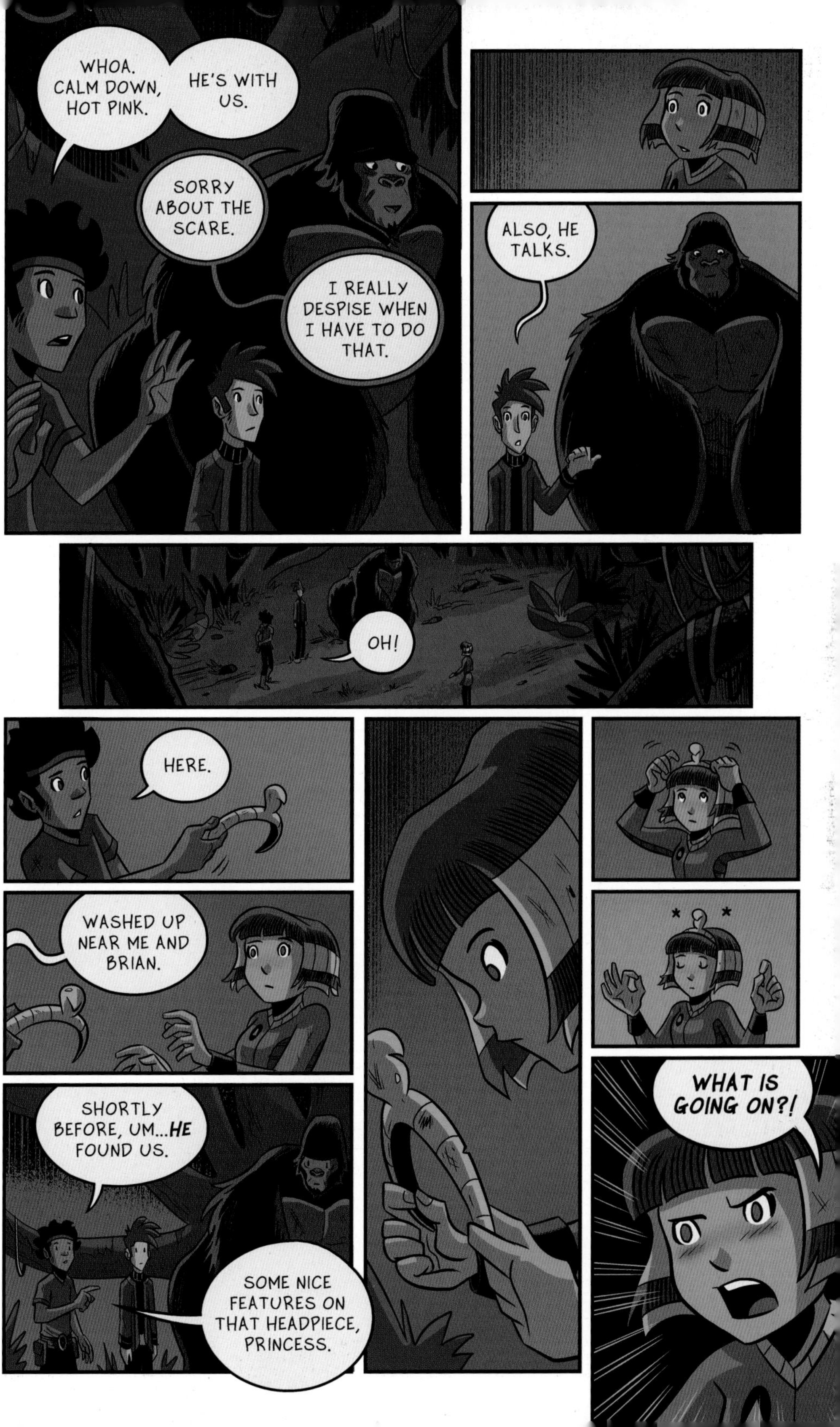
WHOA. CALM DOWN, HOT PINK.
HE'S WITH US.
SORRY ABOUT THE SCARE.
I REALLY DESPISE WHEN I HAVE TO DO THAT.
ALSO, HE TALKS.
OH!
HERE.
WASHED UP NEAR ME AND BRIAN.
SHORTLY BEFORE, UM...**HE** FOUND US.
SOME NICE FEATURES ON THAT HEADPIECE, PRINCESS.
WHAT IS GOING ON?!

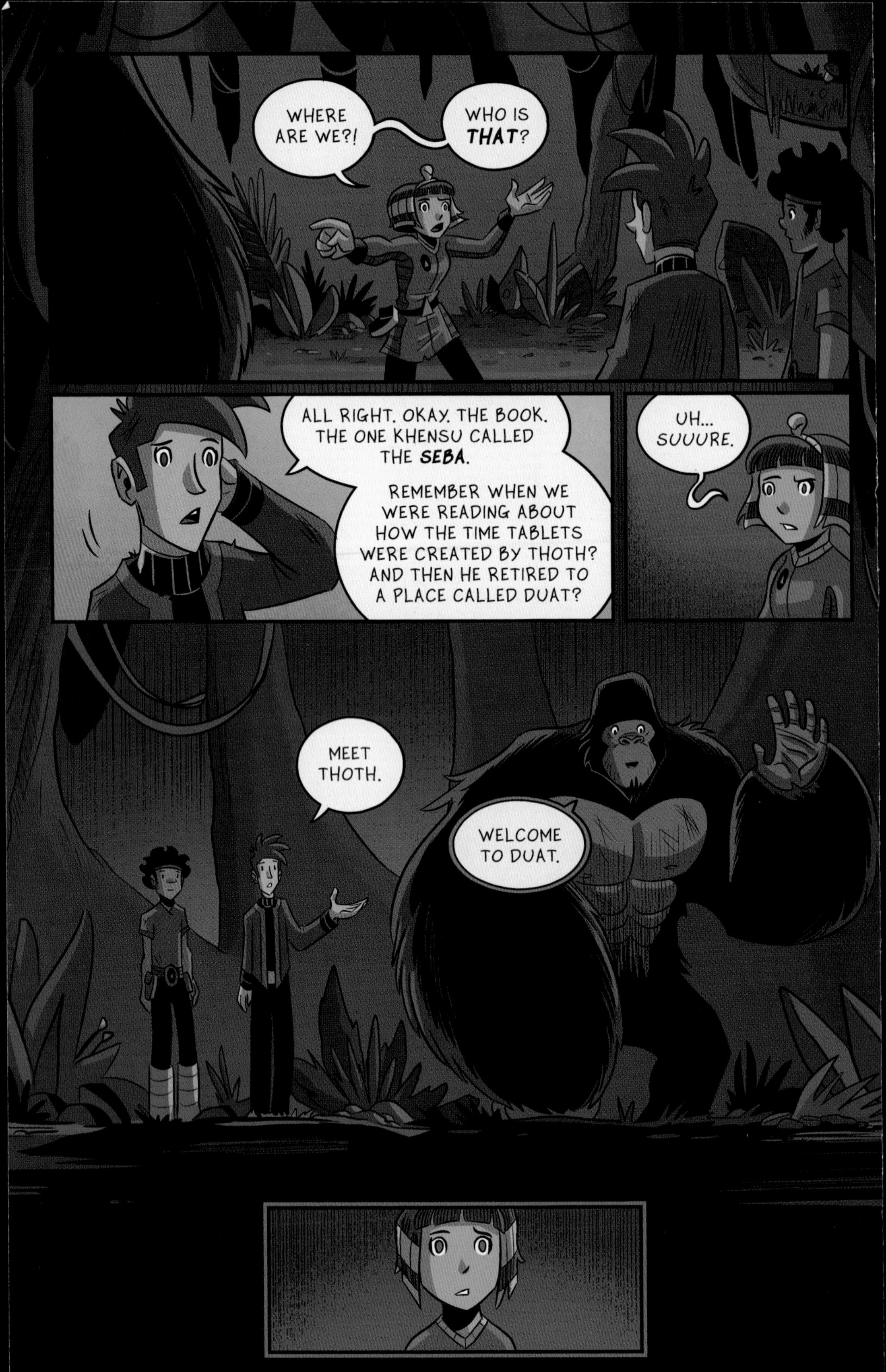
WHERE ARE WE?!
WHO IS **THAT**?
ALL RIGHT. OKAY. THE BOOK. THE ONE KHENSU CALLED THE **SEBA**.
REMEMBER WHEN WE WERE READING ABOUT HOW THE TIME TABLETS WERE CREATED BY THOTH? AND THEN HE RETIRED TO A PLACE CALLED DUAT?
UH... SUUURE.
MEET THOTH.
WELCOME TO DUAT.

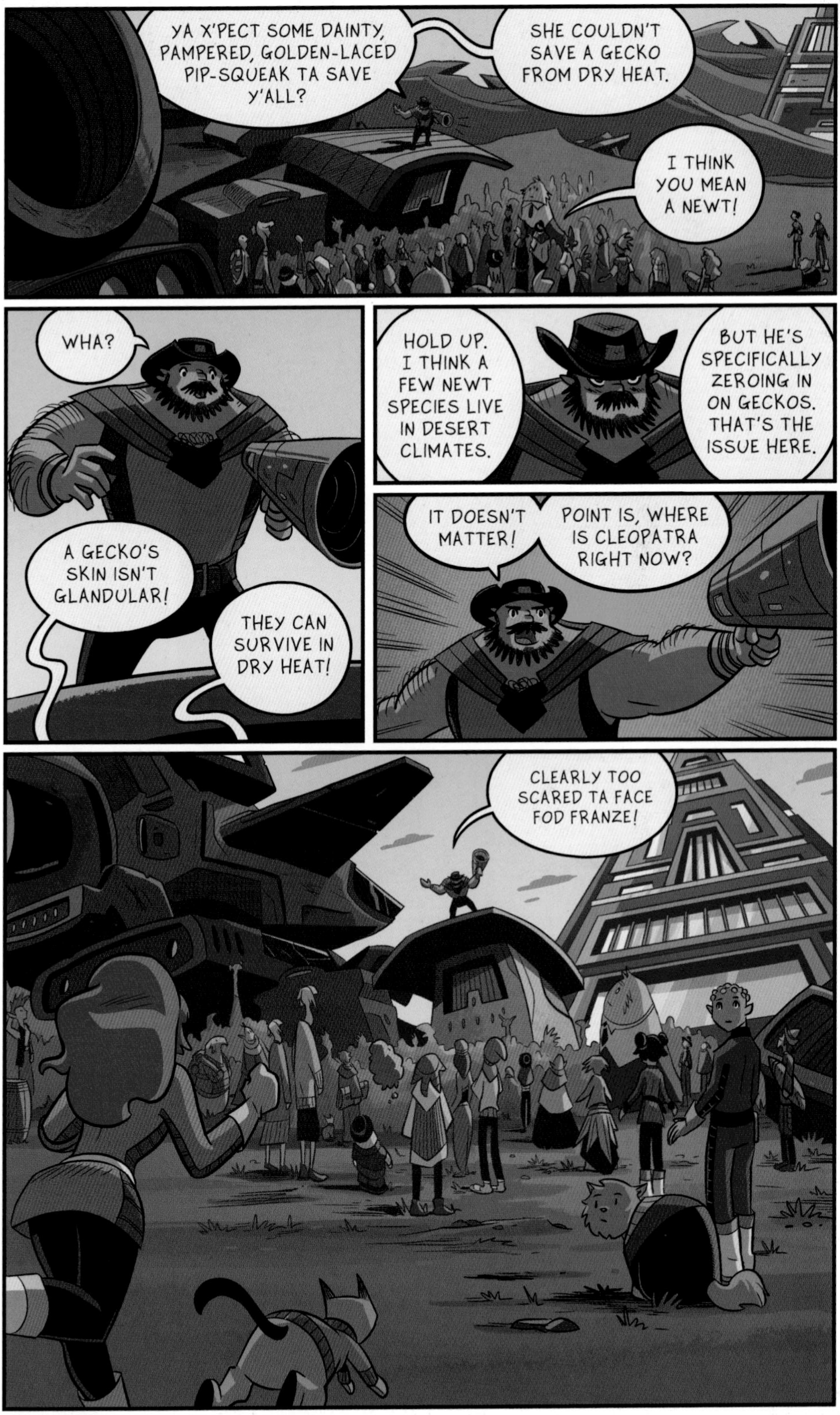
YA X'PECT SOME DAINTY, PAMPERED, GOLDEN-LACED PIP-SQUEAK TA SAVE Y'ALL?
SHE COULDN'T SAVE A GECKO FROM DRY HEAT.
I THINK YOU MEAN A NEWT!
WHA?
A GECKO'S SKIN ISN'T GLANDULAR!
THEY CAN SURVIVE IN DRY HEAT!
HOLD UP. I THINK A FEW NEWT SPECIES LIVE IN DESERT CLIMATES.
BUT HE'S SPECIFICALLY ZEROING IN ON GECKOS. THAT'S THE ISSUE HERE.
IT DOESN'T MATTER!
POINT IS, WHERE IS CLEOPATRA RIGHT NOW?
CLEARLY TOO SCARED TA FACE FOD FRANZE!

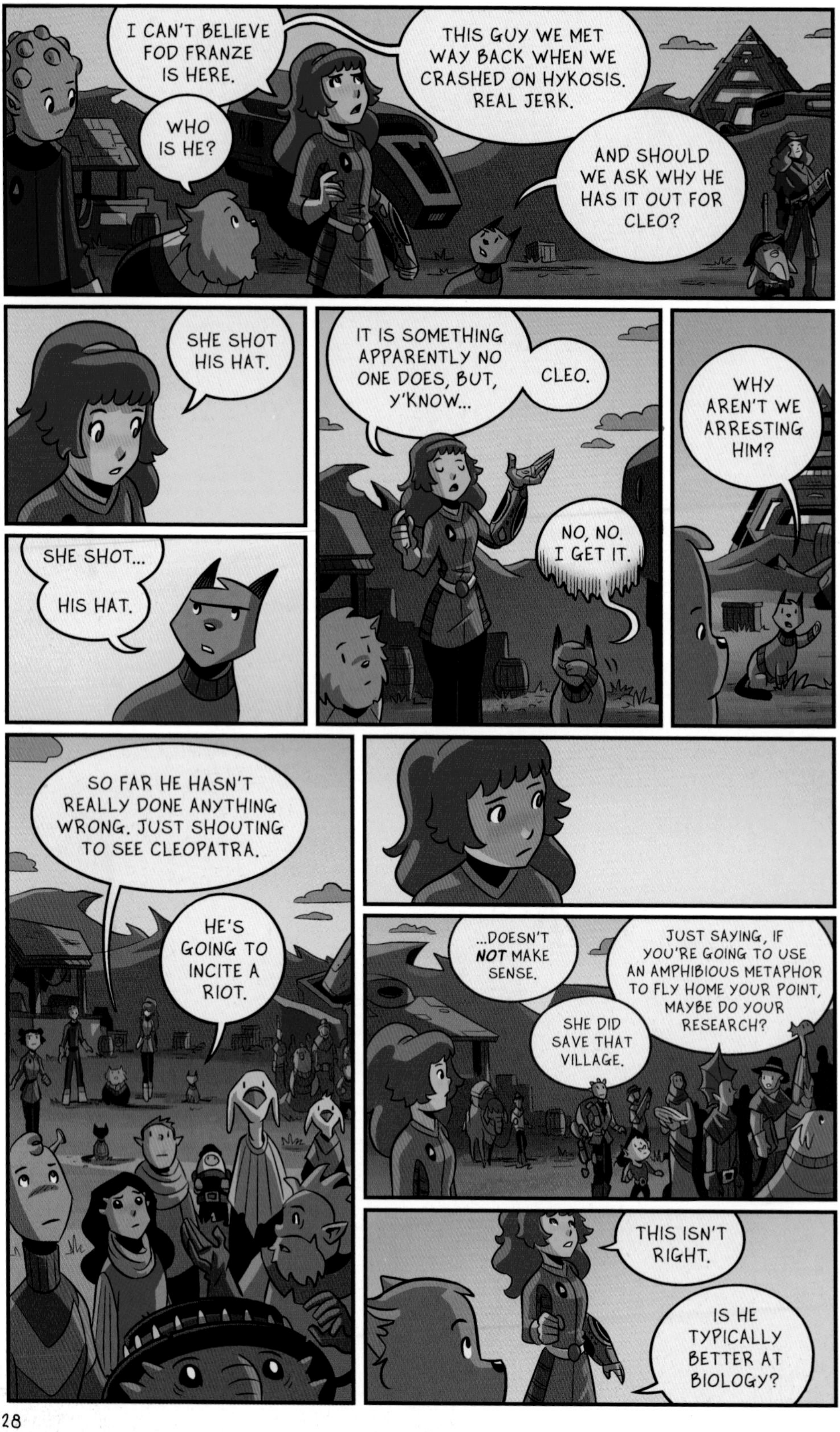
I CAN'T BELIEVE FOD FRANZE IS HERE.
WHO IS HE?
THIS GUY WE MET WAY BACK WHEN WE CRASHED ON HYKOSIS. REAL JERK.
AND SHOULD WE ASK WHY HE HAS IT OUT FOR CLEO?
SHE SHOT HIS HAT.
SHE SHOT...
HIS HAT.
IT IS SOMETHING APPARENTLY NO ONE DOES, BUT, Y'KNOW...
CLEO.
NO, NO. I GET IT.
WHY AREN'T WE ARRESTING HIM?
SO FAR HE HASN'T REALLY DONE ANYTHING WRONG. JUST SHOUTING TO SEE CLEOPATRA.
HE'S GOING TO INCITE A RIOT.
...DOESN'T **NOT** MAKE SENSE.
JUST SAYING, IF YOU'RE GOING TO USE AN AMPHIBIOUS METAPHOR TO FLY HOME YOUR POINT, MAYBE DO YOUR RESEARCH?
SHE DID SAVE THAT VILLAGE.
THIS ISN'T RIGHT.
IS HE TYPICALLY BETTER AT BIOLOGY?

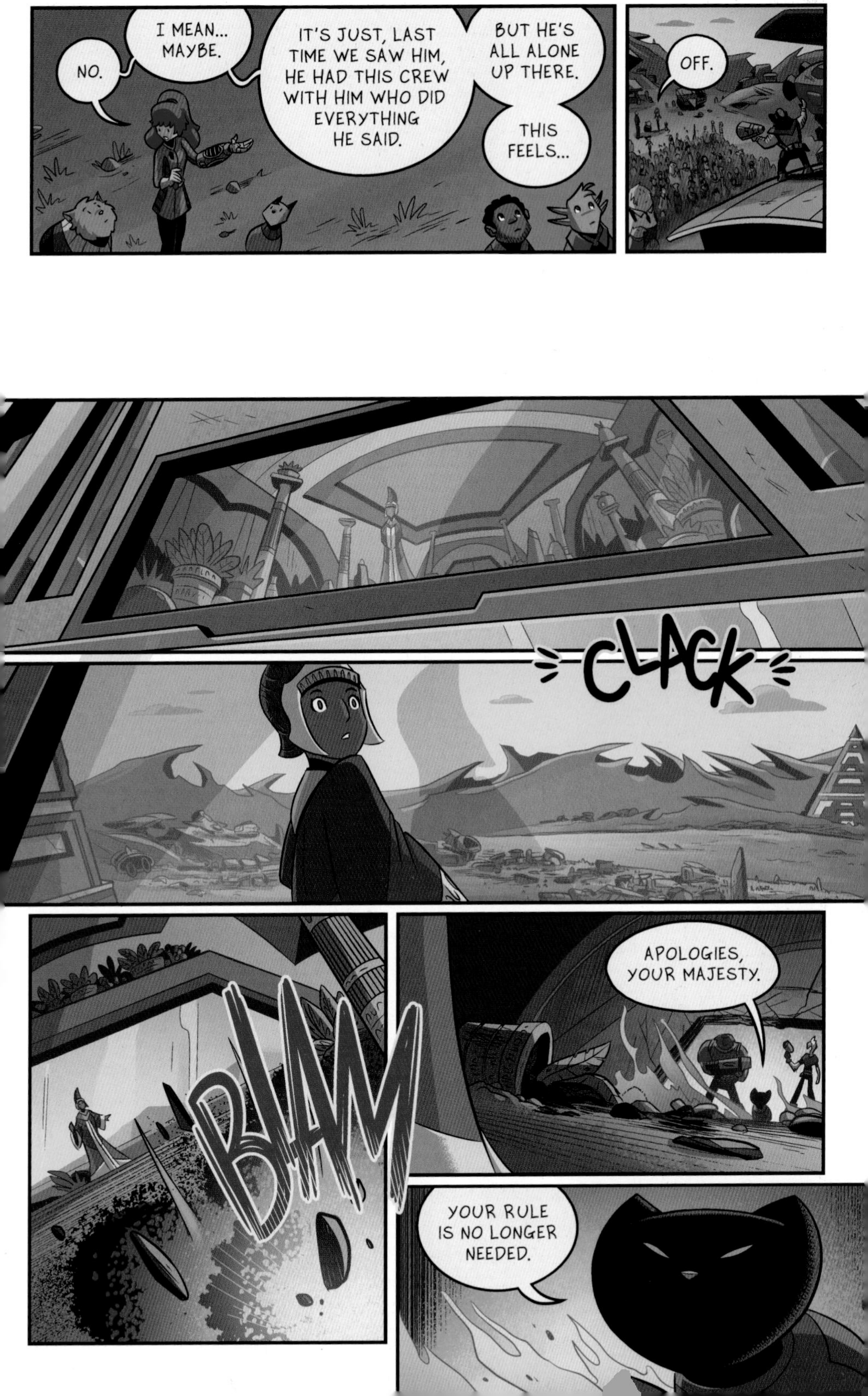
NO.
I MEAN... MAYBE.
IT'S JUST, LAST TIME WE SAW HIM, HE HAD THIS CREW WITH HIM WHO DID EVERYTHING HE SAID.
BUT HE'S ALL ALONE UP THERE.
THIS FEELS...
OFF.
CLACK
BLAM
APOLOGIES, YOUR MAJESTY.
YOUR RULE IS NO LONGER NEEDED.

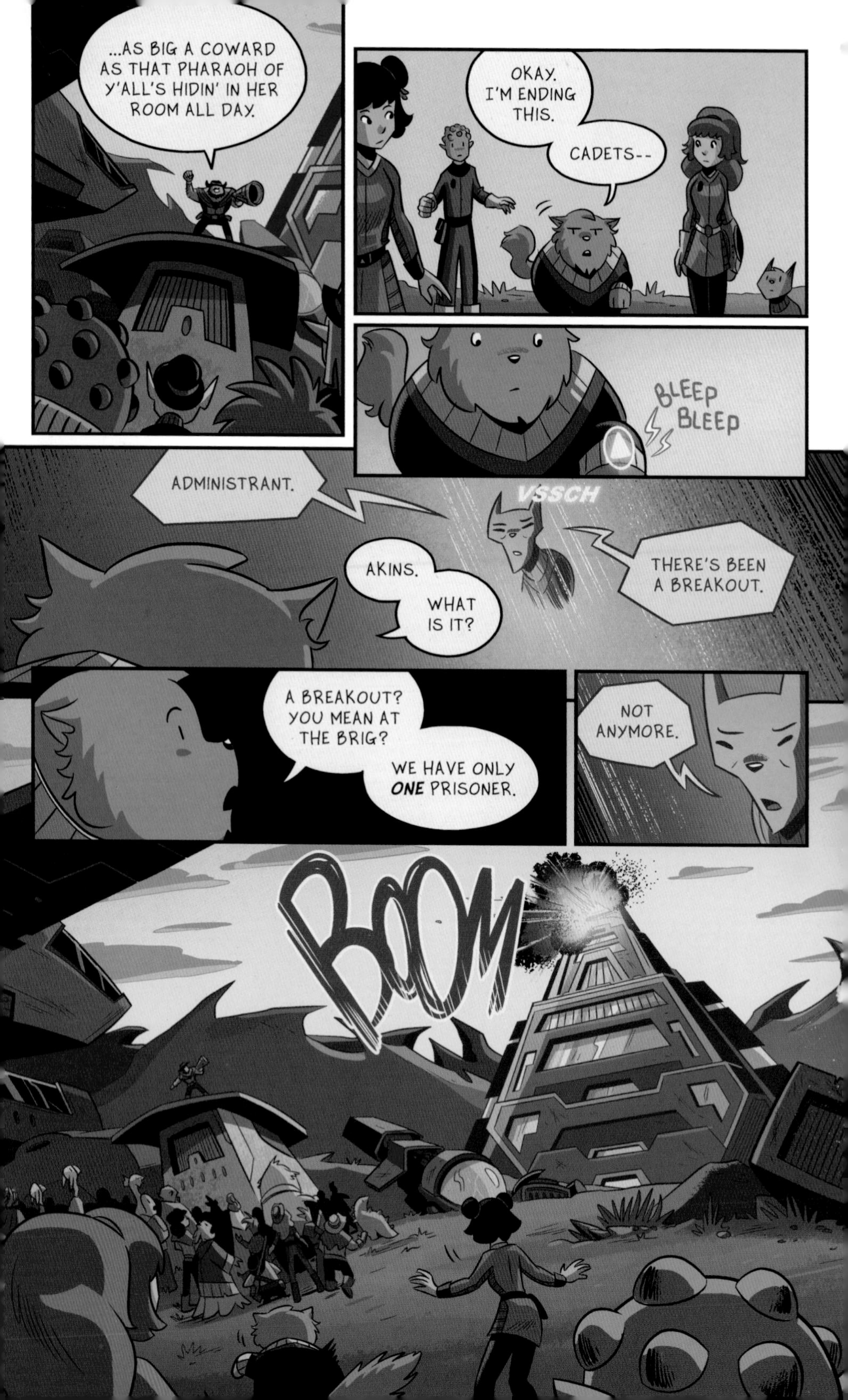
...AS BIG A COWARD AS THAT PHARAOH OF Y'ALL'S HIDIN' IN HER ROOM ALL DAY.
OKAY. I'M ENDING THIS.
CADETS--
BLEEP BLEEP
ADMINISTRANT.
VSSCH
AKINS.
WHAT IS IT?
THERE'S BEEN A BREAKOUT.
A BREAKOUT? YOU MEAN AT THE BRIG?
WE HAVE ONLY ONE PRISONER.
NOT ANYMORE.
BOOM

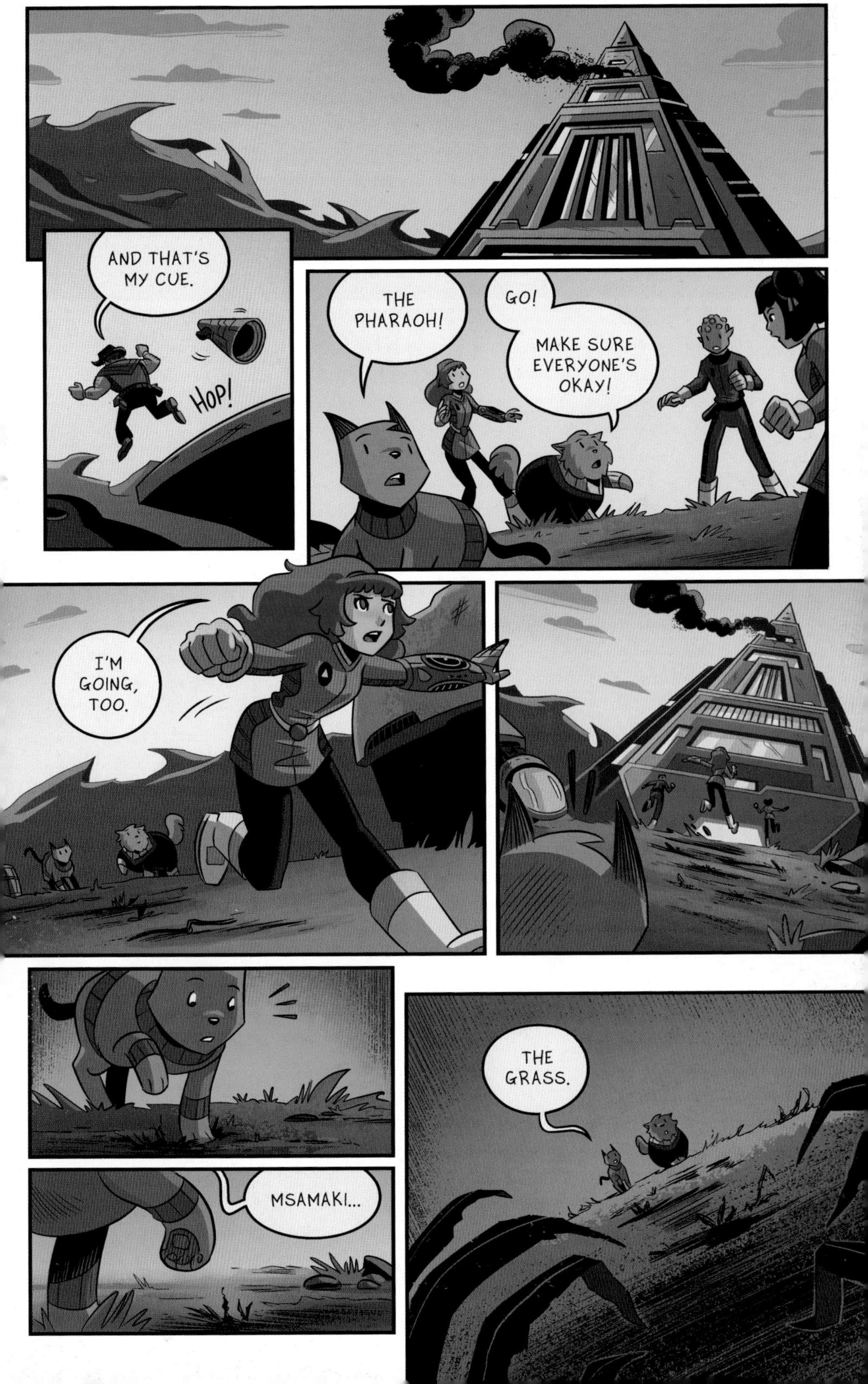
AND THAT'S MY CUE.
HOP!
THE PHARAOH!
GO!
MAKE SURE EVERYONE'S OKAY!
I'M GOING, TOO.
MSAMAKI...
THE GRASS.

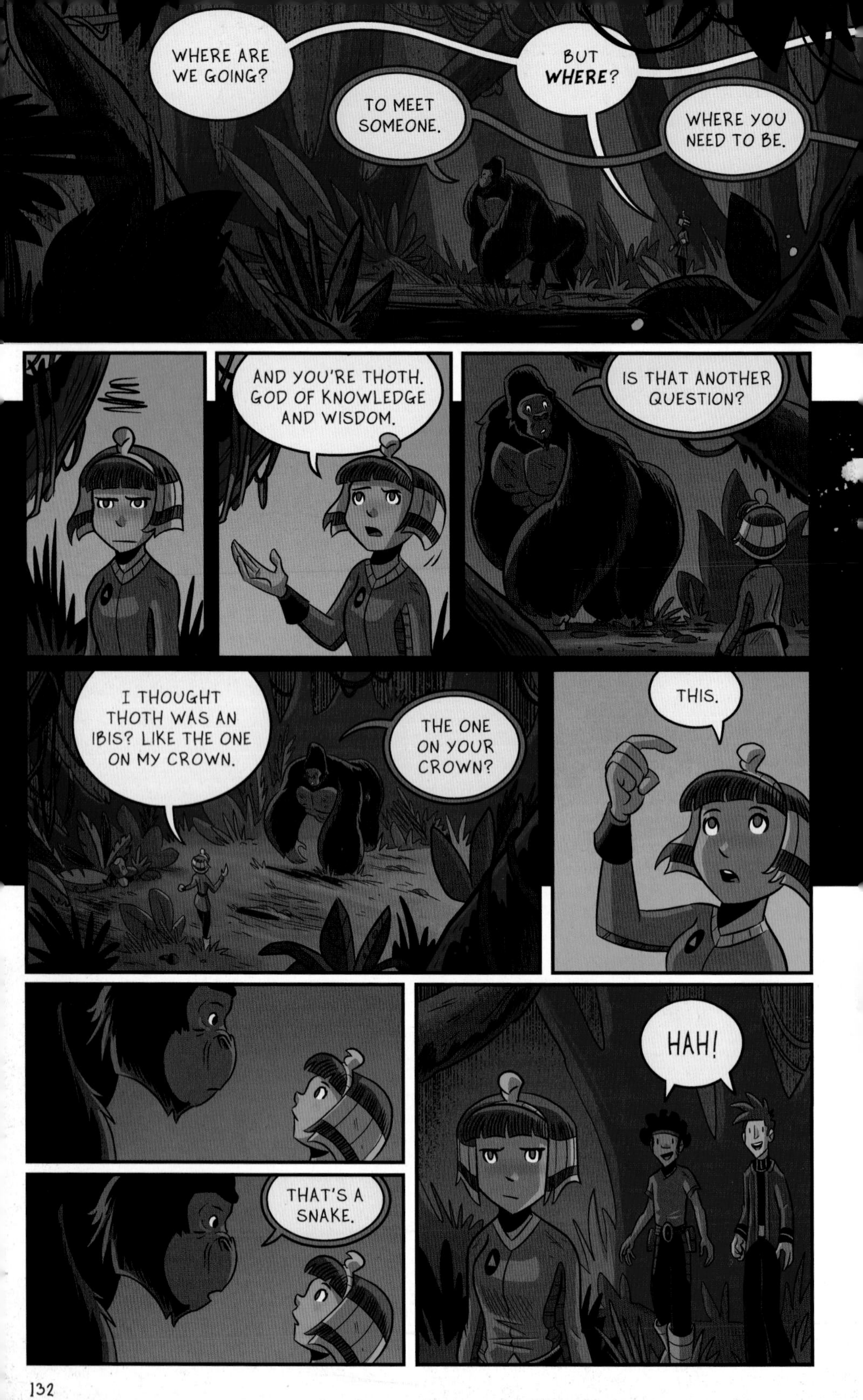
WHERE ARE WE GOING?
TO MEET SOMEONE.
BUT WHERE?
WHERE YOU NEED TO BE.
AND YOU'RE THOTH. GOD OF KNOWLEDGE AND WISDOM.
IS THAT ANOTHER QUESTION?
I THOUGHT THOTH WAS AN IBIS? LIKE THE ONE ON MY CROWN.
THE ONE ON YOUR CROWN?
THIS.
THAT'S A SNAKE.
HAH!

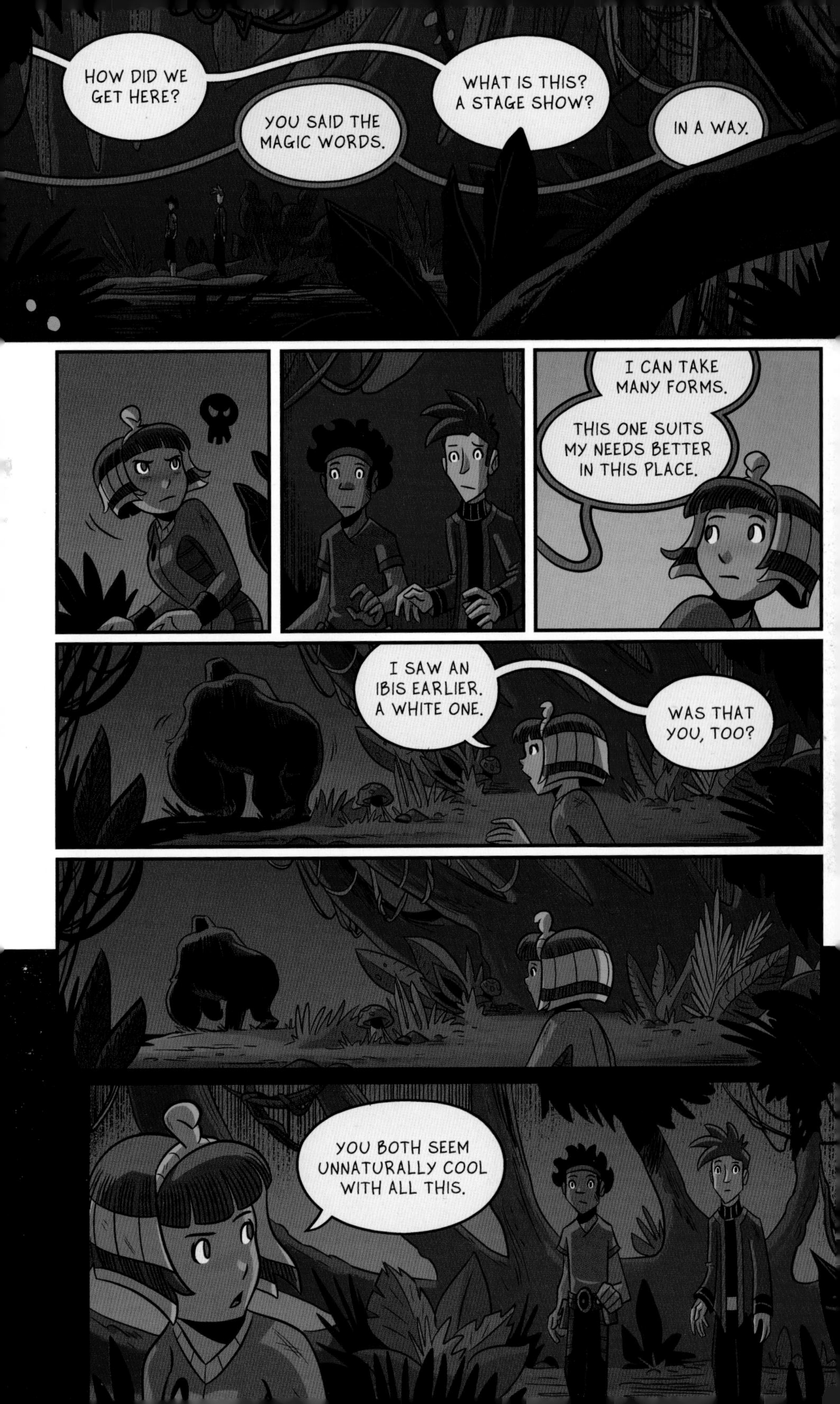
HOW DID WE GET HERE?
YOU SAID THE MAGIC WORDS.
WHAT IS THIS? A STAGE SHOW?
IN A WAY.
I CAN TAKE MANY FORMS.
THIS ONE SUITS MY NEEDS BETTER IN THIS PLACE.
I SAW AN IBIS EARLIER. A WHITE ONE.
WAS THAT YOU, TOO?
YOU BOTH SEEM UNNATURALLY COOL WITH ALL THIS.

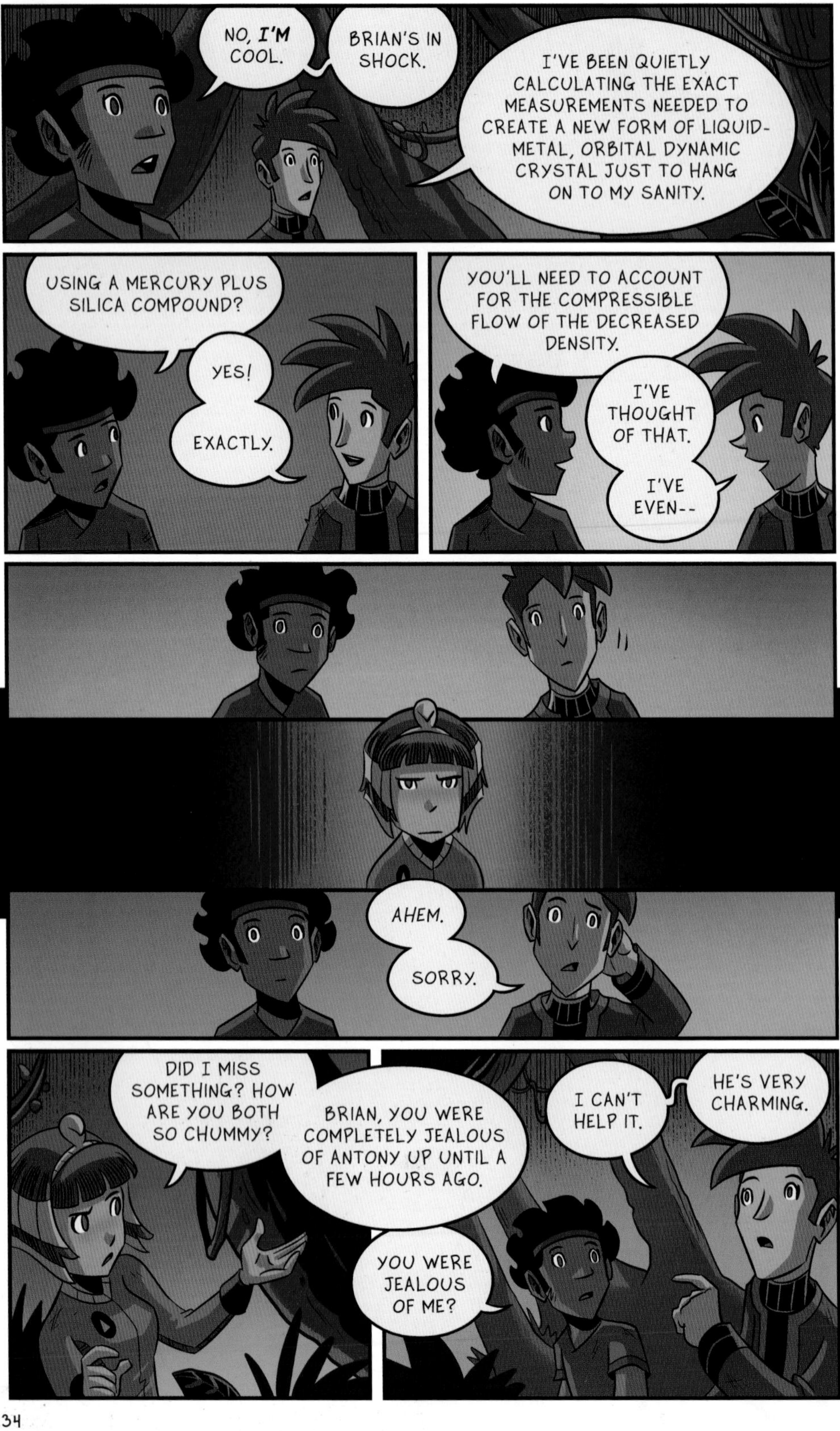
NO, I'M COOL.
BRIAN'S IN SHOCK.
I'VE BEEN QUIETLY CALCULATING THE EXACT MEASUREMENTS NEEDED TO CREATE A NEW FORM OF LIQUID-METAL, ORBITAL DYNAMIC CRYSTAL JUST TO HANG ON TO MY SANITY.
USING A MERCURY PLUS SILICA COMPOUND?
YES!
EXACTLY.
YOU'LL NEED TO ACCOUNT FOR THE COMPRESSIBLE FLOW OF THE DECREASED DENSITY.
I'VE THOUGHT OF THAT.
I'VE EVEN--
AHEM.
SORRY.
DID I MISS SOMETHING? HOW ARE YOU BOTH SO CHUMMY?
BRIAN, YOU WERE COMPLETELY JEALOUS OF ANTONY UP UNTIL A FEW HOURS AGO.
YOU WERE JEALOUS OF ME?
I CAN'T HELP IT.
HE'S VERY CHARMING.

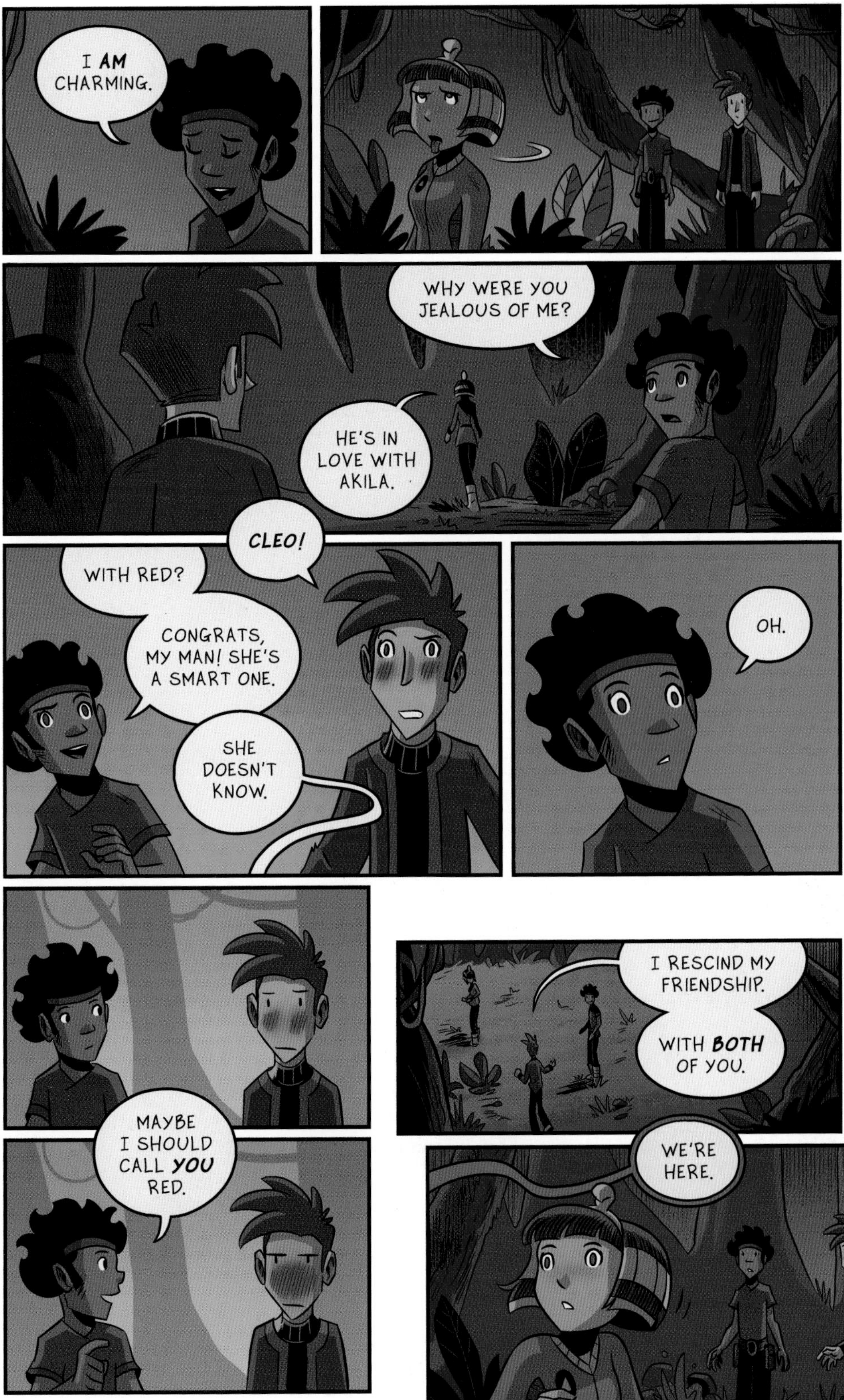
I AM CHARMING.
WHY WERE YOU JEALOUS OF ME?
HE'S IN LOVE WITH AKILA.
CLEO!
WITH RED?
CONGRATS, MY MAN! SHE'S A SMART ONE.
SHE DOESN'T KNOW.
OH.
MAYBE I SHOULD CALL YOU RED.
I RESCIND MY FRIENDSHIP.
WITH BOTH OF YOU.
WE'RE HERE.

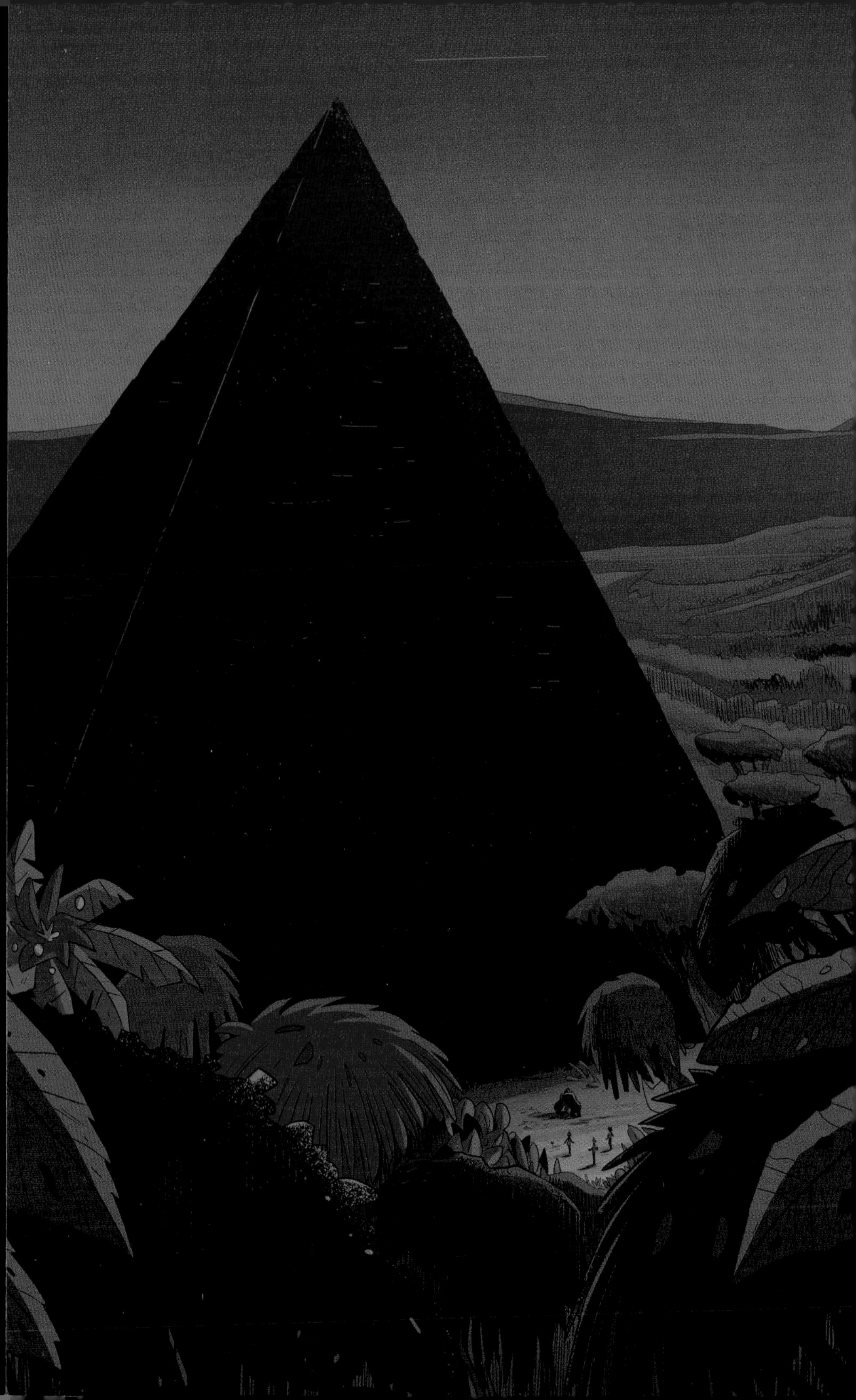

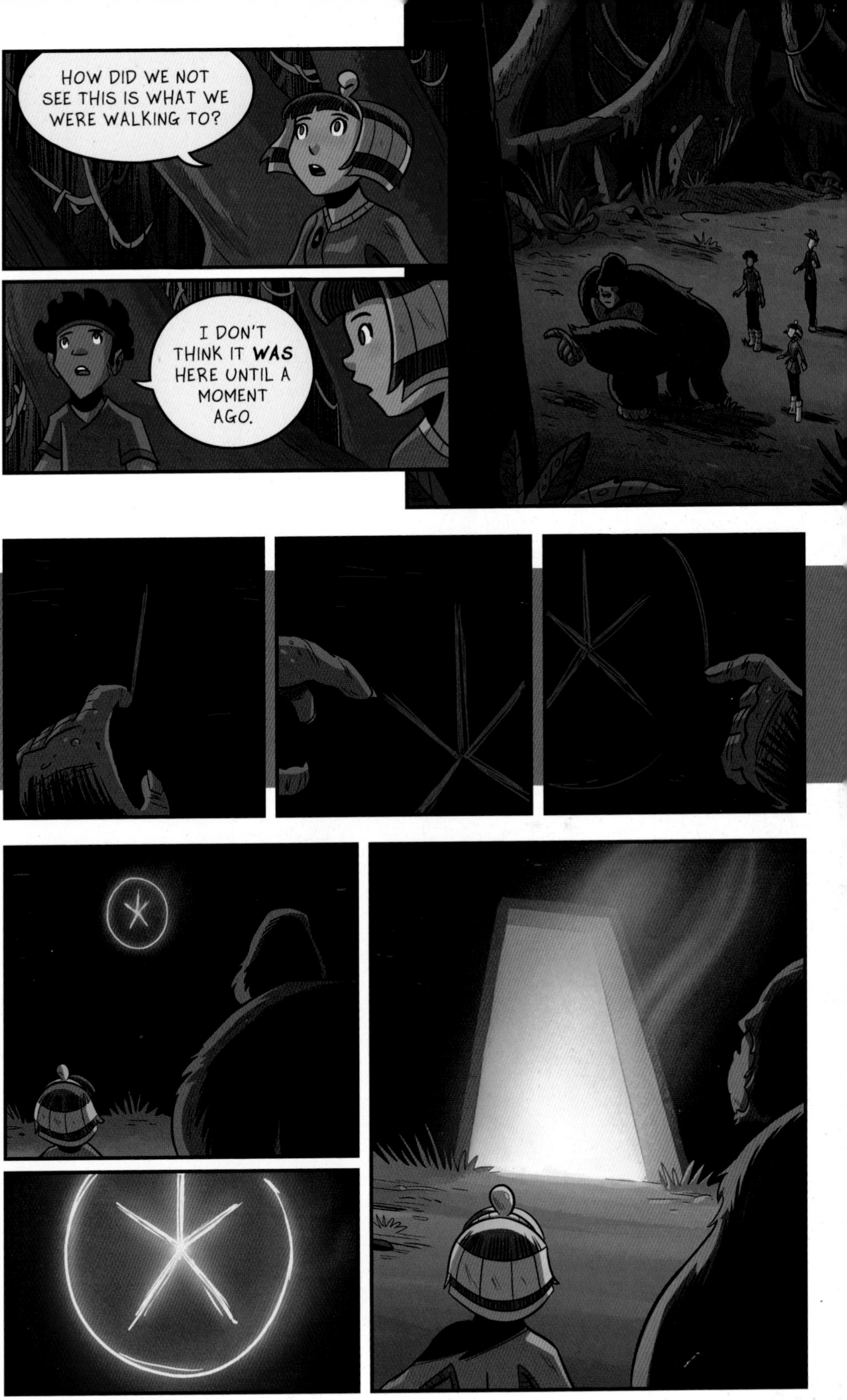
HOW DID WE NOT SEE THIS IS WHAT WE WERE WALKING TO?
I DON'T THINK IT **WAS** HERE UNTIL A MOMENT AGO.

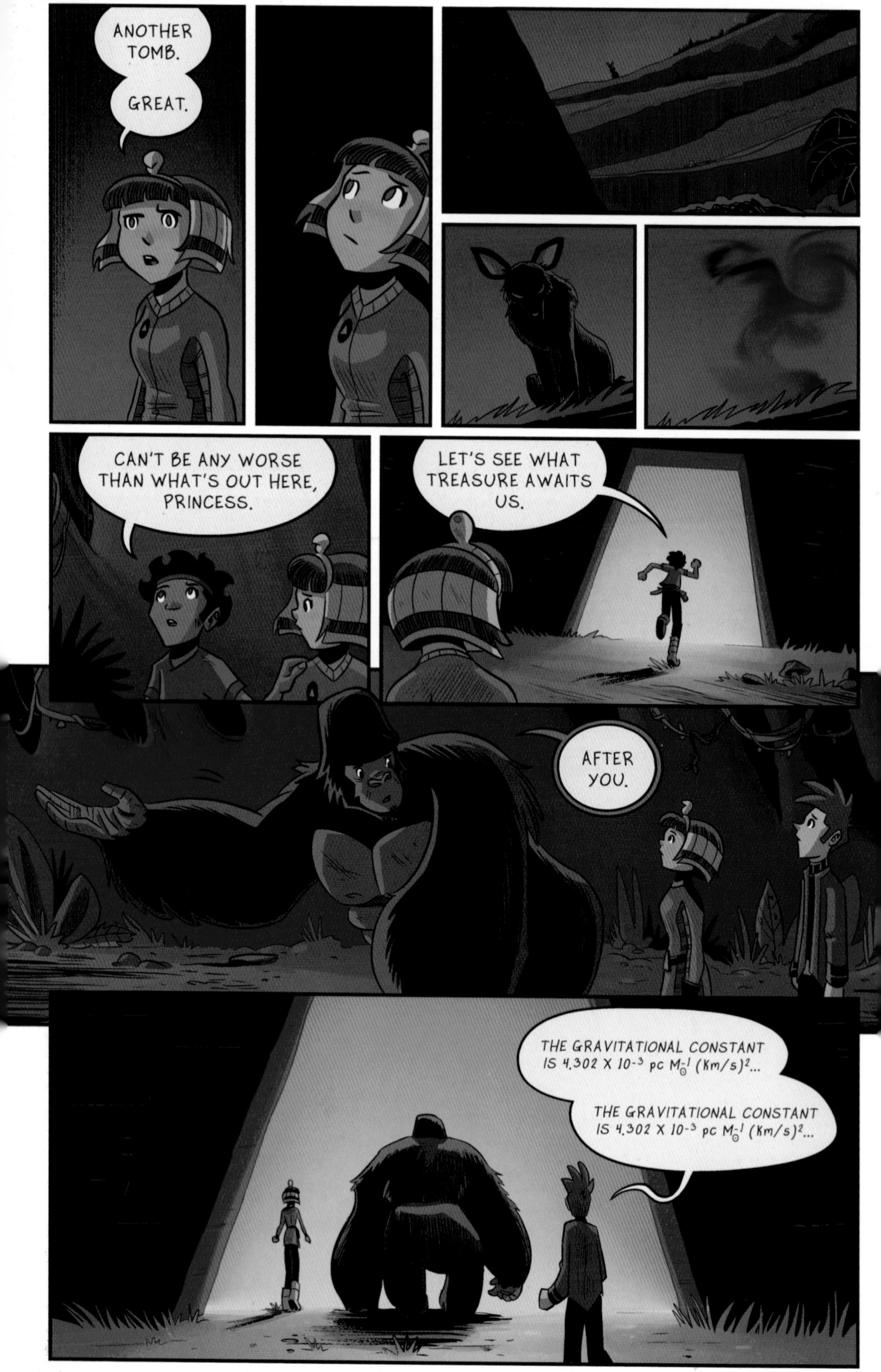
ANOTHER TOMB.
GREAT.
CAN'T BE ANY WORSE THAN WHAT'S OUT HERE, PRINCESS.
LET'S SEE WHAT TREASURE AWAITS US.
AFTER YOU.
THE GRAVITATIONAL CONSTANT IS 4.302×10^{-3} pc $M_{\odot}^{-1}$ $(Km/s)^2$...
THE GRAVITATIONAL CONSTANT IS 4.302×10^{-3} pc $M_{\odot}^{-1}$ $(Km/s)^2$...

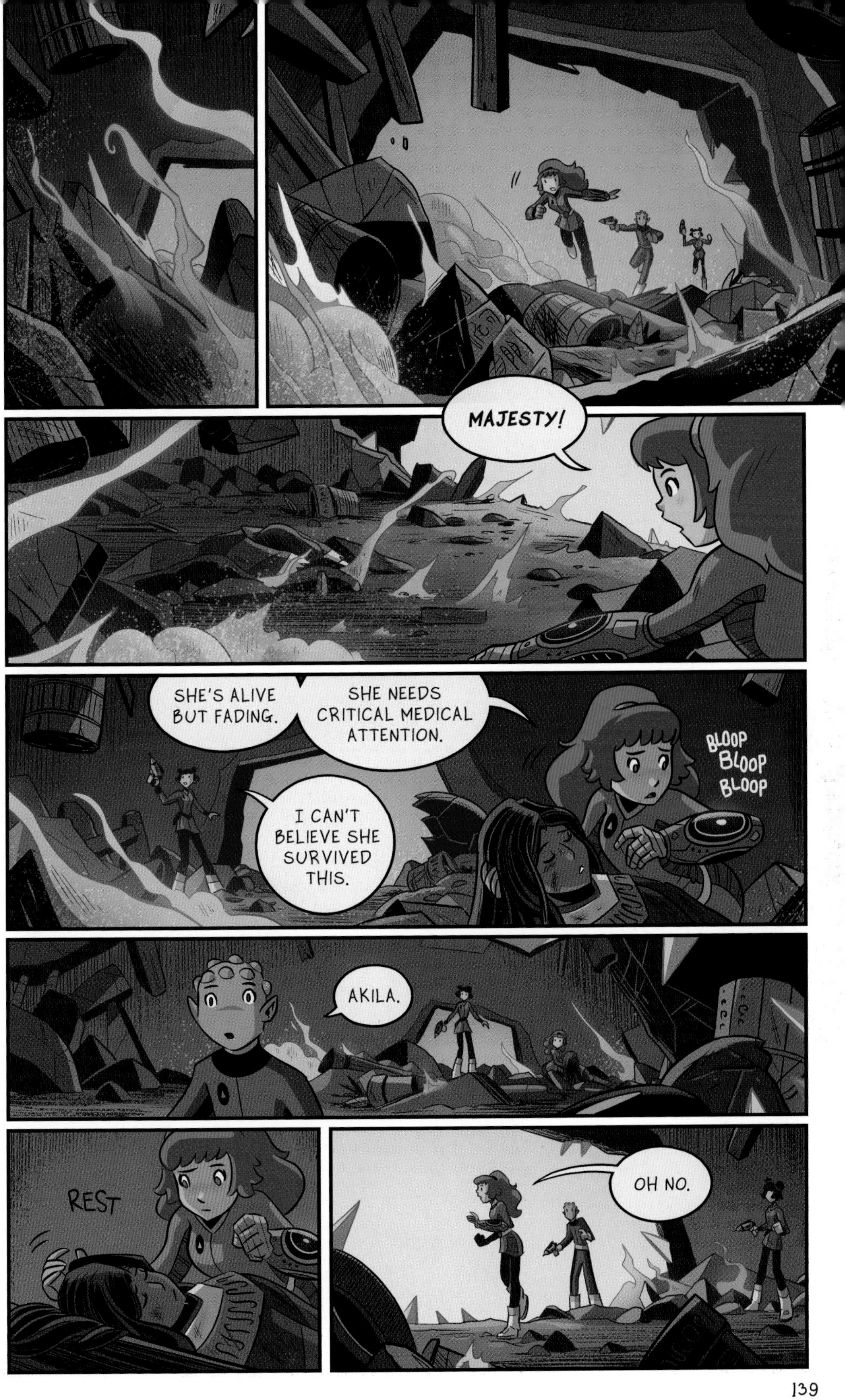
MAJESTY!
SHE'S ALIVE BUT FADING.
SHE NEEDS CRITICAL MEDICAL ATTENTION.
BLOOP BLOOP BLOOP
I CAN'T BELIEVE SHE SURVIVED THIS.
AKILA.
REST
OH NO.

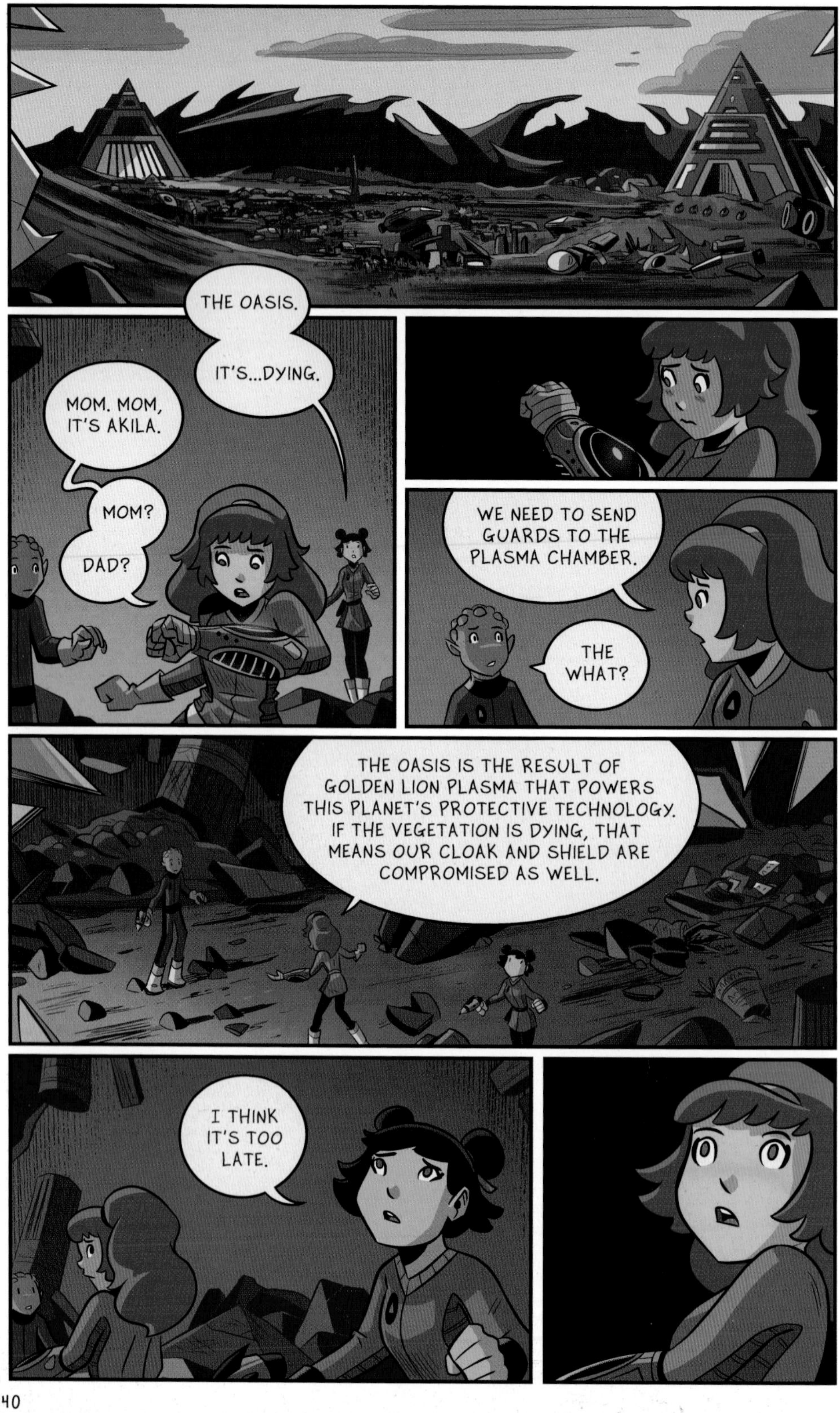
THE OASIS.
IT'S...DYING.
MOM. MOM, IT'S AKILA.
MOM?
DAD?
WE NEED TO SEND GUARDS TO THE PLASMA CHAMBER.
THE WHAT?
THE OASIS IS THE RESULT OF GOLDEN LION PLASMA THAT POWERS THIS PLANET'S PROTECTIVE TECHNOLOGY. IF THE VEGETATION IS DYING, THAT MEANS OUR CLOAK AND SHIELD ARE COMPROMISED AS WELL.
I THINK IT'S TOO LATE.

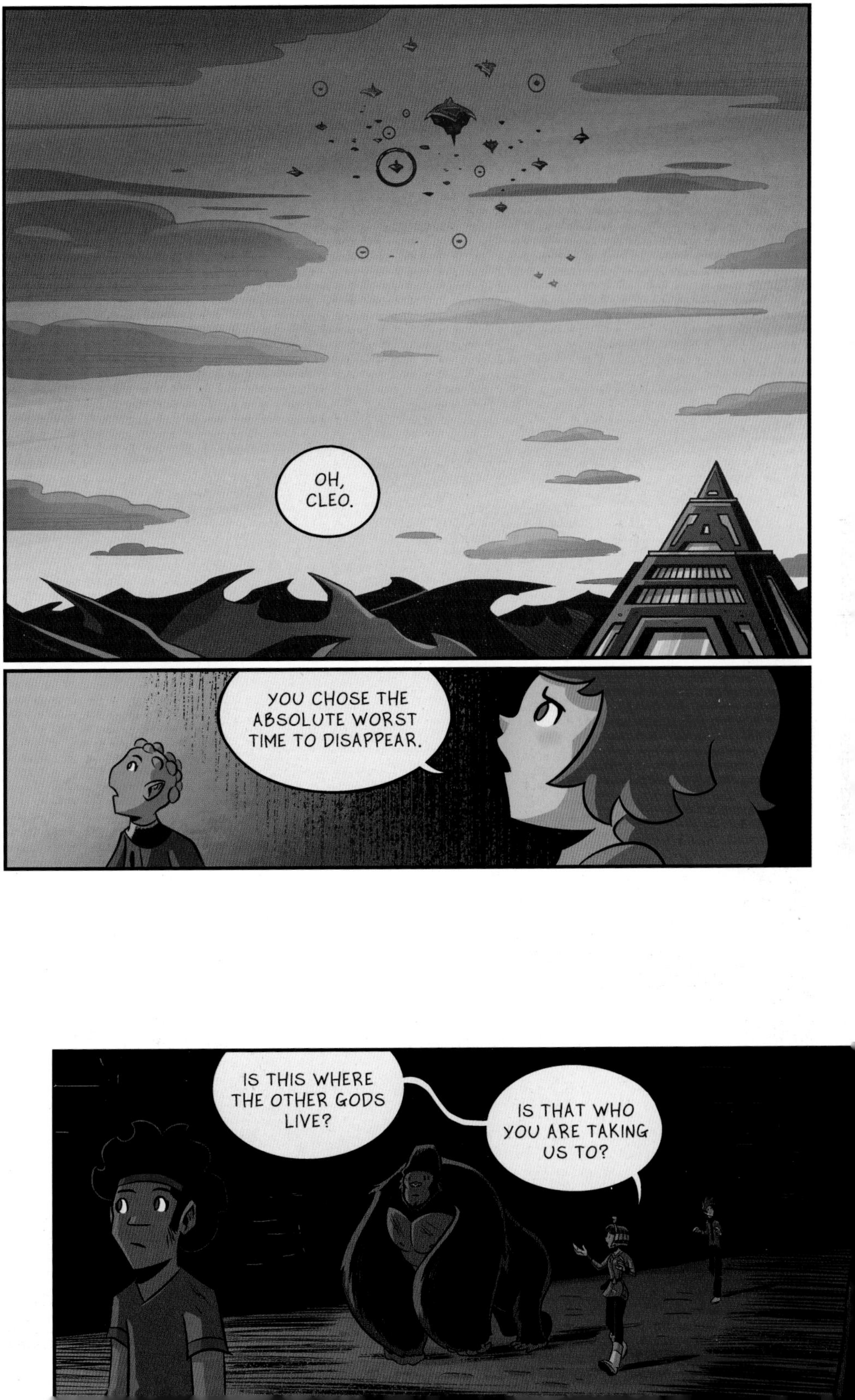
OH, CLEO.
YOU CHOSE THE ABSOLUTE WORST TIME TO DISAPPEAR.
IS THIS WHERE THE OTHER GODS LIVE?
IS THAT WHO YOU ARE TAKING US TO?

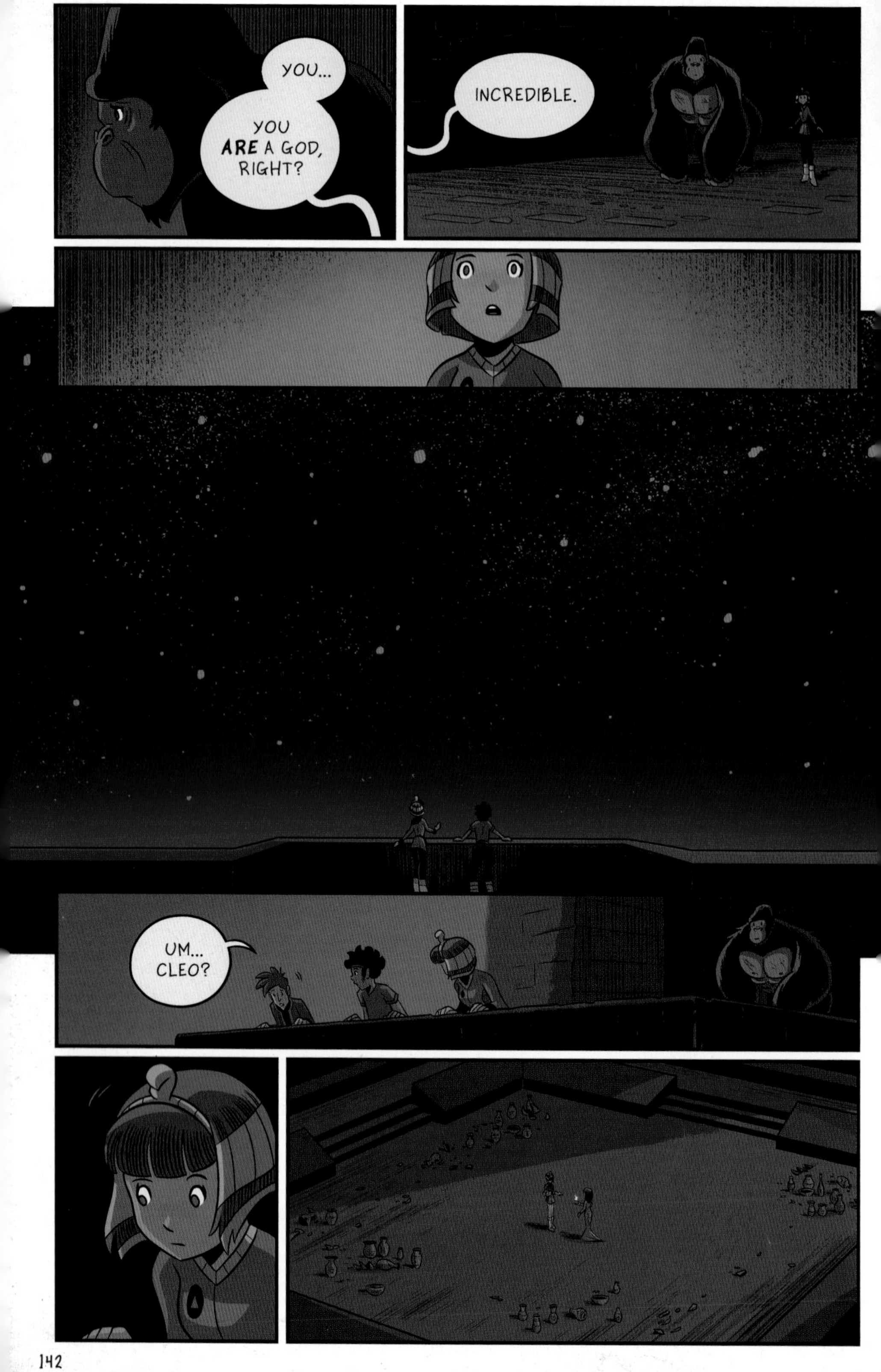
YOU...
YOU ARE A GOD, RIGHT?
INCREDIBLE.
UM... CLEO?

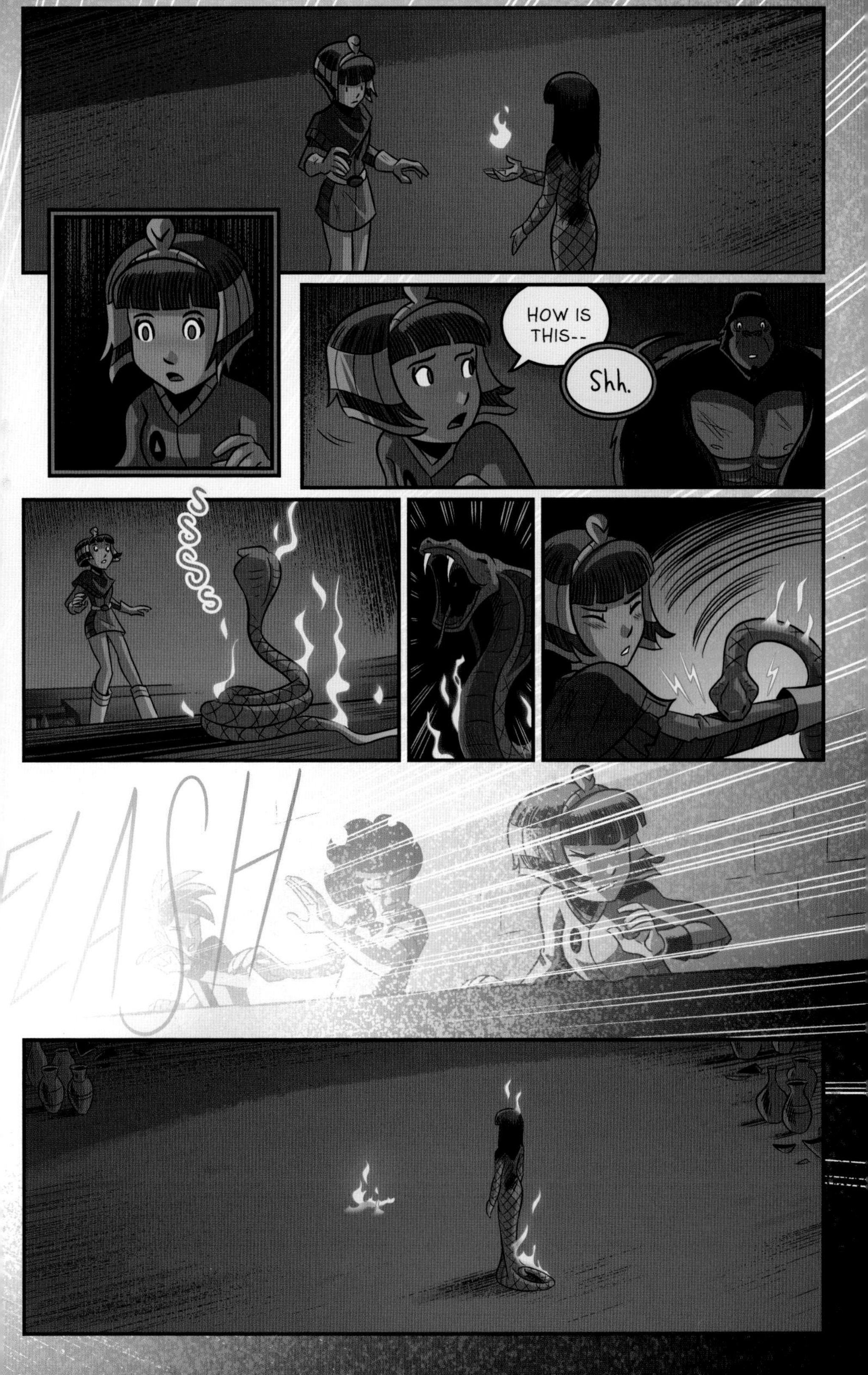
HOW IS THIS--
Shh.
SSSSS
FLASH

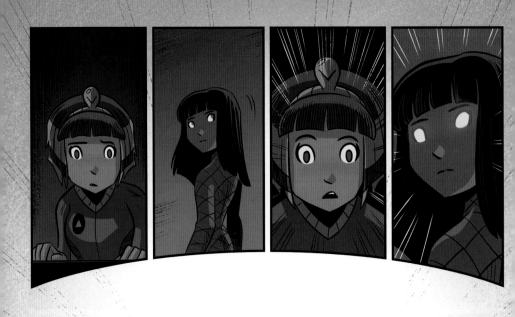

FLASH

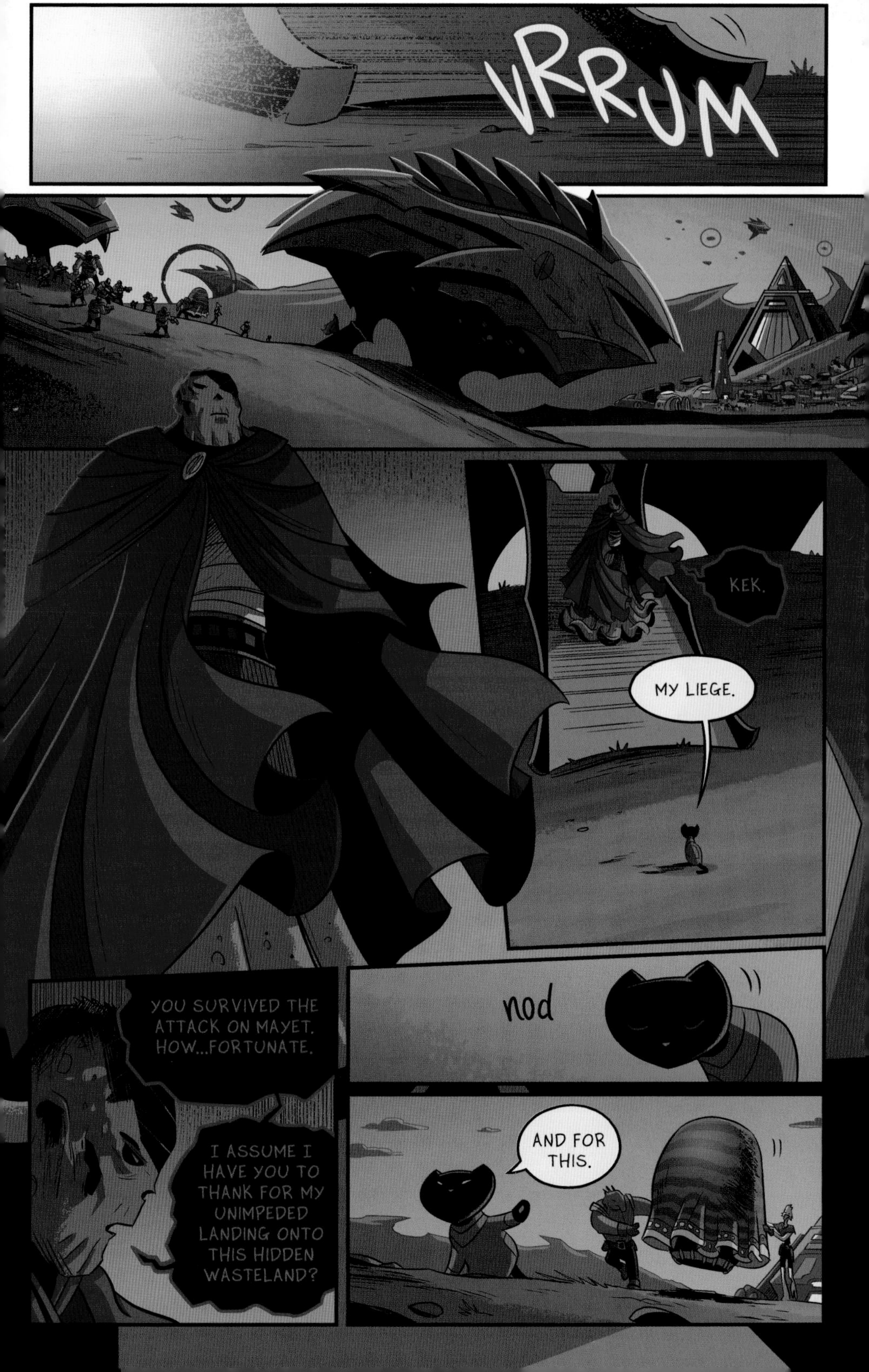
VRRUM
KEK.
MY LIEGE.
YOU SURVIVED THE ATTACK ON MAYET. HOW...FORTUNATE.
nod
I ASSUME I HAVE YOU TO THANK FOR MY UNIMPEDED LANDING ONTO THIS HIDDEN WASTELAND?
AND FOR THIS.

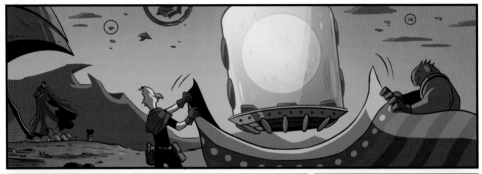

THE PHARAOH HAS ALSO BEEN TAKEN CARE OF. WE'RE ROUNDING UP THE REST OF P.Y.R.A.M.I.D.'S COUNCIL AS WE SPEAK.

I'M IMPRESSED.

HOWEVER, NONE OF *THEM* ARE WHO I WANT.

TH' PRINCESS, CORRECT?

CLEOPATRA?

NOT A FAN, EITHER.

FOD FRANZE. WE 'AVEN'T MET, BUT AH'M THRILLED TA BE IN BUSINESS WITH YA.

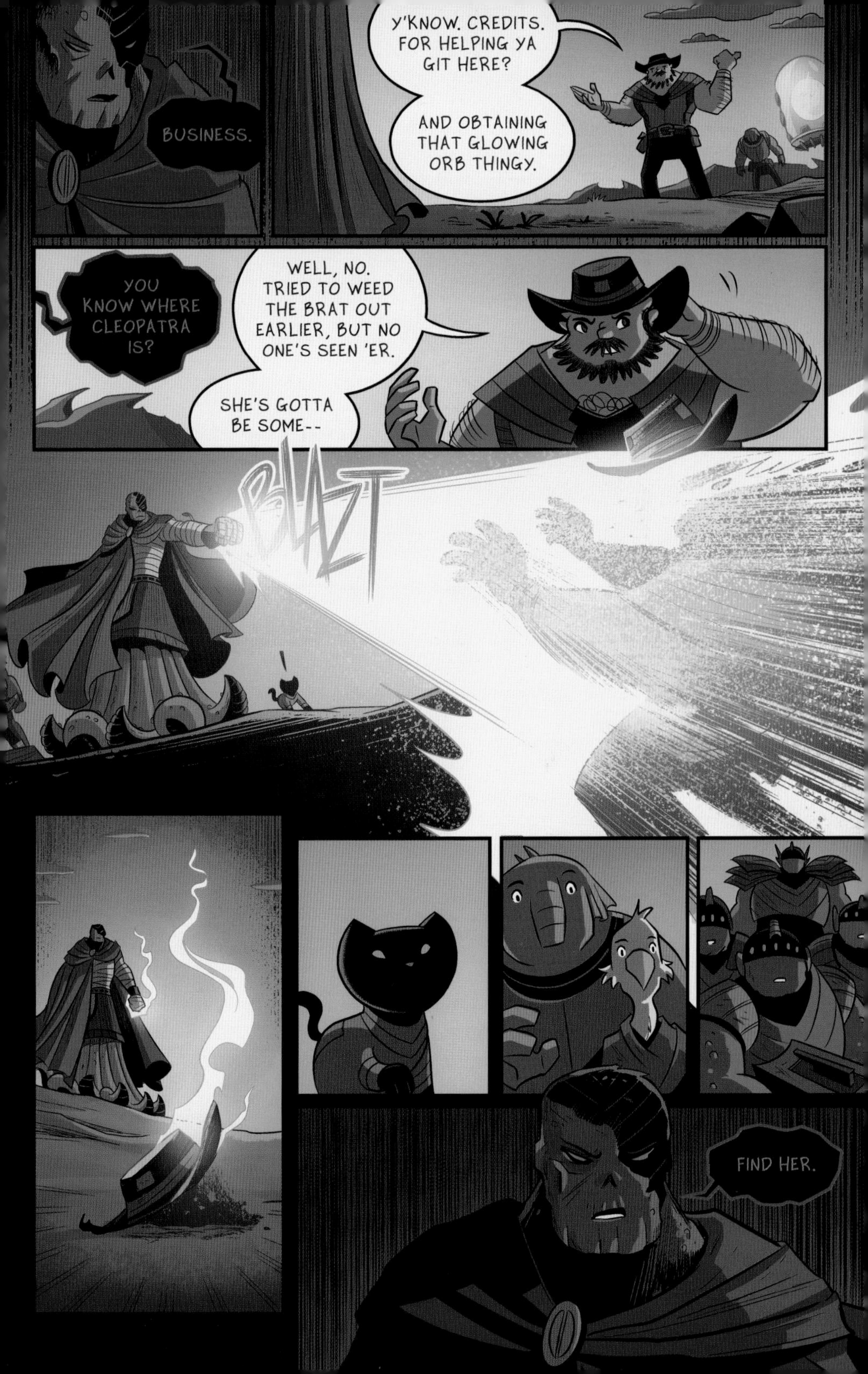
BUSINESS.
Y'KNOW. CREDITS. FOR HELPING YA GIT HERE?
AND OBTAINING THAT GLOWING ORB THINGY.
YOU KNOW WHERE CLEOPATRA IS?
WELL, NO. TRIED TO WEED THE BRAT OUT EARLIER, BUT NO ONE'S SEEN 'ER.
SHE'S GOTTA BE SOME--
BLAZT
!
FIND HER.

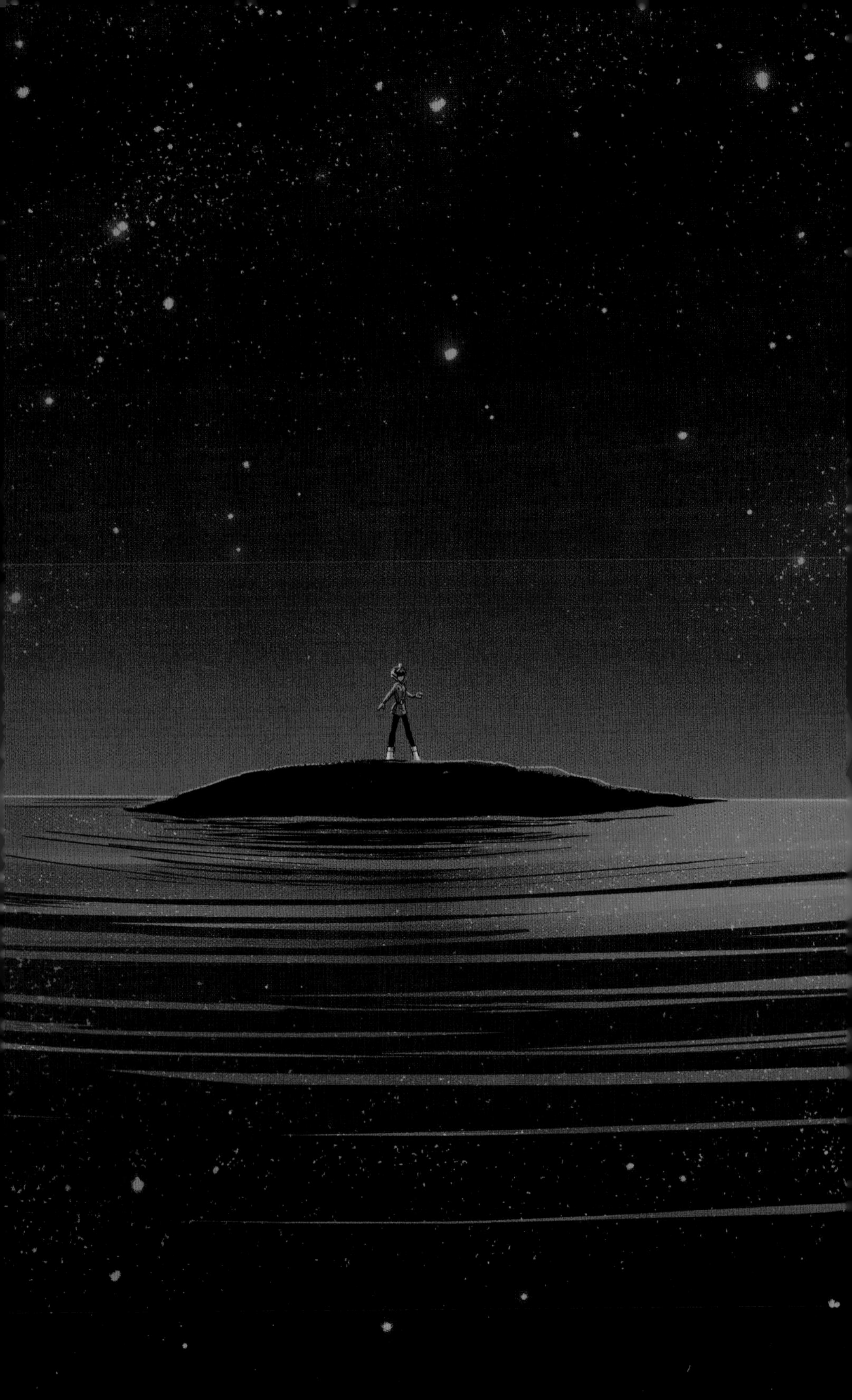

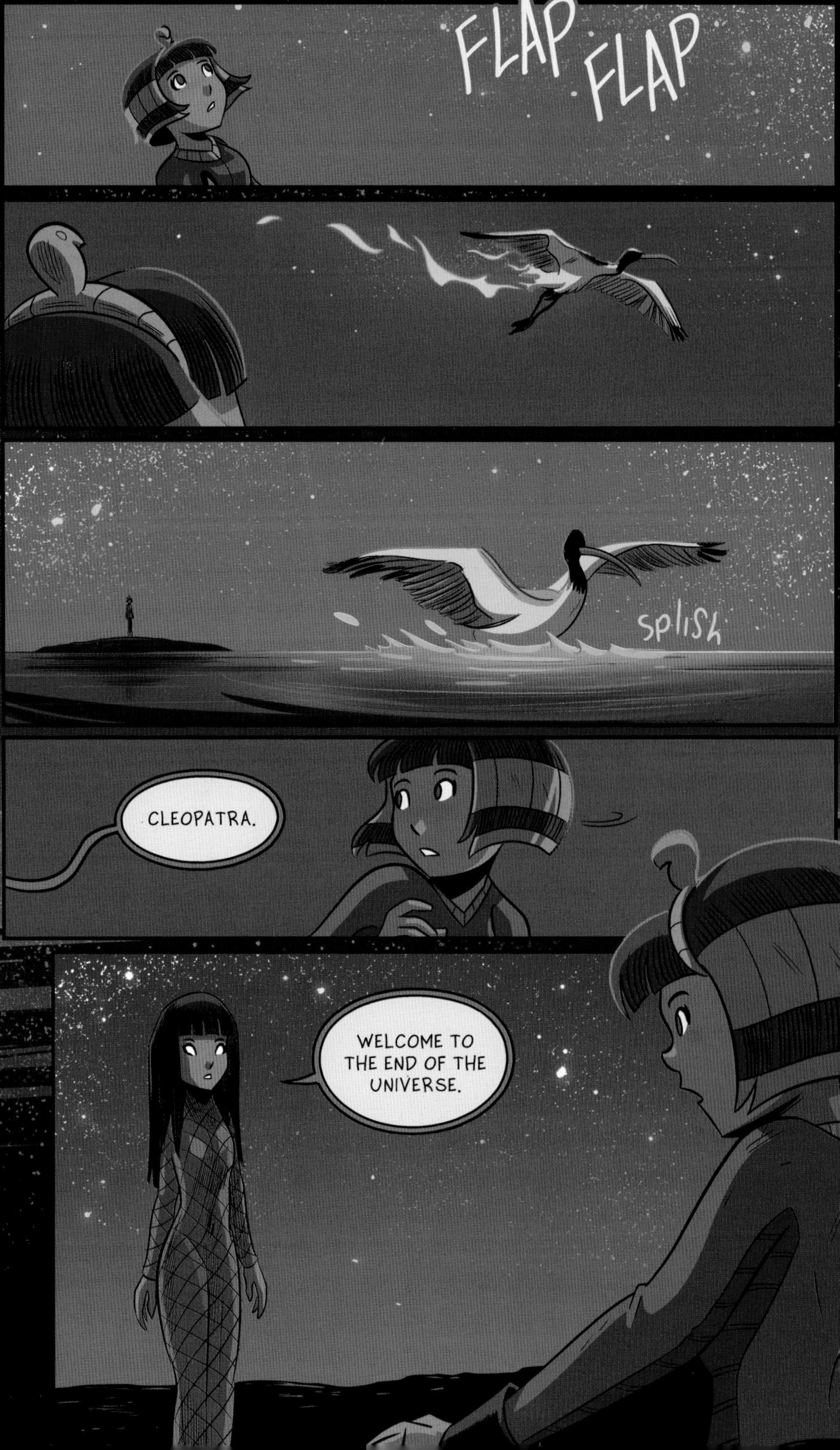
FLAP FLAP
splish
CLEOPATRA.
WELCOME TO THE END OF THE UNIVERSE.

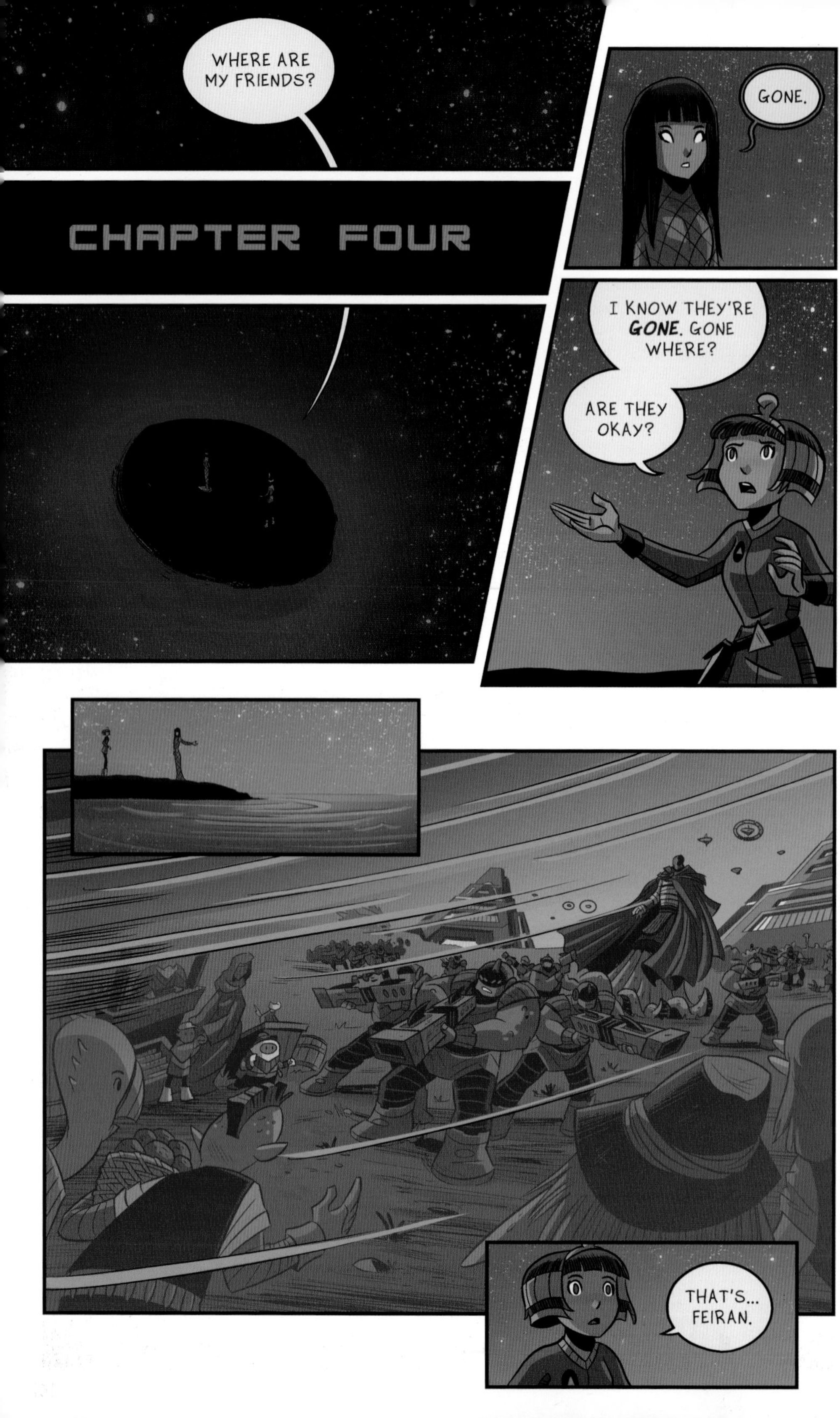
WHERE ARE MY FRIENDS?
CHAPTER FOUR
GONE.
I KNOW THEY'RE **GONE**. GONE WHERE?
ARE THEY OKAY?
THAT'S... FEIRAN.

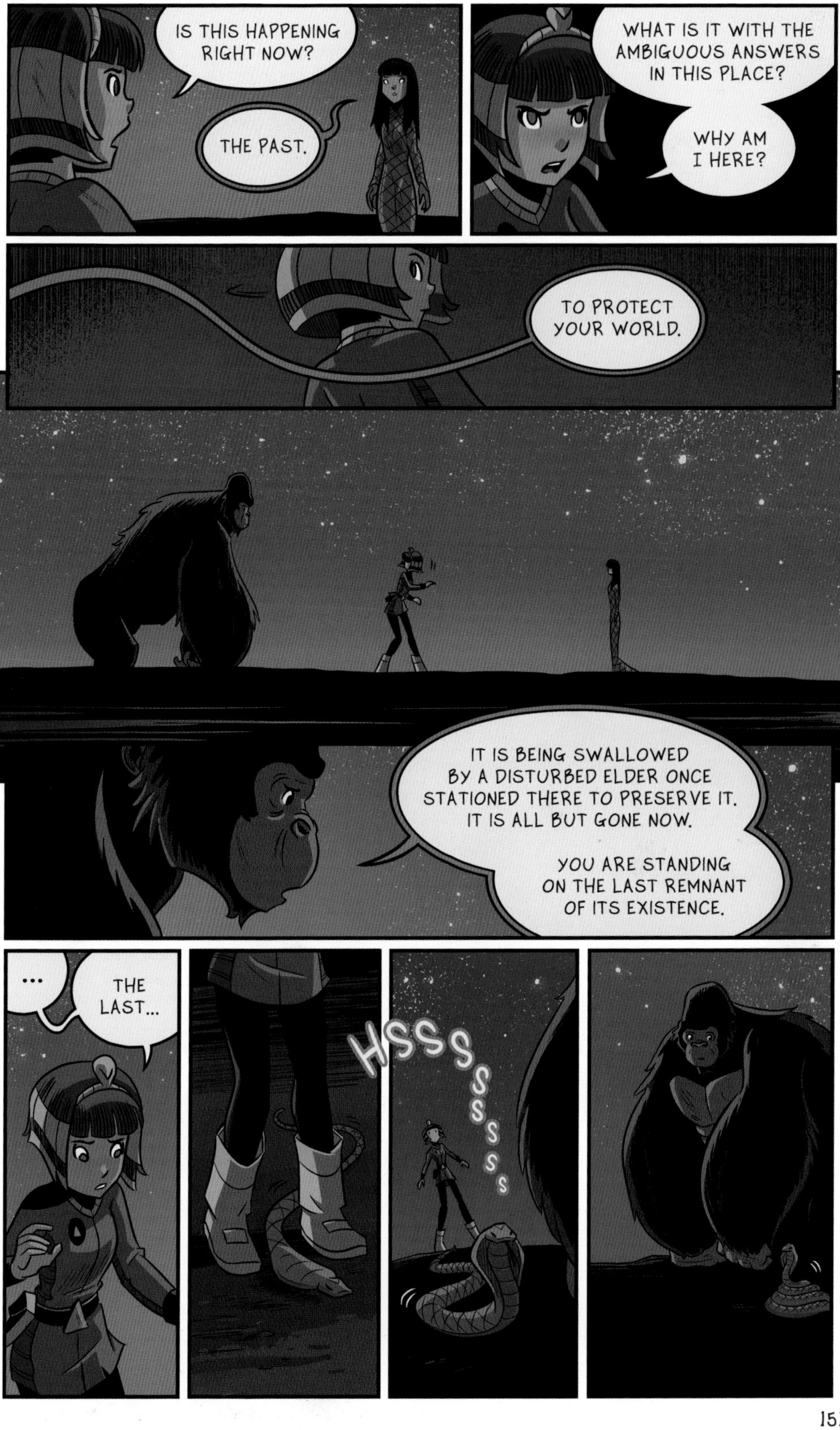
IS THIS HAPPENING RIGHT NOW?
THE PAST.
WHAT IS IT WITH THE AMBIGUOUS ANSWERS IN THIS PLACE?
WHY AM I HERE?
TO PROTECT YOUR WORLD.
IT IS BEING SWALLOWED BY A DISTURBED ELDER ONCE STATIONED THERE TO PRESERVE IT. IT IS ALL BUT GONE NOW.
YOU ARE STANDING ON THE LAST REMNANT OF ITS EXISTENCE.
...
THE LAST...
HSSSSSSSS

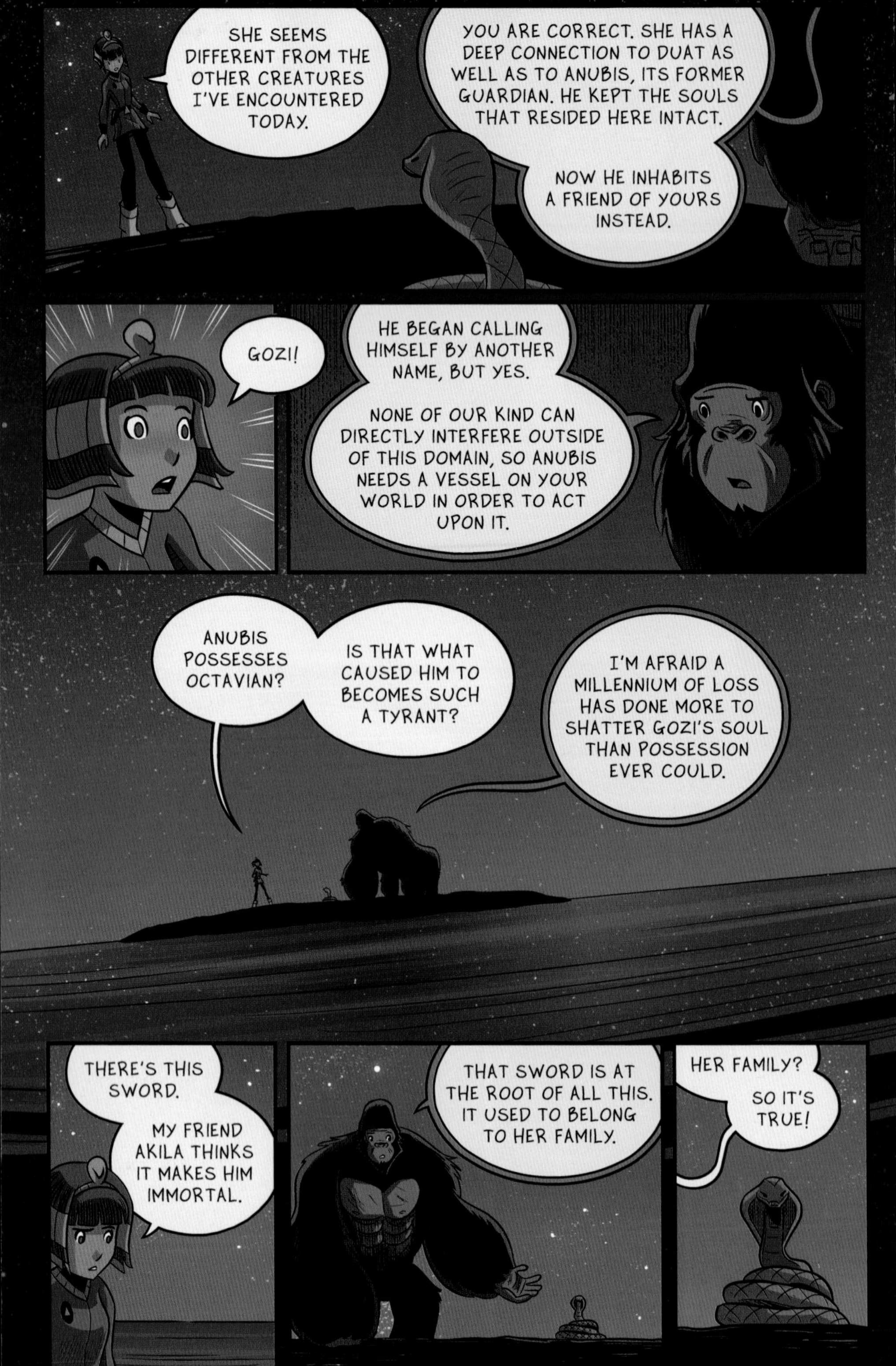
SHE SEEMS DIFFERENT FROM THE OTHER CREATURES I'VE ENCOUNTERED TODAY.
YOU ARE CORRECT. SHE HAS A DEEP CONNECTION TO DUAT AS WELL AS TO ANUBIS, ITS FORMER GUARDIAN. HE KEPT THE SOULS THAT RESIDED HERE INTACT.
NOW HE INHABITS A FRIEND OF YOURS INSTEAD.
GOZI!
HE BEGAN CALLING HIMSELF BY ANOTHER NAME, BUT YES.
NONE OF OUR KIND CAN DIRECTLY INTERFERE OUTSIDE OF THIS DOMAIN, SO ANUBIS NEEDS A VESSEL ON YOUR WORLD IN ORDER TO ACT UPON IT.
ANUBIS POSSESSES OCTAVIAN?
IS THAT WHAT CAUSED HIM TO BECOMES SUCH A TYRANT?
I'M AFRAID A MILLENNIUM OF LOSS HAS DONE MORE TO SHATTER GOZI'S SOUL THAN POSSESSION EVER COULD.
THERE'S THIS SWORD.
MY FRIEND AKILA THINKS IT MAKES HIM IMMORTAL.
THAT SWORD IS AT THE ROOT OF ALL THIS. IT USED TO BELONG TO HER FAMILY.
HER FAMILY?
SO IT'S TRUE!

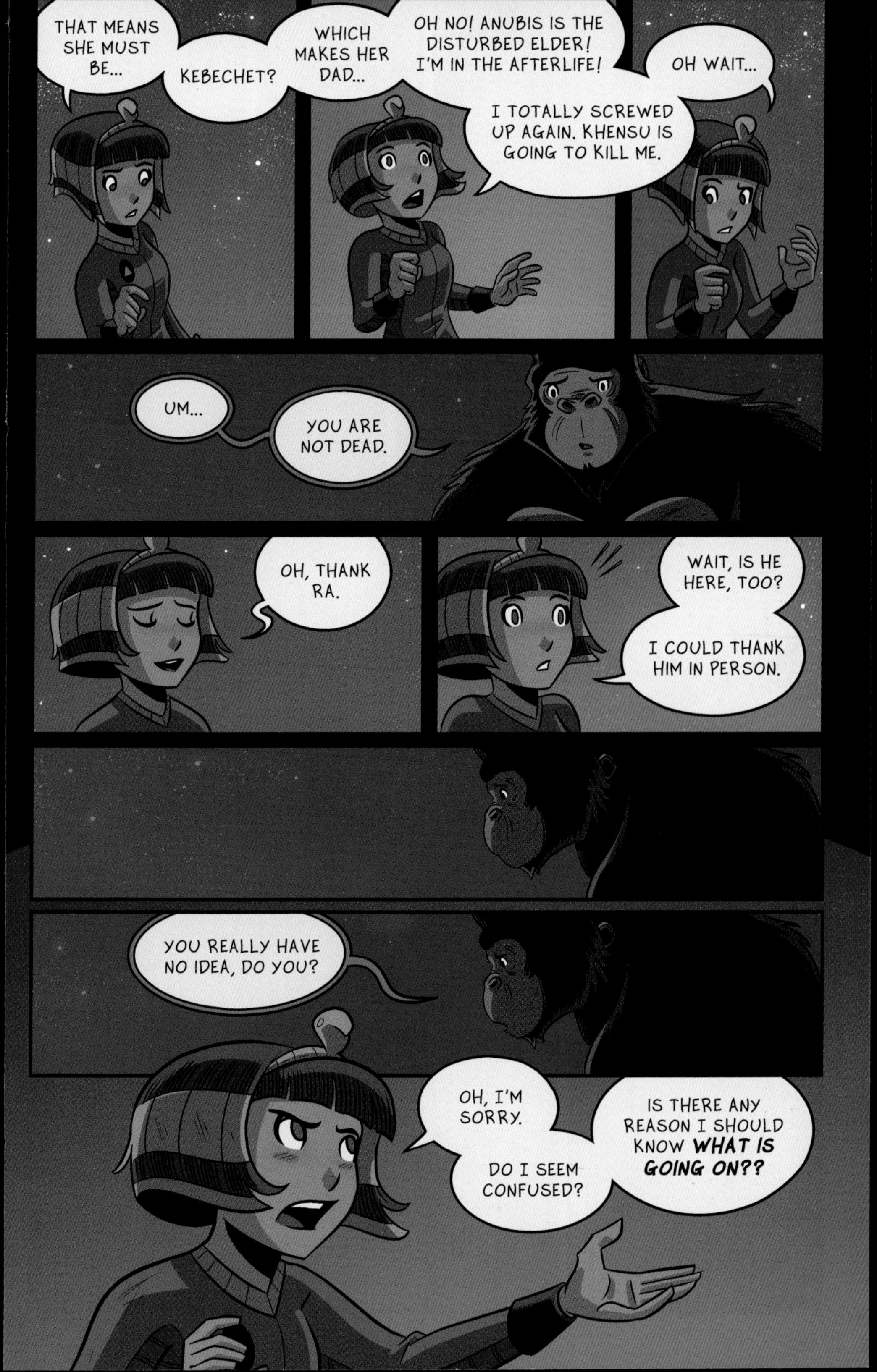
THAT MEANS SHE MUST BE...
KEBECHET?
WHICH MAKES HER DAD...
OH NO! ANUBIS IS THE DISTURBED ELDER! I'M IN THE AFTERLIFE!
I TOTALLY SCREWED UP AGAIN. KHENSU IS GOING TO KILL ME.
OH WAIT...
UM...
YOU ARE NOT DEAD.
OH, THANK RA.
WAIT, IS HE HERE, TOO?
I COULD THANK HIM IN PERSON.
YOU REALLY HAVE NO IDEA, DO YOU?
OH, I'M SORRY.
DO I SEEM CONFUSED?
IS THERE ANY REASON I SHOULD KNOW **WHAT IS GOING ON??**

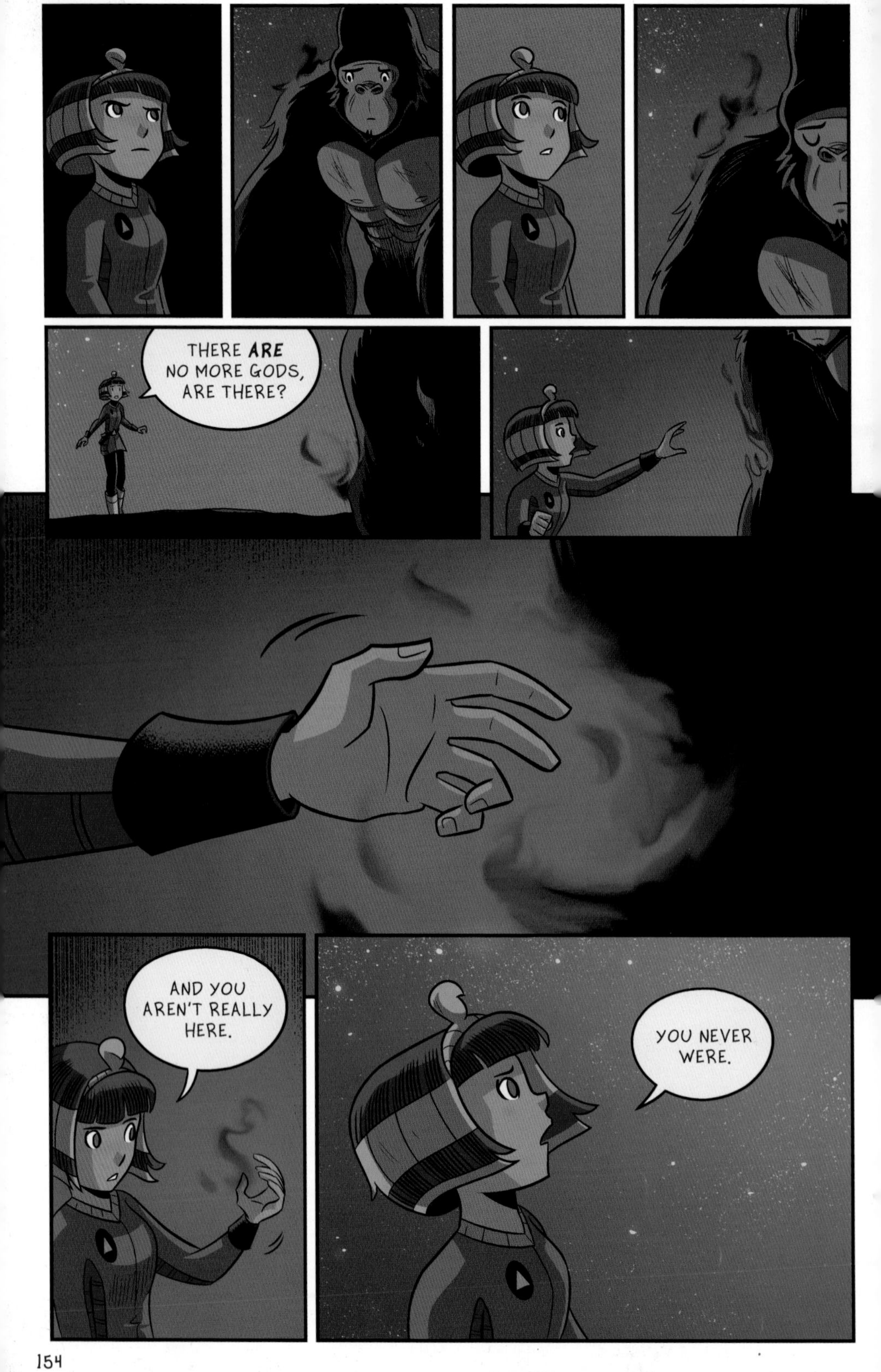
THERE ARE NO MORE GODS, ARE THERE?
AND YOU AREN'T REALLY HERE.
YOU NEVER WERE.

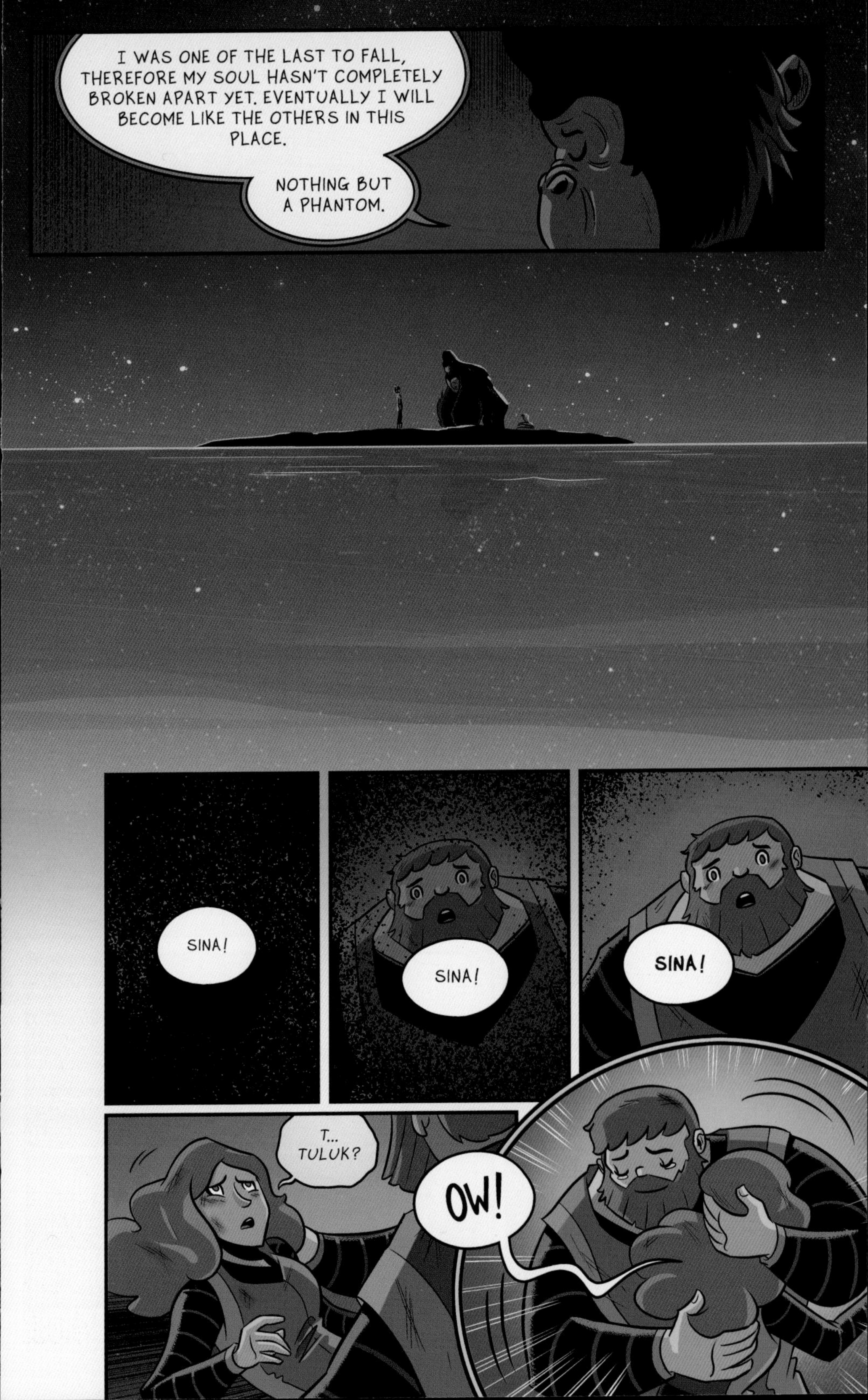
I WAS ONE OF THE LAST TO FALL, THEREFORE MY SOUL HASN'T COMPLETELY BROKEN APART YET. EVENTUALLY I WILL BECOME LIKE THE OTHERS IN THIS PLACE.
NOTHING BUT A PHANTOM.
SINA!
SINA!
SINA!
T... TULUK?
OW!

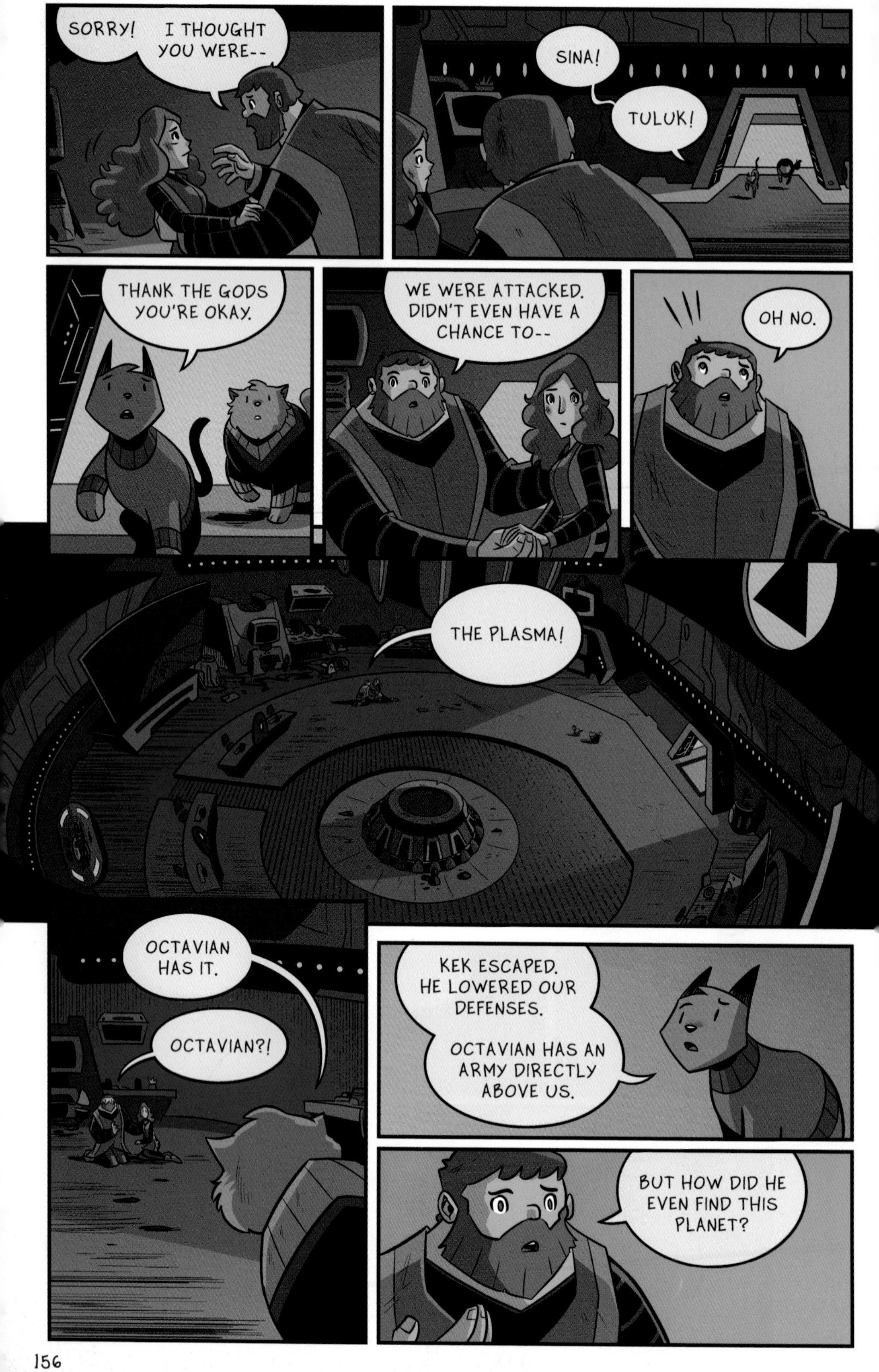
SORRY! I THOUGHT YOU WERE--
SINA!
TULUK!
THANK THE GODS YOU'RE OKAY.
WE WERE ATTACKED. DIDN'T EVEN HAVE A CHANCE TO--
OH NO.
THE PLASMA!
OCTAVIAN HAS IT.
OCTAVIAN?!
KEK ESCAPED. HE LOWERED OUR DEFENSES.
OCTAVIAN HAS AN ARMY DIRECTLY ABOVE US.
BUT HOW DID HE EVEN FIND THIS PLANET?

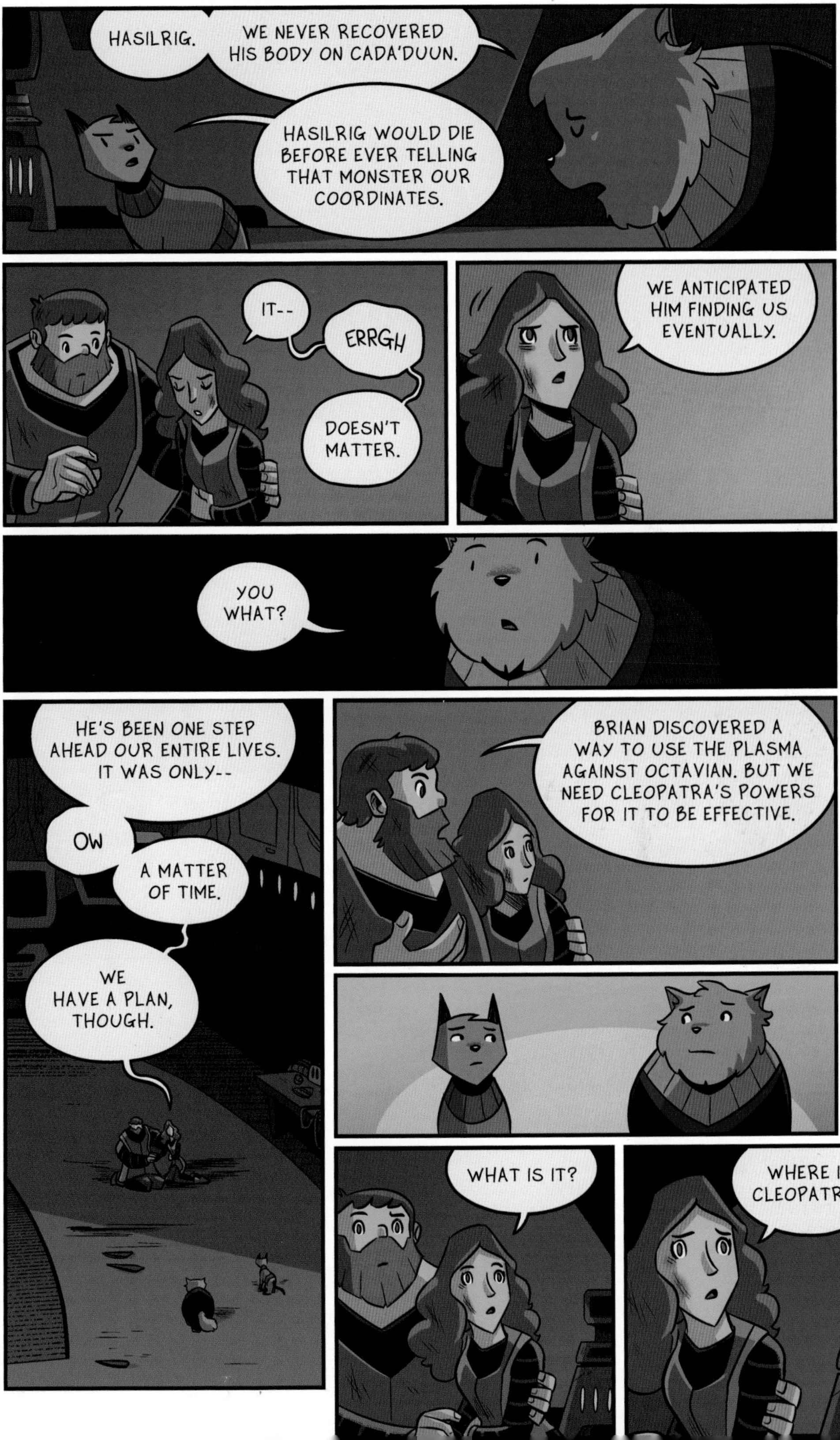
HASILRIG.
WE NEVER RECOVERED HIS BODY ON CADA'DUUN.
HASILRIG WOULD DIE BEFORE EVER TELLING THAT MONSTER OUR COORDINATES.
IT--
ERRGH
DOESN'T MATTER.
WE ANTICIPATED HIM FINDING US EVENTUALLY.
YOU WHAT?
HE'S BEEN ONE STEP AHEAD OUR ENTIRE LIVES. IT WAS ONLY--
OW
A MATTER OF TIME.
WE HAVE A PLAN, THOUGH.
BRIAN DISCOVERED A WAY TO USE THE PLASMA AGAINST OCTAVIAN. BUT WE NEED CLEOPATRA'S POWERS FOR IT TO BE EFFECTIVE.
WHAT IS IT?
WHERE IS CLEOPATRA?

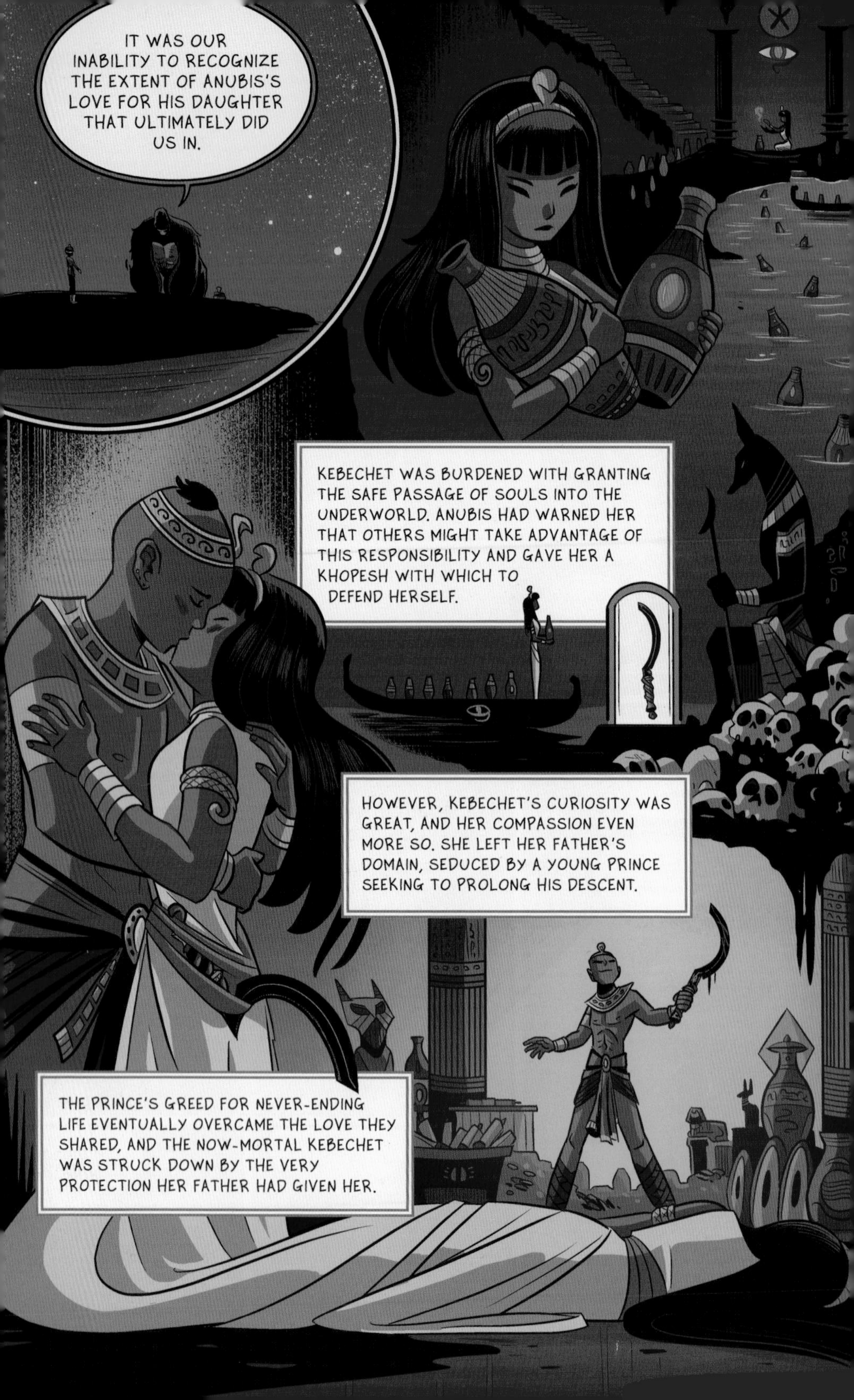
IT WAS OUR INABILITY TO RECOGNIZE THE EXTENT OF ANUBIS'S LOVE FOR HIS DAUGHTER THAT ULTIMATELY DID US IN.
KEBECHET WAS BURDENED WITH GRANTING THE SAFE PASSAGE OF SOULS INTO THE UNDERWORLD. ANUBIS HAD WARNED HER THAT OTHERS MIGHT TAKE ADVANTAGE OF THIS RESPONSIBILITY AND GAVE HER A KHOPESH WITH WHICH TO DEFEND HERSELF.
HOWEVER, KEBECHET'S CURIOSITY WAS GREAT, AND HER COMPASSION EVEN MORE SO. SHE LEFT HER FATHER'S DOMAIN, SEDUCED BY A YOUNG PRINCE SEEKING TO PROLONG HIS DESCENT.
THE PRINCE'S GREED FOR NEVER-ENDING LIFE EVENTUALLY OVERCAME THE LOVE THEY SHARED, AND THE NOW-MORTAL KEBECHET WAS STRUCK DOWN BY THE VERY PROTECTION HER FATHER HAD GIVEN HER.

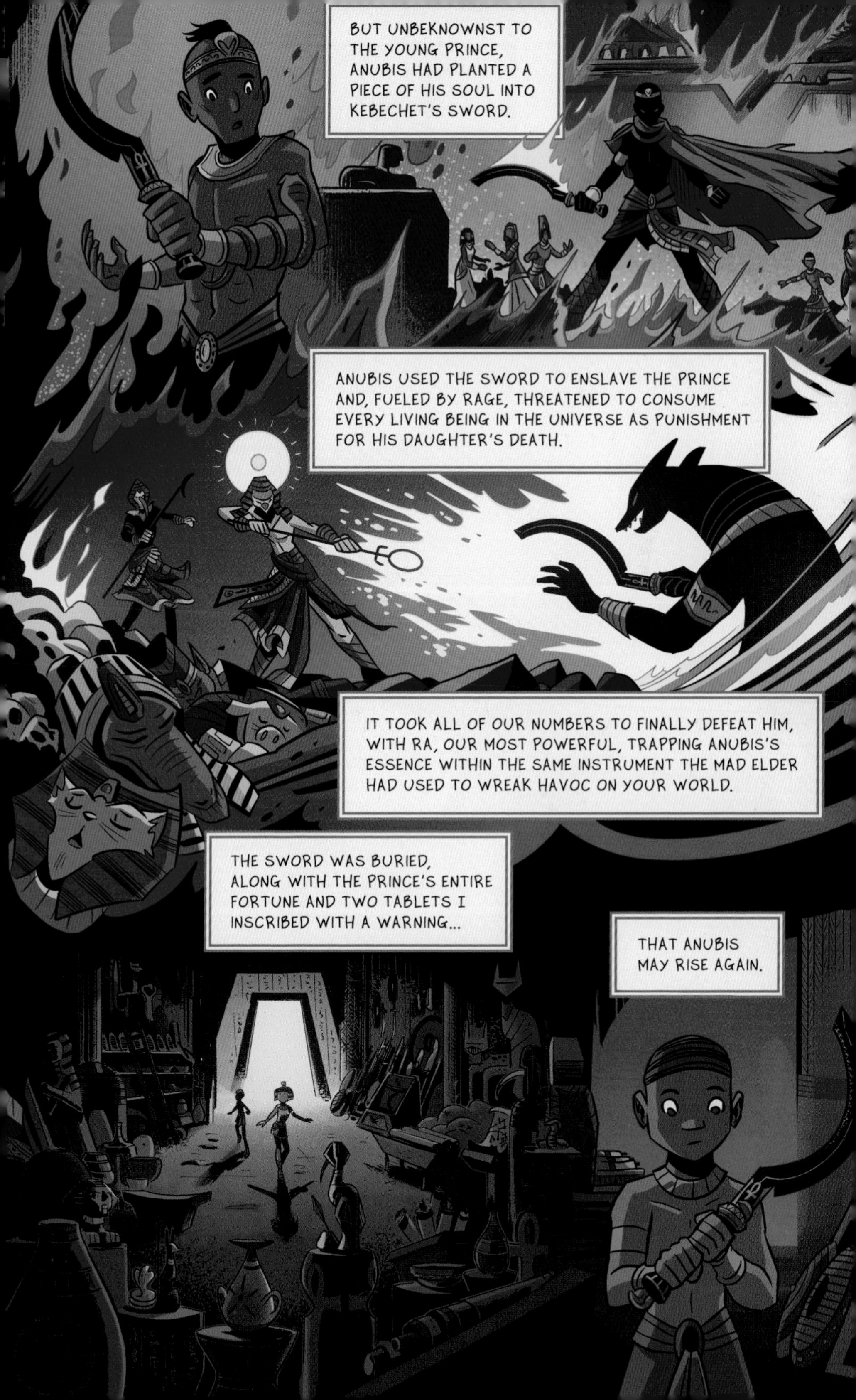
BUT UNBEKNOWNST TO THE YOUNG PRINCE, ANUBIS HAD PLANTED A PIECE OF HIS SOUL INTO KEBECHET'S SWORD.
ANUBIS USED THE SWORD TO ENSLAVE THE PRINCE AND, FUELED BY RAGE, THREATENED TO CONSUME EVERY LIVING BEING IN THE UNIVERSE AS PUNISHMENT FOR HIS DAUGHTER'S DEATH.
IT TOOK ALL OF OUR NUMBERS TO FINALLY DEFEAT HIM, WITH RA, OUR MOST POWERFUL, TRAPPING ANUBIS'S ESSENCE WITHIN THE SAME INSTRUMENT THE MAD ELDER HAD USED TO WREAK HAVOC ON YOUR WORLD.
THE SWORD WAS BURIED, ALONG WITH THE PRINCE'S ENTIRE FORTUNE AND TWO TABLETS I INSCRIBED WITH A WARNING...
THAT ANUBIS MAY RISE AGAIN.

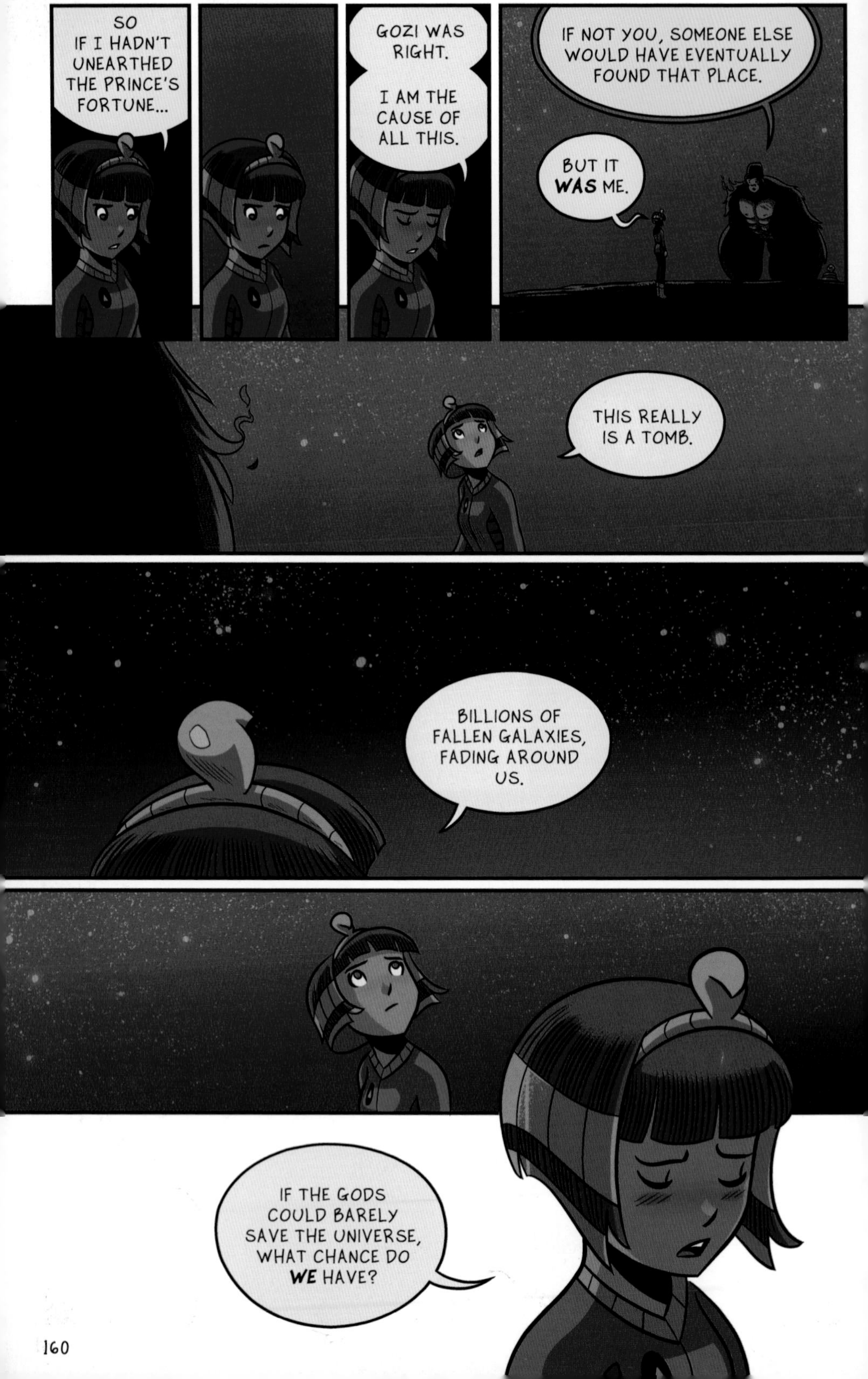
SO IF I HADN'T UNEARTHED THE PRINCE'S FORTUNE...
GOZI WAS RIGHT.
I AM THE CAUSE OF ALL THIS.
IF NOT YOU, SOMEONE ELSE WOULD HAVE EVENTUALLY FOUND THAT PLACE.
BUT IT **WAS** ME.
THIS REALLY IS A TOMB.
BILLIONS OF FALLEN GALAXIES, FADING AROUND US.
IF THE GODS COULD BARELY SAVE THE UNIVERSE, WHAT CHANCE DO **WE** HAVE?

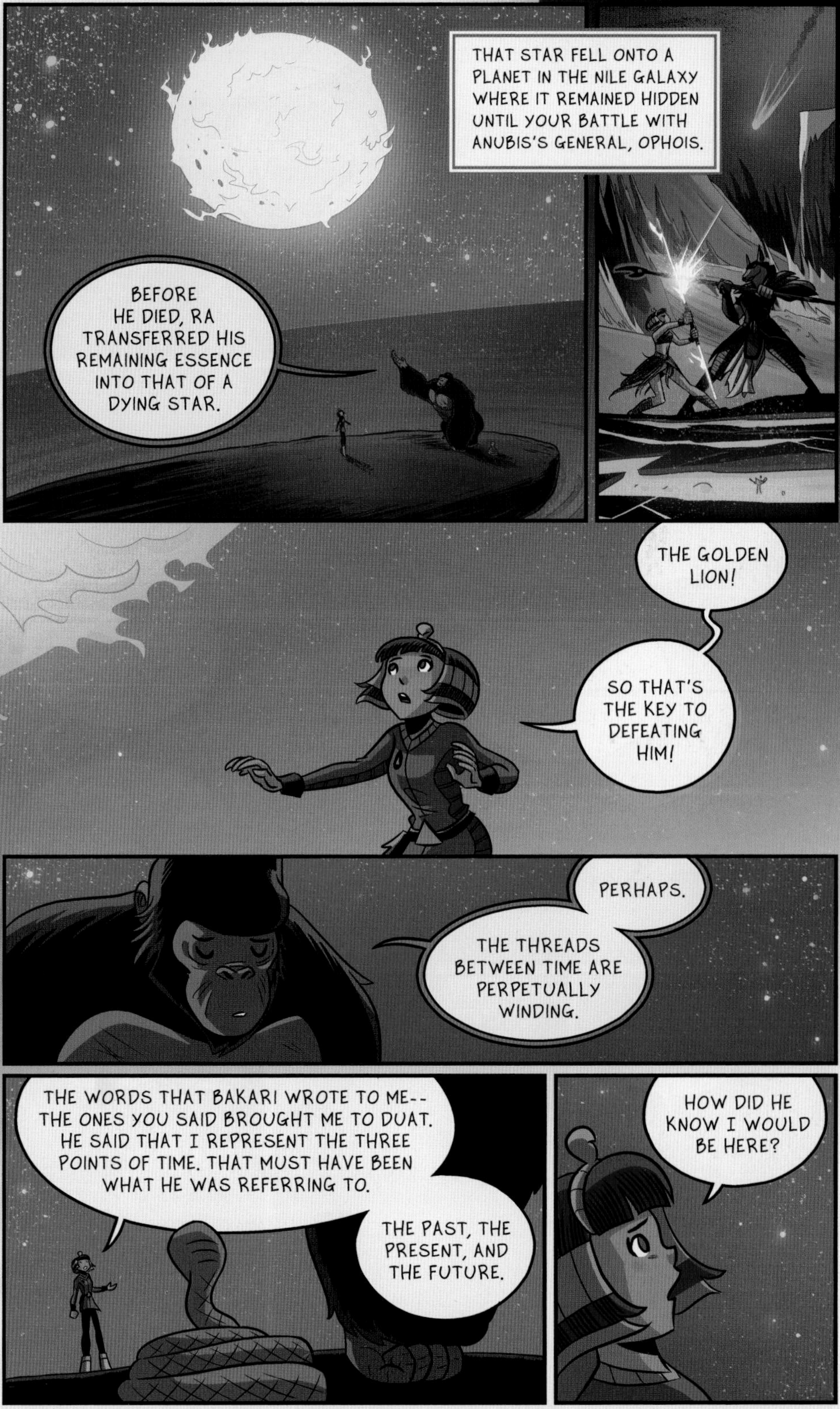
BEFORE HE DIED, RA TRANSFERRED HIS REMAINING ESSENCE INTO THAT OF A DYING STAR.
THAT STAR FELL ONTO A PLANET IN THE NILE GALAXY WHERE IT REMAINED HIDDEN UNTIL YOUR BATTLE WITH ANUBIS'S GENERAL, OPHOIS.
THE GOLDEN LION!
SO THAT'S THE KEY TO DEFEATING HIM!
PERHAPS.
THE THREADS BETWEEN TIME ARE PERPETUALLY WINDING.
THE WORDS THAT BAKARI WROTE TO ME-- THE ONES YOU SAID BROUGHT ME TO DUAT. HE SAID THAT I REPRESENT THE THREE POINTS OF TIME. THAT MUST HAVE BEEN WHAT HE WAS REFERRING TO.
THE PAST, THE PRESENT, AND THE FUTURE.
HOW DID HE KNOW I WOULD BE HERE?

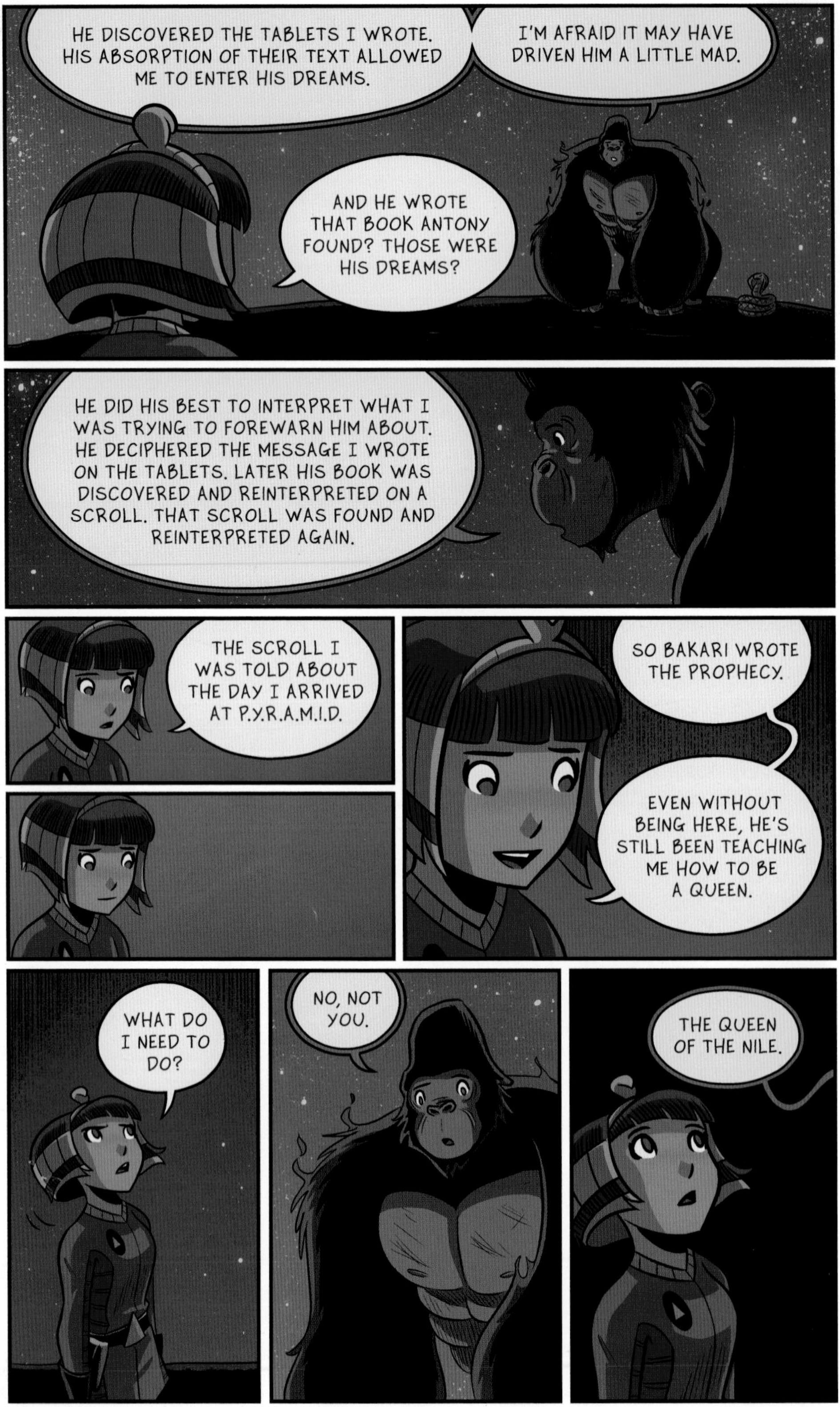
HE DISCOVERED THE TABLETS I WROTE. HIS ABSORPTION OF THEIR TEXT ALLOWED ME TO ENTER HIS DREAMS.
I'M AFRAID IT MAY HAVE DRIVEN HIM A LITTLE MAD.
AND HE WROTE THAT BOOK ANTONY FOUND? THOSE WERE HIS DREAMS?
HE DID HIS BEST TO INTERPRET WHAT I WAS TRYING TO FOREWARN HIM ABOUT. HE DECIPHERED THE MESSAGE I WROTE ON THE TABLETS. LATER HIS BOOK WAS DISCOVERED AND REINTERPRETED ON A SCROLL. THAT SCROLL WAS FOUND AND REINTERPRETED AGAIN.
THE SCROLL I WAS TOLD ABOUT THE DAY I ARRIVED AT P.Y.R.A.M.I.D.
SO BAKARI WROTE THE PROPHECY.
EVEN WITHOUT BEING HERE, HE'S STILL BEEN TEACHING ME HOW TO BE A QUEEN.
WHAT DO I NEED TO DO?
NO, NOT YOU.
THE QUEEN OF THE NILE.

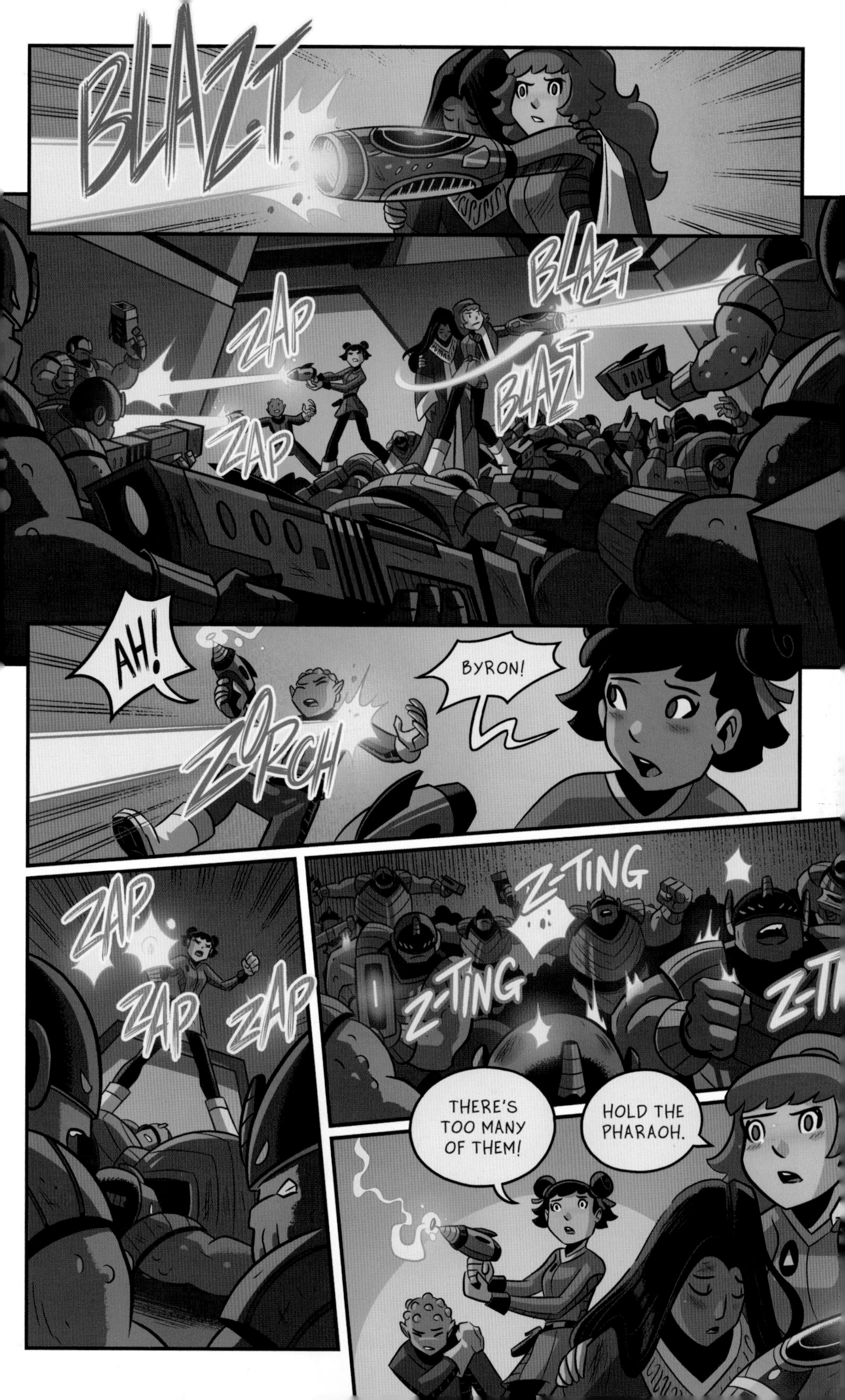
BLAZT
ZAP
BLAZT
BLAZT
ZAP
AH!
ZORCH
BYRON!
ZAP
ZAP
ZAP
Z-TING
Z-TING
THERE'S TOO MANY OF THEM!
HOLD THE PHARAOH.

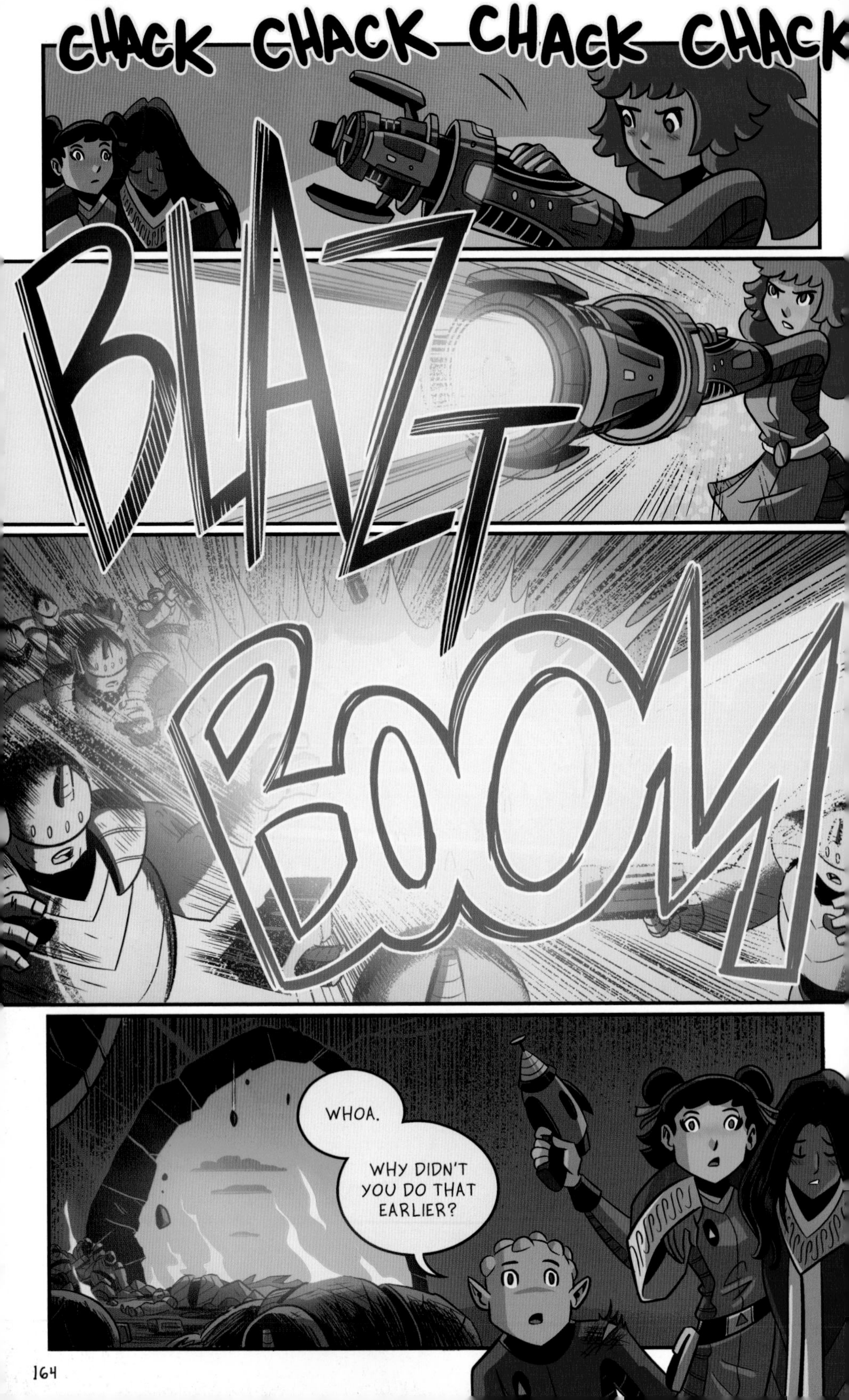
CHACK CHACK CHACK CHACK
BLAZT
BOOM
WHOA.
WHY DIDN'T YOU DO THAT EARLIER?

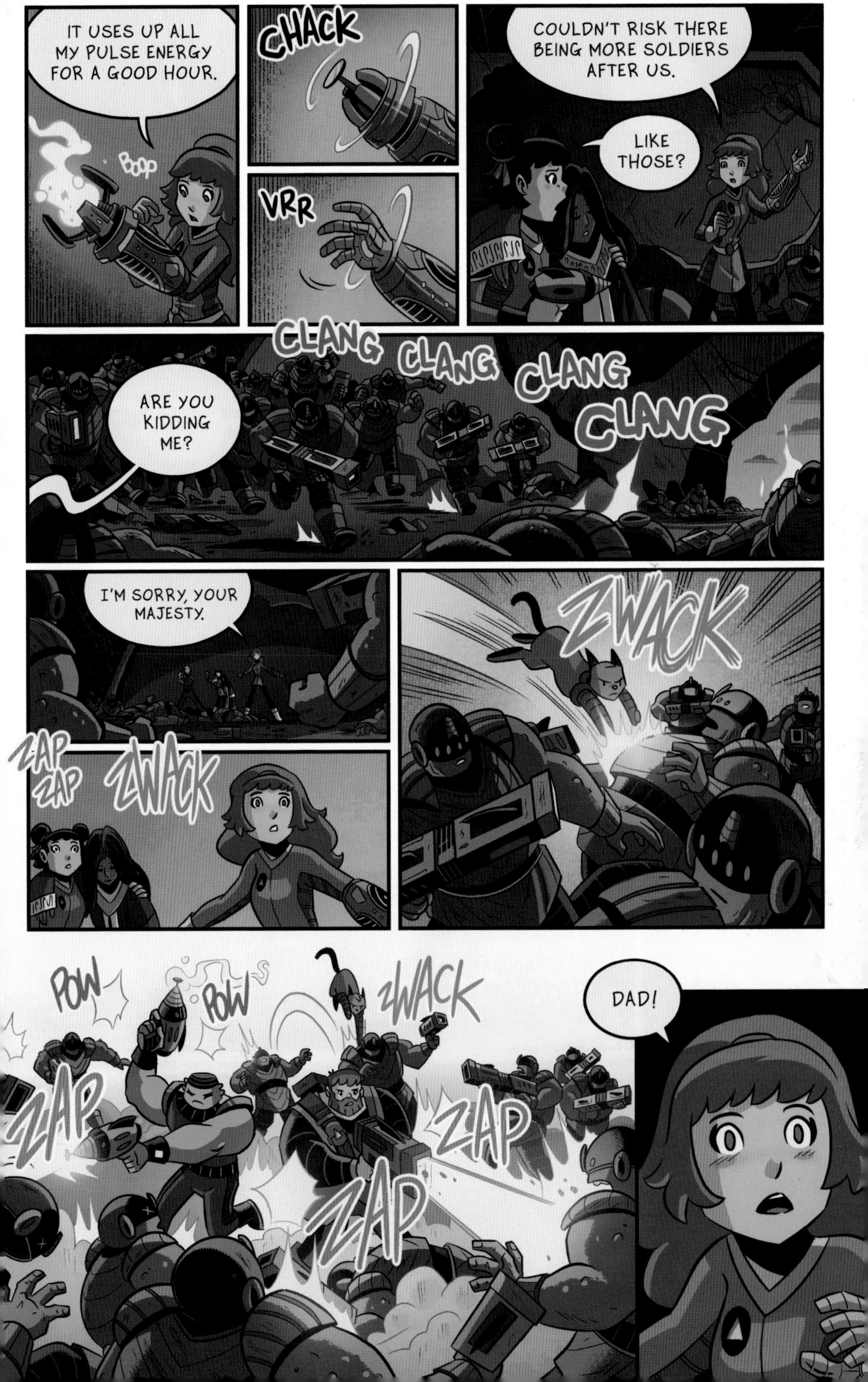
IT USES UP ALL MY PULSE ENERGY FOR A GOOD HOUR.
BOOP
CHACK
VRR
COULDN'T RISK THERE BEING MORE SOLDIERS AFTER US.
LIKE THOSE?
CLANG CLANG CLANG CLANG
ARE YOU KIDDING ME?
I'M SORRY, YOUR MAJESTY.
ZWACK
ZAP ZAP ZWACK
POW POW ZWACK
DAD!
ZAP ZAP ZAP

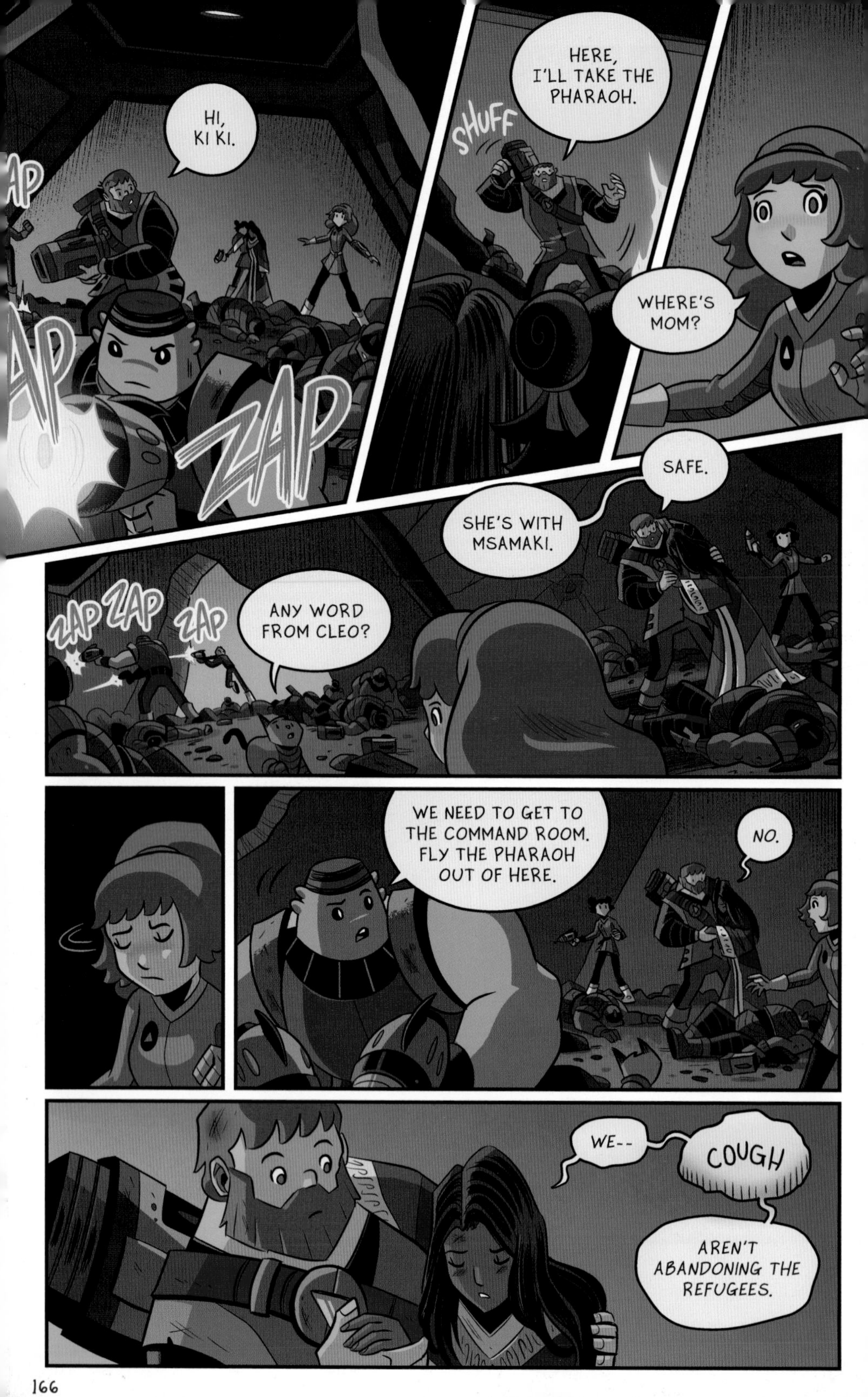
ZAP
HI, KI KI.
ZAP
ZAP
SHUFF
HERE, I'LL TAKE THE PHARAOH.
WHERE'S MOM?
SAFE.
SHE'S WITH MSAMAKI.
ZAP ZAP ZAP
ANY WORD FROM CLEO?
WE NEED TO GET TO THE COMMAND ROOM. FLY THE PHARAOH OUT OF HERE.
NO.
WE--
COUGH
AREN'T ABANDONING THE REFUGEES.

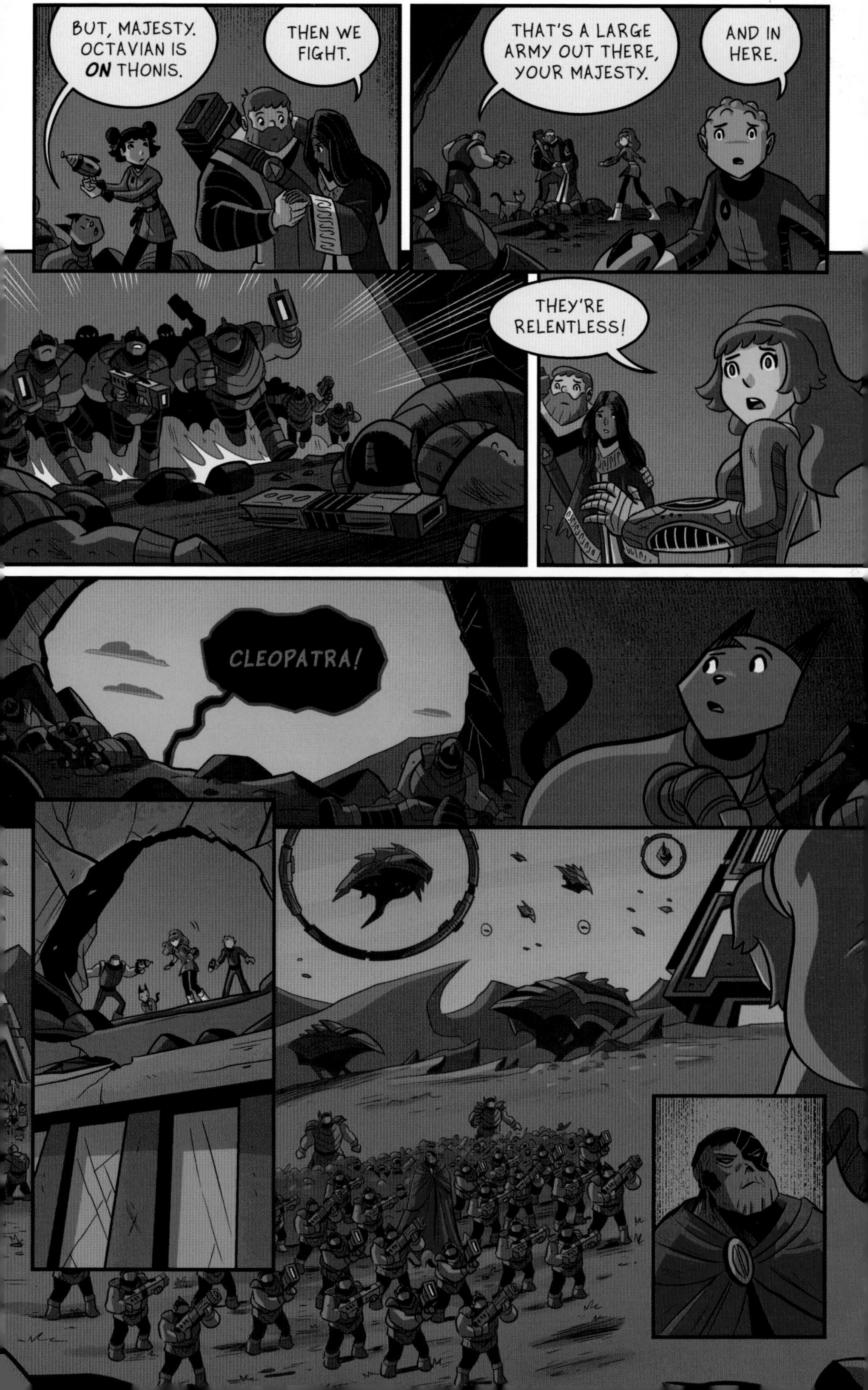
BUT, MAJESTY. OCTAVIAN IS **ON** THONIS.
THEN WE FIGHT.
THAT'S A LARGE ARMY OUT THERE, YOUR MAJESTY.
AND IN HERE.
THEY'RE RELENTLESS!
CLEOPATRA!

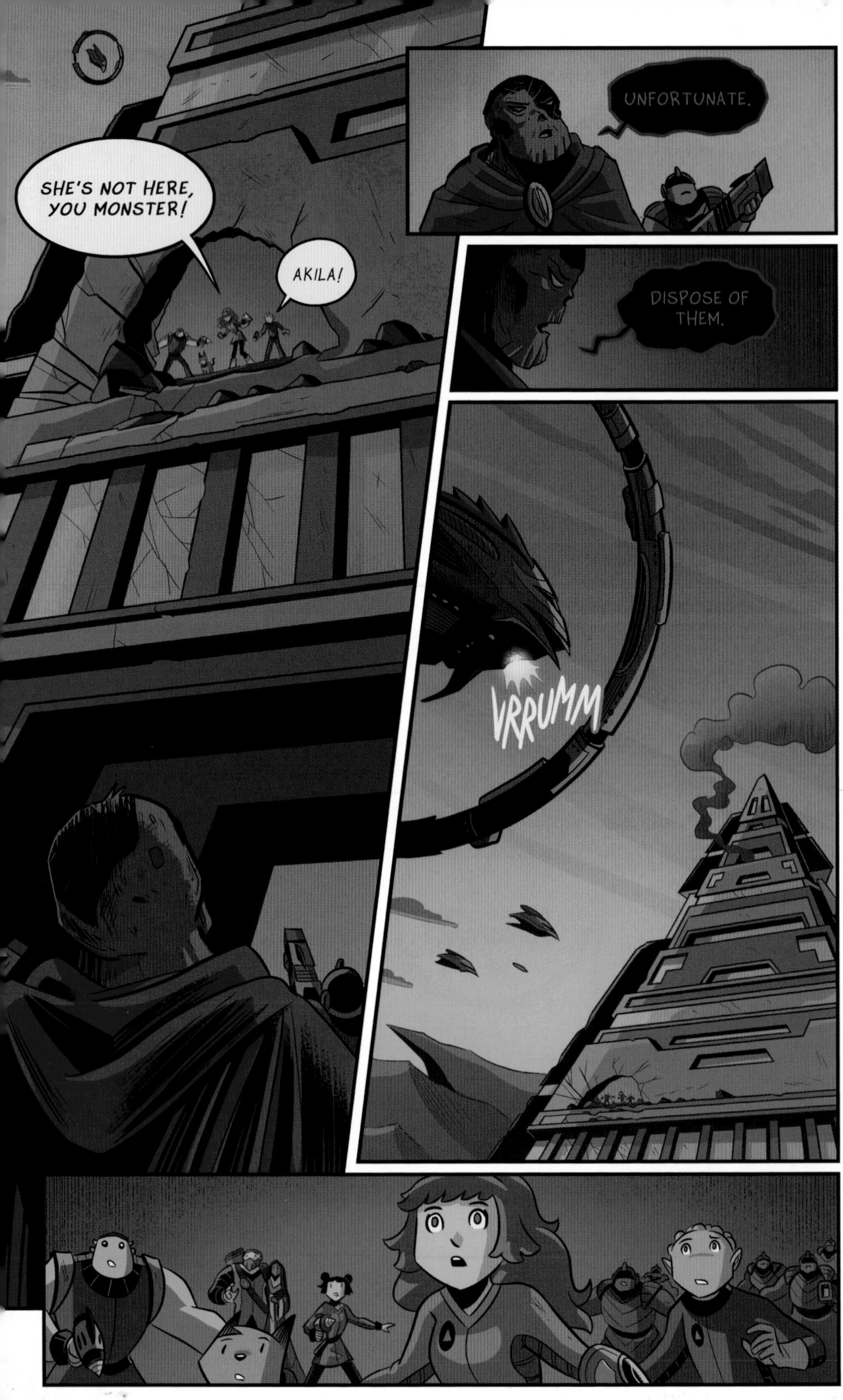
SHE'S NOT HERE, YOU MONSTER!
AKILA!
UNFORTUNATE.
DISPOSE OF THEM.
VRRUMM

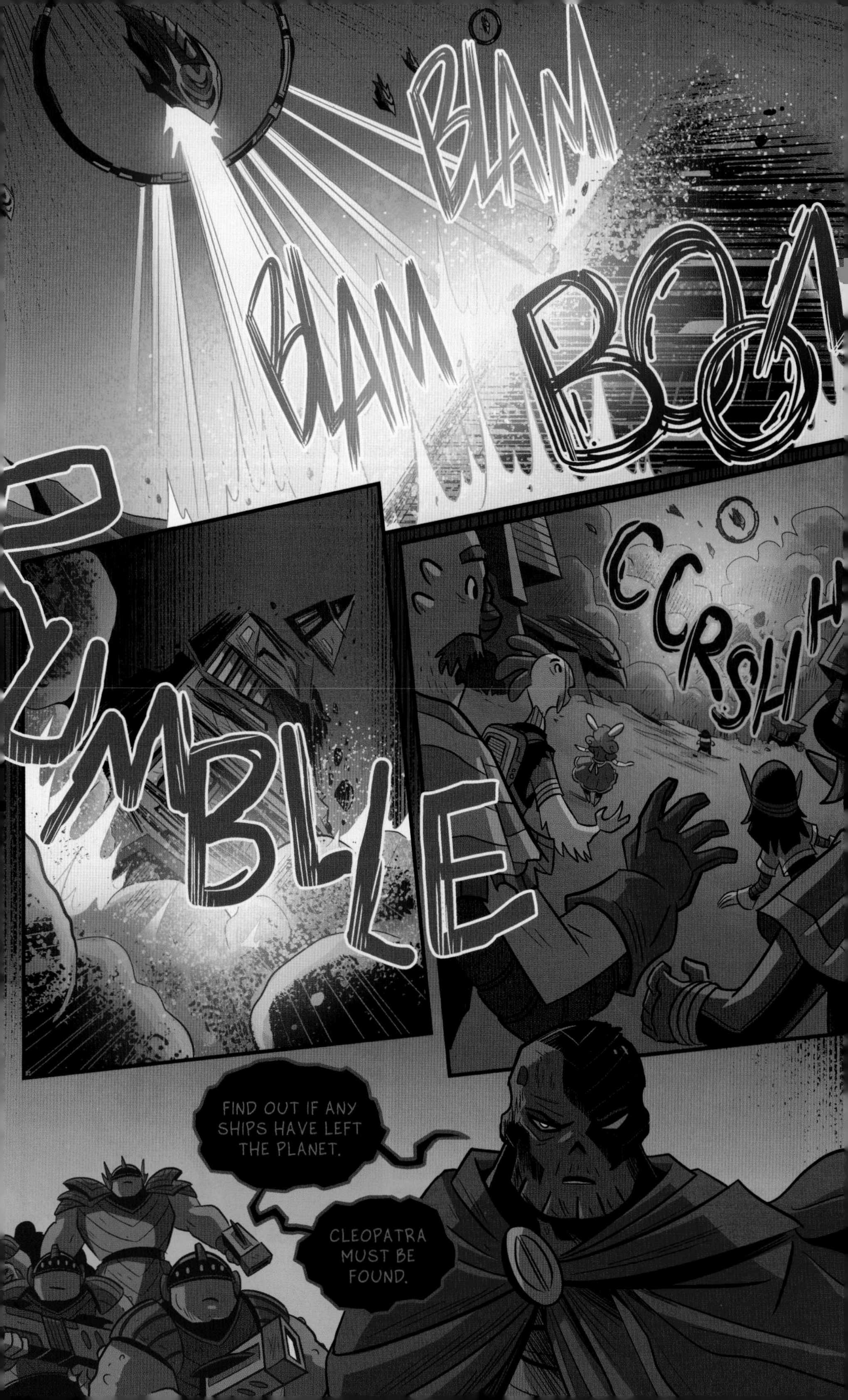
BLAM
BLAM
BOOM
RUMBLE
CCRSHH
FIND OUT IF ANY SHIPS HAVE LEFT THE PLANET.
CLEOPATRA MUST BE FOUND.

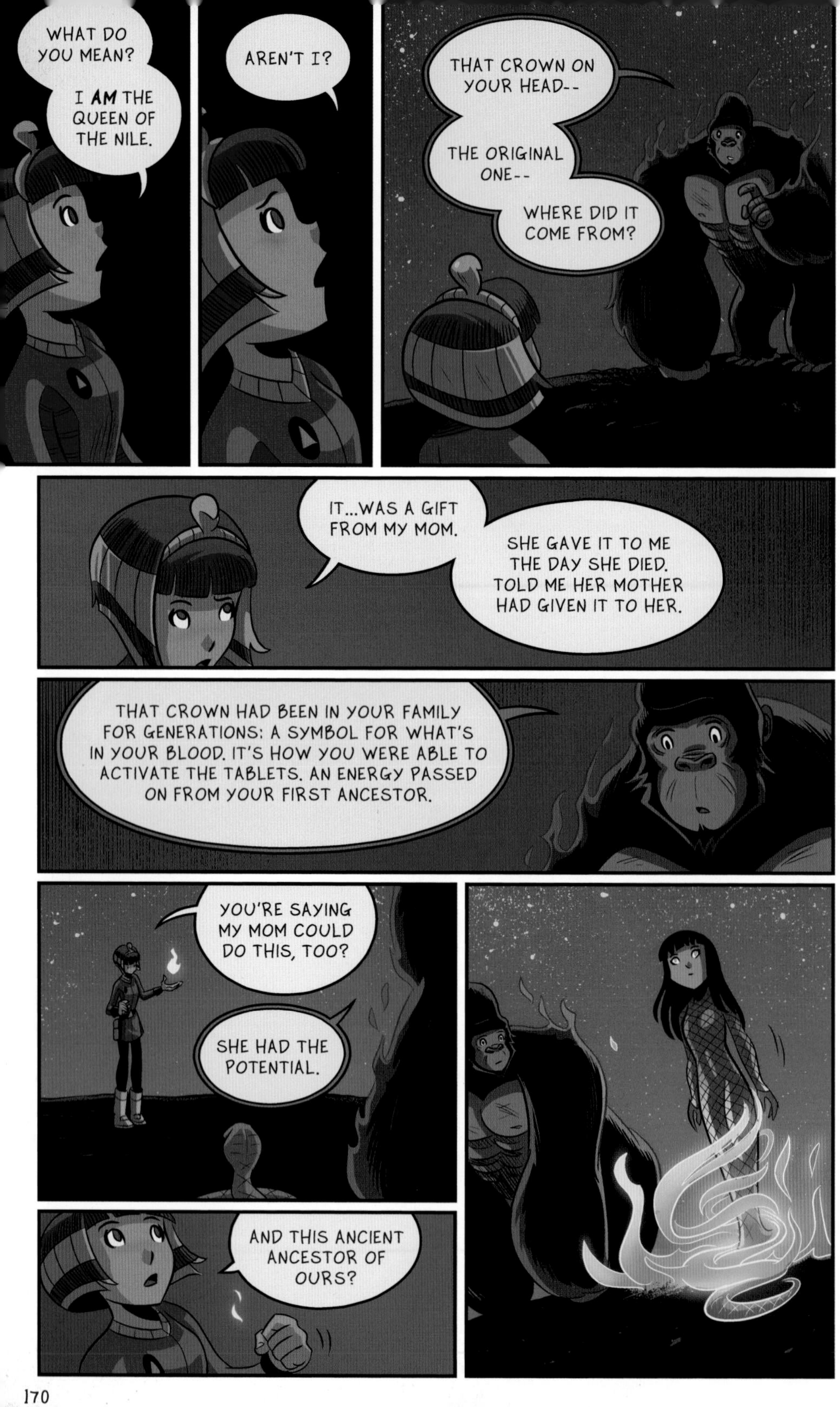
WHAT DO YOU MEAN?
I AM THE QUEEN OF THE NILE.
AREN'T I?
THAT CROWN ON YOUR HEAD--
THE ORIGINAL ONE--
WHERE DID IT COME FROM?
IT...WAS A GIFT FROM MY MOM.
SHE GAVE IT TO ME THE DAY SHE DIED. TOLD ME HER MOTHER HAD GIVEN IT TO HER.
THAT CROWN HAD BEEN IN YOUR FAMILY FOR GENERATIONS: A SYMBOL FOR WHAT'S IN YOUR BLOOD. IT'S HOW YOU WERE ABLE TO ACTIVATE THE TABLETS. AN ENERGY PASSED ON FROM YOUR FIRST ANCESTOR.
YOU'RE SAYING MY MOM COULD DO THIS, TOO?
SHE HAD THE POTENTIAL.
AND THIS ANCIENT ANCESTOR OF OURS?

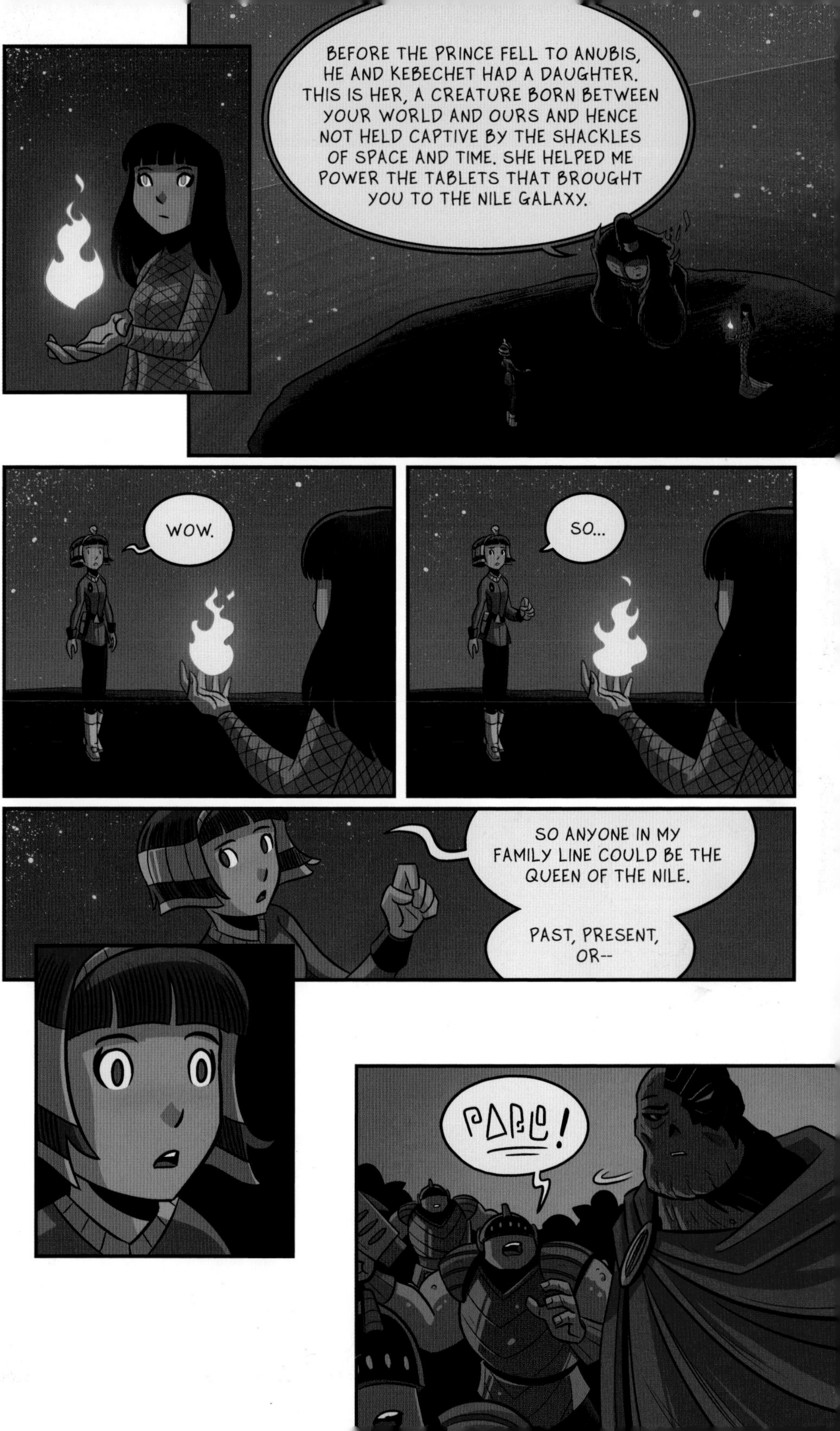
BEFORE THE PRINCE FELL TO ANUBIS, HE AND KEBECHET HAD A DAUGHTER. THIS IS HER, A CREATURE BORN BETWEEN YOUR WORLD AND OURS AND HENCE NOT HELD CAPTIVE BY THE SHACKLES OF SPACE AND TIME. SHE HELPED ME POWER THE TABLETS THAT BROUGHT YOU TO THE NILE GALAXY.
WOW.
SO...
SO ANYONE IN MY FAMILY LINE COULD BE THE QUEEN OF THE NILE.
PAST, PRESENT, OR--

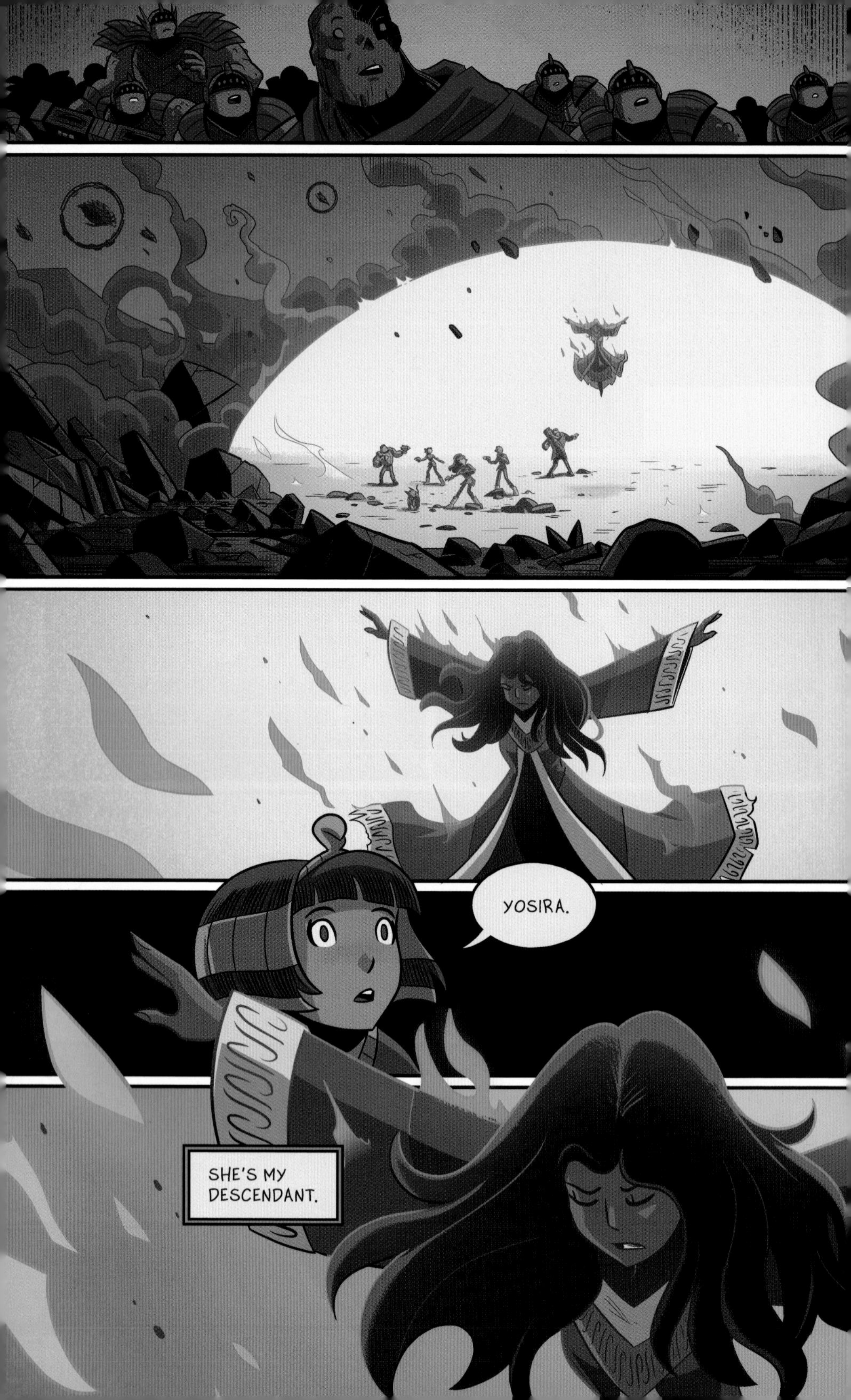
YOSIRA.
SHE'S MY DESCENDANT.

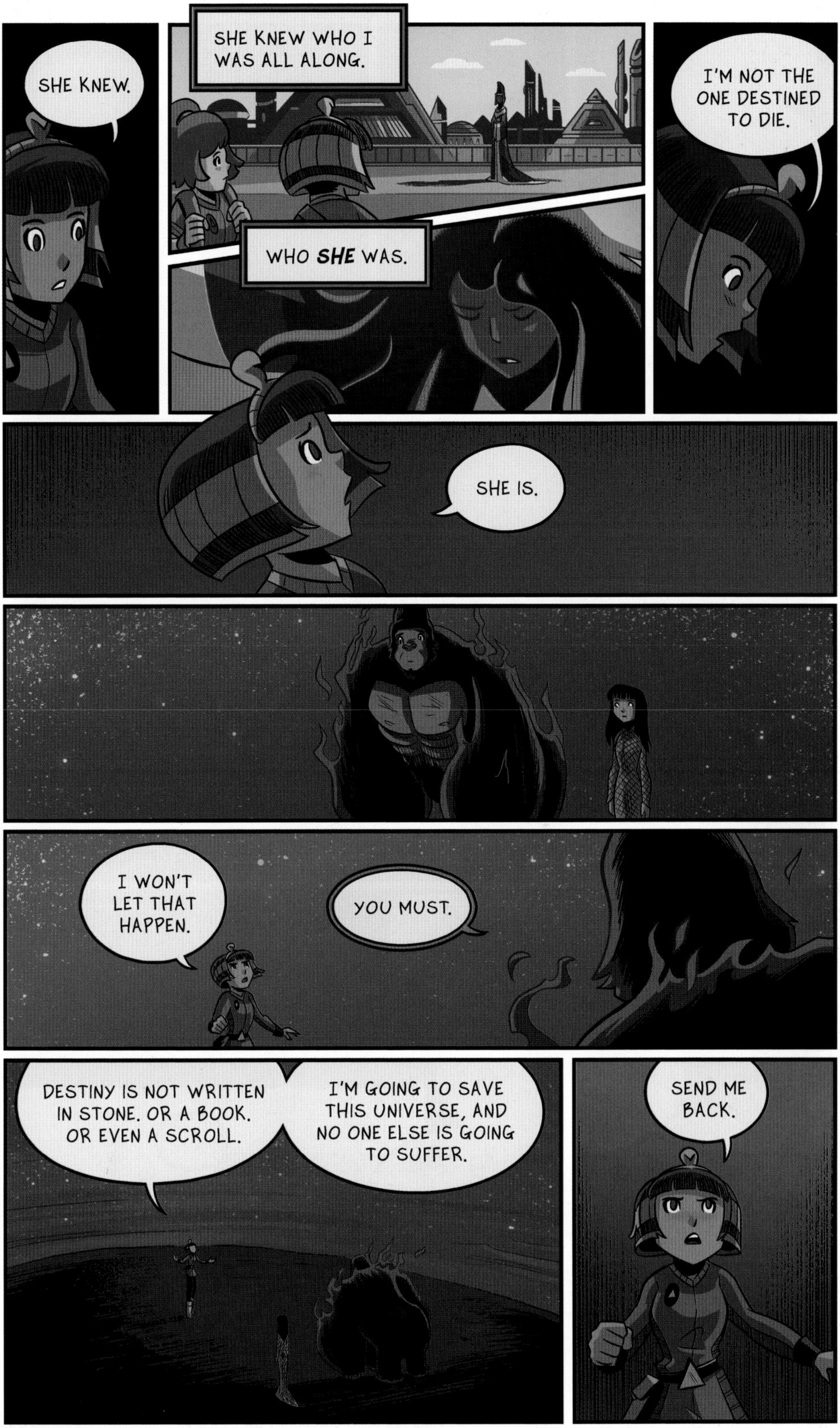
SHE KNEW.
SHE KNEW WHO I WAS ALL ALONG.
WHO **SHE** WAS.
I'M NOT THE ONE DESTINED TO DIE.
SHE IS.
I WON'T LET THAT HAPPEN.
YOU MUST.
DESTINY IS NOT WRITTEN IN STONE. OR A BOOK. OR EVEN A SCROLL.
I'M GOING TO SAVE THIS UNIVERSE, AND NO ONE ELSE IS GOING TO SUFFER.
SEND ME BACK.

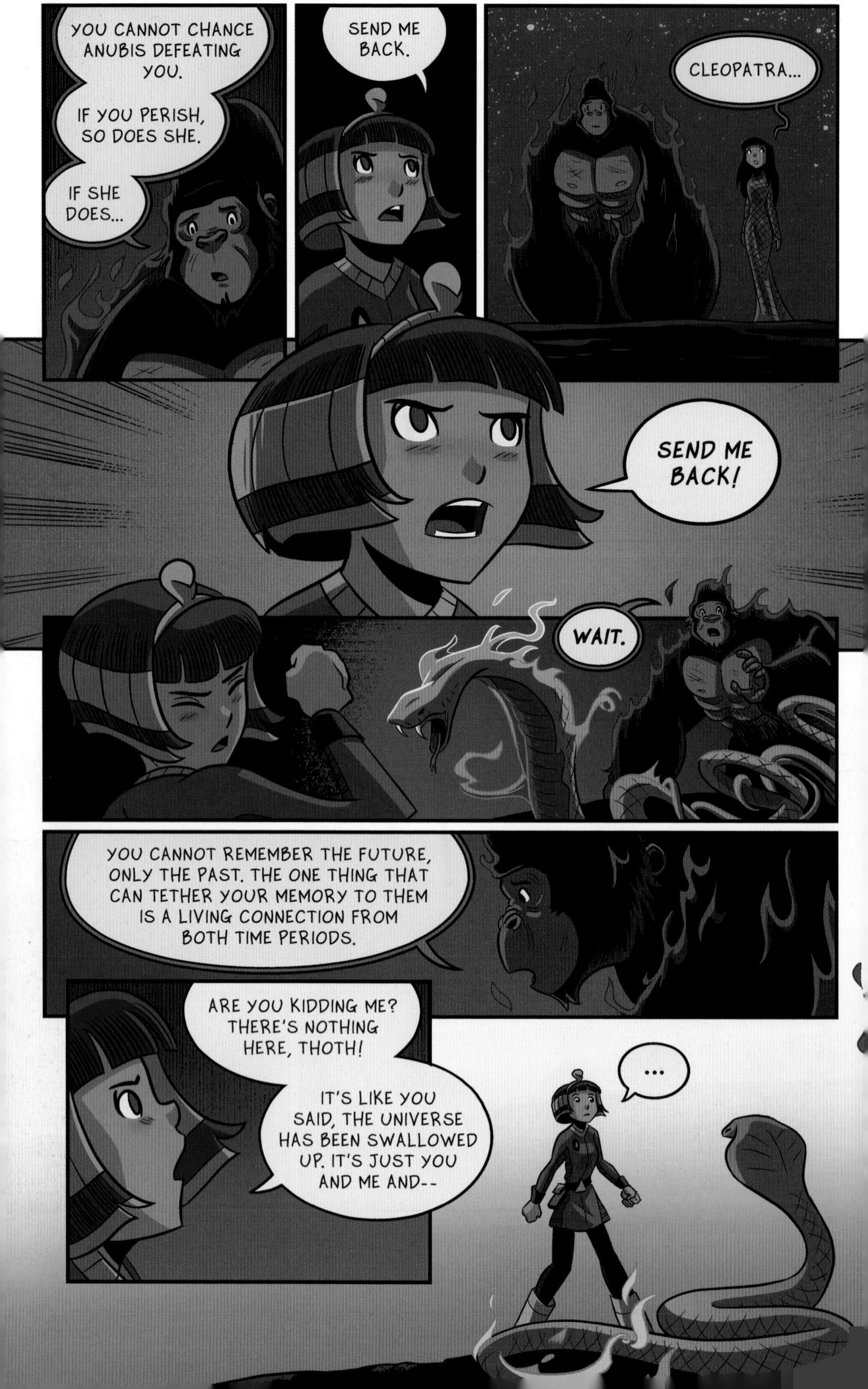
YOU CANNOT CHANCE ANUBIS DEFEATING YOU.
IF YOU PERISH, SO DOES SHE.
IF SHE DOES...
SEND ME BACK.
CLEOPATRA...
SEND ME BACK!
WAIT.
YOU CANNOT REMEMBER THE FUTURE, ONLY THE PAST. THE ONE THING THAT CAN TETHER YOUR MEMORY TO THEM IS A LIVING CONNECTION FROM BOTH TIME PERIODS.
ARE YOU KIDDING ME? THERE'S NOTHING HERE, THOTH!
IT'S LIKE YOU SAID, THE UNIVERSE HAS BEEN SWALLOWED UP. IT'S JUST YOU AND ME AND--
...

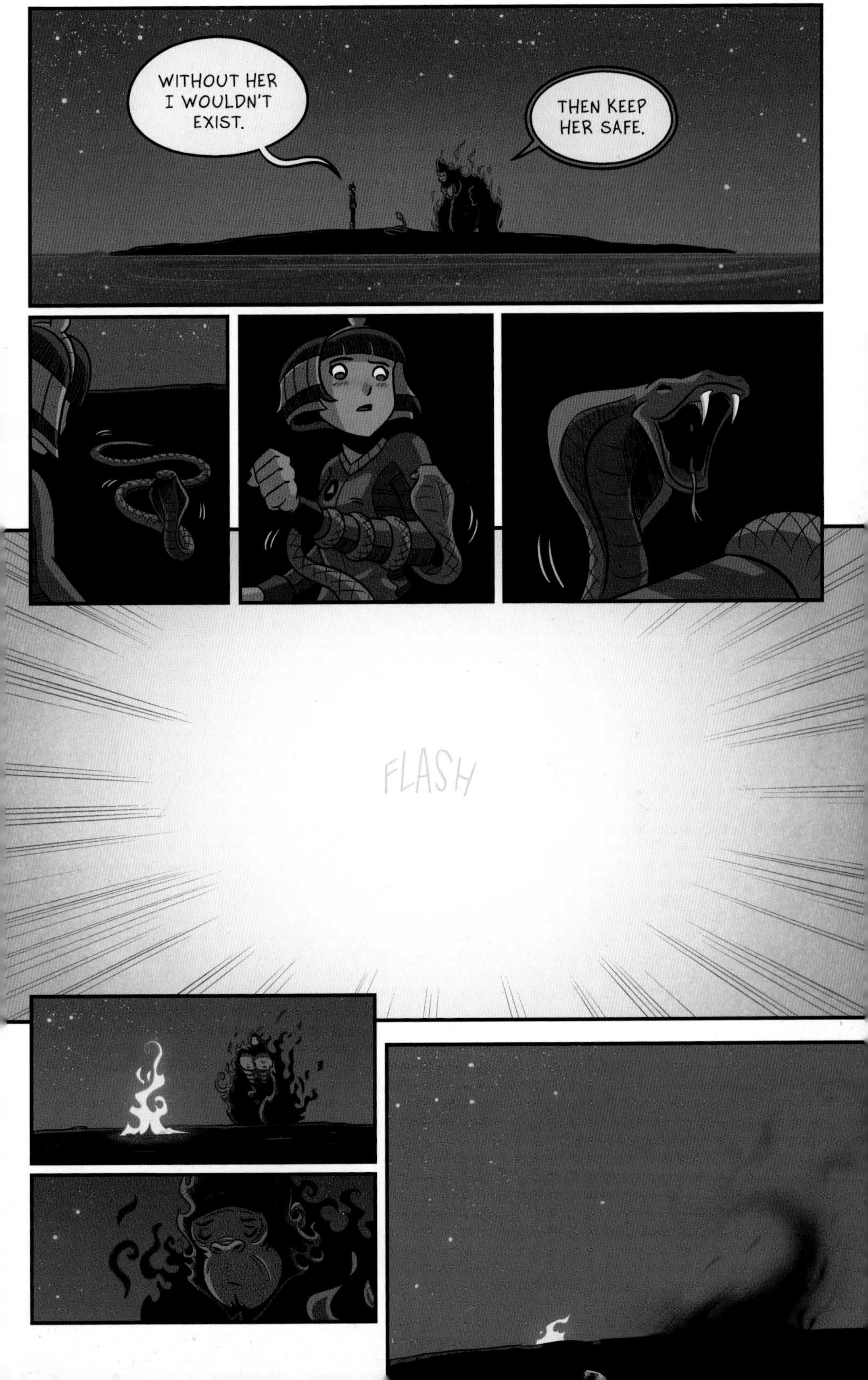
WITHOUT HER I WOULDN'T EXIST.
THEN KEEP HER SAFE.
FLASH

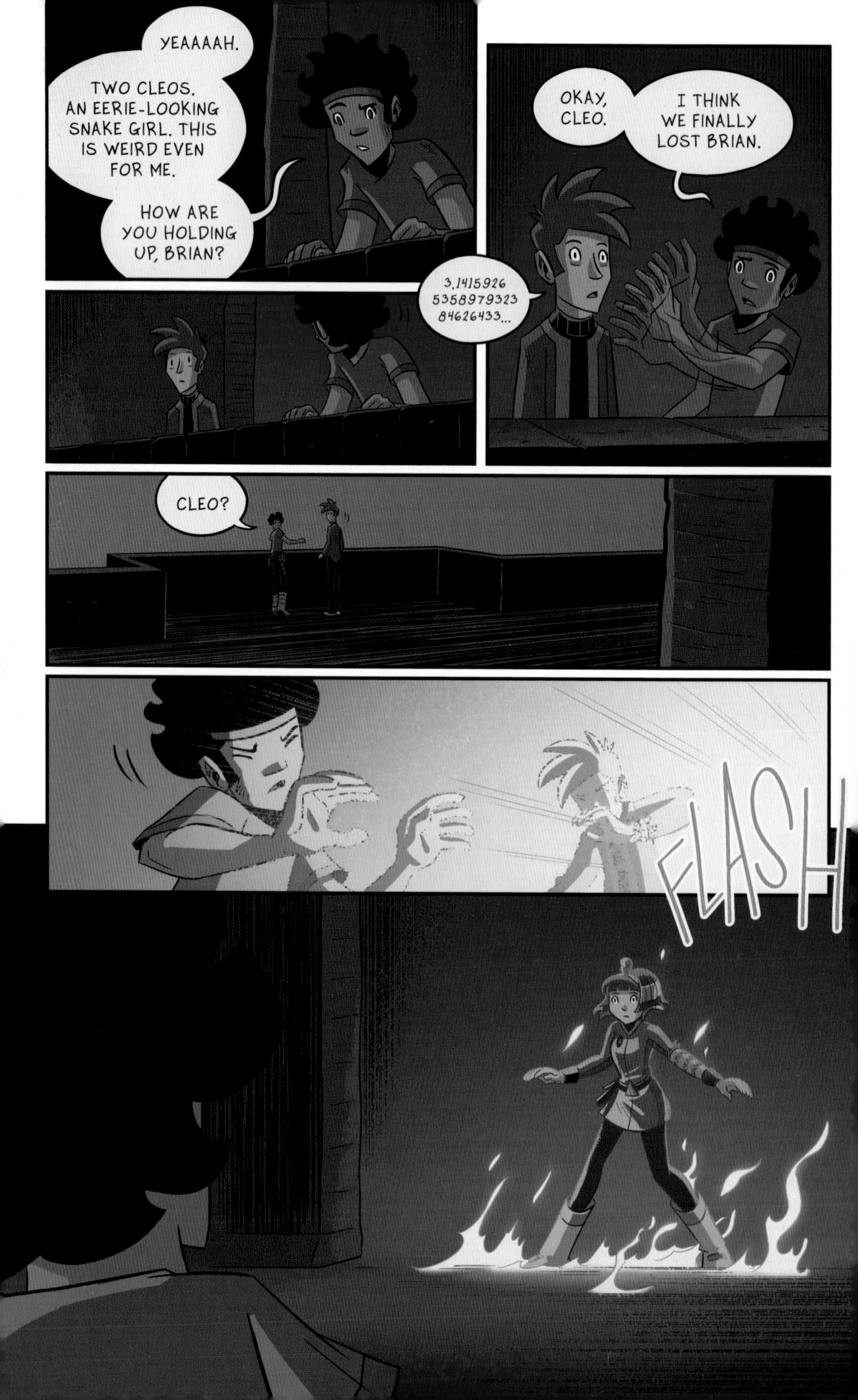
YEAAAAH.
TWO CLEOS. AN EERIE-LOOKING SNAKE GIRL. THIS IS WEIRD EVEN FOR ME.
HOW ARE YOU HOLDING UP, BRIAN?
3.1415926 5358979323 84626433...
OKAY, CLEO.
I THINK WE FINALLY LOST BRIAN.
CLEO?
FLASH

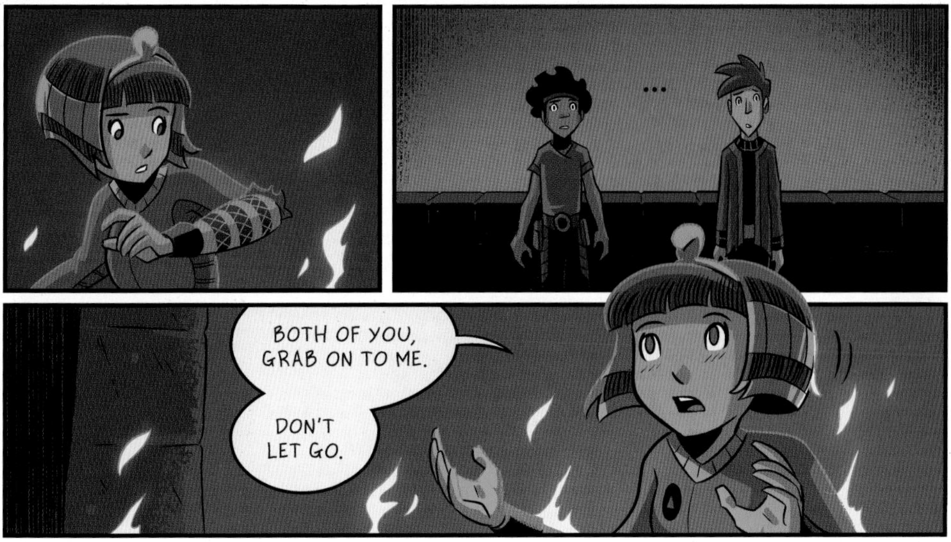
...
BOTH OF YOU, GRAB ON TO ME.
DON'T LET GO.

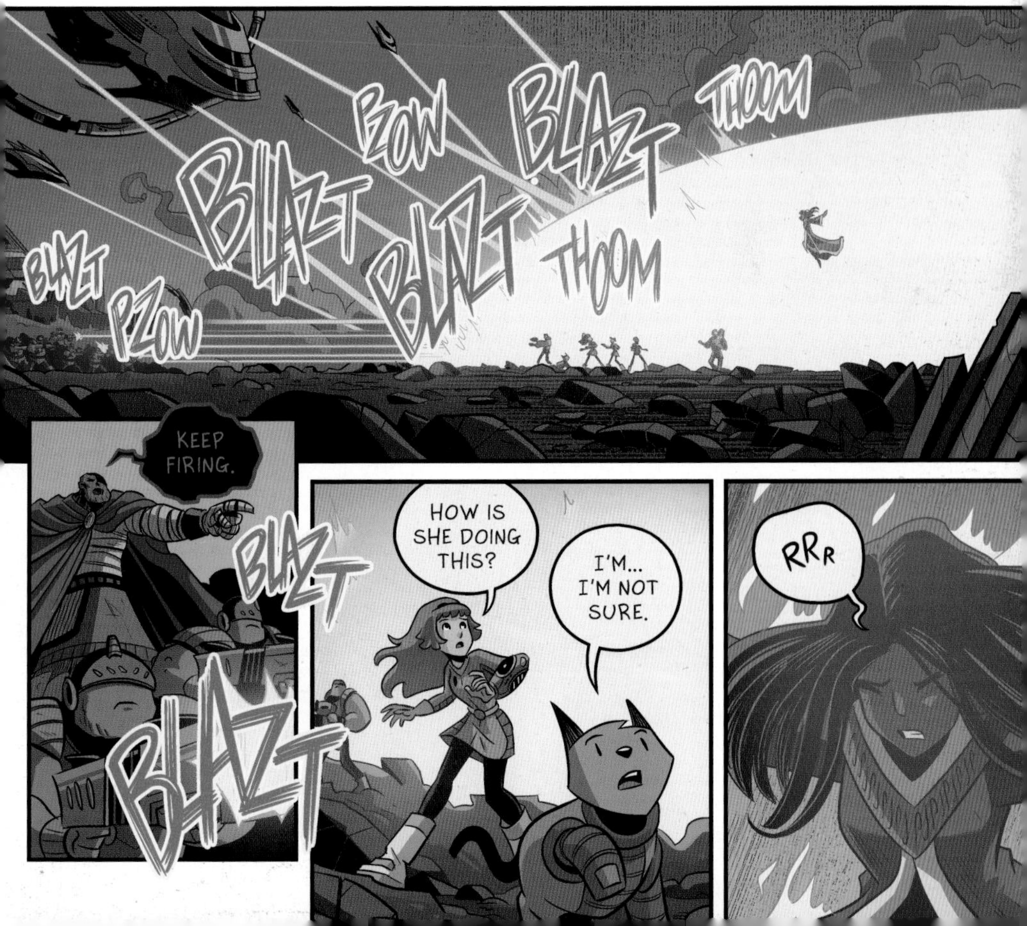
PZOW
BLAZT
THOOM
BLAZT
BLAZT
BLAZT
THOOM
BLAZT
PZOW
KEEP FIRING.
BLAZT
BLAZT
HOW IS SHE DOING THIS?
I'M... I'M NOT SURE.
RRR

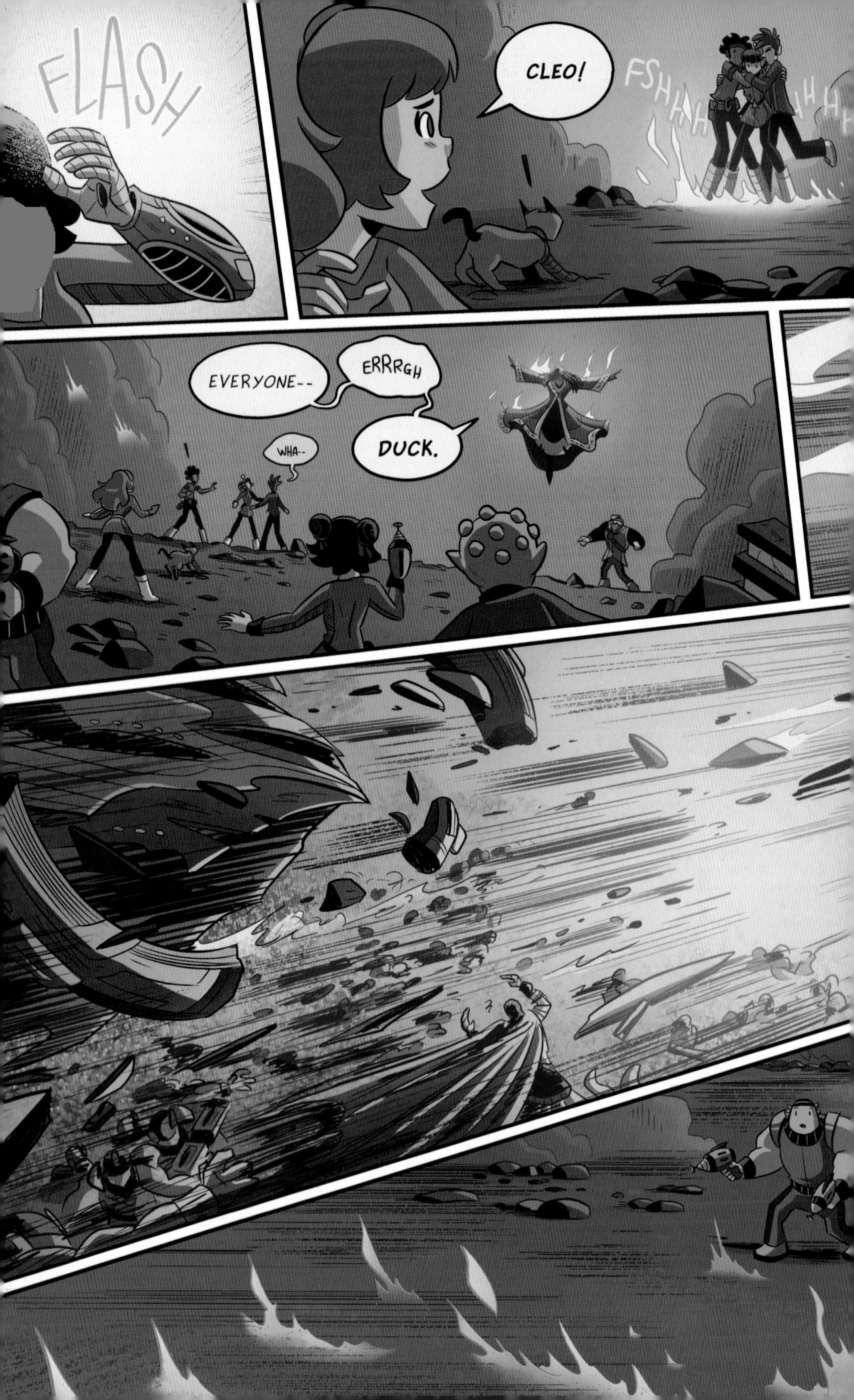
FLASH
CLEO!
FSHHHH
EVERYONE--
ERRRGH
DUCK.
WHA--

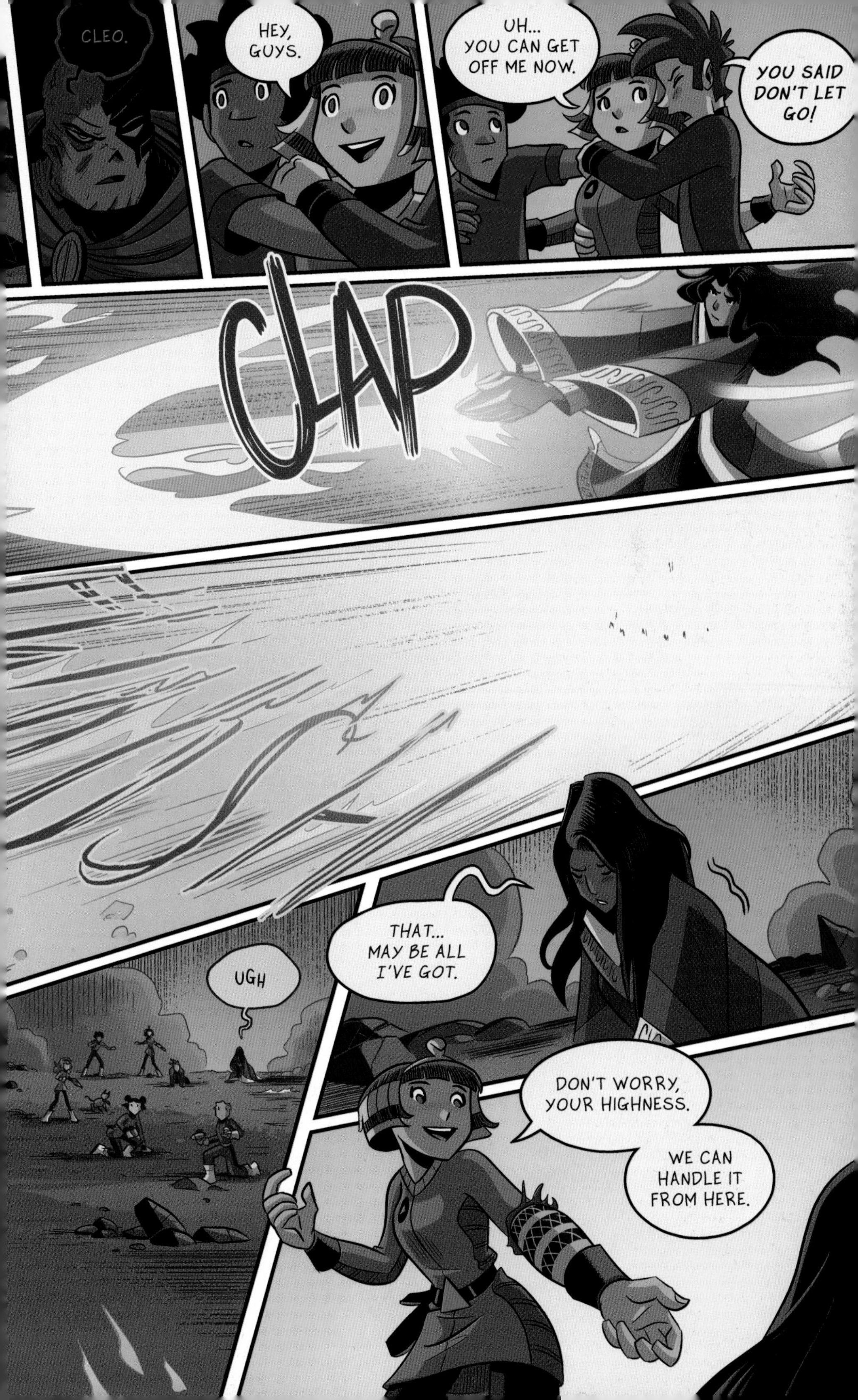
CLEO.
HEY, GUYS.
UH... YOU CAN GET OFF ME NOW.
YOU SAID DON'T LET GO!
CLAP
THAT... MAY BE ALL I'VE GOT.
UGH
DON'T WORRY, YOUR HIGHNESS.
WE CAN HANDLE IT FROM HERE.

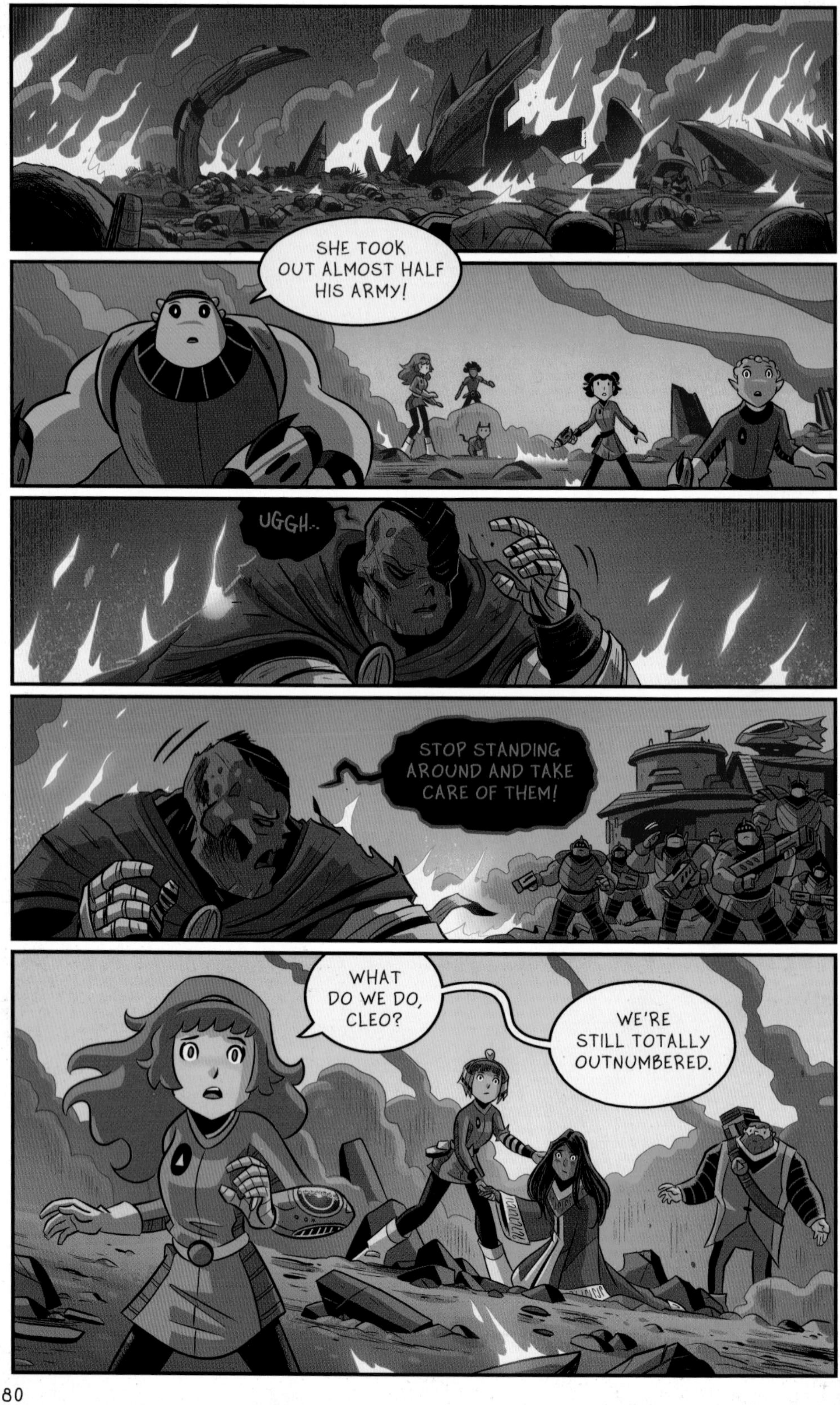
SHE TOOK OUT ALMOST HALF HIS ARMY!
UGGH...
STOP STANDING AROUND AND TAKE CARE OF THEM!
WHAT DO WE DO, CLEO?
WE'RE STILL TOTALLY OUTNUMBERED.

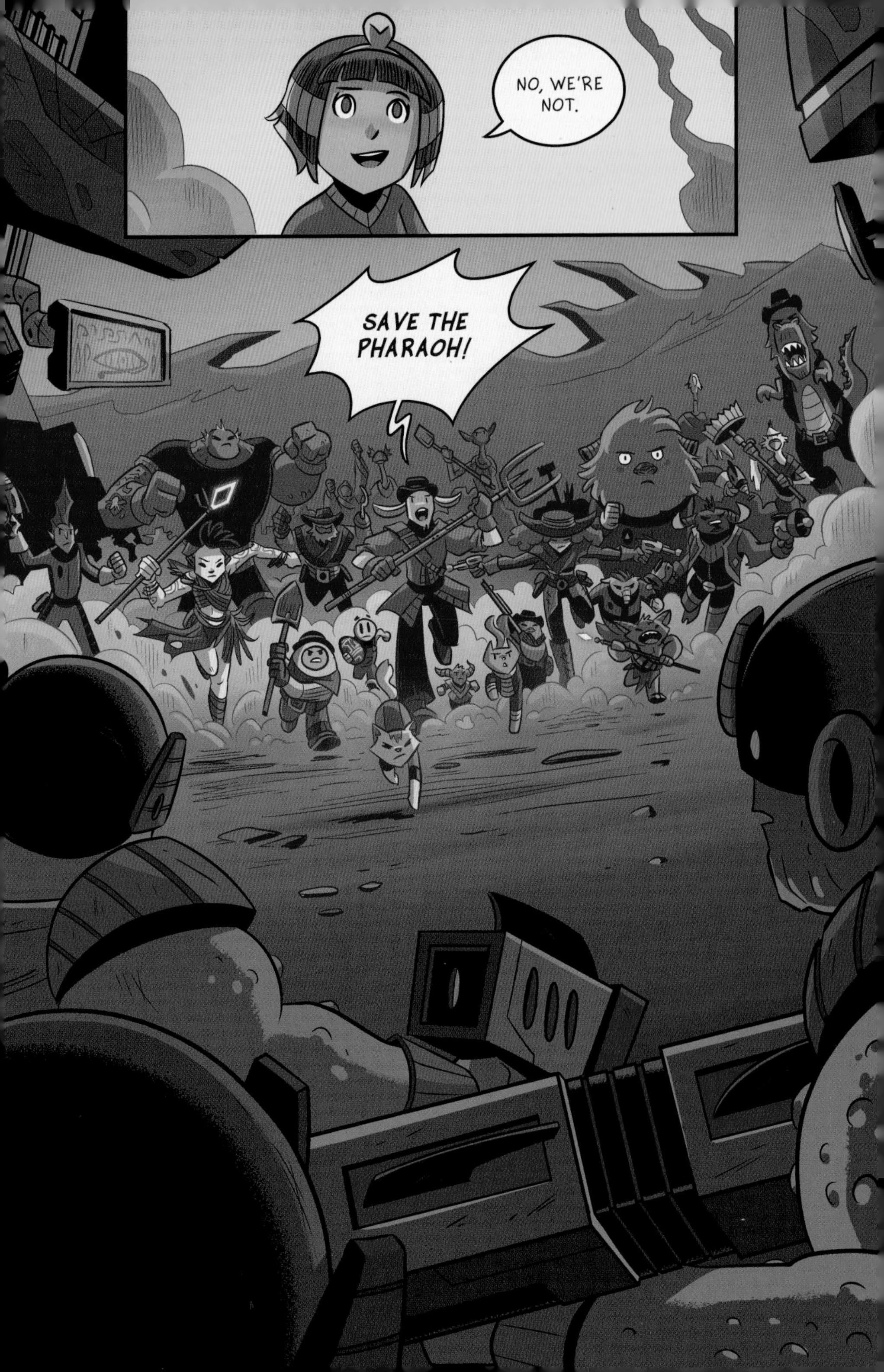
NO, WE'RE NOT.
SAVE THE PHARAOH!

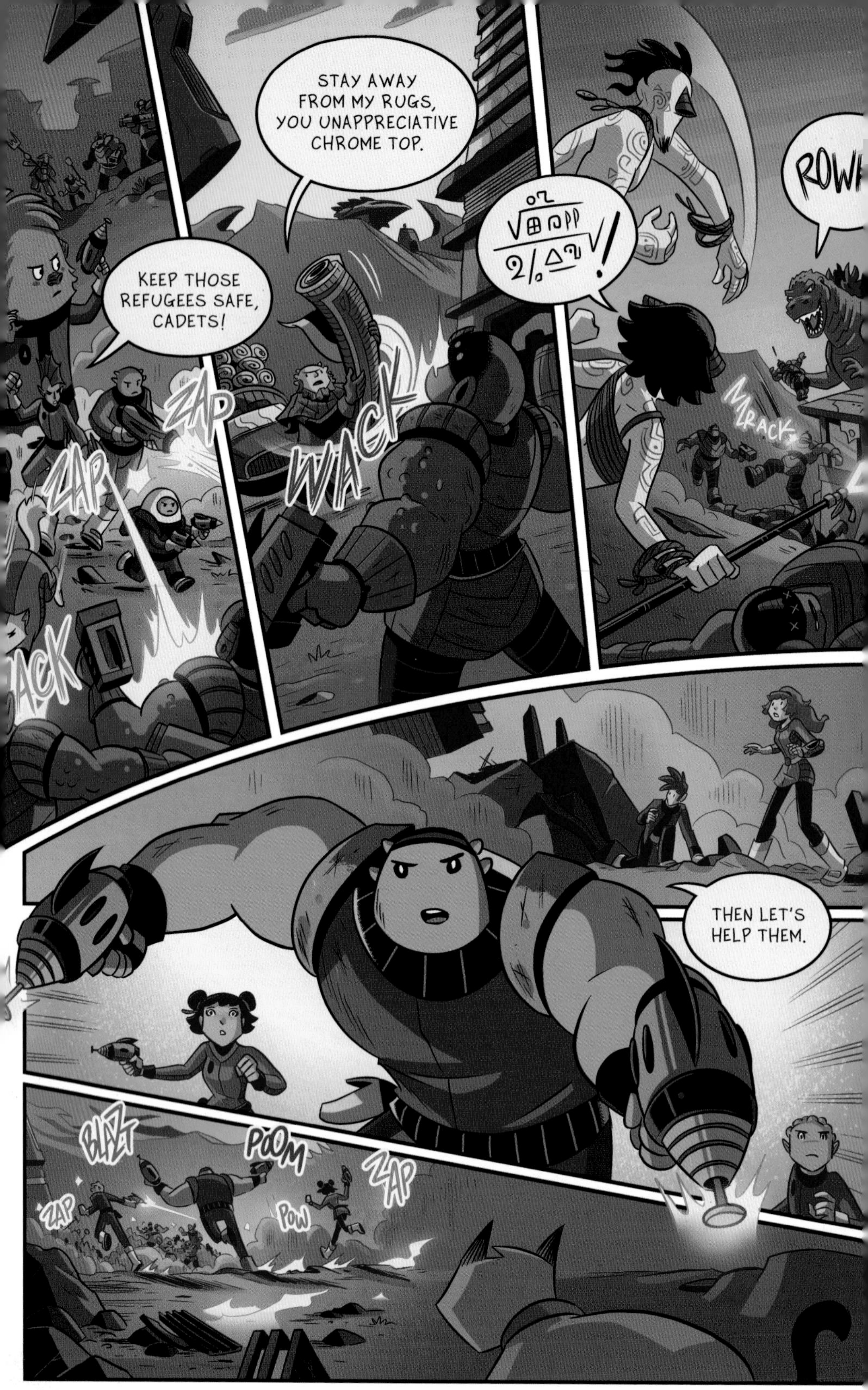
KEEP THOSE REFUGEES SAFE, CADETS!
ZAP
ZAP
STAY AWAY FROM MY RUGS, YOU UNAPPRECIATIVE CHROME TOP.
WACK
KRACK
THEN LET'S HELP THEM.
BLAZT
POOM
ZAP
ZAP
POW

FOR HYKOSIS!
POW
POOM
GRAB
BLAZT
BAM
BLAZT
ZORCH
POW
THEY WON'T BE ABLE TO HOLD THOSE XERX OFF FOR LONG.
HEY...
WHERE IS ANTONY GOING?

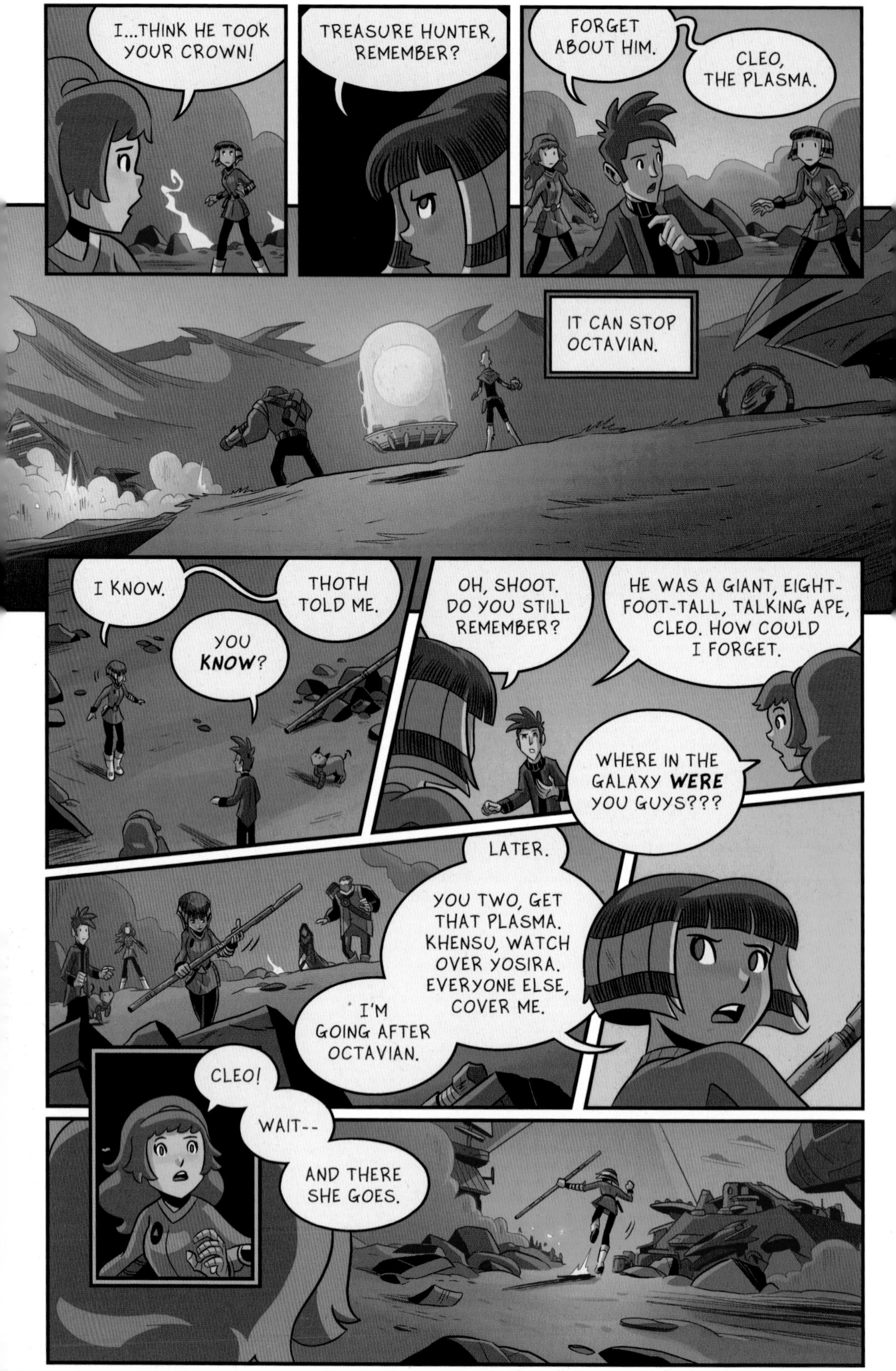

I...THINK HE TOOK YOUR CROWN!
TREASURE HUNTER, REMEMBER?
FORGET ABOUT HIM.
CLEO, THE PLASMA.
IT CAN STOP OCTAVIAN.
I KNOW.
THOTH TOLD ME.
YOU KNOW?
OH, SHOOT. DO YOU STILL REMEMBER?
HE WAS A GIANT, EIGHT-FOOT-TALL, TALKING APE, CLEO. HOW COULD I FORGET.
WHERE IN THE GALAXY WERE YOU GUYS???
LATER.
YOU TWO, GET THAT PLASMA. KHENSU, WATCH OVER YOSIRA. EVERYONE ELSE, COVER ME.
I'M GOING AFTER OCTAVIAN.
CLEO!
WAIT--
AND THERE SHE GOES.

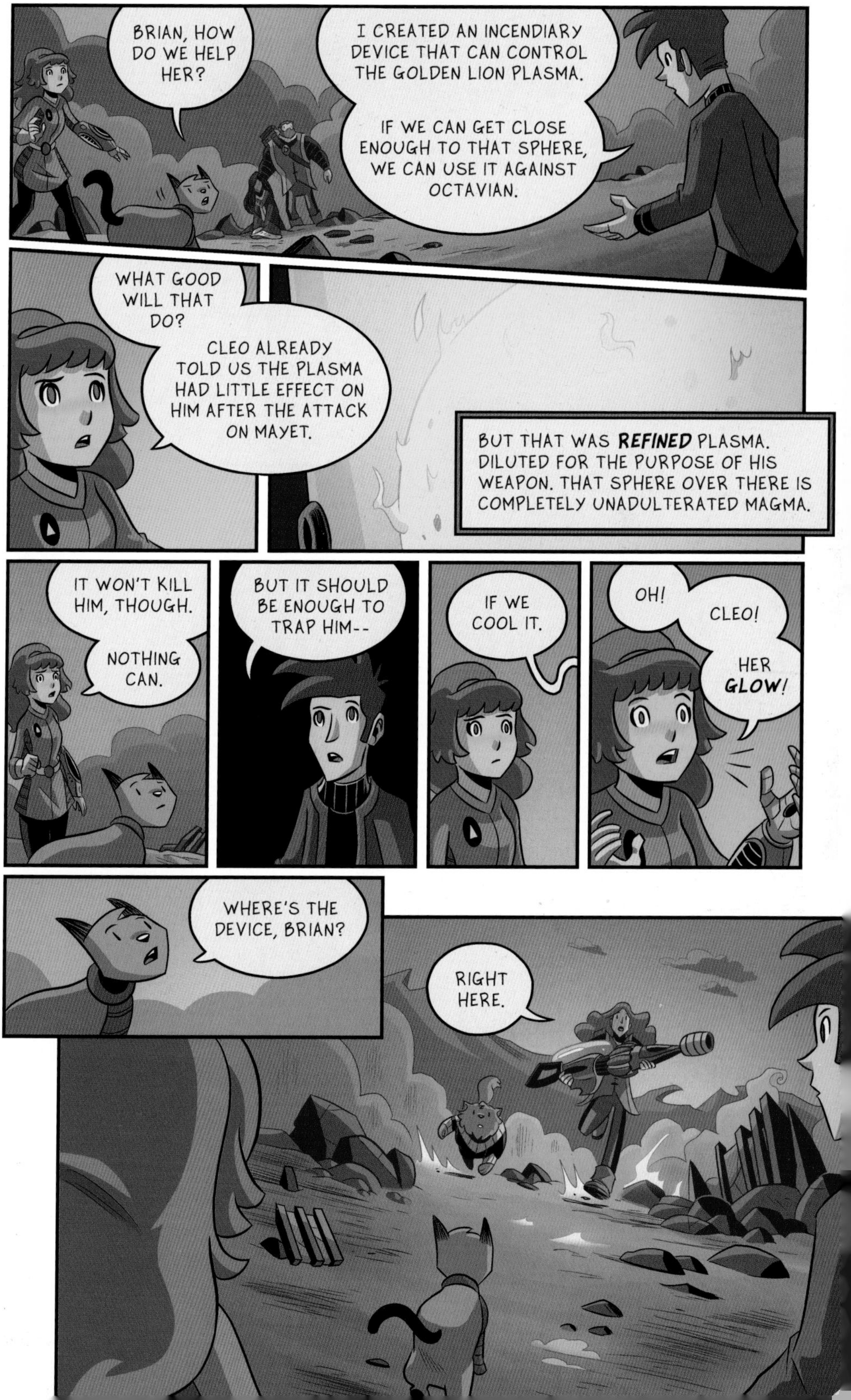
BRIAN, HOW DO WE HELP HER?
I CREATED AN INCENDIARY DEVICE THAT CAN CONTROL THE GOLDEN LION PLASMA.
IF WE CAN GET CLOSE ENOUGH TO THAT SPHERE, WE CAN USE IT AGAINST OCTAVIAN.
WHAT GOOD WILL THAT DO?
CLEO ALREADY TOLD US THE PLASMA HAD LITTLE EFFECT ON HIM AFTER THE ATTACK ON MAYET.
BUT THAT WAS **REFINED** PLASMA. DILUTED FOR THE PURPOSE OF HIS WEAPON. THAT SPHERE OVER THERE IS COMPLETELY UNADULTERATED MAGMA.
IT WON'T KILL HIM, THOUGH.
NOTHING CAN.
BUT IT SHOULD BE ENOUGH TO TRAP HIM--
IF WE COOL IT.
OH!
CLEO!
HER **GLOW**!
WHERE'S THE DEVICE, BRIAN?
RIGHT HERE.

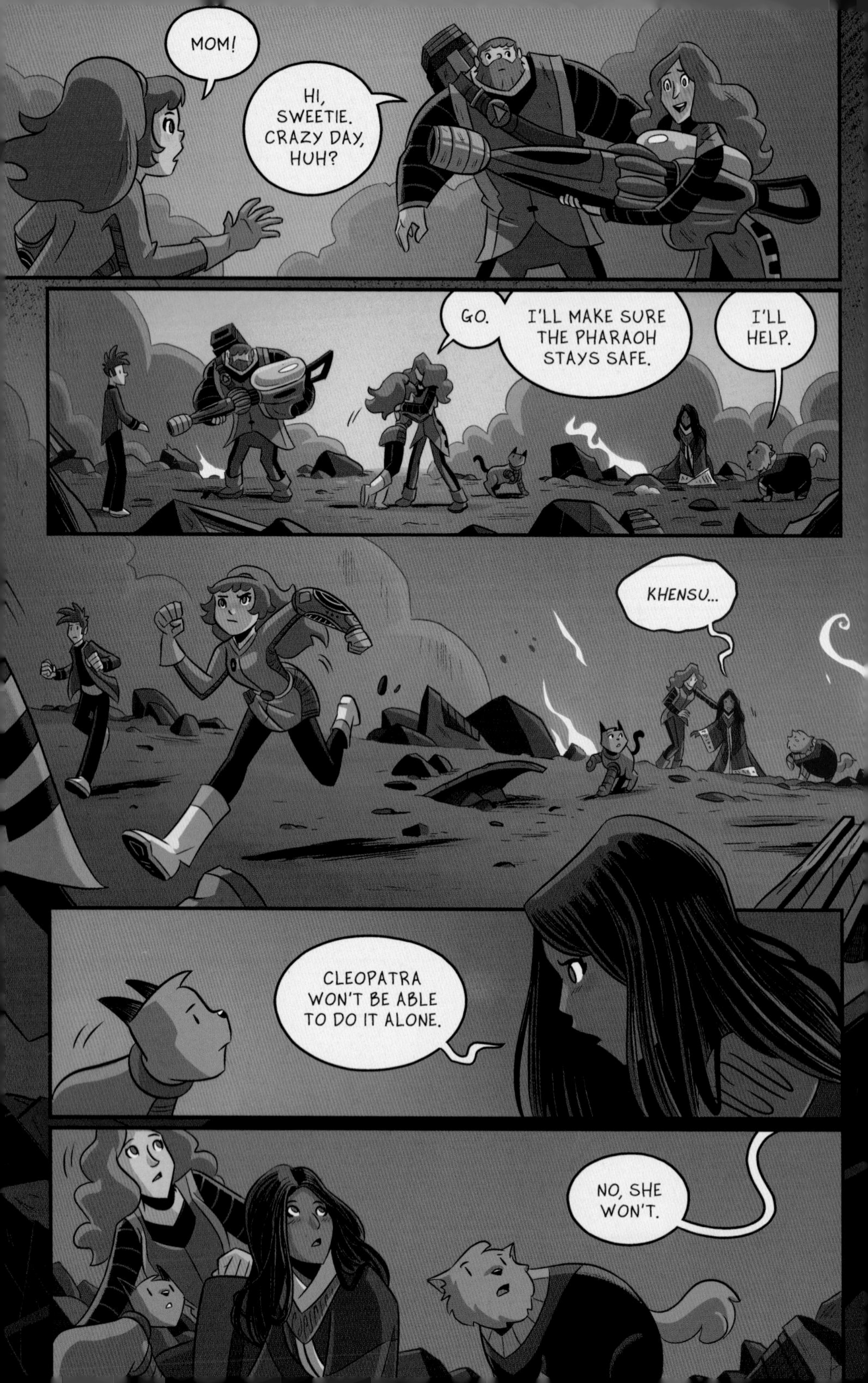
MOM!
HI, SWEETIE. CRAZY DAY, HUH?
GO.
I'LL MAKE SURE THE PHARAOH STAYS SAFE.
I'LL HELP.
KHENSU...
CLEOPATRA WON'T BE ABLE TO DO IT ALONE.
NO, SHE WON'T.

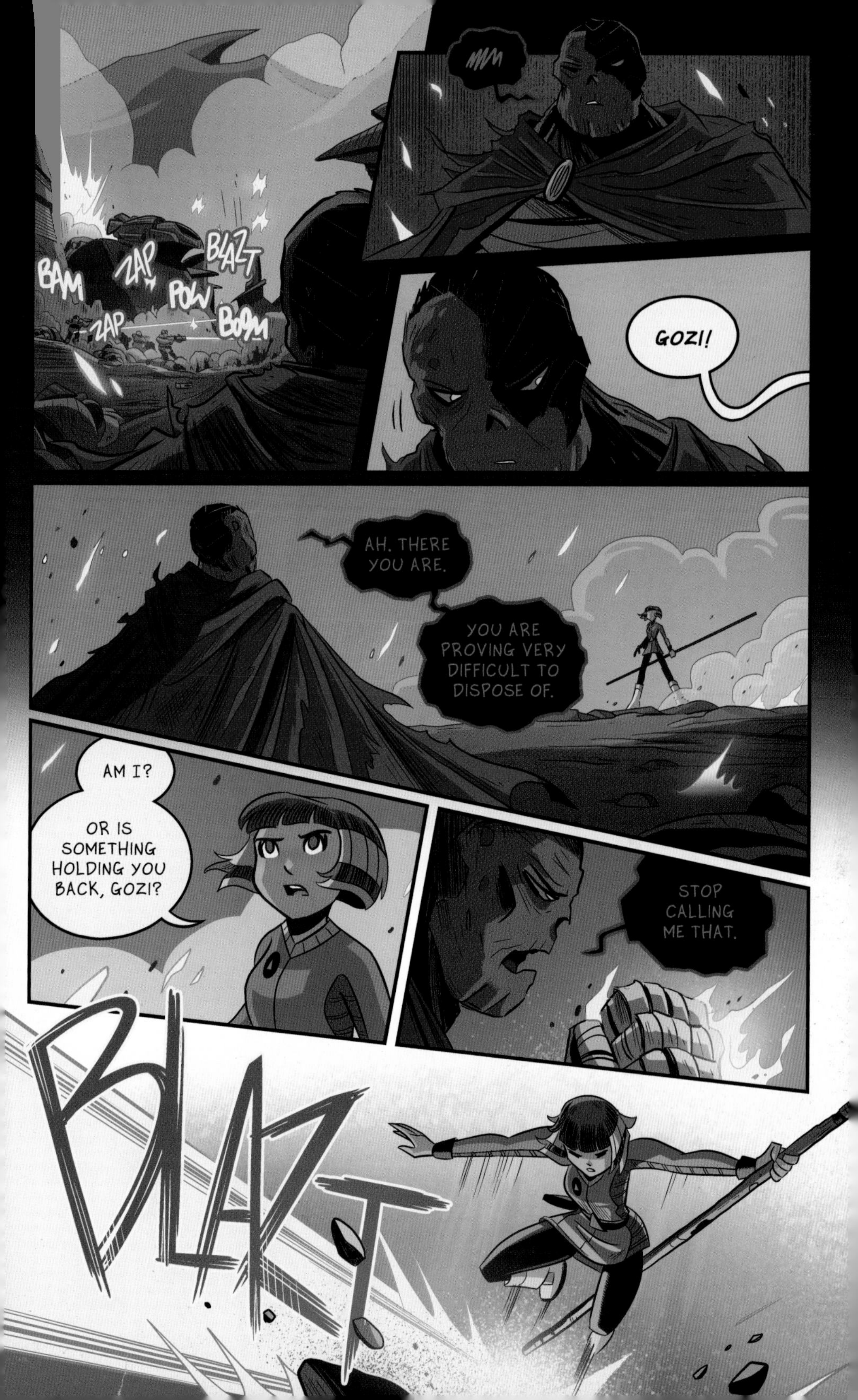
BAM
ZAP
BLAZT
POW
ZAP
BOOM
MM
GOZI!
AH. THERE YOU ARE.
YOU ARE PROVING VERY DIFFICULT TO DISPOSE OF.
AM I?
OR IS SOMETHING HOLDING YOU BACK, GOZI?
STOP CALLING ME THAT.
BLAZT

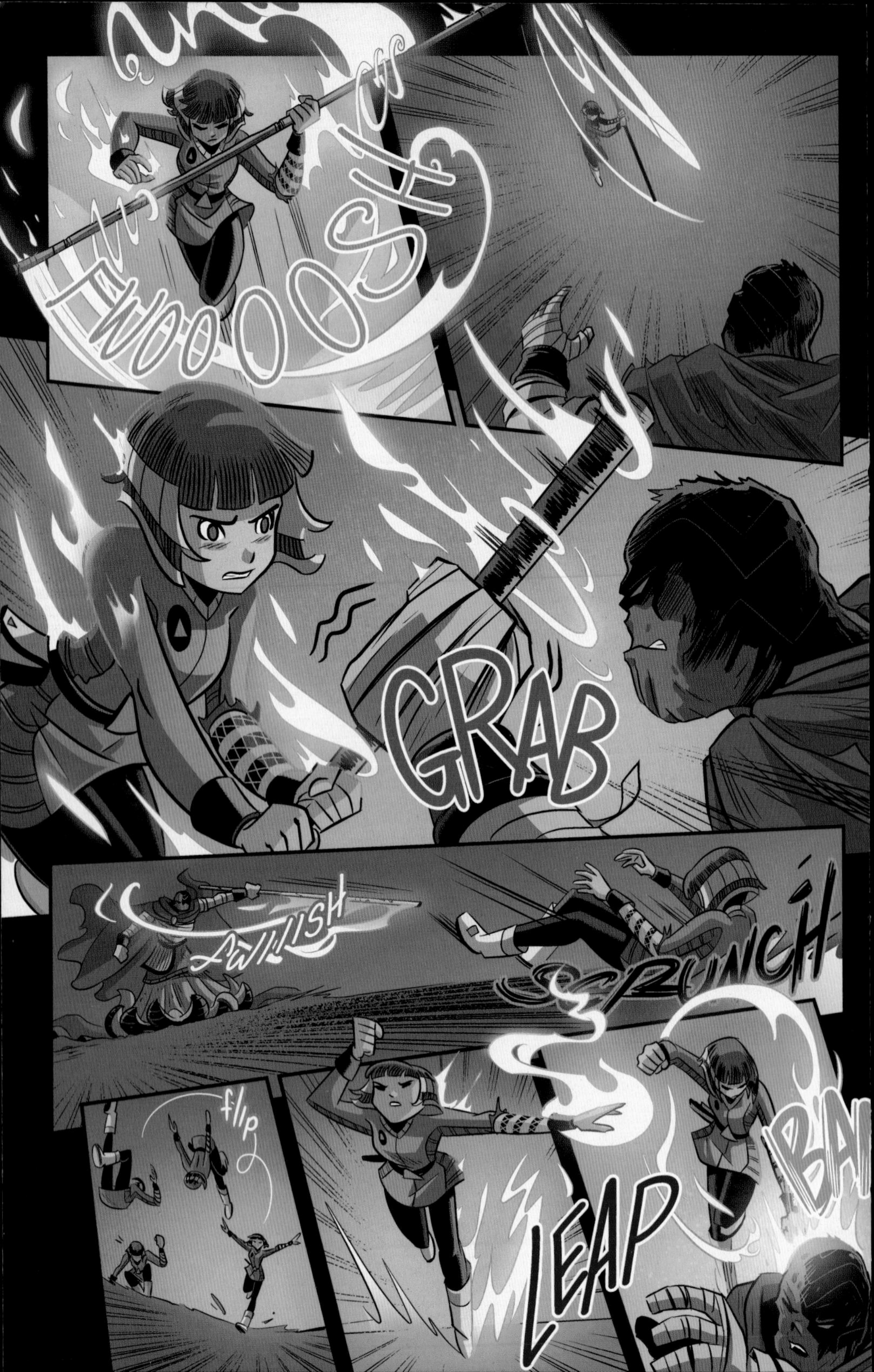
FWOOOOSH
GRAB
FWUSH
CRUNCH
flip
LEAP
BA

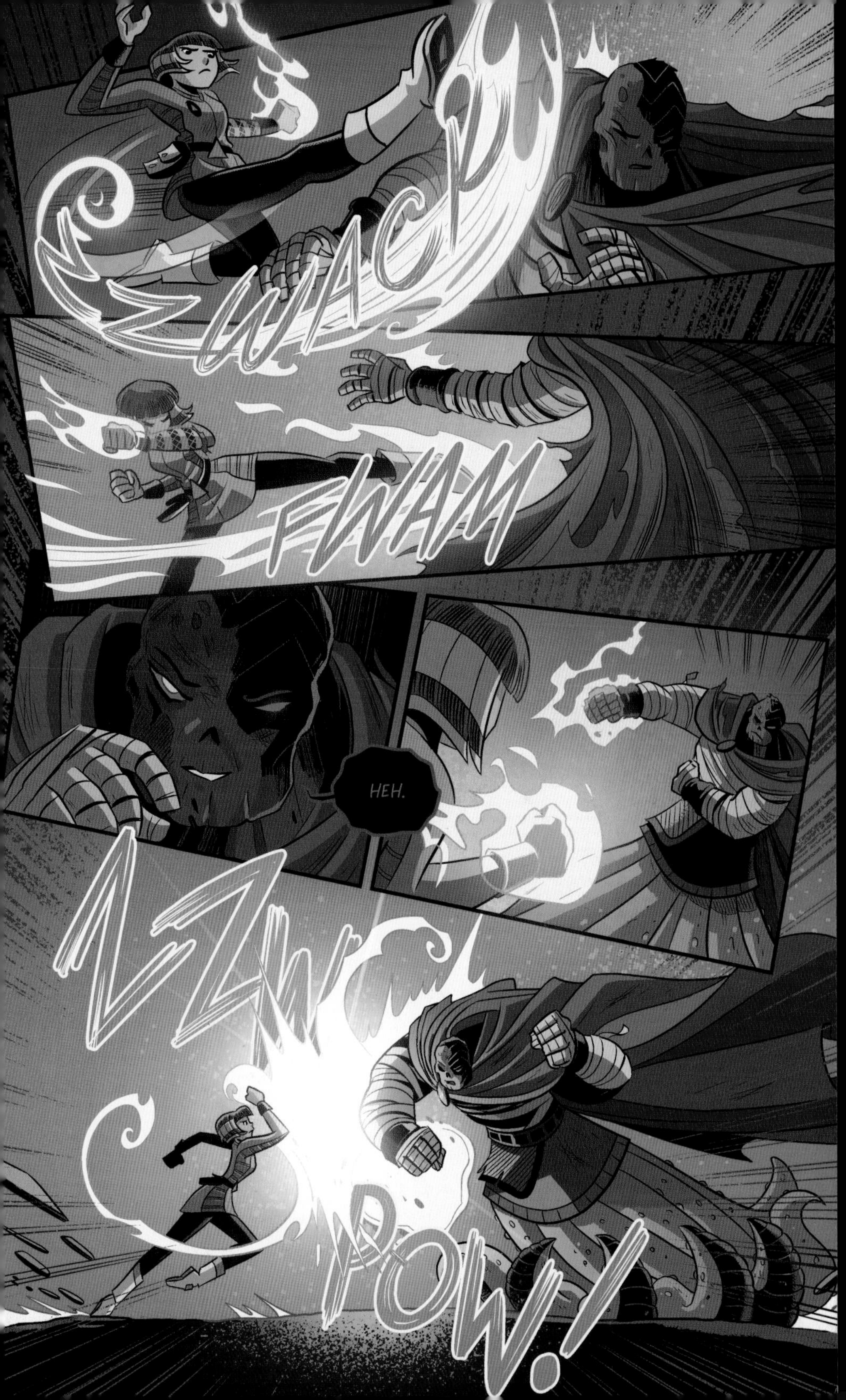

ZWACK
FWAM
HEH.
ZZWAM
POW!

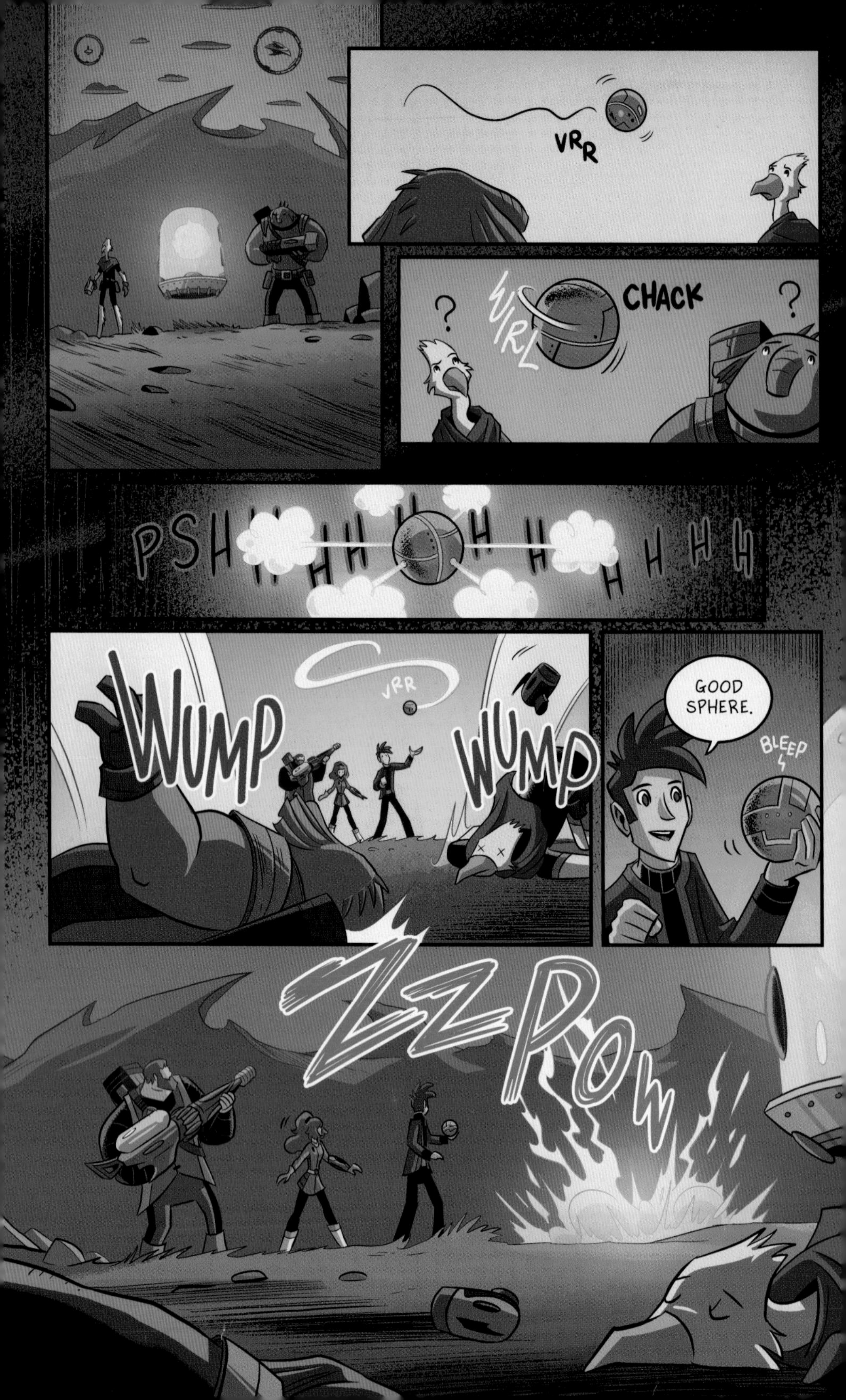
VRR
?
WIRL
CHACK
?
PSHHHHHHHHHHHHH
WUMP
VRR
WUMP
GOOD SPHERE.
BLEEP
ZZPOW

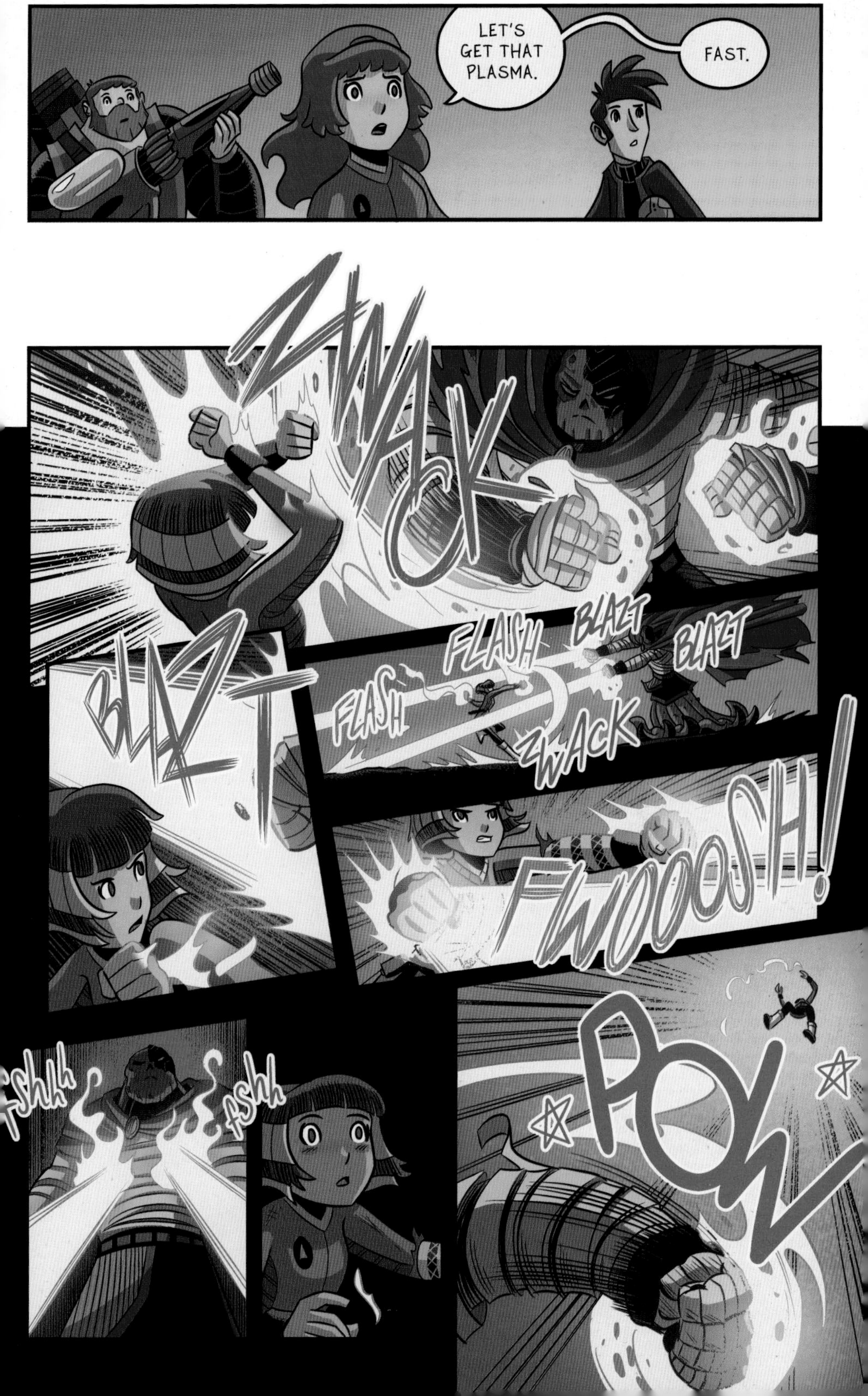
LET'S GET THAT PLASMA.
FAST.
ZWACK
BLAZT
FLASH
FLASH
BLAZT
BLAZT
ZWACK
FWOOOSH!
fshhh
fshh
POW

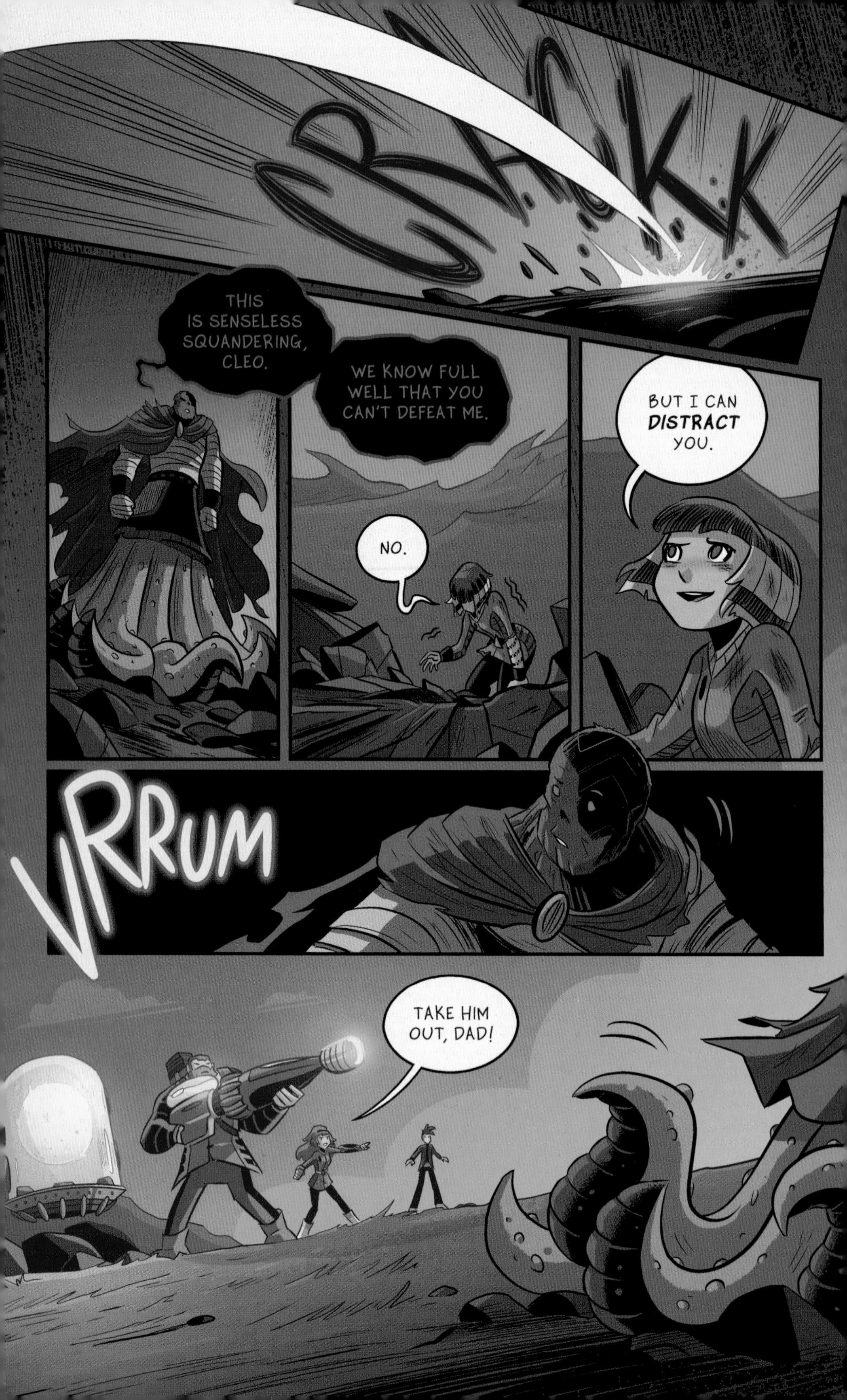
BACKK
THIS IS SENSELESS SQUANDERING, CLEO.
WE KNOW FULL WELL THAT YOU CAN'T DEFEAT ME.
NO.
BUT I CAN DISTRACT YOU.
VRRUM
TAKE HIM OUT, DAD!

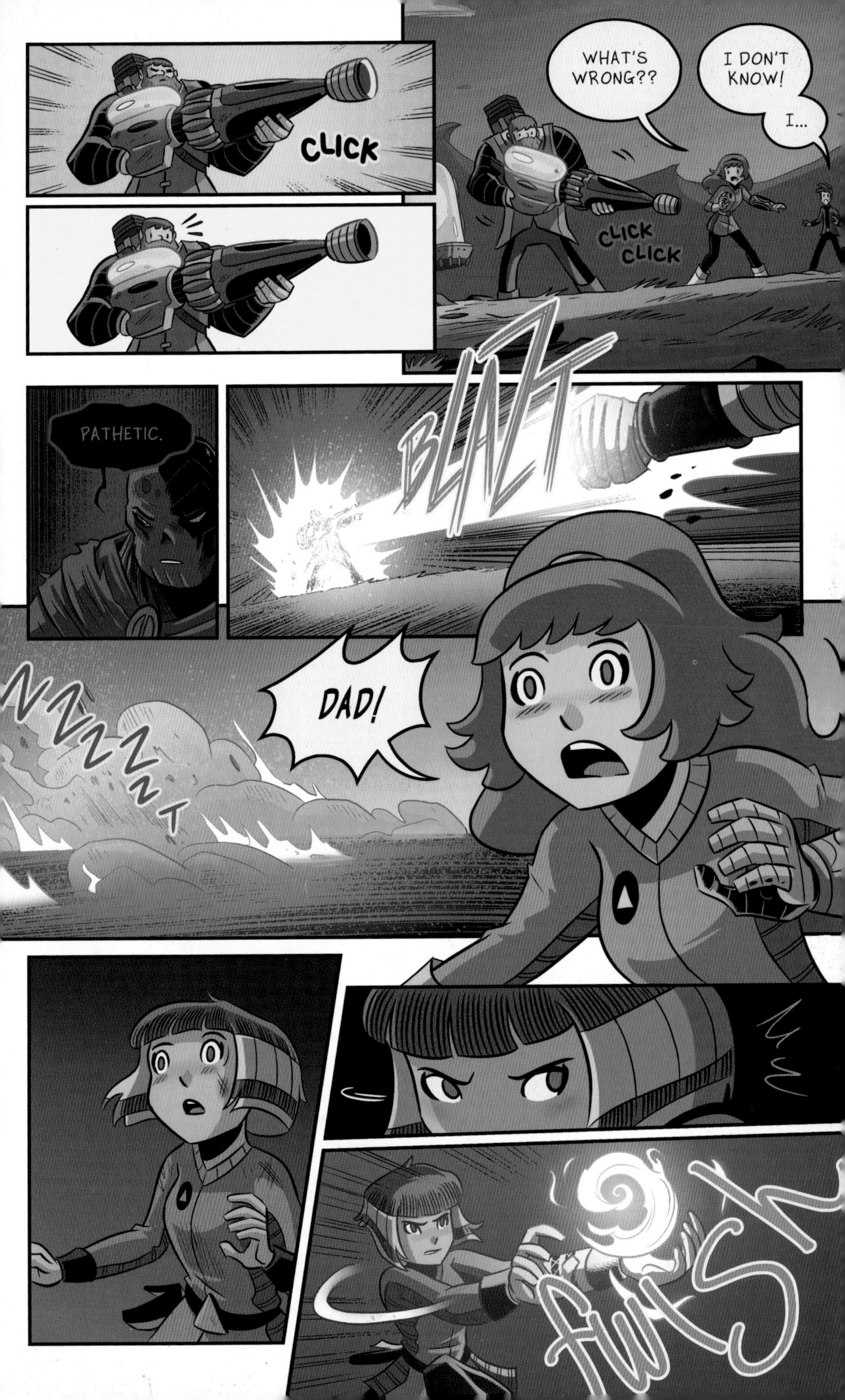
CLICK
WHAT'S WRONG??
I DON'T KNOW!
I...
CLICK CLICK
PATHETIC.
BLAZT
DAD!
FWSH

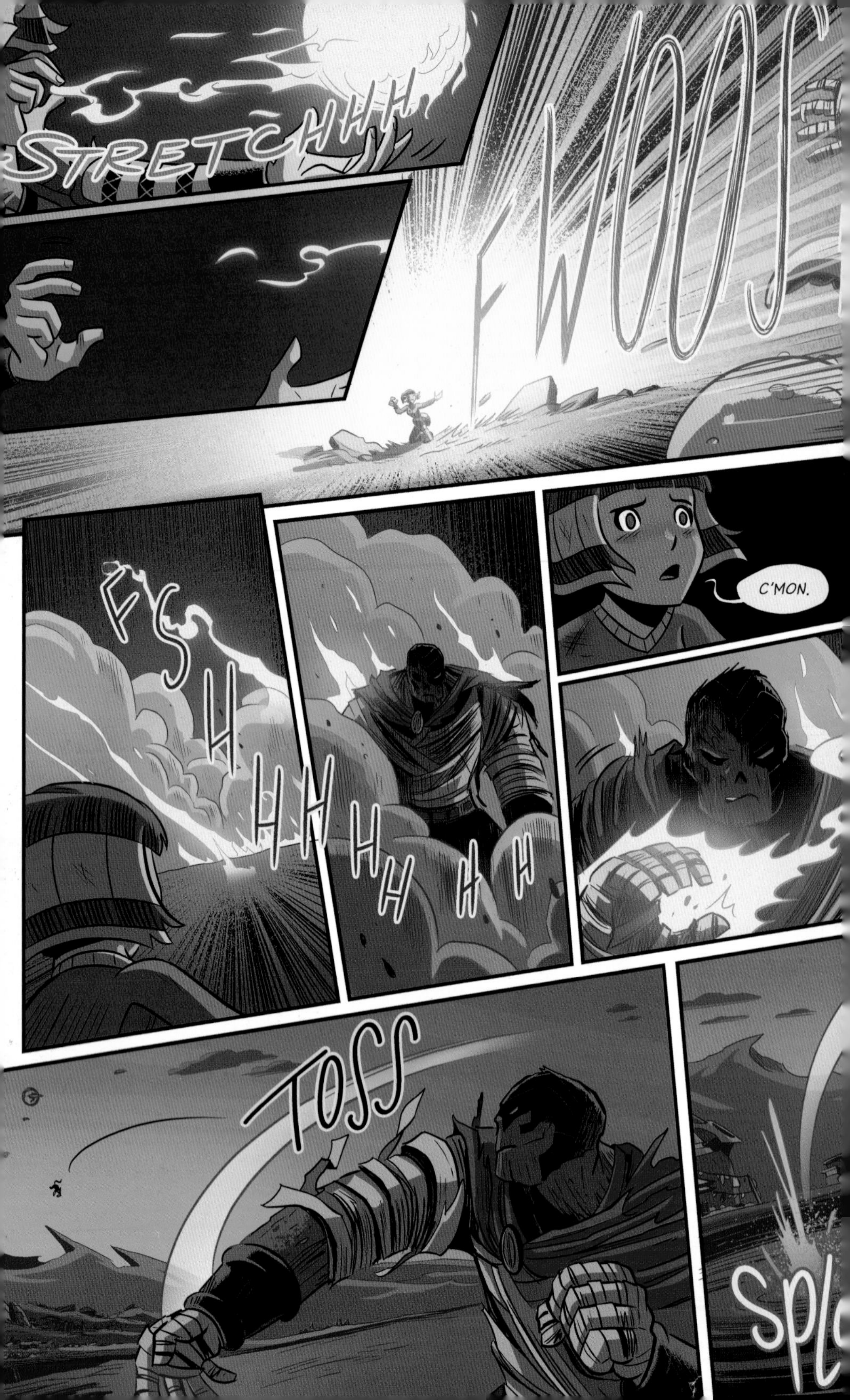
STRETCHHH
FWOOSH
FSHHHHHHH
C'MON.
TOSS
SPL

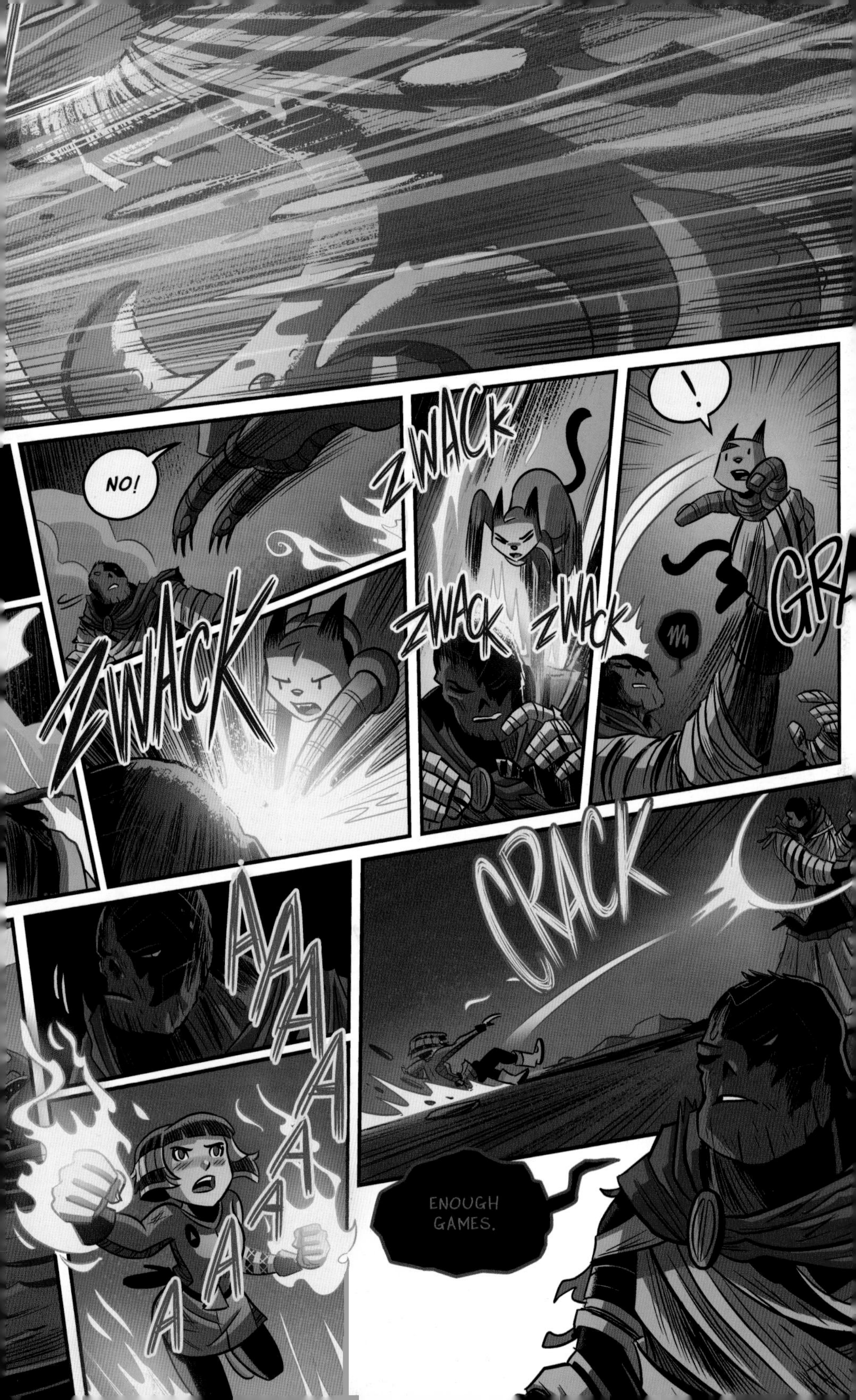
NO!
ZWACK
ZWACK
ZWACK
ZWACK
!
GRA
CRACK
AAAAAAAAA
ENOUGH GAMES.

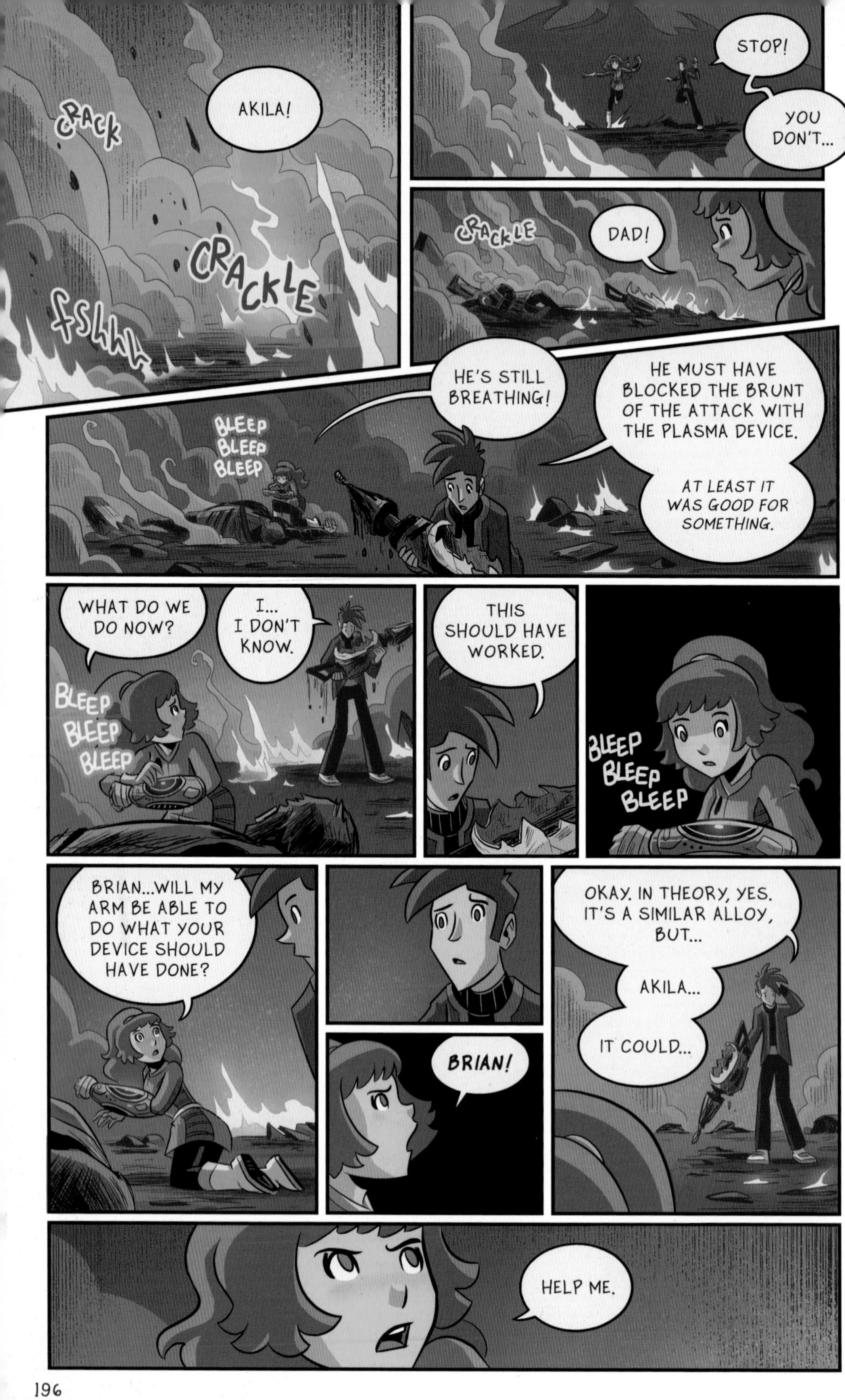
CRACK
AKILA!
CRACKLE
FSHHH
STOP!
YOU DON'T...
CRACKLE
DAD!
BLEEP BLEEP BLEEP
HE'S STILL BREATHING!
HE MUST HAVE BLOCKED THE BRUNT OF THE ATTACK WITH THE PLASMA DEVICE.
AT LEAST IT WAS GOOD FOR SOMETHING.
WHAT DO WE DO NOW?
BLEEP BLEEP BLEEP
I... I DON'T KNOW.
THIS SHOULD HAVE WORKED.
BLEEP BLEEP BLEEP
BRIAN...WILL MY ARM BE ABLE TO DO WHAT YOUR DEVICE SHOULD HAVE DONE?
BRIAN!
OKAY. IN THEORY, YES. IT'S A SIMILAR ALLOY, BUT...
AKILA...
IT COULD...
HELP ME.

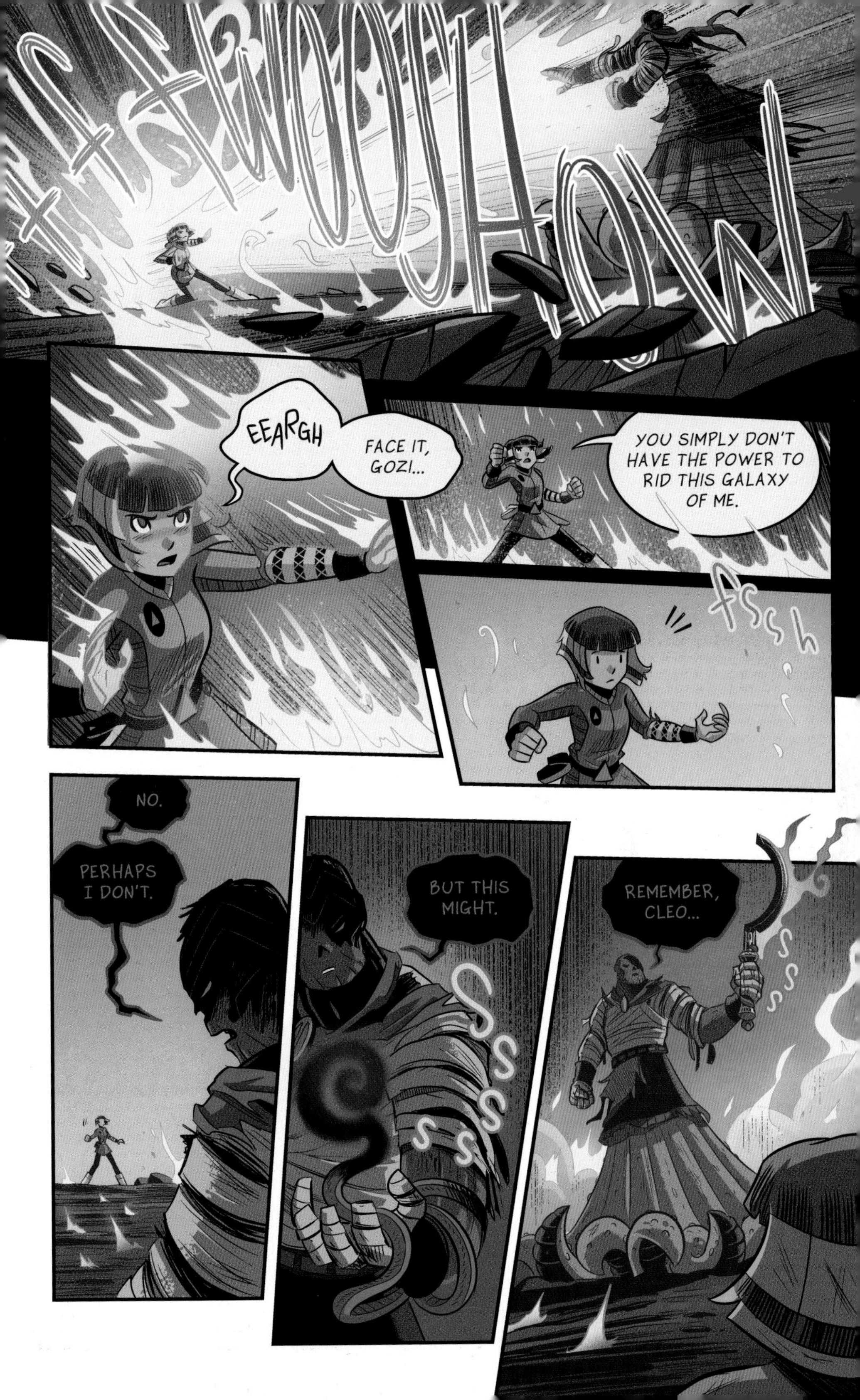
FFWOOSHOW
EEARGH
FACE IT, GOZI...
YOU SIMPLY DON'T HAVE THE POWER TO RID THIS GALAXY OF ME.
fssh
NO.
PERHAPS I DON'T.
BUT THIS MIGHT.
SSSSS
REMEMBER, CLEO...
SSS

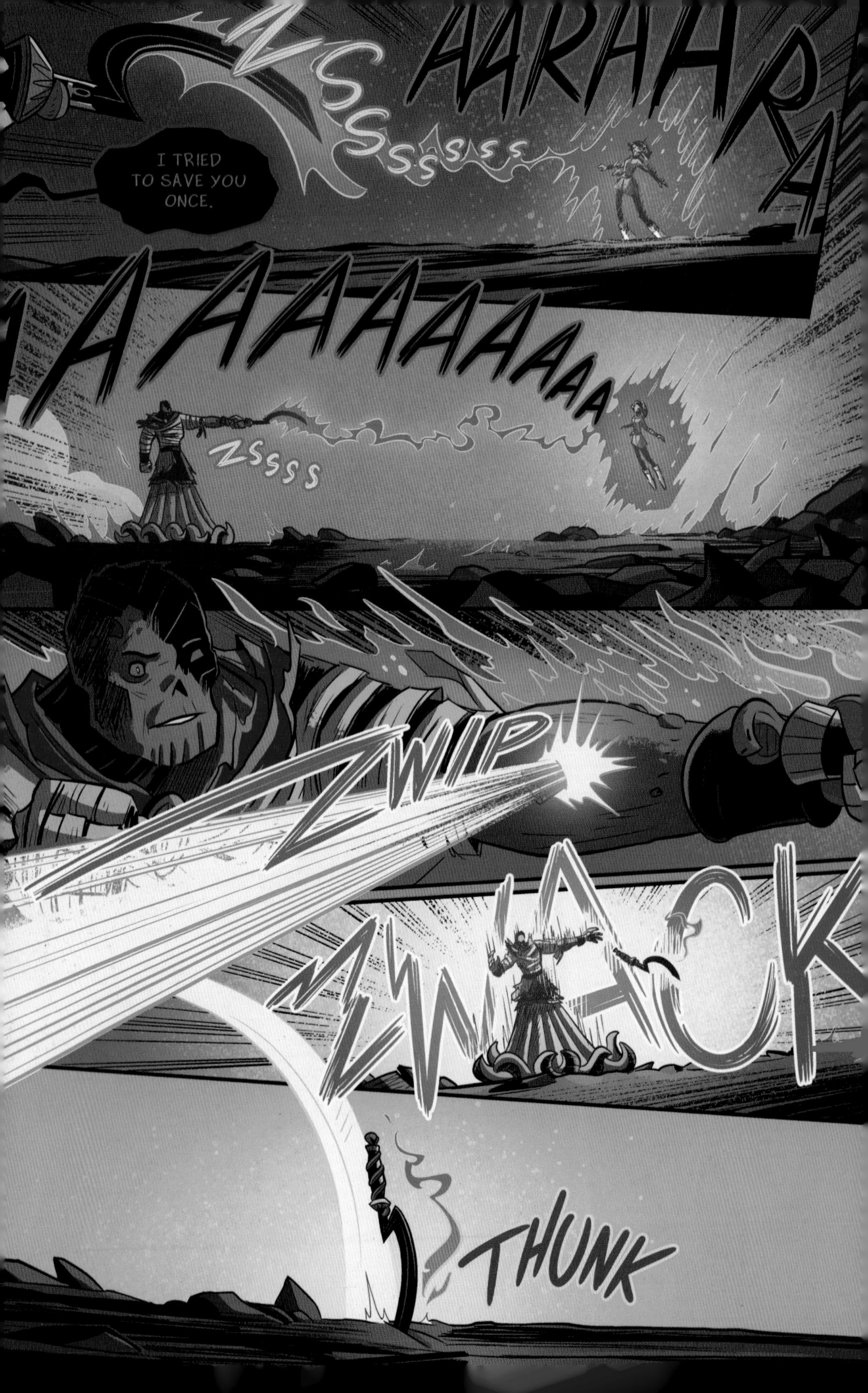

VSSSSsssss
AARHHRA
I TRIED TO SAVE YOU ONCE.
AAAAAAAAAA
ZSSSS
ZWIP
ZWACK
THUNK

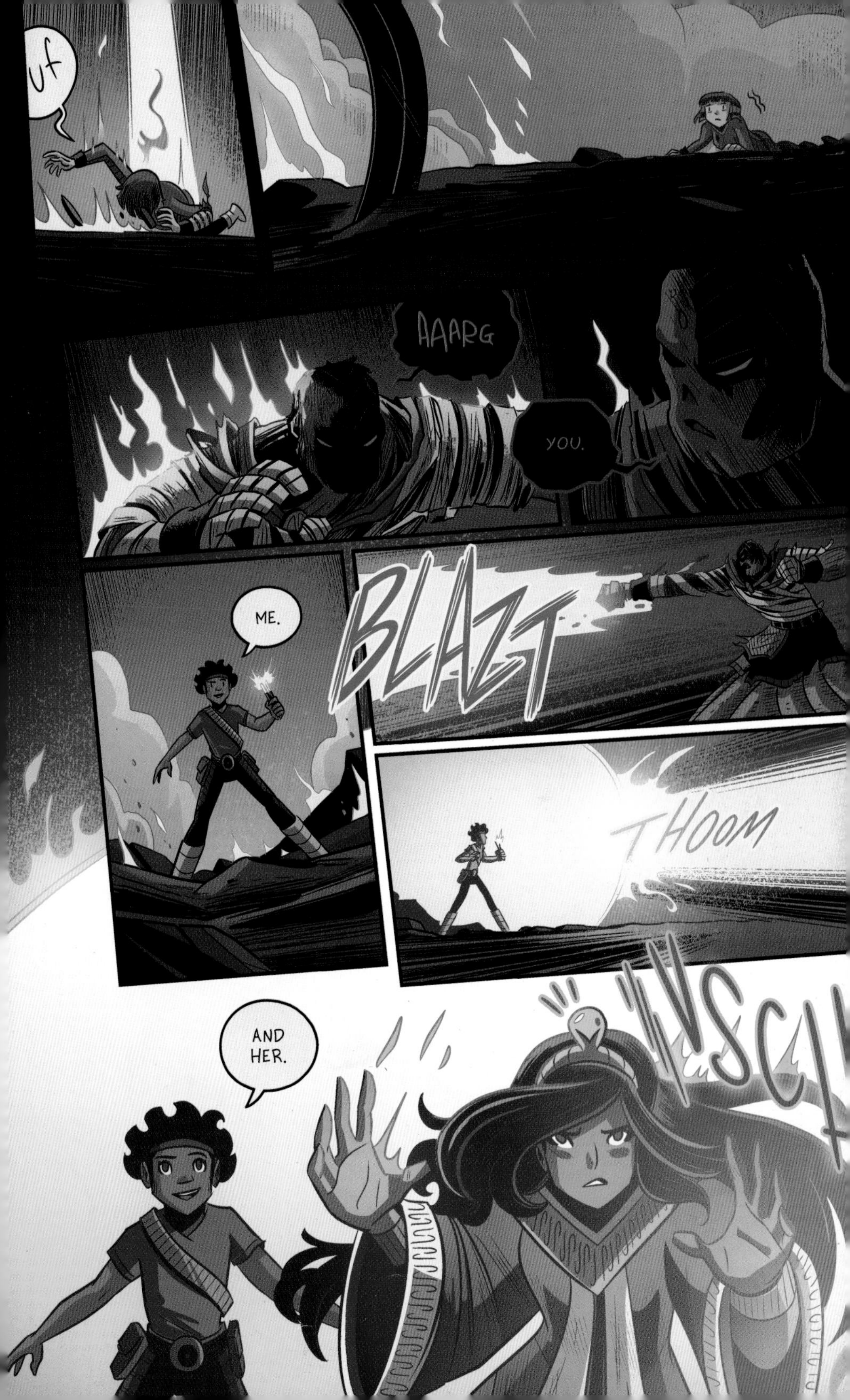
uf
AAARG
YOU.
ME.
BLAZT
THOOM
AND HER.
SCH

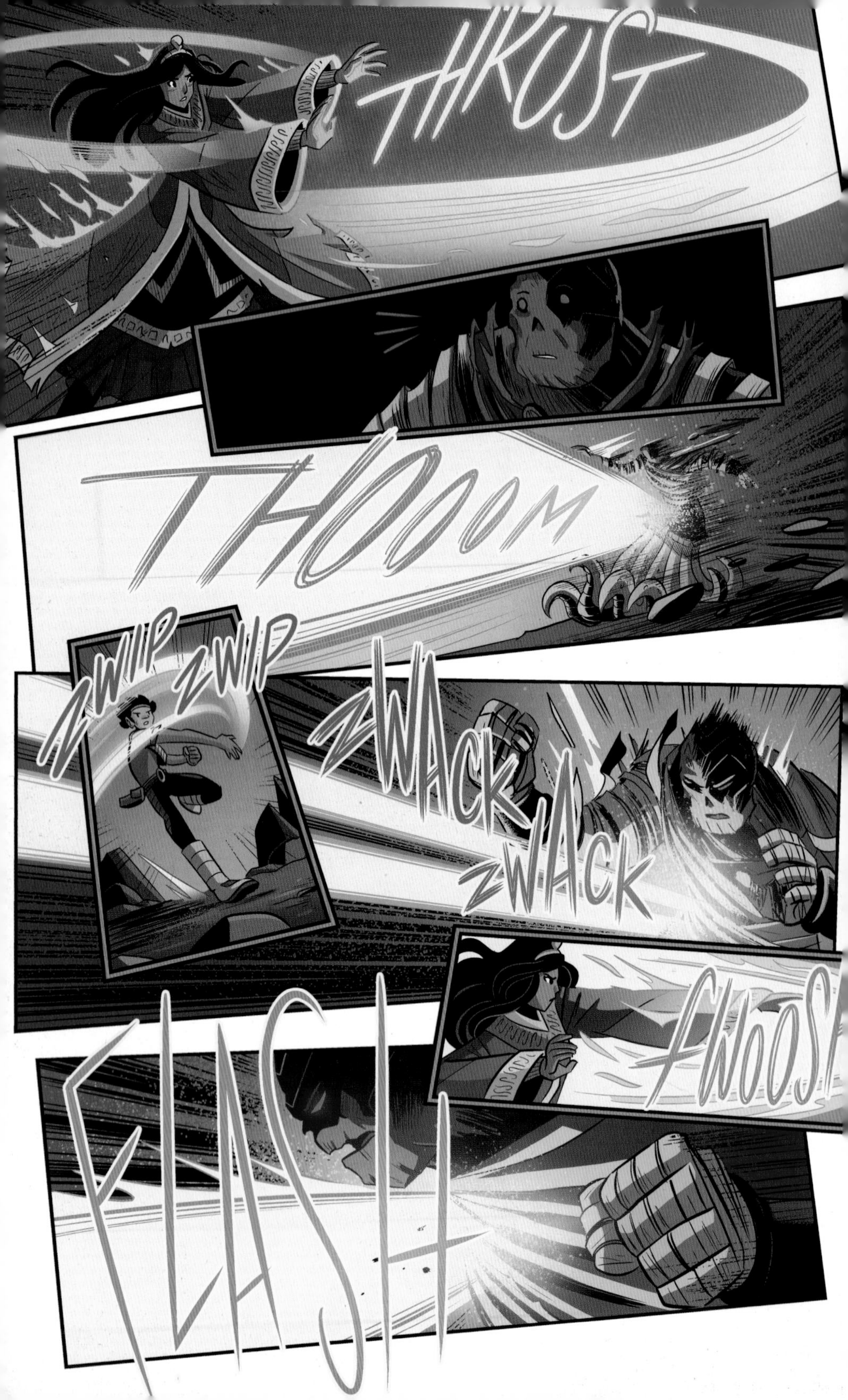
THKOST
THOOOM
ZWIP ZWIP
ZWACK ZWACK
FWOOSH
FLASH

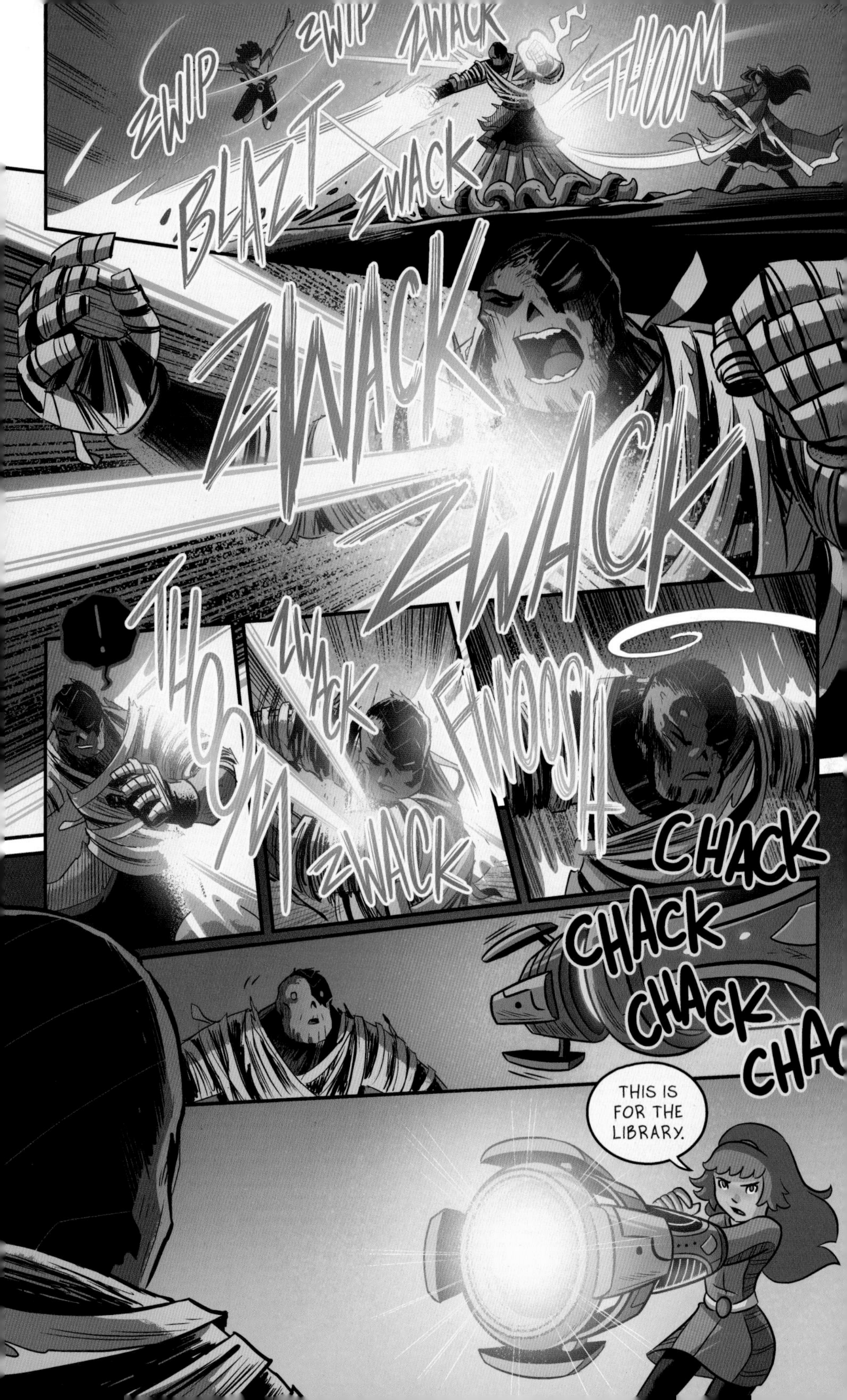
ZWIP
ZWIP
ZWIP
ZWACK
THOOM
BLAZT
ZWACK
ZWACK
ZWACK
!
THOOM
ZWACK
FWOOSH
ZWACK
CHACK
CHACK
CHACK
CHAC
THIS IS FOR THE LIBRARY.

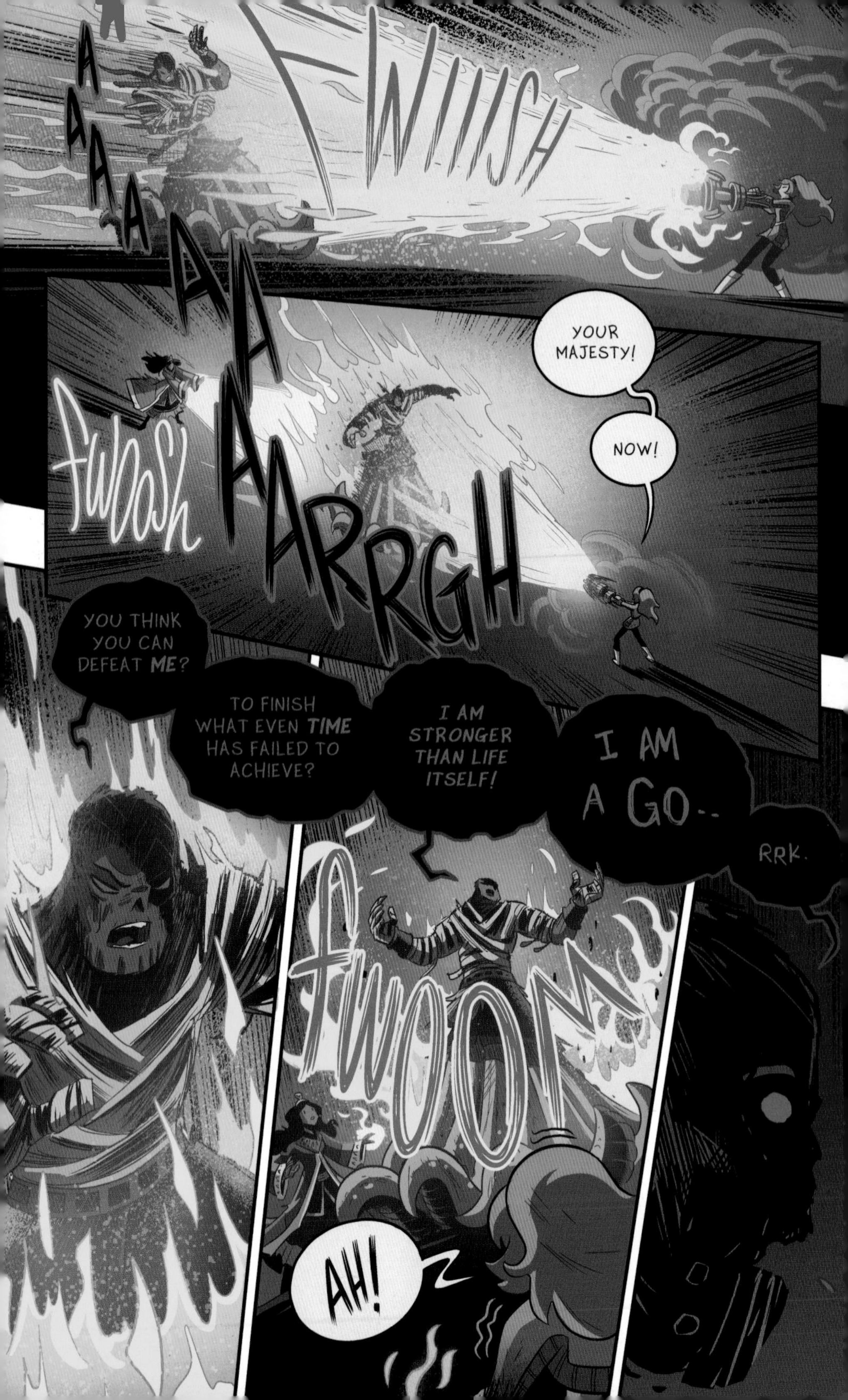
AAAAAAAAAARRGH
FWIISH
YOUR MAJESTY!
NOW!
FWOOSH
YOU THINK YOU CAN DEFEAT ME?
TO FINISH WHAT EVEN TIME HAS FAILED TO ACHIEVE?
I AM STRONGER THAN LIFE ITSELF!
I AM A GO--
RRK.
FWOOM
AH!

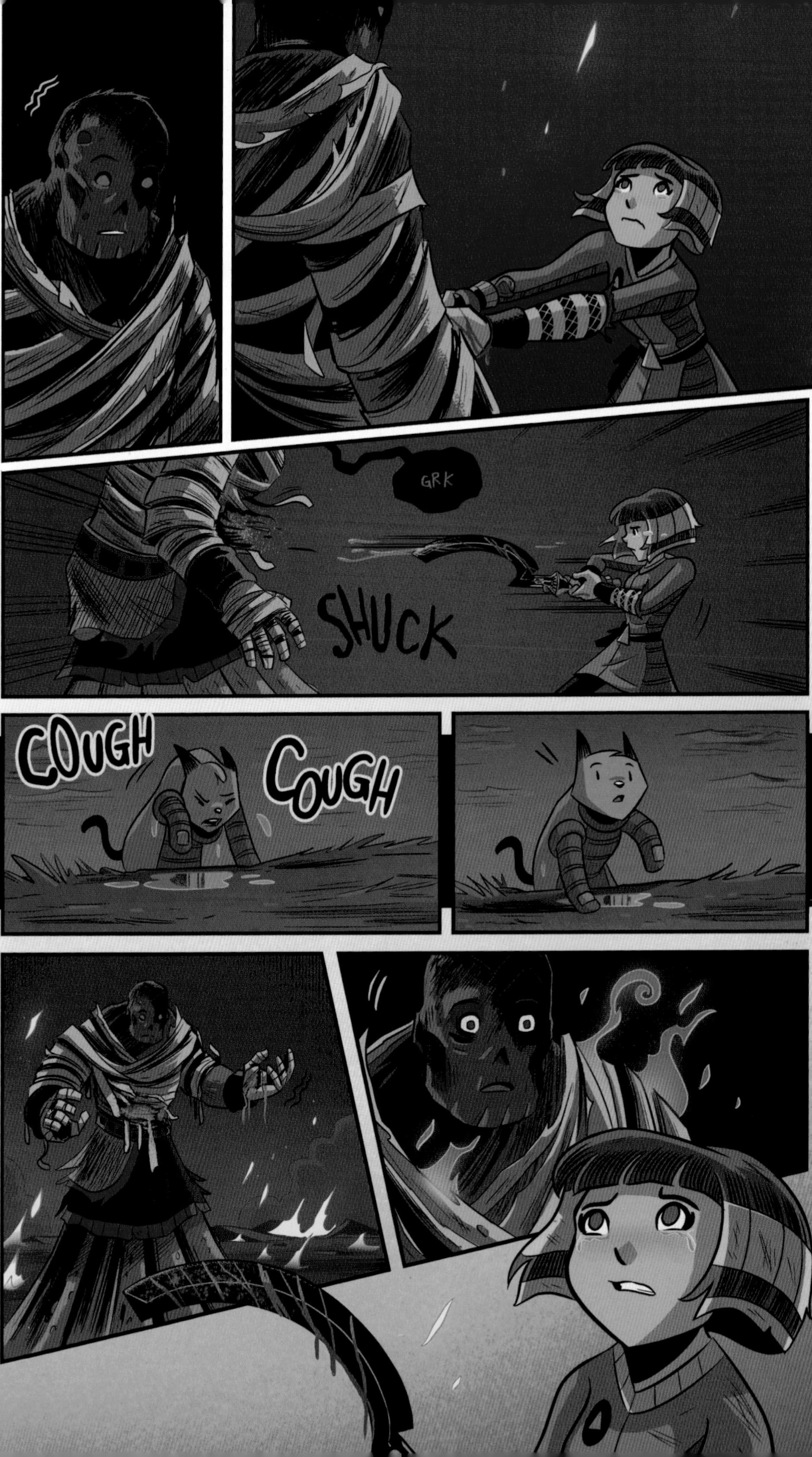
GRK
SHUCK
COUGH
COUGH

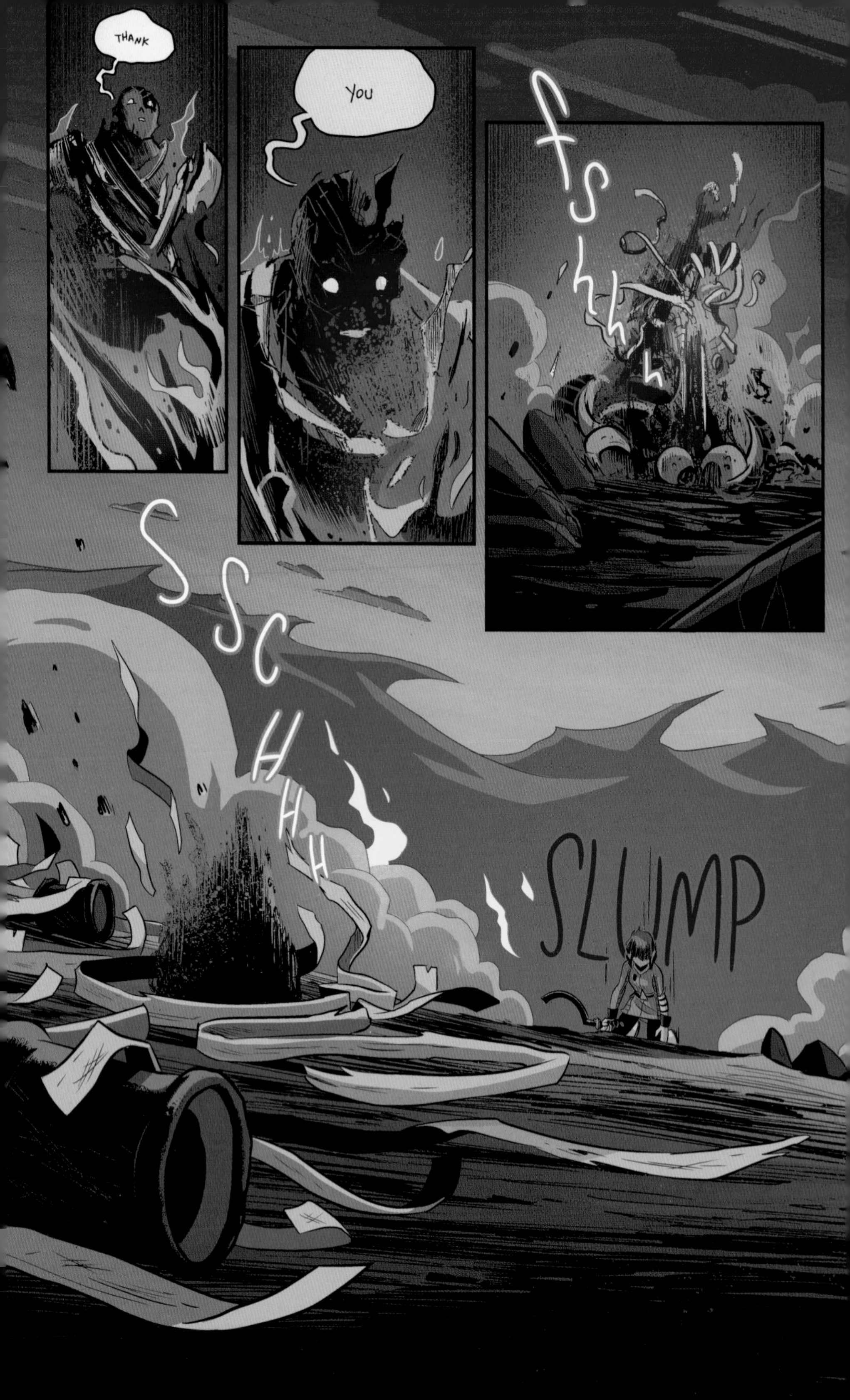
THANK
YOU
fsshhhh
SSCHHHH
SLUMP

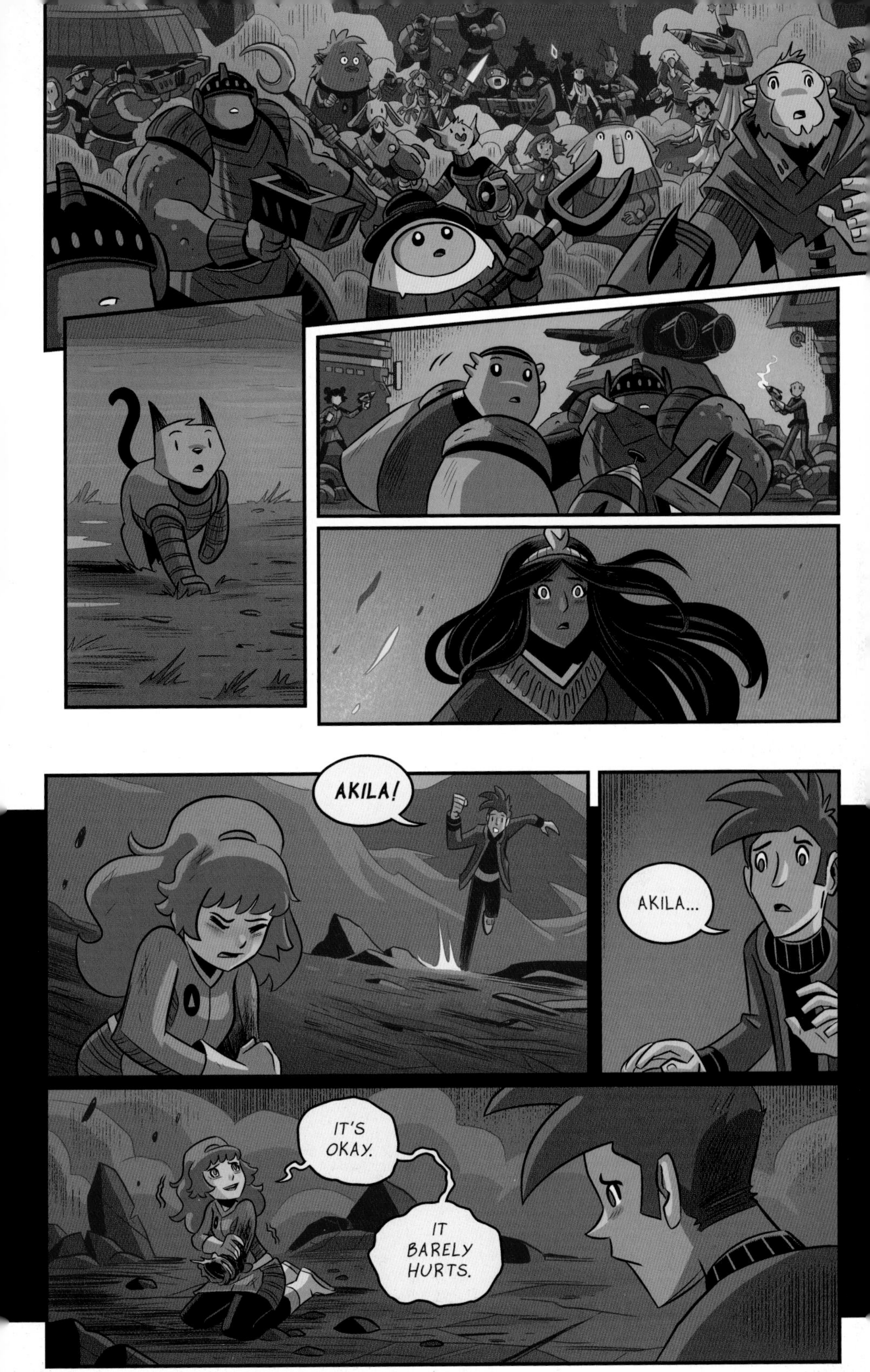
AKILA!
AKILA...
IT'S OKAY.
IT BARELY HURTS.

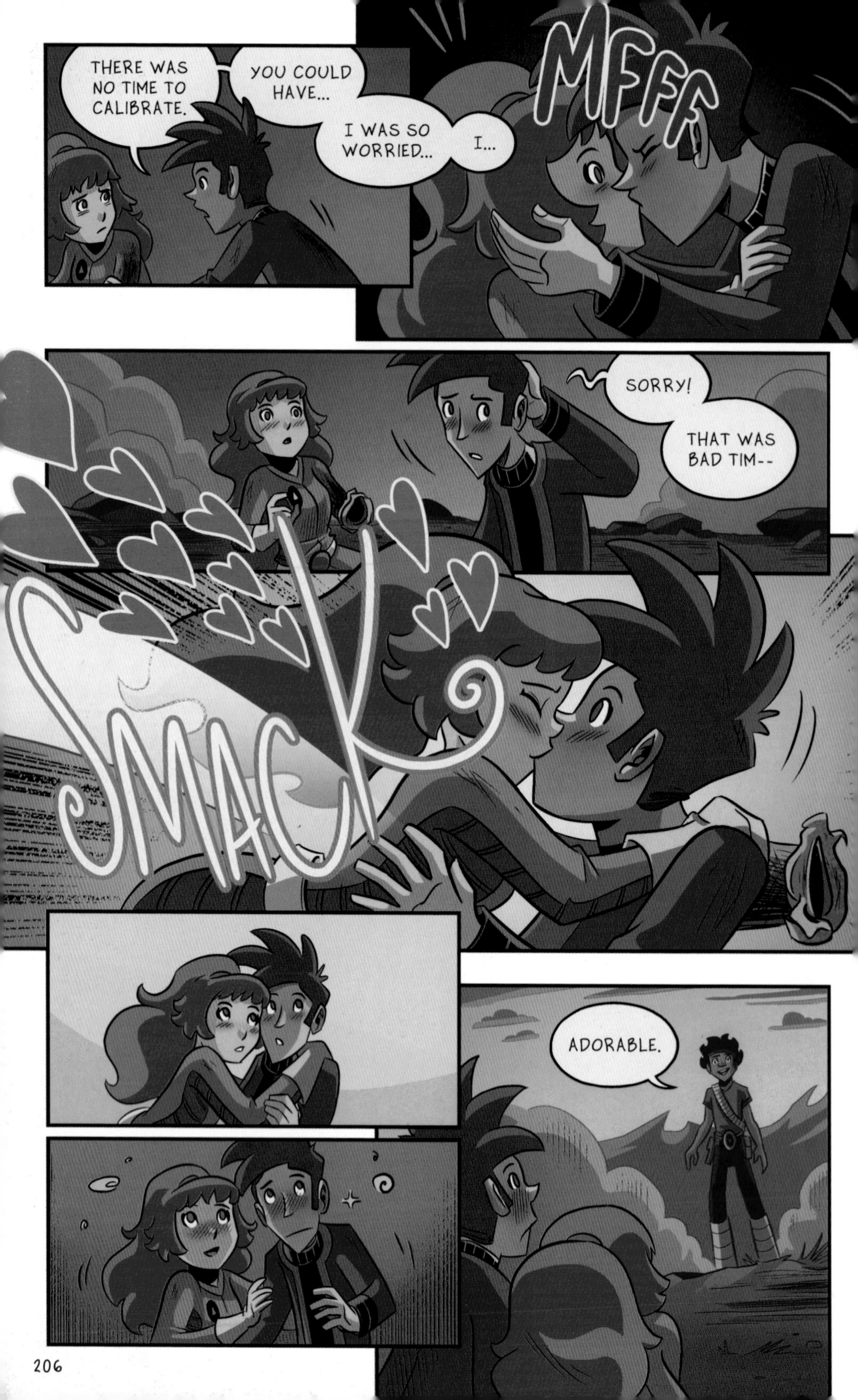
THERE WAS NO TIME TO CALIBRATE.
YOU COULD HAVE...
I WAS SO WORRIED...
I...
MFFF
SORRY!
THAT WAS BAD TIM--
SMACK
ADORABLE.

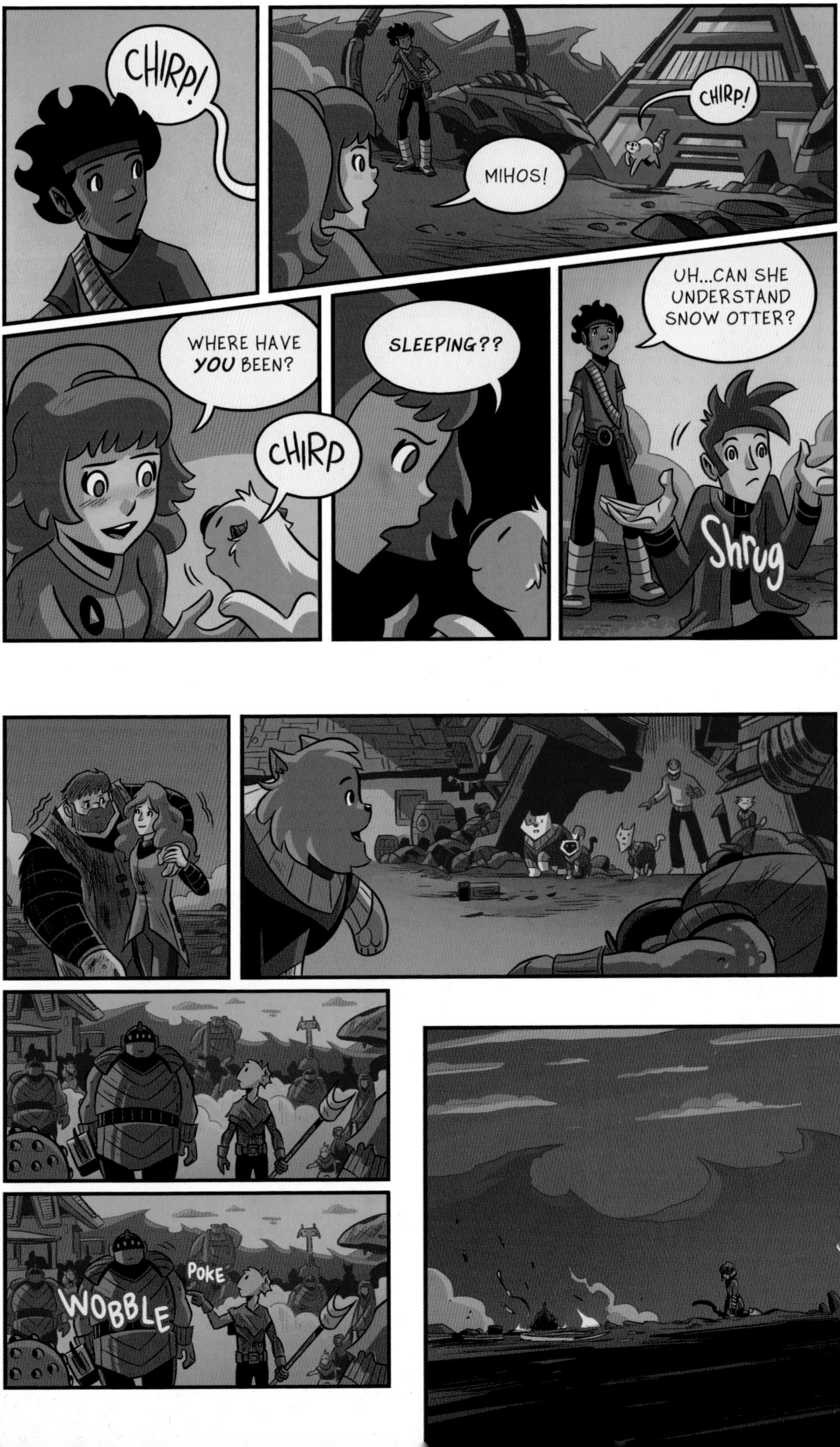
CHIRP!
CHIRP!
MIHOS!
WHERE HAVE YOU BEEN?
CHIRP
SLEEPING??
UH...CAN SHE UNDERSTAND SNOW OTTER?
Shrug
WOBBLE
POKE

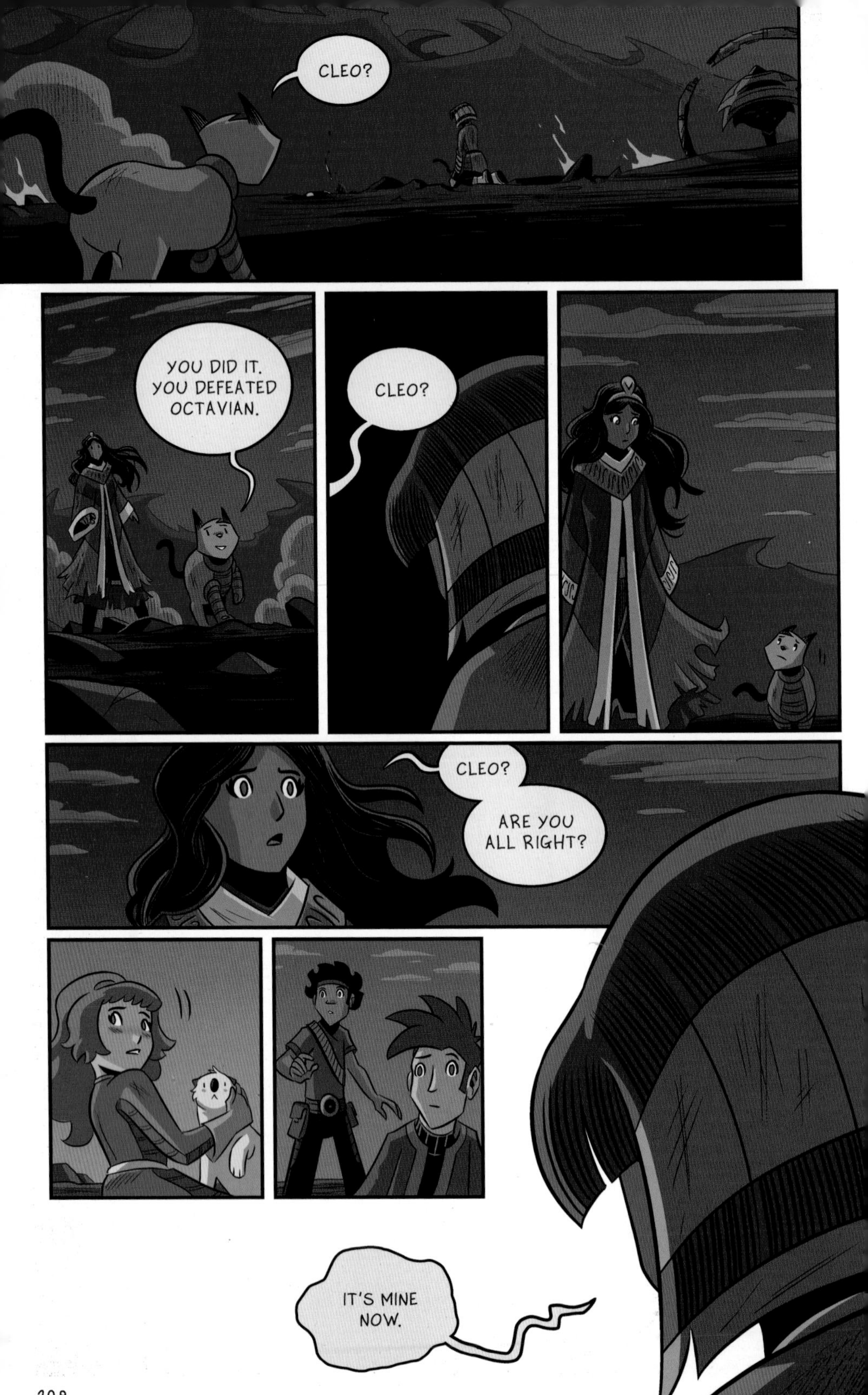
CLEO?
YOU DID IT. YOU DEFEATED OCTAVIAN.
CLEO?
CLEO?
ARE YOU ALL RIGHT?
IT'S MINE NOW.

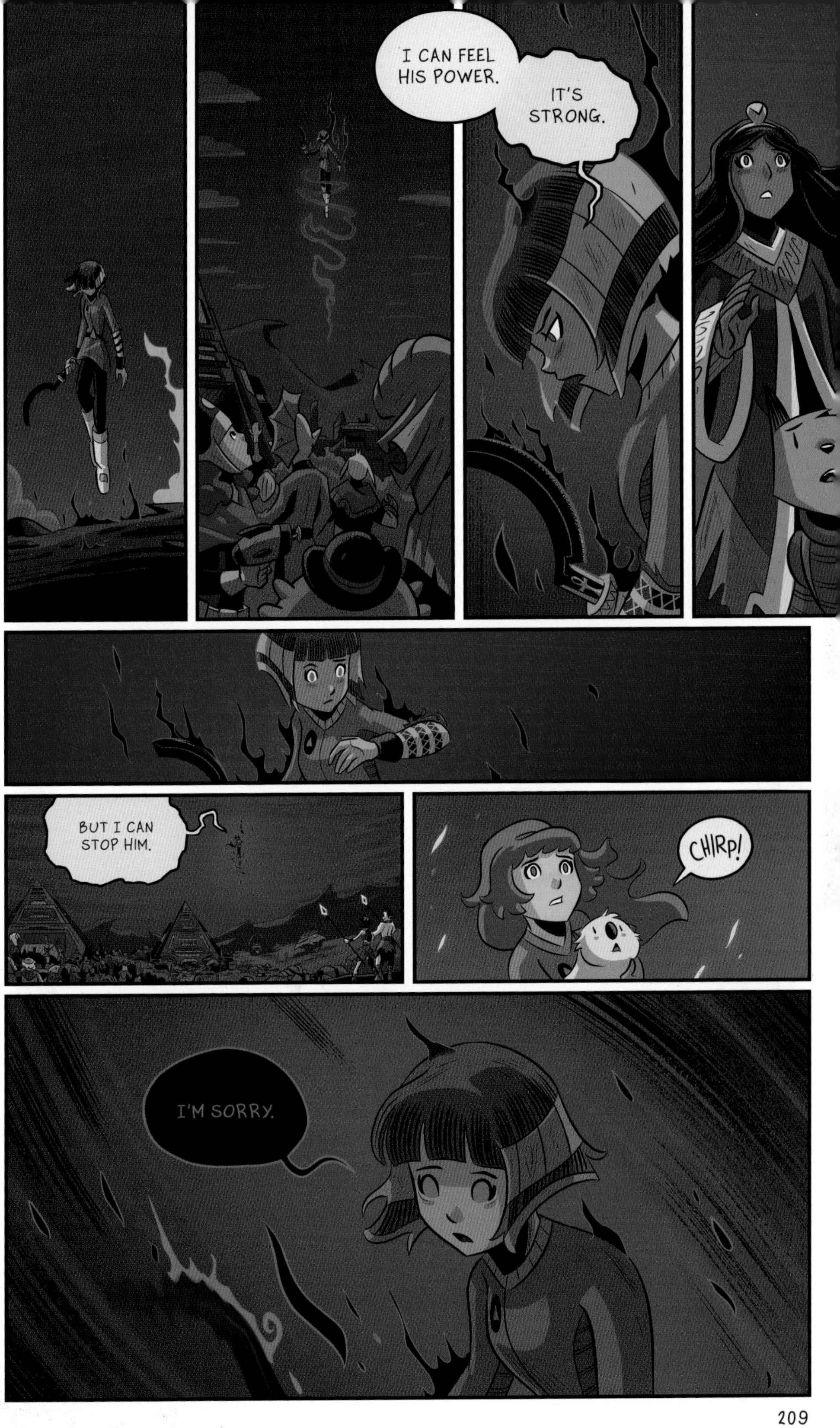
I CAN FEEL HIS POWER.
IT'S STRONG.
BUT I CAN STOP HIM.
CHIRP!
I'M SORRY.

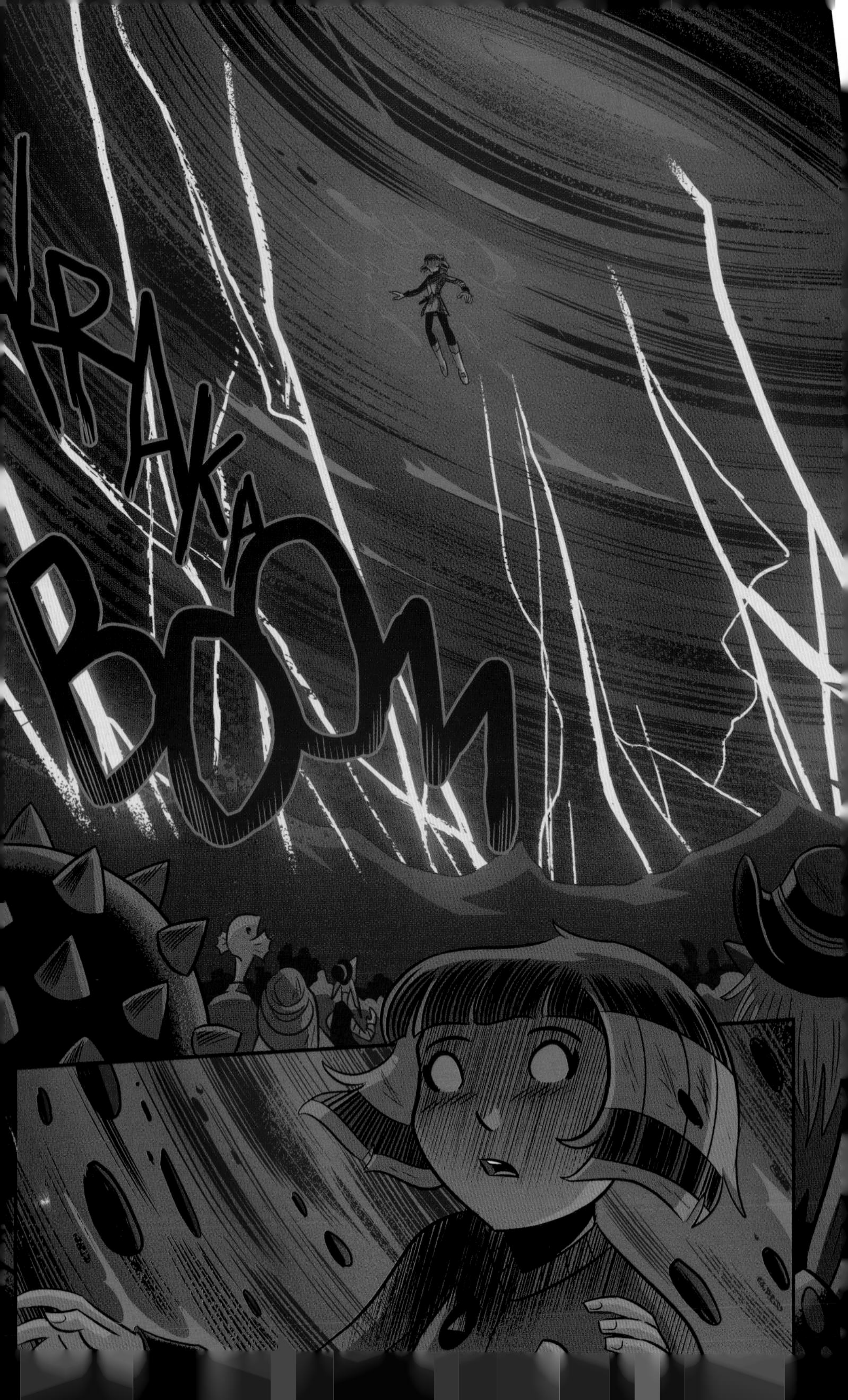
RAKA
BOOM

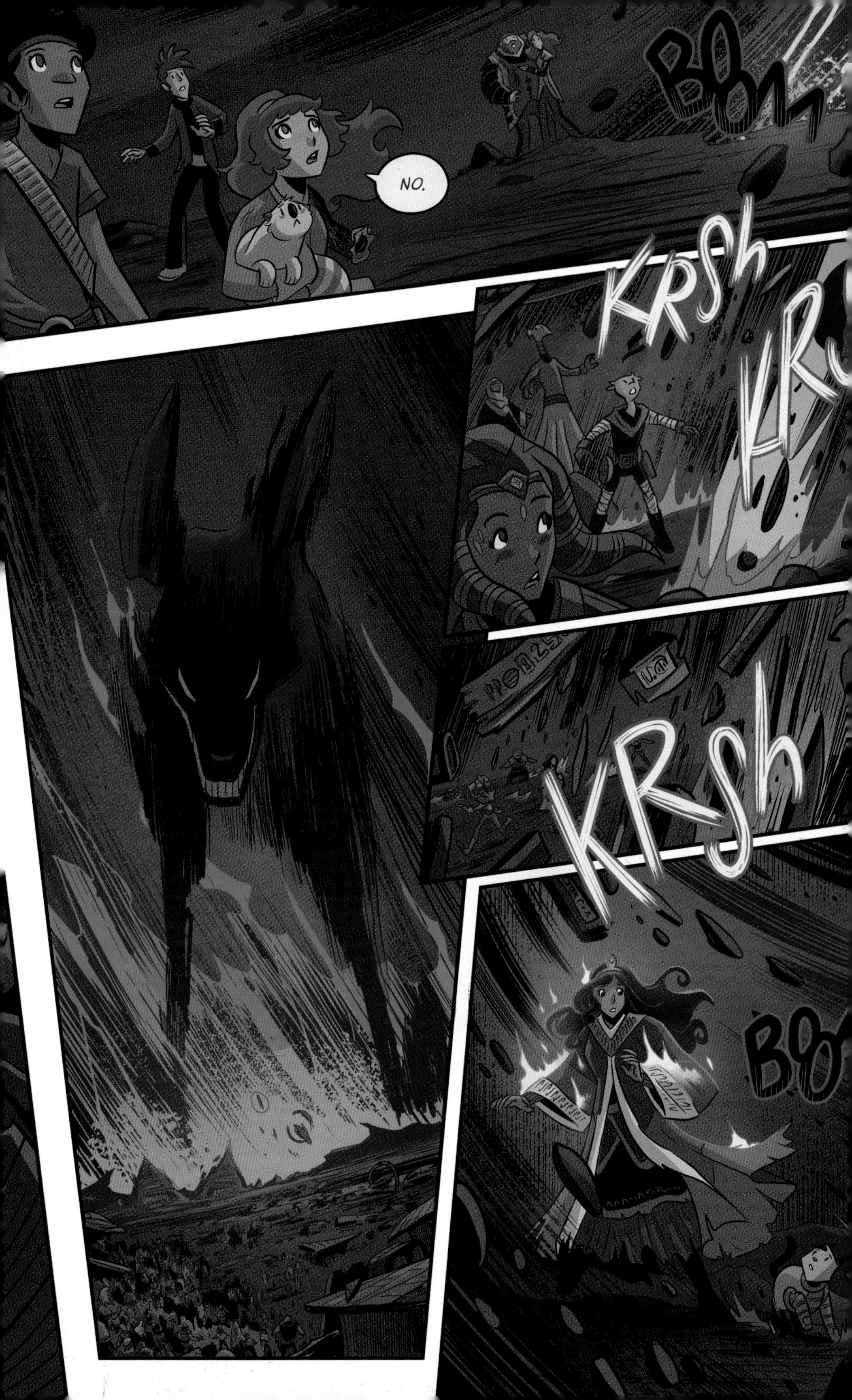
BOOM
NO.
KRSH
KRSH
KRSH
BOO

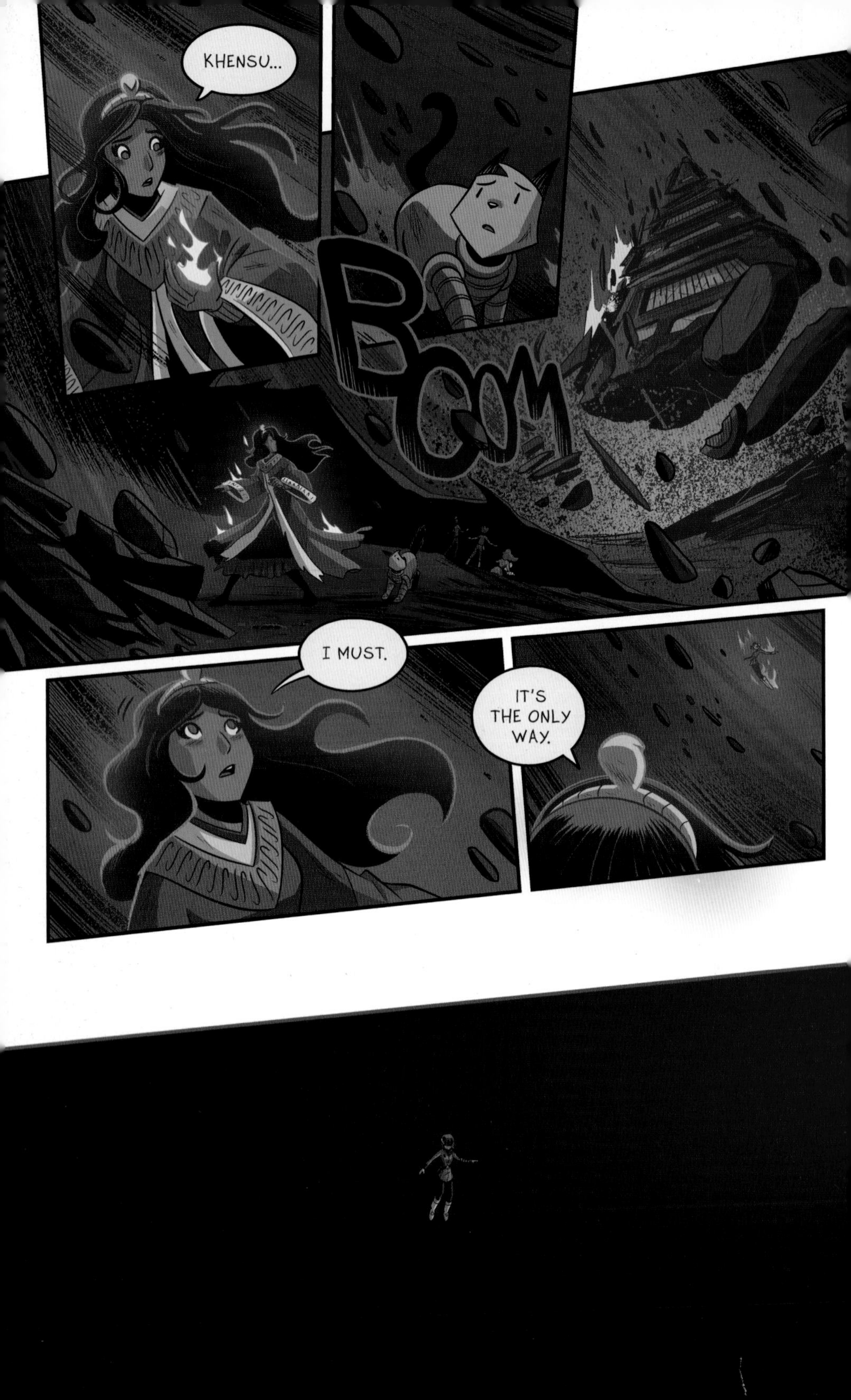
KHENSU...
BOOM
I MUST.
IT'S THE ONLY WAY.

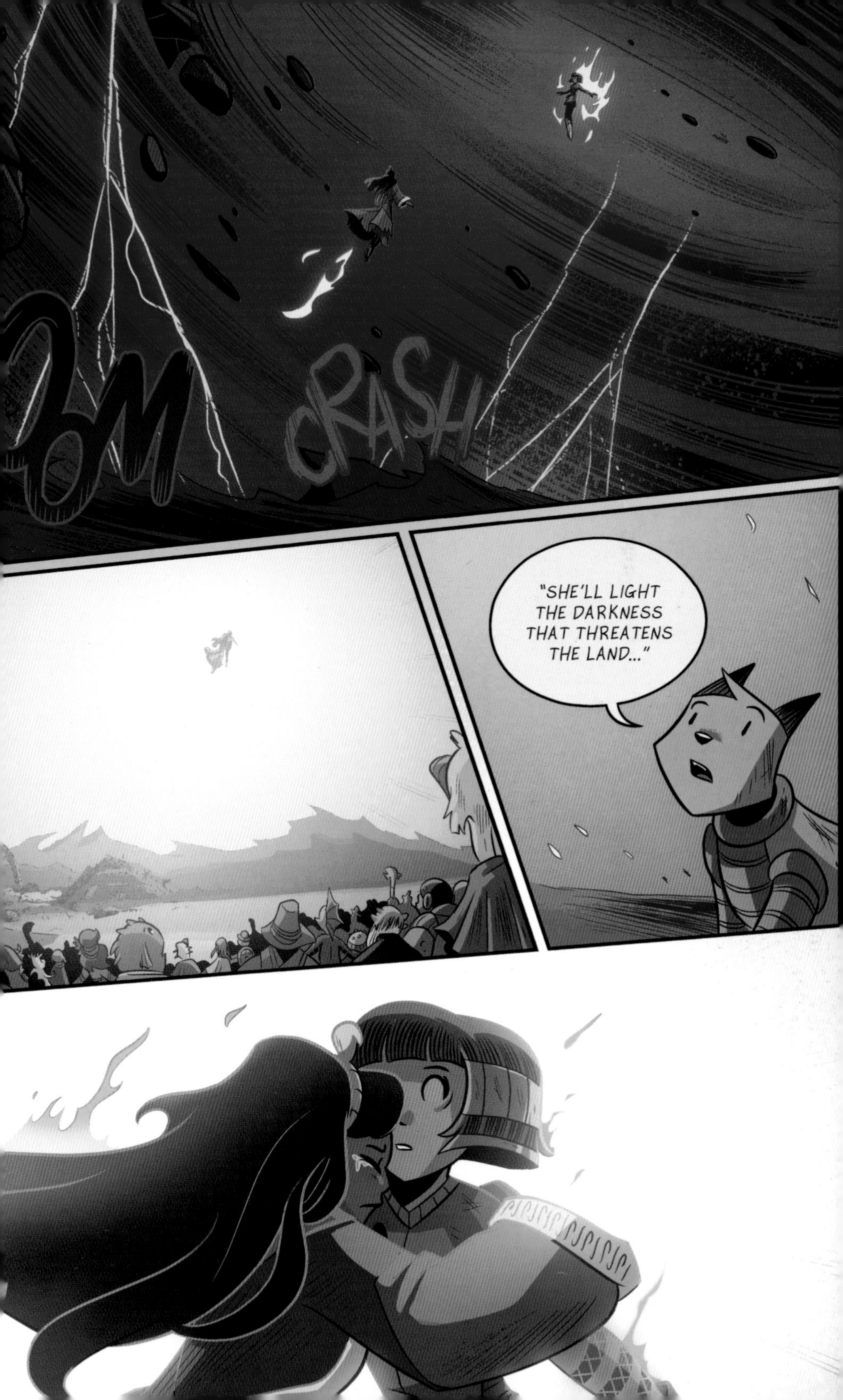

CRASH
"SHE'LL LIGHT THE DARKNESS THAT THREATENS THE LAND..."

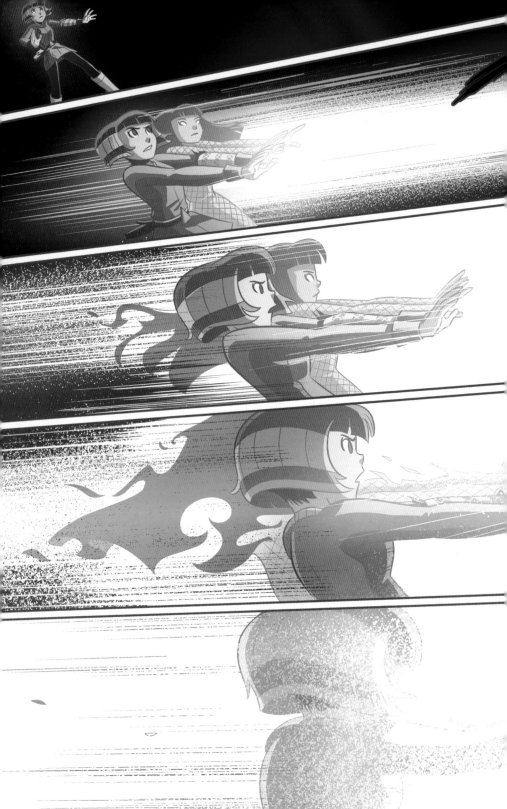

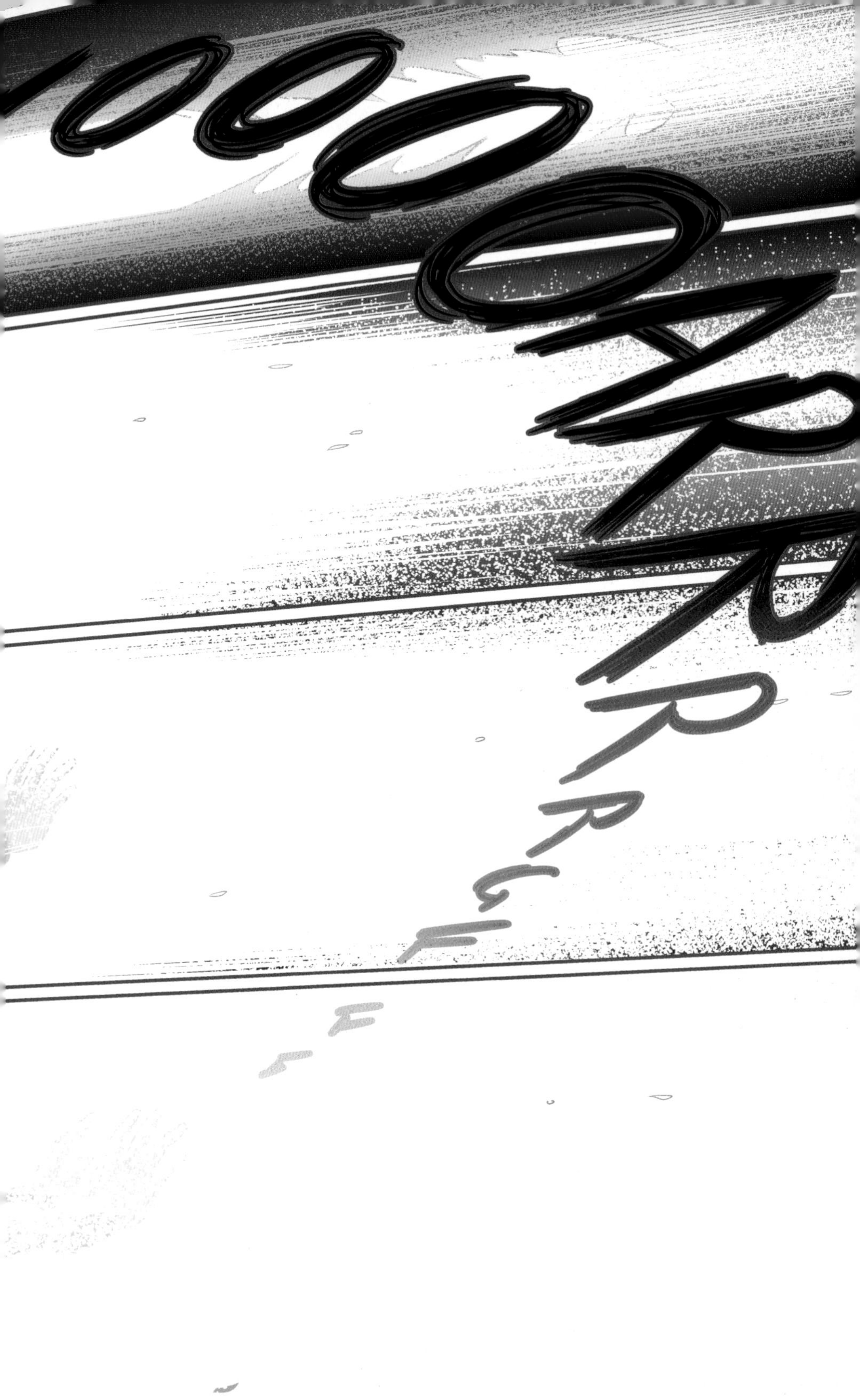
OOOOARRR

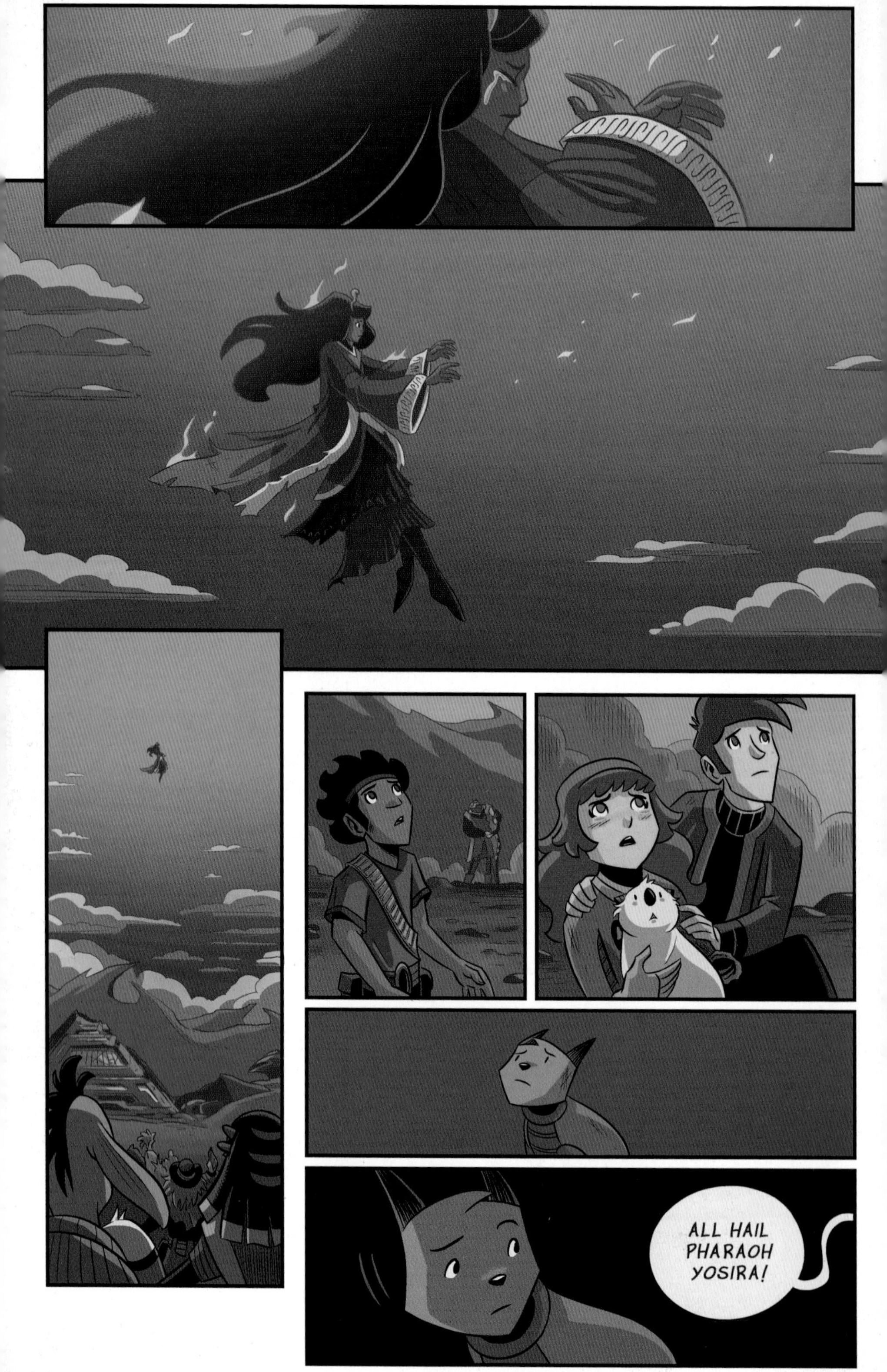
ALL HAIL PHARAOH YOSIRA!

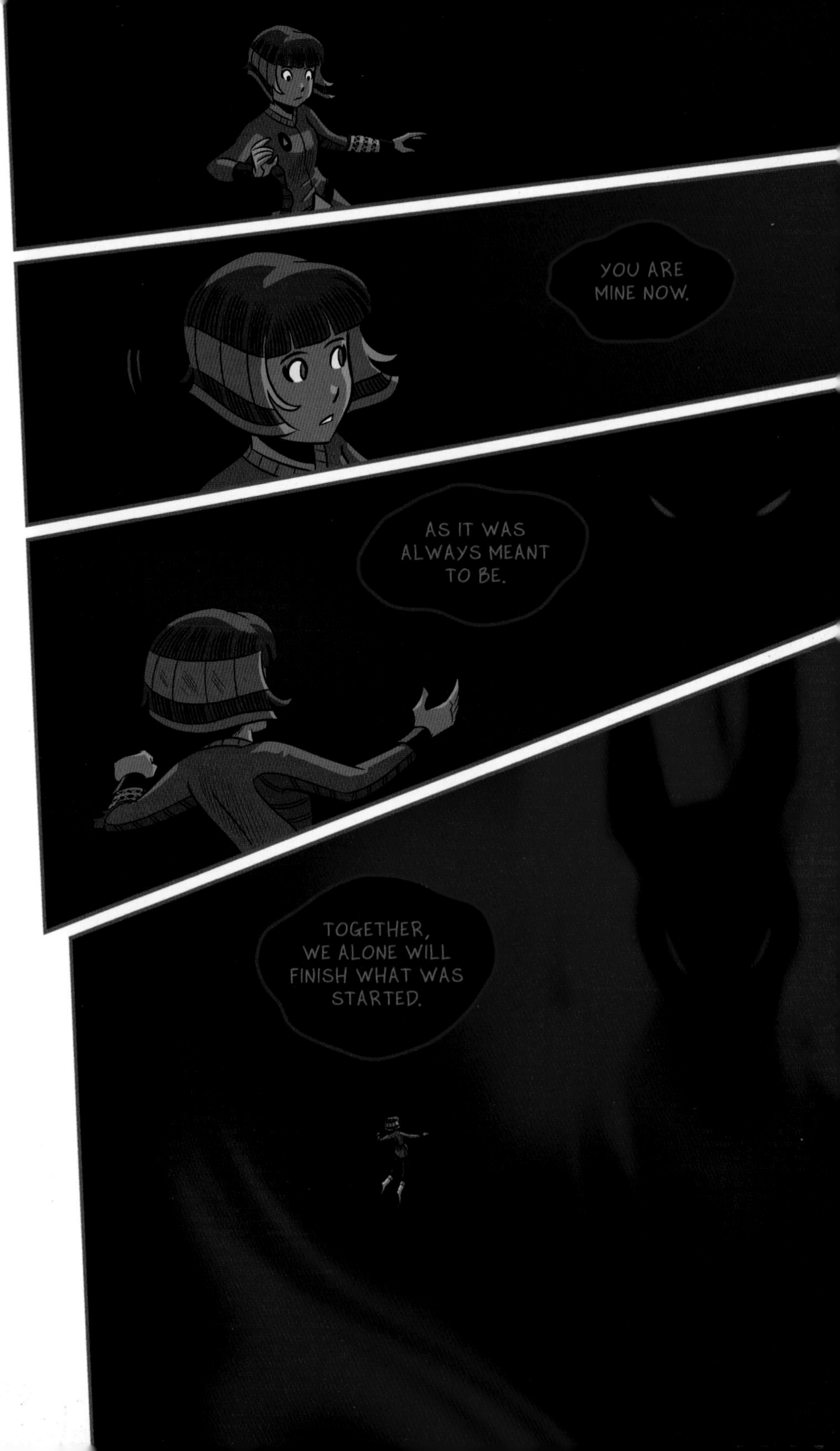
YOU ARE MINE NOW.
AS IT WAS ALWAYS MEANT TO BE.
TOGETHER, WE ALONE WILL FINISH WHAT WAS STARTED.

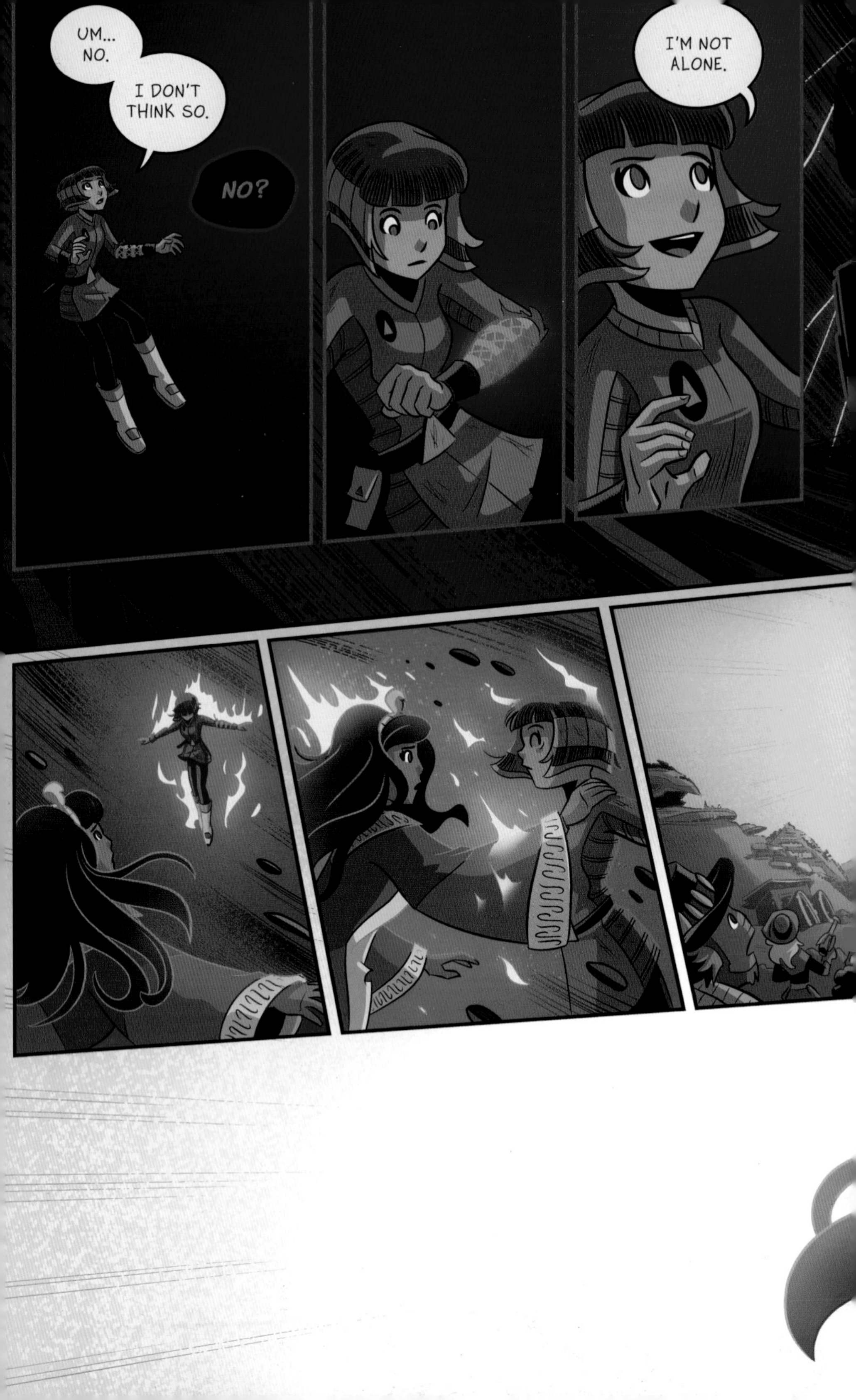
UM... NO.
I DON'T THINK SO.
NO?
I'M NOT ALONE.

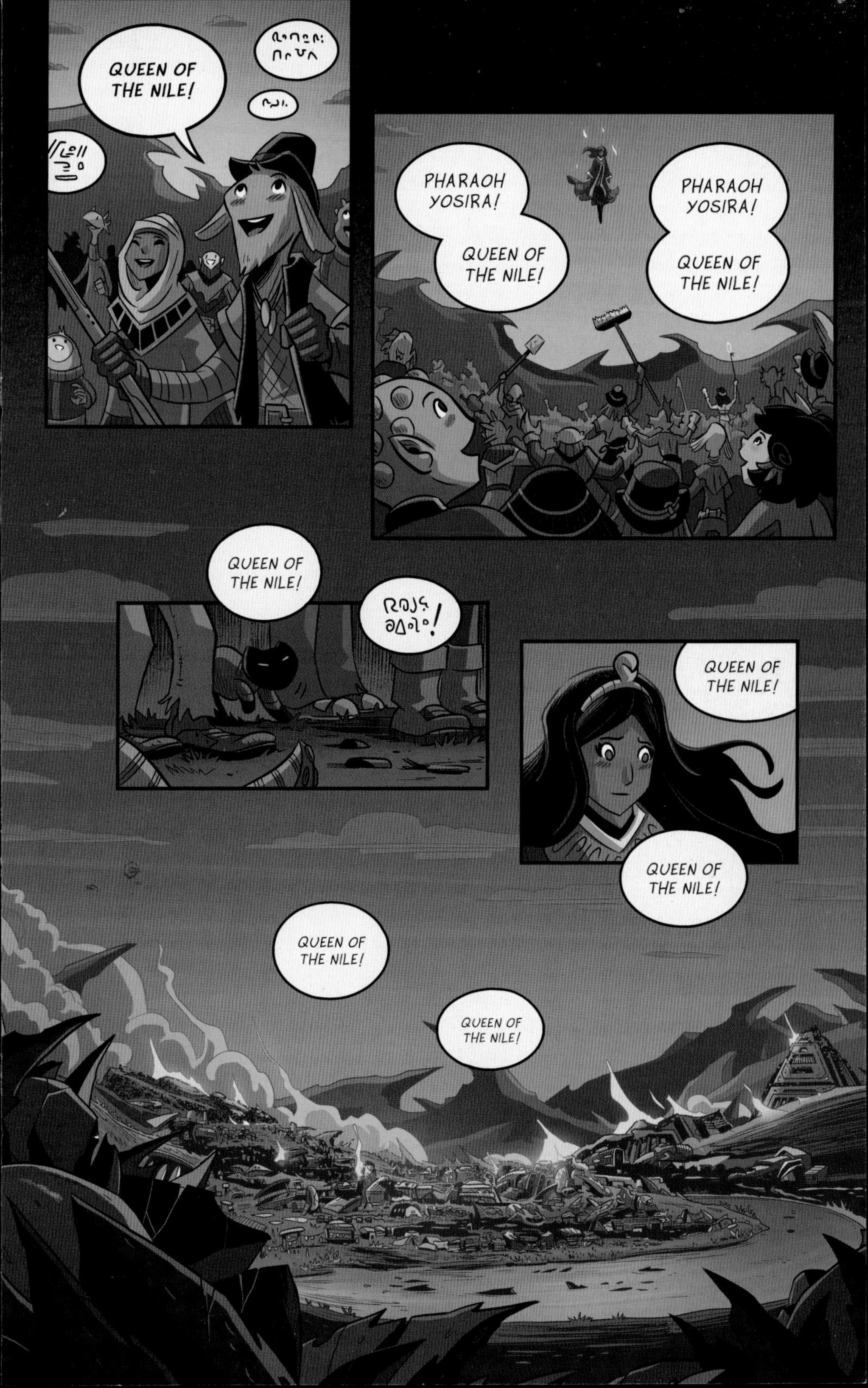
QUEEN OF THE NILE!
PHARAOH YOSIRA!
QUEEN OF THE NILE!
PHARAOH YOSIRA!
QUEEN OF THE NILE!
QUEEN OF THE NILE!
QUEEN OF THE NILE!
QUEEN OF THE NILE!
QUEEN OF THE NILE!
QUEEN OF THE NILE!

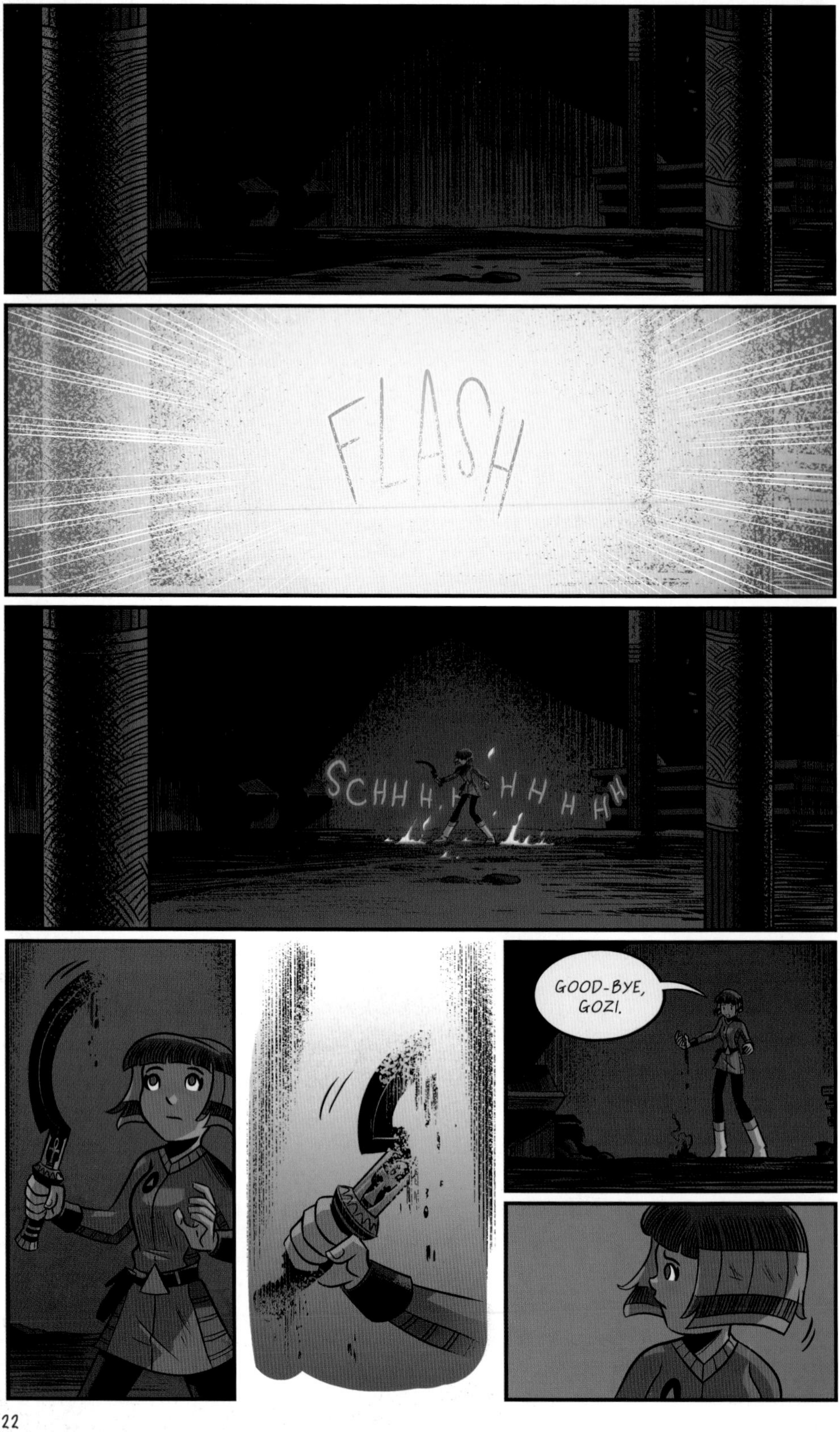
FLASH
SCHHH...HHHHHHH
GOOD-BYE, GOZI.

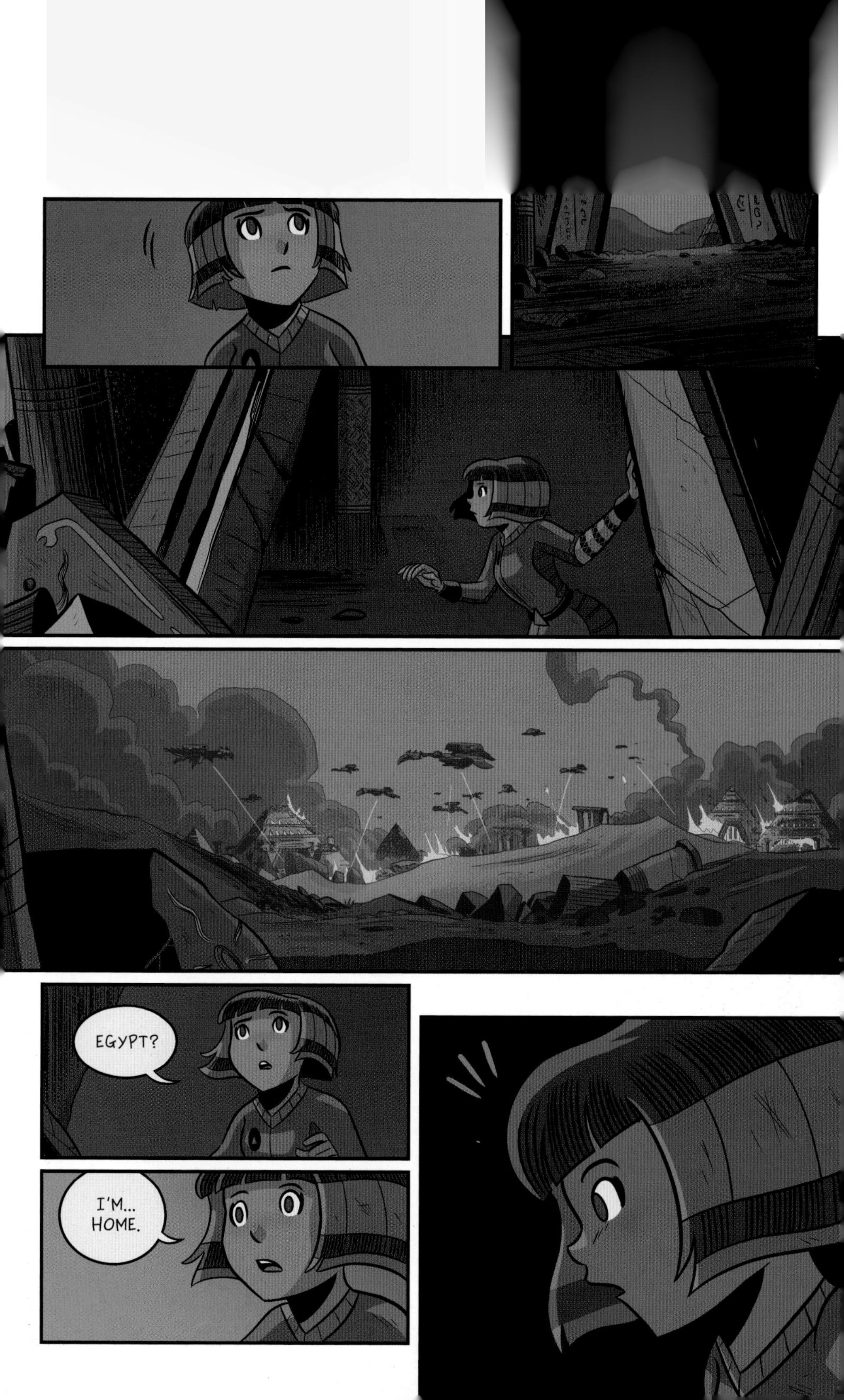
EGYPT?
I'M... HOME.

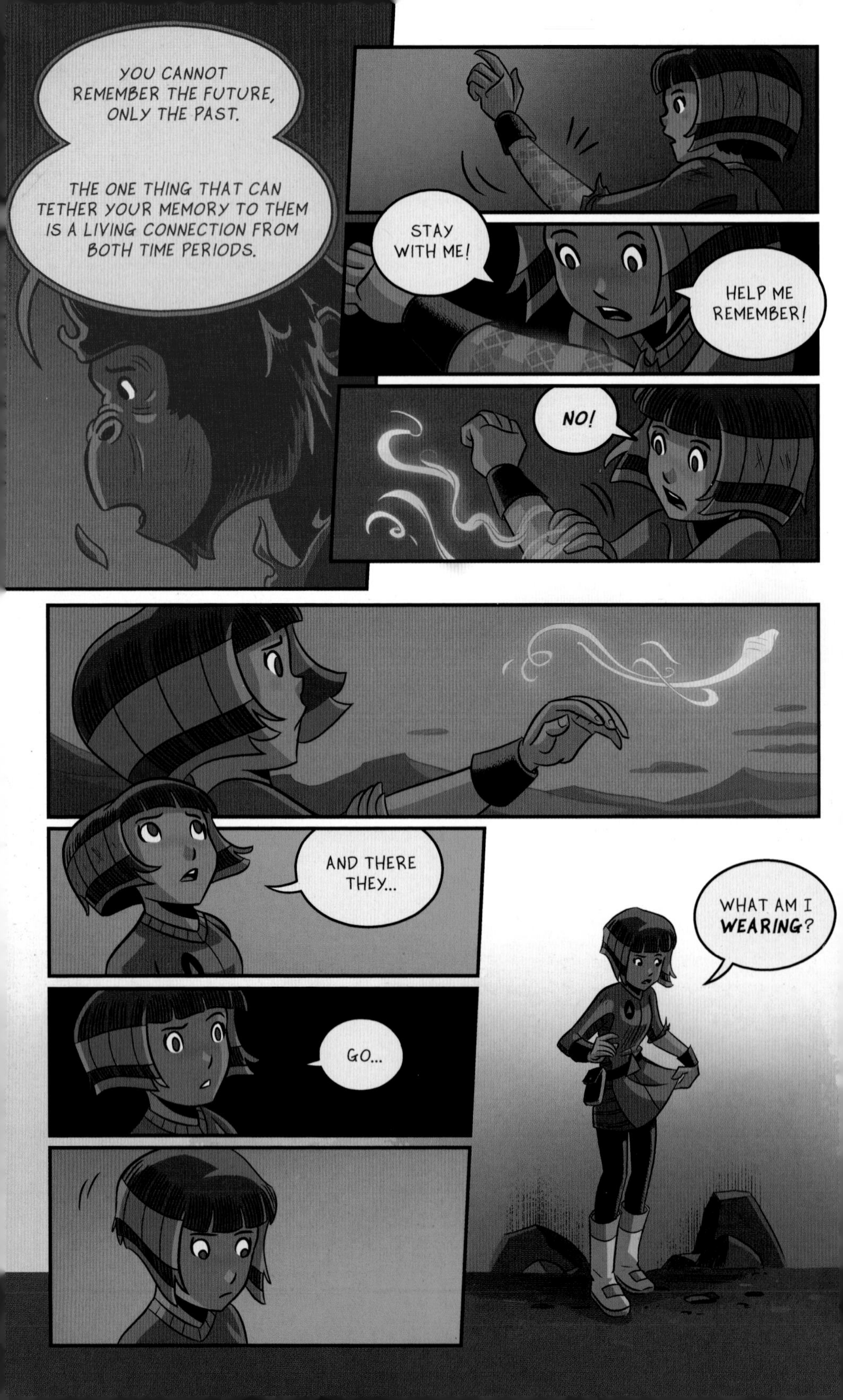
YOU CANNOT REMEMBER THE FUTURE, ONLY THE PAST.
THE ONE THING THAT CAN TETHER YOUR MEMORY TO THEM IS A LIVING CONNECTION FROM BOTH TIME PERIODS.
STAY WITH ME!
HELP ME REMEMBER!
NO!
AND THERE THEY...
GO...
WHAT AM I **WEARING**?

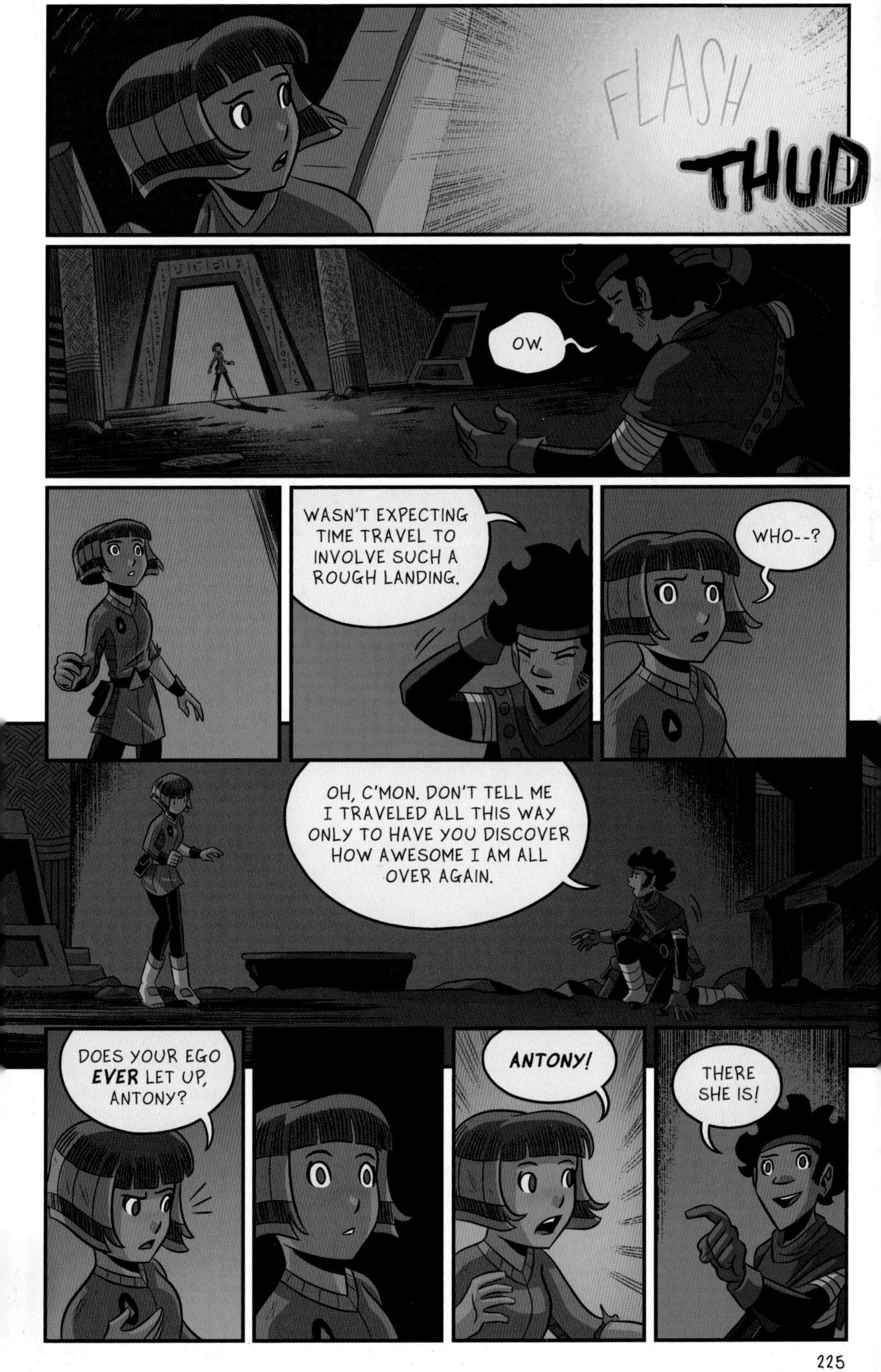
FLASH
THUD
OW.
WASN'T EXPECTING TIME TRAVEL TO INVOLVE SUCH A ROUGH LANDING.
WHO--?
OH, C'MON. DON'T TELL ME I TRAVELED ALL THIS WAY ONLY TO HAVE YOU DISCOVER HOW AWESOME I AM ALL OVER AGAIN.
DOES YOUR EGO **EVER** LET UP, ANTONY?
ANTONY!
THERE SHE IS!

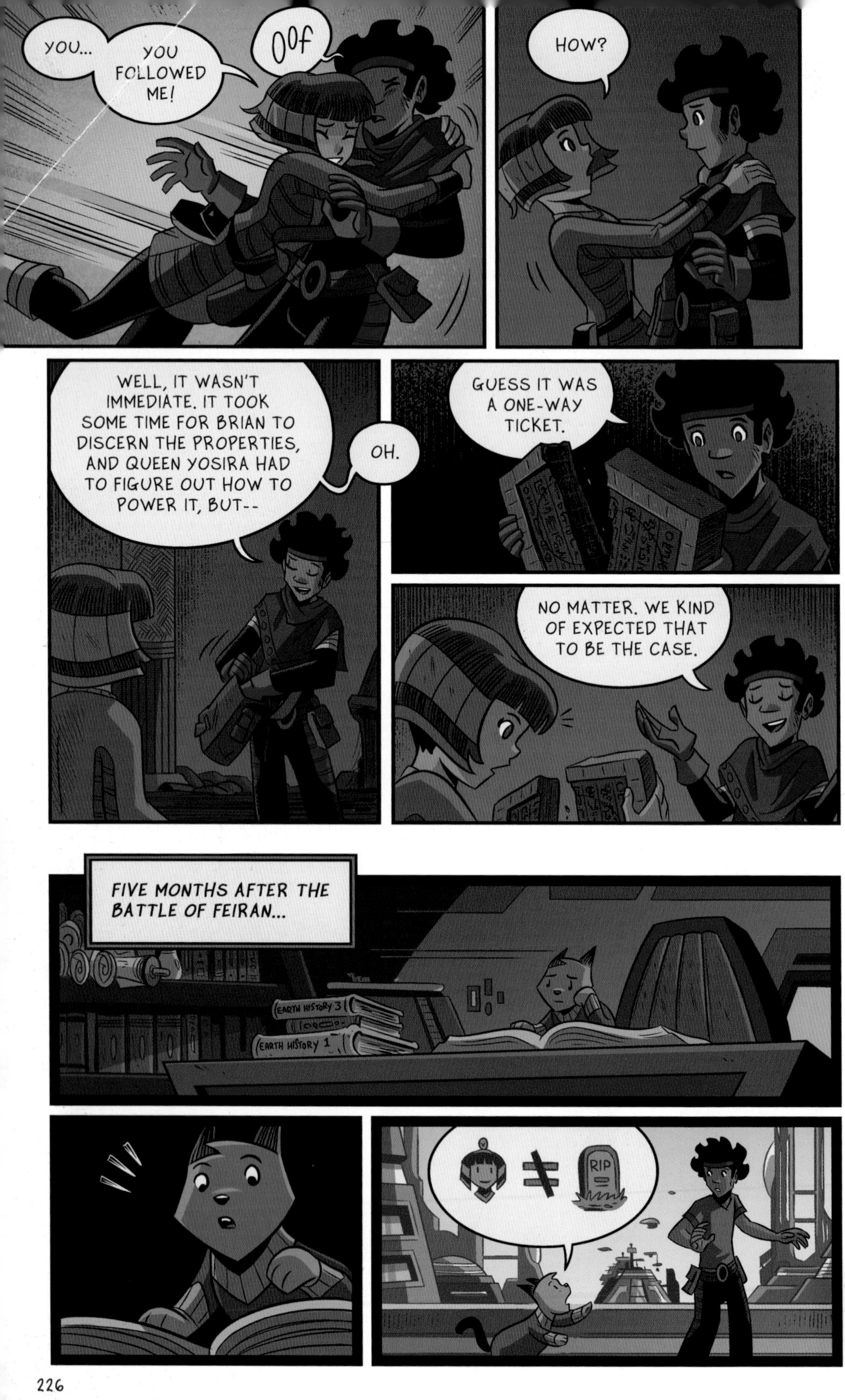
YOU...
YOU FOLLOWED ME!
OOF
HOW?
WELL, IT WASN'T IMMEDIATE. IT TOOK SOME TIME FOR BRIAN TO DISCERN THE PROPERTIES, AND QUEEN YOSIRA HAD TO FIGURE OUT HOW TO POWER IT, BUT--
OH.
GUESS IT WAS A ONE-WAY TICKET.
NO MATTER. WE KIND OF EXPECTED THAT TO BE THE CASE.
FIVE MONTHS AFTER THE BATTLE OF FEIRAN...
EARTH HISTORY 3
EARTH HISTORY 1
RIP

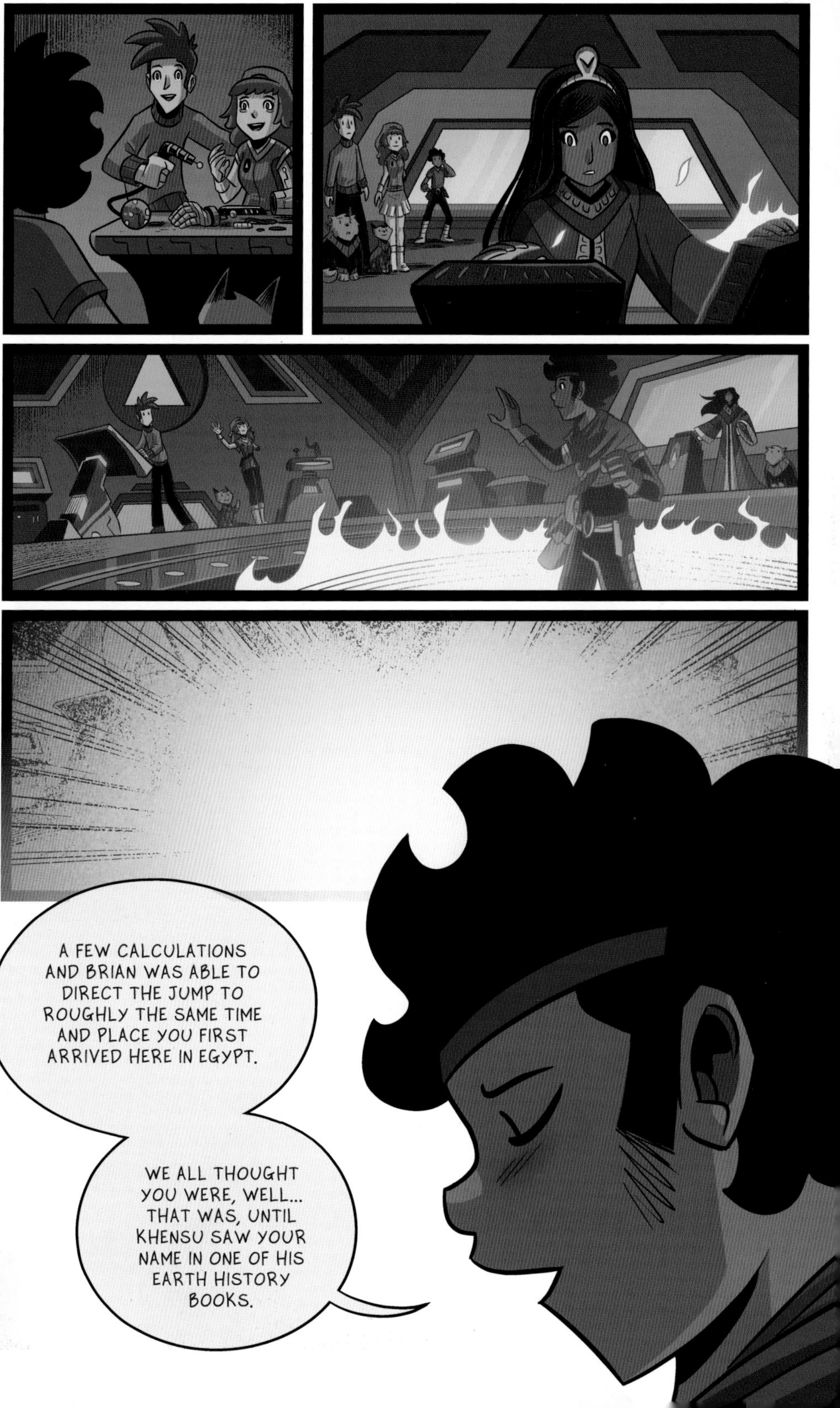
A FEW CALCULATIONS AND BRIAN WAS ABLE TO DIRECT THE JUMP TO ROUGHLY THE SAME TIME AND PLACE YOU FIRST ARRIVED HERE IN EGYPT.
WE ALL THOUGHT YOU WERE, WELL... THAT WAS, UNTIL KHENSU SAW YOUR NAME IN ONE OF HIS EARTH HISTORY BOOKS.

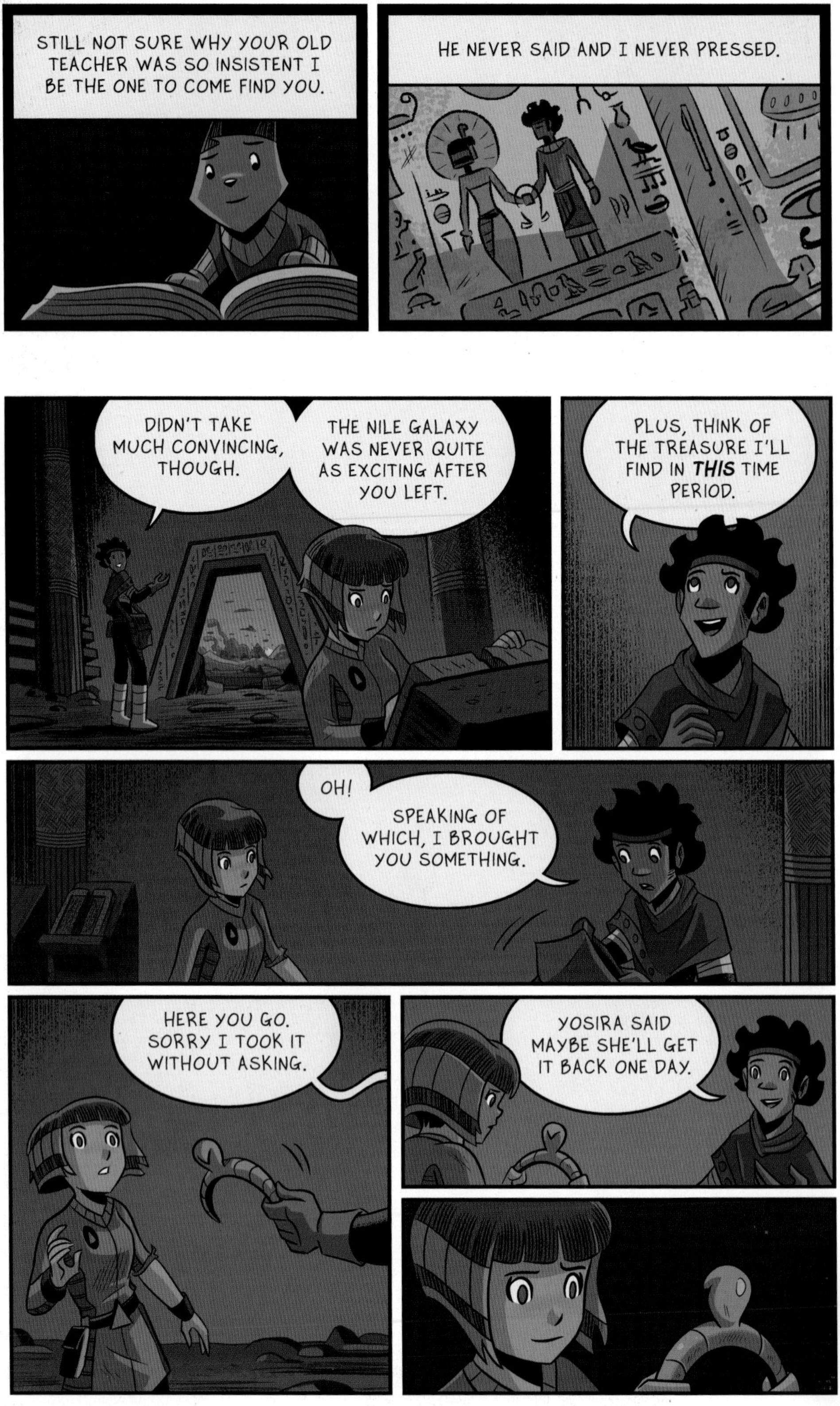
STILL NOT SURE WHY YOUR OLD TEACHER WAS SO INSISTENT I BE THE ONE TO COME FIND YOU.
HE NEVER SAID AND I NEVER PRESSED.
DIDN'T TAKE MUCH CONVINCING, THOUGH.
THE NILE GALAXY WAS NEVER QUITE AS EXCITING AFTER YOU LEFT.
PLUS, THINK OF THE TREASURE I'LL FIND IN ***THIS*** TIME PERIOD.
OH!
SPEAKING OF WHICH, I BROUGHT YOU SOMETHING.
HERE YOU GO. SORRY I TOOK IT WITHOUT ASKING.
YOSIRA SAID MAYBE SHE'LL GET IT BACK ONE DAY.

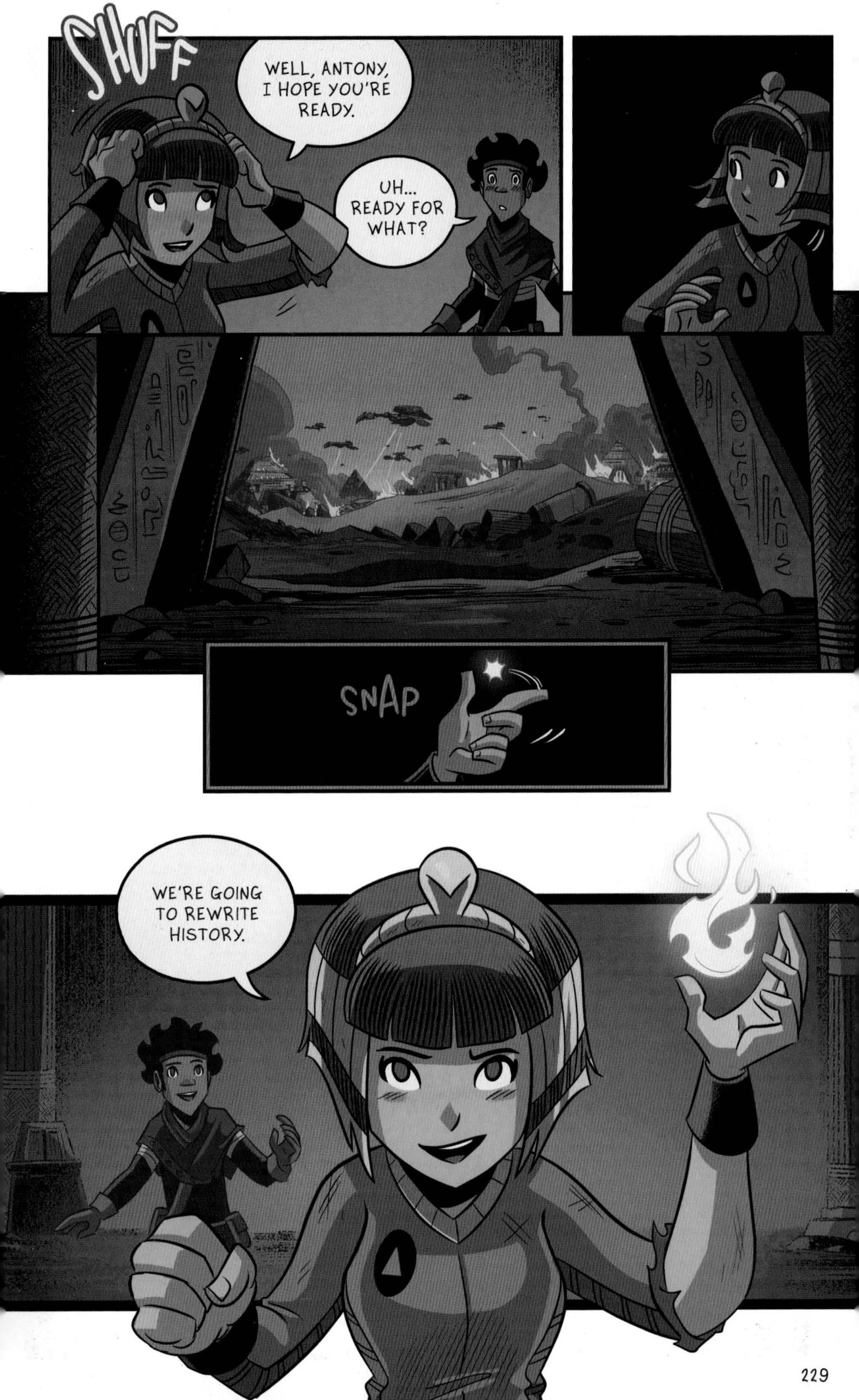
SHUFF
WELL, ANTONY, I HOPE YOU'RE READY.
UH... READY FOR WHAT?
SNAP
WE'RE GOING TO REWRITE HISTORY.

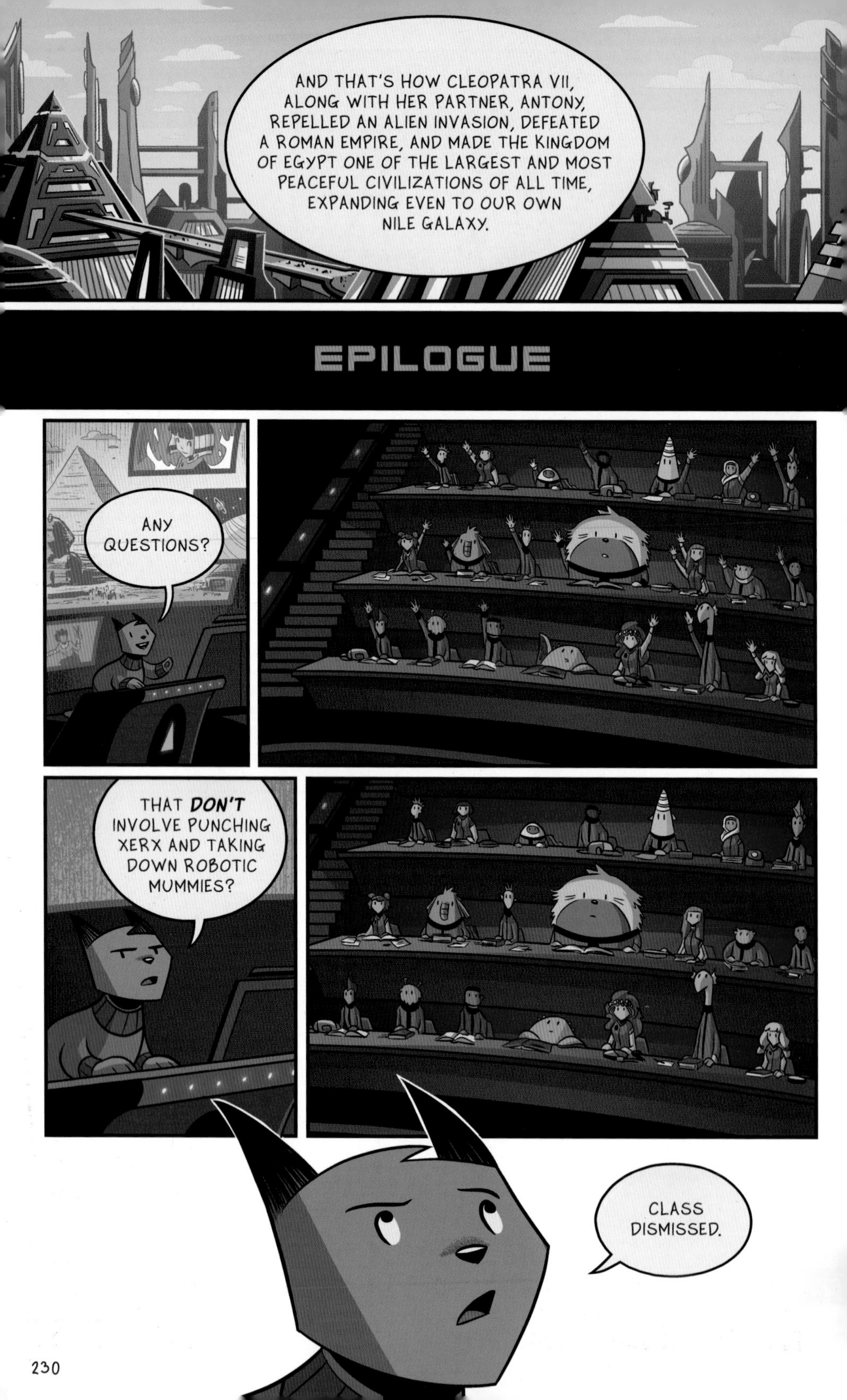
AND THAT'S HOW CLEOPATRA VII, ALONG WITH HER PARTNER, ANTONY, REPELLED AN ALIEN INVASION, DEFEATED A ROMAN EMPIRE, AND MADE THE KINGDOM OF EGYPT ONE OF THE LARGEST AND MOST PEACEFUL CIVILIZATIONS OF ALL TIME, EXPANDING EVEN TO OUR OWN NILE GALAXY.
EPILOGUE
ANY QUESTIONS?
THAT **DON'T** INVOLVE PUNCHING XERX AND TAKING DOWN ROBOTIC MUMMIES?
CLASS DISMISSED.

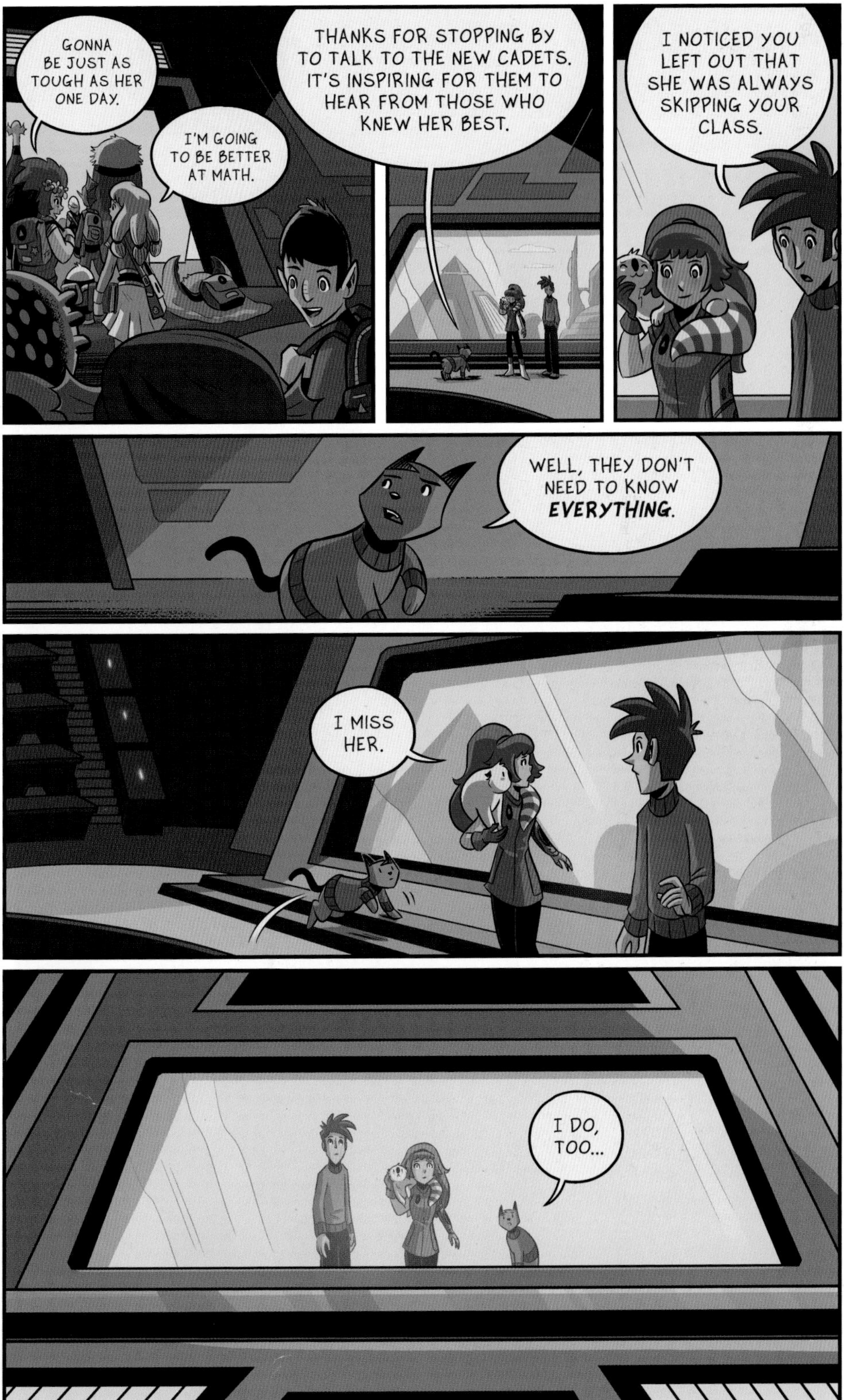
GONNA BE JUST AS TOUGH AS HER ONE DAY.
I'M GOING TO BE BETTER AT MATH.
THANKS FOR STOPPING BY TO TALK TO THE NEW CADETS. IT'S INSPIRING FOR THEM TO HEAR FROM THOSE WHO KNEW HER BEST.
I NOTICED YOU LEFT OUT THAT SHE WAS ALWAYS SKIPPING YOUR CLASS.
WELL, THEY DON'T NEED TO KNOW **EVERYTHING**.
I MISS HER.
I DO, TOO...

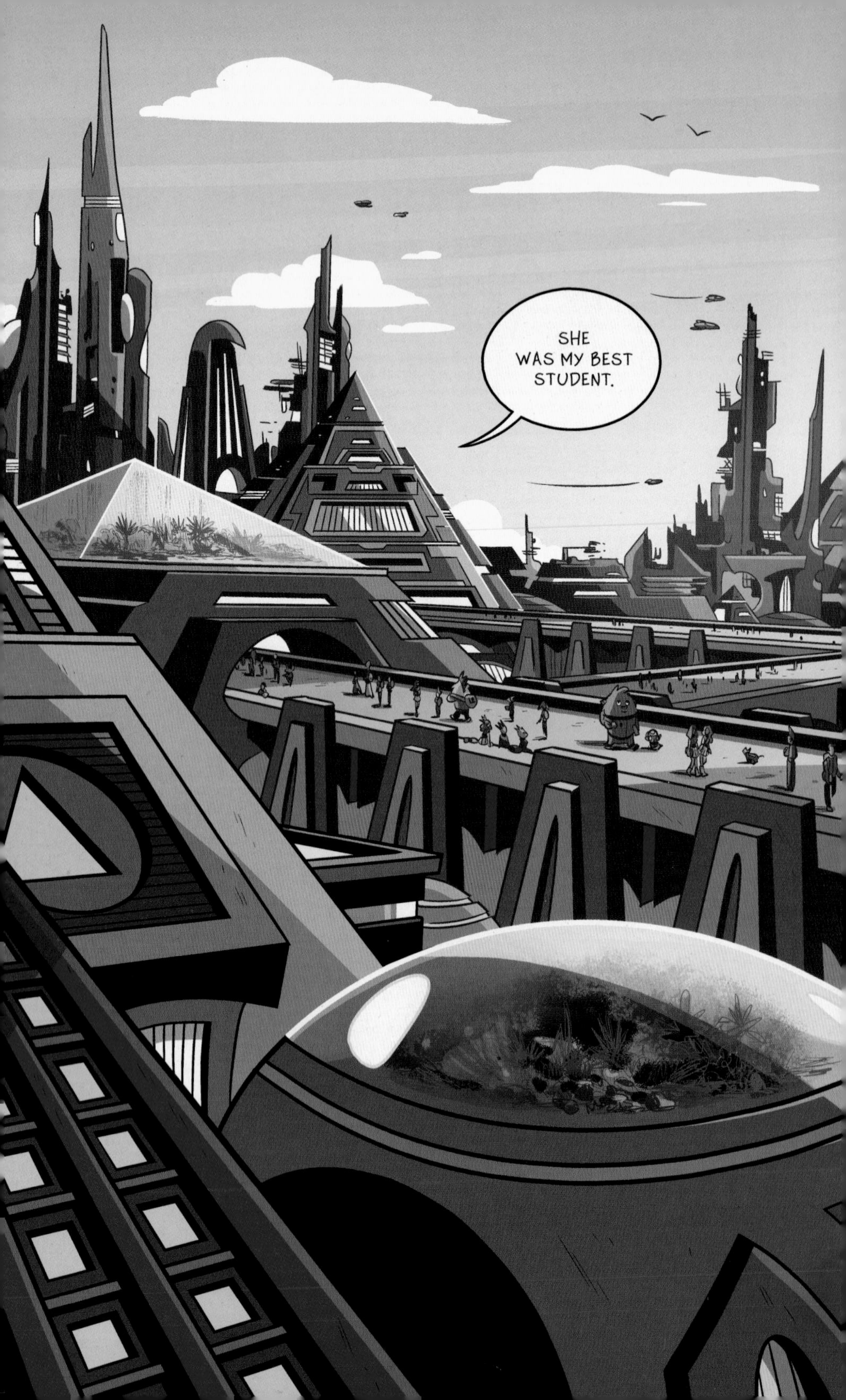
SHE WAS MY BEST STUDENT.

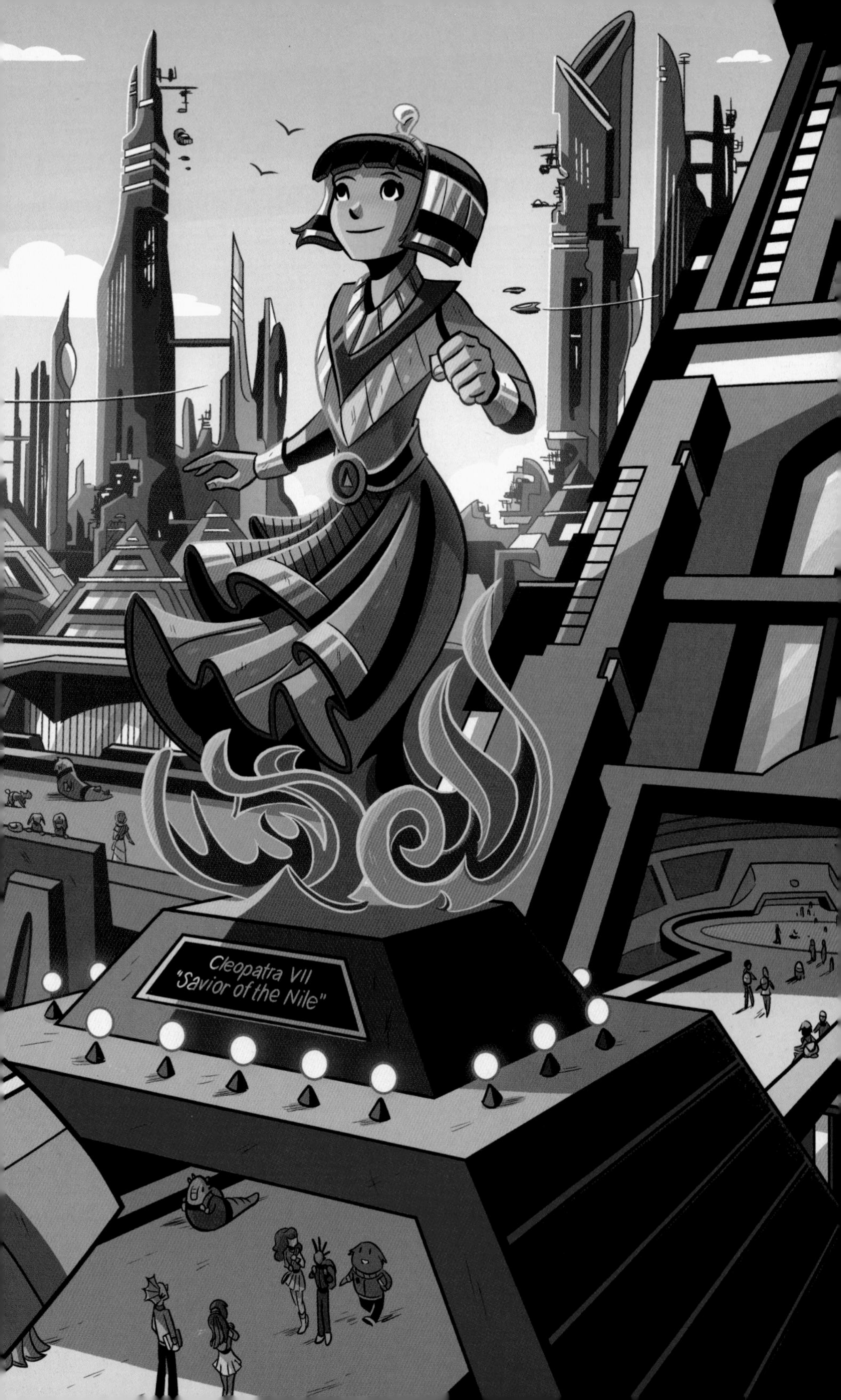
Cleopatra VII
"Savior of the Nile"

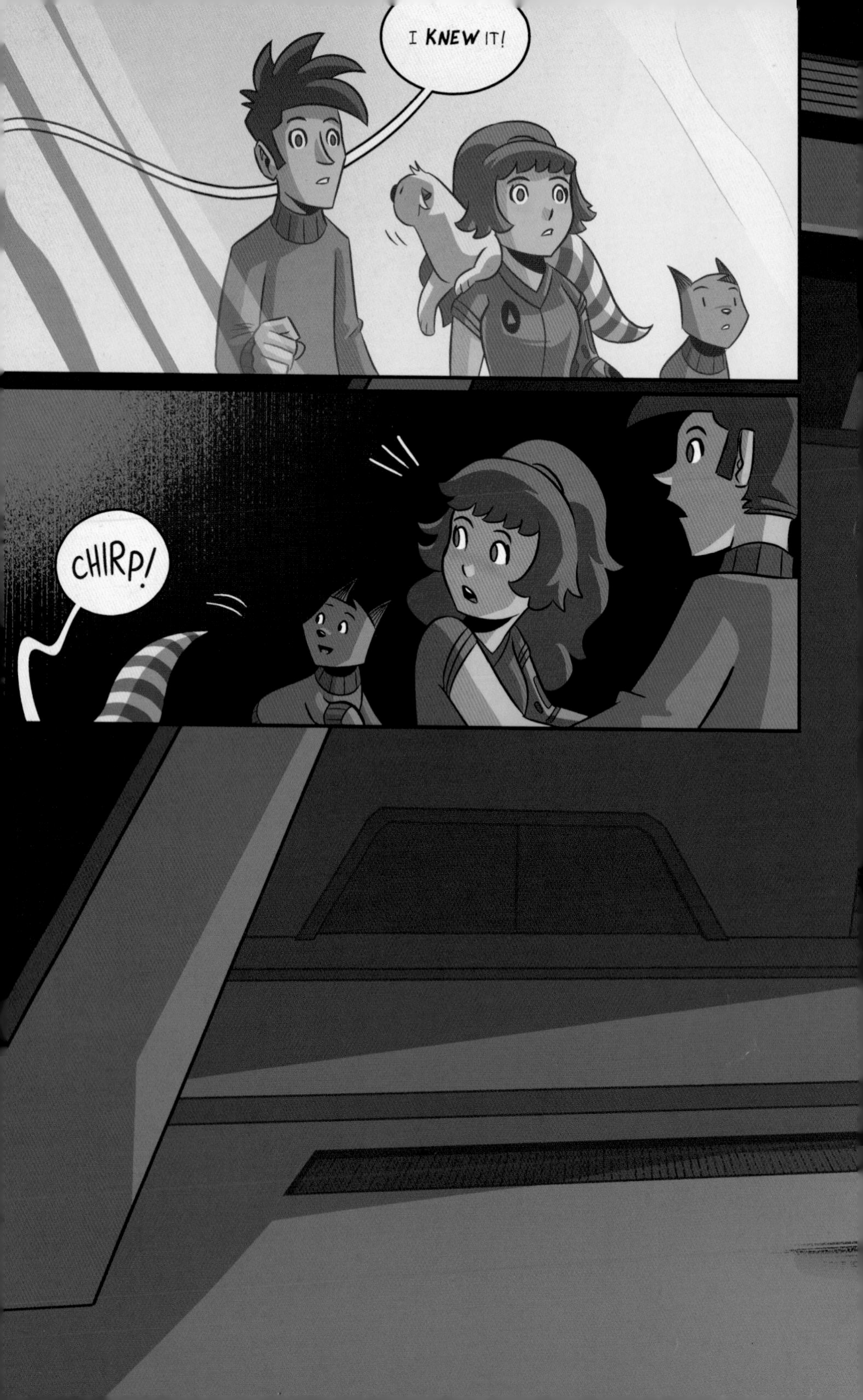
I KNEW IT!
CHIRP!

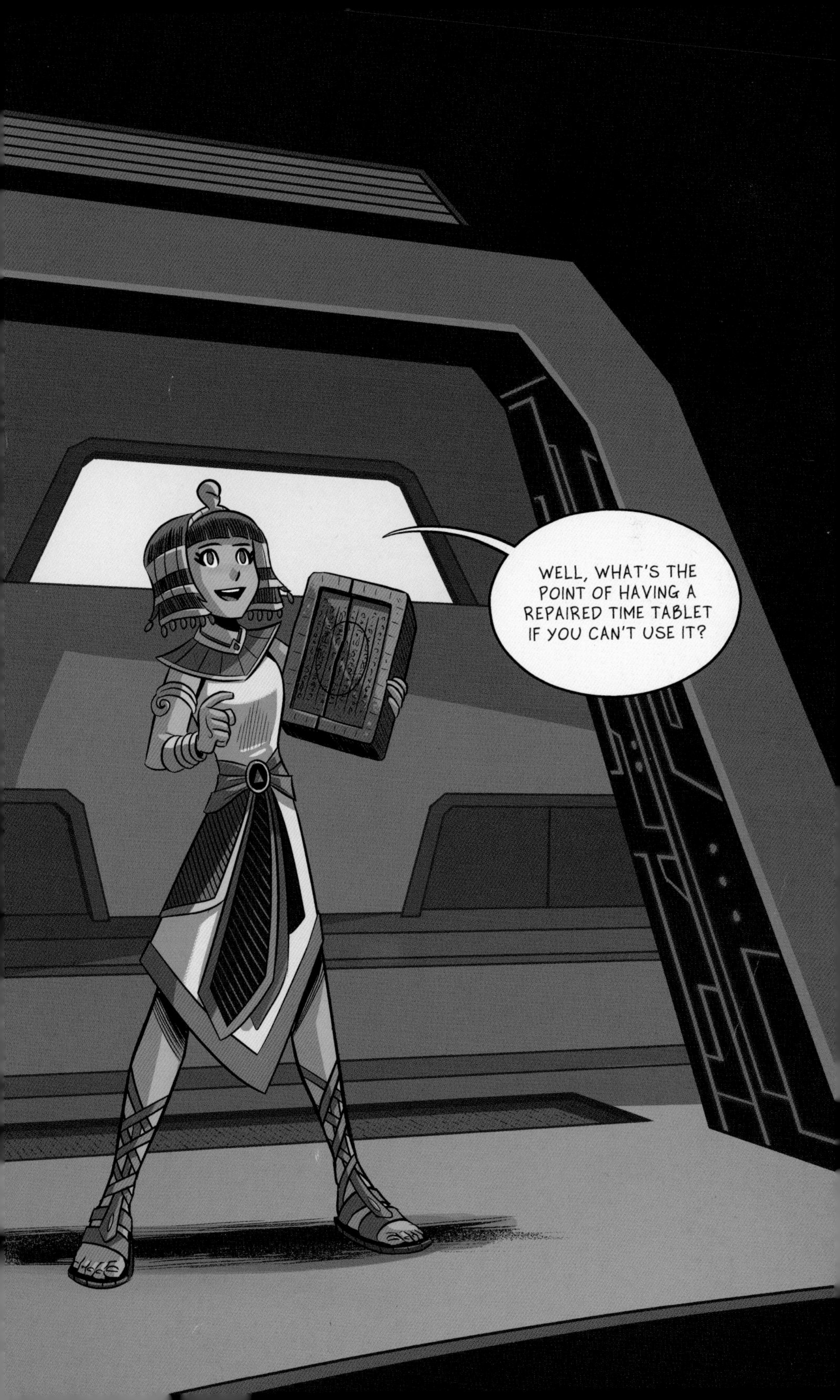
WELL, WHAT'S THE POINT OF HAVING A REPAIRED TIME TABLET IF YOU CAN'T USE IT?

THE END